A Song to Wake a Thousand Sorrows

MICHELLE MANUS

For Skyla.
Thank you for believing in my weird trauma books.

PROLOGUE

The creature in the swamp could not remember being a woman, though its form remained that of a human female. It drifted, dead moss and ooze squelching between bare toes as it walked, and though the denizens of this swamp were not kind, nothing dared approach it. For the swamp's inhabitants had long ago learned that to touch the creature was to die.

It walked the same path it had walked endlessly since its arrival two years ago, a serpentine loop through the murky depths, the bare footfalls withering anything that had managed to grow since last its feet had tread upon that ground.

It could not remember being a woman because in this moment it was only a shell, a form sustained not by food and water and shelter, but by pure, burning power. It was a husk, a container inside which two forces warred, each as determined as the other to be the victor in this contest of wills. The one was ancient and eternal, a primal force that whispered, every second of every day, *Give in, give up, give over.*

But the second force, the one that had existed for a mere fraction of time compared to the other, did not know the meaning of the word *give*. That force—the one that *had* once been a woman—had not survived to adulthood merely to lose herself to something *else*.

She had not clawed her way out of hell only to be erased by this thing that lived within her. But she was lost, and she could not remember her way back to herself. She had a vague memory of something snapping inside her, and she thought it might have been that path, that way back to *her*.

Whoever she was.

But since she couldn't find it, she was the thing and not the girl, the war and not the person. So the creature walked. Around and around, through and through, over and over, the same words shattering off themselves inside her skull.

Give in, give up, give over, that eternal voice beckoned, lapping like waves against the woman's will.

I won't, I can't, I never will. And unlike a rock beneath the ocean's waves, the woman did not erode. She did not give. She didn't know *how* to give. It was, after all, why the power had chosen her.

The bones of some dead animal crunched beneath the creature's feet as it walked, rounding a bend that brought it close to the swamp's edge. A flicker of light caught the creature's attention and it halted. For the first time since it had come to this place, it *halted*. There was something mesmerizing about that light. Something... warm, when the creature had not even realized it was cold.

It stood hypnotized as the light came closer, and as that brilliant warmth splashed over it, that path the woman had been looking for unfurled inside her, as if it had only been hidden by autumn's leaves, and a good wind had finally blown them clear.

Woman and primal force saw the way out at the same time. But that path—it belonged to the woman, not the force. She knew it better, and it was she who stepped foot upon it first, spiraling back into herself in a burst of effort and triumph and pain; she who gathered the threads of power that had leaked free into her and shoved them back into the cage she had built for them so long ago, slamming the door shut.

For a moment, the silence inside her skull was so absolute she thought she might have gone deaf. But then she heard the slow approach of wagon wheels, and that light that had brought her back to herself drew closer, bringing with it the soft murmur of voices.

She had the desire to fling herself into its path, to seek some kind of connection...and yet she found herself backing away. Because people weren't safe. People had never been safe.

Thick ooze squelched beneath her feet, and without the power running rampant through her body, the cut that opened on the bottom of her foot did not seal itself. Cold lashed her as the wind stirred.

Winter in a swamp was still winter, if not as cold as it might become in other, less temperate climates, and she shivered, teeth chattering, because she was naked. The wagon rumbled away and she told herself it was best to let it go.

But even a starved and beaten creature craves company, even if they know that company cannot be trusted. She found herself slinking along the edges of the swamp, following the rumble of those wagon wheels. She yearned for the soft, steady light that kept pouring from within the wagon. Where was it traveling? It didn't seem to be going anywhere, only…rambling.

Eventually, when night fell, it stopped. The two voices she had heard earlier began speaking again, soft and companionable. Easy. The crackle of a fire stirred to life and laughter floated to her. They sounded…happy, whoever they were, and she had the desperate urge to run to that fire and curl up there.

She had actually taken a step toward it, almost out of the cover of the trees, before she caught herself. Her mind, once quick-witted and calculating, stretched its claws and woke. She was a naked, filthy woman in a swamp. If she went out to that fire, she would be lucky if they didn't kill her.

But as she remembered exactly how she had come to be here— and how far from civilization she likely still was—she knew she couldn't let this opportunity walk away from her, either. She was human again, no longer capable of living off anger and burning power.

Her stomach twisted and she was intensely, painfully hungry. But that, at least, was nothing new.

Something—a half-forgotten memory—drew her gaze to the left, where it snagged on something that did not belong in a swamp. A hard case rested beside a tree. It had a long, thin neck that burgeoned into an oval body.

A desperate need stirred and she ran for it, falling to her knees and running her fingers over the battered case. Battered, but perfectly dry, untouched by two years in this humid environment, kept pristine and sheltered from time by the very power she'd shoved back into a cage. As if that power had known, when they came to this place, that if she ever came back to herself, losing this one thing would break her as nothing else had.

That was the problem with the thing that lived inside her—it could be kind. That made it difficult to remember that it did not, in the end, have her best interests at heart.

She unlatched the case with trembling fingers. It was designed for an instrument larger than the one it carried, and so there was room also for the meager clothing she'd shoved into its compartment when she'd fled here.

She grabbed the first things that came into her hands and pulled on a pair of leggings, so patched and tattered the original cloth was only a memory. A tunic in similar condition followed. The only other items—two dresses, one plain but serviceable, the other so fine it made her want to vomit for reasons she refused to remember—she placed into the open half of the lid, revealing the instrument in the bottom.

Reverently, she ran her fingers over the guitar, her skin touching lacquered wood grain. She swallowed past the rush of emotions the sight of it, the feel of it, evoked. She had run, with nothing but *this*, determined to become something with it. Something no one could ever harm again.

She swallowed and shoved down the tide of emotions that threatened to choke her, to turn her into a sobbing mess on the filthy swamp floor. She tucked the dresses back around the body of the guitar, so the material would keep the instrument from rattling in the extra space inside the case.

Latching it closed, she hefted it into her hand, walked back to the treeline, and looked out at the crackling fire. She had no mirror to let her know her appearance, but running her hands through her hair proved the power that had raged through her body for...however long she had been here, had at least kept her hair clean.

She could do nothing about her lack of shoes or the grime that covered her bare feet. But she would think of something. She always did.

Gripping the handle of the guitar case in her hand, she walked out of the swamp and to the edge of the fire's warmth. Two men sat on the end of a covered wagon that was parked by the fire's edge.

One had dark black skin, his head shaved on the sides, the thick hair in the middle styled into short twists. The other man seemed his mirror opposite, his pale skin and long blond hair a sharp contrast.

And yet she knew, looking at them, that they were less opposites than they were different sides of the same coin. Complements.

They looked at her, and that soft light that had drawn her back to herself washed over her again, beckoning her forward. She dug her heels in and stood. She couldn't tell which of them the light came from. They were too close, the blond leaning back against the other man's chest.

The short-haired man spoke, his voice deep and melodious, and she didn't understand a word he said. Had she forgotten how to speak? Did words only make sense in her mind, in her thoughts? Hesitant, she opened her mouth. Her throat, disused to speech, made a single hoarse word. "Hello."

"Hello," the man replied, and this time she understood it. Because, her brain put together, there were more languages than one in the world, and he'd switched to the tongue she'd used after her greeting.

Common, the universal language of the Faelhorn Provinces.

"I'm Marquin," he continued, "and this is Verol." He indicated the blond who still hadn't spoken. "Do you have a name?"

For a heart-pounding second, she didn't have an answer. Then her spine steeled and the name came to her lips. "Clare. I'm Clare Brighton."

"Well, Clare Brighton, if you play that"—he nodded at the guitar —"you're welcome to travel with us. We're going to Veralna City."

It couldn't be this easy, this simple, to get to somewhere new. And yet she felt no fear, no danger from the two men before her. That they *were* dangerous, she had no doubt. But it was easy enough to read that, so long as she didn't come between *them*, they were not a danger to her.

She licked her dry lips, hesitant. But she had a promise to keep. One she'd made to herself from years of blood and pain and enduring. If she was going to keep it, she needed something she didn't have. Something she intended to gain in the capital city of the Faelhorn Provinces. She licked her lips again, her tongue catching on the rough, peeling cracks in them. "I'm going to Veralna, too."

Shadows flickered in the depths of Marquin's eyes, as if he'd known she would accept their offer, but had hoped she might not.

"Then come sit by the fire"—he nodded to the empty chair that indeed sat by the flames, as if waiting for her—"and play us a song."

CHAPTER

ONE

THE HAWK AND SCEPTER

The life Clare Brighton remembered as she stared at the door to the Hawk and Scepter, willing herself the courage to enter, was not her own. It was some other young woman's life, one to whom cities and inns and civilization were ordinary, expected things.

She sank herself into the normality those memories offered, even as a small part of her wondered if the woman whose life she'd donned like a cloak had actually existed. Were these real memories, taking the edge off her uneasiness, or were they simply a pretty dream she told herself? A pretty dream that steadied her nerves as she grasped the handle of the inn's door. A pretty dream that let her paste a bright, unworried smile on her face as she stepped into the inn's tavern, guitar case clutched in her left hand.

For all the loftiness of its name, the Hawk and Scepter huddled in Veralna's Midtown, and the bad edge of Midtown, at that. Still, the quality of the carpets in the dining area, the rich mahogany of the bar and chairs, the ornate attention to detail in the fixtures, showed the innkeeper hoped to earn a clientele to match the majesty of the inn's name. He had even paid for magelights that glowed pure white, when the yellow ones cost a quarter of the price. They shone from within small spherical cages of white stone, and though she knew it *wasn't* quellstone, it looked so like it that the sight tore her from the pretty fictions she'd told herself to get through this door.

The cloak of civility fell away and she wasn't some farmer's daughter who navigated city streets on market days and dreamed of happy futures. She was a nameless, feral thing, one whose closest brush with stability had come at a cost no human should pay, and she was mad to have come here. To the capital city of the Faelhorn Provinces, with its rules that were so different from those in the place she had survived. It mattered little that she'd been trained for this place, this society. She didn't think any amount of knowledge on how to act and dress and speak could ever truly make her belong here and it would be easy—so easy—to leave.

The innkeeper was nowhere in sight, the only patron an early afternoon drunk. Her hand clenched tighter on the guitar case. Her resolve wavered and in that instant the Song struck, sinking hooks into the opening her hesitation provided, raging its fury against the cage she had locked it inside. The force of its anger blossomed as heat in her head, as if Ferrian's own flames licked at the insides of her skull.

The taste of dirt coated the back of her tongue, the smell of moss and swamp water thick in her nose. The stone floor beneath her worn boots gave way to the feel of brittle bones snapping underneath the bare soles of her feet. Her vision doubled, the bright interior of the inn overlapped by hanging vines and murky water. She could almost hear the call of a marsh loon, or the soft swish of something rising from deep water long enough to break the surface before disappearing once more into its depths.

Madness clouded her thoughts, comforting in its familiarity, its power, its safety.

Come back. The Song's voice swam through her mind, a soft, resonant contralto. She had fought it, she had betrayed it, and she had caged it, but it would welcome her back.

All she had to do was let go.

The drunk coughed with startling loudness, the roughness of the sound shocking Clare back to the present. She grabbed hold of the momentary clarity with lion's jaws, reciting the words that had become her mantra for sanity.

You are Clare Brighton. You fled Renault County and lived, and you are in control.

The mantra strengthened the bars of the Song's cage and the power quieted, her senses emptying of everything save the sight of the rich interior of the inn, the sound of the drunk's throat clearing another time. Clare did not make the mistake of hesitating again. She forced herself to be a woman and not the madness. She would not turn back now. She had made a promise, and to keep that promise, she needed power. To gain power, she needed money, and to gain money, she needed adoration. Adoration required an audience.

She clutched the guitar case more firmly in her hand and took a seat at the bar. For a woman who needed the world to fall in love with her, she was grateful the establishment was almost empty. The soft corners of civilization rasped irritatingly against her skin, and she did not think she could handle a crowd. Later she would have to, but for now she had only to contend with the middle-aged drunk three seats down.

His stomach strained at the edges of a shirt he apparently refused to admit no longer fit. His bleary-eyed face hung over his wine tankard. The cut of his clothes was expensive, though the fabric's wear told Clare he was not as well-off as he had once been.

The tavern door opened and Clare turned, a smile on her lips in case a smile should prove useful. The newcomer wore the blue and white uniform of the city guard and his gaze alighted on Clare with a cruel brightness indicating fate had proffered him a particularly delightful amusement. His eyes traveled over her, malice lurking in their depths.

Clare had seen the look before—in other guardsmen on the journey here, in waste-street things, in embittered souls who blamed everyone but themselves for problems of their own making—and knew the guardsman did not see *her*. He saw the traveling clothes laden with ingrained dirt, their quality one step up from rags. He saw the beggar-thinness of her figure, the sun-tanned skin and the loose fall of deep brown curls.

In short, he saw a poor girl from one of the poverty-stricken holdings in the outer reaches of the Faelhorn Provinces, and likely thought she ought to have had the sense to *stay* in the outer reaches. If she had come from such a place, perhaps she would have. But Renault County was worse than any Faelhorn holding, and no one would ever believe she'd escaped from *there*.

Clare forced her smile wider. "Afternoon, sir."

He did not return her smile. The severity of his expression deepened, as did the dark enjoyment at the corners of his eyes. He walked to her.

"Papers."

It was no small miracle that Clare's papers had survived her foray into madness, and the miracle was one she did not examine too closely. She simply pulled them from the outer pocket of her coat, instinct more than conscious thought causing her to reach slowly, deliberately. As her fingers brushed the folded edges, a half-forgotten memory surfaced of a guardsman's fist striking her cheekbone. It wasn't her memory, and it wasn't the farmer's daughter's memory either. It was as if her thoughts of holdings girls had summoned one from the aether for her, sending her the memory to gather stray thoughts and reasonings in her mind, linking them together so she would know that you moved slowly because it was safer.

Clare clamped down tighter on the Song—it needed to stay the hell out of her head. To stop sending her all of these *helpful* thoughts. She didn't think guardsmen took kindly to poor women who couldn't remember their own name, much less if they were a farmer's daughter, or a poor holdings girl, or something else altogether.

Clare let him look over her information several times before asking, voice mild, "Is there a problem?"

The papers were real. They weren't *hers* but they were real, and they shouldn't have even mattered. Ever since El-Dennon had fallen under the relentless onslaught of the Jackal King's armies, every pocket of civilization belonged to Faelhorn. What was her place of birth meant to prove, now that they all belonged—in theory—to the same kingdom?

The guard grunted. "Shop across the street had a break-in last night. You know anything about it?"

"No, sir. I only arrived in Veralna this morning." Her papers were clearly stamped to that effect.

"What brings you to the city?"

"I sing." Clare indicated the guitar case propped underneath the bar.

"And you just got here this morning?"

It was an effort not to grind her teeth, to keep her smile in place. "That's correct."

"'Cause bystanders say they saw someone matching your description fleeing the shop last night."

"I wouldn't know anything about that." She tried to coax her voice into the timid obsequiousness he no doubt expected, needed, but the best she could manage was a bored indifference. The Song strained against her, trying to make her palms dampen, make a nervous panic flutter in her stomach to remind her that it didn't matter whether she had or hadn't done anything wrong—it wouldn't stop the guardsman from arresting her if he felt like it. When it all came down to it, it wasn't her gender or her looks or her clothes that gave him the ability to mistreat her. Those things only made it easier. It came down to power and means, and the fact that Clare had neither.

But she had survived far worse than him, and though she recognized she *should* fear him, she was still too disconnected from her emotions to take him seriously.

He scanned her papers yet again, then tapped them carelessly against his palm as he raised his gaze. "You staying with family in the city?"

She wanted to say yes and be done with him. But the very fact he'd offered her an easy answer, instead of asking her what she was doing in the city, made it clear he wanted her to take it. She thought of giving him the names Verol and Marquin, the two men who had let her travel in their wagon the last two weeks, and who were the only reason she'd reached Veralna City before true winter hit. They had obviously had money and, having money, their word might count for something on her behalf. And they were kind enough that if a guardsman dragged her to their door and demanded to know if she was staying with them, they would invite her in with a smile and demand to know where she'd been.

The only problem was, she had no idea where they lived. She didn't even know their last names, or if they openly lived together, and the very reason she had felt safe traveling with two male strangers would likely be a reason for the city guard to cause the men trouble if he did manage to find them. They had been kind to her, at a time when kindness had seemed many lifetimes off.

She might be cold-hearted and ruthless and all but dead inside, but Clare Brighton didn't repay generosity in unlike kind.

She responded to his query with a simple, "No."

Irritation sparked in his eyes at her reply. At the lack of explanation. "Where are you staying?"

She set her teeth, knowing precisely where he was going with this line of inquiry. The guards at the city's gate had made it very clear that Veralna had strict laws on vagrancy. "Here."

"I'm going to need to see your room key."

Ferrian's hells. "As soon as the innkeeper returns and rents me the room, I would be delighted to show it to you."

Where *was* the damn innkeeper, anyway?

That cruel, dark amusement kindled in the depths of his eyes again. "You are aware that vagrancy is punishable by imprisonment, and anyone without a room once the afternoon bell tolls is considered a vagrant?"

Clare's smile thinned, but she held it in place. The afternoon bell couldn't be more than fifteen minutes off. She didn't have a single coin to her name. If the innkeeper didn't let her sing for her room tonight, she had no doubt the guard would take great delight in hauling her out of here.

Prison. A cage. Trapped again, her life once more in someone else's hands. Bile rose in her throat. She wouldn't do it.

She forced her mouth to open. "I assure you, I will have a room here before then."

The guardsman smiled, a sick twisting of his lips that sent waves of revulsion down Clare's spine. "Now that, I very much doubt. But I'll be sure to wait for Crenn to get back, so you can ask him."

So the guard knew the innkeeper, then. Knew him well enough to think he wouldn't give Clare a room.

The inn's door banged open and she turned at the unexpected noise. A middle-aged white man stood in the doorway. He was well-dressed and possessed of enough money to allow him to age well, despite the salt-and-pepper color of his hair. His gaze landed on the guardsman and his lips compressed into a thin, angry line.

"Moretz."

The guardsman straightened. "Master Guire."

Master Guire's eyes narrowed. "See here, when my daughter said she saw you coming in here, I told her that certainly the guardsman in charge of the safety of this quarter wouldn't be in his friend's inn, waiting for a pint when our shop's been broken into for the fourth time this month."

Moretz reddened. Clare observed the change in color—it wasn't the flush of embarrassment, but that of anger. He wasn't chastened, he was angry that this man held power over him. That the shopkeeper had enough clout or money that it mattered how Moretz responded to him. "I was questioning a suspect in your case, Master Guire."

"Yeah?" The shopkeeper's gaze flicked over Clare, dismissing her. "She doesn't exactly look like an athletic blond man. Pretty sure that was the description my clerk gave."

"Master Guire, I assure you—"

"Your assurances haven't recovered my wares or secured an arrest. They haven't made my wife feel safe enough to sleep for more than two hours a night. I've half a mind to take my complaints to the Guardsman's Council."

Moretz gave Clare a look clearly intended to make her stay put, and walked over to the shopkeeper. If they took the conversation outside, she could slip around the counter, through the kitchens and out the back door. Her gaze locked on Moretz's left hand, where her papers carelessly dangled from his fingers, and her teeth clenched. She couldn't run without those. Not that it mattered, because Moretz never went outside, only pulled the man over near one of the windows, his gaze flicking to her every couple of seconds.

The innkeeper chose that moment to return to the bar, his expression dark. When his gaze landed on her, Clare thought that expression turned just a shade darker. She didn't let it deter her from smiling and asking, her voice bright, "Do you have any music this evening?"

The innkeeper grunted. "I did, only the Musicians Guild tells me the girl I hired's sick and they've no one to replace her. As if I give a damn she's got the sniffles when the Duke of Merlain's nephew's staying at my inn tonight, and everyone knows how he likes his music."

The tightness in Clare's chest eased a fraction. This might be the first good luck she'd had since leaving Verol and Marquin. The singer the man had hired was ill, and he desperately needed a new one. Clare racked her brain, forcing old knowledge to surface.

Knowledge she had never wanted to gain, but had done so anyway. Merlain was a small holding within Trin Province, but to an inn like this one, clearly trying to gain some manner of prestige, the duke's nephew would be a fine catch.

Almost *too* fine a one. It didn't make a great deal of sense for the duke's nephew to travel all the way to Veralna City only to stay at this inn, of all places. She tucked the oddity away in her memory in case it should prove useful later—for now, it didn't matter.

"I sing, and I play the guitar and the piano." The inn didn't have a piano but she hoped her knowledge of the instrument would boost her respectability, and if the innkeeper managed to produce one out of thin air, she *could* play it. She could play any instrument he cared to drop before her, but she doubted he wanted a recitation of them.

"I had intended to rent a room for the night," she continued, careful to keep desperation from her voice. That voice that wasn't *quite* hers whispered that nothing turned a potential employer away like desperation. "But I should be happy to save the coin and cover the evening's entertainment in exchange for the room, if you like."

The innkeeper's expression shifted and, for a moment, Clare thought he was considering her offer. In the second before he spoke, Clare recognized she had misjudged the emotion on his face. What she'd thought was consideration was actually derision.

"You?" He gave a short bark of laughter. "I'd sooner lose the Duke of Merlain's favor than have an outer holdings whore on my stage."

Sick heat pooled in Clare's belly, followed by a flush of anger in her cheeks. She was so, so tired of people thinking they knew her. So tired of men looking at her and proclaiming her *anything*, as if their words and their judgment were the culmination of her worth. The Song answered the rising tide of her anger, flooding her chest and limbs and demanding release.

Clare closed her eyes. She would be damned to Ferrian's hells before she would allow that she had survived Renault County only to rot in prison or be brought low by someone as insignificant as *this* man. She didn't stop to think as she unspooled the thinnest tendril of the Song, letting a fraction of the power escape from its cage. She told herself that she had no choice, that it was the Song or jail, but part of her—and not a small part—felt a fierce elation as the Song's power lit her veins.

She grasped the innkeeper's forearm and locked his gaze, her heart pounding with the clamor of a barely contained storm. When she spoke, she spoke not only with her voice, but with the Song's soft contralto as well. "You would be honored to have me sing for your guests tonight."

The innkeeper gasped, his eyes slipping out of focus. "I…would be honored to have you sing here this evening, Miss…"

"Brighton," she supplied. "Clare Brighton. You would be honored, and you will pay me the fee that was to have gone to the Musicians Guild, along with supplying me with a room for the evening."

"I—of course, Miss Brighton." He pulled two silver coins from his pocket and handed them to her. "Your fee. And your room. Please be down by eight." He handed her a brass key on a ribbon, the number twenty-one embroidered on the red cloth.

She took the key, her hand trembling as the Song inundated her, pulsing in her veins and demanding *out, out, out*. Such a dangerous thing, this taste of freedom she'd given it, and she struggled to put it aside as it battered at her will. With a grunt of effort she sucked the tendril of power back down and let the innkeeper go. He stumbled a little but didn't fall, looking blearily around as if he didn't quite know where he was.

Too late, Clare remembered the drunk three seats down. A quick glance confirmed he still slept, oblivious to the world around him. Her shoulders eased a fraction, and yet…something about him bothered her.

She shook her head and stood, nearly running into Moretz. Her pulse raced, slamming hurtfully against the barrier of her body. Had he seen?

"Going somewhere?" he asked.

"Yes." Heart drumming against her ribs, Clare held up the key. "To my room."

Moretz's eyes narrowed. "Crenn, this girl staying here tonight?"

The innkeeper grunted by way of affirmation.

"I thought you was all booked up for the night."

"She's a singer, I needed a singer. Gave her the singer's room."

Crenn's voice held the flatness Clare recognized as the aftereffects of the Song's influence, and the empty tone wasn't lost on Moretz.

"Doesn't seem like you to take on someone like her without any references."

"Duke of Merlain's nephew'll be here in less than an hour. What was I supposed to do?" He slapped a towel on the bar, wiping at invisible stains on the gleaming mahogany. "Ain't you got a break-in to investigate?"

"Yeah." Moretz drew the word out, turning it into two syllables, his gaze never leaving Clare. "Suppose I do. Have a nice evening, miss. Maybe I'll come back later and see the show." He tapped her papers against the tip of her nose before he dropped them onto the bar. She refused to so much as blink—at the thinly veiled threat or his actions—and a scowl darkened his face as he turned abruptly. She didn't do more than breathe until the door swung closed behind him. Then she very calmly gathered her guitar case and ascended the stairs to her room, each footfall measured, graceful, precise. She turned the lock, set the case down with the care it deserved, and made it to the washroom before she vomited.

Her stomach, empty, heaved up only yellow bile, the harsh liquid burning her throat as it rose. The aftereffects of the Song shuddered through her, but it was not its use that sickened Clare. It was the ease, the delight, she had felt in using it, the rush as heady as the first time it had shown itself to her.

It had taken her only the one time, the single use, to understand the consequences of giving that power free rein. To understand that if that power ever raged freely through her again, it would burn and burn until it burned her out. The magic inside her could save her from nearly any fate, if allowed—but there would be nothing of *her* left to be saved.

Clare closed her eyes against the memories that were now only too eager to return to her, but the physical action did nothing to staunch the flow of images that followed, blood and bloated corpses rioting behind her eyelids. The memory of something inside her snapping as she disconnected from herself, because it was that or die or let the Song have control. The scent of swamp water hit the back of her throat and she retched again.

Two years. She'd lost two years to the madness in that swamp.

And if Verol and Marquin hadn't come along when they did…she didn't think she would ever have found her way back.

Clare scraped her hair from her face as the dry heaves abated. Her mouth tasted of acrid sand. She stumbled to the washbasin and stared at her reflection in the small oval mirror above it, eyes rimmed a harsh red and filled with a short but bitter lifetime of knowledge. Few things were uglier than knowledge, and Clare so hated ugly things. Hated them, and yet her life seemed destined for them.

She dipped a towel into the washbasin and dabbed it at her eyes, at her slightly puffy cheeks. She stared straight into the green irises looking back at her, unblinking, until the knowledge and the ugliness faded.

Her face blank, Clare took every emotion writhing inside her and imagined slipping each one into a bag, then cinching the bag closed tight. She envisioned a well, cold and dark and deep, so deep that if one dropped a boulder into it, one might listen for days and never hear it hit water.

Down this well Clare tossed the bag, and as emotion fled her, so did the remnant powers of the Song.

CHAPTER

TWO

THE STRANGE MATTER OF THE DRUNK

An hour before Clare was due to perform, the innkeeper recovered from his exposure to the Song enough to send a maid to her door with a list of songs he expected her to play that evening, and some thinly veiled threats about what would happen to her if her performance embarrassed him. Clare didn't bother to even glance at the list before she crumpled it into a ball and dropped it on the bed.

Even if she was inclined to play whatever Crenn had instructed —which she wasn't—she wouldn't have been able to read the list. The only language she could read was music, notes and lines and melodies, and letting anyone know of this deficit in her knowledge didn't appeal. Besides, only a fool tried to pick a musician's set *for* them. Crenn's was probably full of overly complex, classical pieces he thought would impress a duke's nephew. But since Clare's memory served that the man in question was barely nineteen winters—somewhere in the vicinity of her own age, though she didn't know hers for certain—she suspected pretty classical music would bore him to tears.

And angering the innkeeper was far less of a concern than boring the audience. She didn't care what Crenn tried to do to her at the end of the performance, because he didn't matter. *They* did, and she needed every single one to end the night in love with her.

Needed them to talk about her and *keep* talking, because she needed another engagement after this one, and another after that.

She surveyed her meager dressing options, though there was little point; she only had the one option. A dark green gown embellished with silver embroidery that cinched tight at the waist. She hated it, and the thought of putting it on again…

She'd never intended to wear it, had brought it because it was fine enough that she could trade it for something else. But she'd had no opportunity to make such a trade on the journey here, and now this was the only presentable thing she had to wear.

Appearances mattered, a fact that irritated Clare to no end, for one of her first lessons in life had been that appearances held no intrinsic value. The body one was born with and how one chose to dress it gave no true insight to the soul, held no moral value, and yet it was by these things that one was judged.

But because they *did* matter, she gritted her teeth and put the dress on, tightening the strings that ran down both sides of the gown's bodice, straightening it by feel rather than sight. She didn't look at herself in the mirror as she picked up her guitar and went downstairs.

The stage in the common area was small yet tastefully decorated, and Clare immediately realized she had a problem. The acoustics in the room were terrible, and the inn had no voice crystal. Likely because any member of the Musicians Guild would travel with their own.

She took the small stool on the stage and started warming up, strumming through a series of notes and chords and simple melodies. There was hardly anyone in the room—just the drunk from earlier, who looked a little less bleary-eyed, and a handful of others—but her heart fluttered with nerves anyway and her stupid fingers wanted to tremble.

She closed her eyes and lost herself in sounds as her fingers found a familiar pattern, strumming a song that had no words and never would, because it was *hers*, and like her it was always changing. It had started as a simple thing when all she knew how to do was hum it inside her mind, because giving it actual voice was too dangerous. Had morphed into something she'd clumsily picked out in single notes on her first guitar, an instrument so broken it barely deserved the name.

Had grown now into *this*, something intricate and yet clear, chaotic and yet grounded, and as she played it changed again, gaining a new layer of depth born from her nervousness. She gave that feeling to the song, and as her fingers wove it into the music, it left her body, the pulse of her heart evening out, the unsteadiness in her hands disappearing. She played until this new part of her had found its place in the song of her life and, when she was ready, she let the notes fade out.

Silence greeted her. Not the absence of people talking, but the pure silence that came from a frozen world. And when she opened her eyes, she discovered the world had indeed gone still. Every eye was trained on her, from the innkeeper and the drunk at the bar, to the group of five men who'd halted at the bottom of the stairs, as if mesmerized, and that—that ability to enrapture, to ensnare—*that* was power.

Her shoulders straightened and her muscles relaxed. She let a soft, slow smile spread across her face, and greeted her world. "Hello. I'm Clare Brighton."

CLARE PLAYED FOR HOURS. Each song drew someone new into the inn, until the common area was packed and people had spilled out into the halls. Crenn was doing a brisk enough business behind the bar—with three women now in the fray with him, serving drinks— that she expected to hear nothing from him on her failure to play his song choices.

She played anything and everything, songs that had dug their way out of her soul over every year she had survived, songs born of hope and fear and determination. She sang plenty of common tunes, interspersed with her own, but it was *hers* the crowd came alive for and she...she hadn't realized how much she'd needed that acceptance until she had it. Hadn't realized the dark void inside her could be sated by their attention. It didn't matter that they didn't know *her* and never would. It only mattered that they stood before the stage that was her altar and worshipped.

She finished her current song and reached for the glass on the little table by her stool. The table had appeared by way of a serving woman when someone from the crowd had bought her a drink. It had been ale, so she hadn't drank it, but once the guests realized she didn't drink alcohol the offers had turned to sweetwater and iced teas, and she hadn't wanted for a beverage all evening.

The ice alone—so common in Veralna and so scarce in a place like her own Renault County—would have made the evening worth her effort. And yet she'd gotten so much more. The crowd called for another song—just one more—even as the first of the night's warning bells rang, alerting Veralna's citizens that it was only one hour until the city's curfew laws went into effect. Her fingers itched to touch the strings again, to give the crowd that one more song. But that need—to give what they asked for and bask in their adoration—felt a little too much like dependence.

So instead she told them her name one more time and slipped off the stage, confident that by tomorrow afternoon enough word would have spread of her to gain her an engagement—and a room—at another inn. This one a little further into the *good* part of Midtown. She could see it lining up for her, moving further up in the city day by day, until she caught the right eye. It wouldn't take much—playing the right festival, the right noble's nameday celebration, could be enough to grant her the firm foothold she needed in society.

She dodged invitations to talk, avoiding them with the little smile she knew would make her look either playful or shy, rather than rude, her gaze trained cautiously on the bar. Leaning against the end of it, where he'd been all night, was guardsman Moretz. He'd stared at her with an eerie focus all evening, and she knew the look. Earlier, she'd been a fun distraction for a petty man who liked to feel important. Now he'd heard her play and that pettiness had morphed into something darker, something that was predatory in a different way. It was desire and possessiveness, in the way so many broken people seemed to want beauty and grace only to hold it in their hands and destroy it.

His gaze didn't stray from her as she walked, and when he pushed off the bar and took a step toward her she stopped and turned, passing a smile and a hello with a girl who had danced every song of Clare's set, whether she'd had a partner or no. She was a plain girl but her smile and that energy that beat from her was extraordinary. Clare found it easy to keep up a discourse with her and it was…strange and heady, how special it seemed to make the girl feel that, of all the people in the room, Clare had stopped to talk with *her*. Clare's attention had never been that important to anyone before. It had been commanded and demanded, but it had never been…cherished.

The feeling was so unsettling that the second Moretz's eyes slipped off Clare she made her excuses and turned quickly around the corner, moving past the kitchens and down a service hallway. But once out of Moretz's line of sight she couldn't stop herself from pausing to look back at the girl.

Something harsh and savage bit into Clare's chest and she realized, with unwelcome clarity, that it was envy. Envy, because the girl looked carefree and happy, as if her life was an easy, simple affair, and in this moment Clare was tempted to settle for easy and simple. But her life had never been either, and no passing temptation could lead her to settling.

Besides, looks were so often deceiving. Give the girl an hour, a day, a year, and she wouldn't be carefree or happy anymore. Nothing lasted forever.

Clare turned from the girl and the emotions she'd stirred, moving further down the hallway. Six feet from the stairs she passed a window, soft light spilling out, and her eye caught on a familiar form within. The drunk from the bar lay on a small couch in what was probably Crenn's office, snoring away at a volume easily heard through the walls, his hand cuffed to a rail above.

So this was where he'd ended up, then. About halfway through Clare's set, the man had picked a harmless enough fight with the Duke of Merlain's nephew. She'd have wondered at him having the bad sense to choose a minor noble, of all people, to engage in misbehavior with, if she hadn't seen a brief flash of silver slip from noble to drunk during the fight, one that had disappeared quickly enough into the latter's pocket.

A drunk, yes. But one that was adept at thieving. Something about it didn't add up to Clare, in the way something about his snoring from inside the room also bothered her. She just couldn't place her finger on what precisely the irritation was. Nor had she expected to have the chance to find out. The duke's nephew, in a fit of kindness uncommon to the nobility, hadn't wanted to press charges, just wanted the man thrown out. Crenn had, of course, loudly objected to letting go of what he perceived to be a major grievance. In all likelihood he'd tried to get Moretz to arrest him and Moretz, being off duty for the evening, had refused.

So now the drunk was here, languishing in Crenn's office until the innkeeper convinced Moretz to do something with him.

Clare eyed the door and its lock. She could pick it easily enough. No more than a few seconds and she would be inside, and whatever it was about this situation that didn't make sense and tugged at her could be solved. But opening the door brought risk—the risk of being caught once inside, the risk of inviting suspicion if someone came across her while she was at the door. She could not afford suspicion.

She swallowed down her curiosity and left. She was halfway up the stairs to her room before she realized what it was about the drunk's snoring that had bothered her so. It had been too perfect, too much precisely what one expected to hear when one said the word "snore." It was so real that it lacked reality.

She turned the thought over in her mind as she slipped into her room. It wasn't a particularly small room but it *felt* small, the way all enclosed spaces felt to her, the walls seeming to grow closer the longer she stayed within them. The window to the outside beckoned and she went to it, pushing the glass panes open, exhaling in a rush as the evening air drifted inside. The breeze was frigid but she drank it gratefully, even as it teased at the annoying wisps of hair near the front of her scalp that were forever too long to simply cut away, and too short to remain tethered in any hairstyle.

The night air caressed and enticed, calling to the wildness in her. Clare wanted to be down on the streets with it, running until her muscles ached, then further until the ache in her muscles stretched into her bones, so that by the time she returned to her rooms she wouldn't need to hide her feelings down an imaginary well because she would be too exhausted to feel anything at all.

She let the dream go with the next sigh of the wind and set about pulling off her dress. She did it with her eyes closed, so she didn't have to see it, and wished she couldn't *feel* the texture of the fabric as she carefully rolled it into a bundle that wouldn't wrinkle and shoved it into the case with her guitar.

Her pants and tunic from earlier that evening might have the dirt of travel permanently ground into the fabric, but they felt cleaner than the dress. More honest, even if Clare didn't necessarily appreciate the honesty they told. Crossing to the window, she leaned her head out and looked down just as the final curfew bell rang.

The streets were empty save for the occasional carriage—Veralna's nobility were exempt from the curfew, as was any family with enough money to pay the exorbitant fee for an annual exemption. The office the drunk had been locked in was on the same side of the inn as her own room, and she'd seen that the interior window in the office had an exterior twin.

A culmination of thoughts and desires led her to swing her leg out the window and carefully climb her way down the wall. The stones of its facade, conveniently staggered unevenly for aesthetic appeal, provided far better handholds than she required. It wasn't that Clare particularly cared about the drunk. While he *had* ironically been the one to deduce she didn't drink alcohol, and his purchase of an iced tea for her the only reason the rest of the crowd understood to make the switch, that wasn't enough to endear him to Clare on any meaningful level. Wasn't enough to make her risk being caught breaking curfew.

It wasn't even that she felt sorry for him. He had gotten himself into this mess, and her capacity for sorrow required a great deal more to stir than a once-wealthy drunk fallen on hard times. Nor was it entirely that the drunk's disappearance would anger Crenn and perhaps, by extension, Moretz.

No, mostly it was Clare's curiosity that had her nimbly working her way to the office window. It was those things about the drunk that didn't add up in her mind, that too-perfect snoring. She might not learn anything from him for letting him free, but then...she just might.

She was ten feet from the ground when the creak and rattle of another windowpane opening made her freeze. Carefully, she looked down. The drunk climbed out of the window, looking remarkably nimble for a man who had been drinking heavily since well before the evening bell. He dropped the five feet from the window's sill to the ground, landing in the alleyway below without a trace of a stumble.

He walked away in a drunken zigzag-pattern, but having witnessed his graceful exit from the window, Clare saw the zigzag as just that—a pattern. His bothering to keep up the pretense, and the slow, careless manner in which he did it, told her another thing about him that didn't add up. Her supposedly broke-enough-to-steal-from-nobility drunk could afford a curfew exemption.

The decision to follow him was not a decision at all. Curiosity called her, and no threat of guardsmen or city curfews could keep her from knowing what secrets this man hid. Secrets were decent enough currency, and had too often been the only currency Clare could put her fingers on. Not that they had helped much, in the end.

She waited until the drunk rounded the corner of the next building then quickly finished her descent. She hit the ground and ran quietly for the alley corner, confident the man would not be too far ahead given his dedication to his feigned drunkenness.

It only took two blocks for Clare to grow irritated at the slow pace, and she wondered that he kept to the act despite the fact she had not seen a single soul about to witness it. Clare herself had none of the innate patience of the predator stalking her prey but managed, as she managed most things in life, by sheer stubbornness.

The lack of guards on their path made her suspect he knew their night patrols, because they traveled at least a mile into Lowtown before the man rambled into an inn. She counted the time in her head she estimated it would take him to reach a room, then circled the building, waiting for a magelight to flicker on in one of the windows. When it did, she was surprised to find the light on the second floor, having thought such a man would take a room on the first for ease of entry and escape. But perhaps he preferred the greater privacy afforded by the higher level.

Determined not to let a matter of height waste her evening's work, Clare looked for a way up the smooth walls and found it almost immediately, for a drainpipe was secured next to his window ledge. She wondered at its ready availability—if he'd chosen his room because the pipe could provide a quick escape should he need one, or if he'd simply been careless. Or perhaps he hadn't considered it too much of a risk, since it took a certain amount of practice and determination to shimmy up a drainpipe, and a fair bit more of both to do the task quietly. In short, it was a skill few sane people bothered to cultivate.

Clare Brighton knew all too well that she was *not* particularly sane. She shimmied up the drainpipe and out onto the window's ledge, peering through a gap in the window's curtains just in time to see the drunk, looking very much sober and collected, remove a slim silver tube—the item stolen from the duke's nephew?—from his pocket and unroll a small slip of paper from inside. She could just make out red ink on the page.

The man read, and his lips twisted in distaste. He did not bother to re-read, as people so often did when they learned bad news, but simply rolled the paper back inside the small silver tube, storing it inside a cleverly hidden compartment of a leather case of men's travel accessories.

Item hidden, he went to work with the case's accessories. First, he removed the grayed beard on his face to reveal the smooth, unblemished skin of a man in his early twenties. The long, lank hair came away next, revealing a slightly shorter crop of silky black, untouched by gray, that fell just past his chin. And the eyes, when he wiped away the yellow staining beneath that had given his skin its dull pallor, were a brown dark enough to be nearly black.

His face, shorn of its disguise, was now completely at odds with the rest of his middle-aged body. This mystery lifted when he removed his shirt, the garment cleverly padded to give its wearer the appearance of added weight. His torso was lean and lined with the sort of subtle, practical muscle garnered from activities like shimmying up drainpipes.

Clare might have spent half the night staring into the room, retrieving more pieces of this interesting new puzzle, had the man not suddenly frowned and strode to the window, twitching the gap in the curtains closed.

Mercifully, he did not look out.

Quiet and nimble, Clare descended the drainpipe, wondering just what in Ferrian's hells she had stumbled onto this evening.

CHAPTER

THREE

KINTHING

Rain pounded against the carriage window, stirring up the old ache in Verol's left knee as the carriage thundered down the empty night streets. Marquin felt that ache, as if it were his own, through the heartstone that glowed red within the clutches of his ebony staff. He rolled the staff idly between his hands as Verol's tension poured through it, Marquin's own tension kept at bay by the ruthless practicality that had seen him through his forty-eight winters on this planet.

On the bench seat across from him, Verol let out a string of curses. It always surprised people that, of the two of them, Verol was the one with the filthy mouth. Marquin waited until Verol was finished with his litany of insults to the night and commented, wryly, "I thought *I* was supposed to be the pessimistic one in this relationship."

Verol shoved a curtain of long silver-blond hair out of his eyes, and Marquin had a feeling he was on the verge of finally cutting it all off, like he'd been threatening to do for years. Hair out of the way, he leveled *that* look at Marquin, the one that said Quin was being intentionally obtuse. "It isn't a matter of pessimism. She's in danger." The howling wind rattled the carriage, adding emphasis to the growl in Verol's words.

"If she is, then we will reach her before it strikes." Marquin's voice held the calm born from thirty years of following where

Verol's instincts led. If Quin did not remain calm, Verol would lose all semblance of restraint.

"There is no if. She's in danger."

Through the heartstone, Quin felt the Kinthing roaring the certainty of that danger in Verol's chest. It did not like the thought of the girl in danger, liked Verol speaking of it even less. In the Kinthing's mind, the young woman Verol and Marquin had shared the last two weeks of their trip back to Veralna City with already belonged to its circle. She was the Kinthing's to protect, and it *would* protect her. It had failed, once, to protect one of its children, and Verol had been too heartbroken afterward to hear the call of any others who needed him.

Until now. Until they had found a near-feral young woman on the edges of the Valedon Swamps, a woman whose eyes had at times seemed to bore right through him, as if she was made of fire and could set the world alight with a single touch. He'd watched her claw her way back to civility with each passing day of their journey, until she had gone from a barefoot, half-wild thing to someone who spoke and held herself as if she were the daughter of a duchess, someone who could make herself look regal in nothing but tattered clothes and Verol's spare boots.

The effect had been…disturbing.

"I'm sorry," Verol gritted out. "It hasn't gripped me this strong since…" He didn't finish the sentence. He didn't have to.

It hadn't gripped him this strong since Marie. Twenty years dead and Verol still couldn't speak the child's name.

Marquin's hand tightened on the heartstone staff, the deep black of the wood only the barest shade darker than his skin. The heartstone, held in place at the top by thin veins of silver, flickered again, this time with Marquin's anger and concern.

He wished, not for the first time, that Verol had been born without the Kinthing inside him. Wished, with an uncharitableness he had not felt since he was a much younger man, that they had never met the woman at the edges of the swamp.

Ferrian's hells. Verol wouldn't survive another Marie.

"I never should have let her go," Quin's husband was saying. "I knew it wasn't safe for her, I felt it."

Marquin snorted. "Sympathetic as I am, a wall of horses could not hold that young woman if she did not wish to be held."

Clare Brighton had been a force unto herself. Half the time when Marquin looked into her eyes it was as if something besides *her* looked back at him as well. Something dark and ancient and endless. Something Marquin was very much afraid he knew the nature of.

"I could have explained," Verol insisted.

"Explained what? That you have a magic entity inside you that claims certain people as its hoard, and so now you cannot leave her alone until you are certain she is safe?"

"Family, not hoard."

Marquin made a dismissive noise. "*You* call it family. Your magic simply calls it 'mine'. And trying to explain that to a woman only works if you are roughly her age, have smoldering dark eyes, the body of a god, and are madly in love with her."

The faintest hint of mischief flickered through the heartstone before Verol asked, innocently, "You don't think I have the body of a god?"

Marquin barely had time to register that Verol had managed an honest-to-Ferrian *joke* in the full thrall of the Kinthing's grip before his husband banged on the roof of the carriage and it jerked to a stop. Through the carriage window they looked up at an inn. A sign hung from its eaves depicting a hawk with a scepter clutched in its talons.

"Here." Verol exhaled harshly. "She's here."

"Wait." Marquin caught hold of Verol's elbow, refusing to release it until he looked him in the eye. "*How* like Marie is she?"

He regretted the pain that flashed across Verol's face at mention of the girl's name, regretted the resounding tremor than ran through the heartstone in his staff, but the question had to be answered.

"She is exactly like her. Only stronger."

Marquin let go, following Verol out of the carriage. From his perch on the carriage box, Fitz Draven made as if to come with them, but Quin motioned for him to stay. Verol had taken the return of his former apprentice in stride, but Quin still had misgivings about the man, and there were things that had to be said that Verol needed to hear, and Fitz did not. He kept his voice low. "She is twenty winters. Have you considered how she managed to survive this long on her own?"

Verol's jaw clenched. "She is clever."

"Oh, she is that."

"What is the point you wish to make, Quin?" He threw open the door to the inn, thunder rumbling through the heartstone.

Marquin sighed. There was no reasoning with Verol about these things, because there was no reasoning with his magic. Perhaps if Marie hadn't died...

He shook his head. "I mean simply that you may find she is much more like me, than like you. And given what she carries inside her, that is *not* a good thing."

Predicting how people would react to various situations was a skill, one Marquin had honed over the decades, one he prided himself on. All of his knowledge, all of his observation of the human condition, told him that Clare Brighton was not looking for anyone to save her. Unlike little Marie, Clare was not looking for fathers. He suspected she had only accepted their offer to take her to Veralna because she was smart enough to realize she had no other options, and his and Verol's obvious attachment to each other made them rank low as a threat in her eyes.

During the trip she had avoided learning anything about them almost as diligently as she had avoided answering questions about herself. Once through Veralna's gates she had promptly—if politely —abandoned them. She hadn't told them where she was going, nor asked where they were going, and her attempt to return the boots Verol had given her for the trip told Quin she disliked even the possibility of being indebted to someone.

Whatever danger they were about to rescue her from, she wouldn't thank them for it. Or rather, she probably *would*, in a brisk, efficient manner that pointed out she hadn't *asked* for rescuing and therefore didn't owe anything for it.

Then she would disappear on them, and Marquin would be left with the difficult task of explaining to the upset magic overriding Verol's rational senses that her leaving was a perfectly reasonable reaction.

CHAPTER

FOUR

AN UNWELCOME GUEST

Returning to her room took Clare twice as long as leaving had, because she had to spend chunks of the journey hiding from the night patrolmen now sweeping the previously empty streets. It convinced her more than ever that the not-drunk had known the guard rotation. When a light rain began falling, soaking through her clothes and chilling her skin to a numbing point, she wished *she* knew the guard rotation.

She took a few alternate streets when she felt confident in doing so, but she didn't know this city, and retracing her steps was the only sure way of finding her way back to the Hawk and Scepter. But she didn't mind the wait, the distraction, even the fear of getting caught. Fear, and the fine edge of danger that hovered by her throat and sometimes nicked her skin, was the most constant thing in her life. Its return settled her in a way the safety of the past two weeks had not. As if her baseline of normal was so far from other people's that she didn't know how to exist without the constant rush of danger.

After rubbing warmth into her fingers, she scaled the wall to her room, finding the handholds easily, the climb soothing. She'd always liked climbing, had never had a fear of heights. There were so many other things to be afraid of that a simple matter of height seemed a silly one to worry over. And at least when she climbed, the possibility of her death was in her control. Her skill, her nerve, her determination. Once, she'd descended the cliffs at the northern end of Renault County to Siren's Cove, just to see the skeletons of ship-wrecked hulls there, and to wonder if it wouldn't be better to stand on the rocky outcropping and let the salt spray numb her until she fell asleep and never woke again.

After a few hours, she'd climbed back up, her fingers so numb she almost hadn't made it. And then, for years after, she'd *wished* she hadn't. But by then the stubborn streak in her was too well-defined, and she'd refused to die out of sheer defiance.

She reached the open window of her inn room and froze. Guardsman Moretz sprawled across her bed, a wine bottle dangling from his fingertips, spilling a drop or two of red liquid onto the cream bedspread.

Clare could climb back down, could do it quietly enough that Moretz wouldn't wake. But while she might escape with her life—provided she remained hidden from the night patrols until morning—her life alone was not worth much. Everything she owned was in this room. Her *guitar* was in this room. Without it she might as well be dead.

Dead, or lost to the madness again.

For all that the night's payment—the two silvers tucked into her breastband—were more money than she'd ever possessed, they weren't enough to replace the guitar. And even if they were, she... couldn't leave it. She had the absurd notion that her soul was somehow bound within its wooden frame, woven into the metal strings, and if she lost it there might be nothing of her left. There was so little of her to begin with—so little that was truly *her*. She couldn't lose this, too.

She grasped the window ledge and swung herself inside, light and silent. Moretz didn't move. Clare's fingers crept to the inside of her left boot, to the knife hidden between the outer shell of leather and the soft inner lining. It was a near invisible opening, this makeshift sheath, the edges sewn carefully so they wouldn't continue to fray, the stitching decorative. A useful thing she'd been pleased to find in a pair of boots not originally her own, though she doubted it had been made to hold a blade.

The one she'd slipped into the opening only fit because it wasn't what most people would think of as a knife, wasn't sharpened steel melded into a thick, clunky hilt. It was a short, thin strip of bone honed to a sharp point. True knives could be wrapped in the elegant artistry of their making, could be things of such beauty and craftsmanship that people forgot what their purpose was.

There was no forgetting the purpose of the bone knife in Clare's hand. For a moment she simply stood there, staring at the rise and fall of Moretz's chest and thinking how very easy it would be to end him. She had no doubt of precisely what he had come to her room *for*.

But the cold calculations always running behind her eyes reminded her that he would bleed straight through the mattress, and while she might manage to hide a body, she didn't know how she could hide *that*.

Get her guitar, get out the window, hide until morning. It would have to be enough. Her hand curled into a tighter fist around the bone. It *wasn't* enough.

But someday it would be. Someday her life wouldn't be...*this*. She clung to the thought, even as a part of her whispered that maybe it never changed. Maybe, no matter how high she climbed, the situation would always be the same. She culled that whisper of doubt almost the second it appeared.

Things would be different. She would *make them* be different.

She crept across the floor on silent feet. Her guitar case was already packed out of habit. All she had to do was grab it and she could be gone.

Moretz let out a loud snore and jerked in his sleep. The wine bottle slipped from his fingers and hit the ground with a loud *thunk*. He jolted upright, his eyes snapping open.

He didn't notice the wine bottle, or the quick movement as she slipped the hand holding the bone knife behind her back. His gaze went to her face, as if he hadn't even realized he'd fallen asleep, and thought he'd been vigilantly waiting for her all this time.

"We-ell," he slurred, "look who decided to wander in." He lifted his hand to his mouth and he did notice the wine bottle was gone then.

"What are you doing in here?" It wasn't that she didn't know. It was that part of her wanted him to say it. Because now that he was awake, there was only one way this was ending, the consequences be damned to Ferrian's hells.

Never again. I said never again.

Moretz's eyes narrowed in that way particular to men when they didn't like a woman's tone. "You're a smart-mouthed little bitch." He reached for the wine bottle on the floor and hurled it at her. It was a calm sort of violence with which Clare was well-acquainted.

She didn't flinch, didn't move, didn't even breathe. The drunken toss sent the bottle wide of her and it broke open against the wall, shards of glass and red droplets raining down. But even if the toss hadn't gone wide, even if the bottle had flown straight at her face, she wouldn't have flinched then, either. Because there was a power in stillness, too, in refusing to bend.

Men like Moretz thrived on forcing reactions, on feeling people like her cringe, or struggle, or fight. So she stared him down calmly, knowing her eyes were dead and empty to him, lacking the fear he craved, and that that lack would frustrate him beyond reason. He wanted a reaction. And while she would give him one, it was one he wouldn't see until it was too late.

He rose from the bed, taking shuffling steps until he was close enough she could scent the sour mix of wine and ale on his breath.

"You got a pretty voice for all those songs." His words slurred together at the end, a nearly unintelligible stream. "An' as holdings whores go, you ain't bad to look at."

Clare adjusted her grip on the bone shard. It was more difficult than most people realized to stab a man in the heart. To do it effectively, the angle had to be just right, slipping between ribs and up into the muscle. She knew just where to strike, but satisfying as it would be, the bone shard in her hand wasn't long enough to handle the matter. She was better off going for a gut wound. That, or the carotid. Less satisfying, but more…dead.

She settled on the carotid while his drunken ramblings devolved into a string of syllables she didn't think formed actual words. When he tired of talking and made a lunge for her, she struck.

CHAPTER

FIVE

THE LORDS ARRENDON

Clare's blade never reached its target. The door to her room flew open, wood splintering as the lock gave, and Moretz was jerked back. Clare herself stumbled, as there was suddenly no body to absorb the force of her thrust, the bone knife cleaving only empty air.

It took her a moment longer than it should have to accept the scene before her, because it made so very little sense. A tall, lean man with pale skin and a waterfall of straight blond hair loomed over Moretz.

"Verol?" She had never had occasion to sound so incredulous in her life, but she couldn't fathom how one of the men she'd traveled to Veralna City with had come to bust down her door.

"Are you all right?" Verol didn't take his eyes off Moretz as he directed the question at her, and there was an edge to his voice that said he was on the verge of violence. He had not struck her as a violent man.

She nodded in response, her eyes catching on fresh movement in the doorway as a man with dark skin, his frame wide and corded with muscle, stepped into the room. He carried a black staff with a glowing red stone clutched by silver tendrils at its apex, and he stopped in between her and Verol.

"I think," Marquin said, his voice a deep rumble, "it would be helpful if you could *tell* him that you are all right."

It seemed an unnecessary request, until she understood that something was not quite right with Verol. The air around him felt heavy and charged, like the air just before a storm hit, and that was when she realized that not only was Verol's boot pressing down on Moretz's throat, it was doing so forcefully enough the man couldn't breathe.

Clare didn't particularly give a damn whether he could breathe, given the situation, but if Verol killed him...hiding a body and pretending nothing had happened would be a great deal more difficult now that her door was broken and the crack of it happening had likely woken the entire hall.

How in Ferrian's hells were they going to get out of this mess?

Moretz tried to cough and couldn't, his hands flailing ineffectually at Verol's boot. It irked her to have to intercede on his behalf, even if it was, in the end, really on *her* behalf. She sighed and told Verol, "I am fine."

The air around him stopped being silent with such ferocity that it stole breath. He lifted his boot and Moretz rolled onto all fours, coughing and spluttering. He sucked in three breaths that sounded excruciatingly painful. He found enough air to wail in outrage as he gained his feet. "You dare attack—" He cut off abruptly as his eyes met Verol's. Interestingly, his face blanched of all color, and he practically fell down in his haste to bow. "L-Lord Arrendon?"

Lord?

Marquin stepped forward. It put him at Verol's side and slightly in front of Clare. She couldn't decide if he was supporting Verol, shielding her, or both.

Moretz's gaze shifted to Marquin, and while he didn't have any color left to lose, his lips pinched together as he bowed again. "*Lords* Arrendon."

There went that "L" word again, and Clare took in the two men's appearances anew. They were much better dressed than they had been on the road, their clothes finer. Traveling, she had recognized they were well-off, as their clothing and supplies were all of good quality, if plain, their wagon was in impeccable condition, and their horses were happy and well-fed. But certainly nothing about their dress or behavior had said *lords.*

Not in the way their bearing and the gold stitching running

down Verol's coat arms now did. Not in the way neither of them batted so much as an eyelash at Moretz deferring to them.

Clare's gaze narrowed on the guardsman. He was, she realized, *terrified*. And she thought it had more to do with Verol, specifically, than it did with simply being in the presence of aristocracy. Having addressed the two of them, he now seemed at a loss to say anything else.

When it became clear he would not fill the silence, Verol did. "What are you doing in this young woman's room?"

"She—I—that is, I had reason to believe she was involved in a crime. You…know her, my lord?"

"A potential apprentice of mine."

That was a pretty lie Clare hadn't expected. Apprentice to what, precisely? The words had the effect of making Moretz lose any fortitude he'd managed to regain.

"What crime is she meant to have committed?" Marquin asked.

"It was only an inquiry, my lord. A matter of a shop burglary."

Verol's gaze hadn't once left Moretz since he'd come into the room, and it did not do so even now, as he asked, "Clare?"

"He questioned me about it earlier, when I explained that since the burglary occurred last night, and I was still traveling with you and Marquin at the time, I couldn't possibly be responsible." She waited a beat, decided that, yes, Moretz *did* deserve the verbal knife driven in further and added, "I also believe the suspect was described as a man."

Verol's expression went practically glacial. Soon, she would require an explanation for precisely what the "Lords Arrendon" were doing in her room, and why they were defending her, but for the moment, she chose to enjoy the fact that it was happening.

"Clare explained this to you and yet you still felt the need to… investigate?"

"She didn't say she was traveling with *you*, my lords."

And thank Ferrian's fire she hadn't. She remembered that impulse she'd had to give Moretz their names earlier. If she'd told him that she'd traveled here with two lords, he would never have believed her.

"I don't believe our names should have been necessary," Verol growled. "Nor do I believe it should have been necessary, if you questioned her earlier, for you to do so again late at night, in her room, alone."

Verol advanced on the guardsman and Marquin put a gentle, restraining hand on his arm. Verol halted, but the fury on his face did not abate.

Moretz took the intercession and scrambled to explain. "She broke curfew, Lord Arrendon."

"I see. So you found her wandering the streets and, instead of arresting her, brought her back to her room?" The dangerous edge in Verol's voice intensified.

"N-no. I came here to question her and she was gone. Look at her, she's soaked from the rain."

"Miss Brighton?" Marquin asked mildly. It was the kind of mild that politely suggested she lie through her teeth. As if she needed the prompting.

"I love the rain. I opened the window to see it and then *he* came in." She let a tremble enter her voice. "He didn't even knock and I" —she shivered, rubbing her arms— "I was so startled I almost fell out."

Verol appeared barely to hear her, Marquin looked like he was trying desperately not to laugh—she'd had the suspicion, on the road, that he saw right through every lie she told—and Moretz was gaping at her, like it had never occurred to him that she could lie and be believed over him. Because it likely *hadn't* occurred to him. He was the one accustomed to telling the lies and being believed.

She watched that glint of pure hatred surge in his eyes before he remembered that she was—apparently—Verol's potential new apprentice to *something*, and snarling that she was a lying bitch wasn't in his best interests.

He went back to ignoring her and went with a pleading tone to the men. "She left through the window. I watched her come back in that way as I waited."

Marquin laughed. It was a low and dangerous sound, reminding Clare of the jaguars that prowled the marshes. "Surely you do not expect us to believe that this young woman climbed out the window from two stories up? Much less that she climbed back in that way?"

"I..." Moretz looked from Verol to Marquin, finding no sympathy in either face. The word of even the lowest lord would overrule a street guardsman.

Power, Clare thought. The only story that mattered was the one told by the person in the room with the most power. It was a lesson she'd learned at an early age, but she'd never been in a position to benefit from it before. It was a heady feeling, knowing you didn't really even have to pretend that a lie was the truth, just let it roll off your tongue and wait for everyone around you to trip over themselves in their eagerness to proclaim you correct.

"What is your name?" Verol asked the guardsman.

"M-Moretz, my lord."

"And does anyone else know you are here, Moretz?"

"No."

"How did you gain entry to this room?"

Moretz paled, and a few seconds passed before he answered. Before something *made* him answer, a thin tendril she could barely sense stretching from Verol to Moretz.

A mage, then. She'd suspected. Between the red stone in Marquin's staff that practically screamed magic, and the glow she sometimes caught from Verol—one she was certain most people couldn't see, one that had drawn her out of a swamp and to their campfire—of *course* she'd suspected. But she hadn't known, and while she hadn't known, she could pretend.

Mages. She suddenly understood just what sort of potential apprentice she was supposed to be. Fear worked its way under her breastbone, but Verol and Marquin…they couldn't *know*. Not about the Song that even now laughed within the confines of its prison, the ripples leaking out through the hairline fractures in the cage walls.

They couldn't know. The apprentice nonsense was just that, an excuse, except…except why were they here? *How* were they here? The answer to that question was vitally more important than it had been minutes before.

Something touched her elbow and she jerked, whirling on instinct and slashing out with the bone knife still in her hand.

Marquin slid out of the path of her weapon with liquid grace. He didn't so much as raise an eyebrow at her attack.

"I'm sorry if I startled you. But I was saying I think it would be best if we waited downstairs."

Clare's gaze flicked to Verol and Moretz. The one was glaring murder at the other, and since Verol and Marquin were both lords and mages, she no longer felt it her responsibility to be worried about them facing the repercussions of any actions they might take.

She gathered her guitar case and followed Marquin out. She'd expected the noise of the door breaking to have woken other guests, but the hallways were empty, her path down unlit stairs guided only by the red glow from Marquin's staff. She stared at the stone as they descended the steps. There was something...not entirely natural about it. Not even natural by mage standards.

The main floor was dimly lit as well, the night clerk slumped over at the bar. She cleared her throat. The clerk didn't move. Marquin stopped and she arched an eyebrow at him, nodding at the clerk. He shrugged innocently and headed for the door, which was when Clare realized he had no intention of waiting within the inn's confines for Verol to finish...whatever it was Verol was doing.

Marquin pushed the door open, revealing a waiting carriage on the road beyond, its driver sitting casually, as if the torrential rain didn't bother him. Marquin looked back, marking her hesitation. "I feel it would be best if we did not linger and draw notice. The carriage will not go anywhere without your permission. We may, of course, simply wait outside, however..."

However, the rain was coming down in sheets now and if she *did* actually like the rain, she wasn't keen on standing in it until her skin pruned and her guitar ruined. She glanced around the empty interior of the inn. Thus far, Marquin and Verol had done the impossible and not drawn attention. She would prefer it remained that way.

She nodded and walked briskly to the carriage, which was notably finer than the wagon she'd traveled in with them. But the mismatched horses pulling it—a stocky bay and a palomino—were the same. The bay nickered at her. She might have had a habit of feeding it the sugar cube that was meant for her tea each morning on the road.

She climbed inside the carriage without further hesitation. It wasn't that she trusted Marquin and Verol—she liked them well enough, but trust was another matter—it was that she trusted in her ability to run, if necessary, and the ability of the Song to protect her from magery. Even caged, as it was, what little magic existed in Renault County had had a tendency to simply slide off her. She hadn't been oblivious as to where that protection came from. It made her wonder, sometimes, if she had as much control over the Song as she thought.

The cushions padding the carriage benches were so fine they made her uncomfortable. She hid it, but Marquin's warm brown eyes, watching her, flickered as if he noticed. She'd either completely lost her touch, or he was one of those people it was extremely difficult to fool.

Maybe it was hubris that made her suspect the latter, but she settled further into an easy, relaxed manner, as if nothing about the evening was in the least bit troubling, even though every stray sound rasped against her nerves. She was calmly sitting in a carriage as if waiting in the street wasn't dangerous. In Renault County, even someone with the connections to possess a carriage would not be foolish enough to remain idle with it unguarded in the streets.

You aren't in *Renault County,* she reminded herself. *And if you can't get that through your head and stop jumping at every noise, you'll never become anything here.*

She wanted to close her eyes, didn't because she didn't want Marquin to see. She'd been staring him down this whole time, both because it gave her something to focus on, and because she wanted to see if he would blink.

He didn't.

She smiled at him, wide and brilliant, and he offered her an amused shake of his head in return. *Where did you come from, Marquin Arrendon?* Because she would bet the two coins she'd earned tonight that he hadn't been born with the title "lord".

"Why did Verol claim I was his apprentice?" It was the least important of the questions she could have asked, which made it the perfect starting one.

"Verol once had several apprentices. Though he has not had any for some time, your being a new one was yet a plausible enough reason for us to be arriving at your room so late in the evening."

"And why *did* you arrive at my room so late in the evening?"

"That is difficult to explain."

"Did you follow me?"

"No."

"Have me followed?"

"No."

Clare narrowed her eyes when he offered no further information. Silence was a weapon in the right hands, and his were clearly the right hands. She wished she were having this conversation with Verol instead. He was easier to read, had an openness to him that probably caused him no end of grief. Or, more likely, caused Marquin no end of grief. Because while one would always know when Verol was sincere, when he was happy, they would likewise always know when he lied, and when he was so sad he could fill a room with his unhappiness.

Marquin was different. He had been no less kind to her than Verol, but he was more...distant. He was more like *her* than like Verol. More calculating, slower to trust. They were traits she understood and respected, traits that kept a person alive. She was not certain how he and Verol had come to be here, but she was certain that, while Verol's interests upstairs had been in keeping her safe, Marquin's had been in keeping Verol safe. Marquin would help her insofar as helping her helped Verol.

Verol. *He* was Marquin's pressure point. She pasted her sunny smile back on. "You don't want to answer my questions, but I take it you *would* prefer if I waited here for Verol to return."

Marquin didn't answer. Not that she'd expected him to.

"Well, then. If it is of no consequence to you, I'll be on my way." She rose.

"Your guitar will ruin in the rain. That case isn't waterproof."

"I'll bear that concern in mind." She turned and reached for the door handle.

"You'd do it, wouldn't you?" he asked. "Disappear into the rain with nowhere to go, curfew be damned despite what almost happened to you in that room."

What almost happened. It sounded practically civil when he put it like that. So proper and politic. So very *not* what it was. She shoved her anger down and calmly replied. "Of course I would. I've never found a bluff productive. If someone calls it, you either look like a fool, or have to make a choice you didn't want to make. I find ultimatums far more effective."

A soft sound that might have been a laugh escaped him. "That they are. Very well, then. If I explain, you'll wait until Verol returns?"

"Yes."

"It is an…unusual explanation. You may not believe me."

Clare settled onto the bench once more. "How fortunate for you that my belief was not part of our bargain."

He sighed. "I do not suppose you have ever heard of the magic called Kinthing?"

Clare had not heard of much in the way of magery at all. She had gathered what information she could on magic, back when she'd still wanted to know what the thing inside her—the Song—was. But reliable information had been difficult to find in Renault County, and even more difficult to trust.

Still, an answer floated into her mind, as answers sometimes did, even when she was certain she hadn't known them before. "It's some type of familial magic, yes?"

"In a way. Kinthing magic is very specific, almost an entity on its own. At its core, the Kinthing is a protective force. It feels an affinity for those who may be a danger to themselves, or those who are in danger from others, and it pulls the mage who possesses it towards those people." He gave Clare a meaningful look.

She laughed at his suggestion that this Kinthing had dragged Verol and Marquin across the city to *protect* her. "Every person is a danger to themselves. And every person is a danger to everyone else. Safety is an illusion to all but a powerful few. If this Kinthing operated as you say, Verol would never sleep for its constantly dragging him about."

"But there are some who are *more* a danger to themselves, or who are in a different type of danger than others. The Kinthing is… selective. It does not pull him towards everyone."

Tightness gripped Clare's spine and suddenly it was difficult to breathe. Better to be one of a thousand than one *in* a thousand. An unwanted voice rose in her mind, and try as she might, she couldn't shove it down, couldn't stop it from whispering old words.

I am very selective, min quellea. *I am not drawn to everyone.*

A roaring sounded in her ears as her blood pounded, trying to drown out a voice she'd never wanted to hear again. The interior of the carriage and the soft cushions disappeared, replaced by cold walls and concrete floors and the ever-present skitter of things she couldn't see in the darkness.

Not there. She wasn't there, she *wasn't*. But she couldn't remember where she was, and the roaring in her ears was growing louder and louder, and she knew when it grew loud enough it would drown her, and—

"*Clare.*"

Soft warmth heated the cold in her veins and she snapped back to the interior of the carriage. That gentle white glow that had led her out of the swamp two weeks ago filled the carriage, emanating from Verol, his concerned face hovering inches away but he wasn't, thank Ferrian, touching her. The soft glow—was *it* this Kinthing? Was that why she'd been so drawn to it, had been so willing to travel with the two of them?

"Are you all right?"

Her gaze snapped up. Verol's worried green eyes stared back at her.

No, she wasn't *all right*. She needed out of this carriage, away from the warmth of that light and Verol's concern and Marquin's silent judgment, and the lassitude stealing over her that told her she was *safe* here, and she should stay. Away from the contentment seeping out from the Song, that ancient power humming as if this was the best place in all the world for it to be.

"Will the guardsman be an issue?" she asked.

Verol clearly wanted to press the question of whether she was all right, but he didn't. At mention of the guardsman, thunderclouds appeared in his eyes. "He won't remember anything, and he is currently rethinking his choice of professions."

Mindmage, her memory supplied. A Mindmage could mess with a person like that.

"Is he still in my room?"

"No. Are you—"

Her mouth spouted words while her heart beat faster and faster behind her chest, demanding she get away, get out. "Your assistance, though unasked for, is appreciated. I have a long day tomorrow and I'm afraid I need to sleep."

She grabbed her guitar case and flung the carriage door open.

"Have you given *any* practical consideration to how you will—" Verol cut off mid-sentence as she leapt out into the rain. He undoubtedly would have followed, but she heard Marquin's low voice telling him to, "Let her go, Ver. Let her go for now."

For now. As if it was inevitable that she would come back to them.

Inside the inn, the night clerk was still hunched over asleep. She sprinted up the stairs and into her room, checking every inch until she was convinced it was as empty as her soul. The broken door refused to latch. She shoved a chair against it, levering it beneath the handle to hold it closed. It wouldn't keep anyone out, but it would give her warning if anyone tried to enter.

She stared at the room. She wasn't going to sleep tonight. Not on the bed that had turned her stomach even before she'd found Moretz sprawled across it. Not on the floor where broken glass and red wine splattered the floorboards and rug. Not in the bathroom where she'd hurled her stomach up earlier.

Sleep. Ferrian's hells, she wanted to sleep. Sometimes, she thought she hadn't slept in lifetimes, and she wondered if the lack could drive a person mad. If maybe nothing lived inside her at all, and the Song was a figment of her imagination.

It sparked inside its cage, clearly irritated at her dismissal of it. And annoyed that she'd run from Verol and Marquin.

"Be as irritated as you want," she snapped at it. If the Song wanted something, then she didn't. It was as simple as that. It *should* be as simple as that.

So why did she feel...lonely? Why did some part of her wish she hadn't left that carriage? Why did she miss the camaraderie she'd felt on the road, from two people who had never asked anything of her, and only ever helped her?

Because people can't be trusted, answered the practical side that had kept her alive. *Because people are never fully what they appear and the moment you* want *them to be...that's when they are most dangerous to you.*

She found a corner of the room that gave her a good view of the window, the door, and the bathroom, slid down against it and pulled out her guitar. She settled it on her lap, fiddling with strings that didn't need tuning before her fingers found the position she wanted.

She'd passed so many nights, *survived* so many nights, by writing songs in her head she'd never actually played, because she'd only ever wanted to play them for herself. Because they were her soul and she hadn't wanted to give it away.

Now…now she'd give away every last piece of it if it bought her what she wanted. So she strummed the guitar and heard aloud the notes that had only ever existed in her mind and she sang, softly, the words that went with them. Sang and played, until the chaos in her mind went quiet, and the night rolled through to dawn.

CHAPTER

SIX

THE ANSWER TO A QUESTION

Numair Tolvannen had far more urgent things to do than follow a woman he didn't even know through Veralna's Midtown. A fact he reminded himself of more than once as he watched Clare Brighton flit from vendor to vendor as the morning light eventually gave way to early afternoon.

But he was tired, an aching exhaustion that dragged at him every second of every day, and watching her haggle over prices with half the city's vendors while never once buying a thing was distracting in an oddly soothing way. It didn't take away the feeling of enervation that had ridden him the last few years but it did... move him sideways of it.

Let him forget, for a time, as her voice had let him do last night. He'd never heard anyone sing like that. It wasn't her words or the chords she'd strummed or even her voice itself. Someone else with a pretty voice could sing and play the same things, and he wouldn't have felt what he had. It was something about *her*. It was the voice and the words and the songs but it was more. It was in the way she sang, defiance in every line of her body, as if she wanted them all to love her, but she would hate them for it when they did.

And that—that was why he was here, truth told, even if he told himself he followed her because of that hot flame of power that had slipped from her yesterday in the Hawk and Scepter, when her voice had shifted and she'd calmly informed the innkeeper of how honored he would be to have her sing for him...and he had agreed.

What she'd done wasn't unheard of. It was something well-within the abilities of a diamond-ranked Mindmage, but there was only one diamond Mindmage in Veralna, and Clare was *not* Lord Verol Arrendon. Besides which, Numair had seen Verol work and what Clare had done—it was the same end effect, but not the same means of getting there. She was something different, and he didn't know what it meant.

Didn't know where she'd come from, when every mage was required to register with the Mages Guild under Faelhorn law. People slipped through the cracks here and there, defying royal decree, but the only ones who ever managed it long-term were those with minimal ability. Or those who, like himself, had dual abilities of equal power, the one able to mask the other.

She entered the marketplace and he drifted closer to her, absently picking through a display of brightly colored scarves—Ferrian's hells, he was probably going to have to wear something like this soon, they were coming into fashion—while at the next stall over Clare pulled out the dress she'd worn during her performance last night.

And standing this close to her, a handful of feet separating them, he wondered if his sanity was going and he'd imagined the entire encounter with the innkeeper yesterday. Not a single trace of the magic he'd felt from her then escaped her now. There was something else—a soft wash of magic, but it wasn't the storm cloud he'd sensed before.

The scarf merchant asked a question and he answered absently, unable to convince himself he hadn't witnessed what he had at the Hawk and Scepter. Yet the more he watched the woman, the less sense she made to him.

She was finally trading the dress. He'd watched her go back and forth with no less than a dozen other clothing dealers and she'd settled on this one? He respected wanting to get the best bargain for something, but he was certain at least one of the others must have offered her a deal of similar value.

So why this one? Why now? She didn't look tired, as if the morning's efforts had exhausted her and she was taking the deal because it was here and she was tired of haggling. No, her calculating gaze was sweeping over the vendor's wares as she pointed out the garments she clearly meant to have in the dress's place, not a trace of exhaustion in her face.

He ran back through what he'd seen of her that morning. She hadn't only gone to clothing vendors. She'd been through similar bartering exchanges at almost every shop she'd gone into, picking up items and inquiring about prices.

So many shops she'd gone into, yet she'd never bought anything, and the items she'd looked over had little in common. As if she hadn't wanted any of them. As if…as if she had no idea how much anything should cost, and she was gathering a baseline in the most expedient way possible, without revealing to even the most casual passerby the gap in her knowledge.

The certainty of it settled into him. It made as little sense as the power he'd felt that was nowhere to be found in her today. The last of the known world had come under the Jackal King's control eleven years ago, and where the king conquered, his institutions followed. Only one currency remained. There was nowhere she could have lived in the last decade that would prevent her from knowing the value of money…nowhere except one.

His stomach clenched, but he discarded the ludicrous thought as soon as it came into his head. No one had ever left Renault County and lived.

Clare finalized her selections and Numair bought the scarf, turning his back to her. She walked past him a moment later, a careful hand on her purchases, as if she knew precisely the best way to steal from someone walking through a crowd, and therefore precisely the best way to ensure it didn't happen to her.

He should let her walk away. He'd seen nothing this morning to indicate she was anything other than what she appeared. If a Hound from the Mages Guild stood before her, Numair doubted they would sense anything more than that soft wash of power he'd just felt. Nothing dangerous, though they would no doubt take great pleasure in tossing her into indentured servitude in the Mages Guild and charging her a backlog of fees, no matter how insignificant the power she possessed.

That was the law under the Jackal King's rule: every magic was found, every magic was trained, and every magic was known, however unimportant it might be.

Numair meant to leave. His feet followed her instead, through the winding crowd, and when she slipped down an alleyway he went too, as if he didn't damn well know better. He *did* know better, yet he was still surprised when he rounded the corner, the alley stretching empty before him, and an arm came around his shoulders, a blade pressing to his throat, another to his back.

Surprised, but not afraid. It wouldn't be so terrible, to slip away into whatever waited past this life. He hadn't found much good in this one yet.

"WHY ARE YOU FOLLOWING ME?" Clare asked.

She'd had the sense of being watched all morning, but it wasn't until she'd seen him at the scarf display that she'd been certain. He'd looked a little too long through the sheer green slip of fabric he'd even gone so far as to purchase. It dangled carelessly from a bag in his left hand. His fingers hadn't even tightened around it, nor had he tensed up, as if the blades she held to him were of no concern.

He was either extremely confident in his ability to get out of this situation, or the prospect of his own death mattered little to him.

He didn't answer her. She pressed the bone knife more sharply against his back and repeated the question. He shrugged, and something wet and warm trickled over her fingers as his movement sent the tip of the knife at his throat slicing through delicate skin.

His silence woke the anger that always slept just beneath her surface. Because his refusal to answer, his complete lack of concern for the physical danger she held him in—it made her feel helpless. And she hadn't come to this city to feel that way.

The Song perked up for the first time that day, reminding her that *it* could make him talk. That with the Song, she would be in control.

But I wouldn't be.

She would become helpless in *its* grasp, mastery of her life given over yet again to something else. Maybe not right away, but in time, it would consume her. She denied its offer and strengthened the internal song that shored up the walls of its prison.

The man in her grasp remained still, not so much as a twitch of a muscle. No words.

Doubt crept through her. She didn't recognize him—sandy, almost-blond hair and a medium build, his clothes common but well-made—and it made no sense for anyone to be following her. She knew no one here, save Verol and Marquin, and since they were lords, if they had changed their minds about letting her go, they would hardly have needed to hire a man to follow her. A man who, furthermore, was doing his best to impersonate a statue beneath her hands.

A man who still hadn't spoken, and his silence was so easy she wondered if perhaps he couldn't speak. If he was so compliant because he'd learned that, for him, compliance was the safest path out of danger.

Every lesson life had taught her urged her to kill him anyway. That it was safer that way. Except this wasn't Renault County, and the rules that had kept her alive there would not do the same for her here. Not in this city that slumbered under a veneer of civility, where people had attachments and families who would be surprised if they didn't come home rather than surprised if they *did*.

Her fingers twitched, the action to twist the one knife or drive in the other habitual, instinctive.

She dropped the blades and shoved him to the ground, her knee driving into his low back as she twisted his arms behind him. He didn't struggle, though she'd dropped him hard enough his breath came out in a harsh, forced exhale.

"Once," she told him, "we'll call a mistake. I don't want to see you again." She hammered a punch to his throat and he moved *then*, the struggle to suck in air sending him lurching to all fours. Which he could do because Clare was already off him. She spied only one of her knives and swept it up along with her guitar case and then she was running without looking back, the choking noises behind her a soothing assurance that she wouldn't be followed.

When Numair could finally breathe again, he laughed, though his bruised throat protested. Full-on raucous laughter, the kind of unhinged noise one would expect from a madman. Which he very well might be.

He swiped the blade she'd dropped from the ground. It was an odd, primitive thing, and he would wager it was made from bone, though human or otherwise, he couldn't tell. He found himself slipping it into his pocket, a small memento of this moment. Because he'd had a question battering at his head for months, and that blade pressed to his body had finally allowed him to see the answer. The relief coursing through his veins had him nearly high. Not relief that he hadn't died, but relief that he knew what to do.

He had her to thank for that, for the clarity that had come to him. She would never know it, would never understand it, but in that moment, he was indebted to her. He never left his debts unpaid, but he didn't have much time to pay this one.

Five days. Not even a week. He had five days to discover what Clare Brighton wanted and find a way to give it to her.

SEVEN

THE PRICE OF CHASING A DREAM

Three days. That was how much time Clare wasted. Three days of watching her two silver coins turn to lesser ones to pay her lodging and buy her food.

She blamed the damn curfew for the necessity, even if she knew she'd have spent the money anyway. She'd made herself a promise that she would never go back, not willingly, and if she knew how to sleep in the streets and survive, well, that was going back.

So she spent the three days exploring Midtown and learning precisely why she couldn't find another engagement. The Musicians Guild had a stranglehold everywhere from here up to Hightown. The inns wouldn't hire any musician unaffiliated with them, so non-guild members were relegated to playing in the streets and the outdoor spaces, dependent on whatever meager offerings passersby chose to throw their way. Which from Clare's observation wasn't much.

Finally seeing no way around it, she found the guild's office nearest her inn. The clerk sat just inside, a bored-looking middle-aged man with skin so white Clare wondered if he knew the sun existed. She approached the desk. He was scribbling into a notebook and didn't look up.

"I'm here to inquire about membership." The polite words weren't the ones she wanted to say, but they were the ones she made herself speak.

He pointed to a sheet pinned to the wall beside him without ever bothering to actually look at her. "Rates and information are all here."

She glared at the sheet, the letters and numbers swirling together in her mind into a useless mess, and willed the Song to *actually* be helpful. But it was still sulking after her refusal to allow it to help with the man in the alley, and it refused to give her a temporary glimpse into the life of some other person who *had* known how to read.

She stared at the sheet for another minute anyway, willing the scratchings there to make sense. They didn't. Her gaze shifted back to the clerk. "Explain it to me."

He finally looked up from his notebook, disgust on his face. "Fail your way out of primary education, did you?"

Clare smiled. It was her habitual response to almost every situation. If she was sad, she smiled. If she was in pain, she smiled. If something horrified her, she smiled. And if something monumentally pissed her off, she smiled all the sweeter.

It had the effect of making him sit up a little straighter as the brilliance of it washed over him. She'd always had that effect on people when she smiled, even if the end result wasn't always to her liking.

His gaze wandered over her but he talked, making it abundantly clear that the guild's aim was not to protect its members from exploitation, but to exploit the members themselves.

Memberships were sold by the month or the year, and varied in cost according to the artist's talent. The higher one was ranked, the more expensive it was to *be* ranked. And she suspected if you could string two notes together, where you ranked after that was entirely dependent on your financial state.

At first, she couldn't understand how the guild continued to function. There couldn't be *that* many people who could afford these fees. A monthly membership cost twice the money she'd earned at the Hawk and Scepter, and she'd only earned *that* rate because she'd demanded the fee that would have gone to the Musicians Guild singer in the first place.

"And if you can't afford that," the clerk said, his gaze hovering just south of her collarbones, "you can buy a single-use license."

When he told her the cost of it, her rage nearly exploded. It wasn't that the single-use license was outside of the ordinary person's reach. It was that it was just inside it. And while her grasp on math might be nearly as shaky as her grasp on letters, hours spent each day in the markets had taught her the value of Veralna's currency. An average person *could* afford the single-use license and, if they were lucky, they would find an engagement that would pay just enough to cover another one the next day, along with a meal.

By the time you totaled up a month's worth of fees for doing so, not to mention the labor and the constant uncertainty of making it from one day to the next, the single-use license was nothing short of charging a person to take their money.

A liquid cold spilled through her veins as she listened to the man explain, in bored, precise terms, how much it would cost her to try and live under this system. She saw her life playing out before her, an endless repetitive loop of barely making enough money to buy another temporary license, each time hoping that next time, *next time*, would be the time that made a difference. The time things changed. The time she'd gained enough of a reputation that someone paid her even a fraction of what she was worth. The time she caught the eye of a patron, or anyone with enough standing to hire her for an engagement that would make her name known.

Each time hoping, but knowing it wouldn't happen.

"Your guild is a parasite." The words fell out of her mouth. If she hadn't been so furious, maybe she wouldn't have spoken them.

The clerk sneered at her, a deprecating glance that more than said how little he thought of her, and everyone like her. "If you're worth the license, it'll pay for itself."

She laughed. "No, it won't. It never *could*. That's what you count on." The guild didn't need to peddle in anything so mundane as drugs, when they could sell hope instead.

The Song finally perked up as it felt the rising tide of her fury. It was ever-hopeful, when she was angry, that she might let it out to play. The tired ache in her bones whispered, *Maybe you should.*

So she did. "Who runs this guild?" Her words were whips of power that lashed around the man and squeezed.

"M-Madame Aria, miss."

"And where can I find Madame Aria?"

He was wild-eyed now, struggling to breathe in the grasp of the Song's power. It was not persuasive and lulling, as it had been with the innkeeper at the Hawk and Scepter. Now it was harsh and demanding.

"She keeps her office in the Hightown branch," he gasped.

"Thank you." She yanked the Song free of him with a brutal pull, and he sucked in a breath, his gaze mutinous, head tilting at that angle that said he was about to call for help. "One more thing," she said icily, the Song curling lovingly around her words, dripping from the syllables. "You won't mention anything about this, or me, to anyone by any means at your disposal."

She exited the building, the Song slithering over her body in giddy serpentine movements. Her fury didn't dim in the slightest in the two-and-a-half hours it took her to exit Midtown and make her way through to the north end of Hightown.

Here the buildings were all glittering white stucco, as if crushed crystal had been mixed into the aggregate solely to catch the sun's brilliance and reflect it. No doubt most people found the statement dazzling and impressive. Perhaps on a different day, Clare would have as well. At the moment she was sweating from exertion despite the cold, and her shoulders and back ached from having hauled her guitar in its over-sized case so far on foot.

The case still contained everything she possessed in the world, and she still had no permanent, safe place to leave it. She fingered the worn, frayed strap, knowing she must look half-wild. She wore a clean tunic and one of the respectable pairs of leggings she'd purchased, but her face was flushed and her feet were still stuffed into the too-large boots Verol had given her on the trip here.

She felt the oddest pang of longing as she remembered the mage and his husband. The second-guessing sense of *Maybe I should have stayed with them.* She shook her head. She didn't second-guess. This unusual sense of attachment, this brief wanting for human companionship, was the Song nudging her toward the outcome it wanted. There could be no other explanation.

The Song's power still whipped around her, and people took subconscious notice of it, giving her a wide berth on the crowded streets. She did not yet rein it in, halting a passing pedestrian for directions to the building that housed the Musicians Guild. Only once she stood outside its glossy mahogany doors did she finally temper the Song.

She had been hasty and furious in Midtown. She was *still* furious, but she could no longer afford to be hasty. She didn't fully know how this world outside Renault County worked—knew even less than she had imagined she did—but she didn't need to in order to understand that publicly displaying the power that lurked within her was a sure bet for drawing the kind of attention she did not want.

Had she the slightest bit of sense, she would walk away and consign herself to that fate she had seen splayed out before her earlier as the clerk had explained the guild's fees: that fate of working herself to the bone day in and day out, pouring her heart and soul into an endless sucking chasm while she hoped for that singular moment that would change everything.

A *tsking* sound burst forth from her memory, and for a moment the mahogany doors in front of her swam, replaced by a different set carved of sun-bleached white stone. A familiar and wretched weight pressed at her back, a hand reaching over her shoulder to stroke bony fingers across her cheek.

You were not made to live and die in the quotidian mundanity of the masses, min quellea. *You are so much more.*

Revulsion was a churning sea in Clare's stomach. She stomped booted feet on the memory, grinding it beneath her heels, scrubbing at her cheek to erase the feel of phantom fingers.

"Clare Brighton," she whispered. "Clare Brighton, Clare Brighton, *Clare Brighton.*" Not *min quellea.* Not *his.* Never that. Never again.

She hadn't been *made* for anything. She was making herself. So that one day she could walk back through the horror palace of her past and make the perpetrator of so many atrocities scream—make him scream *her* name, as he pleaded for mercy.

She squared her shoulders and walked through the guild's doors. This wasn't smart. But she refused to sink into obscurity here just as she refused to play by the Musicians Guild's rules.

With every footstep she took she drew on all those unasked-for lessons that had been drilled into her. Lessons that corrected her posture, her bearing, her gait. Lessons that had her face softening into a beatific expression, so that as she strolled across the glossy marble foyer, she drew every eye in the room. She was not attired like a court lady—the battered guitar case on her back should have marked her as contemptuously beneath notice—but everything about her manner and bearing screamed that she was important. That she was to be respected.

She approached the clerk at the licensing desk. "I'm here to see Madame Aria." Not a single trace of power limned these words. Clare wouldn't allow them to, wouldn't allow that anything she did here today was anything other than herself.

The clerk blinked, startled, but she recovered a moment later. "Of course. Follow me."

The woman led Clare to a large, airy office, sunlight filtering in from the outside windows. The woman within looked up sharply as the door opened, arching a single eyebrow in questioning command.

The clerk fidgeted beneath the weight of that glare. "I have..." She trailed off, as if just realizing she had never asked Clare's name. Swallowing, she tried again. "Your appointment is here."

"I have no appointments."

"You do now." Clare stepped past the clerk into the room and shut the door in her face, absolving the poor woman from any further attempts to explain herself.

She took the chair across the desk from Madame Aria, settling her guitar case carefully beside her. It was an effort not to sigh in relief at the temporary reprieve of its weight. The head of the Musicians Guild watched all this with silent, condescending boredom, and waited. She kept waiting. Clare didn't speak. She simply sat in her chair, her legs crossed, her hands clasped lightly over her knee, holding the other woman's gaze.

Finally, Madame Aria leaned back in her chair. "You have guts. I'll grant you that. But I am not a man, to be amused by a pretty face and a display of bravado. I won't listen to you sing or play or whatever it is you do. But if you leave now, I won't call the city guard on you for trespassing."

"I am not here to sing or play. I am here because I have recently had the pleasure of having your guild's fees and practices explained to me, and I wanted to put a face to the name of the woman who makes her living preying off people's hopes."

Madame Aria's expression didn't shift from its bored calm. "We provide licensing and a reasonable standard for quality of product. If you haven't the talent for the guild, I'm sure you'll find Lowtown much more to your liking."

Clare uncrossed her legs and leaned forward, bracing her forearms on her thighs. "The place I come from isn't a kind one. But it is, I suppose you could say, an honest one. If someone robs you, or extorts you, they do not attempt to claim they are doing anything other than that.

"But you—you put a price on the chasing of a dream. You've convinced this entire city that your seal of approval is necessary for the right to even pursue that dream and you've institutionalized the taxing of it. It's despicable."

"Do you expect me to respond to this, you foolish child?" She laughed. "Did you imagine you could come in here with borrowed airs and an idealistic notion of *fairness*, and make me see the errors of my ways?"

Clare shook her head, displaying none of the anger or embarrassment Madame Aria had no doubt intended to make her feel. "No. I had no expectations you would make even the slightest concession. I came here for one reason, and one reason only."

"And what is that?"

"For you to know my face, as I came here to know yours. For you to know my *name*. It's Clare Brighton. Remember it."

Madame Aria snorted. "I'll remember you, girl. If only so when my carriage drives by the sewer ditches, I'll have a name to put to your face. Now get out, before I have you thrown out."

Clare smiled and stood, reaching for her guitar case. "If you look for me in the sewer ditches, you'll be disappointed. I'm going to take something from you. Something as important to you as what you steal every day from the artists in this city. So when you're standing there, wondering how it all went wrong, remember me. Remember me just as I am now, and know that *I* am to blame."

She swept from the room, Madame Aria's laughter following her out. She didn't mind it, mocking though it was. She would remember that laughter. She would remember the disdain. But most importantly, she would remember the promise she'd made.

CHAPTER

EIGHT

A STARING PROBLEM

Having made her declaration, Clare wasted no time in setting it into motion. She'd been bereft of a concrete purpose ever since she'd discovered the difficulty of being hired outside the blessing of the Musicians Guild, and having now given herself a new one, the entirety of her being had settled.

She spent the next two hours wandering Hightown, asking casual questions to gain information and locate what she wanted. What she wanted turned out to be Rosalita's. A cafe in the music district known for exotic teas and a lively atmosphere, it catered to Veralna's elite musical patrons. At the mid-afternoon bell she found it still doing a brisk business, though the lunch hour had surely gone and the evening rush was yet to come. She supposed that was what came from visiting a part of the city in which money bought one's schedule, rather than the work most people did to earn that money.

A quick inquiry about entrees had her foregoing food entirely and opting for a cup of tea, even though her stomach was growling from the walk here. The money she had wasn't going to get her far. She certainly couldn't afford to sleep in Hightown tonight, and would have to walk back to Midtown or Lowtown before curfew to afford lodging.

She took the tea—which cost four times what it would have in

Midtown—in its ridiculously delicate porcelain cup, to a table outside. The day's chill was kept at bay by the warming spells on the chair seats and the fires that burned in small pits in the centers of the tables.

Clare sat in the chair, her entire body warmed, the chair conducting warmth through her skin, her fingers wrapped around the hot cup so not even they went stiff or numb.

She wanted to laugh. Or cry. Or scream. She wanted to shove her chair back and demand to know how every happy, oblivious person here could stand it. The easiness, the lack of fear or need or urgency. No one here had anywhere to be, and the absence of a purpose stemmed from an abundance of wealth rather than a lack of it.

It was everything she'd ever aspired to—and she hated everyone here for having it, including herself. Even if she was only an imposter for the hour.

Two men dressed in severe black stood on opposite sides of the outdoor seating area; both of them took in her guitar case and her single cup of tea and watched her carefully, as if she might disturb the affluent atmosphere merely by existing in it. Their entire purpose was likely to keep people like her from approaching the cafe's other patrons, the ones who could actually afford to be here. She doubted she was the first aspiring musician to think that coming to this district of Hightown could be beneficial to her career.

But she wasn't here to do anything as foolish as approach someone in an attempt to gain their patronage. For one, that was guaranteed to end in failure, and for another, everyone here likely paid homage to the Musicians Guild. So no, she wasn't here to socialize. She was here to listen to the chatter around her and verify that it confirmed everything she'd already learned wandering the music district.

She'd been sitting for half an hour, cataloging the people around her, catching snippets of conversations, and plotting, when she noticed *him* watching her. She wouldn't have—he sat at a table behind and to the right of her—had a server not placed a silver pitcher on the table in front of hers. Its shining surface reflected his face, and if the image was too distorted to give her any idea of who he might be, the intensity with which he watched her was undeniable.

She didn't give any outward sign that she'd noticed the attention until she'd made up her mind to confront him rather than walk away. This was hardly the place anyone would cause a scene, and after the event in the marketplace a few days ago, when she'd been so certain she was being followed and then *not* so certain—well, better to confront this man here, where the public eye of Veralna's elite gave her a reason to control herself.

She lifted her cup in one hand, guitar case in the other, strode to his table and sat down across from him.

He didn't look much older than her, perhaps in his mid-twenties, with straight brown hair that fell to his shoulders and an exceptionally pale complexion. She wanted to say there was something off about the skin color, but there wasn't a centimeter of skin exposed anywhere else on him for her to compare it to. His shirt was high-necked and fashionable, as were the thin white gloves that covered his hands.

"You seem to have a staring problem," she told him.

His mouth split in a slow grin, a flash of amusement dancing in his eyes. "Indeed I do." Something about his voice didn't match him, in the same way his skin tone and his hair didn't quite match him. There was nothing she could point to that was wrong with them, and they all fit together, even the pale blue eyes, except... there was a faint sheen of magic over those eyes, so thin she almost missed it. But she didn't and, as always happened for her, once she noticed a glamour she was underneath it. His eyes weren't blue, but so deep a brown they might as well be black.

A shadow loomed over their table as one of the black-clad men who'd been stationed at the perimeter of the cafe asked, "Is she bothering you, sir?"

Clare stiffened, but it wasn't at the question, or the knowledge that she would be escorted off the premises if the man wished it. No, she stiffened because she'd recognized the deep, almost-black eyes beneath the man's glamour. She'd seen them reflected in a mirror inside a hotel room, and now she understood why nothing about him seemed quite right.

His disguise was as perfect as the first one had been, but now that she'd seen what lay underneath, she couldn't make the face he wore today fit him. Only those eyes, that hadn't yet broken from her gaze, belonged to him.

The cafe attendant cleared his throat, and the man across from

Clare waved a dismissive hand. "She's not bothering me. Quite the opposite, in fact."

The attendant dipped his head in acknowledgment and retreated, shooting Clare a warning glance as he did. She bared her teeth at him as he left, and the man across from her laughed.

"Tell me, do you threaten everyone on principle?"

She widened her eyes in feigned innocence while her heart raced, her brain scrambling to figure out if he'd seen her that night on the ledge and had somehow followed her here. "Threaten?"

Amusement crinkled the corners of his eyes. "If that smile wasn't a warning, I don't know what is."

She ignored the obvious invitation to banter. "Why have you been staring at me? I don't know you." The statement was a challenge, daring him to tell her that *he* knew *her*. That he'd seen her that night, knew she knew what he looked like under this facade he wore, and he was here to ensure the knowledge went no further than her.

"You'll have to forgive me." He gave her a smile that invited confidence and trust, a little bashful, his tone repentant. "I saw your performance the other night and it was..." He looked off into the distance, as if remembering. As if her music had actually meant something. "I've never heard anything like it."

She snorted and leaned back in her chair. She might know he'd been there, but if she hadn't recognized him, she'd have said it unlikely. "And you'll have to forgive *me* if I don't believe anyone from Veralna's Hightown had cause to find themselves in a Midtown inn three days prior."

He put a hand to his heart. "Why, Miss Brighton, are you prejudiced against the wealthy and bored?"

"To an extent you could never comprehend."

His gaze took on a hard edge. "Oh, I might comprehend more than you think."

"And yet, here we both are."

The hardness left his eyes as if it had never been there, and he grinned again. "And yet, here we are," he agreed.

"You have me at a disadvantage. You know my name, but I don't know yours."

He shrugged. "You told everyone your name. Half of Midtown knows it by now."

She stared him down and didn't respond. It was a stare that had, quite literally, driven men to madness. The one across from her didn't even blink.

"You can call me Taius," he said finally.

"That isn't your name." She didn't know why she bothered pointing out the obvious. It didn't matter what she called him. She wouldn't be calling him anything for long. As soon as she confirmed he had no idea she knew his secret—and she was more and more certain by the second that he didn't know—her interactions with him could cease.

"Maybe not. Is Clare Brighton really yours?"

"It is."

CHAPTER

NINE

YOU'RE STARING AGAIN

Numair rolled the name over and over in his head. "I didn't find a Clare Brighton registered with the Musicians Guild." He hadn't found her registered with the Mages Guild either, but the latter hadn't surprised him.

She leaned back in her chair and offered him another smile, one slightly less feral than the one she'd tendered to the cafe's security staff. A stupid man might take that smile for an invitation, but Numair had a wealth of experience telling him that flirting was the last thing on this woman's mind. If he had to guess what *was* on her mind, he would wager it was murder-adjacent.

"You asked after me. Should I be flattered or concerned?"

He shrugged. "Dealer's choice, I suppose. Your performance left an impression."

"I see." She sat unnaturally still. Most people, if faced with someone they didn't know, especially someone who appeared to be of a higher status than them and had unclear motives, tended to fidget. To shift in their seat or tap their foot or wring their hands under the table where they thought no one would notice.

She did none of it. She was like an immovable rock the sea could batter but never break, could swallow but never consume. In that moment, he was struck with the certainty that she could bring all of Veralna to its knees, and he wanted to watch her do it.

"You're staring again," she said.

"I never stopped staring."

"You never stopped *looking*," she argued. "There's a difference. So why are you staring again?"

She was unsettlingly direct and he…liked it. Because it allowed him to be the same. "I'm wondering if you're a woman or a hurricane, and what I have to give you to bring this city to its knees."

She was the one staring at him now. For a long, long minute, she stared. Then she threw her head back and laughed. He waited until she was done and then lifted one eyebrow in silent question.

Dark mirth dripped from her words like poisoned honey. "I find that when people say they want to give you something, what they mean is that they want to tie strings to you and pull you about, but they want it done in such a way that you feel glad to be their puppet.

"If you want to give a person something, there is nothing to stop you. The only reason to tell them of your intent to give is if you wish for something in return. In which case you don't actually want to *give* me anything—you want to make a deal.

"I won't be put in pretty chains and made to dance. So tell me what you want, and I'll tell you if it's a price I'm willing to pay."

He opened his mouth to tell her she was wrong—because she'd already paid a few days ago in an alley—but the words never left his mouth. Because he realized he *did* want something else. One last thing.

"I want to be there. That's my price."

She narrowed her eyes. "Want to be where?"

"Wherever you are when you make your opening gambit."

"You seem quite certain I have one."

"Are you telling me you don't?"

There was a pause before her answer, as if she was weighing what to reveal. "It's in the planning stages," she finally said. "And whether I tell you anything more than that depends on what you're offering."

"Whatever you want. Money. Introductions. Information." He grinned at her. "Pick something. First one is truly free. Take it and walk away, and I won't bother you again." He expected her to ask for money. Barring that, an introduction would have been the likely second choice. But it told him more about her when she asked for the third and perhaps, in learning that, he decided he wasn't even giving her the first thing freely, after all.

He suspected she knew it, knew what she was revealing with the answer, because it took her so long to give it. "I want a name," she said. "I want the name of the best musician the guild has."

"Best as in the most artistically gifted, or best as in the most popular?"

"Best, as in the most beloved. I want the person every noble has seen perform at least once, the one so comfortable in their position they are certain no one can oust them from it."

Easy enough. "Estrella Vane."

"Tell me about her."

"She's a singer. She used to play the piano at her performances but now she has someone else do it for her." She'd been good, once. Before the guild sank its claws into her. The change had been easy enough to see, if one was looking. The way all the creativity went out of her and she began instead churning out the same types of songs over and over, her voice and her charm and her small talent for Songweaving carrying what lacked in the music itself. "I have to tell you—if you plan on rivaling her professionally, it will be a long, thankless, and expensive campaign to even arrive in the same circles as her. You're talented, but the Musicians Guild runs things a certain way, and they're exceptionally good at weighting down progress."

"So I noticed. I met the head of their guild today. And I made her a promise."

"I'm dying to know what that was."

The corner of her lip quirked up. "I promised her I would take something important from her."

"And you think Estrella Vane qualifies?"

"Don't you?"

"She is Madame Aria's golden child." He didn't feel even the slightest guilt at confirming it. Once, he'd thought Estrella might have been a friend. Once, he'd thought there was a person behind the singer's pretty face. But if there ever had been, that person had disappeared once she'd run in high circles long enough that she became just like all the rest, and she'd sought to use him in the same way everyone did.

Just once, he wanted someone to see *him*. Not the mask that so obviously was one that it never should have hidden anything. He thought he'd given up the longing for that when he'd realized that if anyone ever *did* see through to him, they wouldn't live very long after. But he was human beneath it all, and dreams died hard.

He shoved the thought down. Apparently, having made the decision that had been haunting him for months, he was now to be subject to all sorts of fun clarity he'd avoided.

"But," he continued, "she won't be easy to go after, and I'm afraid I can only give you two days of assistance," he found himself saying. "I'll be gone, after that."

He braced himself for the questions—he wasn't fooling himself into believing that once she realized he was on the hook, even if he'd put himself on it willingly, she wouldn't try to keep him wriggling there for as long as possible. He didn't even blame her. It was in her best interest, and she owed him absolutely nothing.

"I don't need two days to take her down. I only need one."

He blinked. "One?"

"Yes. Estrella Vane is playing at the Rival Theater this evening. I need you to get me in."

"If you already know that," he said slowly, "then you'd already decided she was the key to getting what you want."

She shrugged.

"You could have asked me for anything and you asked a question you already had the answer to. Why?"

"Because if you gave me anyone else's name, you would either be a liar, or incompetent. I can work with both, but I needed to know what I was dealing with. Can you get me in, or not?"

"Yes." He studied her for a moment, but she only waited, so he continued. "Am I to take it you know *why* it's called the Rival Theater, then?"

She flashed him another smile in response, and the way her eyes shifted when her lips curled up—he was half convinced she lost a sliver of her soul each time she smiled.

"If you're doing what I think you're doing, you need a better dress."

She looked ready to snarl, as if he'd inexcusably insulted her intelligence. "I wasn't planning on wearing this one."

"I meant you need something better than anything you have."

"And you know what I have?" she asked, a dangerous edge to her voice.

"I can guess." He pulled a pen and a small notebook from his pocket, scratched a series of characters across the back. "There's a tailor near here. Chalen Mora." He rattled off directions, trusting she'd remember them. "Tell them what you need the dress for and give them this." He tore the page out and offered it to her. "They'll get you what you need."

She eyed the paper with obvious distrust.

"And Clare? This does come with a condition." She relaxed, now that he was giving stipulations. He was beginning to realize she was the sort of woman who didn't trust anything unless the price was stated up front, and perhaps not even then. "I respect Chalen. Don't insult them. And it is *them*."

He could tell by the blank look on her face she didn't understand what he meant. She was clever. She'd figure it out. And if she didn't —or if she had a problem with it—Chalen would throw her out, and Numair would get an earful about it.

He stood, which was the signal for a server to approach with the food he'd ordered earlier, setting it down and retreating.

Clare eyed the food, then him. "You aren't staying to eat?"

He shrugged. "I have things to do. You're welcome to it if you want. Or leave it and the staff can throw it out." He walked away with the feel of her scorn heating the outdoor courtyard far better than any of the warming spells.

If he'd told her he'd bought it for her, he was relatively certain she would have refused it. But his wasteful dismissal of it had pissed her off, and he was equally certain that pissing Clare Brighton off was a good way to get her to do things.

And she needed to eat something. She'd found clothes that hid it well, but the woman was more than half-starved.

TEN

I DON'T BITE

I f Veralna's Hightown could be said to have a poor side, Chalen Mora's shop resided in it. Clare stopped at the mouth of an alley—still a very clean alley compared to any previous one Clare had known—tapping Taius' card against her thigh.

On the one hand, this could be a trap. On the other hand, there was little point. The man had money, and therefore far easier ways of gaining control of her if he wanted to.

He didn't want to. She knew the look men got when they wanted to own her, was all too familiar with the sick, obsessive *need* that could stare out from the depths of someone's eyes. Taius didn't have that. Whatever reason he was helping her for, it wasn't actually for *her*, and that was a relief.

She moved down the alley to a door made of gleaming black metal that looked too smooth and perfect to be iron. The looped, swirled symbols it twisted into seemed to shift before her eyes, serpentine and mesmerizing. She put her hand on the metal and found it hot to the touch, like solid fire. It felt old and powerful, and the Song rumbled inside her in response, perking up in its cage.

Clare removed her hand, but her touch had been enough to summon the building's occupant. The outer door slid to the side, revealing an inner security door and the person standing behind it. Clare looked into golden-yellow eyes, tilted ever-so-slightly at the corners, and black hair that fell in shining sheets to either side of one of the most arrestingly beautiful faces she had ever seen.

Chalen Mora stared at her suspiciously. "Yes?"

She held up the card. "I need a dress."

Chalen motioned and Clare slipped the card through the bars of the security door. She wanted to know what it said, but even if she'd been able to read Common, she wouldn't have been able to read this. It wasn't written in letters as she knew them, but characters that were an art form in their own right.

Whatever might be on that paper irritated her, in the same way her satisfied stomach irritated her. She'd seen how fast the service at the cafe was. The only reason for Taius's meal to come so late was if he'd *asked* for it to come late. Then he'd gone and made her angry to ensure she'd eat it.

She almost hadn't, just out of spite. Because no one had ever so neatly understood how she would react before, much less someone who barely knew her. It was unsettling and she didn't like being unsettled. But she was, more than anything else, practical.

So she'd eaten the food and come to see the tailor. If the tailor ever decided to let her in.

Their—and Clare had no idea why it was "their", had no past experience for the usage, but it cost her nothing to think of them that way—gaze kept flicking from the note to Clare and back. "What are you to" —they looked at the note again and settled on— "him?"

Clare snorted at the insinuation. "Clearly nothing important enough to warrant his real name."

A ghost of a smile broke Chalen's face and they slid the security door open. "Come inside then, Nothing Important."

Clare hesitated. Mostly because the Song was giving little contented rumbles inside her, as if it had found a person it particularly liked. They weren't as strong as the ones it had given off around Verol and Marquin, more like the Song had walked into a room it hadn't entered in years, and run across something it had forgotten about that used to bring it great joy.

"I don't bite," Chalen said.

"I doubt that," Clare answered, finally stepping inside. "Only foolish people don't, and you don't strike me as foolish." Entering the inside of Chalen's shop—or was it their home? Or both?—felt like entering a lair. A cozy, inviting lair, yet a lair nonetheless. The interior lighting was muted, which was the opposite of what Clare would expect from someone who presumably spent most of their time making small stitches into expensive fabric.

The room was perfectly circular, a third of the wall to Clare's left taken over by a fireplace with sleepy flames crackling in its depths. Suits and dresses and all manner of fashionable pieces draped over surfaces, hung off racks, or posed on wooden models.

Chalen went to a rack and started flipping through options, glancing at Clare every now and then before discarding this or that. Clare wandered the room, inspecting the pieces on display, but stopped just shy of running her hands over the fabrics when Chalen snapped, "Don't touch that," without ever taking their eyes off the dress they were considering.

Clare *didn't* touch, but she ached to. She had never cared much about the way clothes *looked*. Most of her life had been spent simply hoping for any garment that would keep away winter's chill or summer's wealth of insects. As for the years spent in finer garments...she'd wanted to burn them. Every drape of fabric, every stitch.

She had walked into this shop braced, expecting her stomach to turn, her hands to sweat, her heart to race. She had walked into this shop unsure of whether she could wear anything nice in the way Veralna's elite meant "nice" without hating herself.

But the clothes in Chalen's shop were different. Every design, every stitch, every embellishment felt born of some grand vision, born of...dreams. Because that's what the clothes were. They were dreams, in the same way Clare's songs were dreams, the only light that lived inside her poured into the notes and the lyrics and the hope that someday she would understand what any of it meant.

Chalen was doing the same thing through a different medium, and Clare lost herself in looking at the patterns and the designs, until she came to one that arrested her. It was a waterfall of dark red silk that was...not precisely dangerous, but sharp. Sharp cuts, sharp edges, sharp asymmetry in the skirt. She knew that wearing it she would *feel* dangerous, as if she wore... "Battle armor." Her whispered words carried to Chalen, who came to stand beside her.

"Ah," they said softly, "so that's its name. Battle Armor."

And it made perfect sense to Clare that Chalen should name their works, in the same way Clare named her songs.

"It would look perfect on you." Chalen drew their lower lip into their mouth, let it go. "It's Althenian silk," they said finally. "The fabric alone cost a fortune. He can easily afford it, but I'd prefer to send a courier to confirm the amount before we settle on it."

Clare was so busy trying to figure out what Althenian silk was—there was no province in Faelhorn named Althenia—that it took her a moment to process the rest of what Chalen had said. "Why would *he* be affording anything?"

Chalen gave her a wry smile. "What did you think was on that paper? A letter of introduction? It was an approval to charge whatever you need to his account."

"I don't need his account." It wasn't that Clare had a problem spending his money. It was that she had a problem spending his money when someone else *knew* that was what she was doing. If he'd handed her a purse of coins, she'd have been all too happy to hand it over in turn in exchange for a dress. This way felt...not traceable, precisely, but less...clean. Less easy to sever ties and pretend they'd never been there.

Chalen sighed, their gaze slipping pointedly over Clare's current clothes. "Unless I vastly underestimate your financial situation, you very much need his account. I'm not cheap. You might be able to afford a pair of socks, if you put all your change together."

Clare bristled, mostly because Chalen was likely right. But that didn't mean she had to accept the situation. "Why is your shop here?"

Chalen narrowed their eyes at the abrupt question and didn't answer.

"You aren't in the clothing district and no one is going to find you here without the very specific directions I was given," Clare continued. "And anyone who can afford you isn't going to make the trip. If I had to guess, I'd say Taius is your only customer and he spends enough to keep you afloat."

The annoyance in Chalen's eyes told Clare she'd gotten it right so far. "What's your point?"

"My *point* is that I don't think someone who makes things this beautiful made them so they could languish in this house forever."

"I design things for myself," Chalen snapped. "Because I like them, because I—"

"Need to," Clare finished for them. Chalen couldn't stop making things any more than Clare could stop writing songs in her head. "And if that's all you could ever do with them, you would keep doing it." The way Clare wrote songs in the dark, for only herself to hear. "But you want more. They're made to be worn. So why are they here? Why are *you* here?"

"I'm a designer, not a shopkeeper."

Clare waited. And waited.

"I tried," Chalen whispered. "When I first came here, I tried. No one wanted to buy from me." Their lips twisted into a snarl. "Well, some of them did. The clothes are good. But they expected me to sell everything for nothing, as if I should be *grateful* for their business. And I should have been. I should have swallowed it down and done what they wanted until I established enough of a name to finally charge what I was worth, but I couldn't.

"If Nu—If *Taius*—hadn't bought out everything I had I would—" They cut off, shaking their head. "It doesn't matter. I *can't* sell to anyone. That's why I'm here. Are you happy, now?" They were angry, as if they couldn't understand why they'd told her what they had.

Clare had always had that effect on people. It was in her voice, in that ripple of magic that flowed in her words that wasn't the Song, but was something all her. Something that had people telling her truths they'd rather not and frequently blamed her for.

"So that's why you're here. Now what do you want?"

"I want them to know my name. I want them all to want something I've made and when I refuse, I want them to beg, and maybe *then* I'll make them something."

"And Taius can't make them know your name?"

Chalen snorted. "Not in any *good* way. The only reputation I'd gain from that wouldn't be a useful one."

"What if I can do what he can't? Lend me a dress for this evening. No charges to Taius. Give me a dress for one night, and I guarantee that by tomorrow evening, everyone in Hightown will be knocking down your door."

Chalen studied her, and Clare swore small twists of flame flickered in their eyes. "How do I know you can deliver on that promise?"

"What do you have to lose?"

"Hope," Chalen said at long last. "But I suppose I've already lost it once, so a second time can't hurt as much." Their fingers skimmed over Battle Armor. "You can't have this one. It should only be worn by one person, who intends to keep it. But I'll give you another." Her gaze flicked down to Clare's boots. "And shoes. Return them by tomorrow evening and don't cross me. You won't like the results."

"You'll have it back. And Chalen? I'd triple all your prices."

CHAPTER

ELEVEN

THINGS SHE NEVER EXPECTED

Clare stood inside the empty Rival Theater. The main stage, where Estrella Vane would sing in less than three hours, lay far to Clare's left. It was a large stage, the one intended as the focal point of the audience. All the seats pointed toward it, the stage lavishly decorated, its chosen accoutrements meant to enhance the singer and draw the crowd further into the performance.

A few feet to her right, at the opposite end of the spectator's seating, stood the rival's stage. It was less than a third of the size of the other, more a dais than a true stage, and until a moment ago it had been hidden from view by thick, black velvet curtains. The theater attendant who had drawn back those curtains looked nervous to have done so. He wiped his hands on his thighs, a slight whine in his voice as he addressed Taius like Clare wasn't even present. "You sure about this? Miss Vane's a platinum member of the Musicians Guild, and this girl don't even have a one-use license."

"I'm sure." Taius sounded bored. Or annoyed. Possibly both.

The attendant crept in closer, lowering his voice, as if that would keep Clare from overhearing when she stood less than two feet from him. "I know he's the biggest supporter of the arts in Veralna, but does he know what he's doing? If she isn't any good, I could lose my job."

Given his anxiousness, Clare guessed he hadn't had the job very

76

long, and that it was a sight better than any he'd had before. It didn't stop her from being irritated with him, or hoping he was just nervous enough to slip up and reveal who the "he" was whose name Taius had used to get her into the theater. Mostly because she suspected "he" was probably Taius's actual identity.

"Think back to what you just said," Taius said. "Remember whose judgment you're questioning and ask yourself what's more likely to end in you losing your job—a disastrous performance tonight, or me explaining to him that I couldn't make this happen because *you* thought he didn't know what he was doing."

The attendant paled. "I didn't mean that I just—I need this job."

Taius sighed. "You aren't going to lose it."

"But—"

Clare sang. It seemed like the most expedient method of shutting them both up and allaying the attendant's concerns. She chose the song she instinctively knew would speak to him, about a person who'd just come into a newfound security, and was both happy and terrified of it. She sang of easing those fears, and painted a nice pretty picture of a nice pretty life.

By the time she finished, the attendant's color had returned and his posture relaxed, a slack look dominating his face. Taius was giving her another one of those looks she couldn't read. The inability frustrated her, and she reminded herself that it didn't matter. That she was never going to see him again, so whether she could or couldn't decipher his expressions was of no consequence.

The attendant didn't awaken from his daze until Taius snapped his fingers in the man's face. He startled, blinking.

"Any further concerns?" Taius asked.

"N-no." The man shook his head. "No. The dressing room is through here." He led them past the dais to the hidden door at its back. "Will you want the stage curtains open or closed?"

"Closed," Clare said without hesitation. Half of a performance was how good you were. The other half was presentation, and an element of mystery, of surprise, never hurt. She didn't want anyone in this theater tonight—especially Estrella Vane—knowing she waited behind the curtains until she opened her mouth.

According to the theater rules, no one was supposed to announce a rival. It was meant to be a true test of an artist's skill, to respond in an improvisational manner rather than with something rehearsed.

But the Rival Theater hadn't actually hosted a rival to a significant performer in over fifteen years. According to the gossip she'd acquired in the music district, the last few rival bouts had been near-disasters, devolving into chaotic performances, rather than the grand displays of musical talent they were meant to be.

Clare had a suspicion the Musicians Guild might have had a hand in that—because the sudden onset of poor performances had coincided with the guild's rise to prominence. The theater was in a bind because their business license was founded on the rival performances as a core component of their business and, as such, they couldn't be discontinued. So the Musicians Guild had struck a deal with the theater to vet their performers, in exchange for the theater being the first to require that all musicians performing for them be licensed by the guild in the first place.

Now they hosted rival nights once a month and by all accounts Clare had heard they were fun enough if one didn't attend them very frequently. They were never bad and they were never surprising. Which said, to Clare, that they were scripted. That, and the fact that to take the rival stage against a prominent performer, such as Estrella Vane, an artist was supposed to win three successive rival nights.

Taius's ability to circumvent that requirement on so little notice practically proved his true identity was that of the mysterious patron of the arts the attendant had mentioned. Her curiosity burned to know that identity, but she set the desire aside. The only thing she needed to care about, the only thing she *could* care about, was that she was here. And she would ensure that, after tonight, no one would be able to forget her.

This wasn't a performance in a small inn, where no one expected to remember the performer. This was where Veralna's elite came to be seen and entertained. Where they wanted to spend their money to feel like they knew an artist. They *would* remember her.

And because she was a surprise, because she was a novelty, they would want to possess her. And one didn't need a Musicians Guild license to be hired by the wealthy for their private parties. Clare would play for them, and she would take their money into the rest of Hightown and she would do what she'd promised Madame Aria she would. Because despite what she'd allowed Taius to believe, Estrella Vane was not the important thing Clare intended to take from the guild owner. Estrella was simply the beginning.

"Miss?"

Clare had stopped listening, at some point after the attendant led her into her dressing room, as he told her things she already knew, and it sounded like this wasn't the first time he'd tried to gain her attention. She looked at him. Her lapse in focus had him wringing his hands nervously again.

"The room is yours until the performance begins. I'll be here to lead you to the stage a quarter hour before the start. Do you need anything? Water? Tea?"

She started to answer nothing, until she realized the offer was simply the standard one given to any artist singing at the theater. "Tea," she said, and because she might as well, added, "with lemon."

The attendant left and she was alone with Taius. She prickled with the awareness of their isolation and no small part of her waited, calmly, for him to make a move she didn't like. Didn't want.

But he only shoved his hands into his pockets and leaned against the door frame, keeping well back from her, a shadow of a smile on his face. "Well, it seems as if our partnership is concluded."

"So it seems," she agreed, because it sounded like the casual kind of response an ordinary person would make. A person who wasn't constantly expecting everything in her life to go wrong. A person who could say something that didn't have to have a double meaning, or a threat, or a taunt beneath the words.

She wanted to be that person. Wanted to feel like she had an identity beneath her drive to survive. And somehow, in the oddly peaceful space that existed between her and Taius in this moment, she felt like that person was slowly being born inside her.

That's the stupidest thing you've ever thought, the practical side of her nature warned. It was. More stupid was her desire to ask him if he would be there tonight, in the crowd. He'd said he wanted to be and...*she* wanted him to be. Because she'd never had anyone do something *with* her before, and even though this wasn't a true partnership, wasn't anything more than a transaction where they were both getting something they wanted, it felt different.

And it scared her more than anything in her life ever had. So she didn't ask. After a moment he straightened, that smile fading from his lips. "I'll say good luck, because it's what I'm supposed to say, but you don't need it. It was…nice to meet you, Clare Brighton."

He turned and walked away, leaving her alone in the dressing room trying to deal with emotions she'd never expected to have.

CHAPTER

TWELVE

HAS SHE?

Saying that Verol was tense was like saying a Taella Province monsoon was a storm. Technically correct, but it didn't come close to encompassing the ferocity of the actual thing.

Marquin studied his husband as their carriage once again thundered through Veralna's Hightown. The anxiety had been building in Verol since morning, strong enough that Marquin didn't even need the connection through the heartstone to feel it. The Kinthing had a wild energy when it got worked up, and it had pushed them out of the house half an hour ago, the carriage taking the winding streets from the countryside to town at inadvisable speeds, rough turns steadied by the careful touch here and there of Marquin's magic.

"Any idea of our destination yet?" He didn't think Verol would have an answer, but the question had the intended effect of making his husband stop boring a hole into the carriage floor with his eyes.

"No." The short syllable was hoarse. "It feels different this time, though. Last time the danger was physical. This time it's something different. Something worse."

Something magical. He didn't say it, but that was the only *something worse* there could be, where the Kinthing was concerned.

"The king's Hounds have focused their attention in the south," he said, telling Verol things he already knew, because the look in his eyes said he needed the reminding. They had spent the last three days working to ensure the bulk of the Hounds were as far away from Clare as possible. Until they could convince her that being with them was the safest place for her.

Except he wasn't entirely certain Clare *wanted* to be safe. Not if it meant depending on another person. If it weren't for the Kinthing's infallibility, Marquin didn't think he could be convinced that the same power that had lived in Marie now lived in Clare.

Marie had been such a sweet child—quiet but open. Completely trusting. Clare was her opposite in almost every way. Which was likely why she was still alive. A fact Verol needed reminding of.

"She has made it twenty winters on her own. She has hidden from the Hounds her entire life. She won't do anything foolish."

"Has she?" Verol asked, finally lifting his head to truly focus on Marquin.

"Has she what?"

"Hidden from them all her life?" He shook his head. "It doesn't make sense that she could have managed it for so long. *She* doesn't make any sense. The way we found her... She'd obviously been through some kind of trauma. I thought that's why she acted so strangely, but what if..." Verol trailed off, the only sounds the steady rolling of the carriage wheels.

"What if?" Marquin prompted.

"What if she wasn't hiding from them? What if she doesn't even know what the Hounds are?" Verol licked his lips. "What if, this time, the power was smart enough to be born somewhere not even the Jackal King can reach?"

Every muscle in Marquin's body tightened. Because Verol was suggesting...

"We found her in the Valedon Swamps," Verol whispered. "It's the closest ecosystem to the Deadlands."

The Deadlands. The ten-mile-wide circumference of Reaped ground that surrounded Renault County. The ground the Jackal King had vented so much of his fury on that nothing that touched its surface survived.

"It's not possible. Nothing leaves Renault County and lives." But even as he said it, Quin knew that if anything *could*, it would be her. And if she had come from Renault County, if she didn't understand how the Jackal King's kingdom worked...

Verol knocked on the carriage roof and it came to a halt. Marquin's unease intensified as they exited the carriage and he found himself staring up at the glowing lights of the Rival Theater's mage-lit sign. "She can't be singing," he said, unsure of whether he was trying to convince himself or Verol. "Vane is the performer tonight, and Clare would have had to be in town three very successful months to qualify as a rival."

Verol didn't look convinced, but he nodded, and the two of them went inside. They didn't typically attend the theater, so they didn't have reserved seats, and ended up with two in the row farthest back from the main stage. Closest to the rival stage.

Its black curtains were firmly drawn, and Quin exhaled a sigh of relief as they sat. The rival curtains weren't open. She wasn't singing. Because he hadn't missed, during two weeks of Clare singing softly by their campfire on the road, that she was not only the ancient power that hungered in her veins.

She was something simpler, too, something she would have been even without the power—she was a Songweaver. And if that ability was no danger to her or anyone else, it *was* a danger simply for its being unregistered with the Mages Guild. And if Clare *had* grown up in Renault County—as impossible as that seemed—she wouldn't know how dangerous it would be to let even that harmless talent slip. That in letting it slip, she might allow the other one to be found.

He told himself, as they sat, that the Kinthing had finally gotten it wrong. No branch of magic they knew of could truly tell the future, so how the Kinthing knew where and when to send them was a conundrum he'd never been able to solve.

Murmurs rippled through the crowd, and it only took a single glance toward the entrance to discover their origin.

"What is *he* doing here?" Verol's voice held the world's worth of vitriol. To say that Verol disliked the second prince of the Faelhorn Provinces was an understatement.

"He does own a permanent seat," Marquin said mildly. That seat was, naturally, the principle one at the very front of the theater facing the main stage, placed dead center of the aisle that cleaved the other two halves of the theater's seating. "And he is a renowned patron of the arts."

Verol snorted. "He's been too drunk to *patronize* the arts outside of the bedroom any time in the last half a decade."

Quin made a noncommittal noise. He was more ambivalent where the prince was concerned, but he was unable to shake the feeling that the man's sudden renewed interest in theater attendance wasn't a coincidence. And that it wasn't a good thing.

They waited in tense silence until all the lights except those on the main stage fell, the curtains drew back, and Estrella Vane began to sing. When two songs went by without incident, Quin relaxed. Verol didn't, and he should have known right then it would all go to hell.

Estrella began her third song. And a mere handful of seconds into it, a second voice joined in, one Quin had heard many times over a smoky campfire. Excitement rippled through the audience as Clare's voice twined with Estrella's, the two working in tandem—until Estrella *noticed* the other voice and faltered.

It was a brief stumble, a quarter beat at most, but it was all Clare needed. Her voice rose in volume as she took the lead on the song, transforming it into something *hers* as the magic of the theater came to life under her voice.

Every head in the crowd turned as the curtains on the rival stage parted. Clare sat on a tall stool, her guitar resting on her lap, hands in position though she didn't yet play, her head bent so no one could see her face. In the bright dome of light shining down on her, catching in shimmering ribbons on her silver dress, she looked like a goddess of old.

Estrella's voice rose in volume, aided by the voice crystals scattered throughout the room that, for now, still answered to her. But though her voice was louder, it wasn't as beautiful, as raw, as hypnotic as Clare's. The look on the prominent singer's face was nothing short of murder, and her magic slithered out of her like vipers from a den, her talent for Songweaving rippling through her words, willing the crowd's attention, their adoration, back to her.

Marquin knew it was over the second Estrella's magic poured out. Because if there was one thing he'd learned about Clare in their short time together, it was that she didn't back down. Magic kin to Estrella's spilled out in Clare's voice, but where Estrella sought to coerce the audience to her side by brute force, Clare's magic wove into her song. It gave her words—the ones that twined with and yet challenged the other singer's, flowing in perfect harmony and perfect opposition at the same time—a raw truth that couldn't be ignored.

That power rippled through the crowd like water—and the second prince of Faelhorn drank it down like wine. He rose. For a moment he simply stood there, as if wanting to make certain that every eye in the theater noticed he had stood. Then, slowly and deliberately, he turned his back on Estrella, lifted his chair in one hand, and carried it down the aisle. He placed it in front of the rival stage, less than five feet from Marquin's own chair, and sat, staring up at the vision that was Clare Brighton as she finally lifted her head to let the crowd see her face.

Marquin's gaze remained on the prince. Because in that first moment the man looked up at the stage, his expression wasn't the bored indifference or drunken confusion Veralna knew him for. It was…peace. As if Clare's music had reached into a tortured soul and pulled out tranquility.

Then his dark eyes flickered briefly to Marquin, noticing the attention, and that glimpse of a person beneath the prince disappeared. He leaned back in his chair and his expression cooled to one of indolent amusement.

The two rows of seating closest to the rival stage followed the prince's example, standing practically as one to turn their chairs to face Clare, Quin and Verol turning their seats with the others.

The theater, designed to absorb the shift in the audience's favor by the physical turning of chairs, took the corresponding number of voice crystals scattered throughout the auditorium away from Estrella and gave them to Clare. Her voice intensified as the magical aid granted it new sway.

He felt Verol's magic as the Mindmage opened a channel between them.

Go, he told Verol, mind-to-mind through the connection. *I will ensure her safety, if you are not back by the time the performance ends.*

They had been together too long for hesitation, too long for Verol to waste time with objections when he knew very well that what needed doing outside this theater was something only he could do. And that if Clare needed a physical defender, Quin was better suited to the task.

Take care of her, he said.

You know that I will.

Don't let the prince get his claws in her. She's too young.

Marquin didn't bother reminding Verol that the prince was hardly older than Clare, or that he suspected it would take diamond claws to pierce her skin. He only repeated his reassurance. *I'll take care of her. Go. The sooner you return, the better.*

THIRTEEN

THE RIVAL THEATER

Clare felt the magic of the theater shift as a man walked down the center aisle and placed his chair before her dais. The lights shining on her were too bright for her to make out in detail anything past the darkness that lay beyond her stage.

She saw the chairs, the rows, but not the faces. But she didn't need to see them. Her voice amplified as the two rows nearest her turned their chairs to face her. Across the theater, Estrella's magic turned the other singer's words into battering rams.

But Clare had been a cliff wall too long to let something as unrefined as brute power and anger dent her exterior, and the vehemence of the attack failed to knock her off stride. Besides, Estrella was putting all her confidence in her magic—she wasn't paying enough attention to the song she sang, the one she was hitting all the right notes on with soulless precision.

Clare took the added weight given her by the voice crystals and strummed the first few notes on her guitar. It was no simple task, stealing a song from another. They had an intention of what they were doing, of where they were going, and by virtue of being the first one to the stage, they carried the most weight, in the beginning.

But as Clare wormed her way deeper into the melody and the lyrics, as more chairs in the theater turned to hear her voice, she slowly became the dominant in the song, her chords on the guitar turning the melody into something new, something the piano player accompanying Estrella failed to follow.

They failed to follow it so badly that Estrella cut them off with an irritated flick of her hand, all but shoving them out of the way as her own fingers found the keys and the piano's notes flowed once more into the auditorium.

But the short lapse had turned more chairs in Clare's favor, and control of the song had shifted to her, leaving Estrella to blend. And it became all too clear that Estrella did not blend well. Her voice and song continued to hammer against Clare's, creating an unpleasant dissonance and this—this was why the Rival Theater had done everything possible to shut down rivalries on major performance nights. Because when a singer took a brute force approach, there was nothing fun or unique in the musical exchange. There was nothing *created*.

Of course, it was the rival the theater expected to perform so badly—not the reigning queen—and Clare wasn't going to let Estrella ruin this night through her own failure to remember that this moment wasn't about winning or losing—not truly—it was about performance and creation. Clare took a breath between notes as more chairs turned toward her, and that magic that had always been a part of her song when she willed it, the magic that felt like *her* and not the Song, poured out of her in a wave.

It swelled as it moved across the audience, so soft and gentle its true size and danger went unrecognized until it crested—and broke over Estrella. Clare's words and the power wrapped in them didn't try to convince the other woman to quit—she could likely have achieved that only by imbuing the world's wealth of hopelessness into her song, and if she had no doubt she could do it, hopelessness was not what she wanted this crowd to feel. It was not what she wanted them to remember, when they thought of her.

Instead, she gave Estrella what her career had made her forget— the rush and joy of first discovery, the love of the music first and not the fear of losing it, the reminder that Estrella had started down this path in life because she *was* good. Because she had once been extraordinary.

Estrella's hands stilled on the keys, her voice dropping to a mere accompanying hum for two beats as she fought the insistent push of Clare's magic. Then her own magic snapped, no longer trying to beat Clare's into submission. Her fingers found the keys again but this time when she played, it was as Clare had sung in the beginning—a joining, an accompaniment, biding time while she looked for an opening.

Estrella Vane was finally playing the Rival Theater's game.

CHAPTER

FOURTEEN

HOPE IS A TERROR

Numair could hardly breathe as the music crested around him. There had been a moment when he'd feared Estrella's stubbornness would ruin everything. He'd known she'd react badly to the rivalry but he'd counted on her adeptness with music and her unwillingness to look like a fool to carry her through.

Apparently, he'd overestimated her intelligence. But just when he'd feared she was going to push forward with that obstinate, blunt-force approach, the one that had the theater's staff looking as if they were about to step in and fabricate some emergency that required the ending of the performance, Clare's Songweaving wrapped around the other singer. And for a brief time, Estrella Vane became again the singer Veralna had once adored and still pretended to.

Even though he knew how it would end, now that Estrella was trying and the performance would be allowed to run to its conclusion, he couldn't relax. Every push and pull between the two, as they vied for dominance in the song, was something he felt in his core. That dead place in his heart, where he hadn't felt anything but numbness and a cold-burning anger in years, stirred and he felt, for the briefest of moments, something else.

Something foreign, and horrifying, and unwanted: hope.

He knew it was only the song, the mood, the power of Clare's

Songweaving ensnaring everyone in its path. But it made fear pulse through his veins all the same. He couldn't hope anymore, was done with imagining he could. Because hope was the thing that made a person keep living through the worst humanity had to offer, and he was done surviving.

He sat there, in the grip of terror and hope and futility, as the song Clare and Estrella wove together built toward its inevitable conclusion.

CHAPTER

FIFTEEN

HIS NEW APPRENTICE

Clare knew she'd won long before Estrella accepted it. The woman was good, but her performance was a last-ditch resurgence of effort given in an attempt to cling to something she'd lost long ago.

Clare's performance was a battle cry, a gauntlet thrown down before all of Veralna, daring them not to love her. She wanted everything they were willing to give her, and everything they weren't, and her words and her voice and the notes she strummed on her guitar were a staggering display of brilliance meant to blind them.

And blind them she did. She could *feel* it, their bated breath, the way they hung on each syllable that rolled off her tongue. The way each give and take between her and Estrella always came back more heavily to Clare, until the final chair in the auditorium turned to her and Estrella simply quit as Clare's voice rose in a resonant, haunting note that echoed through the theater and held its occupants enthralled.

The voice crystals held her last strum on the guitar, her final word sung, for a handful of seconds. For a moment after they faded the world hung in perfect stillness, as if the hand of a god had stretched forth and frozen time.

Then movement broke the spell, Estrella striding off the stage, down the aisle. Clare couldn't see her face with the bright lights still shining in her eyes, but she didn't need to see it in order to feel the fury radiating from the woman. Didn't need to see her to hear the vehemence in her voice.

"You fucking *bitch.*"

Clare lifted her face, her expression schooled into serenity, the kind of expression meant to make her look angelic to everyone around her, and guaranteed to anger her rival even further. Because the only thing that might make her *more* beloved of the audience right now was if Estrella decided to slap her in an act of unprovoked rage.

But then the occupant of the chair nearest her, that first person to not only turn his chair but walk to her, stood, blocking the other singer's path.

"Really, Estrella, you can't want to embarrass yourself any further." The voice was deep and low and amused, in a bored way, and something about it made Clare wish she could see the speaker's face. Or see the expression on Estrella's in response.

Clare did see the woman's hands curl into fists—but then Estrella's gaze shifted to the left and she laughed, like she'd won even though she'd lost.

Clare followed her gaze, could just make out three brilliant red uniforms steadily coming toward the rival stage. Her spine steeled, every instinct in her body going on alert, telling her she'd missed something, some danger she hadn't been aware of, and it was too late to repair the damage.

Hounds, the Song whispered as the red-clad figures approached. *Magic hunters.*

But then another person was moving, reaching her first, Marquin Arrendon's large frame entering the circle of light surrounding the rival stage. He extended a hand to her and she didn't need the Song's push to act as if she'd expected him all along, didn't need its urging to place her hand in his and allow him to help her from the stage.

Her eyes took a moment to adjust to the dimmer light. Once they had, she noted that the red-uniformed individuals had halted five feet from Marquin, that the man who'd blocked Estrella's advance was gone, and that Estrella herself was staring at Clare with a look of tight-lipped fury.

Clare gave the other artist a shallow bow, as if she hadn't heard Estrella's earlier words. The woman jerked back like she'd taken a blow, and her gaze snapped to Marquin. "I hadn't realized the Lords Arrendon were taking in strays again."

"She is yours, then, Lord Arrendon?" one of the red-garbed figures asked, stepping forward. There was something hard in his gaze, and Clare had the distinct impression that nothing would make him happier than an excuse to cross Marquin.

"Mine, actually." Verol's voice preceded him as he approached, and Clare didn't miss the way Marquin relaxed a fraction, as if he'd been preparing for a battle that no longer needed to be fought.

Mine, Verol had said. His *what,* exactly?

If Clare had thought the red guardsman looked hard before, it was nothing compared to the dislike that dripped from him at Verol's approach. "I trust you have her apprenticeship papers and a dispensation for this…performance."

Verol simply handed the man a roll of papers in response. He took his time looking through them while the theater crowd remained, whispering and speculating on a situation Clare didn't understand.

When he handed the papers back it was wordlessly. He left with the other guardsmen as if Clare and the theater were beneath his notice.

CHAPTER

SIXTEEN

A VERY FAR THING FROM HAPPY

The specter of Clare's supposed apprenticeship to Verol stole the afterglow of her performance. It was not that she'd expected to bask in the glory of her triumph—her working of the room afterward had always been intended as a calculated thing—but she'd intended to revel in each strategized word and smile and manner that left her lips as she circulated among the theater's attendees.

Instead, she was looking for quick remarks and easy manipulations, for a way to leave as quickly as possible so she could understand why the word "apprentice" was suddenly attached to her name. Why she had to be grateful that every time someone else asked a similar question about it, Verol was there to answer it.

Even so, she remembered to drop Chalen Mora's name every other conversation, and by the time she followed Verol and Marquin outside to a waiting carriage, she was certain the tailor's name would indeed be spread through Hightown by the next day's midafternoon bell. The same driver from the night outside the Hawk and Scepter held the horses' reins now, his eyes narrowing as she approached.

When she'd traveled with Quin and Verol on the road, they had taken turns driving. But she supposed lords, however nontraditional she suspected they were, didn't drive themselves in town. Marquin held the carriage door open and Clare got in because

95

yelling at lords in public did not go well with the image she was working to cultivate.

They settled across from her, and as soon as the carriage door closed, she spoke. "Explain."

"You aren't registered with the Mages Guild."

"And?"

"And it is illegal to possess or use magic without being registered. Had Verol not arranged your apprenticeship papers, back-dated to your arrival in Veralna, you would have left that performance in the custody of the king's Hounds."

Clare stiffened. "You might have mentioned that law before I entered town, if you were so concerned."

They shared a glance. Verol spoke next. "That stipulation on magic use isn't particular to Veralna but to all of the Faelhorn Provinces. Until the Kinthing prompted us to attend this evening, we had no reason to suspect you wouldn't know of it."

There was a question under the words, one Clare had no intention of answering. She didn't precisely know if it was illegal to leave Renault County, but she did know that no one was ever *intended* to leave it.

"So you decided to take it upon yourself to make me your apprentice? Without the slightest consideration from me?"

Verol winced. Marquin held her gaze. "No, he decided to ensure you didn't end the evening in the clutches of a person whose custody I can assure you, you do not wish to be in. Here." He pulled from the inside pocket of his suit the roll of papers Verol had handed the Hound earlier. "Your signature agreeing to the apprenticeship is obviously forged. All you need to do to get out of this situation is tell the guild it's so and they will dissolve this contract."

Clare didn't take the roll of papers from Marquin's hand. She couldn't have even recognized her own name on the contract, much less signed it, so there was no point in looking. "And if I do that?"

"Then you will face repercussions for magical use on the public without proper dispensation. Depending on how that goes, the guild will then test your magical inclination without the protection of having present a mage who has your best interests at heart, and *they* will assign your apprenticeship. You can refuse an assignment, of course, but you *must* have an apprenticeship before you leave the guild testing, and you might not end up with someone you like.

"In addition, you will owe the back payment due to the guild for every year of your life that your magic has gone un-reported to the guild since Faelhorn annexed El-Dennon. Verol has paid it, but only masters are allowed to take on financial obligations in the Mages Guild for their apprentices. Should you dissolve this arrangement, they will refund Verol's payment even should he ask them to keep it."

Clare's fingers curled around the carriage's plush seat, as if she could strangle the finery from it. Did *every* guild in this place attempt to force its members into indentured servitude?

You couldn't have warned me about this? She snapped the thought at the Song, felt its maddening contentment in response, and understood. Yes, it could have warned her, so she would have known about the law, and the dangers, and she would have perhaps rethought using magic in the performance against Estrella.

But if the Song had done that, she wouldn't be where she was right now—backed into a corner where her only *good* choice was accepting Verol's help. Putting her right where the Song had wanted her all along. Right where *Verol* had wanted her. Because it was impossible for him to have arranged all of this in the span of her performance. Yes, her battle with Estrella had been a lengthy one, but no matter how powerful Verol's magic was, he must have already had the pieces in place to accomplish so much in so short a time.

She didn't like being manipulated. She liked making poor choices even less. And taking an unknown over a known—especially when she *liked* the two knowns inside the carriage—would be a poor choice. But she was a very far thing from happy about it.

She lessened her grip on the seat cushions and choked the anger down. As she always did. Sometimes she thought her entire life had been nothing but choking on fury. "What does this testing involve?"

"You will sing for a master Songweaver. They will verify you possess the ability and adequate control over it to pose no danger, after which any misuse of your gifts becomes my responsibility." Verol paused, waiting for a response Clare didn't give him. The less direction you gave a person, the more they tended to talk, and Clare wanted him to talk. But he was apparently familiar with the game because what he said next wasn't terribly illuminating. "We will be at the guild in a quarter hour. You should make your decision before we arrive."

The carriage was rolling to a spot when she finally spoke. "Why didn't you falsify the testing?"

Verol frowned. "What?"

She nodded at the roll of papers now resting between Verol and Marquin. "You falsified my application, my signature, all of the documentation. Why not the test, too?"

"All magic leaves an imprint—a signature, if you will. That signature can be recorded, and is during a mage's initial testing. I can't falsify that for you."

"How is it recorded?"

"Various mediums can catch an imprint, but for rankings, the guild settled on gemstones. There are fifteen primary ranking levels, from amber at the bottom, to diamond at the top. Even the lowest level mage can imprint on amber, while very few make it to diamond."

"And where do you rank?"

He brushed his hair back from his face, revealing the gem that dangled from his left ear. "Diamond."

Of course he did. Her gaze flicked to the matching earring Marquin wore. She had noted them before, in the habitual way she noted anything worth stealing, and had wondered if they were some kind of alternative version of wedding rings. Now she understood the ornaments had nothing to do with who they were to each other, and everything to do with *what* they were.

Both mages. Both diamonds. Like so often called to like. She wasn't entirely certain what that said about her.

Brushing the thought aside, she reached for the carriage door. "Let's get this over with."

<hr>

THE MAGES GUILD was an impressive building that overshadowed its surrounding neighbors. The painstakingly carved engravings on its facade spoke to years of labor and an excess of wealth readily available to spend on architectural whims. As did the sharp spire jutting from its top like the horn of some mystical creature of old.

She followed Verol and Marquin through the front doors and the mostly empty lobby. But mostly empty wasn't entirely empty, and the six people—mages—who were present had an…interesting reaction to their entrance.

Two left immediately. The remaining four observed Verol and Marquin as if the lords might bite without the slightest provocation. Two of those four had badly disguised hatred worming its way through their features, but overshadowing that was a baser emotion: fear.

She hadn't noticed any similar response among the theater crowd as Marquin and Verol shadowed her after the performance. Was the elite of Veralna's society simply better at hiding their reactions, or did the city's mages have a different reason to dislike the Arrendons?

Either the Mages Guild did not do a brisk business at this time of night, or else word had preceded them and the halls had cleared accordingly, because she didn't see another soul as they wended their way through labyrinthine hallways and up several flights of stairs.

Her breathing quickened the deeper they went into the building, not from physical exertion, but from an ever-increasing fear that she wouldn't get out again. The further she walked the shallower her breaths came, until she kept stopping after she exhaled, her lungs empty, forgetting to take that next breath in.

The soft cream-colored walls insisted on bleaching themselves to white in the periphery of her vision, the sandstone tile becoming gleaming, glossy white, until she was deep in the bowels of another building, in another time.

She hadn't gotten out. Of *course* she hadn't gotten out. No one did. No one left Renault County. No one left *him.*

"Clare?" The voice pulsed in her fading vision like visible sound, unfamiliar and teasing at the edges of her panic. "Clare?"

She didn't know a Clare, but she didn't know the names of most people she met. There was little point in the familiarity. People either used you, betrayed you, or died, so it was only worth learning their name if doing so gave you some advantage over them.

But Clare was a nice name. Clare felt…bright, like sunshine. She wasn't bright. She was darkness and pain but she *wanted* to be bright someday. That was why she'd given herself a name, one she whispered in her head where only she could hear it. But she couldn't remember that name right now because she hadn't gotten *out* and—

"Clare Brighton?" The high, imperious voice cut through the chatter in her head.

Hard fury jerked her back to the present. Because she *had* gotten out. *She* was Clare Brighton. That was the name she'd given herself in the dark—and that was Madame Aria speaking it with so much disdain.

Memory's desperate clutch fell away and Clare stood once more in the cream-colored hallway of the Mages Guild while the woman whose *other* guild infuriated her walked toward her.

Clare straightened. Marquin's and Verol's worried expressions smoothed over as Madame Aria's morphed into one of cruel delight. "If you're here to take that something precious from me you promised, I'm afraid I'm busy at the moment."

Clare pulled confidence around her like a cloak, superiority the broach with which she held it pinned. "I already accomplished that task. Have you spoken to anyone from the Rival Theater in the last hour? Because I just knocked Estrella Vane from her pedestal."

Madame Aria's lips thinned.

"The two of you have met, I take it?" Marquin said.

"If you could call this *child* threatening me a meeting, then yes, we have met."

Clare's lips curved into the most condescending smile in her arsenal. "I see it's true what they say about memory fading with age. I didn't threaten you, I challenged you. It's not my fault if you can't hold on to your things."

Madame Aria took a step toward her. "You little—"

"*Madame Aria.*" Verol's stern voice halted her. "Whatever history you may or may not have with my apprentice is of no concern at this moment. You are not here as yourself but as a representative of the Mages Guild. Are you capable of performing without prejudice the function you have been tasked with, or should I have you replaced?"

For a brief moment, Clare thought the woman might actually back down. But in the end, Clare followed the three mages into a room down the hall. It was a soft room—that was the only word

Clare could think of to describe it. Soft floor, soft colors, soft furniture.

Not a very good room for acoustics, and she wondered if that wasn't part of the test. Madame Aria proceeded to explain what Verol and Marquin already had. Clare would sing. She would use her Songweaving talent to weave what emotion she could into the song. Madame Aria would judge her control, and the gemstones would judge her strength.

Clare looked at the row of stones sitting atop the piano in the center of the room. Only ten of them there, amber through garnet. Her lip curled. "You're missing a few."

Madame Aria made a *tutting* sound under her breath. "Songweavers rarely rank above chalcedony. Only one has ever reached garnet."

Since that very gem hung from Madame Aria's ear, Clare took great pleasure in leaning closer to the other woman and saying, "Then I suppose I'm knocking two Songweavers off their pedestals tonight, because I rank higher." Clare didn't doubt the words as she spoke them. She could feel the power that wafted off Madame Aria and it was nothing compared to her own. Before she'd known who her tester would be, she had considered hiding the full extent of her power. Appearing less than—common—to avoid scrutiny. But now? Now she was angry. "Get the other gemstones."

Madame Aria turned on Verol. "You are wasting my time with this? Honestly, if you intend to have an apprentice you might try teaching her some manners first."

Verol's gaze hardened. "You have a responsibility to *accurately* test her abilities. If she had only a grain of power, she would still have the right to a full range of testing. Do as she says."

The woman scowled, but she left the room and came back a moment later, setting the rest of the stones down in a row, plunking the diamond down last with a harsh thud. She turned, crossing her arms. "Well, then, let's hear you sing."

Madame Aria didn't move to take a seat at the piano, nor did she allow Clare to do so. When Clare undid the first latch on her guitar case, the woman snapped, "Without accompaniment. If you can't sing without it, you can't sing."

Clare bristled, but it was at the snapped order, not at the fact she was to sing without an instrument. That wasn't the disadvantage Madame Aria thought it was.

Clare set the guitar aside. "What would you like most to hear?"

"I should *like* to hear 'The Summer Song' from De Monin's *Reckoning and Dissonance*. However, since it is unlikely you even know of the song, I should settle for—"

Clare sang. She had no interest in hearing what Madame Aria would have settled for. The derision in the woman's tone, the assertion that Clare would not even know "The Summer Song", much less be capable of singing it, fanned the ember of anger that was always, always smoldering in Clare's chest.

Maybe if Clare hadn't nearly broken down in the hallway earlier, or if she wasn't trying to navigate a world she barely understood, or if Madame Aria hadn't been so dismissive of her, both at the Musicians Guild and now, Clare could have shown the restraint logic begged for.

Instead, she closed her eyes and dove into the song's depths. "The Summer Song" was arguably the most famous song of any in De Monin's works, and unquestionably the most difficult. Likening a loss of innocence to the fading of summer, it covered the full range of voice, from bass to highest soprano, and the erratic tempo was difficult to keep properly, especially if one sang without accompaniment.

In melody and style, the song was undeniably beautiful, but its message—Clare hated its message. As if a girl faded forever from summer into winter once her first blossom was plucked. Why was it that the songs never sang of a *man's* innocence fading once he first came inside a woman?

She couldn't instill in her voice and song the sadness the character of Sofraya was meant to be feeling. Instead, the power that spiraled into her words was filled with bitterness; bitterness toward the song, toward De Monin, toward a society that bound women in glittering chains of purity and declared a woman's worth depended on those chains, or at least on the illusion of them.

The gemstones atop the piano rattled and shot into the air, surfaces etching as Clare's power surged. Her anger fueled it, had it coalescing into wide ribbons she wove into her words. She entered the mid-point of the song, her voice dropping a note with each word, down toward the low end of a second tenor's range, the room filling with the power radiating from her.

The amber stone exploded. Then the jet and the coral and the malachite, stone after stone pulverizing as she finished the descent and began the climb out. There was a brief reprieve in intensity as the song demanded, and the final four gemstones—emerald, ruby, sapphire, diamond—hovered, waiting, the first three etched, the diamond as yet untouched.

The reprieve ended, and though Clare hated the song's message, she couldn't stop her musical appreciation of the piece itself as she entered its zenith. For the sounds, the bones, were beautiful. Words could always be changed. Skeletons, less so. The first eleven stones, she had broken with bitterness. These next three, she broke with adoration. With love. With everything in her that wanted those things.

When she hit the final note—when she held it, ringing out in the room—and the etching shot across the diamond's surface, she wasn't bitterness *or* love, but a bright column of anger. There was a moment, holding the final note, when she could have shattered the diamond, too. But as the gem clouded over, darkening from clear to gray to deepest black, she pulled her magic back. Because right now, she still fell within the range of the guild's understanding of power. She'd been foolish enough to excel at their test—she wasn't so foolish as to break its boundaries altogether.

She let the song die. The now-black diamond clattered to the piano top. Her anger remained in the room, past the fading of the last notes, past the silence that followed, past the reasonable limits of what the song should have awakened in her. Discontent roiled within her and she was not just angry about the song, but about everything she had ever been through, everything that made the world as it was, and everything that was yet to come.

Her vision darkened to a haze that she was unmotivated to clear. In the haze, the space between the here-and-now and the rest of the world, everything was hot and pure and simple. A flicker of the true Song licked up from its prison. She had diverted too much of her power from holding it caged, and it stretched seductive tendrils toward her, whispering that she should open herself up to the rage. Open up, and let the Song embrace her. Let its power mix with the purity of her fury and create a force whose desolation would far surpass anything this guild could offer.

It would be easy.

So pitifully, painfully, easy.

Verol coughed.

Clare opened her eyes, bolstering that inner song that held the *other* Song at bay. She looked to Verol, to see if she had given herself away, if he had sensed the otherness within her. He looked…sad, and yet something else, as well. Hopeful, perhaps. Proud.

No.

No, she was reading him wrong, *must* be reading him wrong. Because no one in the whole of her life had ever been *proud* of her.

Madame Aria wore, of all things, a smile. There was something off in her expression, something feverish in her eyes as she walked to the diamond and plucked it from the piano. She rolled it between her fingers, as if trying to memorize the etchings, or as if she was looking for some hidden meaning in them.

She closed her fist around it and turned back to Clare. "A diamond-ranked Songweaver. A *black* diamond." Jealousy in the words, but hunger too. Hatred and desire. The woman moved closer —and Marquin stepped between them.

"We expected as much," he said smoothly. So smoothly she couldn't tell if it was a truth or a fiction. *Had* they expected this when they'd brought her here? Was that—and not this Kinthing— the true reason they'd interceded for her? Or had this been a surprise to them as well, and Marquin was even now downplaying the severity of it?

"We have all had a long day," he continued, "and now that the formalities are concluded, we should be going."

Clare turned, eager to get away from that look in Madame Aria's eyes, to retreat and soothe the scraped-raw wound she'd become. She'd poured too much of herself into that song, felt as if she'd laid bare a part of her soul, and now all she wanted was to hide away in some forgotten corner and cover it back up.

"Wait." Madame Aria's hand latched onto Clare's shoulder, pulling her back.

It took everything she had not to respond with violence. But ordinary people did not hit someone at the mere provocation of being touched. Instead, Clare glanced pointedly at the hand on her shoulder, but the woman didn't remove it. A predatory air hung over Madame Aria, one Clare was all too adept at recognizing.

"Are you sure you want to apprentice to them? They know much about magic, yes, but their strengths aren't in music. Mine are. We had a difficult beginning, but it's nothing that cannot be smoothed over."

"Thank you," Clare said, in a voice that conveyed anything but appreciation, "for the offer. But I will stay with Verol."

Madame Aria's eyes narrowed, cracking the facade of beneficence. "I could have you singing for the king within three months. That's what you want, isn't it girl? Patrons? A quick rise to fortune? Stay with him and you'll find yourself begging to be allowed to sing in the Lowtown's winter festival."

Anger was a hot rush inside her. "I don't need you, or them, or anyone to get what I want. I have myself. And I haven't forgotten the promise I made to you. Prepare yourself, Madame Aria. Because I haven't taken nearly enough from you yet."

The fingers on Clare's shoulder tightened, the grip a force Clare knew from experience would bruise, would leave thin finger-like lines of purple that would remind Clare of this moment. Life was always, always reminding.

"You think *you're* too good for me?" Harsh, whispered words. "You shouldn't even be alive. You're an abomination, a—"

"*Madame Aria.*" A whip of power cracked through the room alongside Verol's words. "A moment of your time."

Clare barely registered the color leaving Madame Aria's face, her hand dropping, the way her, "Of course," came out a little too monotone. She barely registered Marquin guiding her out of the room, his soft, "Let us wait downstairs, so Verol and Madame Aria may…talk."

They weren't going to talk. Verol was going to do whatever Verol did because of that single, cold-spoken word. *Abomination.*

A noise like rushing water pounded through Clare's ears. She never should have come here. She should have run the second Marquin gave her the option. But where would she run *to*? Where was she going to go that things wouldn't be exactly the same as they were here? Her only option for staying hidden was the same one she'd always had: hiding in plain sight.

If she hadn't just ruined that.

Step by step they moved out of the bowels of the building, the pressure on her chest easing as the guild's labyrinthine halls lost their grip on her. Outside, the frigid night air cutting easily through the fine fabric of her dress, the rushing in her ears finally dimmed. Enough for her to notice how calm Marquin was, as if nothing at all was the matter, and that calm made Clare question her initial reaction to that word.

Abomination.

Had the woman recognized that something *other* lived inside Clare? Or had it only been a word, spoken in anger against someone the woman had already proved she looked down on? Madame Aria had thought Clare nothing on their first meeting. And now that she had shown she was worth something, the woman wanted to own her.

What was more likely—that the word was an indictment, or merely an insult? She hadn't imagined that whip of power from Verol but maybe…maybe that was just anger too, Madame Aria's reaction only the recognition that she'd overstepped in the presence of two men the entire Mages Guild seemed to fear.

Their carriage pulled up and she followed Marquin into it, out of the chilled air, and finally made herself look at him. He wasn't looking at her any differently than he had before, wasn't looking at her like Madame Aria's word had *meant* anything. And surely, in a guild full of mages who knew precisely what Verol could do with his talents, the man wasn't in there realigning a woman's memory.

Still… "What is Verol talking to her about?"

Marquin grimaced. "Her conduct. I am sorry you had to be exposed to that."

Clare laughed. "I have been called far worse, and far more often."

Marquin gave her an odd look, and she reminded herself that probably wasn't something normal people would say. And she needed to know those things so she could act normal because she wasn't normal.

Abomination. How many times had Clare wondered it herself? Images flashed through her mind. The endless swamp, lost so deep within that the light could not penetrate the canopy. Muck and bones crunching beneath bare feet. A memory of madness.

The carriage door swung open. Verol claimed the space next to

Marquin, his face a mass of thunderclouds. He handed her a small box, which she opened to find a black diamond in a setting identical to the ones Verol and Marquin's diamonds were clasped in. A sign, to everyone who saw her, that she belonged to the Mages Guild now.

She touched her fingertips to her earlobe, the skin unmarred by any opening.

"We can have your ear pierced tomorrow," Marquin said. "If you will be remaining with us."

He'd understood, then, when she came to the Mages Guild tonight that she hadn't accepted anything. Verol hadn't, if the way he tensed was any indication.

Her thumb stroked over the stone. "For now. We'll see how things look in the morning."

Silence held sway the rest of the ride, until the carriage halted. The two horses hitched to it, Ginger and Skye, stomped their hooves impatiently, and it eased a little of her tension. They'd had a tendency to express their impatience in just such a manner every time the wagon had stopped on the two-week journey from the Valedon swamps to Veralna City, and she found it comforting that the horses, at least, had not changed.

She followed Marquin and Verol out of the carriage, noting it had stopped outside the barn, rather than by the front door of their home, as she'd expected. Either she had an unfair opinion of what the nobility were like, or Verol and Marquin were every bit as unconventional as she suspected.

A young woman, perhaps a couple winters older than Clare, stood by Ginger, helping the driver unhitch the gelding's harness. The first thing Clare noticed was that her clothes—breeches and a long tunic, well-worn but quality boots—didn't match her. It was the way she carried herself, like clothes were an ornament and she was the main fixture, except this wasn't the type of clothing that accentuated anything.

The second thing Clare noticed was the scar that started at the top of her left temple. It slashed across her left eye, leaving a distorted iris in its wake, ran just shy of her nose to cut across her lips to her chin. And Clare shouldn't have been able to see it.

Glamour covered the mark, and wasn't that strange? Glamour wasn't cheap—her day of comparing prices in the market had taught her that—and here someone was, wasting it to cover a scar in the middle of the night.

Except…Clare blinked, humming a note under her breath and her vision shifted again. Oh, the glamour was good. The first tug of it, should anyone with the ability care enough to look beneath, only revealed the scar. And it was so obvious why someone might hide it that likely no one bothered looking any further. But if they did, as Clare did now, they would notice that the first glamour masked a second. One that subtly changed the features of the woman's face.

Instead of auburn hair the world would see a common brown. Instead of high pronounced cheekbones and an angular face, the glamour showed one less sharp, rounder and fuller, still pretty but nothing like the true face beneath.

The woman's eyes—hazel from the glamour but blue beneath it —swept over Verol and Marquin, fell on Clare. She stilled. "My lords?"

"This is Clare," Marquin said. "She will be staying with us. Clare, these are Fitz"—he nodded to the carriage driver, who only grunted in response—"and Alys." A nod to the woman.

The look Alys gave her made it clear her battles weren't over for the night.

"Hello, Alys." Clare spoke with neutrality so perfect that it was difficult to say her tone sounded like anything at all, and yet the deep hollows and crevices of the neutrality were filled with the nuanced subtleties of warning, impossible to point at directly, yet present all the same.

"Hello, Clare." Alys's voice, higher in pitch than Clare's own rich alto, was nonetheless a studied thing as well. Just as polished, as hidden, as Clare's, and it held an accusation Clare liked not at all. Though Marquin's and Verol's relationship was obviously known, it seemed that fact held little value when they showed up with a young, attractive woman in the middle of the night.

But then, the way Alys was looking at her…perhaps it was not Verol's and Marquin's intentions the woman mistrusted.

Verol glanced between Clare and Alys, seeming to sense the unspoken challenge hanging in the air and yet unable to pluck it from the four words that had passed between them. Marquin was not so lost.

"Clare is Verol's new apprentice." His voice was gentle, but it brooked no room for misinterpretation.

Alys's gaze did not turn any friendlier as she studied Clare. "You're a mage?"

"That *is* why one apprentices to a mage, is it not?"

"You're a little old for an apprenticeship."

"I had an unconventional upbringing."

Alys's gaze flicked to Verol. "Could I have a word with you, Lord Verol?"

Verol nodded, taking Skye's halter as Alys took Ginger's, and walked with her into the stable.

"Does something amuse you?" Marquin asked, noting Clare's smile.

"Only that your stablehand doesn't hide her roots nearly as well as she thinks." That 'Lord Verol' had rolled off her tongue so easily, so familiarly. Marquin made a noncommittal noise, as if he didn't understand what she meant, which told her he did.

She followed him across the stretch of lawn from the stable to the house. An ancient, towering tree stood sentinel midway between the two. Its silvery trunk was easily as wide as she was tall, and as she passed it a great rent in the width made her halt. The gash was a vertical four-foot slash, out of which oozed a viscous black sap, as if the tree was slowly bleeding out. She stared up at the wide branches, gnarled and barren of leaves, and was struck with a sense of profound unease.

She hurried past it, up a short series of stairs to a raised porch, and through the doors of the Arrendons' home. The starlight only afforded her the impression that the house was large and made of stone, and she was not to get a much better view of the inside. Marquin guided their way with a soft magelight, though why he did not turn the primary magelights on she could not guess. The expense would be next to nothing for a lord, but she did not ask him about it. Something in the way he moved, confident and silent in the near-dark, gave the impression that he was both comfortable in the shadows, and found the shadows comforting.

The magelight lit just enough of their way for Clare to see the ornately threaded runner covering the hardwood floor of the hallway they walked, and to keep her from banging the guitar case into the corner they rounded before coming to an abrupt halt in front of a set of ebony wood double doors. She was relieved to be on the ground floor, relieved there were no stairs to climb. Relieved, if her mental mapping of the home's layout was correct, that this room was on an exterior wall.

Marquin pressed a small metal key into her hand and gave her the magelight. "This is the only key to your room. Sleep. We can figure everything else out in the morning."

Clare stood before the doors, listening to the fading of Marquin's footsteps, and she did not turn the small key until she could not hear them anymore. Inside, she closed the door softly behind her, and locked it. She settled her guitar case on the floor and let the magelight guide her to a tall-backed chair set in front of a solid wooden vanity table. Turning the chair so it faced the door, Clare sat, the magelight a soft warmth nestled between her palms, held delicately in her lap, and waited.

What she was waiting for, she did not know, and she did not find out. Exhaustion, so long staved off, overcame her, and she fell asleep in the tall chair, magelight softly glowing.

CHAPTER

SEVENTEEN

WE ARE NOT GOOD MEN. AND OTHER LIES
PEOPLE TELL.

Clare jerked awake to the scritching and scratching of insects scrabbling over the cellar floors and wall. She jumped to her feet, brushing furiously at arms and clothes to shake off the scratchy, feathery feel of little legs crawling on her skin, her face, poking at the corners of her lips, burrowing beneath folds in her clothes. A scream tore at her throat but she choked it off to a strangled whimper.

Couldn't scream, couldn't *ever* scream. If she screamed it would draw his attention and once *that* happened… Couldn't scream. But Ferrian, she couldn't stand the bugs in her hair again, frantic trapped legs kicking and clawing at the tangled locks. She would have to finger-comb the hair to get them out, the little creatures skittering across her hands but there was no help for it because they had to come *out.*

She reached for her hair, the reflection of her hands trembling in the room's mirror.

Mirror.

She'd only ever seen one mirror in Renault County, and this was not that floor-length monstrosity. Her reflection looked back at her, face drained of all color, and it wasn't just her hands trembling but her entire body.

She grasped the back of the chair she'd fallen asleep in and leaned heavily. She forced a breath in and held it, let it out slowly.

Mirror. Vanity. Chair. For a moment, the things sent a wave of revulsion through her. But these were not made of pale almost-white material. These were a glossy cherrywood, shiny and comforting. The large bed was not a soulless white, but covered in sheets and blankets and pillows in varying shades of soft green.

It was all luxurious, yes, but it didn't feel twisted, as the only other luxury she'd ever known had. It felt tasteful. Comfortable. It felt…clean.

Clare's head dropped to where her hands curled around the back of the chair, and she gave in to the heaving, shuddering sob that was the aftermath of panic and fear and relief. But no matter how tight she grasped the finely carved chair, how much she stared at the differences between this room and that other room, she couldn't quite shake the feel of her own skin crawling.

Swallowing the panic that threatened to build again at the thought of what she *wasn't* living in, she forced herself to straighten, to find the small washroom that was partially separated from the rest of the room by a half-wall. An honest-to-Ferrian marble tub graced the center of the space, mercifully clean, the taps above it showing its connection to the aqueduct system.

She wouldn't have cared if the water came out cold as Renault County's winters, but heating spells kicked in when she turned the left tap. The need to have the crawling feeling off her body was strong enough she didn't even take a moment to marvel that the lords could afford to keep heating spells in place for a room that presumably was not in frequent use.

She peeled the layers of her clothing off, fabric sliding roughly over the old scars on her back, her buttocks, her thighs. She shed the rest of her clothes and stepped into the water, closing her eyes as the bliss of its heat rolled over her ankles, up her calves. She sank into the tub, letting the hot water seep into her bones, until it turned her pleasantly numb.

She took the cloth and little cake of soap that rested on the marble ledge and scrubbed at herself, until she felt she had stripped every stray bit of old skin from her body. Then she scrubbed harder, fixating on some imagined speck of dirt on her leg, until the skin rubbed away entirely and the water turned pink with blood. Sometimes, she thought the only way she could ever truly be clean would be to strip all the flesh from her body and start anew. Sometimes, in the dreams she so often had of other lives, she thought something of the kind might have happened to her once.

Shaking, Clare put the cloth down, staring at her leg until it finally clotted and stopped bleeding. She didn't get out until the water turned cold.

AFTER TOO MUCH INTERNAL DEBATE, Clare put on one of the dresses she'd bartered for in the market. She'd gone for dresses because they were a safe choice for performing, but she didn't like them. Unfortunately, her travel clothes were past their limit on dirt, and her only other pair of breeches had been patched so many times the original material likely only existed in someone's memory.

She couldn't go out in public wearing them. Not in Veralna.

She retraced her steps from last night until she found Verol and Marquin—and Fitz—in the home's dining parlor. It was a large, airy room with arched windows lining the eastern wall, letting in the morning sun. Plants dangled from hanging baskets anchored into the exposed wooden beams overhead, making the space feel alive and inviting.

Not even the scowl Fitz gave her could break the charming, sunny atmosphere. Finally seeing him in the daylight, she determined he was somewhere in his early thirties. With a medium build, light skin and muddy brown hair, he was, in all physical ways, fairly unremarkable. But there was an intelligence lurking behind the washed-out blue eyes.

"Good morning." Verol waved at her, calm and easy, as if her being here wasn't strange for them. Maybe it wasn't. Maybe it was only strange for her. "Did you sleep well?"

What the hell kind of question was that? Certainly not one she'd ever been asked before, and she found herself looking to Marquin. Because she'd known, instinctively, that he would understand her confusion.

"Sleeping in a new place can be trying," he said, offering her a response, the ability to piece together what Verol's tone alone should have told her. The question wasn't an interrogation—it was a meaningless pleasantry. "I hope the bed was comfortable."

She decided telling them she'd fallen asleep in the chair and awakened thinking she was in a lightless, bug-infested cellar was not the sort of morning chatter they were aiming for.

She answered without answering. "Thank you for the room."

Marquin nodded. "We weren't sure if you would be awake for breakfast, but we made you a place, just to be safe."

Marquin and Verol sat across from each other, neither one at the traditional head of the table. The seat Marquin pointed out for her was one down from Verol, and across from Fitz. As she approached it the latter rose, shoving his chair back, and left.

"You'll have to forgive Fitz," Verol said. "He's dreadfully antisocial in the hours before noon."

"He is also," Marquin added, "dreadfully antisocial in the hours *after* noon. Try not to take it personally."

"And…who *is* Fitz?" He certainly wasn't simply their carriage driver if he was eating at their breakfast table.

"Whoever he needs to be. If he feels like telling you, he will."

She doubted that would be likely any time soon, but she could find it out on her own.

The tantalizing aromas of the morning's breakfast, laid out on platters in the center of the table, drew her to it. She hadn't eaten since the food Taius had ordered at the cafe and left for her yesterday afternoon.

She wondered if he'd been at the theater last night. He'd said he wanted to watch the performance and yet she hadn't seen him in the crowd, after. He could have been wearing a different face, but at this point she was pretty sure she would have recognized him anyway, had that been the case.

Midway to the table she halted, a tremor running through her body. She forced herself to take another step but then her mind slid sideways, trying to go somewhere else. Somewhere in the past.

"Clare?" Marquin's voice snapped her partially back to the present and she resumed walking. But the closer she came to the table, the more wrong it seemed. Like it wasn't real, like it was a dream.

A happy, bright room. A table laid with food she was allowed to eat. Two people she wasn't afraid of sitting there, welcoming, like this was every other morning for them.

Her fingers brushed the chair back and her heart kicked up its beating. Her stomach wanted her to sit down and eat everything laid out before her. The rest of her wanted to turn and flee. Out of the room, out of the house, out of Veralna City. To run and keep running until civilization was gone again and so was she, her mind given back over to that blank haziness she'd drifted in while she wandered the swamp.

It was a heavy thing, this world. Its institutions, its violences. Her body like a prison chaining her in it, and this half-wild need for vengeance—for security, for triumph—the only thing that made her strong enough to keep going.

She pulled the chair out. The moment she sat she knew this wasn't going to work. Her entire body trembled. Sitting at the cafe's table hadn't invoked this feeling in her because it had been small, and outdoors. But here, inside, at a formal table meant for far more people than the three of them—there was only one other place she'd ever sat at a table like this.

Her palms pressed against the layered wood grain, ready to push her away, when the Song shifted and a kind of happy warmth stole over her. She remembered sitting at a table, larger than this one, filled with people—her parents and aunts and uncles, young children darting around and underneath, giggling, everyone happy.

It wasn't her memory but that didn't matter to her body, which took the new information and settled, muscles easing. She wanted to scream and rage, or maybe cry, none of which she could do out loud.

This isn't helping, she snapped at the Song. *I don't care if some other girl had a happy fucking life where a Ferrian's cursed* table *didn't send her into a panic, she* isn't me.

Layering the girl's memories over Clare's wasn't going to change her. And yet she had a feeling that was exactly what the Song was trying to do. It gave her these bits and slices, things that helped her in the moment, but she couldn't shake the feeling it was trying to erase her. To mold her, to soften her, because it was her resolve that kept it caged.

Only since she'd left Renault County, since doing so had sent a jagged crack through that cage, had it been able to crowd her mind with other people's lives. As if it was looking for the right one, the perfect one, the one Clare would want so much that she would let it overtake her own. And once she was someone else, someone happier, someone more pliable, she wouldn't have the resolve that kept the Song at bay.

And if that happened, she—both the Clare that she was now, and whatever happier identity the Song convinced her to give herself over to—would cease to exist. Because the Song would break free and obliterate her, until all that was left of her was a body for it to control. A vessel.

"Are you all right?" Verol leaned toward her, concern on his face.

Clare snapped out of her internal thoughts and pasted on a smile. "Perfectly fine." As if to prove it to herself, she made selections from the array of food carefully, delicately, as if she were not hungry at all.

Control. Control had to be the master of her life, of her thoughts.

So she selected a single roll, buttering it with the delicate little silver knife in the pretty butter tray, took two slices of bacon, and a small portion of eggs and browned potatoes. She wanted more. She wanted everything here and could have eaten it all too. But then she'd find herself hurling her guts up as soon as she was done.

That was the funny thing about the body—once it had been starved long enough, it had a tendency to reject the very thing that could keep it alive.

The three of them ate in the companionable silence they'd shared at mealtimes on the road. Clare ate half of what was on her plate and then reached for the clear glass coffee carafe, knowing what memory it would evoke and needing to prove to herself that she could handle it.

The smooth glass handle fit the cradle of her palm, and she poured a cup of the deep brown liquid with graceful movements, careful not to let the carafe clatter as she set it down. She had almost lost her hand once, letting a different carafe clatter, and the scar on her right wrist gleamed up at her. He had been so angry for marking her there, where the scar would be visible. Angry at her, for driving him to it.

She let the memory wash over her in a detached way, as if it had happened to someone else, and her hand didn't shake as she lifted the coffee cup and took a careful sip. She'd never actually tasted it before, and it lived up to the promise of its scent. Rich and warm, silken smooth even with the slight bite of bitterness at its core. She'd never minded bitter things.

It slid down her throat in a hot line, warming her from the inside as it settled. She decided she liked it. She also decided this wouldn't be the last time she had it. It wouldn't be the last time she had more food than she could eat. It wouldn't be the last time she sat in a nice house without shaking in fear.

Whatever it took, whatever she had to sacrifice or pretend to be, she would mold herself into the person *she* wanted. Even if she had no idea who that person was. Even if the only thing that kept her going was a half-cooked dream of vengeance she had no idea how to achieve.

She placed the coffee cup on its saucer. She slipped the small box containing her earring from the pocket of her dress and placed it on the table, lid open, black diamond nestled on silver cloth.

"It's black," she said, pointing out the obvious. "Is that going to be a problem?"

"It's going to cause interest," Marquin said. "There hasn't been a black diamond mage in over two-hundred years. If you were anything but a Songweaver, it might be a problem. But Songweavers, though rare, are…"

"Not considered serious magical talents?" Clare guessed.

"It is a blessing, in this case. But given your performance last night, once news of your ranking spreads, you are going to be of interest to everyone." He waited a beat and added, "But that *is* what you wanted, isn't it?"

"One doesn't put on a performance to go unseen. The question is, what do *you* want of *me*?"

"You understand about Verol's magic."

"And I'm to understand that all you want is to help me? For nothing in return?"

"Is that so difficult to believe?" Verol asked.

It wasn't difficult to believe. It was impossible. No one did anything for free.

"We do like you, Clare," Marquin said. "We would keep you from harm when it is easy enough for us to do."

She sensed truth in the words, just as she sensed that it wasn't a complete truth. The way Verol's Kinthing magic was a truth, and yet not a complete one. There was something they weren't telling her and yet…and yet she had survived Renault County by trusting her instincts. And if logic was telling her not to trust them, her instincts were telling her the opposite.

She'd spent two weeks on the road with them, no one else around, and they had done nothing to her. They had let her go when they reached Veralna City, had let her go after coming to her aid at the Hawk and Scepter. And she knew that if she walked out of this house right now, they wouldn't try to stop her with anything more than words.

She was *tired*. Of running, of hiding. Hadn't she come here to stop doing both?

"This apprenticeship. How long is it?"

Verol exhaled audibly. "In your case, given your age and the fact your innate control of your ability is already strong, the guild has opted for the minimum one-year apprenticeship with a test of your control at the end of the one year. Should you pass that, the apprenticeship will be dissolved. Should you fail, it will extend another year."

"And what are the terms?"

"I am responsible for providing you with food, clothing, and living accommodations for the duration of the apprenticeship, as well as adequate instruction of your talent."

"And in return?"

"Nothing."

"That doesn't make any sense." Verol had already paid the guild the back payment she owed. He was now to provide all the basic necessities of her life and spend his time teaching her, and that was to come for free? Perhaps he might do it for her—but the rest of the mage population could not possibly be so altruistic.

"Under a typical contract," Marquin said, "a master has complete control over the apprentice's schedule, including any projects the apprentice hires out for. Eighty-percent of an apprentice's income during the apprenticeship goes directly to the master. Additionally, once the apprentice passes guild certification, ten percent of their earnings return to their previous master for the next fifteen winters, or twice the length of their apprenticeship, whichever is shorter."

"That's hardly nothing."

"That's a *typical* contract. Yours is modified." He rose and returned a minute later with the roll of papers he'd tried to hand her in the carriage last night. "Read it for yourself."

She waved the papers away. "Just tell me." Maybe she could force the Song to give her an identity that would let her read what was written there. But she still wouldn't know how to read at the end of it. Not unless she held on to the identity after.

She was loath to give the Song a temporary ingress to her mind simply to read a piece of paper. Because if she couldn't trust Marquin and Verol to tell her the truth about what was on it, she couldn't trust them at all.

"There is no financial obligation on your end. Either during or after your apprenticeship ends. You may choose to work or not, and any income you receive will remain yours.

"Your schedule, likewise, is your own to determine. All apprenticeships require at least five hours a week of dedicated instruction. You may decide when you wish those to occur, though of course they will have to work around Verol's schedule as well."

"You're telling me the obligation—the entirety of the obligation —is on Verol's side."

"Yes."

"Why?"

"Because," Verol said, speaking up again, "it's the only way you'll stay."

As if they knew the only leash that could hold her was one so thin she hardly felt it. She had a choice: leave their house and leave Veralna too—because no other mage would offer her so favorable an apprenticeship—and spend the rest of her life hiding from the repercussions of that action. Or, accept the offer, and have a stable place to live. Food to eat. Clothes to wear. The protection that came from being apprenticed to a lord of Veralna.

It wasn't a choice, it was a godsend. She trusted it all the less for it.

"There are two more things you should know before you make a decision," Marquin said. "One is that Verol and I are not loved by this city."

She glanced between them, but neither offered further elaboration, so she hazarded a guess. "Is it because of your relationship?"

Verol laughed. "No. I'm sure that doesn't help matters, but

believe it or not, our marriage is probably the least controversial thing about us."

"Then why?"

He sighed. "A long time ago we had to make a decision. We made the best one we could at the time, one most people will likely never understand and others will never forgive us for. We would make it again—but we have done terrible things in the name of that choice. We…are not good men."

It was Clare's turn to laugh. "If you think *I* am a good woman, then you will be sorely disappointed in me." It all came down to what a person thought of as good, she supposed. Whether you thought all choices carried the same weight even when you were boxed into a corner and forced to make them. "What's the other thing I should know?"

Marquin answered, this time. "The king requires the members of his court to live in palace quarters five days of each week for half of each year. We have just begun that half of our year. All mage apprenticeships require the apprentice to live under whichever roof the master happens to reside under. You will have to stay at the palace when we do."

She could only think of one reason why Marquin might feel the need to point this out to her, and humiliation made heat rise in her cheeks. "I am capable of conducting myself in the court's company without embarrassing you."

"Embarrassment is not our concern," Marquin said. "There is a reason the king forces the living requirement on the proconsuls and nobility of every province. There is a reason even his most syco-phantic courtiers watch how loudly they tread in his presence. The Jackal King's court is not a safe place."

Years of training had her opening her mouth to pacify his concerns. To tell him that she could bend and bow and go beneath notice. The words stuck in her throat. Because she hadn't come here to live the same way she had before. Her life had been a contortion-ist's act of fitting herself into a mold small enough so that she wouldn't be a threat or an embarrassment or an inconvenience. But she had taken herself out of the mold, had grown into a different form and could never fit herself back into the old one without cutting off the pieces of herself that no longer fit it.

So she told the truth. "If life has taught me anything, it is that there is no such thing as a safe place, and I have lived in the farthest thing from one I can imagine. I do not fear your king's court."

Verol looked ill at the pronouncement. Marquin looked resigned. "Do we have a deal, then?"

"We do."

EIGHTEEN

WORTH IT, AND MORE

Apparently, if one ousted Veralna's reigning queen of music in a public display, followed that up with an apprenticeship to the Lords Arrendon, and then ranked a black diamond with the Mages Guild, word of it would spread through Veralna's elite by high noon the next day. No less than thirty letters had arrived at the Arrendon manor, and Fitz, who seemed to be the Arrendons' shadow in town, had taken up permanent residence at the front door to prevent the runners from knocking endlessly.

Verol took one look at the growing pile of correspondence, one look at Clare's wardrobe, and announced that they were going into town. Since Clare had a dress to return, she didn't argue, and Verol didn't comment when she asked him to take her to the cafe she'd eaten at the day before, because she only knew how to get to Chalen Mora's shop from that location.

He did balk when she opened the carriage door onto the alleyway that led to Chalen's shop. "Are you sure we're in the right place?"

"Quite sure. I'll only be a moment." She grabbed the dress, trotted down the alley to Chalen's door, and knocked.

A man opened the door. He was of a light build, soft black hair framing his face, his dark eyes narrowed. They fell on the dress in Clare's hand and he relaxed. "So you're the reason Chalen left at the morning bell with every finished item we have."

"Am I?" Clare asked innocently.

He snorted. "When Chalen told me they'd loaned out that one" —he nodded at the dress— "for a promise you could do in a night what ten years of work hasn't, I thought they'd lost their mind. For that matter, so did they."

"And now?"

"Now I think you're the reason I'm going to have needle pricks on all my fingers for the next month." But he was smiling as he said it. Clare held out the dress, but he shook his head. "Chalen said if you came by to tell you to keep it. You more than earned it."

She didn't argue. If Chalen was moving their entire stock into town, then Clare *had* earned it. Unfortunately, it meant her secondary motive in coming here—namely the one that meant buying the wardrobe Verol insisted she needed from Chalen rather than from a shop in town—wouldn't be possible.

"Does Chalen take requests?"

"For you? Sure. You need something made?"

"I need a lot of somethings made. With some…modifications I'd like to discuss with them."

He shook his head. "Modifications. Why do I have a feeling you're going to be a lot like our *other* private client?"

Taius. He had to mean Taius, and she almost asked. But it was better not to. Cutting ties the second they were formed—that was the safest way to live. She already had two ties she couldn't sever for a full year. There was absolutely no sense in adding a third.

"When do you think they'll have time for me?"

"Come back in a few days. Any time between the morning and noon bell."

She nodded and turned away.

"And Clare?"

She looked over her shoulder.

"Thank you. Chalen hasn't—they haven't had hope. Not in a long time, and I didn't think anyone could give it to them again. But you did. I won't forget that."

Clare wanted to laugh at the idea of *her* giving hope to anyone. Hope wasn't a word she entertained, wasn't something she had, something she'd *ever* had. She had determination, and stubbornness, and a refusal to be broken past the point of mending, but she didn't have *hope.*

Yet this man—she didn't even know his name, or what he was to Chalen—was looking at her like she'd plucked a star from the sky and given it to him. It felt like a joke Ferrian herself might have made—as if the hopeless could ever bring hope to anyone.

She made herself nod and walk away before she could say something stupid, or callous, or intentionally hurtful. She got in the carriage and let Verol pick their next destination.

***

DAYS OF WANDERING the streets in Veralna had still not accustomed Clare to the wealth of glass in the city's buildings. The only glass in Renault County had belonged to *him*, and even he hadn't had all that much of it, because what was the point? All it did was get broken.

Here, glass dripped from structures as if it was as common as stone and just as easily replaced, but the store she currently stood before outdid all the others. The entire storefront was not only glass, but a glass so perfectly clear she could see through to the clothes displayed within.

She stood on the sidewalk, taking it in. Trying to decide if it was beautiful or obscene, a marvel or a waste. That, and she didn't want to go inside. Verol had gone two stores down with promises of returning with tea, and told her to go ahead and start looking.

The problem was, Clare hadn't ever shopped in a store. Not one like this. The market in Midtown had at least been familiar—if still leagues in quality and variety above anything Renault County had to offer—so she'd understood how things worked there.

But this place…she didn't know how she was supposed to act once she went inside. She loathed not knowing how to act. If she couldn't pull on the facade the world expected to see at any given moment, then she was left with only herself. And she didn't know who that was.

So she told herself it was the sheer wall of glass that held her entranced, made her linger rather than enter. But she lingered too long. A woman strode out of the shop, her lips twisted in a moue of distaste. She crossed her arms as she looked at Clare.

"Didn't you read the sign? You can't loiter here."

Clare glanced at the sign she couldn't read. The word "loiter" wasn't familiar to her either, save that it clearly meant "existing unwanted in the space outside this shop."

"I was just coming inside."

"No, you aren't. You want to get out of the cold, you do it somewhere else."

Clare bristled. Her shoulders drew back and she shifted from Renault County gutter child to the woman she'd been molded into when her life had ceased being her own. She looked down her nose at the shopkeeper. "I was coming inside to *shop*."

The woman hesitated at the haughtiness in Clare's tone, but then her eyes raked back over Clare's dress—the one that was a hundred times better than anything Clare had ever procured on her own before, and yet still marked her as less-than-nothing in this part of Veralna. "You can't afford anything in my shop and I won't have you upsetting my actual customers. Now leave, before I—"

"Is there a problem?" Verol's shadow fell over Clare.

The shopkeeper gave a hasty bow. "Lord Arrendon?" She sounded genuinely confused about his presence, as if she hadn't realized that Verol's question was directed to Clare, and thought he'd inserted himself into an argument between two random women in the street.

"There does indeed appear to be a problem." Clare turned to Verol, holding her hand out for one of the two paper cups of tea he held. He handed her one. She wrapped her fingers around the warmth and waited until the light of realization dawned in the shopkeeper's eyes before saying, "According to this woman, you can't afford anything in her shop."

"I didn't say—I didn't mean—that is, I didn't know she was with you, my lord."

Clare continued on as if the woman wasn't still stammering and tripping over herself. "And since I am loath to make you spend outside your means, I think we should take our business across the street."

Verol, bless him, didn't say a word until they were on the sidewalk opposite the previous shop's. He glanced up at the sign they now stood beneath. "I'm curious, was the selection of this store an impulse, or did you know Galina's is Theresa's largest competitor?"

"I wouldn't be very observant if I didn't," she answered breezily, opening the door and stepping inside. She might not have been able to read the name of either shop, and she might have been a little dazed at the glasswork, but she was still a child of Renault County. She could mark the movements of people on the street in her sleep, and all that foot traffic had told her the most expensively dressed people milling about either went into this shop, or the one she'd just come from.

A young woman glided forward to greet them, an innocent, charming smile on her face. She was impeccably put together, hair sleek and twisted into an elaborate up-style, her gown a silky fabric of a deep, rich blue. Clare drank in the woman's appearance, memorizing the twists and turns of her hairstyle—she thought she could probably replicate it on her own—the artful stroke of blush, high on the woman's cheekbones, the way the brows had been darkened to look fuller and more defined.

She was going to have to purchase cosmetics at some point, and sincerely hoped there were better ones here than what she'd worn before. She had never particularly enjoyed the feeling of her face being literally painted on.

"Lord Arrendon." The young woman gave a graceful dip of her head in deference. "Welcome to Galina's. My lady is out, but I can assist you with anything you need. I'm Cynthia." She was devoid of the fear so many people had thus far exhibited in Verol's presence, but Clare didn't think the woman knew him, even if she obviously knew *of* him.

Her eyes sparkled with curiosity as she took Clare in, none of the other shopkeeper's condescension in her gaze. The hard, uncharitable part of Clare couldn't help but wonder if that condescension *would* have been there had Clare not walked in with Verol at her back.

"Cynthia, this is my new apprentice, Miss Clare Brighton."

"Pleased to meet you, miss." The woman dipped her head to Clare, the keen interest in her eyes conveying she'd already heard the rumors and Verol was merely confirming them for her. "What are you looking for today?"

"Everything," Verol said.

"Everything?" Cynthia's brow furrowed in confusion.

Clare swooped in. If she didn't cover Verol's misstep in admitting her lack of wardrobe, the *next* rumors running around Veralna would be that the Lords Arrendon had taken in a penniless waif as an apprentice. She didn't need everyone knowing that that was precisely what she was. "I lost everything on the journey here," Clare confessed. "The carriage had a broken axle, which I don't think was accidental. It was right after we stopped for a rest in a passing town, and then shortly after it broke we were *robbed*."

Clare's performance was, to her own mind, a little on the over-dramatic side, but Cynthia drank it down like water. "Oh, that must have been awful. But weren't you with her, my lord?" Cynthia asked Verol. She had a little bit of hero-worship in her eyes where Verol was concerned—which was opposite every other reaction Clare had seen to the mage thus far—and she clearly thought it impossible Clare could have been robbed with him near.

"I was traveling in on my own," Clare said, before Verol could damage the story she was concocting, the one she needed to be viewed as fact by the end of the day. "Fortunately, Verol and Marquin did worry when I didn't arrive in town on time and were able to find me. I barely made it into the city in time for the theater performance, and thank goodness Chalen was able to find me something to wear on short notice."

As Clare had hoped, Cynthia took the three gossip points she'd been given—the performance, Chalen, and the fact that Clare called Verol and Marquin by their given names—and ran with them, chattering excitedly as she drew Clare into the store, steering her toward this or that item. Verol followed, obviously uncertain about what to do with himself.

"If you have other business to tend to, I'm sure you don't need to stay. Cynthia can take care of me," Clare offered. Gossip was a valuable currency in its own right, and Clare suspected she could get a lot out of Cynthia if Verol wasn't around.

"Oh, yes," Cynthia agreed. "If you come back in three hours or so, I think we should have everything sorted out."

Three hours? Ferrian's hells, did the woman mean Clare to look at every dress in the store?

Verol allowed himself to be ushered out with very little persuasion. Once he was gone, it only took Clare half an hour—and an offhand comment about how excited she was for her apprenticeship —to steer Cynthia to the topic Clare most wanted to know about.

"Who wouldn't be excited, apprenticed to Lord Arrendon? You know he hasn't taken an apprentice in over twenty years?" The woman fussed with the sleeves of a dress she'd convinced Clare to try on.

"Twenty?" It was roughly Clare's own age, though she couldn't be sure. Namedays were not the type of thing celebrated in Renault County, and Clare didn't even know when hers was.

Cynthia nodded. "Not after the dreadful business with that girl dying. He had another apprentice at the time, and of course he did his duty by them, but since then? Nothing. You can see why news of you is spreading like wildfire."

So one of his apprentices had died. And he'd another, too. It made her wonder. Fitz was a mage—she'd noted the sapphire dangling from his ear that morning—and of an age to have been apprenticed twenty years ago.

"But if it's true what they're saying about you, it's no wonder he wanted you." When Clare didn't respond to this prompt, Cynthia blushed, but she must have really wanted to know because she pushed forward. "*Is* it true? Are you really a black diamond?" Her eyes were practically riveted on Clare's un-pierced, unadorned ears.

Black diamond. She'd *almost* managed to forget all about that business. But if she had to be an item of gossip in this particular manner, proving it to Cynthia would make it more likely the girl would tell her what she wanted to know. She reached into her pocket for the small box that bore the earring and opened it.

The predictable amount of gasping and rushing of chatter followed, until Clare clicked the box shut and tucked it away again. Then, leaning into Cynthia, as if confiding in her was a special thing, she said, "I'm embarrassed to admit this, but I don't know much about the Lords Arrendon. I grew up quite sheltered, you see. Lord Verol was very kind to me, when he discovered my talent, and I felt he would treat me fairly as an apprentice, but I had no idea he was as well-known as you seem to indicate."

"Oh." Cynthia's eyes widened—they did so with disturbing frequency. "*Everyone* in Veralna knows them. They earned their lord-ships during the Mages War. I wasn't even born then, but Father says it was a terrible time. He says they were instrumental in restoring Veralna to peace, and that without them we'd all be enslaved to the Mages Guild.

"The king himself gave them their titles for their loyalty. Father says they're the sole reason there's never been another uprising. No one wants to go against the Butcher and the Barbarian." Cynthia's hand flew to her mouth, a deep blush coloring her cheeks. "Oh, I'm sorry! The monikers are so common, but I know I shouldn't use them. You won't tell, will you?"

Clare had to work hard not to laugh—as if she was going to stride out of here and demand Verol punish Cynthia for calling them *names*. But then, the woman seemed as if her viewpoint of the world was one handed to her by her father, so maybe she was.

"Don't worry, I won't say anything." She was far more interested in how they'd gotten the names, and why two men who had already warned her about the dangers of the Jackal King had apparently supported him in a war waged by their own people. At least the hostility and fear she'd noticed at the Mages Guild last night made sense now. "Lord Verol's last apprentice," she said, moving the conversation forward to smooth over Cynthia's discomfort, "the one who died. What were they like?"

Cynthia's eyes saddened. "I didn't know her, but she was a Songweaver, like you. She was murdered when she was six. Lord Verol didn't leave his estate for an entire year afterward. Called for the High Court to do an official inquiry and everything, but they never found out who did it. Most people think it was some kind of revenge, trying to get back at him for the Mages War."

Cynthia was getting that pinched look around her lips that told Clare the conversation had grown tiresome, and it never did good to irritate an easy source of gossip. So she made an appropriate, "That's dreadful," comment, and pulled a random nearby dress up to the light. "What do you think of this one for me?"

Cynthia brightened immediately. "Oh, it's *perfect*, do try it on."

Two hours later, Clare's interest in finally having a wardrobe had been dulled considerably by the number of times she had slipped in and out of dresses—as for the pants and shirts she preferred, Galina's was sadly lacking in many options on that front. Clearly, she was going to have to pay Chalen Mora to do something about the lack of functional clothing in her life.

"Oh, you should wear this one home, Miss Clare," Cynthia gushed, beaming at the light green dress Clare stood in. "You'll feel ever so much more like yourself in something respectable."

Something respectable. In Renault County's streets, the dress she had worn into this store was damn near as respectable as one ever came. But since she'd gone to the difficulty of pretending to be a woman and not a street urchin, she vowed not to ruin the illusion by snapping at the woman. Instead, she suggested that Cynthia choose what shoes she was to wear home, and the woman ran off in her eagerness to acquiesce. Clare had probably just bought herself an entire quarter hour of blessed silence.

She smoothed the dress—it was practical and comfortable enough for her tastes, with wide straps at the shoulders that left her arms free of hindrance. The fabric was smooth, soft and evenly woven, and she marveled at how different it felt—how different it made *her* feel—to wear something that had never been worn by anyone else. Living with *him* there had been nice dresses of course, but she had had no choice in the wearing of them. They were not things she had chosen for herself, but things that had been picked out for her so she could be dressed like a doll.

Looking at herself in the floor-length store mirror she felt, almost, like a human being.

She turned, getting a feel for the garment's maneuverability—the need to run, quickly and nimbly, was one Clare liked always to be prepared for—when a flash of red in the corner of her eye caught her attention.

She moved toward it, toward the window it was displayed in, some instinct driving her forward. She had avoided all of the window displays because they held the most expensive items, and while Verol hadn't set a budget for this venture, Clare had. Maybe Verol truly wouldn't view her as owing him anything once this apprenticeship was through, but *she* would. Nothing was free, and a sense of obligation was one of the most dangerous weights a person could carry. She didn't have to carry it if she intended to pay him back.

The closer she came to the dress, the more certain she was, until she came to its front and found herself staring at Battle Armor. It was as perfect as she remembered. Every part of her wanted it, and she couldn't fully explain *why*. Only that it once again evoked that feeling of power and danger in her, the feeling that if she stood before all of Veralna in that dress, she would hold the city in the palm of her hand.

"I confess myself dying to know what it is about that dress that puts such a look of consternation on your face." The words carried as if they were murmured in her ear, slow and lazy like a cat basking in summer sunlight, amusement evident in the lilt and cadence of the stranger's voice. But intimate as the words sounded, no lips brushed her ear as the stranger spoke, no breath graced her neck, so he—whoever he was—stood a respectful distance away.

There was something about the voice—she was almost certain she'd heard it before, though she couldn't place where. She answered serenely, refusing to be shaken by her failure to recognize someone had approached until they'd spoken. Either she was growing complacent already, or he was very good at sneaking up on people. "I cannot decide if it's a dress, or a weapon."

He laughed and the deep, rich sound had her turning as he said, "Didn't you know? The best clothes are both."

It took everything in Clare not to give recognition away when she saw him. Because her stranger was none other than the not-drunk thief she'd seen at the Hawk and Scepter, Mr. Call-Me-Taius himself, and looking nothing like he had either of the previous times she'd seen him.

This was the face he'd revealed in the mirror that first night, after taking off his disguise. If she'd thought that half-reflection pretty, it was nothing compared to standing a handful of feet away from him. He was the most beautiful man she'd ever seen, and it had nothing to do with the clothes he wore—fine clothes she suddenly recognized Chalen Mora's careful hand in.

No, take away the clothes and he would still look like an artist had set out to sculpt perfection and created its living embodiment instead. His skin was a shade darker than her own, a rich warm brown she wondered how he'd ever passed off as a lighter color in that last disguise she'd seen him in. Arched cheekbones led up to those almost-black eyes he'd tried to hide under glamour as Taius, and his slightly-too-long black hair was tousled, as if he ran his hands through it often.

But his allure wasn't in any of those things. It was simply *him*—the way he stood, the way he smiled, the way he *looked* at the world. Like existence was a joke and he was waiting for the punchline.

And he was staring at her with the self-assuredness of a man who knew she had no idea who he was. Her lips curved into a smile, because it was always more fun knowing something when a person thought they had it hidden. "Forgive me if I say *your* clothes don't look particularly dangerous."

"Maybe they're like this one." He stepped past her and tapped a tented piece of paper that rested on a small table before the dress. "Battle armor."

Chalen had kept the name, then. "Armor, hmm? Are you a man in need of defense?"

He laughed again, and she liked the sound. "You have no idea."

"And is that what brings you in here today? Your need of defense?"

"Perhaps." He leaned back against the wall, slipping his hands into his pockets. "Or perhaps I heard you sing last night."

That was where she'd heard his voice. He'd spoken differently in his Taius persona, an altered accent then, a shaper edge to his consonants. But this voice was *him*, and she'd heard it last night, from the man who had walked his chair across the room to her. The one whose face she hadn't been able to see through the brilliance of the stage lighting. The one who had stopped Estrella from approaching Clare and told the other singer not to further embarrass herself.

And there was that feeling in Clare's chest again, the part of her that had wanted him to be there and was glad to discover he had been, but still didn't understand why. It was more effort than it should have been to keep her voice light and unconcerned. "Did you? I don't recall meeting you after the performance."

He shrugged. "I didn't stay."

"Not worth it?"

He grinned. "Worth it, and more. Is it true you apprenticed to Verol?"

She didn't miss his failure to put a title before Verol's name. "Yes."

A minuscule tightening of his lips, but she caught it. "How did that happen?"

"In the usual way," she said evasively. Because it had just occurred to her that here was a man who knew the truth about her performance at the theater—that it hadn't been her apprenticeship to Verol and his acquisition of a dispensation from the Mages Guild that allowed her to play there. That those things had come *after*, not before.

That knowledge was a danger she hadn't understood before

she'd learned that what she'd done at the Rival Theater was illegal without that dispensation. And he might not even have to give up his disguises to use it, since she suspected she was looking at the "patron of the arts" who had secured her ability to sing in the first place.

Who in Ferrian's hells *was* this man? "I'm afraid I didn't catch your name," she said sweetly.

"I didn't give it." He pushed off the wall. "Are you buying the dress?"

He didn't look like he was taunting her, though he had to know she couldn't afford it. Except, of course, that Verol probably could. "No."

"That's a shame." He moved past her, swiping the paper for Battle Armor as he went, so smoothly she almost missed it. "It was…interesting talking to you."

"If you don't tell me your name," she called after him, "I'll have to find it out on my own."

He turned, walking backward long enough to say, "I look forward to your efforts," before slipping out the shop's front door.

Cynthia chose that moment to return with Clare's shoes, staring out the glass front of the shop with a flustered look on her face. "Was that…" She trailed off, staring out the window at the retreating form before shaking her head, as if she'd made a silly mistake.

No amount of teasing or prompting could convince Cynthia to give up the name of the person she'd thought the man might be.

CHAPTER

NINETEEN

BATTLE ARMOR

Two hours after her encounter in the dress shop, Clare walked back through the doors of the Arrendons' manor, unable to stop fidgeting with the black diamond that now hung from her left earlobe. As Faelhorn law would have it, she was required to wear the irksome thing, which had necessitated having her ear pierced. Apparently, if you were apprenticed to mages possessed of considerable means, voluntarily punching a hole in your body was preceded by a healer numbing the area, and followed by them speeding the typical healing process.

She'd never witnessed so much fuss expended over so small a hurt. She kept tugging at the earring, expecting to *feel* something, some small pain or swelling, but there was nothing. The matter was done with, and she would grow accustomed to the dangling weight soon enough.

She'd barely taken a step toward her room when the sound of clattering hooves caught her attention, some innate sense urging her to wait with Marquin and Verol in the living area. A knock sounded and a few moments later Fitz led a short brunette woman inside, a paper-wrapped bundle cradled carefully in her arms.

"Madame Galina," Verol said, surprise in his voice. "Did we forget something at the shop?"

"No, my lord," Galina answered. She shifted, her eyes sliding from Verol to Clare. "I have with me an item that was purchased for a Miss Clare Brighton."

"I am Clare Brighton."

After waiting for a confirming nod from Verol—which Clare found mildly insulting—Galina handed Clare the bundle. She took it cautiously, unreasonably concerned it might sprout fangs and bite her.

Madame Galina didn't leave. "I have instructions to make certain you open it."

"I wasn't aware Galina's took such…unusual requests from its customers," Marquin said lightly. "Or that you were in the habit of making deliveries personally."

The woman swallowed. "I do for this client."

It was that, more than anything else, that made Clare certain of what she'd find inside, even before she pulled the paper wrapping apart to reveal the first hint of red fabric. She made herself finish, methodically unwrapping, until she held Battle Armor in her hands.

The silk was exquisite against her skin, soft and cool. She felt the thinnest sliver of magic in its threads, as if Chalen had poured their heart into the making with something more than talent and passion.

"A gift," Galina said softly, "from His Highness, Numair Tolvannen."

Numair Tolvannen. The second prince of the Faelhorn Provinces.

Clare barely processed it before Verol snapped out, "She cannot accept it."

Galina nodded. "He said you would say that, and I am to reply that *she* may choose not to accept it, but no one else may do so on her behalf."

"I see." Clare ran her fingers carefully over the dress before draping it across the back of the living area's sofa.

"I will not tell you what to do," Verol said, "but I would urge you not to accept this. There is no good reason for a man you have never spoken with to—" He cut off, a new and, if the look on his face was anything to go by, terrible thought occurring to him. "*Have you spoken with Prince Numair?*"

She was beginning to suspect she had. "That depends. What does His Highness look like?"

It was Marquin who finally gave her a description, because Verol's version did not contain actual physical attributes but rather impolite defamations of character that Madam Galina grew more and more visibly horrified at being subjected to hearing. Lord Verol might be of a position to speak about the second prince that way, but she most certainly was not.

Once Marquin took over, any doubts Clare had held were gone. "Apparently we did share a brief conversation."

"Where?" Verol asked tightly.

"In the shop."

"About?"

"Dresses." She turned to Galina. "I will accept it."

"Clare—" Verol started, but Clare and Galina both ignored him, the latter obviously eager to conclude the business at hand.

"I am so pleased, and certain His Highness will be, as well." She held out two envelopes, one black, one red. "The red one is for you alone." She bowed and exited the manor with more haste than elegance.

In the silence that followed, Clare found herself under twin inquiring stares. There was a weight of concern in the air she was unfamiliar with, because it almost felt as if it was concern for *her*. She broke the awkwardness by thrusting the black envelope at Verol. "You may as well read it aloud for us, as it looks like your curiosity may choke you otherwise."

Marquin narrowed his eyes at her, and she told herself he couldn't possibly be deducing *already* that she didn't know how to read. Verol extracted the card from the envelope and scanned it. His eyes closed, as if seeking reserves of patience he had tucked away for just such a moment, and he handed the envelope to Marquin.

"Well?" Clare asked.

Marquin's brow furrowed. "It is a request for you to sing at his nameday celebration."

Ever practical, her first question was, "And how much is His Highness offering to pay me for this honor?" Marquin named a sum that made her eyebrows creep up. "Is that...a typical engagement fee?"

"If you were a platinum-ranked member of the Musicians Guild, yes."

"Ah. Well," she said brightly, "since I've already outperformed a platinum-ranked member of the Musicians Guild, I suppose I must be worth it." The money would go a long way toward making her feel less dependent on the Arrendons. Seeing as how she'd schemed her way into singing at the Rival Theater, she hadn't actually made any money off that venture, and she hardly had anything left of what she'd earned that first night at the Hawk and Scepter.

She was busy enough running calculations in her head, already weighing necessary expenditures against how long she might need to make the money last, that it took her a moment to realize Marquin and Verol were not nearly so pleased by this offer of employment as she was. Rather, they looked worried by it.

"Is it so unexpected he would make the offer?" she asked. Perhaps she hadn't expected to go straight to a member of the royal family, but the entire point of her performance last night had been intended to achieve a result similar to this one.

Verol answered. "Prince Tolvannen's nameday celebration is tonight. And Estrella Vane was engaged to perform at it."

Clare managed not to laugh, but only because Verol looked so very pained by the situation. "I see. How fortunate then that he bought me a dress and I needn't find something appropriate to wear on short notice. What time is the party?"

Marquin glanced at the card again. "If you accept the engagement, he will send a carriage for you at the eighteenth bell. That would give you approximately two hours to set up and rehearse before the celebration begins."

"You cannot be thinking of accepting," Verol said.

"On the contrary, I cannot well be thinking of refusing. I may be new to this, but even I know you don't turn down a prince and then sing for someone else. Who am I to work for if I slight the royal family?"

Verol opened his mouth, then clicked it shut.

"Precisely," Clare said. "You made your opinion of Lord Numair quite clear" —she hadn't known there were that many creative ways to call someone a drunk, philandering idiot before Verol's earlier diatribe— "but I assure you I am perfectly capable of taking care of myself. And unless you intend to renege on an agreement we made only this morning, then it isn't your decision."

Verol exhaled audibly. "No, it isn't. And you are correct. You can't refuse. That's what I don't like about it." He strode for the door, pulling his coat off the rack as he went.

"Where are you going, love?" Marquin asked.

"To inform Lord Numair of the code of conduct I expect he will adhere to while engaging the services of my apprentice."

"Since you're going, do pick up my payment in advance," Clare called.

Verol turned, his face a mask of incredulity. She gave him her most beatific smile and he shook his head, muttering something about youth and early graves. A second later the door slammed shut behind him.

"You shouldn't antagonize him so," Marquin admonished.

"On the contrary, I rather thought I was distracting him from his irritated rage." That, and she truly did prefer being paid in advance. "Does he often talk to the second prince of Faelhorn in the manner I suspect he is about to?"

"Typically, they avoid each other like the plague. But when they do converse? Yes. It's about as pleasant to be around as being stabbed in the eye with a needle."

"And Verol is allowed to talk to him that way?"

"Verol and I are granted a certain amount of leniency given our history of service to the crown."

She thought of the monikers the shopgirl had called them by —the Butcher and the Barbarian. Not kind titles, even from a girl who had seemed in awe of them. "And that history would be?"

"A tale for another time."

She narrowed her eyes.

"Of course, I might be persuaded to tell it earlier, if you want to tell me what you and Lord Numair actually talked about in Galina's."

"Sometimes, a conversation about dresses is only a conversation about dresses."

Marquin made a noncommittal noise.

"Did he actually see my performance last night?"

Marquin gave her a look that said he knew she was smarter than that question. And she was. But she still wanted to hear him confirm it. She didn't relent.

He sighed. "Who do you think carried his chair across the theater so he could stare up at you like he just found a god?"

She answered, in order to cover the smile that wanted to break out. "Well, at least he shouldn't be disappointed tonight, then."

"Clare, I know the kind of attention he's offering you is heady—"

"You needn't bother with whatever speech you're about to give. Even if I was foolish enough to have aspirations that high, I didn't come to Veralna looking for a husband."

"Prince Numair will never be king," Marquin continued, as if she hadn't spoken. "So even if he marries, which I must inform you it is unlikely he will ever do, his wife will never be queen."

Clare's emotions went flat, all former lightness and humor leaving her body. *Queen.* Ferrian's hells, she hated that word. "I assure you, if there is anything I want less than to be someone's wife, it is to be someone's *queen*." She gathered Battle Armor from the back of the couch, careful with it despite her anger. "If you're quite finished insulting me, I have a great deal of preparation to do and very little time in which to manage it."

MARQUIN WATCHED Clare storm out of the room and wondered precisely when he'd lost *all* of his ability to trust anyone who wasn't Verol. He couldn't even say he'd pushed her about Numair because he was concerned for her, like Verol was.

He had no doubt she could take care of herself. No, he'd pushed her just to find out how she would react. If that iron control she had would slip and allow a glimpse into the power she carried.

It hadn't. She'd felt as much like nothing as ever. If it weren't for the fact that he'd looked into her eyes the two weeks they'd spent on the road and seen something ancient in them, he'd think Verol was wrong about her. That two decades of guilt over Marie's death had made Verol look for any surrogate he could protect.

But he didn't truly believe Verol was wrong. And Clare's control hadn't slipped.

He told himself it was still something he'd needed to know—because if she *did* slip that easily, they were all dead—but it didn't make him feel any better. Because he'd seen that short, sharp bite of hurt and fear in her eyes, hidden beneath her anger.

He hadn't thought she cared anything for his or Verol's opinions. Cynical to his core, he'd been so certain he knew exactly what kind of person she was, what kind of person the world had made her to be. The kind who would take Verol's protection without considering the consequences, the kind who wouldn't hesitate to move on a perceived opportunity like Numair Tolvannen.

The door to her room slammed shut. He rubbed his forehead and went into the kitchen, staring blankly out the window, trying to decide if and how to apologize. He was surprised, a few minutes later, to see her striding across the lawn behind the manor, her hands curled into fists. His surprise wasn't because she'd left her room, but at the fact that the ward on her window hadn't sent him any feedback that she'd opened it, and that had to have been how she'd exited the house.

She'd changed into the tunic and pants she'd worn on the road, the ones that were little better than rags, and Verol's old boots. It was a wonder the grass didn't catch fire under the fury of her footfalls, she moved with such determination. Just when he thought he was going to have to follow her—Verol would kill him if he had to explain that Clare had left because he was an insensitive prick and now he had no idea where she was—she ducked into the barn. He relaxed—she'd spent hours with the horses on the road, clearly preferring them to human company—before he remembered that Alys was in the barn, but it was too late to curtail that interaction.

Alys could handle herself.

He hesitated, then went out the back door to Clare's window. She'd closed but not latched it—and there wasn't a single trace left of the magic from the ward that should have been there. He tested the other windows, the doors, but every other ward on the home's openings was in place.

Only hers was gone, and he hadn't even felt it disappear.

Clare walked toward the barn, the steady pulse of anger thrumming beneath her skin, her clunky too-big boots beating the frozen winter ground. The dozens of seams connecting the patches on her breeches crawled across her legs like spiderweb scars, ugly and uneven, but comforting against her skin. She'd have thought she'd burn the clothing at the first available opportunity but here she was, sliding them on like they could remind her of who she was.

Like she would even *want* to be reminded.

But maybe she did want it a little, because Marquin had rattled her. She'd known he didn't really like her—he tolerated her for Verol's sake—but she'd thought they understood each other. She'd thought they were, in many ways, the same, and she'd been comfortable in that similarity.

Now she thought maybe he didn't understand her at all if he could think... She stopped in the barn doorway, her brain clicking pieces into place. Her anger mounted, not at him but at herself, for failing to see until this moment what he'd been doing—prodding at her with words to see where her pressure points were.

And how easily she'd handed them over.

She glanced over her shoulder, saw him outside, inspecting the window to her room. A smile curled her lips. The magic lining the window frame had pulled away easily, sliding under her skin like water through a crack. She hadn't enjoyed the satisfied feeling of the Song after she'd taken it, as if the entity inside her was having a snack, but she did enjoy the obvious confusion the missing magic was causing Marquin.

She could consider them even, now, she supposed. And she would know better than to let him rattle her in the future.

She walked into the barn, noting idly how small it was for a lord's stable. There was only the one barn and it consisted of a paltry six stalls, each one empty. She spotted Ginger and Skye in a paddock on the back side of the barn, and it was beginning to seriously appear as if they were the only two horses the Arrendons owned. It was also beginning to seriously appear as if Alys was the only stablehand the lords employed.

Unless Fitz doubled as a stablehand too. She found the two of them in the tack room, both seated on opposite ends of a wide bench, polishing saddles that didn't require polishing. They weren't talking, so there was no reason to sneak up on them, save Clare wanted to see how they would react.

She stepped silently, moving so as not to block the light streaming in from the door, and rapped smartly against the wood frame.

Fitz looked up, displeasure creasing his brow. He stood, placed the saddle back on its rack, and silently brushed past her. She felt more than displeasure coming off him as he left, she felt...hostility. He *really* didn't like her.

But that was a problem for another time. For now, she turned her attention back to Alys. The woman had startled at Clare's knock, though the movement had been slight, easily missed if one hadn't been looking for it. Clare had, so she'd noted the woman's surprise, but she appreciated Alys's quick recovery, the practiced nonchalance with which she finally deigned to look up. Her gaze swept over Clare, taking in the patches on the breeches, the threadbare areas of the tunic. Then she looked back to her work.

"What can I do for you, Miss Brighton?" She drawled the words, but though her delivery was admirable, the drawl did not have quite the right cadence for someone born to the lower dialects. It would fool anyone of higher rank, as Clare suspected it was intended to do, but it would not fool anyone lower.

She was going to have fun figuring out who Alys really was, and why she was hiding out in the Arrendons' barn. And, for that matter, why they were letting her. But right now she had more pressing issues.

"I need to borrow your cosmetics, and I need your help with my hair for an engagement this evening."

Alys snorted. It was a pretty, artful sound, and she tossed her head as she made it, a habitual movement that flicked her hair neatly. "As if I know hair or have cosmetics."

"You do, on both counts."

Alys looked up, irritation written across her face. "Even if I did, I'm not helping you. Hire a maid, if that's what you need."

"I don't want to hire a maid. I want your help."

"How unfortunate for you that you aren't going to get what you want."

Clare smiled. "Oh, but I am. Because if you don't help me, I am going to start asking around to find out who you really are."

Alys's fingers clenched on the rag in her hand. She relaxed them quickly, but not before Clare saw. "Ask away. Women like me are a dime a dozen."

"Stable girls with brown hair and forgettable faces are a dime a dozen," Clare agreed. "But women who move like they're court-trained, with auburn hair and blue eyes and scars that run across half their faces? Those are much less common."

Alys went completely still.

"I'm singing at Prince Numair's nameday celebration this

evening," Clare continued. "I wonder, if I very loudly keep asking about a woman with that description, who there might be able to give me your name."

Alys set the saddle aside and stood, stalking toward Clare. "The Arrendons said you were a Songweaver."

"I am."

"Songweavers don't see under glamour." Her gaze caught on the jewel in Clare's ears, and sarcasm limned her voice. "Not even black diamonds."

Clare resisted touching her fingers to the earring newly pierced through her lobe. Her only response was a careless shrug.

Upon deducing Clare wasn't going to respond, Alys snapped, "What do you want?"

"I already told you. Hair. Cosmetics. Current popular topics of conversation."

"That's it?"

"Well...that, and a supply of the glamour that hides your scar." The glamour was the real reason she needed Alys. Her help with appearance would be useful, but Clare could manage that on her own. What she couldn't manage on her own was the number of scars that would be visible given the backless nature of her expensive new dress.

Alys gave her a considering look, as if she was putting Clare's true purpose together. "It won't make you prettier. It isn't that kind of glamour."

"How fortunate, then, that I'm pretty enough."

Alys didn't answer.

Clare turned and made to walk out. "Well, if I don't look quite right tonight, at least I'll have the very interesting topic of *you* to keep people from getting bored with me."

She was halfway out of the barn before Alys called, "Wait."

Clare halted and turned back.

"I make you look good tonight and you'll leave it alone? Leave *me* alone?"

"I won't promise not to find out who you are—curiosity's in my nature—but I promise to be discreet about it, and can keep it to myself, once I do. I have no interest in being your enemy, Alys. But I do need your help and I am pressed for time, so I'm getting it the guaranteed way."

Alys shook her head. "You're a strange woman."

Clare shrugged. "You'll do it, then?"

Alys looked like she'd rather strangle her. "I'll do it."

Clare held out her hand. "Glamour now, then meet me in my room in half an hour."

CHAPTER

TWENTY

ALIKE IN THAT WAY

Alys's glamour came in a small, clear jar etched with vines and flower buds, and this told Clare that however much Alys might have left the physical realm of the privilege she obviously came from, she had not left its means or its suppliers behind. Only those who catered to the wealthy would see the necessity of putting an expensive item into equally expensive packaging.

On the one hand, it irked her. The frivolous, stupid beauty of a *container* when she'd spent her entire life starving. On the other hand, she loved it. Because it was something simple and pretty and nice, and it made her feel that way too. Because, having spent so much of her life surrounded by ugly, broken things, the jar was precisely the type of trivial luxury she aspired to.

People with abundance seemed to think the miserably poor should want only for food and shelter and should, if such things were provided, never want for anything more, because they were so much better off than they had previously been. But the basic necessities of food and shelter were but the lowest rung of human decency, and if obtaining them was a necessity of great relief, they alone did not make a person feel wholly human. They certainly did not cause *others* to view a person as fully human. Luxuries—the ability to have something that was not strictly necessary for one's continued existence—were what made people feel human. The access to excessive luxury, to frivolous waste, was—however morally reprehensible one

145

might consider such activity—what made others view a person as better than them, even if they abhorred the person for it.

Clare could withstand abhorrence. She had been hated for the depths of her poverty in a poverty-stricken place. Even the poor hated the poor, because they needed *someone* to view as lower than themselves, and so they chose the easiest target in close proximity and struck. But if there was no escaping being hated, Clare had every intention of being hated for lush excess rather than abject want. Because she was tired of being considered *less*.

So she gazed upon the pretty etchings on the glass until, rather than thinking of the waste—the pointlessness—of them, she saw only the beauty. Because she was never going back, and a pretty jar was only the start.

She applied the paste with calloused fingers, covering the scars that crisscrossed nearly the whole of her back. She didn't bother with the ones that were lower—they wouldn't show.

As the cream soaked into her skin, she found *this* benefit of wealth one she could appreciate without trying. She had worn a glamour once before and, though it had done its job, it had been a harsh, abrasive thing to apply to the skin, tingling and irritating. This glamour came in a smooth cream. It smelled of honeysuckle and vanilla, and its application felt more like a balm meant to sooth and moisturize the skin than one meant to conceal atrocities. By the time Clare had covered the entirety of her back, Alys's "one month supply" was almost empty.

Clare considered the remaining contents. They were not enough to cover her back again, and since she was likely to be under much more scrutiny tonight than she had been under the previous one, she supposed the rest of her might as well look as flawless as her back. She scooped the remainder out and dotted it over the plethora of long-healed-over cuts and burns that littered her arms.

She finished and surveyed the results of her work, the room's mirror reflecting skin that was beautiful and flawless. She hated the sight of it. Each scar, each *flaw*, was a memory. None were pleasant, but she never focused on how they had been made, only on the fact that she had survived them. Were she a man, she could bear them proudly and people would respect that she had survived them, that she continued to live. She would be considered strong. But she was a woman, and people cringed from women's scars. Society held that women were supposed to be soft and delicate—unblemished—and horrified by what scars they did possess. When they were not, people did not quite know what to do with them.

Battle Armor was draped across her bed. She gathered the dress and pulled it on. The silk slid over her like water, delicate as a spider's web, smooth as the kiss of a soft breeze. As it settled, that little sliver of magic she'd felt in its threads settled as well, molding the dress to her, tightening and loosening where it needed to, until the end result was a creation that looked as if it had been tailored to her.

The dress did its name justice. Was it Chalen's magic that made Clare feel powerful in this moment, or was it a different kind of magic? The magic of cunningly cut fabrics placed together just-so. The way they could tell a story and project an image that made their wearer feel as if they belonged in the same level of society the clothing did.

She was still observing the startling effect when Alys entered the room. The door had made no sound when the woman opened it, and Alys moved quietly, but no amount of quiet could fool someone whose life had continually depended on the ability to sense a person's mood before seeing them. There was a presence, a heaviness, that people carried with them, and it was something that, once one was attuned to it, could not be disguised no matter how silent a person became.

"Hello, Alys," she said without turning.

"Hello, Clare," Alys answered, matching Clare tone for tone, as she had in their very first introduction.

"I trust you are pleased with the glamour, as I can't see a possible thing you would be wanting to hide."

"That," Clare turned to face Alys, "*was* the idea."

"Your back, then?"

"Or perhaps my arms?" Clare held them out, close enough that Alys would catch the delicate scent of the glamour on them. "Or my chest." Clare traced her finger across the exposed flesh above the low neckline of the dress.

Alys's eyes narrowed. The expression seemed to be as close to a frown as the woman would allow herself. "Did you really waste glamour on *all* of your bared skin simply so that I would not know *where* you glamoured?"

Clare shrugged. It was a delicate, perfect mimicry of the way Alys performed the action. "If you tell me who you are, I will happily tell you the answer to your question."

"The secret is not worth *that* much."

"I assure you, it is worth much more."

Another might have taken Clare's words as an invitation to casual flirtation. Alys narrowed her eyes in consideration. "You find me interesting because of my secrets. Take care that I do not start to find *you* interesting for yours. You might find you dislike the attention."

"The threat hardly holds the same weight. Your secrets are knowable. Mine are not. But if you wish to try, I do enjoy a good game."

Alys shook her head. "You may not have been born to the court, but you certainly are inclined toward it. Now we simply have to make you look the part." She pointed at the chair before Clare's vanity. "Sit."

Clare did, letting Alys settle a small cape around her shoulders to protect the dress from any stray cosmetics.

"I do hope you are not prone to headaches," Alys said sweetly.

For the next hour, Clare was uncertain whether this "hope" had been uttered in reference to the amount of brushing and twisting and pinning her hair underwent, or in reference to the unending stream of information that came out of Alys's mouth.

Clare had chosen her tutor well. Alys was confident in her knowledge of everyone who would be at the celebration that evening, and furthermore was capable of listing them and their families three generations back. She mercifully only did the last of these for two lineages—Numair's and the king's—because the sheer volume of information was otherwise overwhelming.

It was not that Clare hadn't understood that the court of Veralna was large—though her own information was outdated, she knew the more prominent names Alys rattled off already—it was that her mind still had difficulty understanding that the world could support so many individuals possessed of obscene incomes, idle time, and comparatively idle concerns.

Clare memorized it all absently. She had never been certain if her adeptness at memorization was a natural occurrence, or if it was some side effect of the Song's presence. Because most of the time, when she learned things, it felt more like remembering something she had known long ago, but had cause to forget until recently. Whatever the case, committing things to memory never required the whole of her attention.

So it was that half of her focused on filing information while the other half focused on the unsettled feeling in her stomach. The fluttering of unease inside her was on a level she had not felt since the day she'd left Renault County. The certainty thrumming through her that this was a moment of change that could not be undone—much like the prior one. Now, like then, she found herself on a precipice, and now, like then, the Song thrummed inside her coaxing, cajoling, and begging for release.

She had granted it, then. She could not afford to do so now.

"Clare, are you paying attention?"

She willed her nerves to settle. "Quite."

"Then what is the name of Lord Abbott's dog?"

Willed the Song to quiet. "His prized hunting hound or the little one his wife carries to balls?"

Alys's lips twitched.

"The hunting hound is Gibraltar and the little one is Ina."

"One day you must explain to me how you can be in two places at once. It seems a useful skill."

"More a curse than a skill."

"How so?"

"If one's mind can focus on two things with equal devotion, then it takes twice the distraction to get out of one's own head."

"I believe that is why people began dancing."

Clare frowned—she supposed she should break the habit, as Alys never seemed to perform it herself. "Dancing is nothing but memorized steps in time to music. A task performed without thought as easily as walking."

Alys laughed, then. "If that's what you think, you haven't done dancing correctly at all. I'll give you a hint—half of it is finding the correct partner."

There was clearly some underlying entendre there Clare was meant to understand, but didn't. The Song nudged at her wanting, as always, to grant her that understanding. She shunted the offer aside.

"One more thing about tonight." Alys finished applying the

paint to Clare's lips and pulled back to study the final result. "I do not know what you did to land yourself this engagement and truthfully, I do not care. But I *do* care what you reflect back on Marquin and Verol. Do not embarrass them.

"You are not only there as entertainment, but as Verol's apprentice. The first he has taken in nearly two decades. It will generate interest, as will that pretty new gem in your ear. But do not delude yourself. They are not interested in *you*. Only in using you. And if you are foolish enough to allow them to, it is the Arrendons who will pay the price."

Clare clamped down on the fiery retort that wanted to leave her mouth. Her temper, restrained for nearly the entirety of her life, kept wanting to rip out of her these days. But instead of telling Alys the many unpleasant places she could shove her advice, Clare arched her eyebrow and said, "Careful now. One might get the wrong impression from *your* concern."

A knock sounded on the door before Alys could reply. In the vanity mirror's reflection, Clare saw Marquin standing on the threshold of her room. His gaze focused on her back for a second too long, as if he could see her true skin beneath the glamour.

Some mages could, in the same way *she* could see beneath it, but if any of those were at the party tonight, she was counting on them not caring enough to look past it. In her wanderings through Hightown she'd caught the scent of glamour on practically everyone— for clearer skin, shinier hair, different colored eyes—and she expected it would only be more prominent at a celebration like the prince's. Her glamour should simply be one in a hundred.

She stood and turned, daring him to say anything about her scars. "Aren't you going to tell me I look pretty?" she finally asked, when the silence grew awkward.

"You look beautiful," he said dutifully. "But you already know that. Could I speak with you alone for a moment?"

Alys needed no further urging to depart, giving Marquin's shoulder a friendly squeeze on her way out.

"She offered to help you?" Marquin asked, clearly doubting that was the case.

"Something like that. What did you want to talk about?"

"I wanted to apologize. For what I said earlier."

She made a noncommittal noise and walked to the window,

waiting until she saw Alys's tall, lithe form striding toward the barn before she answered. "It isn't necessary. I can understand how embarrassing it might be for you if the apprentice in your home started throwing herself at the prince."

"That isn't why I said it. I care very little for people's opinions."

Clare folded her arms across her chest, unable to parse out if he hadn't taken the easy explanation she'd given him because he truly wanted to be honest with her, or if it was all just another manipulation. "Then did you find out what you wanted to? Have you figured me out?"

He shook his head. "I don't want to be at odds with you."

"We got on well enough before, didn't we?" In truth, on the road to Veralna, she had felt much more at ease with Marquin than Verol. She understood Marquin better.

"Yes. But that was before."

Before she was here, in their home.

"I don't...trust easily," he said. "I think you and I are alike in that way."

"And you trust less when you must trust other people with Verol."

"You matter to him. You have the potential to hurt him more than anyone save myself."

She knew, by the way he said it, exactly what he was thinking. "I'm not trying to be his daughter. I don't need a father, I'm not a child."

"No. You aren't. But to him, you might as well already be his family."

"It's not my fault how he sees me. I didn't *ask* for him to want to help me."

"I know. And while he can't control the Kinthing's insistence that he do what he can to protect you, he would never try to force you to feel any way about him. Nor would I ask you to."

"Then what *are* you asking?"

"For you to try and be patient with *me*. There was a time I almost —" He broke off, rubbing a hand over his face. "Twenty-one winters ago, Verol had another apprentice. A little girl named Marie. She was killed. It broke him and I lost him and it's taken me two decades to bring him back. Two decades where the Kinthing was buried in so much misery he didn't hear its call. Until you."

"So that's why you hate me," she said softly.

"I don't hate you."

"But you wish I wasn't here."

"Yes," he said. "And no. You've brought him back to life, in many ways. I just need time. To adjust to you."

"Take all the time you need." Clare retrieved her guitar case, holding onto it like a shield as she stepped past him into the hall. "It won't take him long to discover I am nothing anyone would want to call family."

She hit the end of the hall and nearly ran into Verol. He stopped with a mildly stunned expression on his face. "You look very nice."

"Thank you." Clare dredged up a smile because smiles were her currency. "Your husband had to be prompted to say the same."

Verol's lips tilted up in an answering smile. "He was never good with compliments. Made figuring out he liked me very difficult."

Behind her, Marquin snorted. "You didn't need compliments. Your ego was the size of Drake Mountain when I met you."

She couldn't help herself from wanting to know. "So how did you figure it out?" Relationships—all of them—were strange to her, but romantic ones the most. Because the only love she'd ever known was the kind that lived in between the lines of song lyrics, and then she'd met *them*, and she'd seen it between them. But she didn't understand how it existed. How it came to be.

And she wasn't prepared for Verol's answer.

"I broke a wine bottle over his ex-boyfriend's head."

Clare blinked. "And how did that tell you he liked you?"

"It didn't. It told him that I liked him."

"You might have found a better way than bludgeoning poor Anderson with a perfectly good vintage."

"Oh he's *poor* Anderson now? He was saying the most awful things about you at the time."

A throat cleared and she turned to see Fitz standing in the front doorway, customary scowl firmly in place. "The prince's carriage has arrived for Clare."

All the easy humor left Verol's face, and she found herself wanting to bring that lightness back. She didn't understand why, especially given the conversation she'd just had with Marquin, except that it was impossible not to like Verol. Which was going to make it that much harder when he figured out that she wasn't going to turn normal in the blink of an eye. That she wouldn't ever make good family.

She pushed the thought away and forced her voice to be light and easy. "Will you tell me the rest of the story, sometime? I'm thinking it would make the perfect ballad."

He gave her a quick half-smile. "Of course. Put on your cloak and I'll walk you out."

The cloak she'd forgotten because she was so utterly unused to having one. And because she hated it. While warm enough, it was a cream affair entirely too close to white. She'd tried to opt for a gray or black one by pointing out that white stained so easily, at which point Cynthia had replied, with complete sincerity, "Stains are what servants are for, and you don't want to look all drab in dark colors." Clare had relented only because Galina's hadn't actually had any cloaks in darker colors.

She turned for her room, intending to retrieve it, when Verol said, "Oh, I nearly forgot. Your payment. In advance, as requested." He dropped a coin purse the size of her fist into her palm. The weight was heavy and solid, and she barely managed to restrain herself from opening it before she reached the solitude of her room. The wealth of coins that glittered back at her was mesmerizing, and she quashed the voice that said she hadn't earned this. The voice that said other artists would work years, maybe decades, to dream of earning this much in a single night.

But the system itself wasn't fair, and she *was* worth it. She would earn every coin before the night was through. She closed the purse and stowed it in the armoire, tucked into the toe of her boots. She would have to find a better hiding place for it later, but this was the best she could do on short notice.

Grabbing her cloak, she put it on and returned to Verol. Apparently, when he'd said he would walk her out, what he'd meant was that he would march out of the house ahead of her, fling open the carriage door—much to the bewilderment of the carriage driver—and peer inside. It didn't take supreme powers of deductive reasoning to guess what he was doing.

"If you're looking for His Princeliness, I don't think men of his station typically come to collect their hired singers in person," Clare teased. Verol shot her a look and returned to the carriage interior.

"Make sure you check under the cushions," she added. "I understand cushions are very good at hiding princes."

She leaned her guitar case against one of the wheels, picked up the hem of her dress and cloak so they wouldn't drag, and further bewildered the poor carriage driver by walking up to the horses. The way animals reacted to people was a good indicator of what kinds of interactions they had with humans, and Clare was interested to discover how Numair treated his.

These two were a matched set of palomino mares, obviously well-fed with gleaming coats. She approached them both with an outstretched hand. The mare on the right wasn't interested, bored by Clare but without any hint of fear. The mare on the left stretched her head forward eagerly, sniffing at Clare's hand and then lipping at her harmlessly.

"She doesn't bite," the carriage driver said quickly.

"Of course she doesn't," Clare cooed at the mare before turning to the driver. He'd scrambled down from his seat and now stood beside her, clearly at a loss as to what to do now that he was here. She supposed he probably didn't pick up many women in formal wear who decided to go pet the carriage horses. "What's her name?"

"The horse?"

Clare nodded.

"Butterscotch, miss. And the other one's Daisy." He hesitated a moment, then: "Do you like horses, miss?"

"Very much so," she answered.

"Prince Numair has the finest horses in the kingdom." He paled a bit and amended, quickly, "Excepting His Majesty the King, of course."

"Of course," Clare echoed, trying hard to hide the amusement tugging at the edges of her mouth. And then, because it appeared the man feared she might actually take his unintended offense against king and country to heart, she prodded, "Prince Numair likes horses as well, then?"

"Oh, indeed. He purchases each one himself."

"Yes, well," came Verol's voice, in a caustic tone she would not previously have suspected him capable of producing, "he is a gentleman of *leisure* after all. And it is hard to have difficulty with it when you're Deirdren Blessed."

Deirdren, the patron goddess of horses and the hunt. Those whose magic gave them an affinity for horses were often called Deirdren Blessed.

Something akin to anger flashed in the carriage driver's eyes, but it was quickly swept away by a mask of deference. The driver, it seemed, bore a loyalty for his liege that was oddly incongruous with Verol's opinion of the man.

"Are you certain you do not wish me to accompany you?" Verol asked.

Clare waived him off and made for the carriage doors. "I think you'd find a musician's setup somewhat dull." And she would never learn anything interesting about Numair with Verol hovering over her shoulder.

She held out her hand for Verol to help her into the carriage, as if she had been accustomed to being so helped since she could walk. Verol, conditioned as he was to respond to such unspoken societal requests, settled her onto the bench without uttering any of the arguments or warnings that were no doubt on the tip of his tongue.

Marquin appeared next to him and handed her guitar case to her. She settled it onto the opposite seat, and she blamed all the nonsense Marquin had put into her head for the fact she asked, "You will be there, won't you?"

"We will be there," Verol assured her.

Then the door shut and the carriage slid smoothly away, and Clare was staring out the little window, watching Verol and Marquin grow smaller and smaller, and wondering why she suddenly felt like she wanted to throw up.

TWENTY-ONE

LIFE IS DROWNING

As it turned out, the Arrendons and Prince Numair were neighbors—though enough land lay between the two estates that the ride still took nearly thirty minutes with the horses moving at a fast walk. A woman met her at the front of the manor and led her down a path that skirted the outside of the house.

Clare wondered at the outdoor route, but figured maybe she was to be taken inside through a door in the back. The abhorrent cream cloak kept the cold at bay, but the thin, pretty slippers she'd chosen would do little to keep the chill of the ground from seeping into her feet.

She braced herself for it—it wasn't like she hadn't gone barefoot in lower temperatures than this—but the cold never came. It took her a moment to realize why. The walkway was heated, the smooth stones coated with warming spells.

Warming spells. On an outdoor walkway in the middle of winter. Because why not?

The walk itself was black stone, smooth and shiny as glass, and swept clean. No one stone matched any other in shape or size, though they were fitted together so seamlessly that Clare could not find the grouting between them. The end effect was a sort of ordered chaos made eerie by the inky dark hue of the glossy stone.

When she looked up and found precisely the same effect

mirrored in the towering manse, where even the balconies appeared to jut like elegant outcroppings on some steep mountainside, it had the overall effect of making one feel as if they had wandered into the lair of a dark mage straight out of the old legends. It was an abode that said, in no uncertain terms, "You are unwelcome here."

Even the landscaping kept with the message. Not for Lord Numair were the carefully pruned rosebushes, and hedges trimmed into lions and horses she'd seen adorning estates on the ride into the city that morning. Here, flowers ran wild, and every single one was the kind that bloomed at night.

Datura and moonflower. Night-blooming jasmine and wisteria. Queen-of-the-night and tuberose. There were dozens more, far more than she knew the names for. They claimed the terrain for their own, climbing plants woven into trellises here, scaling walls there, while the ground-ridden ones sprawled about in such perfect chaos that the hand behind their tending must be a masterful one indeed.

Not a single one of them should be alive in the dead of winter, much less all of them growing together in harmony, as if it didn't matter that they had their origins in disparate climates. Clearly, Prince Numair had an army of nature mages he paid a small fortune to.

She wanted to be irritated about that, but the scent coming off the blooms was heady, intoxicating. The only thing she really wanted was to wander off the pretty, heated path, lie down in the mass of blooms and sing, not for the gilded nobles soon to be here, but for herself and the sky, and no one else.

"Is something wrong, miss?"

The voice jolted Clare back to the present. She'd frozen, staring out at the grounds, one slippered foot hovering off the edge of the heated path. Her guide was looking at her with a mix of disapproval and concern. Clare didn't think the concern was for her so much as about her.

"Nothing wrong. It's only a distracting view." She resumed walking, though this time she kept her stride next to the woman's, rather than behind it.

The path wound around the eastern corner of the house and split into two branches. One trailed around a small pond, the waters covered in night lily, small fish darting about beneath the surface. The other branch, the one they followed, trailed alongside the house. When they reached the back, Clare had the impression of being in a wide alley—hemmed in on the left by the back wall of the house, and on the right by a twelve-foot-high wall of living greenery.

Her guide stopped between two archways. The left, made of black stone, led to an inner courtyard of the house, its path blocked by iron railing. The right archway was formed of living, growing things, and it was through it that the woman led.

She entered into a wide, open space, easily large enough to fit two ballrooms, all enclosed by walls of green. The middle area of the ground was covered in temporary flooring that had been pieced together in seamless fashion to create a dance floor. At the far end of where she stood, on the other side of the dance floor, a stage had been constructed, vining plants trailing about and around it, leaving just enough space for one to stand or step between them.

On either side of the dance floor, carved wooden tables waited for the food and drinks that would no doubt be set out closer to the beginning of the festivities. Beyond them, in the remaining space, the living walls appeared to open here and there into a maze that Clare itched to explore.

"The sound crystals are on the stage. Will you require any assistance?"

Clare forced her gaze from the mesmerizing intricacies of the plants and found her voice. "No, thank you."

She barely noticed when the woman left. She walked across the dance floor to the stage, because some primal part of her thought that if she didn't move, she would remain rooted to the ground forever, until she became a part of the landscape, just another tree or bush.

She had the sudden image of people trapped inside the living walls, bodies still, gazes forever frozen as vines grew over them, grew into them, until they no longer knew if they were plant or person. With the image came the certainty that just such a thing had happened. Not here, not now, but in a past time, in one of those lives whose memories were always pressing at the edges of her consciousness when she least wanted them to.

She shook the feeling away, taking in the multitude of life teeming around her, still unable to fathom how it thrived in the middle of winter, or how the air in this space was far warmer than it should be. Warm enough that she shrugged out of her cloak as she climbed onto the stage. She took out her guitar, found a little hideaway beneath the stage to stow the case, and slipped the guitar strap over her shoulder. A sound key rested on the stage, a beautiful deep indigo stone. She took it and slid it into the nook on the guitar designed for such things. It flared to life with a soft, pleasant glow, and she looked around the enclosure for the accompaniment stones. They were spaced evenly in the area around the dance floor, soft blue light clutched by vines here, sitting on tree trunk pedestals there.

She strummed her fingers over the strings. The accompaniment stones fed off the sound key, taking the guitar notes and spreading them evenly throughout the space. Beautiful though the enclosure was, it should have been an acoustical nightmare, but the sound flowed perfectly, soft and delicate, somehow blending with the space rather than being hopelessly absorbed by it.

She looked about the stage for the voice key, but didn't find it. She probably should have asked the woman how to call for someone if she needed something, but she hadn't wanted to admit how out of her depth she was here. Not with the music, not even with talking to people, necessarily, but in knowing all the minutiae, the habits, that any other singer in this position would know.

For instance, who to summon to find lost voice keys. If she was meant to still be standing on this stage when guests began to arrive, or if someone would come to give her instruction before then. It felt a little strange that she'd been left entirely unattended. Didn't princes worry about security and thievery? She hadn't seen a single guard, hadn't seen anyone other than the woman who'd led her here.

Her fingers brushed over the stiletto tucked into her hair. If things turned strange, she had a lifetime of practice stabbing things when the occasion called for it. The thought settled her, and she began plucking the guitar strings, idly working her way through comfort songs, ones she knew so well that she could play them in her sleep. Her fingers warmed and settled into the rhythm. She sang low, soft, and without a voice key, the song was only for her. She descended the stage and wandered as she played, getting a feel for how the music would carry in each area.

She stopped on the left side of the dance floor, where an opening led into the maze beyond. Her fingers stilled on the strings, gaze drawn by the twisting walls. It seemed darker inside the maze than it had any right to be without a roof, even given the severe overcast nature of the sky. She found herself gently setting the guitar against a chunk of wall, one foot taking a slow step forward.

"Do you like it?" The soft, velvet voice sounded pleasantly in her ears, dark and rich and entirely at home.

She halted and turned. Prince Numair stood behind her, just far enough away not to trigger her personal boundaries, his black eyes at once warm and distant. He wore all black, as if dressed for his funeral rather than his nameday.

"Yes." She met his gaze as she answered him, looking for that hint of mischief, that readiness to verbal sparring she'd seen from him earlier. But the only thing she found in the black depths of his irises was endless melancholy. She glanced at the maze entrance, then back to him. "It's...oddly peaceful."

He raised an eyebrow. "Most people tell me it is wild and disturbing."

"And yet you invite Veralna's nobility into its heart for the evening. Tell me, do you enjoy making them uncomfortable, or is it that you do not wish to have people in your home? Or," she continued when he remained silent, "is it both?"

He shook his head. "You ask a lot of questions."

"Because they tend to get me answers, whether people give them or not."

He laughed and the melancholy in his eyes receded a little. He was young, she realized, hardly older than herself. If she had to guess, she would not put him at more than twenty-five winters. Yet he seemed—like she felt—centuries older.

And he was nothing like she'd expected—nothing like she would expect a prince who had a pretty woman alone in a secluded place to be. For a man who'd paid an extraordinarily large sum of money to put her in the dress she now wore, his eyes had never once left her face.

"Why did you bring me here tonight?" she asked softly. She was not quite certain when they had moved closer together, nor which one of them had done the moving, but they stood a mere foot apart. The air between them had taken on a charged quality, as if a storm would break at any moment.

Shadows clouded the prince's eyes, and she had the horrifying sense that whatever words came out of his mouth would be the absolute truth.

His lips parted and, like most truths, the answer he gave didn't readily appear to be a response to the question she'd asked. "Have you ever seen a place that has been utterly ravaged? Razed to the ground until nothing is left alive? Not a person, nor plant, nor any living creature?"

She hesitated, not because the question was strange, though it probably was, but because she wanted to answer with the truth, and her truths could not be told in full. "I've seen…something like that," she hedged. Renault County wasn't razed, wasn't obliterated, but she wouldn't call it *living* either.

"I saw El-Dennon after it fell."

El-Dennon. The last kingdom that had resisted falling under the control of the Faelhorn Provinces.

"I was fourteen at the time. My uncle butchered it." He swallowed, a harsh bob of his throat. "He didn't do it because he needed to. He did it because their defiance infuriated him. And he did it well.

"I wandered through the wreckage for hours. I don't know why. There was nothing to save, nothing to be done. But I felt like I owed it to the dead. To remember they'd existed. I was in the remnants of the town square as night fell, and in the center of so much dust and death, a single night orchid unfurled its petals. Everything around it was beaten and broken. It had seen what happened, been exposed to it, and yet somehow it lived. It bloomed." A brief hesitation clouded his eyes before he plunged ahead. "Seeing you was like seeing that orchid all over again."

If anyone else had spoken those words to her, she would have laughed. To compare her to a single spot of beauty in a sea of destruction was the type of thing poets did to flatter court women. But no one standing in Numair's orbit, hearing him talk, feeling the intensity that rolled off him, could take his words for contrivance. He looked at her like he was a drowning man and she something to cling to.

Foolish, foolish man. Didn't he know that she was drowning too? That life was drowning, and that if two people clung to each other too tightly in rough seas, they only drowned faster?

"You asked me why I wanted you here," he said finally, when the silence between them had stretched long enough that it risked growing into something else. "I answered. It's your turn. Why did you accept?"

"Do you want honesty?" she asked.

The right corner of his lip curled up in a half-smile. "If such a thing can be said to exist, yes."

Smart man. Because she wasn't going to give him honesty. At least, not all of it. "For one, you *are* the prince of Faelhorn."

"Second prince," he corrected.

"Why is that?" Everyone seemed always to point out that he was second, yet she hadn't heard tell of a first.

"My cousin is first." There was something in the set of his jaw that spoke of unpleasantness.

"Does it bother you? Being second?"

"Hardly. I wish there were a thousand princes in front of me. What other reasons do you have?"

"You didn't bore me to tears in Galina's."

"And?" He was closer now—or she was closer, she wasn't sure which.

"Because," she said softly, so softly her voice barely carried to him, close though he was, "you have not yet realized that I'm not the orchid. I am the wreckage left behind in the aftermath."

"Don't sell yourself short—I see no reason you can't be both."

A throat cleared at the edge of the enclosure.

Clare turned to look at the woman who stood in the archway. It was the guide who had met her at the front walk earlier.

Numair's gaze had yet to leave Clare's face, even as he asked, "Yes?"

The woman held up her left hand, dangling a silver chain with a single black icicle stone. "We couldn't find the voice key earlier, but we've located it now."

Numair crossed to the woman and stood for a moment, talking to her in low, measured tones that Clare could not pick up. The woman left and Numair returned, holding the voice key out to Clare.

Her lips stretched into a wry smile. "You aren't going to offer to place it about my neck yourself?"

Amusement danced in his dark eyes. "Forgive me, but you seem like the type of woman who might snap at a man for doing so."

"I see you aren't entirely without intuition." Clare took the voice key from him, securing the chain about her neck, twisting the crystal at the base so the spell remained inactive.

Numair's staff arrived, filing in from the archway, bearing trays laden with meats and vegetables, fruits and nuts and other delicacies. The trays bore the telltale engravings of containers spelled to keep their contents hot or cold, and the people carrying them arranged them on the polished wood tables with the kind of careless efficiency born from years of practice.

She'd never seen so much food in one place.

Clare took staff and bounty in against the backdrop of the enclosure and the mansion towering behind it. Her mind's eye juxtaposed the scene with the grime of dirt streets and half broken-down, mold-infested quarters, of rats and people scrabbling about in the streets, and it not always obvious which was which.

Restlessness overcame her, the desire to flee gripping her hard enough to leave invisible bruises.

Impossibly, Numair seemed to notice. "Do you want to get out of here?" he murmured.

Yes.

Except she couldn't.

"The guests will start arriving in less than an hour. I can't be late."

"The joy of being the evening's centerpiece is that the celebration doesn't start until *I* arrive. And even then, tradition demands the damn minstrels play their nameday song before we cede the stage to you. So you see, it is quite impossible for you to be late."

It was a terrible idea. "Lead the way."

He slipped around a bend in the maze and she followed. Out of sight, the need to run reached a fever pitch. As if, by virtue of the fact she couldn't be seen, she was now even more likely to be caught. Mad laughter bubbled up in her throat. She pulled the light, silken skirts of the dress to an improper height and *ran*. The muscles in her legs sang, the breath in her chest coming freely as the wind caught the stray curls of her hair and sent it streaming behind her.

Clare loved to run. It had often been a necessity, a means of fleeing pain, but when it was not—and even sometimes when it was

—nothing compared to the feel of muscles bunching and relaxing, propelling her forward, of the way the world seemed to spin around her, as if for just that moment she was its center, and everything else simply drifted about her.

Just when she thought she would have to slow, a solid wall of greenery ahead, vines and branches curled in on themselves, creating a space just tall and wide enough to leap through. She cleared it in a single bound, landing on the other side to find a world filled with trees. Their canopies reached endlessly towards the sky, their trunks wide enough to fit twenty of her inside one. She looked back and saw Numair on her heels, the hole in the greenery closing behind him.

She didn't realize she was grinning until she recognized that his smile matched her own.

She stopped abruptly beneath the towering overhang of a tree, its exposed roots curving to form a perfect, smooth seat, which she took.

"Do you always run like Ferrian herself is chasing you?" Numair asked, gliding to a stop a foot away.

"What makes you think she's not? I notice you had no difficulty keeping up. For a reported drunk, you seem quite easy of breath."

"Ah, well. Cherish this moment of my sobriety, for once the festivities start you won't see it again."

The clouds were back in his eyes, gloomy and overcast, and for once Clare regretted her insistent need to figure everyone out, to merge the man she had met with the rumors she kept hearing. She had gotten nothing for her troubles, and she had lost the energy from his soul, the lightness that had matched her own as they ran. It was as if while they ran Numair had slipped a set of chains, and her words had allowed them to bind him once more.

"It seems that we have run, but we have not quite escaped," she said softly.

"Do you think anyone ever does?"

She looked away, trying to peer beyond the depths of the endless forest. Whatever spells kept the elements at bay within the maze's enclosure were not in effect here, and she shivered against winter's chill, wishing she'd grabbed her cloak. "I don't know."

It was a lie. She already knew no one ever escaped. Not really.

TWENTY-TWO

SMART WOMEN NEVER DO

Numair Tolvannen was a selfish prick. If he wasn't, he wouldn't have brought her here tonight. He hadn't intended to. Just like he hadn't intended to walk into Galina's that morning, or buy that damned dress, but Clare Brighton seemed to have a way of dragging him into her orbit.

Rationally, he knew he hadn't altered the course of her life. From the moment he'd heard her sing in that Midtown inn, he'd known her path was a straight trajectory here, to the height of the kingdom's attention.

All he'd done with his interference was speed her journey. Hasten an already guaranteed thing.

"What would you do if I said I'd brought you here for selfish reasons?"

She stiffened for a moment, until she realized he'd taken two steps *away* from her as he asked the question. She relaxed. "Congratulations, you're human?"

"Sometimes I wonder if that word means anything," he murmured.

"So do I."

What had she seen of their kind, that her voice held such bitterness? He didn't blame her. He'd seen enough to think that if humanity did mean something, it wasn't anything good. And yet he *was* human, so he kept on hoping that someday the species would prove itself worth something.

They lapsed into silence, and that silence was such a relief. He couldn't remember the last time he'd stood with someone and not felt the need to fill the emptiness between them with false things. It almost made him regret how this night was going to end.

But he was tired, and the only thing he regretted was that she was going to be here to see how the evening played out. Somehow, he hadn't thought of that when he'd sent her that impulsive invitation. Somehow, in the rush of sending it, he'd forgotten what the *point* of this evening was. He'd only thought that Clare deserved the notoriety of being hired for this event far more than Estrella Vane ever could, so he'd given it to her.

"Should we go back, then?" she asked, when enough time had passed that even he couldn't ignore they were going to be *too* late, soon. Or rather, *she* was.

He nodded, and the walk back was like walking into a deep forest as opposed to out of one, every shadow and oppressive height hanging over him. When they neared the enclosure, he took a slightly different path than they had left by, leading her to the back of one of the enclosure walls.

"The stage is on the other side." His hand gently brushed the wall, and the foliage rearranged itself, opening a path for her.

"Clare?" She looked up at him, and he almost didn't say the rest. With the cunning that lurked in her eyes, he doubted she *needed* him to say the rest. But he was never going to have the opportunity again. "My uncle is not a good man."

"I should hardly think anyway needs a warning that the *Jackal King* is not a good man."

"I know. But whatever you think he may be, I can promise you he is worse."

"I didn't think even princes spoke so openly of their kings."

He gave her a smile, the practiced one that made people see a charming, empty-headed fool, and watched it bounce right off her. "I'm my uncle's favorite. Everyone knows I get away with everything."

She shook her head. "True favorites never get away with anything. People with power only value people they can control."

He laughed, a short, uncalculated sound that surprised him.

"True enough." He gestured to the opening. "My apologies in advance. You'll be waiting a while."

"Why?"

"Because the party truly doesn't start until I arrive. And if I'm not late, I'll deprive them all of their favorite pastime of betting on precisely how late I will be. If you want to make a small fortune, you can throw your money in on an hour and a quarter."

"You intend to be *that* late?"

He grinned. "I do." He gestured through the opening. "After you."

She looked through to the stage, hesitated. "What am I supposed to do until you arrive?"

He wondered how much it cost her to ask it—to admit she didn't know what to do. She clearly hadn't admitted it to anyone else, as someone could have told her how these things went.

"Mingle. Eat. Drink. Be charming. We have to let the royal minstrels open with the traditional nameday song or else they feel unloved, after which you'll be called to the stage." Not that the evening would progress that far, but...well, at least she would know for her next event.

She nodded and walked through.

"It was nice to meet you," he said softly.

She turned and gave him a sharp look. "You say that as if we will never speak again."

She saw too much by half, so he gave her the answer that would be true if this were any ordinary night. "Once the night is through, I doubt you should ever desire to speak to me again. Smart women never do."

A whisper of his magic drew the wall of foliage closed on any response. He walked away before he could change his mind. Before that brilliant defiance burning in her eyes could make him think that maybe, just maybe, what he'd decided to do tonight wasn't the right answer after all.

TWENTY-THREE

COURT JESTER

Clare wasn't in the mood to mingle after her conversation with Numair—his melancholy was infectious—but as it turned out, she didn't have to talk to very many people. As soon as Verol and Marquin arrived, merely being in their company put an invisible boundary around the three of them. It wasn't that no one approached them, it was that everyone who did so performed the act with the resolve of someone who had an unpleasant task before them that needed carrying out.

They approached, they made polite noises, and then they left. Even if she'd been inclined to throw money into the betting pool that was indeed accumulating, she wouldn't have gotten anywhere near it with the Arrendons at her side. She was going to have to find a tactful way to ask them about those monikers Cynthia had called them by.

Beneath the inane chatter of the crowd and the increasingly less-good-natured betting, she caught snippets of conversation.

"—how long does the prince intend we wait for him?"

"Honestly, I know the king dotes on him, but—"

"—gives him far too much leeway, if you ask me."

"—probably passed out drunk."

"More likely in his bedchamber entertaining the newest thing to catch his fancy."

Irritation built in Clare's chest for no valid reason. It was only chatter, only rumors, both of which were good social currency. She knew better than to take people's speculations to heart. The truth of a thing was often of less value to her than how it could be used.

Abruptly the mood in the space shifted. Clare felt the change, felt the thing that had caused it—like a swarm of locusts had at once darkened the horizon—as the announcer at the archway straightened and said, "His Majesty Alaric Tolvannen, Commander of the Four Armies, Uniter of the Realms, Lord of the Southern Reaches, and King of the Faelhorn Provinces." At this exhaustive list of titles, Clare half-expected a carpet to magically unfurl in front of the king so his boots would not have to touch the bare ground.

Power rippled through the space and the knees of everyone present hit the ground. Heads bowed, eyes lowered, and Clare barely managed to mimic it all in time, grateful she and the Arrendons stood at the very back of the crowd. Because while the magic rippling off Alaric Tolvannen forced obedience from everyone it touched, it washed over her as if she wasn't there.

In its wake, the Song's rage boiled. The phantom taste of blood, hot and coppery, hit the back of her throat. Her world swam in pain and fear, screams demanding release, and for a moment she was *not* Clare Brighton, but someone else. Someone much smaller and younger and deeply, deeply terrified, before terror became nothingness.

It took her a moment to understand that she was not that person. She was *not* dead. But she knew that whoever that person had been, the man—the king—who stood before her, had killed them.

The sheer wealth of power that radiated off him was staggering. Magic soaked into every thread of his clothing, thrummed in the jewelry anointing him, hid in the lotion rubbed into his skin. As if a dozen mages had poured the wealth of their power into him. Or as if he simply had that much of his own.

And that was only what coated the surface. Beneath it, something foul and oily lingered, as if hundreds of souls clung to his skin, the residual energy of their lives feeding into him.

Instinct screamed at her to run. Run far and run fast, and never come within a thousand miles of this man again.

"Uncle!" Numair's voice rang out, overly loud and boisterous. "You made it." He appeared at the far end by the stage, stumbling a little as he made for the king, to all appearances delighted to see him.

Alaric moved toward his nephew, far enough away and with his back to Clare that she lifted her head enough to see them. Enough to see that every other form in the room had their heads tipped so far down they wouldn't see past their own laps. Even Verol and Marquin to either side of her were immobile.

King and prince embraced. Numair's left hand thumped the king hard on the back, disguising the quick jerk of his right hand that had a flash of silver catching Clare's eye as a knife appeared in it.

Everything came together in her mind in an instant—Numair's assertion, as Taius, that he only had two days to help her. His earlier melancholy and the sense that when he'd said it was nice to meet her, what he'd really been saying was goodbye.

Numair wasn't trying to kill the king—that much magic around Alaric meant a knife had no chance at all of accomplishing the deed —he was committing public suicide. And if Clare was smart, she would remain kneeling and let him do it.

Except everything in her rebelled and she was already on her feet. Numair caught her movement, looking at her over Alaric's shoulder, and his eyes flared wide. Everything else happened in the blink of an eye. The knife in Numair's hand vanished, so smoothly she didn't see what he'd done with it. Vines thrust from the ground to either side of her, ensnaring her wrists and ankles, pulling her down.

She went easily as Numair's now-empty hand thumped Alaric's back. In the jostle of the movement he mouthed a single word at her: *Bow.* She held his gaze for a defiant second before lowering her head as deeply as everyone else's. The vines let her go, disappearing into the earth as if they'd never been.

Numair and Alaric broke apart, the king releasing them all with a lazy, "Rise." His magic came back to him like tentacles curling inward, and in its absence his courtiers gained their feet.

She ignored the heightened energy pouring off Verol and Marquin. Maybe everyone's eyes had been too downcast to see that brief moment she'd been vertical when no one else could manage the feat, but the Arrendons had been right next to her. They'd *felt* her stand.

The chatter of hundreds of voices resumed, the laughter a little more brittle, the easiness a little more forced. And Clare was the only one who noticed how rattled their prince looked before he shuttered it behind the appearance of a man drunk off his ass.

The king laughed off Numair's antics as his nephew stumbled away, as if he did indeed find him amusing rather than embarrassing. Then he turned and walked straight for Clare. Verol and Marquin tensed, a readying she felt rather than saw. Twenty feet away, Numair's gaze found her again. For a moment the four of them—Clare, Marquin, Verol, and Numair—waited in suspended collection to see if the Jackal King had noticed Clare's earlier defiance. That his magic hadn't held her.

She cataloged him as he approached, the familiar routine of doing so easing the flight response in her body. He didn't look as old as she had expected. The title of king always made her think of an old, wrinkled man grown fat off privilege and luxury, but this man bore no semblance to such a caricature. He was large, broad but fit, with tanned skin and brown hair lightly peppered with gray. He appeared to be in the early half of forty winters, though that didn't *feel* right. Perhaps it was only the power wrapped around him, but he felt far, far older than he looked.

He smiled as he approached. It had the effect of making Clare's skin crawl and the Song vanish. The power that was always a steady annoyance inside her buried itself so deep in the cage she'd built for it, she couldn't feel it at all.

"Is this your new apprentice, Verol? Do introduce us." The voice was deep and resonant.

Verol put a hand on her shoulder, the gesture unmistakably protective. She allowed it where normally she would have brushed it away, because she understood the reason for it in this moment.

"My king, this is Miss Clare Brighton. Clare, His Majesty King Alaric." Verol's voice floated between them, crisp and perfectly polite, in the same way a venomous snake might be perfectly beautiful if one paid attention only to the colors of its scales.

"A pleasure to meet you, Your Majesty."

The king's face broke into an amused smile. "Please, all of this Your Majesty business grows tiresome."

Says the man who just forced all of his subjects to their knees, she thought.

"I have been Alaric to Verol and Marquin for some time. I see no reason their ward should not call me the same." He smiled wider, his teeth glinting between red lips.

Ah yes, Your Majesty, I see your jackal teeth. Verol's grip on her shoulder tightened, but she did not need his warning to know the invitation to familiarity was one she shouldn't take. "That is…a very kind offer, Lord Tolvannen."

"But you must refuse me?"

"I must acquiesce to the customs of the country, lest they fall apart in our failure to observe them."

"I see."

Clare could not discern if he was amused or annoyed, nor which of the two would be more dangerous for her.

"You are a Songweaver, yes?" She barely had time to nod before he continued. "Verol does seem to have an affection for them. I think his last girl was a Songweaver. Odd, when it is not a particularly *useful* talent, wouldn't you say?"

Tension sparked between Verol and the king. For whatever reason, the king was trying to rile Verol by goading her—and doing a damn good job of it, if the way Verol's fingers dug into her shoulder was any indication.

Clare smiled and answered eagerly, as if she thought he'd meant the question as a serious, philosophical one. Just like a hopeful, naive girl might in the presence of the king. "I do not find it odd at all, Your Majesty. After all, useless talents are often the most enjoyable."

"Oh?" he said, his tone bored now that she hadn't played into his hand as he'd intended. "Do enlighten me."

"If a thing is useful, it must be practiced and honed only for the purpose of what it can produce. As such, it becomes tiresome, if for no other reason than it *must* be done. One grows to resent it, over time, for its necessity. For instance, if one is a skilled carpenter and makes a living in such a fashion, the joy of crafting eventually becomes lost in the drudgery of being required to craft in order to make a living. If, however, one possesses a less useful skill, something as silly as an ability to arrange a drawing room, or a dinner setting, in an aesthetically pleasing fashion, well, no one expects a person to make a living from such a skill. It is not a necessary one, and therefore it never becomes a required one. For that reason, the person retains the joy of doing it, and it brings joy to others who benefit from its performance. In such a way, the latter skill is inherently more enjoyable than the former."

The king stared. She wasn't sure if it was because he hadn't expected her to be able to string an intelligent sentence together, or if it was because she'd really just given him an articulate argument on an arguably pointless subject.

"A Songweaver and a philosopher, I see," he said finally. "I'll have to bow to your wisdom in this matter. If your talent is so enjoyable, will you be Songweaving this evening?"

"Clare has only just been apprenticed, Alaric." Warning limned Verol's voice.

"Oh come now, we have already discussed the trivial nature of the talent, surely you do not mean to tell me it requires such skill of practice that she should be incapable of performing it this evening? Especially when she came out a black diamond?" He put his thumb and forefinger together and flicked the gemstone hanging from her ear.

She didn't give him the satisfaction of flinching. Could she hear Verol's teeth grinding together, or was it her imagination?

"Just one song, perhaps?" the king prodded.

"One song," Clare answered for Verol. "The first."

"And you can make a person feel anything when you sing?"

"Anything at all. What would you like most to feel?"

"Heartbreak."

"An odd choice."

He shrugged, his eyes so devoid of emotion it was like looking into the fabled void of Haidaera, where lost souls were said to roam eternal. "I have never felt it before. Every Songweaver I've met has failed to make me. I am…interested in experiencing what I am told is a common feeling at some point in a person's life." The words 'common feeling' skittered off his tongue as if he meant common *failing*.

I am not surprised you have never felt heartbreak, King of Faelhorn. You would have to be able to feel love, first.

Therein, Clare suspected, lay the reason no Songweaver had ever managed to make him feel the emotion. They had not understood that first, they must make him feel love—its longings and its trust, its joys and its hopes. Make him feel that, then wrench it away.

Clare's lips curved into a slow smile that bore no trace of warmth. "I have just the song for you, my lord." The perfect song, and she would enjoy making him feel every moment of it. A shame the rest of the crowd would be likewise subjected, but she would make certain they knew who to blame for the choice.

"I look forward to it." The king inclined his head and left them.

Clare turned the full power of her formidable gaze upon Verol and Marquin. "What," she hissed softly, "was that?"

Verol released a long, slow breath. "I wish you had not agreed to Songweave tonight."

"I am aware. Your objection was as painfully obvious as the fact that the king was not going to take 'no' for answer. What exactly are you afraid of?"

Verol opened his mouth, shut it, lips pressing into a thin line. Shook his head. "I suppose there is no chance of you suddenly taking ill?"

Clare narrowed her eyes. "None. *Why* are you worried?"

"He is worried," Marquin said, when it became obvious that Verol wouldn't speak, "that something else might come through when you sing. Something other than Songweaving."

Sick heat pooled in her stomach. They knew. They had known all along that she had something different, something *other* inside her. How long had they known? Since they journeyed together on the road? Before? Was it the reason they wanted her?

The Song woke just enough to offer her an image, a little girl with blonde curls, offering it to her as if it was the answer to all her questions. It wasn't an answer, it was just a girl—a dead girl, she realized. One who'd been dead as long as Clare had been alive. The Song tried to push more at her—memories or knowledge, she wasn't sure—but she pushed back. She didn't want it invading her head, not here, not now.

She stumbled back, even as she had the sense that this sudden revelation was all tied to the king's interest in her, and making a scene right now was a very bad idea. But she only managed a single step away before her back hit a solid warmth, correcting her course in the opposite direction and making it appear that the body at her back had stumbled into *her*.

Hands settled lightly on her waist and a deep, velvet voice whispered, so softly not even Verol or Marquin heard, so softly she doubted his lips were even moving, "Now is a *very* bad time to make that kind of scene. So make a different one instead."

Numair's words in her ear, the brush of human contact, broke through her blind anger and slammed her squarely back into the present.

Make a different one instead. Right. Because she stood in the midst of the most notable people in Veralna, company where it meant something if the prince came up and grabbed her.

She broke away from him and spun around, outrage on her face. "What do you think you're—" She cut off abruptly, as if she'd only just recognized who'd touched her.

Numair looked as disheveled as it was possible to look in expensive clothing, his hair idly mussed, and his face bore a look of priceless consternation. Someone needed to put the man on a theater stage. "You," he announced, loud enough Clare thought the birds three forests over could hear him, the slightest slur in his words, "are *not* Dahlia."

Clare's memory searched and produced Dahlia Klado, a young woman around Clare's age with the same colored hair, and determined that a drunk man might very well mistake her for the Duke of Moria's daughter from behind.

Numair appeared to mull his realization over, then shrugged. "But you're here, so you'll do." He grabbed her hand and tugged her to the middle of the very empty dance floor, at which point Clare realized that she was now to be subjected to the nameday dance under the watchful gaze of every courtier present. With a man who was doing his damnedest to look like a drunken idiot, for reasons she could not fathom. He even smelled drunk, the scent of alcohol rolling off him in waves strong enough to blind a horse.

He pulled her in, clapping one hand to her shoulder. His other hand settled on the small of her back, and that was when both of them went rigidly still. Because while this particular glamour covered appearances, it was not good enough to cover texture, and his fingers had brushed the thick, raised scars that crisscrossed her flesh.

Her body still trembled with anger, unsettled from her interaction with Verol and Marquin, from being touched so much in so short a span of time when she'd avoided it since she'd left Renault County.

Like any creature backed into a corner, she snapped. "Speak a word of it," she growled, "and I will suddenly become very interested in finding out why the second prince of Faelhorn would be pilfering letters off the nephew of a common duke, or getting random singers into the Rival Theater."

Every aspect of Numair turned cold. From the fingertips against her back to the sudden rigidity in his posture, he felt foreign and distant, and it occurred to her she might have miscalculated. A wall of black ice shuttered Numair's eyes, and for the first time in a long, long while, Clare knew she *ought* to feel afraid.

Because like her, Numair had the look of an animal backed into a corner. She'd already snapped and if he did too, the fight was inevitable. Now wasn't the time or the place for a fight. She had no reason to push a man who mere minutes ago had nearly forced a king to kill him. A man who had aborted that move to keep *her* from that same king's notice.

But even knowing all that, she couldn't back down now that she'd launched the opening blow. She didn't have it in her. She'd made her choices and she'd live with them. She rolled her shoulders back and met his gaze.

He stared at her, expressionless, until the first strings of the traditional nameday tune drifted to them, and the ice shuttering him shattered with his quiet laugh as he pulled her into the dance. "Who are you, Clare Brighton?"

She thought of who she'd been. Of who she wanted to be. Of the lives and memories constantly pressing at her mind. "Everything and everyone. Who are you, Numair Tolvannen?"

That dark melancholy moved across his eyes again. "Nothing and no one." His fingers twitched on her back, like he wanted to move them, but he didn't. "I'm sorry."

Every hackle on her body went up. If he was about to apologize for things he couldn't even begin to understand, she was going to walk right off this dance floor. She had no use for baseless pity. "For what?"

"Pulling you up here. It's obvious you don't like to be touched."

"No, it isn't." She was very good at avoiding being touched, at appearing approachable while assiduously dodging any attempt to reach for her. To notice, you had to actually be looking, and most people never did. He was silent as they spun in three slow circles, during which he dutifully stumbled three times, like the drunk he was supposed to be. "What game are you playing?" she asked. "These people think you are a fool."

"I *am* a fool."

"If so, you are not the one they think you."

His only answer was a barely perceptible shrug. Their movements slowed as the song wound down.

"I'm sorry, too," she said softly, surprised to find she meant it.

"For what?"

"You didn't want to stay here tonight, but I wanted you to."

He jerked like she'd slapped him, and she realized he hadn't understood *why* she'd gained her feet when that knife had flashed into his hand. He'd thought—Ferrian's hells, he'd thought she was trying to save the bloody king.

Then all strains of the song died and Numair's real face disappeared beneath a happy, drunken haze. He stepped back, releasing her until he held only the tips of her fingers in his, bowed to her and turned to the guests. He stumbled a little as he turned, looking all around, his features broadcasting that confusion he was so adept at producing on command. He looked at the stage as the minstrels departed, as if waiting for something. Waiting for Clare, because he hadn't yet let go of her hand.

Annoyance swept across his features. "I *did* hire a singer, didn't I?" He looked around. "Clarissa, or something?"

"Clare, my lord," Clare said.

"Oh." Numair brightened, turning to her. "Do you know where she is?"

"My lord," Clare said, playing perfectly into the scene, matching Numair's volume and sparing no exasperation in her tone, "I *am* the singer."

Snickers ran openly through the crowd. Numair's grin widened in answer, as if he thought they were laughing with him as opposed to at him. How had the second prince of Veralna become its court jester?

Numair gave her a thorough once-over, as if trying to put things together. "You look different," he said finally. "You know, without all the lights." He waved his hand above her, as if indicating stage lights.

Another titter ran through the crowd and she had the sudden

desire to incinerate them all. She couldn't do that. But she could keep him from being alone in this farce, if he let her.

She shot him a look that said, *May I?*

He gave her an arched eyebrow in return that said she could have a trial run.

"It's quite all right, my lord," she said brightly. "I have a blinding effect on people." Then she reached up and ruffled his hair as she passed him to take the stage, and all those damnable giggles went quiet.

CHAPTER

TWENTY-FOUR

HEARTBREAK

Clare twisted the voice crystal at her neck and tapped the song key nestled in the guitar's slot, a gentle hum of readiness spreading to the accompaniment stones throughout the enclosure.

"This first song is a request from our king." Clare inclined her head in King Alaric's direction. The song began simply, and if one didn't know what was coming, they would think it sweet enough. It was a story of first love, full of the tenacious certainty that only that first headlong fall into foolishness can bring. She let the emotions she had first captured to build the song flood her words, to echo alongside the guitar chords, insinuating themselves into every listening ear.

Everyone present felt the effect in the way they experienced the song's events as if they had been their own experiences, but none felt it so strongly as Alaric Tolvannen, for Clare sang the song *for* him. She understood, for the first time, what it truly meant to weave emotions, for she interlaced them around the king as if they were a skein of yarn she wove into a pattern of her own devising, binding them tighter and tighter to him. While the other guests experienced the song as a deeply felt tale, Alaric Tolvannen lived it as if it were his own life. By the time Clare had sung through the first half, the Jackal King was in love with a person he did not even know.

Things went badly for the king from there, for he lived as the one

179

he loved drew slowly away from him. When he asked, quite reasonably, for some explanation, she told him that the distance was in his head, that he was becoming hysterical with supposition, until he believed the truth of the words but could not quell the misery he felt inside. He saw less and less of his love, until he grew to hate himself for his own complacency. For the fact that he still loved. For the way his beloved could put him off so easily with slippery words that were impossible to combat when they were spoken, yet easily enough spotted for untruths when she was gone from his sight.

He stayed through it all, until he woke one morning and found his lover gone for good, and he came to understand that heartbreak was a twofold tragedy, both done to him and done to himself.

The final notes of the song whispered softly through the accompaniment stones, bringing an odd peace because the tale had finally come to its end; the heartbreak was finally over.

Clare strummed the last chord and allowed herself to look at her audience. Every last member of the Faelhorn Province's highest-ranked nobility, who prided themselves on being above the petty emotional displays of the lower classes, wept. Some did so openly while others, cognizant at least of their condition, attempted to cover the spectacle.

Yet none struggled quite so much as King Alaric Tolvannen. His beard collected the saltwater of his tears while his face turned bludgeoned red with his attempt to hold them back. Clare doubted he even breathed, and she wondered if he had ever cried before today. His eyes met hers and she knew in that moment that, while the rest of the spectators tonight might pretend this event had never occurred and forgive her for their weakness, the Jackal King would do neither.

She had done what he asked of her, and he hated her for it—hated her more, because her own eyes were dry.

Gracefully, intentionally, the level of humility and deference just perfect enough to be cutting if one knew how to look, she bowed to her king. Rising from that bow, Clare's fingers deftly found a lighter, happier tune and began to play as if nothing at all unusual had occurred. Her audience, skilled at taking advantage of given opportunities, suddenly found themselves eager to dance and prove that *they*, at least, were not shaken.

The Jackal King melded back into the crowd. Now that her song had ended, sorrow fled him and his countenance shifted toward hellfire. Her gaze found Verol and Marquin, the two deftly moving onto the dance floor in calculated avoidance of their king's trajectory.

Clever men, Clare thought, watching them dance as if they hadn't a care in the world. She wondered just *how* clever they were, and how far she could trust them. If, indeed, she could trust them at all. She had cooled somewhat from her earlier rage, and she observed them logically, or so she told herself. The revelation that they knew her power was something *other* was unsettling, but it did not necessarily mean betrayal. They obviously wanted to keep knowledge of it from the king. The question was, did they want that for her benefit or theirs?

She was still angry, and that would not change without explanation. But their acknowledgment of her power opened another door, one she knew she would walk through even though she didn't want to. Because there was now a very good possibility they could tell her exactly what she was.

Abomination, Madame Aria's voice whispered in her ear. Clare silenced the voice, fingers nearly, but not quite, slipping on the guitar strings.

She focused almost entirely on the performance from then on, sparing only the smallest of her attention to observing Numair, who grew progressively more intoxicated as the evening wore on. He flirted with nearly every female in attendance, if such a thing were possible, paying more attention to some than others, but never staying with any one too long.

No one but Clare noticed that his actions, punctuated here and there by the appropriate embellishments and gravitas, were the perfunctory motions of a trained actor. His drunken stumbles were perfectly timed, his inviting smiles so devoid of emotion Clare found it a mystery that women responded to them at all. He was like a spelled creature, carrying out a set of complex, expressly given orders.

Clare sang until she found she could no longer stomach the masquerade playing out before her. She spoke the right words for ending her set, and turned off the voice and sound keys. Later, she would realize she hadn't a clue what words she'd spoken, only that they must have been the correct ones because they elicited the appropriate responses. She left the remnants of the party to the minstrels' tender mercies, descending the stage as they took it. She had only just secured her guitar into the confines of its case when Numair, in a show of spectacular drunken confusion, knocked over an entire table bearing punch and sweets.

The resultant noise was so loud that every head in the party turned and Clare, never one to waste an opportune moment, shrugged her cloak on and ducked silently into the maze with her guitar. She followed the path she and Numair had taken earlier, smiling when she found a narrow stretch between the foliage open. As if he'd known she would exit the party in mysterious fashion, and had left her a way out. The opening was not so large a space as the one she and Numair had leapt through earlier in the evening, but a smaller one that wouldn't be noticed unless one knew to look for it.

She slid through it easily enough and made her way to the front of the house, staying off the main path and following the Pearl of Evening flowers, whose soft blue petals glowed in the darkening night. She found a familiar carriage waiting in the circular drive. Butterscotch and Daisy, the perfectly matched palominos, stood hitched to the same carriage Clare had arrived in. Butterscotch, who had declined to sniff Clare's hand earlier that night, looked bored, stamping a hoof in impatience. Daisy nickered a soft greeting, and Clare returned the recognition by scratching the mare's withers before nodding to the carriage driver.

He smiled warmly. "Home, miss?"

Home. The word had never meant anything before. She wasn't sure it meant anything now. So she simply nodded and climbed into the carriage.

ONLY ONCE CLARE arrived at the Arrendon manor did she realize she had no way to get inside. They hadn't given her a key, and she'd intended to return with them at the end of the evening. She could probably force her room window open, though if she didn't want to ruin this dress getting inside, she'd have to take it off first.

But as she exited the carriage, it didn't move off. "I'll wait till you're inside, miss," the driver said, because that was the sort of thing he was probably paid to do.

She walked to the front door, thinking maybe Fitz was here. She still hadn't puzzled him out—what he really did for the Arrendons. Oh, he answered doors and drove carriages and cleaned tack, but he also had an air about him that felt…lethal. Whatever he was, she didn't think it was anything as simple as a driver or a footman, and she didn't know if he lived in the house or elsewhere.

Judging by the lack of a single light on, she didn't think he was here now. She placed her hand on the doorknob and tried it. At first it held, then a spark of power licked out from the door ward. The magic tasted her, then settled, and the handle turned. As if the home recognized her and now counted her among its own.

She ghosted silently down the dark hallway, not turning on any of the permanent magelights until she reached her room. Her whole body itched with the need to move, to run. To pack everything in here into a bag and leave before she learned anything about herself or Quin and Verol that she didn't want to know.

That feeling was familiar. Less familiar were the equally strong ones wanting her to stay. Wanting the Arrendons to have an explanation that didn't make her want to leave. Wanting to unravel the walking contradiction that was the second prince of Faelhorn.

Practicality decided her in the end, as it so often did. There was no point in running. Everything she wanted, everything she'd sworn to gain, was here. Succeed or fail, she wasn't leaving.

She changed out of Battle Armor, her fingers trailing over the fine silk as she placed it in the carved wooden wardrobe in the corner of the room. She could sell the dress. The material alone would fetch more than enough to ensure her security, and where would she even wear it again if she kept it? Somehow, she doubted Veralna's elite liked it when a person recycled dresses.

It only made sense to sell.

Clare smoothed a nonexistent wrinkle in the gown's bodice, Numair's voice rising in her memory. *"I confess myself dying to know what it is about that dress that puts such a look of consternation on your face."* She finished smoothing the dress and closed the wardrobe door.

For once in her life, she didn't want to be sensible.

Someone had laundered her original clothing and folded it all neatly atop the chest nestled at the end of her bed. She was unsurprised that someone had entered the room and taken the clothing away. She was, however, surprised that they had brought every single piece back, down to the breeches so patched the original material was hardly discernible, and the threadbare tunic worn completely through in places.

Clare ran her fingers over the patches. She hated sewing, had always hated it. Hated it more, perhaps, because it had been so necessary. No matter how often she did it, she always pricked her fingers on the needle, and that was if she could even get her hands on a proper needle for the job. She slipped the patched breeches on, then the worn tunic.

In the darkness that swallowed the rest of the house, she made her way to the sitting room, feeling her way to the large armchair that rested by the unlit fireplace. In the warm, inviting comfort of the chair, she settled in to wait.

CHAPTER

TWENTY-FIVE

ABOMINATION

I t took less time than she'd expected for the Arrendons to find her. She'd barely gotten comfortable before every magelight in the house flared into burning wakefulness, the fireplace next to her crackling to life. Verol practically ran into the room, Marquin on his heels, and Fitz right behind both of them.

"You're here." Verol's surprise was obvious.

Fitz snorted. "I told you she would be. People like her don't throw away the material advantages you afford."

All the fear and confusion Clare had experienced that evening coalesced. Her emotions needed an outlet, and wasn't it convenient that Fitz was here, and it no longer mattered what power she showed the Arrendons? The Song snapped out of her, clamping him tight. "Why do you dislike me so much?"

He strained against her with what power he possessed, but it was as effective as a butterfly fighting a lion. If he'd detested her before, it deepened into rage as words spilled unwillingly out of him. "Because she's dead and you're alive, and you're nothing like her. Because he already looks at you more like a daughter than he's ever looked at me like a son."

She released him. Anger and regret clouded his eyes as they shifted, mortified, to Verol.

"Fitz..." Verol took a step toward him, but Fitz shook his head. Casting Clare a look of pure venom, he stomped out.

Verol looked between Clare and the doorway, torn. Marquin rested his hand on his husband's shoulder. "Fitz will wait."

"I didn't know." Pain laced Verol's features, and Clare suspected she would cause more of it before the night was through.

"I don't believe he wanted us to know." Marquin looked pointedly at Clare. "That was unkind."

"I never claimed to be kind. So she's dead, and I'm alive?" She recalled the image the Song had shoved into her mind at the party, and the glimpses of knowledge that had come with it. "A little girl with blonde hair. She used to live here and she's dead now. Who was she?"

Verol's face twisted in pain and Marquin gave her another hard look. Yes, she'd already pieced together who the girl was. But if Verol couldn't tell her, then she couldn't stay.

Seconds ticked by, but just as Marquin opened his mouth to answer, Verol said, "Her name was Marie."

"The last apprentice you took after Fitz."

"Yes."

"She was...like me?" Because that was what the Song had been trying to tell her with that image. That it had lived in another before. That it was why Fitz hated her. *She's dead and you're alive, and you're nothing like her.*

"She was."

"And that's why she died."

"Yes."

She looked at Marquin. "When you said his Kinthing called him to some more than others, you meant it called him to people like *me*. How many others are there?"

"None," Verol said softly. "There have *been* others like you, but never more than one at any given time."

"What...what am I?"

The question broke Verol's composure. He slumped onto the couch across from her and put his head in his hands. "You're the one who lived. The only one, impossibly, that Alaric never found."

"But *what* am I? What's inside me?"

"A very old power." Marquin pulled a chair close and settled onto it. "Few people know it exists, and of those who do, no one is exactly sure what it is. It is not like other mages' powers we know, which belong wholly to the individual born to them. It is..."

"A being in its own right?" Clare suggested, her voice a bare whisper.

"We believe so."

I know so.

"What does it want?"

"We don't know. What we do know is that every time it surfaces, pieces of the world disappear. Twelve hundred years ago it was born into Illora, the Enchantress of Silence, and the continent of Thieren sank into the ocean. Three hundred years after that, Malryn the Weaver was born, and the Iron Keepings burned until they turned to ash. Two hundred years later marked Karnek the Destroyer's birth and the Deserts of Sorel just...vanished, as if they had never been.

"Things were quiet for a very long time, after that. Until a hundred years ago, when we believe the power began trying to re-enter human form."

"Trying?" And where did it go, when it wasn't *in* human form?

Marquin stood, went to a barrel of scrolls and pulled one out, returning to unroll a map.

Clare stared at it in confusion. Her knowledge of geography was limited, but she knew the names of all the provinces in Faelhorn, and furthermore knew that they were the extent of the world, all clustered together on one continent and one island.

Looking at the map, she saw far more than one continent. A twinge of pain hit in the back of her skull and suddenly the scribblings on the map made sense, the Song always so willing to help her understand things when they were things *it* wanted her to understand.

She took her temporary ability to read and found the continent labeled Thieren, found the Iron Keepings and the Deserts of Sorel. But those were only three. There were easily over a dozen more landmasses, some of them quite large. Marquin pointed to a small cluster of islands labeled *Alawi*.

"These vanished when Alaric Tolvannen was twelve winters."

Clare frowned. Marquin had said the power began trying to re-enter the world a century ago, yet the Alaric Tolvannen she had seen hardly looked more than forty. She filed the thought away, but didn't interrupt Marquin as he continued.

"The event...unsettled him. He read everything he could find on the occurrences, linking the disappearances of past landmasses to Illora and Malryn and Karnek. He grew…paranoid. Because while the three of them each used the power they held in very different ways, they all had one thing in common: they deposed the rulers of their respective nations.

"Five years after the Alawi Islands disappeared there was a boy in the palace, a child of one of the servants, five years old. One day the king, Alaric's father, flew into a rage and beat the boy's father near to death. The boy healed him. Understand that what was done was well beyond the capabilities of even the best healers in the kingdom, and Alaric watched it happen. He was seventeen, by then.

"He killed the boy, and then he killed the boy's father. That same day, the Ice Lands disappeared." Marquin tapped to another place on the map. "Alaric asked his father to have all the children born that day put to death. The order was given, and carried out. When nothing else vanished, Alaric thought he had won. It wasn't until he was leading the army to war in Malrai seven years later and razed a small village, the aftereffects of which caused the Hailaren Jungles to vanish, that he understood the power had simply not rebirthed itself within the bounds of his kingdom.

"That was the day the Jackal King was truly born, though he wasn't king yet, not then. His father gave him command over all four of Faelhorn's armies, and he strove to bring the world under his dominion. As you can see, he succeeded in destroying most of it. By the time Marie was born and the Gaelan Islands vanished, the only thing left outside of Faelhorn and the lands physically connected to it, was the Isle of Miradon. The Isle sank into the sea the day she died."

Clare stared at the map. So many places, so many people, so much of the world, simply gone. It didn't feel real to her. "Marie. What day did she die?" But she knew—of course she knew—what the answer would be.

It was Verol who answered. "The winter solstice, twenty-one years ago."

"I was born in winter," she said softly. She'd never known the exact year, much less the exact day. Only the season. She looked at Verol. "And you've been drawn to these people—people like *me*— your entire life?"

In that moment, Verol looked as haunted as any a person in

Renault County. "Yes. I was always pulled to them too late. Until Marie. She was so little when we found her, barely a year old. Her parents died in the rebellion at Mila's Province. I thought we could keep her hidden. With Fitz helping—I thought we *had* kept her hidden." His hands tightened together. "About Fitz—you have to understand—it isn't *you* he hates. He lost his family very young, and when Marie came to us—he saw her as a little sister.

"He wanted to protect her and I let him try to help. I put too much on him. He was too young. He blamed himself, when she died. Later, he blamed me. Once he finished his apprenticeship he left. He only returned a year ago, it's why I never thought..." He trailed off, as if realizing what he shared was perhaps more personal than Fitz would have wanted relayed.

For her part, Clare was irritated to have the information. It was far easier to coexist in mutual dislike with a person when you didn't understand why they were the way they were.

"So you thought you'd kept her hidden," Clare prompted, when the silence dragged on.

Here, Marquin took up the thread of explanation. "The younger a person is, the less obvious it is what they contain. We think the power manifests as its bearer grows. Alaric seems to be able to find them once they're four or five. We don't know how you survived as long as you did, on your own."

There was a question there, in the lilt of his voice, but she didn't respond. It made sense to her now, why *she* had been chosen. She, a girl from Renault County, a place that on the surface belonged to Alaric, but in reality had its own king. A place Renault County rumor held that Alaric had tried to conquer, and failed.

The Song had chosen to be born into the world again in the one place that was safest for it, by virtue of its terrible danger.

She looked at the map again, at how much of the world had been lost. "There's nothing left but the continent of Faelhorn. If he kills me, does the world end?" And was that what Alaric wanted? Surely, he had to have realized by now what he was doing with each death. Why would he risk the kingdom he'd fought so long to conquer?

"We don't know."

"Does he know it's me?"

A shared glance, then Marquin said, "I don't believe so. It is unlikely he would have let you leave tonight had he any notion of your true nature. With the others—with Marie—it was apparent what they were, if you knew what to look for. They were simply so young that the power had not grown sufficiently strong enough to be a threat.

"As old as you are, Clare, it should be a beacon brilliant enough to draw every mage in the country. But all I feel from you is a bare Songweavers' talent, and I don't always even feel that. Were it not for Verol's Kinthing magic, we would never have found you. I don't understand how that is possible."

Because I built the Song a prison and I locked it away.

Marquin hesitated, then asked, "Does it ever talk to you?"

She laughed. "The Song and I...we used to talk. We don't anymore."

"The Song. Is that what it calls itself?"

Her throat closed up. She hadn't meant to tell them that much. She had never meant to tell anyone anything. "No. It's what I call it."

"Why?"

Because it was the background song of her life. The one she'd always heard, even when she hadn't realized what it was. The one constantly threatening to overwhelm her.

She shrugged. "I had to call it something."

Her indifference didn't deter Marquin. She could feel his excitement, though he tried to hide it beneath careful words. "We have never truly understood what this power is. Why Verol's magic draws him to it. Why it is here, what it wants. If you are able to communicate with it—"

"No." She stood. "I can't. Not anymore."

"Clare—"

"You helped Alaric win the Mage Wars," she challenged, cutting him off. "Why?"

Marquin would have ignored her question and pushed her on the Song, but Verol interrupted him, answering Clare in a tired, quiet voice. "Because the war was already lost. Alaric had enough people within the guild loyal to him that it was only a matter of time before the whole thing came crashing down. We helped him for two reasons. One, to salvage what was left of the mages, and two, because I thought it might keep Marie safe. Alaric has suspected something of what I am for a long time. I thought that if we helped him win a war he simply didn't realize he had already won, he wouldn't look at me too closely. Wouldn't look at *her* too closely. I was wrong."

Clare frowned. "Why hasn't he had you killed?"

Marquin grinned and it was a wicked, lovely thing. "He has tried. Many times. But given that we are the glue that holds the Mages Guild to his service, our deaths are better off not tied to him. And we are not so easy to assassinate."

She stood, too much information crowding her mind, the Song eagerly insistent against its cage now that it wanted her to *understand*, to *stay*. It wanted her to ask all the questions Marquin wanted her to. But she didn't want those answers.

"Will you stay?" Verol asked.

Where else was she going to go? "Yes. But I'm tired and I'm going to bed."

She turned before they could say anything else, her exit as abrupt as her words. All she could see was entire continents disappearing. All she could think of was that the entire world, save a single continent, had been destroyed simply to culminate in the creation of *her*.

Abomination, Madame Aria's voice whispered in her mind. She wasn't certain the woman had been wrong.

***

MARQUIN SLID INTO BED QUIETLY, even though the heartstone in his staff told him that Verol was awake. These little pretenses were part of how their relationship still functioned, after what he had done. Without the heartstone, he would have assumed Verol asleep, so he pretended he thought he was, and let Verol decide what he wanted to do.

After a moment Verol turned over to face him, pressing his forehead to Marquin's. "Is she all right?"

"I don't know," he answered honestly.

"Did you see the scars on her back?"

Marquin nodded. He had not wanted to invade her privacy by glancing beneath the glamour, but he had felt it necessary. Keeping the girl alive beneath Alaric's nose was going to be difficult enough, even if they knew everything about her. And he suspected they would never know everything about her.

"If I might offer a suggestion?" Marquin said. "Don't let her know that you know."

Verol opened his eyes. "Shouldn't we talk to her about it? There are so *many*, I…" He trailed off, uncertain.

"She has survived them, and she doesn't appear to tend toward self-harm. She knows we are here, if *she* wants to talk. Do not take the choice away from her."

Verol was quiet for so long Marquin almost thought he slept. Finally, he said, "I don't want to fail her, too."

"You won't."

"I failed Marie. I apparently failed Fitz."

"We *all* failed Marie. As for Fitz, he had his own pain to deal with. He chose to deal with it by taking everything you taught him about how his magic could protect people and using it to harm them instead. It's hardly a surprise you didn't know the Assassin of Blackrock might have his feelings hurt because you didn't hug him enough when he returned from a decade of wetwork."

"Now who is being unkind? You know what he did was more… complicated than that."

"Regardless, I suspect hoping he and Clare will get along will be *complicated*."

Verol pushed onto his elbow, frowning down at Marquin. "You can't be asking me to send him away."

"No. I am asking you to talk to him. At length. Before we leave for the palace in the morning."

"I'm not sure I know what to say to him. He was barely more than a boy when he left." Regret crossed Verol's face. "And I wasn't really there for him, those last few years. As a mage's master *or* the surrogate father he apparently wanted. Not after…what happened."

"Start there. I suspect you'll find the rest will fill itself in."

Sighing, Verol laid back down. "Unfortunately, I suspect you're right."

CLARE TRIED TO SLEEP. When she failed at that, she tried to read the card in the red envelope, the one Numair had sent with the dress, the one that was only for her. She failed for the third time, the temporary insight the Song had given her when she'd looked at the map now nowhere to be found.

"And you wonder why I don't like you," she muttered. The Song didn't answer. It had been quiet since her discussion with Marquin and Verol, as if it knew that now wasn't the right time to push her. It probably did know that, probably knew her better than any person ever had.

Maybe it was time to change that.

She did not want to be a thing, a *host*, a mere shell born to carry the power inside her. She wanted to be a woman, an artist, a person. She wanted the silly dream she'd had ever since she'd realized the effect her voice had on people, with or without her magic behind it. A dream that with that voice, she could be comfortable. Adored. Untouchable.

It was the dream of a girl who hadn't yet understood what or who or where she was. A girl too young to know that people didn't leave Renault County alive. It was a dream that had gotten her out. And now that she was here, she didn't know if that dream meant anything.

She still wanted to be untouchable, but becoming that wouldn't make her understand herself. It wouldn't sort out the tumult of emotions that kept cascading down on her at every turn now she'd come to Veralna. The girl who'd lived in Renault County hadn't understood that she could ever truly want anything more than survival.

And it had taken so very little—food, a place to stay, a chance to be seen—for her to want everything else. To want to *be* Clare Brighton, when Clare Brighton was only an idea she'd made up in her head, and not a very intricate one, at that.

But she wanted to be her with a fierceness that hurt, and she only knew one person who made her feel like she had any chance of finding her.

She slipped the envelope into her pocket, opened the window, and jumped out into the night.

CHAPTER

TWENTY-SIX

I THINK YOU NEED A FRIEND

A rock hit the sliding glass door of Numair's third-floor bedroom. He sat up, on edge, the black heart vining above his bed responding to his stress. Another rock—just a pebble, really—hit his window. Then another, and another.

He moved to the side of the door, looking out through the one-inch gap between the curtains, and blinked. Another pebble hit glass, thrown with expert aim from the form below. If he had any sense, he'd ignore her until she went away.

He opened the door and walked onto his balcony, resting his elbows on the railing, his chin on his palm in precisely the manner love-stricken maidens always affected in those ridiculous stories where they were locked in towers and rescued by princes. He debated batting his eyelashes at her, but decided she probably wouldn't see it from this far up.

"Are you really tossing rocks at my window?"

She grinned up at him, dropping her remaining rocks and dusting her hands together. "How better to get your attention, my lord?"

"And now that you have it, what do you intend to do with it?"

"Rescue you?" she suggested.

"Ah, I do appreciate a well-planned rescue. What, pray tell, will you be rescuing me from?"

"One of two things, but I do hope, for your sake, that it is not both."

"The first?"

"An interminable stretch of boredom."

"The second?"

"It occurred to me you might have a woman in your bed."

He stiffened, but she didn't seem to mean anything by it. "Most people wouldn't think I would need rescuing from that."

She snorted. It was a rough, unaffected, indelicate sound, and he loved it. "Well, I do. I did, after all, meet the women at your party."

He laughed. She kept making him do that. "As it happens, I only require rescuing from the first of your concerns."

"Excellent." She walked to the wall, found handholds and toeholds.

"I could let you in through the ordinary channels," he called down.

"And have it be said I needed assistance rescuing a gentleman in distress?"

"I think 'distress' might be overstating the situation."

"Princes are always overstating the damsel's distress in those ridiculous stories."

"Fair enough," he conceded. "Should I swoon for the sake equality?"

"I do not think that will be necessary." She started climbing, but he still couldn't believe she actually intended to scale three stories until after she'd passed the first one. His heart thudded into his chest, magic spilling out of him in an uncontrolled way it hadn't since he was young. The moonflower beneath her grew, doubling then tripling in size, ready to catch her if she fell.

She came up alongside the balcony, switched her handholds to the railing and pushed off the wall, legs swinging over to land on the balcony floor. She was dressed in a pair of breeches and a tunic that might be called rags if one was feeling charitable. Her shoes were new, but they were so thin they might as well be slippers. They certainly weren't intended for midwinter.

He tracked the path she'd climbed from the ground to here, and groaned. "There was a drainpipe outside the window at that damn inn, wasn't there?" He hadn't been that careless in years. But he hadn't been this tired in years, either.

"There might have been."

"Why did you follow me?"

She shrugged. "I was curious. What did you take?"

"Nothing that ended up being worth anything. I get how you figured that one out, but how did you recognize me as Taius?"

"Your disguises aren't that good."

"They are exceptional." Taius was one he'd used several times over the years. Taius had an apartment in Hightown, his own bank account, and several influential acquaintances who had never once figured out they were talking to Prince Numair, even though both of his personas knew them.

She gave him a maddening smile. "If you say so."

She really wasn't going to tell him how she'd known.

"I promise to forget your secrets if you promise to forget mine," she said.

"I find it difficult to believe you're the type of person who simply forgets things."

Her expression soured. "On the contrary, forgetting things is how I stay sane."

He was silent for a beat, then: "We have that in common."

"So we will both...forget, then?"

"As much as we can."

The wind blew across the balcony and she shivered. He shook his head. "Come inside, your lips are turning blue."

"They are not," she disagreed. As if she could even *see* her own lips. But when he pushed the sliding door open, she preceded him through it without argument.

CLARE WANDERED through Numair's bedroom, grateful for the room's warmth, no matter that she would never admit it. His room was like the rest of his estate—dark and alive. Dark paint on the walls, black wooden furniture, and growing things everywhere. Tall planting vases, their outer shells painted deep indigo, rested on every piece of furniture save the bed, vines crawling out of them and up the ironwork trellises that covered portions of the walls.

A scrap of green cloth caught her attention, a scarf hanging from his dresser mirror. A *familiar* scarf. One purchased by a man she'd accosted in an alley.

Shit. She'd punched the second prince of Faelhorn in the throat.

"I can explain that," he said quickly. Did he sound...embarrassed?

"Please do."

"I was...curious. You *did* bend a man to your will with a single sentence."

Ice went down her spine. "So you were awake at the bar." Of course he'd been awake. He'd never been drunk in the first place.

"I'll keep your secret, if you keep another of mine."

"Such as?"

"This." A nearby vine grew, reaching for her, threading through her fingers. A bud opened at its tip, a brilliant purple flower blossoming in her palm. The petals, soft like velvet, brushed against her skin.

She frowned. "They don't know you're a nature mage?"

"No."

And he'd shown her that side of himself because he hadn't thought he was going to be alive long enough for it to matter. She wasn't sure how she felt about that. "I'll keep it to myself, for the answer to a question. When you pulled that knife on the king, did you honestly think you had any chance of succeeding?"

"If I said I had no idea what you're talking about, would you forget that, too?"

"Not that one, no."

He was quiet for so long that she turned to look at him. He leaned against the wall, his hands shoved into his pockets, his eyes dark. "You stood," he said finally. "No one stands under his power."

"You weren't kneeling."

"He doesn't use it on me. Not in public. If you decide you want to confess my sins to him, find an anonymous way to do it. If he discovers you can so much as blink without permission under his hold, he'll kill you."

She sighed. "I have no interest in telling him." And from what little she'd learned, she didn't need a reason for why Numair would want to kill Alaric. She just wanted to know if he'd actually thought he could, but she could tell by the set of his shoulders he wasn't going to answer.

Which was answer enough, really.

"I barely know you," she said, "and yet all of our secrets are tangled up together. Should I be afraid of that? Should I be afraid of you?"

"I don't mean you any harm, but many a person has caused a great deal of harm they never intended. Should *I* be afraid of you?"

The Song chose that moment to stir in her chest, a brief flare of heat within before she silenced it, images of islands sinking beneath the depths of cold water filling her mind.

"Yes." She said it with a sadness of certainty that left no room for doubt. She was, to admit a truth she would never admit, afraid of herself, and not only because of the Song. There existed facets of her soul ground long ago to dust and hardened by cold, and when she thought and acted with those parts of herself there were few cruelties she could not imagine, and very little that could move her in the way of tenderness. "If you were smart, you'd throw me out and never talk to me again."

"I thought we established earlier that I'm a fool."

She shook her head. "We established that you act like one." But he obviously wasn't going to throw her out. Before she could change her mind, she pulled the red envelope from her pocket and held it out to him. "What does it say?"

"You didn't read it?"

"No. I…can't."

He looked from the letter to her. "It's for you to read. You'll learn to soon enough."

As if learning were an easy thing to do. She felt at once silly for having admitted her inability, and sillier still for standing there, letter in hand. She tucked it back into her pocket.

"I should go."

He did not move to intercept her path to the balcony doors, didn't try to physically block her exit in any way. But when she drew parallel to him, he stopped her with nothing more than softly spoken words. "Why did you come here, tonight?"

She warred with the safe answer, but safe was far behind her. "Because I think you need a friend. And I think I need one, too." She waited, her hands tightened into fists, for him to laugh at her. However much she kept forgetting the fact, he was a prince. He had better options for friends than the likes of her. Except for that part where she was pretty sure he didn't.

"Clare…I can't change for you. Whatever you know of me, whatever you think you see, I can't change what I am."

"I'm not asking you to."

He studied her, his eyes searching, as if he could tell whether she meant it by whatever he found. "Then I think I'd be a poor friend if I let you walk two miles home when you don't even have a coat."

"I'll be fine."

"You're exhausted. You should sleep."

She arched an eyebrow at him. "Are you offering me your bed?"

"As long as you don't try to drag me into it with you, yes." He sounded dead serious, and she realized she might not be the only person in the room who didn't like being touched.

She should go back to the Arrendons. If she didn't get home before Marquin and Verol woke up, she'd have a fun time explaining where she'd been. But Numair was right about something—she *was* exhausted, and if she went back, she wasn't going to sleep. The silence in the room there was too loud, the bed too foreign, the room too big. She was used to sleeping in small spaces, and though they filled her with a sense of trapped terror, it was yet a feeling she was accustomed to falling asleep to. She could mark every surface of such a space with her fingers and know from which angle danger might approach.

Her room at the Arrendons could not be thus contained. And though Numair's room was even bigger than hers, it felt smaller. Or perhaps not smaller but more…guarded. With Numair in the room and the plants keeping watch…perhaps she would actually sleep.

"I have nightmares," she told him.

"So do I."

"If you need to wake me up, I don't recommend touching me."

He crossed his arms. "Same."

"Perfect." She couldn't tell if he was serious or only agreeing with her to make her feel better. But the fact he would even bother to do the latter was…something. "Where are you sleeping?"

In answer, he dropped down on the chaise that rested against the wall next to a large dresser. She kicked off her shoes, climbed into the bed and pulled the sheets and comforter up to her neck.

"Goodnight," Numair said. The room's magelights winked out, but the darkness wasn't complete. Moonlight shone in through the window, and all around the room, soft blue flowers gave off a faint glow. "I can close the flowers, if you want."

"I like them," she said, and shut her eyes, fully intending to fake sleep in the hopes it would eventually catch up to her. But somewhere between the peaceful glow of the flowers, the steady in and out of Numair's breathing, and the feeling of so much life in the room, like she was sleeping outside under the stars, true exhaustion hit her.

She was almost asleep when she remembered the other thing she'd come here to say. "Happy Nameday, Numair."

NUMAIR WAS glad the lights were low, glad her eyes were closed so she couldn't see the shock he felt stamped on his face.

Three stupid, pointless words.

Happy Nameday, Numair.

Words no one had bothered to say to him in almost a decade. Because he wasn't a person to these people, and his nameday wasn't for him. It was a spectacle for them to come be entertained by and laugh about after.

I think you need a friend.

She had no idea how right she was.

And I think I need one, too.

He hadn't been anyone's friend in a long time, had no idea why she'd want him. Couldn't dare to wonder if she felt the same thing he'd felt since he first heard her sing—like they were the same. Like she could understand the things he'd never told anyone else, because she'd lived them, too. Like he could do the same for her.

He studied her face, the strong arch of her eyebrows, the curve of her cheekbones, and tried to find something in those features that made up a face that could tell him if everything he was thinking, everything he was feeling, was all in his head. But faces didn't quite work that way, and all hers told him was that, even sleeping, she looked dangerous; like the slightest sound could rouse her to vengeful wakefulness. And she would, he was certain, wake with vengeance if disturbed, like Ferrian rising from the Lake of a Thousand Sorrows, flaming sword in hand.

"I am glad you came by," he whispered, knowing she was asleep and wouldn't hear. "And I'm glad you stood up."

CHAPTER

TWENTY-SEVEN

KIALLA

Clare responded to the gentle shake Numair used to wake her by swinging wildly for an adversary that did not exist. He'd already retreated six steps by the time her fist was moving, and when she came awake enough to recognize her surroundings she was already standing, a magelamp clutched in her left hand, ready for use as a bludgeoning object.

"I give you top marks on response time and creativity, but I'm going to have to dock a few points for morning presentation." Numair leaned against his doorframe, looking entirely too awake and smug.

She scowled, trying to make his words make any sense, and placed the magelamp back on the bedside table. "Morning presentation?"

He drew a finger in a circle around his head. She touched her hand to her hair and discovered, if the feeling was any indication, that it had done its best to imitate a squirrel's nest overnight. She glared at him—which made him laugh—and finger-combed it into some semblance of submission while sneaking a glance at the window.

The faintest rays of sunlight were peeking over the horizon. She'd slept the entire night and she hadn't even had nightmares—not in the sense that she usually did. Something new had taken their place, dreams of the world disintegrating until she was the only thing left, her body poised above an endless void, the Song's power lighting her from the inside, as if she were a lantern in the darkness of nothing, until she too began to unravel and only the Song was left, and she *was* the Song, but the Song was not her.

"Come on," Numair said, "I have someone I want you to meet."

"I hardly think I'm in a state to meet anyone."

"You aren't wrong, but it's not my fault you traded a one in a million dress for clothes a beggar would scoff at. But don't worry, you aren't meeting anyone human so I doubt they'll judge your taste." He gestured her toward the door.

She hesitated. "I can go back out the window."

"And why would you do that?"

She shrugged. "If you don't want people to see me."

"How are we going to be friends if people don't see you?"

"Do you *want* to be friends?" Ferrian's hells, she'd never felt more ridiculous in her life, and that was saying something. He hesitated, and she wanted to turn into a living inferno and burn everything to the ground, because that was the exceptionally rational response she had to embarrassment.

"I do, actually." He shoved his hands into his pockets. "But being my friend is not going to be the best thing for your reputation."

She rolled her eyes. "Because women throw themselves at you?"

He winced. "Something like that."

"I'll take it under advisement. Lead on."

She followed him out the door. His home was beautiful, spare embellishments and dark colors and jagged accent pieces. She hadn't known it was possible to be envious of the way a place *looked*. She'd been envious of plenty of homes—the shelter and warmth they provided—but she'd never been in love with an aesthetic before.

They turned a corner leading to a stairwell and it was there, on the wall, that Clare saw the painting and had to stop.

"Is that..." She trailed off, unable to finish the question, the entirety of her attention absorbed by the thick brush strokes spreading across the canvas. Deep, burnt orange waves licked the air, and from their depths rose a woman with hair the color of raven's blood, a sword of forged black metal in her right hand, a bleeding heart in her left.

"Ferrian and the Lake of a Thousand Sorrows," Numair said softly.

Clare reached up, fingers shaking, to touch the flames lapping at Ferrian's body. She half-expected her own skin to burn, but the heat of the lake lived only in the painting.

"Do you think she really existed?" Clare let her hand fall, but her eyes remained locked on the image.

"I do."

"And the lake? Do you think she lived a thousand sorrows, just to tear out Helara's heart?"

"I don't know. I like to think she did."

"Why?"

"Because in stories, everything is simple, even when it's not. Surviving the lake was no easy feat, but Ferrian knew that if she did, Helara would pay for everything she made Ferrian suffer. Life isn't simple that way." His voice hardened. "People do terrible things and they never pay for them. Those who try to make them are often unsuccessful. At least if I believe in the lake, I know that *someone* found justice."

"That is...a nice way to think of it."

"It is not, I take it, how you think of it?"

"Not in such dulcet tones of justice and perseverance." Clare grinned at him. "I thought Ferrian just wanted to tear the bitch's heart out. I respected that about her."

Numair's eyes crinkled at the corners. "You know, I had a friend once who said nearly the exact same thing."

"And here I thought I was your only friend."

The mirth in his eyes dimmed, and he started walking again. "You are, if you decide to stick it out. Even if she hadn't decided a long time ago that my friendship was more trouble than it was worth, she's been missing for six months."

Clare's intuition prickled. "And you have no idea what happened to her?"

He shook his head. "Though if I had to guess, I'd start with her brother. I keep hoping I'll find her before he does."

"You're still looking?"

"Why not? What else am I to do with so much time and money?"

They were quiet for a few steps before she asked, careful to keep her voice neutral, only vaguely interested, "Who was she?"

"Lady Megadari, the Duchess of Wake."

Clare sorted through the names she'd once memorized of Veralna's aristocracy. It took her a moment to arrive at the answer she expected, because in her list of memorized facts, Nera Megadari was the Duchess of Wake. But Nera Megadari's daughter was Alyssandra Megadari.

They reached the bottom of the stairs, exiting through a stone door that fit so seamlessly into its notch when closed, and with no visible handle on the outside, that Clare never would have known it was a door from looking at it.

She stopped and ran her hands along the seams, looking for a mechanism to open it by, but there was nothing readily apparent.

"Don't bother," Numair said, "they're—"

And then the answer came to her, little flares of power that itched for her touch and she followed them with her finger, drawing from here to there, until they sighed against her skin, and the door popped out and slid to the side.

"Oh, I like that." She laughed at the baffled expression on his face. "But you may want to change the locks."

He tapped the door to close it again. "If I did, would it keep you out?"

"No. But your words would." It felt important for him to know that.

He shook his head. "Stop by whenever you like."

They lapsed into an easy silence as he led her around a bend in the path to the west side of the house, where the lush vines and exotic plants gave way reluctantly to stables and horse pastures. He stopped at a paddock in which two horses grazed. The first, a beautiful chocolate brown with a lighter, golden mane and tail, perked his ears at Numair's whistle and ambled over. After a polite, cursory sniff of Numair's hand the horse stuck his head over the fence, shoved his forehead against Numair's chest and rubbed vigorously, as if the prince was a convenient, well-known rubbing post.

Numair's only response was to brace himself for this enthusiastic affection and grin like a young boy until the horse finished. He was an undeniably beautiful stallion, all glossy chocolate and strong muscles, but Clare's attention had been caught by the mare in the enclosure. She was built slimmer and a sight taller than the stallion, her features finer, and Clare guessed her at almost seventeen hands to the stallion's probable sixteen. She stood beneath the arching branches of a wide tree, her coat a glorious dappled gray with a solid dark gray mane and tail.

Beautiful as the mare was, it was the cool intelligence in her eyes, the proud arch of her neck, that drew Clare in. Foreign memories pushed at the edges of her mind, the Song dredging up yet another life Clare hadn't lived, to tell her that *this* horse was one in a thousand. She was proud and fearless, and Clare could see her hooves flying over sand in a desert Clare was certain no longer existed.

But beneath the beauty and the pride, there was a profound sadness—as if the mare was somehow trapped in her own body. As if there was something about her that was missing and she couldn't understand what it was, so she kicked and fought and rebelled.

The Song pushed at Clare, like a child who knew the answer to a question, if only someone would ask them.

"Colin said you like horses."

She frowned, shoving the Song aside. "Colin?"

"The carriage driver." Numair laughed. "You asked for the names of the horses but you didn't get his?"

"Butterscotch and Daisy were prettier." Clare looked at the stallion, then at the mare. "Are you trying to breed her?"

Numair shook his head. "A couple stallions have tried, but she gave them the bloody end of her hooves. Never seen anything like it. She fights like a demon and even when she's in season she won't let any of them near her. She's out with Hellack because he's the only horse she can stand. She picks fights with mares and stallions and geldings alike. Hellack's the only one with enough sense to let her be, so she doesn't mind having him around." He shrugged. "I didn't want her to be alone."

"What's her name?" Clare asked, watching as the mare returned her appraisal with equal scrutiny, ears alert but not back.

"Kialla."

"She's gorgeous."

"Ah, she is that, and well aware of it, too. I thought you might take her for a while. I have a feeling the two of you might be suited to each other."

Clare blinked and said, innocently, "You think me like the horse that kicks out at everyone?"

"Am I wrong?"

She laughed. "Maybe not."

"I think you might do her some good."

"Why?"

"She...isn't happy."

Clare hesitated, looking at the horse. "Verol said you're Deirdren Blessed. You can't...make her happy?"

"No. I can know that she isn't. I can understand her. And if I wanted to be a complete ass, I could make her obey me. But no one can make another living thing be happy if they don't want to be."

The Song pushed at her again, as if insisting that *it* knew how to make Kialla happy, and furthermore it was rude of Clare to keep it from this marvelous creature it had just rediscovered.

Clare bit her lip, looking at the mare. She wanted her. Inasmuch as her brittle heart could be stolen, the casual contempt and defiance in the horse's eyes had already done the work of thievery. She loved horses, had loved them indiscriminately from a young age, though there were few enough in Renault County.

She had known from the start that loving people was a folly. A younger her had thought, foolishly, that loving animals was safe. But loving something, Clare had learned, simply meant that it could be used against you. It could be taken or harmed or killed, and perhaps none of those things would happen to it if only you were not selfish enough to love it in the first place.

But that need, that want for connection, beat beneath her breast. "You honestly believe I could be good for her?"

"I do."

"She cannot be mine." She spoke in a tone of such cold certainty that Numair studied her for a long moment before replying.

"No. But she is an intelligent creature, and easily bored. She needs exercise and stimulation. I fear I have not the time to provide her with either, and she has not yet accepted a rider other than myself. If she accepts you, I would be happy to pay you as her exerciser."

Her exerciser. Oh, that was good. As if Clare, who'd never sat on a horse in her life, was qualified to be an exerciser for one of the prince's horses. Not that she had any intention of enlightening him on her lack of experience. Especially when he'd termed the offer thus to make it more palatable to her.

"Let us call it an even trade for my leasing her, for however long the arrangement should suit us both." It was not an even trade by traditional standards, not close. A mare like Kialla must fetch quite a price, one Clare couldn't hope to afford, but it was not by most standards that she and Numair operated. If she could forge a bond with the horse, she knew that he *would* consider it an even trade.

He left to get the mare's tack and Clare took a brief moment to reflect on what an odd noble he was; if she was not careful, she was soon to think all the nobility fetched and carried for themselves, and furthermore that they were actually people. She took advantage of his absence to respond to the Song's still-pinging insistence inside her.

She had a brief moment to think of how foolish she was being, of how dangerous what she wanted was—and all for a horse. But she did want, and she was tired of wanting and never having. So she thought of that brief flash she'd seen earlier, of hooves flying over sand, and the life that had gone with it. The life of a woman who lived in the desert and knew horses as if she'd been born one herself.

The Song all but tripped over itself in order to fling that other life at Clare. It slammed into her in an assault of knowledge and senses, as so many lives had attempted to overwhelm her at the Song's insistence. So many over the years that Clare was now well-versed in deflection.

The emotions and thoughts of that other woman, Clare fought back. She was not Amori Ha'i'Amoren. Not the daughter of the fiercest war maiden in all the land of Kileen, a land that had ceased existing some two-and-a-half centuries ago. She had never found her peace on the back of a galloping horse as it charged into battle.

But maybe she could take that expertise and find a different kind of peace. The person that Amori Ha'i'Amoren had been, Clare shoved down. There was no room for that personality within Clare's mind, no space she was willing to give another within her own body. The war maiden Amori was long dead.

But her knowledge of horses—of their nature and their training and their needs—she took into herself. The way her body—the same height and shape as Amori's, if less-muscled—would move when astride such a creature. All this she accepted, pulling it away from that other personality, until the connection between them was so tenuous that the right note would cut it. So she hummed that note—

and the Song howled in anguish within her, flinging itself at the walls of its prison as if Clare had destroyed something it loved.

She hoped she had. Ignoring the Song's tantrum, she ducked through the fence and went to meet Kialla. She stopped a few feet from the horse, just outside of the invisible boundary that marked Kialla's personal space, and waited. She continued to wait, long past when she heard Numair return, until the mare, finally, took one step forward and lengthened her neck to sniff curiously at her.

Clare lifted her palm. The mare stepped away, but when Clare did not pursue her she moved forward again, putting muzzle to palm and sniffing delicately, worrying at her with nimble lips. So it went, a slow, step-by-step approach and retreat, until Clare could run her hands over cheeks and forehead and ears. Until when she scratched Kialla's neck and withers the mare stretched her neck out in appreciation.

When Clare turned and walked back to Numair, inviting Kialla to come with her, the mare followed. She retrieved the bridle Numair had brought and offered it to the horse, one hand on the mare's neck, keeping pace with her as Kialla crossed over her front feet, dancing away without running away. When the mare finally came to a halt, Clare let her hand fall from her neck and took the bridle away.

The horse relaxed, and after a moment Clare offered the bridle to her again. Her head went up, nostrils flaring, but she didn't move away this time. Clare just...waited. Waited, until the mare's head lowered the barest amount, her eyes blinking, and then took the bridle away again.

So it went over and over, an offer and a retreat after the horse relaxed, until the moment came when Kialla no longer tensed at all when Clare brought it to her face. It was tedious and repetitive. Horse-training, when done correctly, was a largely boring thing to watch, something the men in Amori's life had never been able to properly accept. They wanted to break an animal—to fight it and conquer it in a flashy display of human dominance and brutality.

But what good was a broken horse? Far better was one who accepted you. Who trusted you. Because a broken horse, while it might be obedient, would reliably give you only half of what it had. A horse who accepted its rider, who trusted its rider, would give that person everything.

Kialla already knew how to wear a bridle—that was not what Clare was teaching her. She was teaching her that Clare would give her a choice. Teaching her that if the mare was not completely comfortable with something, Clare would be patient with her until she was. She was teaching her to trust.

When Clare finally slipped the headstall over Kialla's ears, the mare accepted the bit with the regal resignation of a monarch who has endured much official drudgery with an abundance of calm grace. When Numair approached, saddle and pad in hand, Kialla accepted the placement of these in much the same manner.

"I must admit," Numair said softly, "that I expected you to get on with her. But I didn't expect a Songweaver to move like a horse trainer."

A question lingered beneath the words, one Clare knew she should shunt aside with a mysterious smile and equally mysterious words. But he was—she was—*they* were—trying to be friends. She might be unclear on what the details of friendship entailed, but she thought some measure of honesty was involved in the process.

She couldn't *actually* be honest with him, of course, but perhaps she could…skirt the truth. "I find I can be what I need to be, when I have to."

Shadows swept across his eyes, briefly there and then gone. "That I understand well."

He was, she suspected, adept at doing the same. Though he undoubtedly took a different path getting there.

"Would you like a leg up?"

She would have refused but he was already kneeling, his fingers lacing together to form a step. There was something about the gesture—the openness and almost vulnerability of it—that made her swallow her refusal and place her foot in his hands. Her shoes were so thin, hardly more than slippers—she might appreciation the protection footwear provided against winter's chill, but she also found their bulk cumbersome, and thus had grabbed something utterly impractical last night—and it felt almost as if the bare sole of her foot touched against his palms. Something oddly like the tingling, unsettling nature of a shock traveled up from her foot through her entire body.

He rose, pitching her up, and then she was settled gently astride Kialla's back and the uncomfortable feeling brought on by the physical connection slipped away as her foot left his hand. She had the sudden absurd notion that she wanted it back—only to understand what it was, of course—and in avoidance of that thought her feet found the stirrups with too much enthusiasm.

Kialla pranced beneath her, hindquarters swinging as she pivoted on her front hooves. Clare let the mare fidget, then let her settle. They had time enough to work on the little things. Besides which, a small amount of disobedience on occasion meant the horse still had a personality, and was willing to use it.

The mare stretched out her nose to Numair, as if seeking his permission. A soft smile curved his lips and he rubbed her muzzle, murmuring quiet words Clare couldn't catch. "Well," he said finally, "I don't think she plans on tossing you on your ass, but why don't you try her out here where the landing is soft. I'd have a devil of a time explaining your broken neck to Lord Arrendon."

Clare snorted. "Perhaps the two of you could finally overcome your differences and bond over my tragic death." As if the Song would ever *let* her die. Things broken within her never remained so for long.

She squeezed her legs gently to Kialla's sides and the mare, eager to take Clare's mettle, leapt directly into a trot. Clare tightened lightly on the reins, applying a soft, steady pressure until Kialla slowed to a walk, snorting and tossing her head. Hellack, standing at Numair's side out of the way, looked on almost longingly while Clare took Kialla in a wide, slow circle around Numair. She completed a few circuits until she settled into the rhythm of the mare's gait, then urged her into a trot.

Trotting was frequently an unpleasant gait, depending on the horse, but Kialla's flowed smooth as a calm river, and Clare didn't bother to post it. After a warmup, she tested the mare's canter in a few light circles. For a brief moment she closed her eyes, the supple power of the animal beneath her—the beauty and coordination of the stride—making it feel almost possible to leave this plane of existence entirely.

It was a feeling she remembered having, but those were not *her* memories. This was the first time Clare Brighton had ever felt this way, ever had this experience, and she never wanted it to stop. But she couldn't canter circles around the second prince of Faelhorn forever. Neither could she contain the grin that claimed her face as she loped up to him, the settling of her seat and slight backwards shift of her weight all that was required to bring Kialla sliding to a stop.

Numair grinned. "You like her, then?"

"She's perfect. How does she feel about me?" It was difficult to keep the hesitance from her voice. The horse's good opinion of her mattered far more to Clare than any human's ever had.

He reached out and stroked the mare's face. "She says you don't ride like a sack of potatoes, so you'll do for now." His eyes sparkled.

She scoffed. "Even *I* know the Deirdren Blessed don't hear horses talk in words."

"She likes you well enough. Don't give her cause to regret it and the two of you will do fine."

She rolled her eyes, gathering the reins. "With that glowing praise, I suppose I should be going."

"One more thing, before you do." He pulled the green scarf from his pocket. "You should take it."

She stared at the scrap of expensive fabric. "Why?"

He looked away. "It matches your eyes. That's why I bought it."

She laughed. "Do your court women trip over themselves when you feed them those lines?"

A faint blush of color rose beneath his cheeks, along with a flash of something else. Was that…? Oh, Ferrian's flames. He actually *had* bought the damn thing because it matched her eyes. Quickly, she leaned down from Kialla, snatched the length of cloth and looped it over his neck. "I don't have anything to wear it with. So you can wear it when you think of me."

Before she had to endure any more of this conversation she straightened, a light press of her legs and a kissing noise all it took to send Kialla whirling away at a canter, hooves eating up the ground between them and the fence. As it approached Clare moved into the two-point position, just barely raised off Kialla's back, giving the horse room to gather herself. She did so, muscles bunching then releasing, and sailed gracefully over the wooden slats.

Clare's muscles rejoiced in the feel—so familiar to that other self she had absorbed and severed—of adjusting to keep her seat as Kialla landed, her entire focus caught up in the horse. In the recklessness that hummed along with the mare's stride, one that echoed in Clare's mind.

She did not doubt the mare was a little wild and would show it before this ride was done. But Clare was a little wild, too, and she found the promise of Kialla's wildness only called to her.

TWENTY-EIGHT

THE DUCHESS OF WAKE

Clare climbed through her window just in time for Marquin's polite knock at her door, inviting her to breakfast. She changed and joined the Arrendons at the dining room table, trying to act as if things were normal when she really hadn't a clue what normal was. When they were all trying to pretend they weren't walking on eggshells because of the conversation they'd had last night.

She didn't have to worry about it too long, as a door thudded open and Alys walked into the room, her face an odd juxtaposition of fury and disbelief.

"You told me you put a *horse* in the stables."

"I did." Clare had settled Kialla into an empty paddock abutting the one Skye and Ginger shared, until she could determine if the mare would come around to mixing with the other two horses. "Is there *not* a horse in the north paddock?"

"No, there is not a *horse* in the north paddock. *Kialla N'Marani* is in the north paddock."

Marquin's gaze went immediately to Clare and narrowed, as it so often did when he looked at her. Verol blinked, long and slow, as if trying to dredge up some long-forgotten tidbit that would make him understand why Alys's statement bore importance.

"That mare is the only living descendant of Dragmoir

D'Marani's bloodline, do you have *any* idea how much Numair paid for her?"

"Not in the least." But wasn't it interesting that Alys didn't add a title in front of Numair's name?

"A fortune. No, scratch that, try two or three fortunes. When he finds out she's missing—"

"She isn't missing," Clare said, cutting Alys off calmly. "He's letting me borrow her."

"Borrow her?" Only good breeding, Clare suspected, kept Alys from spluttering. "He's letting you *borrow* her?"

"I don't believe I stuttered."

"Numair doesn't loan out his carriage horses, much less one worth his entire stable combined, who's rumored to be descended from unicorns, for Ferrian's sake."

"Your point being?"

"What did you do to get her?"

"I didn't take *him* for a ride, if that's what you're asking."

Verol choked on his coffee, face turning red.

"But since you're so curious, apparently the expensive would-be unicorn is sad, and he thinks I can cheer her up."

Everyone in the room collectively stared at her.

"What? Horses get sad."

"He's Deirdren Blessed and he can't cheer her up?" Verol asked, an edge to his voice.

"Apparently not."

Verol said, "I would never presume to tell you what to do—

"A wise decision on your part."

"—but have you considered what this is going to look like to everyone else?"

"Of course I have." All she'd done her entire life was concern herself with how she appeared to everyone else. Because however much she hated the fact, appearances mattered.

She'd come here, planning to bend and mold herself however she needed to in order to make appearances work *for her,* for once. But something had happened last night, watching Numair bend appearances to a crowd all too willing to believe them, and she'd realized she was sick of it all.

That she didn't want to play the game—at least, not the one expected of her. That she hadn't come here to bury herself under an image that forced her to smile when she wanted to scream, to defer when she wanted to lash out, to be pretty and quiet and obedient when she wanted to be raw and harsh and unrestrained.

She didn't want to acquiesce to a mold that said she couldn't even have a *friend* because of what other people thought of him, and what they would think of her in turn. He was alone in a sea of would-be wolves, and she could let him drown or she could stand beside him.

It frightened her. Because she had no idea where the path would lead if she took it. Had no idea who she would become if allowed to become *something*.

"But Numair is my friend, and I don't need to care what people think."

"*Prince Tolvannen*," Verol said, by way of correction, "is not your friend. He is not anyone's friend. At best, he's an indolent spoiled brat who refuses to grow up. At worst, he's a depraved, drunken lunatic."

Clare's fingernails dug into the thick lacquer of the dining room table. "You're judging a person you won't look at long enough to know anything about."

Marquin laid a hand on Verol's forearm, preventing whatever angry response he was no doubt about to give. "Perhaps Verol's opinion of him isn't unbiased, but Clare, you've known the man for less than a day."

Clare shrugged. "I've made my decisions. If you're uncomfortable with them, feel free to rescind your offer for my apprenticeship."

Verol said, "That's not what we—"

"And if you are too biased to have a proper opinion of Numair, and I too ignorant, then perhaps we should ask Alys what she thinks of the prince."

Marquin and Verol shared an uncomfortable glance before Marquin said, "What would Alys have to say on the matter?"

"Well, she did grow up with him."

Alys made a choking noise and Clare turned to her. "Do you prefer Lady Alyssandra Megadari, or the Duchess of Wake?"

"How did you...?"

Clare snorted. "It really wasn't that hard." She pointed at the Arrendons. "They're deferential to you, you do a piss-poor job covering up your court bearing, Numair has a childhood friend who disappeared but didn't die, and you forgot to call him by his title instead of his name. Frankly, I'm shocked you've stayed hidden this long. Do you never leave the barn?"

Anger burned in Alys's eyes, but before she could unleash it, Fitz entered the room with an enormous basket of envelopes. He eyed everyone, clearly noting the explosive tension in the room, and said, "I'll just leave this with you." He placed the basket before Clare and left.

Verol paled. "Surely they aren't...all for you?" The look in his eyes was fear, plain and simple. She understood, suddenly, how very difficult it was going to be for him that she intended to make a constant public spectacle of herself.

"The safest place for me," she told him softly, "is in the open." He'd tried to hide Marie. It hadn't worked. Clare was going to ensure it was very difficult for anyone to make her disappear.

He nodded, tight-lipped.

"If you don't mind," she said, changing the subject, "I'd like to talk to Alys, alone."

Marquin nodded and stood. "We will be in the library. Come, Verol," he added, when it appeared his partner might object, "the coffee will taste just as well among the books." With that he grabbed the handles of both his and Verol's coffee cups with one hand, retrieved his staff with the other, and herded his husband out of the room.

MARQUIN DRANK his coffee and watched Verol pace the library floor like a caged tiger.

"You may as well let it out," he said finally.

Verol stopped pacing and faced him. "She doesn't understand what she's getting into with Tolvannen."

"I believe she understands quite well," Marquin replied mildly. "I do not believe she cares."

"Nor do you, it seems."

Marquin settled his cup on the coffee table in response to Verol's caustic tone. "You have...always judged him harshly."

"And you have always judged him more kindly than he deserves."

"Perhaps. But as Clare pointed out, how well does either of us know him? I won't disagree with you on his behavior." But he remembered Numair Tolvannen as a quiet child—before the boy's mother had died and he'd become...whatever it was he'd become. "He is extravagant, he drinks too much, and he doesn't appear to have a faithful bone in his body. But if you honestly think any of that is a danger to Clare, you haven't watched her closely enough."

"The man will sleep with anything that walks," Verol muttered.

Marquin raised an eyebrow. "You know, people said the same thing about you, once."

Verol opened his mouth, clicked it shut. After another moment of recovery he said, "Please tell me you aren't suggesting that Numair Tolvannen can be saved by the love of a good woman."

"No. I'm suggesting that people do need friends, and I'm relieved to see her recognize the fact. Have you forgotten what she looked like when we found her? She looked at this world like it was an alien place worth nothing but damnation."

"Can you blame her? She'd obviously been through hell."

"No, I don't blame her. But I also don't forget what she is. What she is capable of, now she's survived to adulthood, if even a fraction of the old stories are true. I don't forget that if she is pushed too far, I will be grateful if there is a single person on this continent worth a damn to her who might be able to pull her back."

Verol studied him with something like reproach. "She isn't a monster."

"No. But she isn't fully human, either. And I don't think her experiences have left her with much empathy for the state of humanity. Let her find her peace where she can."

***

IN THE EMPTINESS provided by Marquin's and Verol's absences, Clare considered Alys, who considered her in return.

"What are you going to do?" Alys asked.

Clare rolled her eyes. "Don't worry, I don't intend to take the stage at my next event and announce your continued existence to the world."

"You announced it to the entire room."

"I announced it to people who already knew, and only because you attacked me. I don't like verbal assaults. I tend to retaliate."

"I didn't *attack* you."

Clare smiled. "Didn't you?"

Alys settled into a chair with no-longer-disguised courtly grace, looking every inch a noble lady despite her common-made breeches and tunic.

"Perhaps," she admitted. "But if you don't intend to use this against me, why bother figuring it out?"

"I'm curious by nature. And it was too easy to figure out."

"That can hardly be all of it."

Clare hesitated. "I...owe Marquin and Verol. And you are unknown with the potential to have dangerous enemies that could put them in jeopardy."

"Them," Alys asked, "or you?"

Clare smiled. "Why don't we settle on both."

Alys sighed. "No one's actually looking for me. Not anymore. They wanted me gone, so I'm right where I'm supposed to be."

"That isn't entirely true. Numair is still looking for you."

Alys's head jerked up. "He is?"

Clare nodded.

"Idiot man," Alys muttered with long-suffering affection.

"There is a simple solution. If you aren't worried about Numair, just tell him you're fine. He can quit looking."

"It isn't so simple as all that."

"No?"

"No. You were right when you said Numair and I were *childhood* friends. He...changed, around fifteen winters. It was six months or so after his mother died. That is when he became..." She waved a hand airily. "Lord Numair Tolvannen, famous court drunk and male whore. It is as if everything that made him the person I'd known disappeared.

"He was sometimes still himself on the odd occasion we went riding or something, but it surfaced less and less. When we were nineteen, I actually tried to get him to quit drinking." She smiled bitterly. "I told him he was making a fool of himself, and if he didn't stop, he would be this for the rest of his life."

Clare said nothing. He'd fooled everyone. Even Alys. But Clare was more interested in the timing. "You think it was his mother's death that changed him?"

"I thought so at the time. I even asked him outright, thought maybe he needed…I don't know, to talk about it."

"What did he say?"

"Something that didn't make any sense."

When Clare simply looked at her, Alys sighed and said, "He said that it had everything to do with her death, and nothing at all to do with his feelings, so if I thought he simply needed to have a good cry on my shoulder, I was hopelessly mistaken."

Alys straightened, and Clare could tell they were done speaking of memories. "The Arrendons knew exactly what they were getting into when they offered me shelter. So I'll tell you, like I told them, that if I become a problem, I'll leave. Though I really don't think you understand that no one is going to look at the Arrendon household for a runaway duchess."

"Because of that business with the Mages War?"

"That's barely the start of it."

"But *you* trust them?"

Alys shrugged. "Marquin saved my life when I was five. I'd gotten angry with my parents and run away to live in the woods. I got lost, broke my ankle. There was a whole search party out, but it was Marquin who found me. It's kind of hard to be afraid of someone who carried you three miles home and told you stories the whole time." Alys nodded at the basket of envelopes. "Anyway, I suppose what you actually want help with is navigating that mess?"

"Yes."

Alys drummed her fingers on the table, considering. "I'll do it. I'll teach you everything you need to know about navigating the *wonderful* ladies of Veralna's Court. But I need something in return."

"What?"

"A favor. A *future* favor, to be delivered at the time of my choosing."

"I'm not killing anyone for you."

"Don't worry, I'll handle the killing myself. I just need you to… deliver something. A message, when I need it sent."

"Fine. Agreed."

Alys pushed the basket at her. "Tell me which ones you think are important."

"There's another part to this request." Clare forced the next words out. "I can't read."

"You'll want to fix that. For now..." Alys sorted through the envelopes with hardly a glance, making three piles. One contained the majority of the envelopes, the middle maybe ten, and the last, only two. She tapped the large pile. "None of these matter. I'll tell you the names and you can memorize them later. These" —she tapped the second pile— "you need to respond to but don't have to accept. And these" —she tapped the final two envelopes— "you can't politely decline."

"What are they?"

"An invitation to go riding with the proconsul of Taella—in addition to being proconsul, she's also a friend of Marquin's—and this one from Countess Duval, inviting you to have dinner with her at The Musicale House tomorrow evening."

"I'm guessing by the name of the establishment that I don't simply sit there and eat dinner?"

"Hardly. There are seven tables, and each table has to bring a musician. The House pits those musicians against each other. The rules for competition change each month, so no artist ever knows what they're agreeing to when they attend one of these functions, and the results can be...varied. It's the kind of establishment that can make or break an artist's chance of finding good patrons. Especially because sometimes the challenges are set up to make a mockery of the artists."

Clare raised her eyebrows. "The wealthy need their entertainment?"

"Something like that."

"And I suppose I've been chosen because I recently made a spectacle of myself in the name of artistic competition?"

"Yes, and I don't think you've been invited because the countess wants to further your career. She owns seventy-percent of the business, and was on the verge of buying out the Rival before your performance catapulted the theater back into prominence and likely drove the price up. If I had to guess, I'd say it'll be a challenge they don't think anyone can complete."

Clare flashed her teeth. "Please write the countess that I would be *honored* to attend."

"I said you couldn't *politely* decline, not that you shouldn't."

"Well in that case," Clare amended, "please write that I'm honored and looking forward to it, and make it sound like I'm ever-so-naive and very excited to have her attention."

Alys shook her head and retrieved a pen and paper. "You sure you know what you're doing?"

"Of course. Rigged games are my favorite."

Alys had barely finished writing out the responses when Verol came in, knocking on the side of the doorframe to announce himself. "We have to leave for the palace in an hour, so you might want to pack."

She had forgotten, with everything that had happened, about the residency requirement the king imposed on the nobility. With what Verol and Marquin had told her last night, she finally understood why they'd been so worried about it.

Finally understood that simply being Verol's apprentice was likely to make the king suspect she was exactly what he was looking for.

She contemplated her guitar as she packed clothing around it for buffer—she was going to need to buy a case that actually fit it. Last night, she'd used those strings and her voice to make the Jackal King cry. Today…today she was going to have to do something else. He would expect her to be afraid. Or, on the opposite side, expect her to try and charm him. To make him like her.

Which meant she needed to do something completely different. She needed to be obviously indifferent to him. It wasn't the best option—kings, in her admittedly limited experience, did not take well to indifference—but it was the only option she saw.

And the best way to be indifferent to a man was to be loudly interested in someone else. She hoped Numair didn't mind keeping her busy, because she was about to very publicly and animatedly become the best friend he'd ever had.

CHAPTER

TWENTY-NINE

A WHITE THRONE

Nothing in Clare's life had prepared her for the Jackal King's palace. Even calling it a palace seemed inept to describe what was more like a private city. The building itself rested against the cliffs of the ocean's shoreline, and could only be reached via the two-mile High Road that stretched from Hightown directly to the King's Gate. In the first mile between Veralna and the palace the land to either side of the road, stretching to the eastern and western shorelines, could only be owned by those of noble blood. The western side was dominated by mansions and natural forests, while the eastern gave way to the nobles who dabbled in orchards and vineyards, the latter tended to by the lower classes who could never hope to own what they worked by virtue of royal decree.

It was on the western side that the Arrendon's estate lay and, by proximity, Numair's. Since Clare had opted to ride Kialla, Verol and Marquin rode alongside her on Sky and Ginger respectively. Fitz had gone ahead with their luggage in the carriage, pulled by a pair of bay geldings Clare had never seen before. He'd said nothing to her, only shaken his head at her choice of clothing and driven off.

She had attired herself to draw notice. Instead of a riding outfit she'd chosen a lightweight green dress with no waist-boning and a long, flowing skirt with enough material to drape across Kialla's back and sides like a decorative blanket. The hated cream cloak was tied at her neck and similarly draped. The small, hornless saddles favored in this part of the country made the task easy enough without fear of her clothing becoming entangled in the equipment—though she was fortunate she wouldn't need to travel above a walk or her skin would chafe terribly against the saddle leather—and she was certain no one would mistake which horse she was riding once she'd drawn their gaze. Her flashy ensemble was meant to state clearly that she didn't care what conclusions anyone might draw about the fact that she was riding Numair's excessively expensive horse.

For her part, Kialla had taken the fluttering, flowing skirts in stride, without even so much as a hint of a spook, and her unshod hooves now clopped softly on the stone-paved road. They passed through the Outer Gate with only a brief pause at the stationed guards, and as they did so the Song retreated within Clare. It was abrupt, her sense of its departure, as if within the palace grounds it was unwilling to risk drawing notice.

She examined the high Outer Wall as they passed through its gate, marveling at the paranoia that had driven some past king to build it all the way from eastern to western shoreline. The land between here and the palace's Inner Wall ahead was all riding trails and hunting grounds, the forest nearly undisturbed by human inter-ference, save what was necessary to carve out trails here and there. It had a heavy, ominous sort of peace to it that settled in the empty spaces around Clare. She rested easy against its silent weight, lulled into an almost hypnotic contemplation by its companionship and the soothing steadiness of Kialla's gait.

She was pulled from her reverie when the forest ended abruptly, the trees cleared two hundred feet back from the Inner Wall as far as the eye could see. The King's Gate loomed ahead, a monstrosity of twisted iron painted a brilliant white, reflecting the sun's rays so harshly it stung the eyes to look at. They halted at the gate, Kialla fidgeting impatiently while the Arrendons were greeted and cursory questions asked about Clare. The guards were well-trained, and the curious glances they gave her were only noticeable if one looked for them.

Her hands clenched tightly in Kialla's mane as they rode through the gate. Though it did not close behind her, she had the sense of being trapped. She heard the clang of a cellar door, the sound of little insect feet skittering in absolute darkness; heard a soft, sibilant voice telling her that this was her own fault, and for her own good. Fingers traced down the curve of her back and her spine teased tight, her breath coming in harshly audible wheezes through the constriction in her throat.

Not now, she told herself, *not Clare.* The woman in the cellar had never been Clare. That woman had only hoped to become her.

Clare took the memories, shoved them into the darkest room in her soul, and slammed the door closed. The door rattled and shook from the force on the other side, threatened to fly open as she barred it shut. The bar held, and the shuddering eased. One day, she knew, the door would not hold, and everything on the other side would spill over into her present.

But that day wasn't today.

Her hands relaxed, shoulders settling down and back, the set of her body turning fluid and graceful. On this side of the gate the stone road split around a long, rectangular pool over three hundred feet long and a third as wide. Streams of water jetted in arcs from either side, giving the surface of the water the appearance of perpetual rain. The water itself was so blue Clare felt certain it must be spelled, or otherwise chemically altered. Soft, smoke-white tile etched with gold symbols formed the edges of the pool and tall, carefully cultivated rushes lined its edges.

To either side of the path the land gave way to hedge-grown mazes, the greenery towering upwards of twelve feet, and Clare wondered if they were positioned to make visitors feel lost. She followed the carriage as it split off to the left side of the pool and came to a halt at the bottom of the stairs leading up to the palace entrance, the sides flanked with an explosion of greenery wildly incongruous with the season.

Marquin and Verol dismounted, exchanging words with one of the waiting valets attired in the palace livery. The valet's face, which had taken on a taut, uneasy expression at their arrival, glanced from them to Clare. Then his gaze landed on Kialla and he paled.

It turned out that both the horse and Numair had a reputation. Kialla's was for kicking, biting, and bolting, and Numair's was for raining hell down on anyone who mishandled his horses.

She was about to offer to take the mare to the stables herself when a young man ran up wearing the black and green livery of

Numair's stables. He looked terribly familiar, and Clare realized she was looking at a younger version of the carriage driver that had taken her to and from Numair's home.

He gave her a short dip of his head and didn't appear the least bit winded for his run.

"Miss Brighton, I'm Connor. If it's acceptable to you, I'll handle Kialla for you while you're in the palace. She's familiar with me."

The look on the palace valet's face pleaded for her to accept. She was not a complete monster. "Thank you." She slipped her feet from the stirrups, placed her hands on the mare's withers and pushed off gently, swinging her legs up and clear of the mare's body to land fluidly on the ground at her left side, flowing skirts turning the move pretty and artistic.

Kialla bumped her nose into Clare's stomach, and she rubbed her gently beneath her forelock. Her fingers brushed over a ridge she hadn't noticed before. A small circle of raised flesh just beneath the hairline, as if from an old injury. "I'll come visit you soon," she promised the mare, and handed the reins to Connor. Kialla followed him with the resigned air of a monarch who fully recognized that this was all beneath her.

Clare ascended the palace steps, Marquin and Verol hemming her in on either side like a pair of sheepdogs intent on keeping her precisely where they wanted her at all times. The double-doors of the palace, easily twelve-feet tall and curving to form an arch at the top when closed, currently stood wide open, two guards to either side.

Marquin and Verol swept her through the entrance without a word. Neither of them had said much since they'd locked the doors of Arrendon Manor behind them. In fact, Verol had only spoken once, looking over her shoulder at some point in the distance rather than meeting her eyes, to say, "Whatever you may hear at Alaric's court, try not to think too harshly of us."

They were both so quiet most of the time that she still couldn't fathom what they had done to earn their monikers. But she had not missed the air of tense respect, bordering on fear, that had hovered over the valets outside, nor the way the guards at the door seemed to be fighting an instinctual desire to step away as they walked past.

She had also not missed how everything kind and soft about Verol had on the surface disappeared. The fine, almost hauntingly beautiful features of his face had turned harshly so, and he emanated a coldness she would not have guessed he possessed. Marquin, too, had turned stony and silent, but where Verol radiated coolness, Marquin gave off an air of dispassionate boredom.

They entered the palace anteroom, a space so large it could have held half-a-dozen average dwellings. Hexagonal in shape, the ceiling vaulted straight to the top of the building's three-story height, grand six-foot-wide staircases on either side leading to first one, then another, mezzanine level.

Glittering, gold-flecked amber tile covered the floor, cut precisely around a six-tiered fountain that spilled into a shallow pool in the center. The ceiling, situated so high above, was a dome of clear glass through which the sunlight filtered down. The bright rays reflected off the tile and made the falls of water from the fountain shimmer, so that the overall effect of the room was one of almost blinding brilliance.

The white stone walls were uninterrupted bas-reliefs, and Clare's hands ached to think of the hours that must have gone into their carving. Whole sections were of intricate, geometric designs, yet others bore images that seemed to tell a story, though she hadn't the time to look over them and deduce what that story might be.

When Marquin and Verol would have led her through the door directly opposite the entrance, a throat cleared to their right and a stiff, impeccably attired man in the palace colors said, "Lords Arrendon, His Majesty has requested your *entire* party's presence upon arrival."

Clare felt the tightening of the shoulders to either side of her, but Marquin and Verol only turned her in the direction of the door located to the right of the entrance. It was opened for them and closed behind them, and Clare found herself in a throne room, looking down a long gold runner that traveled the length of the rectangular room and up six steps to end beneath a massive throne of carved white marble.

She met the cold, hard eyes of the man who occupied it and she wondered, in the space between one blink and the next, if he *knew* somehow. If he had chosen the color of that throne specifically to torment her. But it was not marble that had made that other throne white, and the man who sat on this one bore no semblance to the man who had sat on the other.

And however much she suspected Alaric wished to be, the man before her was not a god, to see inside her soul with only a look. Even if the Song *did* hide in his presence, so deep within her that not even Clare could sense it now.

Courtiers dotted the room, holding murmured conversations that halted as she traversed the golden runner, locked neatly between Marquin and Verol. The gazes of those courtiers carefully skipped over the Arrendons, an undercurrent of fear rustling through the room as it had when the pair had entered Numair's party. They landed on Clare instead, because it was safe for them to do so, eyeing her openly and speculatively, as if she were on display with a traveling comedy troupe.

She surreptitiously surveyed the room, but Numair was absent. As for the king...he had clearly not enjoyed his brush with heartbreak, if the harsh way he eyed her as she bowed was any indication. A muscle ticked along his jaw, and she read resentment in every inch of his demeanor. Clearly, he'd never learned to be careful about what he asked for.

He let the silence rest a beat before he said, "So, the Arrendons have brought their little songbird to court. What do you all make of her?"

The response was not immediate, and the glances at Verol and Marquin—but mostly at Verol—made it clear where that reluctance stemmed from. Finally, someone answered.

"She sings prettily enough, but I have to wonder if she speaks half as well." The saccharine voice belonged to a pale, voluptuous beauty barely older than Clare, with a river of shining blonde hair collected in artful, cascading ringlets about her face, tumbling over her shoulders and down to her waist. The light tittering that flowed from the other young women told Clare the speaker was popular. That, or she ranked highly enough to merit the response regardless.

The door opened behind her, but Clare knew better than to turn to see who had entered.

The blonde's smile widened, emboldened by either the laughter or the newest entrant. "Given her hasty disappearance last night, one wonders if perhaps she can't speak at all outside of song. Is that the cost of a *black diamond*?" she suggested mockingly. "That one must be mute the rest of the time?"

Clare took in the king's expression before deciding how to

respond. He was bored, and he was watching Clare. He'd invited his court to speak, but he didn't actually care what they had to say. He *was* interested in what she had to say.

A woman who was afraid of him would try to win this situation with politeness—to try and convince this woman, whoever she was, to accept her, in the hopes she might be a buffer between Clare and the king. A woman who wanted Alaric to like her would deliver a cutting remark, but one given skillfully in the hopes he would think her clever.

An indifferent woman was allowed to be blunt. "Even if I only speak half as well as I sing, that's more than twice as eloquent as you. I'd ask your name, but I can't even guess if it's preceded by 'lady' or 'miss'. Or neither."

A dark chuckle came from the back of the room, and Clare knew who'd entered even before Numair said, "It's 'lady', but your confusion's easily understood." He wandered to the front of the room, and—he was wearing that damn scarf.

The king's gaze narrowed on his nephew, but he said, "Indeed. Lady Meraland, it seems as if you owe Miss Brighton an apology."

Lady Meraland had already turned bright red at Numair's words, and her eyes now took on a slight sheen. It wasn't embarrassment that made her flush and tear, but anger. It was a testament to her resolve that her voice was just as pretty as before when she lowered her eyes demurely and said, "Forgive me. I only meant for a bit of fun."

Clare knew when to be gracious. She also knew when to make a battlefield line and draw it—because she suspected that having this woman retaliate head-on was vastly preferable to having her do it in subterfuge. "Try harder, next time."

The crowd that had giggled for Lady Meraland's first cutting comment now laughed for Clare's. It irritated Clare as much to have them laugh with her as it had to have them laugh at her. She had no use for them or their games. The king, it seemed, had no use for any of them either. Including her.

"You may all go." He flicked his hand dismissively. "Except you, Numair."

Numair flinched. It was a small movement, something she wouldn't have seen if she hadn't been looking. But she did see it, and Alaric did, too. Because he smiled, and in that smile were things

Clare had never wanted to see again. She didn't want to leave Numair here, alone, with whatever lurked beneath the king's skin.

But she had no power to stay, and before she could come up with a reason to, Marquin and Verol were herding her out the door as doggedly as they'd herded her in it earlier. They were silent as they led her back through the anteroom and out into the inner courtyard with its latticework of floating walkways over curated ponds, bright orange and white fish swimming lazily in the clear depths.

She followed their example of silence, but in the absence of words, her mind latched onto images. One image, in particular, that would not cease haunting her.

A white throne, pale and gleaming, and the merciless king upon it.

CHAPTER

THIRTY

HOW LONG WILL YOU BE GONE?

I t took everything Marquin had to keep Verol calm. The heartstone in his staff poured Verol's anxiety into him, an anxiety that was a direct result of Clare's own.

One would never know her unsettled to look at her. She walked calmly, almost serenely, as if simply drifting from one place to another while she contemplated some happy ideal. He had seen many a person who was capable of reflecting an outer emotion opposite of the inner one they were feeling. But he'd never seen anyone do it as completely, as perfectly, as she did. Because watching her now, even knowing that only the Kinthing's magic could put Verol in his current state, he almost couldn't believe anything was the matter with her.

They reached the suite of rooms assigned to them in the palace, and the force with which he threw open the door nearly knocked the servant within over. There shouldn't have been any servants in their suite. They'd forbidden even the cleaning staff from their rooms, and only one person in all of Faelhorn could override those orders.

The girl—for she was hardly old enough to be called anything more—shook like a leaf in the wind, her eyes downcast, her hands clasped together. "I'm sorry, milord. His Majesty ordered a room readied for Lord Verol's apprentice."

Marquin wanted to say something kind to her. But even if he

hadn't had a reputation that necessitated maintaining, that very reputation meant that anything he said to her would not be taken in the comforting manner intended. So he held the door open for her without a single word spoken and pointed at the hall.

She ran out, tripping on the rug that lined the hallway floor, and he winced internally at the force with which her knees and palms hit the ground. She scrambled to her feet with the haste of a tripped gazelle fleeing a lion, and disappeared around a bend in the hall a moment later.

Clare watched all this, the false serenity of her previous expression cracking a little to show the cool intelligence that lurked beneath. "You have such an…energizing effect on the staff, my lord."

A snort sounded as Fitz—carrying Clare's two luggage trunks—appeared in the hallway. "Energizing is one word for it." He preceded them into the room, dropped the trunks on the living area floor, and disappeared into his room. For Fitz, it was practically civil.

Marquin gestured Clare and Verol inside, motioning them both —though mostly Clare—to silence with an upheld hand. His magic spilled from him in a cloud. It pervaded the suite, first the common room and then sliding through cracks beneath doors to fill the bedrooms. It searched, hunting, and where it found little tangles and knots of magic that should not be there, it snuffed them out.

Most had been placed in Clare's room, though Alaric had left a token thread or two in his and Verol's. Sometimes, Marquin wondered why they still played this game. Why Alaric bothered when he knew his little traps and listening spells would be found and extinguished.

Except he *knew* why. They were a reminder, ever-present, that Alaric was watching. Not only here and now, but everywhere and always. And that one day, whether in a room or out on the road, Marquin would slip and miss one of those threads, and that would be the end.

He drew his magic back, found Clare watching him with the intensity of someone convinced that if they only stared at a thing long enough, they could take it apart and see how it worked. It was eerie, considering it was *him* she looked at like she wanted to disassemble, but it *had* distracted her from whatever she'd found so upsetting, if the commensurate lessening of Verol's anxiety was any indication.

It was Verol who spoke first, and to Clare. "Lady Meraland can be catty and tiresome, but while she is quite popular, she holds no real sway with those of influence. You need not fear her remarks."

Clare blinked, slow and deliberate, as if certain she had misheard.

It was in moments like these that Marquin found his husband utterly adorable. That, after all the minds Verol had walked through, he could so thoroughly misinterpret a situation—that his first instinct was to be worried Clare might have gotten her feelings hurt because someone was rude to her—amused Quin to no end. Marquin might not know what had unsettled Clare so, but he did know it hadn't been Lady Meraland.

She responded to Verol's assurances with all the cold clarity of a woman grievously offended. "You cannot honestly believe I would be bothered by the vapid declarations of a silly little chit whose brains wouldn't fill a teaspoon."

It was Verol's turn to blink, brows drawing together in puzzlement. "But...you were upset. Extremely so."

"Did your *Kinthing* tell you that?" There was a warning in her voice and Verol hesitated, looking to Marquin.

"He can't help it," Marquin offered. Which were not the words of assistance Verol had hoped for, if his glare was any indication.

"And I suppose you can't help knowing it either?" Clare reached out and flicked a finger against the heartstone clutched in his staff. His surprise must have shown, because she laughed. "I don't know *what* it is," she said in reference to the stone, "but I can sense the two of you in it. What he feels you feel."

"Yes," Marquin answered, because Verol's lips were too tightly compressed to form any response. If they had overcome the issues the formation of that stone had first caused, it was less in the way of having fully resolved an old hurt, and more in the way of having grown around it instead. Marquin knew he would never be fully forgiven for its existence, and he could live with that. Because Verol lived *because* it existed.

"The Kinthing—turn it off," Clare ordered.

Verol rubbed the back of his neck. "I am sorry, but it doesn't work that way."

"I don't believe," Marquin said softly, "she was speaking to you."

"Then who—oh."

Clare had a withdrawn look, as if every ounce of her attention was focused inward. The look shattered a moment later and she shook her head. When she saw the both of them staring intently at her, she scowled. "It's hiding, at the moment, like the coward it is. So the next time your Kinthing decides it cares, just…don't. I don't want its concern."

"And what about mine?" Verol asked softly.

"Can there be any difference between the two?"

Verol opened his mouth, clicked it shut.

"That's what I thought."

It might be what she thought, but it wasn't what was true. Yes, it was the Kinthing that had drawn Verol to Clare—first in the swamp, then again at the Hawk and Scepter and the Rival Theater—but it wasn't the Kinthing that cared. The magic was a compulsion, devoid of human empathy or concern. It was the man who cared. It was the man who had come to know her, as much as he could, on the road to Veralna. The man who would give his life to protect her, if it should prove necessary. It was the man who loved lost wayward souls, who already loved her.

Quin put a hand on Verol's shoulder, squeezing gently. "There can be and there is, but there is no use explaining it to you until you are willing to hear it." He didn't realize how harshly he'd said it until her head snapped back, a crack in her armor appearing for a mere second before it healed over. He wondered if he would ever be easy with her. If he would ever be able to care for her, as Verol already did. If she would even care if he did or not.

It wasn't that he disliked her. Were she removed from their immediate orbit—their immediate responsibility—he would find much to admire in her. Her resilience, her self-reliance, her refusal to bend. But all of those qualities were infinitely more difficult when she *was* their responsibility. When he couldn't even frame it in those terms because she would never accept that she was anyone's responsibility but her own.

The best way out of an awkward situation being the offensive one, he turned the subject. "If you were not bothered by Lady Meraland's remarks, you would have done better to let them go. Making a spectacle of yourself before Alaric will only serve to keep his attention on you."

She looked ready to spit fire at that remark, but there was something beneath the anger, something questing, when she asked, "And why is his attention so much in my direction to begin with? What did you tell him about me?"

The very fact she would think to ask what they might have told Alaric meant there had been something in her conversation with the king—some subtext—that he and Verol had missed. But any attempt Quin might have made to push her toward revealing it was promptly ruined when Verol answered, "Nothing."

Clare narrowed her eyes. "Nothing? Not a single thing?"

Verol rubbed at his temples. "Clare, the only occasion we've had to speak to Alaric since you came to us was last evening. And you were there for the entirety of that conversation."

Her shoulders relaxed fractionally, so Quin pushed, though there was little point now that Verol had reassured her. "What is it you do not wish us to tell him? If you let us know, we can be certain to avoid letting it slip."

She flashed her teeth at him. "I'm certain I have nothing to hide."

For the first time in twenty years or so, Quin felt the urge to roll his eyes. He resisted the impulse.

"Even so," Verol said, worry in every word, "the more you can do to lessen his attention, the better. To that end, avoiding any exchanges like the one just now would be best."

"*He* was the one who asked his court what they thought of me. All I did was respond."

"Yes," Marquin said dryly, "and perhaps if you had given a less interesting response, he wouldn't have asked one of the court's most favored darlings to apologize to you in public. As things stand, he's hardly likely to forget you, nor is Lady Meraland. She may be young but she is indulged and can be spitefully vindictive."

Clare folded her arms across her chest, her fingers digging into her biceps, as if *he* were the one who was hopelessly naive, and she sought patience in dealing with him. "*Nothing* I said or did not say in that room would make King Tolvannen less likely to remember me. The best I can do is attempt to temper that interest, which my responses were calculated to do.

"As for *Lady* Meraland and her vindictiveness, I ensured she will take a public route in her dislike of me, as opposed to a more subtle one, which is how I prefer to fight my battles. So if we are quite done here, I think—"

An urgent knock at the door cut her off. Verol answered it, returning a moment later with a letter. Marquin skimmed the contents, unease tightening his chest. "I'm afraid Alaric has business for us in the south of the province."

Her brow furrowed. "How long will we be gone?"

"*We* won't be. Alaric's orders are nothing you wish to be involved in, even should he allow your presence."

"But I'm Verol's apprentice."

He gave her a pointed look. "You know quite well that of the two abilities you possess, only one would improve from magical instruction. However, it is the one no one is qualified to instruct you on, and furthermore the one you have no intention of taking instruction for."

"Aren't there rules about this? I thought I had to live under Verol's roof or some such nonsense." Her mouth was set in a stubborn line, but behind it he saw something he hadn't expected. Something he didn't think even she was aware of—that she might have fought tooth and nail not to be stuck with them, but she didn't want them to leave her, either.

He found himself, against his will, softening toward her. "The living requirement will not be an issue." He would prefer not to attempt explaining that no one would be able to remember they were gone long enough for it to matter. "We will return as soon as we are able."

She made a dismissive noise in the back of her throat. Verol, who had been largely silent up to this point, said, "*Please* be careful. Alaric can be...charming, when he wishes to be. But Clare, no matter how harmless he may choose to make himself appear, he is not."

When she met Verol's gaze, there was something of that early madness in them that had first been present when they'd found her in the swamp. "I assure you, I know all too well the dangers of powerful men."

It seemed like an opening, an invitation to question, but Marquin knew it was not. Verol didn't.

"Is that what upset you so in the throne room?"

She blinked, as if coming out of a stupor. "I've no idea what you mean."

"It is painfully obvious that something was—"

"What precisely is it you *do* for the king?" she interrupted. The words left her lips sweet as honey, but the look in her eyes was one of pointed triumph. They wouldn't give an answer—not a real one—any more than she would answer Verol's question, and she knew it.

"Whatever is required," Marquin said.

"We will return as soon as we are able," Verol said. "In the meantime, if you need anything, Fitz will be at your disposal. If you have a problem, he will handle it."

"*Fitz* will be at my disposal," Clare repeated incredulously.

"Yes. I've spoken with him and, whenever we are not able to be here, he will be. Though I do think an apology for your actions last night might be in order."

The expression on her face went studiously neutral. Marquin would wager good money Clare had never apologized for anything in her life. Not unless she'd been under duress.

"Consider it," Marquin said. "And please try to stay out of trouble." He took Verol's elbow and steered him to the door, having no doubt that if they let her, Clare could keep them here another hour or two with questions that would never be answered. And the longer it took them to leave, the longer it would take them to get back.

It bothered him more than it should, leaving her here. They didn't make it more than a step outside, the door closed behind them, when Verol stopped. His magic sparked, opening the well-used channel between their minds. *I don't like leaving her. Not this soon. You know this is a fool's errand.*

I don't like it either, and of course I know. Alaric had stripped Veralna Province of all items of magical interest decades ago. Marquin doubted there was a single stone within its boundaries the king had not overturned in his quest for power, so his directive for them to examine a set of ruins in the Duchy of Wake was, without doubt, nothing more than a flimsy excuse to get them out of the palace.

Verol's budding wrath seeped through the heartstone. *He wants her left here without our protection. I should stay.*

Marquin brushed his fingers against Verol's cheek, a touch to take the sting from his words. *He wants to see if you are capable of leaving her. If you contrive some reason to send me alone on this matter, you will ensure his interest in her.*

A muscle tightened in Verol's jaw. *He is already interested. Fitz may aid her if necessary, but he cannot follow her to public functions. She will be alone with those vultures, unprotected.*

That girl is never unprotected. And I do not think she minds being alone. Marquin suspected she wouldn't *be* alone either, not so long as Numair Tolvannen was at court—and he was always at court—though saying as much would only serve to heighten Verol's ire. *If Alaric truly wanted her alone, he would have sent us much farther than Wake, and you know it. This is a test, my love. We can return by tomorrow afternoon. Hardly more than a day.*

Verol's eyes closed. *We left Marie for hardly more than a day, too.*

The sorrow that shot through the heartstone was sharp and deep. It wasn't only Verol's. Quin had raised Marie, too. If he was honest with himself, it was another part of the problem between him and Clare. In this matter, he understood Fitz—Marie had died, and Clare had been born. Marquin thought he'd moved past it, but he was only just understanding that Verol's grief had been so deep that he himself had never had his own space to grieve.

He'd been too focused on ensuring that he didn't lose Verol. Too focused on bringing him back, no matter the cost. Then, on dealing with the consequences of his actions. Consequences that meant he'd almost lost Verol, even though he hadn't lost him to death.

The heartstone throbbed in the clutches of the staff. It was a dangerous, forbidden thing to link one's will to another, and for good reason. But it was that will that had convinced Verol to continue living past Marie's death.

Marquin would never be forgiven—it would, forever, be a betrayal between them. But he had come to terms with that. Just as he now felt Verol coming to terms with what had to be done.

Let us go, then.

THIRTY-ONE

HAS IT ALWAYS BEEN WHITE?

Quin and Verol exited abruptly in a soft rustle of cloaks, and Clare stared at the closed door, disliking the hollow feeling in the pit of her stomach. What did she care if they were gone? She *preferred* them gone. Better to navigate this new landscape without them hovering protectively and badgering her about her choices.

It was only the memory of Alaric's throne that still unsettled her so. Only the dread that filled her at the reminder that the maid who'd exited with such haste had said it was Alaric who had ordered a room readied for Clare. A task that, had it been truly necessary, Marquin and Verol would have seen to.

The door to Fitz's room was closed. Presumably he was in there, if he was to be "at her disposal"—which was, to her mind, laughable. Two other doors branched off from the main living area. Steeling herself, she pushed open the one next to Fitz's room. The space within was done up in soft grays, the furniture polished cherrywood, and bore the telltale signs of inhabitation. Verol's and Marquin's room, then.

She pulled the door shut, the knots in her stomach pulling tighter as she went to the remaining room. Its door was not quite latched, and all it took was the light touch of her fingertips to swing it inward. She didn't enter, couldn't even bring herself to cross the threshold.

The walls were ivory, the smell of fresh paint still lingering in the air. The floors weren't right, but she supposed not even the king could have a floor completely replaced in the span of half a day. And it didn't matter, because placed in the direct center of the room, carved of pale wood and piled high with white linens and blankets, was a massive bed wreathed in gauzy curtains like thin white mist. Pure white fur rugs ran around the perimeter of the bed, stacked two inches deep.

The room wasn't an exact replica of the one that haunted her nightmares, but it was close. Too close.

He knew. Alaric *knew.*

Her heartbeat thundered in her ears like rushing water. He knew, but he *couldn't* know.

She turned, stalked to Fitz's door and pounded on it until he wrenched it open. She considered, given how irritated Fitz looked, Verol's suggestion that she apologize for forcing the truth out of him the previous night. Considered it, and ignored it in favor of asking, "The king's throne. Has it always been white?"

He had a look on his face, like he was trying to be polite. His next words made it obvious he'd failed in the struggle. "Why? Are you thinking of having one commissioned? It's a bit early for delusions of grandeur, don't you think?"

Clare restrained her first—and most natural—urge to grab him by the throat and demand the answers. But he still had that air of something lethal about him that she'd first marked in the stables, and an innate sense told her she would be a fool to threaten him in that way unless she intended to fight for her life.

Since the Song had disappeared the moment she passed onto the palace grounds, it would be no help to her in loosening his tongue this time. She considered, once again, Verol's suggestion she apologize. But she wasn't sorry.

She settled on staring. Directly, unblinking, into his eyes, as she asked again, "Has it always been white?"

He held her gaze for longer than most did, but in the end he blinked, his eyes shifting imperceptibly just to the left of her. "Never to my knowledge, no."

Dread unfurled its tendrils within her, curling around her organs and squeezing. Her thoughts circled round and round the problem of a white throne and a white bed and what they meant. Alaric *couldn't* know. But the dread in her gut said he could suspect. No one who had seen her leave Renault County was alive to tell the tale of it. But *he* would be furious he had lost her, and she could well imagine her description might have found its way to Alaric's ear.

The two had some way of communicating that didn't involve him leaving Renault County, or Alaric entering it. Would he have used it for this? And if he had, what would he have offered Alaric for her return?

Would he have offered enough to make it worth the king's while? It was clearly not enough for Alaric to actually search for her —there were no posters with her likeness on it splashed across the kingdom—but men of power were always curious about the things that interested other men of power and it might be that, having stumbled into his path, Alaric was now curious about her.

Curious if she was who he thought she might be. So all she needed to do was convince him that she was not. The throne, the room, were both a test. She had passed the first, if only because she had not thought it one at the time. She would pass this one, too. Because she was never going back to Renault County, and she had not escaped it only to end up in the same situation in another place.

Fingers snapped in front of her face. She didn't jump, only turned her glare back to Fitz.

"Why does it matter what color it is?"

She answered with the truth, in a light voice that didn't show the nature of that truth. "I detest white. It shows everything." Blood. Dirt. Sickness. It was a blank canvas upon which to paint a litany of sorrows.

Fitz gave her an incredulous look. "Should I write His Majesty a letter, informing him of your dislike of his color scheme?"

She shrugged. "Far be it from me to tell you what to do."

A knock sounded on the door and Fitz's face smoothed over, irritation and incredulity replaced by the calm, neutral mask of a servant. He stepped in front of her when she moved to answer the door, holding up a hand to indicate she should remain where she was. Amused that, despite his dislike of her, he had apparently taken Verol's instructions to protect her to heart, she let him answer the door.

She took only a single step of her own, to the side, in order to make out the visitor. A slim figure—it was impossible to tell the gender—stood clad entirely in dark gray, from whisper-soft boots all the way up to the cloth that covered their entire head. A small window existed around the eyes, though it was layered in a mesh so fine Clare couldn't even make out an eye shape, much less a color. Not a single stretch of skin was exposed.

The individual would have set Clare on alert, except Fitz was so relaxed as to be almost bored, and where she would have expected a weapon, the stranger instead held a rectangular black box with a dark green satin ribbon tied around it.

"The Arrendons are not in," Fitz said

The gray-clad figure only shook their head and pointed at Clare.

"Of course it's for her." Fitz sighed and stepped aside. When Clare didn't move he said, "They literally won't give it to anyone but you."

Cautiously, Clare stepped forward and held out her hands. The gray-clad figure placed the box in them, then bowed and left without a single word.

"Congratulations," Fitz said sardonically, "you've interested someone enough that they went to the exorbitant cost of hiring a Celerian runner."

Clare frowned. Celeria was one of the older goddesses, her domain that of mystery and silence. Of promises made and promises kept.

"What are they?"

"An extraordinarily expensive delivery service. They guarantee absolute anonymity and they've never been compromised in over a hundred winters of operation."

"Could the package be dangerous?"

"They have a strict threshold for the nature and level of magic that can be sent in any package. They don't accept anything with intent to harm, and while that can be manipulated, they won't accept any package containing levels of magic high enough to kill or seriously injure." He shrugged. "Sending such a package also gets you banned from the service for life. Turns out the nobles like having an ironclad way to send letters to their lovers more than they like sending death in a box."

Clare stared at the box in question, wanting to open it but wanting, also, the solitude of a closed door, and knowing there was no way in Ferrian's hells she would step inside her room.

She looked at Fitz. "Switch rooms with me."

"No."

"Do you have a particular attachment to yours?"

"Why? Do you have a particular dislike of yours?"

She gritted her teeth. "Yes. I won't step foot inside it."

He crossed the living area, pushed open the door to her room and surveyed it. She'd expected him to come back with a sarcastic remark, but instead his brow furrowed. "You don't like white, hmm?"

She didn't dignify that with a response. She had already said as much.

He shut the door, and she relaxed a little at having the space closed off. "My question for you is, *why* does the king know you don't like white? And why does he care?"

She lifted her chin. "Will you switch me rooms or am I sleeping in Marquin and Verol's until they come back and make you switch me?"

He studied her. "Have it redecorated."

"I can't. And if you take it, you can't either." Because if anyone came into this suite to "redecorate", Alaric would know. And if he knew it bothered her, his suspicions about her would be confirmed.

"I don't like you," he said.

"I believe we've established that. It's a mutual feeling."

"I don't like you," he repeated, "but I don't want you dead. So if and when you decide the subject of 'white' is one that needs to be dealt with, and if the Arrendons aren't here when that time comes, bring it to me."

He didn't linger to receive her acceptance or refusal. He simply moved his things from his room to the white one, and shut the door between them once more.

"If and when I decide the subject of 'white' is one that needs to be dealt with," she muttered under her breath, "there won't be a damn thing you *or* the Arrendons can do to help me."

Since there wasn't yet a damn thing *she* could do about it either, she pushed it aside, as she pushed aside so many things in her mind, and took her trunks and her odd delivery into her new room. It was a plainer, darker, infinitely more comforting setting than the one she had just left. Soft black rugs covered the floor around a carved oak bed frame, a matching chest at its feet and a wardrobe on the far wall.

The room had a small window, and Clare twitched the heavy black curtains closed before eyeing potential hiding places for the coin purse currently tucked into her cloak pocket. It wasn't that she thought she *needed* to hide it, necessarily. The Arrendons had no need of her money, and she doubted Fitz did, either. But the coins represented the whole of her independence, her security, and that was something she could not leave to chance. In the end, she chose three hiding places and split the coins between them, because her paranoia would allow for nothing less.

Only once she'd completed this task did she sit down on the bed and place her mysterious package in front of her. It could be from anyone, could contain anything. But the black and the green colors said it could only be from one person. A single tug undid the ribbon, and she lifted the lid of the box to reveal a stack of simple leather-bound books. She pulled the first out, turning it over in her hands, wondering what the point was in giving a book to someone who couldn't read.

Then she opened it and understood. The alphabet—for she knew enough to recognize the letters, at least, could still sing the silly song made of them all that had been one of her few pieces of childhood learning—was printed on the inside cover. The next pages bore strings of images. Beneath each image was a word, and when some compulsion tugged her to run her finger across that word, Numair's voice spoke it to her.

She thought of a red envelope, packed carefully between her clothes in one of her bags. Thought of asking Numair to tell her what it said and his easy *It's for you to read. You'll learn to soon enough.*

Her hand shook as she traced word after word, as she made the connection from the spoken word to the written. She leaned back against the pillows, wondering when he'd even had time to make this for her, and listened to him teach her how to read.

Inexplicably, she felt like crying.

THIRTY-TWO

STONE DRAGONS

Clare spent two hours with the first book before she decided she had to go out. She hadn't planned her first day here, because she hadn't planned on being abandoned by Marquin and Verol the moment she arrived. She hadn't planned on a white throne or a white room, and given both of them she couldn't help but wonder, since it was the king who had called the Arrendons away, if he *had* planned on her being alone here.

Yet no one had come to her room to demand her attention since the Arrendons had departed, so she was likely giving herself over to paranoia with that thought. The king had set his snares with his displays of chosen color and, so long as she did not stumble into them and become trapped, he would have no cause to take further interest in her.

She decided she was, for the moment, forgotten. Unemployed, unchaperoned, and likely unwanted by a good number of the palace's guests. What were all of *them* doing now? If Alaric required his court to reside here half of the year, how many of them were now in residence? She supposed that depended entirely on who all was considered part of his court.

Faelhorn was comprised of twelve provinces. Each of those had a proconsul whose fealty was sworn to Alaric, and each of those would have titled nobility beneath them. There were, undoubtedly, hundreds per province. She had no doubt the proconsuls and perhaps the dukes and duchesses fell under the half-year requirement, but surely not everyone did.

She would have asked Fitz, but she'd heard his door open an hour ago, followed by the main one, signaling his exit.

So much for being at my disposal, she thought, though in truth it was a relief not to have to deal with him. No one had ever been *at her disposal* before, even grudgingly, and she wouldn't have known what to do with him. So, though he might have been a speedy—albeit perhaps biased—source of information, she didn't *need* him. Acquiring information unnoticed was her area of expertise.

She changed out of the dress she'd worn, no longer looking to set a scene, but looking instead to blend in. Unfortunately, her options for pants were limited, because Galina's options had been limited. It wasn't that women in Veralna *didn't* wear pants, it was that, since pants were considered practical, women of higher rank clung to their silk skirts with such ferocity that a shop like Galina's didn't see much demand for pants.

She'd managed to find a single pair of soft brown riding breeches that—aside from the overly detailed white embroidery down the sides—was serviceable. She slipped them on, paired with the matching shirt Cynthia had insisted Clare needed—because Ferrian forbid the shirt *not specifically match*—and her new riding boots and slipped outside.

This wing of the palace, clearly residential, was not entirely without activity—servants came and went, and every now and then a door opened to reveal someone of obvious prominence—but no one paid her any mind. She knew how to walk and display herself so that, while no one questioned her right to be here, she didn't draw any interest, either.

She descended to the ground floor, intending to exit and explore the grounds—her mind still equated long stretches indoors with confinement, and she itched for the freedom of open skies—but as she entered the palace anteroom, a rustle of laughter halted her. Something about it—it was the way everyone had laughed at Numair the prior evening. She followed its origin, letting the sound draw her through first one doorway, then another, until she came upon an inner courtyard where Alaric's entourage had apparently departed to after his dismissal of them.

She might have ducked back inside before anyone saw her,

except that Numair lounged at their center, leaning against the low wall of yet another fountain. A young woman with long brown hair nearly the shade and length of Clare's own was doing her best to end up in his lap.

Dahlia of Moria, Clare supposed. She made a snap decision and walked into the courtyard. She ignored Lady Meraland's faux-whispered, "The Black Diamond graces us once more with her presence," ignored too the light ripple of laughter that followed it. Alaric's court was a fickle creature it seemed—they didn't care who they laughed for, so long as they laughed.

She walked straight to Numair, fighting the desire to smile as Dahlia straightened territorially. She pretended as if none of them were there, and addressed Numair. "You promised to show me around the palace. I'm here to collect."

Dahlia stiffened, and Numair gave Clare a look that said, *What the hell are you doing?* Aloud he asked, in a confused voice, "Was I drunk at the time?" That was good for another ripple of laughter.

Clare grinned. "Of course you were drunk, but a promise is a promise, and I'm holding you to it."

She could see him weighing it—whether he should go with her, whether he should stay. In the indecision, Dahlia glared at Clare. "He doesn't have time to—"

Numair abruptly pushed off the fountain, bumping Dahlia and cutting her off. "Never let it be said a prince of Faelhorn doesn't keep his promises." He shoved his hands into his pockets and followed her out of the courtyard. He waited until they were in the empty antechamber to whisper, "What in Ferrian's hells are you doing?"

"Rescuing you. Again."

As he steered her away from the main palace entrance and down a side hall, she had the sense of being watched, and caught the barest flicker of a shadow from the mezzanine above. She casually glanced up, spying Fitz blending in with the shadows in between two seven-foot-tall phoenix statues. So he hadn't entirely left her to her own devices, then. Pity. She couldn't believe he was *that* bad at remaining hidden, if he wished to, so he either meant for her to see him, or he was trying to determine how observant she was.

To let him know she'd seen him, or not?

"Are you going to be making a habit of that?" Numair asked.

She decided on ignoring Fitz, for the time being. "I don't know, are you frequently going to be in need of rescue?"

Numair muttered something under his breath that she couldn't make out. "Did you actually want me to show you around?"

"Yes. Marquin and Verol ran off to do mysterious, no doubt ill, deeds for your uncle, so I find myself adrift in foreign seas."

"And neither of them thought to give you the basic layout?"

She shrugged. "Marquin knows I'm resourceful, and Verol thinks I'm a fragile flower he no doubt hoped would stay in her room all day if he didn't tell me where anything was."

While Numair did not physically lead her through the entirety of the labyrinth that was the royal palace—a tour such as that could have lasted the whole the day—he did show her the areas of it likely to be of interest in her daily life. The sections of the palace frequented by persons of the Arrendons' status included several residential wings, a library, three solariums, a gymnasium, and dozens of other gathering spaces—reading and gaming and dancing rooms, and one that... She stopped, something about the room disturbing to her.

"What is this?" It was laid out almost like an art gallery, wide doors opening onto a long room filled with pedestals, the objects they held covered in glass cases.

"This is my uncle's...personal collection."

She frowned, drawn into the room despite herself. There was no visible theme among the items. Random jewels and accessories, paintings and books, weapons and armor. Too many more things to even list. They were not all beautiful, not all ugly. They did not appear to be from the same era or region. The only thing they had in common was Clare's inability to shake the sense that they were all missing something. That they had all once been something more than the simple objects they had now been reduced to. It felt, oddly, like being in a graveyard.

"Your uncle has odd tastes."

"He has very *specific* tastes," Numair countered. "Can we move on? I don't like being in here."

She nodded and followed him out of the building, to the exterior courtyard. The palace grounds had as impressive an array of offerings as the interior did, from sporting courts and riding arenas, to private gardens and walking paths. It was all glittering and beautiful and so far outside her frame of reference that she found herself blurting out, "You just...grew up in all of this?"

It was a stupid question to ask. Of course he had. The only thing her question did was invite ones about her own childhood in return.

He shrugged. "Not entirely. I spent a good deal of my youth with my mother's people. I didn't permanently reside in Veralna until I was older."

The answer made her realize how little she knew about the royal family's structure. There was Alaric, there was Numair, and there was the first prince of Faelhorn, though she'd yet to hear anyone mention him. Alys had said Numair's mother was dead. Presumably his father was too. She'd heard no mention of Alaric having a single living relative aside from his nephews.

It made her curious, but she didn't ask. Instinct told her these were answers best discovered on her own.

She found her feet heading unerringly in the direction of the stables. "Go riding with me?"

"Where would you like to go?"

She started to say "anywhere" but realized it wasn't true. "I want to see something magnificent. Something that makes men feel small."

A smile tugged at his lips. "Men, but not you?"

She smiled back. "But not me."

He didn't deliberate long. "I think I can manage that."

CLARE LEANED FORWARD in the saddle, feet pushing lightly into the stirrups to make her float the seat, doing her best to aid Kialla as the mare doggedly climbed her way up a mountainside so steep Clare had ceded all control over direction to the horse ages ago. On a loose rein, Kialla bobbed and weaved, picking her way up a hard-packed dirt path littered with sharp rocks, Hellack and Numair following behind.

"Are you sure this is safe for her?" Clare wasn't all that concerned for herself, but a broken leg was all-too-often the end of a horse, and Clare couldn't bear that thought. The desert rider she'd stolen her equine knowledge from had spent her life riding flat lands.

"She's fine. She's having fun," Numair assured her, and since only one of the two of them was Deirdren Blessed, she had to take his bloody word for it.

The path they traversed was a zigzag thing, cutting back and forth in between sharp, jutting rocks the height of her body. She couldn't help but feel as if they wove between spikes on the back of some ancient creature.

Her thighs ached but she refused to admit it or call a stop because, as Numair had said, Kialla *did* seem to be having fun. Like all she'd wanted out of life was a challenge, and now that she had one, she was determined to own it.

The mare wound her way around the last stone, eyed the two-foot incline from the path to the worn-flat top of the mountain. She gathered herself, muscles bunching, and hopped onto it, swinging her hindquarters around and sidestepping to allow Hellack room to follow. Kialla breathed heavily, nostrils flared but head held high as she looked back at the long path they'd cut up the mountainside, and loosed a high, shrill whinny.

"Yes, yes," Clare murmured, stroking the side of her neck, "all the kingdom is yours."

The top was narrower than she'd expected, less than a hundred feet across. Clare spun Kialla around and walked to the opposite edge, where a vertical cliffside dropped to the ocean below.

Except directly across from where the path ended, an outcropping extended from that cliff face. It was wide where it first broke from the mountain top, then narrowed as it pushed out. Its surface was covered in overlapping layers, like scales.

She slipped off Kialla and walked to the side of the outcropping, where she could see that its top formed the broad forehead of a massive face that narrowed to a snout, its great jaws partially open, revealing fangs the length of her body.

Numair came up beside her, stopping just outside that invisible boundary of space he seemed to intuitively know the edges of, the point where she didn't like people coming closer unless she'd invited them. "Welcome to the namesake of Firedrake Mountain."

"She's beautiful."

"She?"

"Definitely." It just felt…right.

"No one knows who carved her. Of course"—he shot her a wide

grin—"legend has it she isn't carved at all. That eons ago, dragons really did roam the skies, and when all the rest were gone, she was lonely and came here to sleep, slowly turning to stone as the centuries passed."

She knew it was supposed to be a story. But some piece of the Song sparked in her at its telling, and she found herself walking onto the broad forehead, lowering herself to place her palms flat against the wide stone scales. The Song perked up again and Clare let it, let it stretch a tendril into the stone, like saying hello. She felt the distant echo of a force, a consciousness, barely noticing that wisp of Song that spoke to it.

A flicker of interest and then it was gone, replaced by an immeasurable sadness. As if the dragon had been waiting for someone all this time, but Clare wasn't them. "I don't think she missed the dragons," Clare said softly, "I think she missed her rider."

And she wasn't going to wake until they came to her.

She stood, dusting off her hands, to find Numair looking at her oddly. But then, to him, it probably seemed like she'd taken a story a little too seriously. He was quiet the entire ride back down the mountain, and every now and then, she would glance over to find him looking at her strangely.

CHAPTER

THIRTY-THREE

ARE YOU THE SECOND PRINCE OF
FAELHORN, OR AREN'T YOU?

Numair contemplated the new and fascinating ways in which he was an idiot. He hadn't been mistaken about that power he'd felt slip out of her at the Hawk and Scepter. It hadn't been some secondary facet of Songweaving, and her ability to stand under his uncle's power wasn't an anomaly some branch of mage theory could explain.

Because he'd felt it again, spearing into existence where before there had been nothing, as she'd placed her hands on a stone dragon he now had the uncomfortable feeling wasn't actually stone at all.

He didn't remember Verol's last apprentice. He'd been too young when she died. But he knew *why* she had died. Knew the truth of it where few probably did. He should have expected that Clare was like her. And if *he* should have expected it, he knew his uncle already had.

If there was anywhere he could send her where Alaric wouldn't find her, he would do it in a heartbeat. But nowhere in this realm was safe, and if Alaric hadn't moved on her...maybe he didn't know.

He thought of saying something to her, but what was the point? Verol would have already warned her. What was Numair going to say that wouldn't make her look at him differently? He selfishly wanted to keep her just like this—the only person he knew who didn't want something from him except himself. And he thought, maybe, that was what she wanted—needed—too. That maybe being that for her was the best thing he *could* do.

You know that isn't true. You aren't good for her. You aren't good for anyone, and you'll only cause her trouble, in the end.

Fingers snapped near his face. He jerked, Hellack flicked an ear back at him in concern, and he looked over to find Clare smiling at him.

"How deeply lost in your head were you?" she asked.

He rubbed the back of his neck. "Too deep, apparently." Since they'd already reached the palace stables and he hadn't really noticed. "You were saying something, I take it?"

"Countess Duval has graciously invited me to sing at the Musicale House tomorrow night," she said, a world's worth of sarcasm in her voice. "I plan to be spectacular. You should come with me."

"I don't believe the countess sent me an invitation."

She gave him a look. "Are you the second prince of Faelhorn, or aren't you? It's not like they're going to tell you *no*." When he didn't respond, she said, "If you don't want to go, you can just say so."

"It's not that."

"Then what is it?"

"This"—he pointed a finger between them—"friendship. It isn't a good idea."

"For me, or for you?"

"I…don't know."

The horses stopped at the edge of the stables and she said, stiffly, "I've made up my mind. Make up yours. I'll be waiting at the Inner Gate at the sixth bell tomorrow evening. Show up or don't. I don't care."

She dismounted and led Kialla inside, her shoulders rigid.

And now he felt like an ass. Wonderful.

CHAPTER

THIRTY-FOUR

GOOD ENOUGH EXCUSES

Clare was still in a bad mood the next morning. The kind of bad mood that had her looking at every new dress she had and not wanting to wear a single one of them that night.

Except Battle Armor, which didn't feel like a dress even if it was. While she was tempted to make a statement by wearing it to every single event she ever sang at, she didn't have any glamour for her back, and even if she could afford to buy it each time she sang, she didn't want to risk that eventually someone with the right abilities might decide to look underneath that glamour.

But what she absolutely wasn't in the mood for was to be captured by long soft skirts and pretty necklines, making her into some kind of doll. That was how she always felt in dresses—like a Ferrian-cursed doll, made up into someone's image of what she should be. No amount of high-quality fabrics, or the fact she'd been allowed to pick these garments out herself, could make her feel any differently.

And when she got into one of these moods, it took a far more dire threat than social disapproval to make her do something she didn't want. Which was how she found herself shoving far too many coins into her pocket, then pulling Kialla out of the stables and riding into Hightown.

She did so unobtrusively, having avoided any further public

appearances in the palace since yesterday. She'd told herself it was because she wanted to observe, unknown, gathering information on this new social world, and because her brief absence before her performance tonight would also serve to generate interest. It also served as a test to see how far the king's interest in her went, and she had felt no small sense of relief when the prior evening had passed without anyone inquiring as to her whereabouts.

These were all good enough excuses, as excuses went, but the truth, as if often did, lay somewhere else. She'd been so irritated with Numair's failure to either deny or accept her invitation—and irritated with herself that it should bother her—that she hadn't trusted herself to maintain a calm public mask if she had to interact with him. His wavering yesterday told her he likely would not come, and she told herself that was fine. That it didn't matter if he'd rethought his association with her. She had never intended to do this—to navigate this new world—with a *friend* at her side anyway. Things would be better—clearer—on her own.

She reached the city, digging in her memory for the streets that would take her back to the Mages Guild. Her apprenticeship to Marquin and Verol allowed her to rent a stall at the stables behind the guild, and she reluctantly left Kialla and walked to Chalen's shop.

When she knocked, she once again got the man who'd opened the door when she'd tried to return the first dress. He smiled warmly at her, like she was some benevolent goddess descending upon his and Chalen's home, and it made Clare feel like a fraud. She hadn't done what she'd done for Chalen to help them. She'd done it because it had benefitted her, pure and simple.

At least, that was what she told herself.

"Come in, come in," he said, ushering her inside.

"I'm afraid I didn't catch your name last time."

"Lian," he said. "Chalen's in the back room working on some new designs, but I'm sure I can pry them loose. Would you like any tea while you wait?"

Clare shook her head and watched him disappear into the back of the house. When Lian returned with Chalen, she once again felt the Song's contented rumble around them, once again had the sense that Chalen was missing something, and they weren't going to be truly happy until they found it. She also had the profoundly irritating sense that she should know what it was they were missing.

"You wanted something custom?"

Clare nodded and explained what she had in mind.

A concentration line appeared between Chalen's eyebrows. "You want fashionable pants?"

"I want extraordinarily fashionable pants. Ones every woman in the city is going to want after I wear them tonight."

"If you want to leave here with something today then you stand where I tell you, you don't move, and you don't complain if I accidentally stick you with a needle."

"I can work with that. There's just one more thing."

Chalen lifted an eyebrow.

"I'd like them to have pockets. Regular ones and…less regular ones, if possible."

"Less regular ones," they repeated. "Would they have the purpose of holding something like this?" A dagger was in Chalen's hand, the movement so quick Clare barely had time to follow it. It was a slim, silver blade, and it was beautiful.

"Yes." Clare suddenly had the feeling Numair didn't choose his tailor solely for their excellent fashion design. Then she promptly kicked Numair out of her head. "I don't suppose you sell those, too?"

She'd lost one of her bone knives in the alley with Numair, and perhaps it was time she had a proper blade anyway.

A glint of humor rolled into Chalen's eyes. "I don't sell this one." The knife disappeared with a flash of silver. "But I sell many others."

<hr>

CLARE LEFT Chalen Mora's shop significantly lighter in coin, and with the outfit they had rushed to completion for her tucked in a package beneath her arm. The new blade she had purchased nestled warmly against her thigh, a comforting weight as she wended her way back to the Mages Guild.

She knew as soon as she rounded the path to the stables that something was wrong, felt it in her bones even before she heard Kialla's enraged cry, before she came to the mare's enclosure and saw the wooden fence broken through. She followed another trumpeting cry around the bend of the neighboring barn and found Kialla run into a corner by three men, two holding the ends of ropes that had been thrown around her neck, and the third a bull whip.

Blood dripped down Kialla's legs from a litany of cuts, no doubt from her flight through the fence, a thin sliver of wood protruding from her shoulder. One long, thick welt rose on her neck, blood dripping from the open gash. She snorted and danced, eyes wide and rolling, then reared.

The man readied his whip.

Clare was already running, package dropped and forgotten. Her muscles burned as the Song flared in response to her anger and she covered a hundred feet in the flicker of a candlelight, throwing herself in front of Kialla as the whip struck. Pain exploded across her face in a bright-hot flash, skin splitting. Her ears rang, sound coming to her distant and distorted. Habit had her refusing to scream, biting down on any sounds that might escape her throat, teeth sinking into her lip until blood washed over her tongue, copper and sick-sweet, the smaller hurt distracting from the larger.

Clare stumbled back into the horse as her hooves hit the ground. Kialla, who could have been forgiven for startling and kicking, did neither. It took a moment, back braced against Kialla's side, for the world to rush back in past the ringing, for Clare's eyes to focus. She raised a hand trembling with adrenaline to her face, touched the blood weeping from the open wound.

"What do you think you are doing?" Her voice came out low and feral, the Song's contralto rumble beneath the words, and the two men holding the ropes dropped them.

Clare knew the fear in the men's eyes should bother her, knew they stood in a semi-public place and she should care about who might see her.

She did not. She straightened and stepped forward, and instead of fighting the rush of power that thrummed through her, she welcomed it. The man holding the whip, the only one who had not stepped back at her words, had eyes that burned with cruelty. His hand twitched on the whip—eagerness, not nerves.

"Damn horse tried to escape, miss," blabbered one of the other two. "We was just trying to get her back in."

Clare didn't need the Song, whispering *lie,* to know the falseness of his words. If Kialla had wanted to leave her enclosure, she would have leapt the fence. To run *through* the fence, she would have to have been driven into a terrified frenzy.

Clare focused on the man who had spoken and slipped the Song's leash another notch, let its power inundate her. He turned and ran. The horror on his face before he fled was a soft stroke of pleasure down her spine.

She turned back to the whip-holder, spun the power of the Song into her voice, and felt her words grip him as surely as any vise. "I asked you a question. What do you think you are doing?"

"That horse is worth a fortune." His words were hollow and monotone, caught as he was in the Song's—in Clare's—fury, but his eyes blazed with undiluted hatred even as he was compelled to answer her. "Lord Tolvannen outbid everyone at auction by double. How much do you reckon he'd pay to get her back?"

"How much do *you* reckon you will pay for harming her?"

The Song squeezed, a phantom hand clenching around the man's wrist, shattering delicate bones to splinters. The whip fell from his nerveless fingers. Even as he opened his mouth the Song stilled his voice, trapping the howl of pain that would have followed.

When had she ever had the luxury of screaming from the pain dealt to *her*?

Another flare of power brought him to his knees, the crack of breaking kneecaps filling the air. The second man tried to flee but the Song brought him down next to the other.

Clare didn't know whether she or the Song was in control, and only that uncertainty held her back when the caress of power coldly and precisely whispered how *simple* it would be to sever the two thudding heartbeats in front of her. Footsteps approached, voices shouted, and the reality of her situation asserted itself viciously. She stood in the *Mages* Guild stables, for Ferrian's sake, wielding a power she didn't even understand.

If anyone discovered that fact, she would be locked in a cage and never released. If the king didn't kill her first.

"Stay here," Clare ground out. "Stay on your knees and tell everyone what you have done to Kialla." The words, and the nuance of power that ensured they would be obeyed, were specific. The men would tell everyone what *they* had done to the horse.

They would not mention her at all. It should be enough of a distraction.

Clare settled a hand on the mare's neck, the Song reaching out to slide the piece of wood painlessly from Kialla's shoulder, to heal over the cuts and take down the swelling. Using the man's shoulder as a mounting block, Clare vaulted onto the mare's back, twined her fingers in Kialla's mane, and squeezed her sides gently. The mare bolted but Clare had anticipated that. She held her seat, using leg cues to guide the horse out of the city, back to the road they had traveled in on.

Only once they were outside the city proper did she lean her head over the side of the mare's neck and vomit, her body aching, her head throbbing.

She was done with the Song, but the Song was not done with her.

Why do you fight me? Its voice, low and hypnotic, filled her mind once more. She'd heard it once as a child, before she locked it away, had the sense she'd heard it endlessly when she'd been lost in the madness. *They are all like those men. You have seen it, time and time again. Let me loose, and I will make them pay. Make them all pay.*

No.

The Song bristled, its fire spreading through her. *Why?*

But Clare didn't answer. She relinquished control of their destination to Kialla and turned her attention to the internal battle that consumed her. She did not in truth care where they ended up. Horses, at any rate, tended to return home when given their head. It was simply a matter of where Kialla considered home.

CHAPTER

THIRTY-FIVE

STILL INVITED

Clare surfaced from thoughts both incoherent and frightening to find herself surrounded by forest, rain tumbling through the trees, tripping off leaves and branches. Kialla slowed to a walk when she found a river and followed along the bank, a distant roaring growing louder the farther they traveled. When horse and rider at last emerged into a small clearing, the roar had grown to a crescendo, its source the waterfall descending from a six-hundred-foot apex.

Kialla relaxed almost instantly, clearly at home enough in the space that neither storm nor rumbling thunder could trouble her overmuch. Clare slipped from the mare's back, feet sinking ankle deep into the growing mud. Kialla, freed of burdens, strode forward and lowered her head to the lake at the base of the falls, drinking deeply.

Clare found a large, flat rock nestled against a larger rock and climbed onto the former, settling with knees drawn up to her chest, letting her back and head rest against the larger rock. She took comfort in the steady pelting of the rain, in the frigid cold that overtook her body with shivers and froze her fingers stiff.

She wanted the cold to freeze the tendrils of Song that still clawed at her. She'd allowed it too much, had given it the most freedom it had seen in years, and it raged against her defenses, wanting to keep it.

No amount of exterior cold could chill the fever in her blood. She tried to ignore it by watching Kialla, the mare leaving the lake for the relatively dry cover provided by a towering evergreen. She shook out her coat and folded herself down, more content than any sane horse without a herd ought to be in such weather conditions.

At some point Clare stopped shivering. She felt like she was floating inside her body, detached, and fear took her. She'd felt this way once before, the last time she'd given the Song any true freedom, and been forced to fight it for control. Then, she had known she was going to lose the battle. That she would lose and the Song would overtake her, and the only way to prevent it had been by descending into the madness. By snapping the tether to herself and entering that place where she hadn't controlled her body, but neither had the Song.

She didn't want to become that empty thing again. Didn't want to trade a swamp for a forest, to give up the life she'd just started to live.

Clare Brighton. She repeated the name to herself, over and over again. She was Clare Brighton. *Not a thing, not a vessel, not a doll, but herself.*

Eventually, the fever cooled a little, but didn't ebb entirely. Her body was an odd kind of numb, and she looked out dazedly at the lake below, watching the rain drops plinking onto its surface in a patterned dance of infinite complexity. She became entranced as she tried to capture the exact moment where they fell through from the world above to the one below.

The lake seemed like a beautiful, serene thing. Here in the storm, the sun hidden, it was enchanting, half-mystic. It called to her. She had a thought of walking into the lake, rain falling, and continuing to walk until the waters slipped over her head, and she found out what kind of world lay beneath them. Maybe there she could find Clare, and leave the Song and the madness behind.

It wasn't until she felt the water lapping at her hands that she realized the impulse had become more than a thought. Dense, icy water lapped over her hips. The water caressed her skin, inviting, and she pushed forward, marveling at how difficult it was to *walk* in water, especially the deeper one attempted to go. Her boots had filled with liquid, the extra weight adding to the strain in her muscles as she moved forward.

She sank to her stomach, her chest, her collarbone. Distantly, she thought she heard someone call her name. The voice sounded frantic, and she wondered if she should turn back. But then the water was slipping over her head, and she was opening her eyes wide, wide, wide, disheartened to learn that in the darkness, she couldn't see what lived beneath the water's surface after all.

She took a breath and found that breathing underwater wasn't pleasant. A small corner of her brain that was not as calm as the rest of her screamed that one didn't breathe underwater at all, and she needed to go *up*. The only trouble was, her feet didn't touch anything anymore, and she had no real concept of which direction *up* was.

Just when she would have tried breathing again, hands wrapped around her arms and she was pulled up against someone blisteringly hot. Or perhaps she was cold? Her head broke the lake's surface and she coughed, her lungs violently rejecting the water in them. She tried to breathe but only coughed again, repeating the painful exchange over and over, until her lungs were finally clear.

The air that rushed into her body brought with it blessed clarity, and she took stock of where she was. Namely, draped across someone's legs, the position keeping her head and torso out of the mud. Strong hands held the wet curls of her hair back from her face, their touch gentle and warm against her skin.

She forced herself up with shaking arms, sat back, and looked into Numair's almost-black eyes. He was angry, in that way only people well-accustomed to hiding their emotions can exude a force of anger by stilling their features into perfect immobility. It was, oddly, that anger—directed sideways of her, for her rather than at her—that melted her irritation at the silence he'd maintained since she'd invited him to the Musicale House.

"What were you doing?" he asked, the pleasant civility in his voice belying his fury.

Clare stared at the water. "Almost dying, I think." Her lips wouldn't move properly. She'd started shivering again, a good sign and likely due to the spelled heat pouring off Numair in waves, reaching for her.

"And you wanted that?" he asked sharply.

"No." She had never courted death intentionally, not even in the darkest periods in her life when she had wished for the strength to wish for death. Some stubborn part of her had always been determined to survive, to keep going, because if she didn't, then what had any of the pain and suffering she had already experienced been *for*? If there was never going to be anything better, why had she bothered enduring?

"Then what were you doing underneath the water in winter in a damn thunderstorm?"

"Discovering that I can." Discovering that she had, indeed, taken some control back from the Song.

"Can what?"

"Die." Because the Song would never have let her come close to drowning, had it been in complete control. And at some point, beneath the icy lake, she had shoved it back into its cage.

Numair stared at her a long moment. "Anyone can die. Are you convinced you're human now you know you can?"

When she only smiled, he shook his head and muttered a curse. "Your lips are bluer than Ferrian's flames." He grabbed a coat off the ground, one he must have discarded before jumping in the lake after her. It was obviously spelled against things as common as dirt and water, looking no worse for wear for having been lying in the mud. He wrapped it around her shoulders and warmth and dryness settled over her, better even than the spelled heat slipping off him.

She slid her arms into the coat sleeves, and after she tried twice to stand and failed, she let him help her. Then he bent down, untying the laces of her boots.

"What are you doing?"

He looked up at her with a glare that clearly said she wasn't allowed to question his actions right now. But he answered anyway. "You don't need to carry the lake back with you. Can I?" He indicated her shin and she nodded, more out of curiosity than anything else. He gripped her leg, bracing her, and pulled the boot off. When he flipped it over, a surprising amount of water dumped onto the ground.

He shook his head, muttering something she couldn't understand because she was pretty sure it hadn't been spoken in Common, and carefully put her boot back on. He repeated the process with the other foot, and there was something about his irritation, at odds with his gentleness, that had a grin curving her lips.

He finished retying the laces and stood. When he saw her face, his scowl deepened. "You cannot be smiling right now."

She grinned wider. He cursed again, and she smothered a laugh while he turned and whistled for the horses. They trotted over, Kialla looking fresh as daisies while Hellack looked miserable, clearly wondering what offense he had given to be dragged out into this downpour.

Numair offered Clare a leg up, and it took her a moment to realize he intended to put her on Hellack with him.

"I c-can ride on my own." Her damn teeth were chattering as she warmed enough to feel again, and she snuggled deeper into the coat's warmth.

"You're half-frozen and Kialla doesn't have a saddle. There's no way you're keeping your seat on her."

"I d-don't want people to know anything h-happened." She would flaunt any social convention that existed, but she wouldn't look weak by letting Numair all but carry her back to the damn palace.

"No one will know. I sent for Marquin and Verol. You can clean up at their house and they'll take you back to the palace."

She shook her head. "They aren't here."

"They returned early this afternoon."

It irked her, that Numair had known this and she hadn't.

Her brain finally warmed up enough to realize she had no idea what he was doing here. "How did you know to send for them?"

He grimaced. "The mages' stables contacted me."

The little warmth that had returned to her limbs fled. "What did they tell you?"

"That two men confessed to attempting to steal Kialla from the stables after you paid for a half day's board, and that the horse was now missing."

"Is that all?"

"That they knew? Yes." His hand reached for the cut on her cheek, stopped short of actually touching her. "I know a whip lash when I see one, Clare. And I know who must have given it to you, but strangely, neither of the men mentioned you at all. They said only that they tried to steal the horse, and she ran off."

"So maybe that's what happened."

"It's not all that happened. I found the third man."

Clare's blood turned as cold as the lake she'd nearly drowned in. So stupid, to have forgotten the third.

"He said he looked into your eyes and saw his death. And the other two? They refused to get off their knees even though one had shattered kneecaps, because they insisted they couldn't leave until they told *everyone* what they had done." His piercing gaze demanded answers, but she had none that she could give.

"I did tell you," she whispered, "that you should be afraid of me."

He looked at her a long moment before shaking his head. "I'm not afraid of you. Now are you getting on Hellack or am I picking you off the ground once you've fallen off Kialla?"

Against her better judgment, she let him boost her into the saddle. He swung up behind her, settling onto Hellack's broad back behind the saddle. When his arms came around to either side of her for the reins, the baffling increase in her heart rate told her that her better judgment would have been a fine thing to listen to. Maybe falling off the horse would knock this strange feeling out of her.

"What *happened*? Not," he continued, cutting off her protest, "what you did. It's already obvious you aren't talking about that. What happened before?"

"They hurt Kialla."

Numair's eyes traveled over the mare walking at their side, no limp or injury evident.

"She's fine."

Clare nodded. "She is now."

His fingers tensed on the reins and she braced herself for his reaction. His voice was almost eerily calm. "Don't breathe a word of it. You never went back to the stables, you never saw her. You were still in the city when I sent word to you of what happened."

Clare exhaled heavily. "Someone had to have seen me."

"It's taken care of."

She decided not to ask. "What did you tell the stables? About the men?"

"That their reaction was the result of a spell I placed on Kialla to protect her from theft."

"And they believed you?"

He shrugged. "Such magics are possible. To warrant investigating the spellwork, the Guild would have to publicly doubt my word." And given who he was, no one was going to do that. "And I am known to be eccentric enough to have done just such a thing."

"And the men?"

"I handled it." They rode in silence a quarter mile before he added, "I know you don't need my advice, but I need to say it anyway. Don't ever let my uncle find out what you did today."

She stiffened, then made herself relax. "I'm just a silly Song-weaver," she said softly, "who got carried away."

"Good."

And then, because she knew it was the kind of "good" that meant he didn't believe a word she'd said, she figured she might as well see if he could tell her something the Arrendons hadn't. "Everyone is so eager to warn me to hide from him. He's the king, but is he not only a man?"

"Once, I might have said yes. After what he did in El-Dennon…I don't know what he is now. There is a reason he has not been deposed, Clare. Don't underestimate him."

"What happened in El-Dennon? What did you see?"

He was quiet a long time before he answered. "I saw the future, and it is a monstrous thing."

They lapsed into silence, the forest passing by to the sound of Hellack's and Kialla's hoofbeats. The closer they came to Arrendon Manor, the more withdrawn Numair became, the more like the empty mask he showed the world.

"How did you find me?"

The question startled him from his brooding, as she had intended it to. "What?"

"Locating me. How did you manage it?"

Clare strongly suspected the shifting of his weight indicated embarrassment.

"You know those eccentricities I mentioned being known for?"

"Yes."

"I, ah, might have had a latent tracking spell on the horse."

"Why, Prince Numair, are you *following* me?" she teased.

"*No.* They're on all my horses. I didn't think to remove it when I gave her to you."

"Oh, of course," she said in her most patronizing tone.

"It's true," he muttered defensively. "But Clare? The spell's used up, and I won't renew it. It was an oversight in the first place, so do me a favor?"

"What's that?"

"What almost happened today, in the lake—promise me nothing like that will ever happen again. Because next time, I won't be able to find you."

If that request wasn't the definition of hypocritical, she didn't know what was. But she looked down at how tightly his hands gripped the reins, and any sharp retort died on her lips. "I'll trade you for it. A promise for a promise. I won't make you jump in for me again, if you don't make me need to stand for you."

He didn't answer until they broke from the forest to the clearing behind Arrendon Manor. And then all he said was, "I'll try."

He stopped Hellack at the edge of the expansive back patio and dismounted. Clare's legs weren't feeling very agreeable about performing the same maneuver. Numair cleared his throat. When she looked at him, he lifted his hands. "I could...you know."

If this wasn't absolutely mortifying, she didn't know what was. She gritted her teeth. "Fine."

"No need to sound so gracious." He gently gripped her waist and lifted her free. "Though I suppose it *is* embarrassing when maidens who rescue princes have to be helped off the backs of their noble steeds."

"One more word and I'll punch you in the throat again."

He laughed as he lowered her down, her feet landing on solid stone, legs wobbling more than she preferred to admit. She was trying to figure out what the odd feeling in her stomach was when the back door slammed open and Verol and Marquin strode out.

Verol's gaze went from Clare's face to Numair's, to Numair's hands on her waist. "I thought I made myself clear when I last spoke with you, Your Majesty."

Obviously, *she* hadn't been clear enough about which parts of her life Verol was allowed to interfere in. Namely, none of them.

"Perfectly clear," Numair answered, his voice as much black ice as ever Clare had heard it.

"Then what are you doing here?"

"I am simply bringing her home."

"Well, you've brought her, and now you may leave."

"Verol," Clare and Marquin said warningly in the same breath, but Verol paid them no heed.

"And you can take that horse with you after the trouble she caused today."

"No." Clare's voice came out harsh enough to grind stone to dust. Her traitorous heart was already panicking at the thought of the mare's loss. *Mine,* it whispered, even though she knew better. But she couldn't make her voice any more human when she said, "Kialla stays."

Verol took one look at her face and clearly knew any argument he might make was pointless. "Fine. Kialla stays." He looked at Numair. "You don't."

Clare opened her mouth to reverse the second order, but the gentle tap of Numair's fingers, where they still rested on her waist, said, *Don't bother. Not for me.*

He let her go and faced Verol. "You have always thought little of me, and that is well enough in the end. But do ponder on some occasion, Lord Verol, how very grateful you ought be that I am not my uncle, for I allow you a manner of speaking to me that *he* would never suffer." To Clare he said, "I'll take Kialla back to the palace stables for you."

But if he hadn't wanted her jumping to his defense, she wasn't capable of letting him leave without making *some* point to Verol. So she waited until he was far enough away to warrant calling after. "Numair?"

Verol's sharp intake of breath at her failure to use any title whatsoever in her address soothed the jagged edges of her pride. Numair paused and turned, an inquiring quirk to his eyebrow.

"You're still invited tonight." Despite trying to convince herself that she didn't need a friend, that doing this alone was, in fact, preferable, she did and it wasn't. She pulled his coat tighter, that spelled warmth washing over her. "I hope you decide to come."

THIRTY-SIX

WE UNDERSTAND EACH OTHER

Clare snuggled into her favorite armchair in the living area, paused to consider the concerning realization she now had a favorite armchair, and folded her legs under her. Sensation was returning to her previously numbed extremities in painful pricks and tingles, needles falling like rain on the inside of her skin.

Marquin sat on the sofa opposite her, the two of them watching Verol pace. He had been pacing for the better part of a quarter hour in absolute silence, clearly attempting to gain some measure of control before he spoke.

The level of his agitation didn't seem warranted, and it wasn't until she felt the power cocooned around him that she realized what was causing it.

Kinthing magic.

Clare found a smoldering coal of anger all her own and fanned its flames. After the ordeal she'd just went through, she'd had enough of the Song pulling strings.

Stop it.

The Kinthing magic *stilled*, the switch from active to dormant so fast Verol jerked his head up, wide eyes finding her. "How did you...?"

Clare shrugged.

"Are you all right?" he asked. "Lord Numair sent word of what happened after the stables contacted him and no one could find you. Obviously, I overstepped outside, but forgive me if I'm angry when I think about the damage that could have been done to you had you been present when whatever fool spell he put on that horse broke."

He looked at her face then and frowned, as if realizing for the first time that she was not precisely a vision of health, and the story he had been told did not line up with the woman in front of him.

If Clare had wanted, she could make the story fit, could fill in the gaps with careful lies. Her face? She had heard about the upset at the stables and in her rush to get there she'd fallen and cut her face open. When she heard how Kialla had run off she had gone looking for her and ran into Numair in the process. Once they found Kialla, they had brought her home. She was sorry she had not thought to send word to Verol and Marquin.

Spoken convincingly enough, any lie could be swallowed in the moment, and Numair had conveniently set himself up to take the blame. To let her walk out of this without telling Marquin or Verol she'd lost control.

She wondered if whatever drove Numair to keep his facade of drunken uselessness in place had cast a shadow over every aspect of his life; if he'd obscured the truth for her, or if he'd done it simply because he didn't know anymore how *not* to be the person to blame.

"There wasn't any spell on Kialla. At least, not the kind he told the Mages Guild." She let the real story come out, no detail spared. "I think I might need those magic lessons sooner, rather than later," she admitted.

Verol hesitated. "What you carry—it isn't magic as we know it. I honestly don't know if anything we can teach you will apply. And despite you being my apprentice on paper, I don't think I'm the best person to help you. The Kinthing is too linked to the power you carry. I think you would fare better with Marquin, but I leave the choice to you."

She thought she would too. Verol would be too easy on her. "Very well." She turned to Marquin. "When do we start?"

"Tomorrow. Meet me here at the tenth morning bell."

Clare nodded in return, and the relief that flooded through her was almost instantly replaced by a fresh wave of anxiety. Nothing had been solved, only delayed, and everyone in the room seemed to know it, so it was as good a time as any for Verol to change the subject.

"I do know I overstepped earlier," Verol began, which told her well enough he was about to do it again. "But I must beg you to reconsider this…friendship with Lord Numair."

"Why do you dislike him so much?"

Verol considered his words before answering. "Because he has everything, and he does nothing," he said finally. "He has social rank, money, and most importantly, he has Alaric's favor. He could use that influence to try to change Faelhorn for the better. I do not believe he is, at heart, a bad man. He is simply a useless one. Had he been born to a lesser family he would be just another drunk dying forgotten in a gutter somewhere as we speak."

It was, Clare suspected, the most unforgiving speech she would ever hear Verol make, and she had to bite her tongue on half a dozen rebuttals, because Numair would not thank her for them. She couldn't tell Verol the king's favor was all for show, that Numair was no more a drunk than she, and that he was far, far from useless. Even if Verol believed her—and he wouldn't—she would not dissemble with a few sentences the charade Numair had spent years building.

But it physically hurt to hold her tongue.

"I can see why you might feel that way," Clare said, "but I'm not you, and I don't. You don't have to understand it, and I'm not asking you to approve. I *am* asking you to leave it alone."

Verol's eyes squeezed gently shut. "What kind of friendship do you think he can offer you?"

"We understand each other."

Verol clearly didn't understand *her*. But he did the right thing, anyway. "Very well. I won't bring it up again."

"Thank you." She even meant it. Because no one had ever tried to convince her to their side by reason instead of force, nor had they ever given in when she told them to.

Verol gave her a half smile. "Only do not ask me to be civil to him. I am not certain I could manage the stress."

"I'll try not to ask it of you." She looked at the clock and groaned. "Do I have time to bathe here or do you need to be back at the palace?"

"You have time," Verol said. "And we need to send for a healer before you return, at any rate."

Clare's brow wrinkled in confusion. "A healer? For what?"

Marquin and Verol exchanged a look.

"For your face," Marquin said softly.

Of course. She had forgotten. It wasn't that the wound didn't hurt, it was simply that she was so accustomed to being in pain from one thing or another, that the state had seemed natural to her, rather than something that needed fixing.

"I don't want a healer."

"Then at least let one of us clean and bandage it."

"There is no need."

"It will grow infected."

Reluctantly, Clare relaxed her grip on the Song, letting it do what it had been clamoring to do since she'd come out of the lake water. It burned the beginnings of infection from the wound, pushing out old blood and foreign particles. Quickly—so quickly the wound seemed to close of its own accord—the Song mended vessels and tissues, knitting them back together. It pulled the sides of her torn cheek to each other and patched between them with new skin, until her face was as perfect as it had been that morning. Not even a scar remained to mark the event.

She leashed the Song before it could move on to the rest of her, before it could take the other scars that marred her body. Before it could destroy her identity, piece by piece. As it was, she was not *quite* quick enough, and she lost the reminder of the first time she'd been caught stealing food.

She gained her feet, ignoring the echo of power that made her feel as if those feet were slipping down into the ground, taking her body with them until she was swallowed up in dirt and roots and the thrumming, pulsing heartbeat of the earth.

"As I said, there is no need." A new thought occurred to her, one that almost made the echoes fade, as she considered the fair amount of coin she had spent earlier and the patch of ground outside the stables where she had dropped her purchase. "I don't suppose Numair found my package and had it sent here?" she asked brightly.

Marquin and Verol, obviously not sure what to make of a sudden miracle healing followed by a happy change in attitude, only nodded and pointed Clare in the direction of her bedroom.

THIRTY-SEVEN

BLITHERING, ROMANTIC FOOL

Numair sat atop Hellack in the shadows just back from the Inner Gate, waiting for his better sense to materialize. He was early, and Clare was not yet here. If he took the forest path, he could return to his room without her ever knowing he'd been here. *He* could pretend he'd never been here.

But every time a muscle in his leg twitched, a precursor to the gentle pressure that would turn Hellack back whence they'd come, he once again saw the water closing over her head and he stopped. He hadn't thought he had it in him to care any longer. If people lived, if they died. He'd cared so much, once, and all it had brought him was pain.

When he was younger and even more foolish than he was now, he'd thought the efforts he'd made in secret would have some effect. Would produce some light in a world drenched in darkness and that, even if no one else would ever know it was his hand behind those efforts, *he* would know. Then he'd watched those minuscule effects, those minuscule goods, drown beneath the sea of death and power and inevitability that was the king of Faelhorn and he'd known that nothing he did would ever matter.

Twice the fool, he'd kept trying, anyway. But he'd stopped caring —if what he did helped, if it didn't. If the people he tried to save lived or died. In truth, sometimes he thought it better when they died. Better that they no longer had to deal with all *this*. All the mess and pain and futility that was living. But he hadn't felt that way when he'd watched her disappear beneath the lake's surface and been unsure if he would reach her in time. He hadn't thought to himself, *At least she'll be free of all this.* All he'd known was a stark, insistent terror. The sense that she *had* to live, because if she didn't… he'd been half-convinced the world would end with her.

He hadn't been such a blithering, romantic fool about anything since his adolescent years, when he'd been lost and dumb enough to think himself in love. Well, that wasn't quite accurate. He *had* been in love—but it had been with an idea of the person, rather than the actual person, and he frequently had cause to be grateful they would never know of the brief infatuation. He was already laughed out of the court with regularity. He didn't want to be laughed off the continent as well.

He didn't want *her,* riding up the path on Kialla, her back straight and her face set, to laugh at him someday too. Experience told him she would. She wasn't the first person to be convinced there had to be something of substance beneath the second prince of Faelhorn's drunken lunacy. She *was* the first to actually find it. A spark of it, a crumb. All that he could give her.

It wouldn't be enough. It couldn't be enough. People *wanted.* It was in their nature, in their biology. They wanted connection, stability, companionship. Some were better at attaining and keeping it than others, but everyone wanted it at least a little. She would too, and when she did, she would realize he was an obstacle to ever having it.

She stopped at the Inner Gate and turned Kialla back toward the palace, watching the road. Watching for him. It was empty here, this time of evening. Most who would venture out had already done so, and there was no one to see her except him, no one to notice the way she sat astride her horse as if readying herself for disappointment.

It took him a moment—longer than it should have, probably—to recognize that the riding coat buttoned up her front was the very same one he'd wrapped around her that afternoon. What drove her to wear it—sentimentality or practicality? The latter, most likely. She didn't seem like the type of person prone to actions of a sentimental nature, and it was a damn fine coat.

Was, in fact, his favorite coat. Not that he had any intention of asking for it back. It looked better on her.

He watched as she waited. She didn't fidget or sweep her gaze across the landscape like most people would if they were waiting for someone and hoping they would come. She simply sat, turning stillness into an art, her gaze fixed on the path. She waited longer than he would have, in her place. A little more than a quarter went past the bell before her fingers tightened on the reins, her eyes hardening, and she offered the night a single word in condemnation of him. "Coward."

Kialla pivoted, took two steps at a trot and then leapt into a canter at the squeeze of Clare's legs, disappearing down the path. Hellack nickered after the mare, muscles tensing in eager anticipation of a chase.

Coward, her musical voice rang in his mind. *Coward, coward, coward.*

Fool, yes. But not a coward.

Not tonight.

He stroked his hand down Hellack's neck and gave the horse his head. "Go get her then, boy."

THIRTY-EIGHT

STORYBOOK FANTASY

Clare was lost in the rhythm of Kialla's gait, her irritation and disappointment thundering along with each hoofbeat when she heard another, faster set of hooves pounding behind her. Kialla stretched her nose out, lengthening her stride, determined to keep her lead. Clare almost let her, but found her fingers tightening instead, applying a gentle pressure to the reins that had Kialla slowing to her previous speed as Hellack and Numair drew even with them.

Man and stallion slowed from gallop to easy canter, keeping pace in a silence Clare didn't break. They slowed as they approached the Outer Gate, though when the guards recognized Numair, they simply waved the pair of them through. Walking now —Kialla bit at Hellack's face when he did so too closely and the stallion, rather than bite back, simply shifted aside, putting another foot of space between them—Clare finally acknowledged Numair.

"You're late."

He didn't answer for a few strides. "Is my invitation rescinded, then?"

"That depends."

"On?"

"On whether I have to worry if you'll accept others in the future." She held up a hand, forestalling him from answering directly. "And before you give me yet another brooding speech about how you aren't a good person to associate with, please remember that I don't give a damn. If *you* don't want to associate with *me*, then fine. But don't act like you can't for my supposed benefit."

He let out a short, sharp laugh. "All right then. Consider me yours. When you regret it, don't come crying to me."

She snorted. "I don't cry. And I don't regret."

He eyed her dubiously. "Never?"

"What's the point? Once something is done it's done, and I find my time is far better spent altering the course of future events than it is worrying about those that have already passed."

"And how will you be altering the course of future events tonight?"

"By proving that the Rival Theater wasn't a fluke and that *this*" —she flicked the black diamond dangling from her ear—"is not a parlor trick."

"About that—Lady Meraland will settle down when she discovers she can't rile you."

She shot him a withering look. "Everyone is so concerned about my fragile feelings where that social blossom is concerned. So let me say first that nothing I do tonight is because that petty creature will no doubt insist on calling me *Black Diamond* until she's on her death bed. Second, my dear prince, it appears that, despite rumored manifold experience, you truly don't understand women."

He snorted. "I understand *you*."

"I hardly count. Now, what can you tell me about Countess Duval that I don't already know?"

"You know she owns most of The Musicale House?"

"So I've been told. I've also been told I'm being set up for dramatic failure, since I've revived the popularity of the Rival Theater."

"You don't seem worried, on that count. You didn't even bring your guitar."

As if she could have carried a guitar on horseback. Certainly not with her current, oversized case for it. Besides: "Everyone knows the guitar is my preferred instrument after the Rival and your nameday celebration. Whatever Duval has contrived for tonight, she'll have been sure to make that affinity irrelevant."

"And what are you going to do?"

"Make *her* irrelevant." At least in terms of the woman being any future threat. It was just a shame she was going to have to do it by making the woman's establishment more popular than ever.

The Musicale House was tucked into the artsy section of the main strip of Veralna Hightown, the buildings all crammed in like trees grown too close together. But where trees would intertwine and grow with one another, would take interesting shapes to make the best of what was available to them, the buildings simply pressed against one another, too close and without their neighbor's consent, mirroring the actions of the humans that had created them.

Like humans, the buildings dressed up their flaws. The Musicale House's outer walls were a flawless white, the doors arched and imposing, the walls adorned with musical notes and instruments painted by some now-forgotten hand deemed inconsequential to the final product. She heard absolute silence on the other side of those doors, a sure sign the establishment's owners had paid for sound-proofing spells both to ensure the privacy of their guests, and to ensure that none who had not paid the entrance fee in money and prestige could partake of even the slightest note of what went on inside.

It made her teeth clench, this world of exclusivity and excess, and yet...she needed it. This was where power lay. Financial, hier-archical, magical—it all rested within the bounds of this glittering facade, and she could not do without it. She would not be *made* to do without it. She understood too well what it was to be power-less, to be subject to this world. Trailing along its outskirts was already an infinite improvement, but she did not intend to trail for long.

Someday—somehow—she would become untouchable. And once she was, she would keep that promise of vengeance she'd made to herself when she'd still been a starved, nameless thing, enduring for a dream of something better.

They dismounted, and in retrospect it was a good thing Numair had come after all, because when a woman came up to take the reins of the horses, Clare didn't think she would have been able to hand Kialla's over had Numair not been comfortable doing so. He gently rubbed Kialla's forehead, murmuring an admonishment to, "Behave, little miss," that was followed by a spark of soft magic. Kialla tossed her head and allowed herself to be led off, while Clare watched her go with clenched fists and worry knotting in her stomach.

"She'll be fine," Numair said, his words as gentle as the touch he'd given the horse. "I promise."

She nodded, unbuttoning her coat. Well, it was technically his coat, but she had no intention of reminding him of the fact. He probably had a dozen of them and wouldn't notice this one was missing. It was too fine to return, with its clever spellwork for repelling the elements, and if it fit her more loosely than it did him, it yet fit her well enough.

She finished with the buttons and Numair's gaze traveled over her newly revealed outfit, taking in Chalen's careful work. Neutrally, he asked, "What are you wearing?"

She gave him a smile of pure rapture and answered, "Pants."

They were nothing like the fitted breeches—riding or otherwise —that were not considered elegant enough for female formal wear. These came up high, to the indent of her waist. Across her abdomen the material was heavy and elaborately embroidered—so much so that Chalen had either taken it from a piece already done, or there truly was something of magic in their sewing—giving it the same look as the corseted waist of a dress. While corsets themselves had, thank Ferrian, fallen out of favor, the *look* of them had not.

This replicated the fashionable aspects without physically constraining her movement. It dipped into a slight V between her hips, and here the heavy fabric gave way to one light and delicate, flowing loose almost like skirts but with just enough form to accentuate, before tapering into fitted cuffs at the ankles.

"And a shirt," she added, as if the question he'd asked was meant to be answered in the most literal of terms. Where the pants were the same red as Battle Armor, the shirt—carefully tucked into the waistband of the pants, that it might billow out above like something vaguely pirate-like, were it not for the fine material and elegant embellishments—was black, as were her satin slippers.

"*I'm* wearing pants and a shirt. You're wearing something else entirely." He shook his head, and he sounded half-annoyed when he said, "You look like a damn storybook fantasy. Chalen isn't going to stop sewing for the next decade. You've likely robbed me of my tailor."

"I doubt that. They seem to have a special fondness for you."

"They liked my business, certainly, but I'd wager that's as far as it goes. Now they've plenty other business to keep them going, I imagine I'll fall by the wayside."

"Everyone is not destined to think of you the way the court does," she said softly. Perhaps Chalen's like of Numair was an indulgent one—a kind that overlooked the faults he so heavily displayed and reinforced for the benefit of his public appearance—but that didn't mean they didn't like him. It didn't mean they weren't grateful to him.

But it was easy enough to see, by the twist of Numair's lips and the set of his shoulders, that trying to convince him of it would get her nowhere. Maybe it was easier for him, at this stage, to think that no one ever *could* truly like him.

So she didn't push the subject, letting him lead the way inside.

CHAPTER

THIRTY-NINE

THE MUSICALE HOUSE

An attendant came forward to take their coats, and Clare reluctantly handed hers over. Impulsively, she pressed a coin to the man's hand. "See that it doesn't get lost. It's my favorite." When Numair's lips curved into a smile, she snapped, "What?"

If anything, her snapping seemed to amuse him more. "Nothing. Only, you have excellent taste in outerwear."

So he *did* recognize his coat, then.

Another attendant came forward, her gaze darting to the gemstone hanging from Clare's ear, clearly having been informed to recognize her from it. "Miss Brighton, your patron is in the courtyard." To Numair, she bowed. "Your Highness, we weren't expecting you this evening."

Clare arched an eyebrow at her. "I trust that won't be a problem for you."

The attendant's gaze snapped between Clare and Numair, as if suddenly realizing they hadn't simply happened to walk in at the same time. "You'll be sitting at the countess's table, then?"

At his nod, a flurry of subtle hand gestures followed, and two other members of the staff slipped down a hallway. Presumably to find the requisite seating for Numair's unexpected arrival.

"Right this way."

Their attendant led them through the building and into a stunning outdoor courtyard, although that was, perhaps, too light a word to describe it. Forming a perfect sphere, the courtyard walls soared to twelve-foot heights, formed of interlocking gray stone that had been polished and lacquered to a hypnotizing shine. The ground between was all set floor, a glory of white marble veined with black and gray, the pieces having been fitted together so perfectly that not even Clare's eyes could find the seams. Tables and chairs sprouted from the marble as if they had grown organically from it, the chairs twisting, beautiful creations, the tables supported only by the most fragile looking stem in the center, yet appearing as if they could withstand the weight of centuries.

Tall trees arched between the tables, towering with such perfection that it took Clare a moment to realize they were not living, but only facsimiles carved from colored glass with so much realism that one could almost hear the wind rustle through their inanimate leaves.

The crowning jewel of the courtyard rose in its center, a twisting silver spire ten feet tall. Water spilled from its tip, traveling down veins that branched off from the spire. The veins twisted and spiraled around each other, little notches cut into them here and there, encompassing the main body and forming a latticework of paths, the water following them down to spill into a basin set flush with the ground. Siren rock, in all its glowing, blue-violet glory, lined the bottom of the basin, covered deeply enough under three feet of water that, as the flowing water from the spiraling veins fell into the basin, it elicited only a soft, beautiful lull from the rocks. Enough sound to impart a slender fraction of the hypnotic calm the rocks were known for, but not enough to truly distract.

She wasn't surprised to find winter's chill banished from this outdoor space. A span of days was, it seemed, all it took to accustom her to the ways in which money bought precisely the setting one desired without any of its natural drawbacks. She followed their guide through the courtyard, grateful for the delicate softness of her slippers that allowed her to move silently across the room, a ghost drifting through shadows. The marble floor slid by, perfectly smooth beneath her feet.

A little *too* perfect, a little too smooth. It would look better shattered, Clare thought. But then, so many things did.

The thought brought the hint of a true smile to her lips, and it was still upon her face when their guide stopped before the table closest to the fountain. Its inhabitants had the look of those recently rearranged and irritated about the fact. Somehow, she wasn't surprised to find the Countess Duval—who fit perfectly Alys's description of a pale-skinned, auburn-haired woman in her early fifties—in the company of Madame Aria, Estrella Vane, and Lady Meraland. She was, however, betting that the last woman had been a more recent addition, made after yesterday's events.

The reasons behind the choice of Estrella were obvious, though how the countess had known to go after Madame Aria, Clare didn't know. Clearly, the woman was extraordinarily put out by her sudden inability to afford the Rival Theater, and had gone digging for anyone who might have a grudge against Clare.

She couldn't help but find a small bit of satisfaction in having managed to produce three such individuals for the countess's picking, having been given only a few days to work with. Making enemies was every bit as much an art as music.

When the attendant indicated the seat next to Estrella Vane for Numair, she felt his loathing to take it. The sentiment wasn't anywhere to be seen on his face—no betraying tightening of his mouth or narrowing of his eyes—but she was certain it was there. Just as she was certain he was going to take it anyway.

She blocked his path, turning to him. "You don't mind if I sit next to Miss Vane, do you? The artists really should stick together."

She felt his tension ease, even as he gave her a lopsided smile in what she now fully recognized as his already-pretending-to-be-mildly-tipsy fashion. "Far be it from me to deny a pretty woman anything."

He held the chair out for her, drawing the curiosity of half the damn courtyard. She took it, ignoring the stares, and ignored everyone else at the table in favor of her patron for the evening.

"Countess, you honor me with this invitation." Her voice held just the right amount of sincere earnestness to convince the table she had no idea this was an evening intended to ruin her, and it brought smiles to every woman's face. "It is a pleasure to meet you."

"Oh, I assure you, the pleasure is all mine." Countess Duval flashed her teeth in a slightly predatory manner Clare might have approved of in other circumstances, then turned to Numair. "Though I admit I wasn't expecting to see you in attendance tonight. After you sold me your stake in this establishment, I was under the impression you had no further interest in it."

Somehow, Clare wasn't surprised to learn he'd once owned part of this place.

Numair answered with an air of affected boredom. "I thought it was time I saw what you'd done with the old place. And Miss Brighton sings so prettily, I'm loath to miss a performance."

"Indeed. I seem to recall another young Songweaver you were once loath to miss a performance of." Estrella stiffened, leaving no doubt which Songweaver that had been. The countess smiled at Clare. "The attention of men is so fickle, is it not?"

"For some, perhaps. I can't say I've ever found it to be so."

Irritation laced Estrella's voice as she said, "I'm sure you will find yourself exposed to the experience soon enough."

Clare made a dismissive noise. "I find several people, of late, enjoy telling me which experiences I can look forward to. Frequently, they seem to be wrong." She turned to Madame Aria. "For instance, it seems highly unlikely I'll be begging to sing in the Lowtown's winter festival, despite my choice of master."

She made the dig pointedly, a deliberate show of hubris intended to nettle. She was determined they should all think her walking blindly into the countess's trap. It would make her victory all the sweeter, for its unexpectedness.

"Give it time," Madame Aria said.

A brief lull descended on the table before Lady Meraland said, her voice thick with false sweetness, "We are all so relieved you were able to attend this evening. The most ghastly rumors are circling that you were brutally assaulted earlier today outside the mages' stables."

So considerate of you to broach the subject with such delicacy. She widened her eyes. "Assaulted? Is that really what they're saying?"

"It is."

Clare laughed. "How dreadfully inaccurate the rumor mills are, then."

Estrella took up the thread of the conversation, refusing to let it die so easily. "I also heard it said it was over a horse, of all things. Kialla N'Marani." She turned to Numair. "But I suppose that would be untrue as well? You never loan out your horses."

"All rumors have some truth," Numair answered flippantly.

The Musicale House's staff poured into the courtyard at that moment, bearing trays laden with the evening's dinner and putting a temporary hush on the conversation. The plate set before Clare smelled divine—and contained nothing she could eat. Even if she'd been willing to risk an entire meal shortly before she was to sing, the contents were entirely unsuitable to be consumed prior to a vocal performance.

A thick-cut slice of pork tenderloin in an aromatic wine-and-cream sauce. Thin rounds of potatoes lightly spiced and covered in melted cheese. It was completed with a selection of summer vegetables only a nature mage could have coaxed to grow at this time of year, and these had been lightly breaded and fried to a crisp perfection.

In short, everything a person should avoid if they wanted to sing well. She pretended not to notice, moving things around on her plate to give a show of eating, and could tell which members of the other tables were the singers by who was doing the same. The meal passed with nothing more of substance in the conversation, little barbs traded back and forth disguised as pleasantries, until the servers returned to remove the plates from the tables.

Their own had just been cleared when Lady Meraland said, "I am curious, Miss Brighton, if you would answer a personal question for me." She didn't wait for a response. "I cannot help but wonder what it's like to live under the same roof as the Butcher and the Barbarian."

There was an edge of something more than malice beneath the question. There was an edge of genuine…well, curiosity was too innocent a word for it, but it was along the same lines. It made Clare wonder how much time Verol and Marquin actually spent at court. If they spent any of that time at all interacting in a social capacity, or if they were shadows lurking in every room, more living myths than people.

Given the rapt attention with which the table waited for her to respond, she knew any response she gave would spread like wildfire through a dry forest.

"Well," she said, pretending to consider the question with great seriousness, "so far I've found the meat selection is incomparable, and having heavy objects lifted is never much of a concern."

The women stared at her. Numair broke out laughing. "You're

funny," he said through the laughter. But what he meant was, "Nicely done."

She was saved from further conversation when a smooth, practiced voice rolled over the courtyard. "I welcome you all, this evening, to the Musicale House. For those of you here for the first time, I am Aurelius Mellifis—"

Clare bent her head toward Numair, murmuring, "If that's his real name, I'll forfeit the competition."

He snorted, causing Estrella to throw Clare a withering look, and whispered, "His real name is Howard Carver. He owns the other thirty percent."

Meanwhile, "Aurelius Mellifis" had continued introducing himself.

"—master of this house and host of the Artists Challenge." He stood in front of the fountain spire in a suit of expensive cut and more expensive indigo coloring, his blond hair slicked back against his scalp. He held an ostentatiously ornamented walking stick clasped in one hand in a manner suggesting he longed to twirl it about. The other hand held a time-glass, which he placed in front of the fountain with a grand flourish.

"We have a *unique* challenge for our artists tonight, something truly special. If I could please have all the artists stand, that everyone might see our competitors and the tables of their patronage."

Clare stood, sliding her chair back silently on the marble floor, and gauged her competition. Nine tables other than her own, nine other artists, the contestants split near even on gender. Four of the group were obviously inexperienced at being in the public eye. They fidgeted, or smiled awkwardly, attempting to look at anything other than an actual person. Three were overly confident, bearings haughty, looking slightly bored at the whole affair. Just two other than Clare knew how to properly bear up under the scrutiny. The trick was to pretend you were not under scrutiny. They and Clare stood as if the entire room stood with them; as if they were merely participants in a thing in which everyone present was also a participant. They kept their attention on the announcer, and they neither smiled nor disdained.

"The rules of tonight's challenge are simple: no instruments are allowed, but that does not mean the performance need be *a cappella*, so long as the artists use nothing outside the fountain area. Each artist will have five minutes to set their stage, and the artist whose song is both the most musically diverse and entertaining to the crowd will be deemed tonight's winner."

Silence of a particular quality greeted this announcement, that kind born of a lack of comprehension, in which everyone was aware they *ought to* understand the brilliance of the setup, but no one did. Aurelius looked at Countess Duval, and there was something of anticipated irritation in his face that Clare suspected she knew the source of: he'd deemed the challenge too difficult, but the countess had insisted.

There was a careful line to tread when running an establishment like this. People could, as Clare well knew, find endless enjoyment in watching people fail spectacularly. But only so long as some others succeeded. Watching nine singers fail in a row would grow tiresome. Aurelius was clearly concerned about the effect of such a failure on his business, while Countess Duval had been more interested in Clare's public humiliation. Since the latter owned the majority stake in the business, she'd forced the issue.

"While we typically choose our first artist at random, tonight we have a special treat for you all. You have perhaps heard by now of the black diamond Songweaver who so delighted the audience at the Rival Theater just earlier this week.

"If Miss Clare Brighton would come forward, I am certain her performance tonight will delight you all no less." There was a threat buried under those words as his gaze landed on her, and she saw that, since he could not hold Countess Duval accountable, *she* was to be personally made responsible for anything his business might suffer as a result of this night.

She stood and walked confidently to the fountain.

"Without further ado, then, let us begin." Aurelius dramatically turned the minute-glass, the trickle of sand counting away the seconds of her time. As he walked away he passed close enough to mutter, out of earshot of their audience, "See that you do not embarrass us all."

She was annoyed that her performance *would* save him the embarrassment he so feared. He was a prime example of why she never saved a person unless the doing of it also benefited her; no matter how desperate a person was for the rescue, they were rarely ever grateful for having been saved. Her gaze went briefly to Numair. Did he hate her, just a little, for saving him?

He noticed her looking and arched his eyebrow, reminding her to focus on the task at hand. She had known which song to sing the moment their host revealed the game. Musical diversity was easy enough to come by, if one had range and a broad enough reservoir of songs to draw on. It was easier still given the instruments at her command. Clare walked alongside the fountain, trailing the tips of her fingers atop the pool of water. The small ripples in the basin caused a ripple in the sound that, up to this point, no one in the audience had noticed.

The glow of the siren rock lining the basin flickered with the change in sound, deeper blue here, lighter violet there. Clare reach into the basin's depths and selected five stones, three large and two small. The size of the stone did not, as was a common misconception of siren stones, change the range or pitch the stone could hold. The difference in size simply made it easier for Clare to remember what each was for.

Water fell from the stones as if repelled, and as they dried, they ceased to glow, changing in color from vibrant blue-violet to dull, ordinary rock.

Into the smallest rock, Clare sang a simple fall from a high note directly down to the corresponding one an octave lower, waited five beats and sang it again. She waited ten beats this time, then sang it in reverse, low to high, repeating again after five beats. She waited twenty precious beats of time and sang a short, high note that would blend with the original one she had started the sequence with. The rock continued to look like a rock, which in turn made Clare look like a simple-minded woman singing a melody to said rock. No doubt it was part of the countess's plan that it was nigh impossible to look anything but silly when setting up to sing using siren rock.

Which was the entire reason Clare wasted the first minute of her setup on the one rock she did not really need. Because no matter how well one sang, if the audience spent five minutes thinking one a bore and a fool, it was difficult to overcome.

Clare held the small stone up on tented fingers for the crowd, like a street magician presenting an object for consideration, then fitted it into one of the notches cut into the veins of the fountain's spire. Water flowed down the spire's veins, slipping over the rock and returning the stone to its brilliant blue-violet hue. As the rock glowed brighter, Clare's voice spilled from it to fill the courtyard, the simple transitions she had sung into it playing back, the drawn-out transitions from high to low, then low to high giving the short sounds a gossamer, haunting feel. It held her twenty beats of silence, then emitted the last, short note she had sang before it started over from the beginning, repeating endlessly.

Her audience did not clap—they were the sort of audience that only applauded once, at the end of a show when it was expected of them, and certainly never with any enthusiasm—but they did sit a little taller in their seats, and the bored expressions fell away.

Clare finished with her remaining four stones, singing the longest melody into the largest stone. She sang a different melody into the second and the third, careful to keep the same tempo on each that had gone into the first. In the last she sang transitions similar to those that had gone into the stone that was currently repeating her initial notes into the courtyard.

As the last grains of sand fell into the bottom of the minute glass, Clare removed the first stone from the spire, replaced it with the largest, waited for the fourth note of the melody, and sang.

Entertaining the crowd was a more difficult challenge than mere musical diversity. But while Clare had only ever had to sing to one audience, that one had been as difficult to sing for as if he were a hundred men in one combined, and she recognized the look in this crowd from one of the myriad she had seen in the other person. The people here had no interest in wild abandon, would not have stood to dance even had decorum allowed it. They were unimpressed by anything and of a mindset to stay that way and yet, at the same time, they desperately wanted someone to prove to them that they still *could* be impressed.

She could sing any number of popular songs and they would clap politely at the end, unable to find any real flaw in her performance, but ultimately unmoved by what they had heard dozens of times before. She could sing any number of songs of her own creation, but none of them fit the mood of the setting she found herself in. People seated at expensive tables, wearing expensive clothes and poised to consume expensive food were not in a state of mind to receive songs born either from the depth of her misery or the height of her hopes for something different.

So she came to them in the only way that she could—with a song old enough that most would have forgotten it and yet its soul, its story, was one that all would recognize. She sang, fittingly, of the man for whom the siren rocks had been named. A man whose name had been lost to time, remembered only as the Siren, for his voice and his attitude and his body had been so beautiful that nations courted him.

He denied them all, wishing not to be caught up in the drama of courts, longing only for the solitude of his youth. He fled to the coastal city of his childhood, certain in the safety of the rocky crags that limned the shore, of the unforgiving cliffs by the sea that would surely be his salvation.

When the ships arrived on the coast, Clare fitted the second siren rock into the fountain's spire, a darker, bleaker melody harmonizing with the first, and she sang of war. War over a man who looked out at gathered ships and understood that it would never stop. That he would never know freedom or peace. That blood would spill and flow until there was nothing left.

So the man known to history only as the Siren climbed to the top of the highest cliff and sang, calling ships and people to him. The ships foundered themselves on the cliffside in their eagerness, their desperation, to reach him. They flailed and sank until the next did the same, until ships piled upon ships along the shore and the desperate inside them clawed over one another, fighting each other to scale the cliff upon which the Siren sang.

When the last ship had sunk and men still scrambled up the cliff-sides, Clare removed the first melody and added the third, the two melodies now harmonizing born only of darkness and sorrow, and as the melodies twined together, the horde of scrabbling humanity reached the Siren. He sang even as, in their desperation to own him, the people tore him apart, fighting for a lock of his hair, a chunk of his flesh, a tooth ripped from his gums. And when they had torn him to pieces and set to the work of killing each other for the bits of him in each other's possession, the rocks beneath them, so sorrowed by the Siren's loss, absorbed his voice and continued his song, singing his eulogy until every man and woman that had come for him, had ravaged him, lay dead upon the rocks at each other's hands.

Clare fitted the last siren rock into the spire and a high, keening note filled the courtyard and lingered, fading slowly as the melody drifted into nothingness, their rocks slid neatly from the spire by Clare's nimble fingers. She removed the last rock before the keening note could repeat again and stood, a quiet form in the midst of the utter silence blanketing the courtyard. The audience sat as if the slightest movement would break the world, as if magic bound them in the rigidity of their forms, though Clare had used no power in the song save her own voice, her own talent.

This, the Song whispered, rumbling deep inside her. *This is why I chose you.*

Clare bowed, breaking the stillness, so no one would see the uncertainty the Song's words had awakened. She had perfected the bow, a beautiful blend of a curtsy and a lord's bow, specifically to set off her choice of outfit, the wide, flowing legs of her pants falling pleasantly around her, and she focused on the perfection of it, the smooth elegance, until the uncertainty fled her face.

Rising, her voice soft, demure, she said only, "Thank you," and returned to her table.

As she took her seat she realized she still clutched the siren stones in her hand and she carefully, soundlessly slipped them into her pocket.

CLARE ALMOST PITIED the artists who followed her. She had done them the service of showing them what the siren rocks did, and the disservice of using them so well that none could measure up against her. A few managed them well enough, though not with Clare's complex blend of melodies and complements. The few that tried to match her intricacy were unmitigated disasters, their unfamiliarity with singing against a melody they were not actively in control of, without the little tells and intros provided by other musicians playing them, throwing them out of rhythm. Two did not use the stones at all, as if accepting the failure that would come of it, and simply sang; they did not impress, but they did not embarrass themselves either.

In the silence that followed the last performance, the brief reprieve in which the members of each table wrote their vote on the little card at their place setting and handed it off to the valets coming to collect them, the countess's irritated gaze remained on her the whole time.

She ignored it, playing off Numair to keep the table's attention occupied. When the time came, she accepted the winning of the contest with pretty words and pretty smiles, her face a beacon of shining appreciation for the honor bestowed upon her. She flitted from person to person in the mingling that followed, noting Chalen's careful hand in no less than half a dozen of the garments worn.

She managed, throughout the endless talking, the trading back and forth of words that didn't mean anything and yet could mean too much, to keep Numair with her. He might have to keep up his usual persona, but she hadn't brought him here to throw him to the court wolves that liked to laugh at him to his face, thinking he was too dumb or drunk to notice they weren't laughing *with* him.

When opportunity arose, she nodded him toward the door, but already she could see the vultures following, knew they weren't going to reach the exit before they were accosted again.

She ducked her head closer to him and said, "Should we go out in…interesting style?"

"What exactly did you have in mind?"

She grinned at him, then sang that note she had instinctively known would shatter the floor. She sang it in the softest of whispers, but the lack of volume made no difference to the intensity of the sound, nor to the cold marble floor beneath her feet, which warmed and shattered with alacrity.

In the confusion that followed, they easily slipped out. She snuck only a single backward glance at the floor. She had been right; it *did* look better broken.

FORTY

TWO WORDS HE SHOULDN'T

Numair shed the weight of Veralna's elite as they stepped out of the Musicale House, if he couldn't yet shed the facade he maintained for their benefit. It was for this reason they ambled out of the city at a walk when he wanted to coax the horses to a gallop, to see wildness and adrenaline overtake Clare's face, instead of the melancholy that had settled there in place of the triumph he would have expected.

She had been spectacular. He had expected no less, and yet she still managed to knock the wind from him every time she opened her mouth. He'd heard the Siren's song before, though it had been years, but he'd never heard it like that. As if every emotion and longing and daring had been drilled into his soul.

They rode past a street musician, her violin case open on the street before her as she played. Abruptly, Clare turned back, deftly loosing her hair to cover the identifying gemstone in her ear. Which was illegal, but he certainly wasn't going to report her.

He followed her lead, staying behind her and hunching his shoulders in that way that could make people look past him. He hated being recognized, and he'd become adept at avoiding it outside the palace. He wondered why Clare had chosen to stop now. They had already passed half-a-dozen such performers, and try as he might, he could find nothing more distinguishing about this one than any of the others.

While she watched the violinist, he watched her face. It was bereft of most expression, showing neither appreciation nor dislike, only a cool calculation. The song finished with a final draw of the bow across the strings and Clare dismounted, a coin in her hand that was far more than any street musician could expect to find tossed into their case at random.

"A beautiful song."

The violinist murmured a soft *thank you* and watched warily as Clare held that coin balanced on her thumb, ready to flick into the case.

"But not perhaps worth quite so much as this, without a word or two spoken as well."

"What kind of words?" she asked warily.

"I'm curious where musicians such as yourself go when they want to…associate with their peers."

The woman hesitated, eyes trained on the coin. "The Musicians Guild has several meeting halls open to its members."

"Ah, but I asked about musicians like you. And you can't afford the Musicians Guild."

Color stained the woman's cheeks—anger, he thought, rather than embarrassment. Perhaps that was why Clare had chosen this one, recognizing a kindred spirit.

"Why do you want to know?"

"I sing a little myself."

"You can afford the Musicians Guild." The words were a little accusatory and a lot bitter.

"I couldn't four days ago. And I'm afraid its mistress made a rather…unfortunate impression on me."

"So, what? You want to associate with us out of spite?"

Clare shrugged. "Something like that."

The woman hesitated.

"I can find it myself"—Clare walked the coin across her fingers before returning it to its prior place atop her thumb—"but it's more lucrative for you if you part with the information."

A hardness snapped into the woman's eyes. "Counteroffer. If you still want to go in two days, I'll take you myself. But you pay now."

"Paying now is a fool's bargain." Clare flipped her the coin. "But I'll make it just this once. What's your name?"

"Amarrah."

"I'll meet you here, two days from tonight, Amarrah." She remounted Kialla and turned. Numair followed, waiting until they were well enough away from the violinist to speak.

"Why her and not the others?"

Clare shrugged. "She was younger and prettier."

To anyone else, it would have sounded like a shallow reason. But he understood her well enough. Understood that often, younger and prettier meant more vulnerable.

"You know she wanted two days so she can warn them all off from you, yes?"

"It's to be expected."

"Then why not find them on your own? Going like this—they'll know you don't belong in their circles."

She didn't answer for several strides, enough of them that he thought she wouldn't. "Because they would eventually put together who I am, even if I tried to hide it." The corner of her lip twitched. "I'm not so good at wearing different faces as you are. It would eventually come out and they wouldn't trust me. They won't trust me this way, either, but they won't be able to feel betrayed. And if word starts circulating that the Black Diamond prefers to spend her time with musicians of no affiliation and refuses to pay any dues to the Musicians Guild, well, I wouldn't terribly mind that."

He shook his head. "Be careful. No matter how long a stick you use to poke that hornet's nest, Madame Aria has a long reach, within the city *and* the Mages Guild. She can be vindictive."

Clare's lips settled into a cold smile. "So can I."

He didn't try to talk her out of it. She wouldn't bend or be persuaded. But unease coiled in his stomach. For a woman who'd come here determined to move up in rank, she seemed equally determined to make as many enemies as possible along the way.

He admired the blunt honesty of her approach—she was unapologetically herself, though he suspected most people would never realize that—even as he wondered how much difficulty it would cause her. He and the Arrendons could only protect her so far. He was limited by the constraints of his role, one he already stepped too far outside of simply by associating with her. The Arrendons were frequently gone, and the members of the Mages Guild disliked them almost as much as they feared them. If they thought they could get at the Arrendons by getting at Clare, they would.

But he suspected if he said any of that, she would only tell him she didn't need anyone's protection.

They passed a mural painted on the wall of one of the nearby buildings and Clare halted Kialla, her eyes going over the vivid strokes of green and red that so perfectly brought the flowering bush they depicted to life.

"It's beautiful." She said it as if it was an indictment. "I like beautiful things. Even if I shouldn't."

He nudged Hellack closer alongside her. "Why shouldn't you?"

"Because they never last. You have to make them ugly, just a little, if you want them to endure."

She wasn't talking about things anymore, he knew. Her fingers had curled into fists around the reins, and there was a hardness in her voice, an anger that didn't want to be tempered.

"Do you want one?" he found himself blurting out.

She looked at him, startling out of that anger. "A mural?"

He shook his head. "How do you feel about taking a detour?" He didn't wait for her to answer, nudging Hellack into a canter and trusting she would follow. They reached his estate soon enough and he dismounted, leaving Clare with a quick, "I'll be right back."

He went in, down the stairs to the basement level, where the rooms were cool and dry and spelled to keep out unwanted moisture. Cabinets lined the walls, hundreds upon hundreds of small drawers, all meticulously labeled. He searched until he found the one he wanted, slipping an envelope of seeds into his pocket before grabbing a small trowel and running back outside, half convinced he'd find Hellack waiting and Clare gone.

But she was still there, wry amusement on her face at his enthusiasm as he mounted Hellack and led them back toward the Arrendons' estate.

"Dare I ask what we're doing?"

"It's a surprise."

"I never like surprises," she muttered. But she didn't argue as she followed his lead.

Outside the Arrendons' manor he asked, "Which window is yours?"

She humored him, pointing out the right one and crouching beside him in front of it. He handed her the trowel.

"What am I meant to do with this?"

"It's a digging implement. One imagines you dig with it."

"One imagines it's also great for hitting princes upside the head with."

"I think you've already caused me enough physical injury for one friendship. And all I ask in return is a *tiny* bit of digging."

"It was *one* throat punch," she objected. "Why am I the one digging?"

Because he wanted to grow something with her. Something beautiful that didn't have to be made ugly to endure.

"Because it's going to be yours. You should have a hand in making it."

She shoved the trowel into the ground, following his instructions on depth with all the good nature of a snarling wolf. He sprinkled the seeds in, gently covered them with the loose dirt. He indicated her hand. "Can I?"

When she nodded, he placed her hand on the ground, covering it with his own. His magic swept through him, through her, reaching to the seeds below. He woke them from their dormancy, coaxing them to sprout, roots burrowing down, growth shooting upwards, breaking the soil, forming stems and leaves and buds.

The bush grew, two feet, then four, the leaves halting just below the sill of her window, the buds bursting open into the lush, red flowers that had been painted on the city mural. Trumpet-like in shape, with five petals, the blooms as wide as his hand.

Carefully, as if afraid she would break it, she stretched her free hand to brush one of the velvet petals. "What are they?"

"Hibiscus. It's from one of the old continents." One that no longer existed, because of Alaric.

She dropped her fingers from the flower. "Why did you grow it?"

That was the question, wasn't it? "Because not everything beautiful has to be marred."

The response seemed to irritate her, and her next words were harsh. "Then it's just going to die."

"I won't let it." Not with his magic feeding it every week. Not when it felt so good to create something again. He looked down, where his hand still covered hers, and some of the high of the feeling left him.

This was dangerous. *She* was dangerous. Not for the reasons she'd warned him of, but still. He shouldn't have come tonight. But he had, and while he was making poor life choices, he plucked one of the flowers and offered it to her, along with two words he shouldn't. "I promise."

CHAPTER

FORTY-ONE

THE LIBRARY IS ON THE GROUND FLOOR

Clare woke to the hibiscus flower staring her in the face from the bedside table, a spot of vivid redness floating in the sea of dark browns and blacks that formed the rest of the room's interior. She'd expected to find it wilting, its decay evidence of her point on the ephemeral nature of beauty.

But it was as plump and unblemished as when Numair had plucked it from the bush, a thread of his magic lingering in its petals, as if he was as determined to prove his own point as she. Curiosity got the better of her and she leaned in to sniff it, disappointed to find it hardly smelled like anything at all. A hint of sweetness, nothing more.

She sat up and cupped it in her palm, transferring it to the drawer of the bedside table, where it nestled beside the still-unopened red envelope Numair had sent with Battle Armor. "Give it time," she told the flower as she slid the drawer closed. "You'll wither and die just like the rest of us."

She dressed and went into the common room. Two things waited for her on the center table. The first was a large wrapped package that proved to contain the first delivery of her clothes from Chalen. The second was a breakfast tray. A tented card rested on it beside the plates and cups. She flicked it open, stared at the scribbles in the bold handwriting she guessed was Marquin's, and growled at the incomprehensible lines. The Song was of no help—she only felt its presence now whenever she stepped outside the palace grounds, so intent was it on hiding in Alaric's presence—and she wondered if it would be such a terrible thing if she admitted to Verol and Marquin that she couldn't read.

A knock on theirs and Fitz's door proved no one was home. The emptiness bothered her in a way emptiness never had before. All her life, emptiness had been an indicator of safety. People couldn't hurt you if they weren't around. The problem, she decided, was that she wasn't afraid of Marquin or Verol or Fitz. And because she wasn't, and because this space was meant to contain them, it felt... lonely, for them not to be here. As if they'd abandoned it.

She carried the tray and the letter into her room and closed the door. Two hours of pouring over Numair's rudimentary reading books and sounding things out later, she managed to decipher the letter.

Verol is in meetings with the king all morning. I have errands to run but I will meet you at the manor at noon, as agreed, for your first lesson. - M

She glanced at the clock—time, at least, was something she could read just fine—and realized with a start that she'd slept in far later than she'd realized. She'd returned late last night, and woken frequently throughout it in little fits and starts. So much of her life had been spent sleeping in stolen snatches of time that the concept of sleeping through the night entirely was foreign to her. She felt safest sleeping in the day, and she'd only settled into true rest sometime around dawn.

All of which meant she needed to leave. Now. She put on the riding breeches and shirt she'd worn two days ago and then, after careful consideration of the items Chalen had delivered, packed a more elaborate outfit for her ride with the proconsul of Taella later that day.

She'd hardly stepped into the hall when she ran into Lady Meraland. Or rather, Lady Meraland ran into *her.* Upon exiting the room, Clare had stopped with the perfect grace and reaction time of someone well-accustomed to being held responsible for any physical mishap. Lady Meraland had kept walking, straight into Clare, and then stumbled back when Clare planted her feet and held her ground.

Clare prepared herself for a tirade of noble outrage but Lady

Meraland—she really had to learn her first name—only stood there with a dazed, confused look on her face, as if finding it impossible to puzzle out what had halted her forward motion. She looked… vacant. As if something had reached inside and hollowed out a part of her, and she was temporarily stunned by the loss.

Grudgingly, Clare asked, "Are you all right?"

Lady Meraland blinked, startled, as if just noticing Clare. But it was as if she'd noticed only the question, and not the person who'd asked it. No hint of antipathy, or even of true recognition, showed on the woman's face.

"I went somewhere I wasn't supposed to." Her voice was smooth and honey-sweet, almost childlike in its cadence.

"Where?"

"I don't remember. Now I must return to my room, and lie down, and in a few hours it won't trouble me." This explanation given, she resumed her forward motion. Clare stepped out of the way just in time, a frown furrowing her brows as she watched the woman walk serenely down the hall, disappearing through a door several rooms down from the Arrendons'.

She took a step towards that door before shaking herself and continuing on her original path. Lady Meraland—and whatever in Ferrian's name was wrong with her—was not Clare's problem. She descended the stairs, intent on reaching the ground floor, but raised voices caught her ear on the landing to the second. She might not have paid them any mind at present—Numair's tour had revealed most of the rooms in this area were for matters of state and business—had she not been fairly certain that one of the voices was Verol's. And there was something about Lady Meraland just now—her confusion and her placid explanation that she would soon be untroubled by whatever had happened—that made Clare suspect Verol's hand in the matter.

A quick glance showed the area otherwise deserted, and she walked on quiet feet toward the sounds of argument. But though she reached the correct door, her proximity to it did not make the words on the other side any clearer. They were garbled, so much so that the words were completely unintelligible, and she felt the hand of magic in the obfuscation. That the one's voice was Verol's, she was certain, and she held little doubt about who the second's belonged to.

The sense of risk thus heightened—and nothing to be gained from the venture—she retreated. She had taken four steps when the door opened behind her. She kept her speed precisely the same, nothing in her step or manner to indicate the increase in her heart rate the door's opening caused. She could be any woman wandering these halls. There was no reason for him to notice her, no reason to fear that—

"Miss Brighton," Alaric called. Nothing more. Only her name.

She could keep walking. There was nothing to say the name was a command, rather than a question as to her identity. Surely the palace boasted dozens of brown-haired girls of her height and build. Except that *everything* the king said was a command, and any one of those other brown-haired girls would have stopped, whether they'd ever heard the name *Miss Brighton* or not.

She stopped and turned, granting him the bow that was his due, and trying to ignore the oily rot of foul magic that slicked off him in waves. How did everyone in this place stand it? Or was she the only one so blessed as to feel its taint?

"Clare." Verol's brow furrowed. "What are you doing here?"

"Well," she said, affecting a chastising manner, "as *someone* left me without a proper tour, I got turned around looking for the library."

"I was under the impression my nephew spent some time showing you the palace." Alaric's words and the tone he spoke them with were pure artwork. So lightly delivered, and yet the intended interrogation in them could not be mistaken.

"Indeed, Your Majesty. Forgive my saying so, but I am afraid your nephew is not the most thorough guide. Especially when he's a bottle of wine into the afternoon."

"Yet I imagine even then he's capable of recalling that the library is on the ground floor." He studied her. "I hadn't realized you were an accomplished reader."

She told herself it was only her own fears that made that statement sound like he *knew* she couldn't read. "I imagine there are a great many things you haven't realized about me, Your Majesty."

"Perhaps I should correct the oversight."

Her heart beat faster in her chest. Her voice remained steady. "That is certainly your prerogative, though I fear that after a few hours spent at the task, you would find my company rather boring. The library was on the ground floor, you said?"

"Yes," Verol answered, "but you haven't time to peruse it. You are, if I am not much mistaken, already late for your meeting with Marquin."

"Of course." She took the provided excuse for a hasty exit and made it. But she felt Alaric's gaze boring into her back, and when one of those foul tendrils of magic snaked after her, licking at the skin of her hand, she *almost* jumped.

CLARE'S HEART was still pounding out an erratic rhythm as she fled to the stables. Much to the relief—and consternation—of the stablehands, she brushed and saddled Kialla herself, the task quieting her scrambling thoughts. She could still feel the oil-slick of Alaric's magic against the outside of her right hand, and she longed to scrub at it until she tore the skin off.

It was ridiculous. He hadn't left anything behind. It had been an inquiring touch, likely to see if she was sensitive enough to notice it, there and then gone in a flicker of time. He was curious about her— because she was Verol's apprentice, and because of whatever knowledge had prompted him to build himself a white throne and her a white room.

He was waiting to see if she would flinch. So she wouldn't.

She mounted Kialla, riding down the path that led to the road out of the palace, and found Fitz waiting for her just beyond the Inner Gate. She glared at him as she passed through, but he nudged his chestnut gelding into step beside her despite it. She wondered if her glare had lost some of its unhinged ferocity since she'd left Renault County, or if Fitz's disdain for her simply made the look bounce off him.

They ambled in silence down the road, moving through the Outer Gate, and she would have happily continued the entire journey in that state. It wasn't that far of a ride, and she was curious to find out if his ability to maintain a silence was as strong as her own. Clearly, it wasn't.

"Verol thinks you need protecting," he said finally.

"Verol, if he had his way, would no doubt wrap me in silk

packing and hide me in a room somewhere until I died of boredom."

"There are worse things in this world than being bored."

She turned a dazzling smile on him. "And how many of those worse things have you perpetrated, assassin?" It was a guess, based on nothing more than the way he moved and watched people.

His jaw clenched. "Verol told you?"

"No, you just did." At the surprised look that flashed across his face she snapped, "I can't be both a conniving bitch here to take advantage of the Arrendons *and* a simpering idiot. Stop judging my intelligence by your general dislike of me. And while you're at it, why don't you go back to murdering people and leave me alone?"

"Can't," he deadpanned. "I made Verol a promise."

"Because of poor, sweet, dead little Marie?"

His eyes flashed with anger. "Because she should have lived and Alaric killed her. Because if anyone can kill *him*, it's you."

She sat back so abruptly, Kialla stopped walking. "I am not here to seek vengeance for your lost would-be sister." She had her own vengeance to see to, and she still hadn't the faintest idea how to accomplish *that*. If Alaric was stronger than the monster she'd left behind... "I am not here to kill him for you."

"I think you'll find, once enough time passes, that he'll leave you little choice but to try. Whether you succeed..." He shrugged. "Well, either you will, or you'll be dead and I won't have to look at you and think of her anymore."

They finished the ride in silence after that, and Clare couldn't stop the niggling doubt now worrying at the back of her mind. The doubt that maybe, just maybe, the Arrendons didn't want to protect her. That maybe she was nothing more than a weapon, in need of care and honing before it was pointed at a previously unkillable target.

Except...Verol *would* hide her away for all eternity if he could. And though she was less sure of Marquin's altruism where she was concerned, he hadn't prevented her from leaving them when they'd first arrived in Veralna, when he'd known all along what she was. They were doing everything wrong, if they wanted to use her.

And yet the doubt remained. She was too much a product of her past for it to not.

CHAPTER

FORTY-TWO

MAGIC LESSONS

Clare, settled cross-legged on the floor opposite Marquin, furrowed her brow and attempted to do as he instructed. As she had been attempting to do for the last hour.

As first lessons went, the day had been a dismal failure, beginning with her balking at the door to the quiet little room they now sat in. Power soaked deep into every inch of the walls, thrumming along the textured stone, stretching across the gaps from door to frame, and reaching up from the floor to caress the feet that walked across soft wooden planks.

She had understood instinctively that it was a room designed to contain, and no matter how patiently Marquin explained that its purpose was to contain power, not people, she could still only think of it as a cage. It had taken her half an hour to force herself inside, and her subsequent attempts to focus on the lesson had been hampered by her general discomfort. It did not help that the Song also disliked the room, if for reasons far different from her own.

Clare feared the possibility of being trapped. The Song held in utter contempt the room's belief that the Song could be held. Clare felt its scorn as if it spoke to her.

Did Marquin really think these pathetic walls could hold *it*? It longed to show him how very wrong he was, and a headache thrummed against Clare's temples from holding it in check.

"This isn't working," she growled. And waited. Waited for

Marquin to tell her she was too impatient, that mastery required time. Waited for him to tell her that she was untrained and so could not possibly know if something was working or not. She waited for dismissal.

"Power has a vibrancy to it, a cadence in the bones that any mage can feel in another," Marquin said slowly, instead. "Over time, a mage may learn to mute that power—to disguise to any curious eyes precisely how much power they have. But they can never disguise, entirely, the fact that they *have* power. Anyone magic-born can feel it. Do you know what I feel when I am around you?"

Her silence was his only prompt.

"Nothing. To mage-sense, standing next to you is akin to dangling one's toes off the precipice of some great abyss. Were it not for the unique nature of Verol's Kinthing, I would never have presumed you possessed power at a casual glance.

"Your problem," he said, softly, "is not that you need to be taught control. Your control is ironclad. You problem is that when that control breaks, you do not know how to negotiate."

"Negotiate," Clare repeated, the word tumbling through her teeth like gravel in a churn-bucket.

"Power cannot be contained infinitely. You must give it an outlet, or it will force its way free. The stronger the power is, and the longer it is contained, the more damaging those outbreaks will be. When yours breaks free, your instinct is to contain it again, when you should be trying to shape it."

"Shape it?"

"Bend it to your will, if you like. Choose what you want it to do."

"And how do I do that?"

"You have to *let* it out, rather than it breaking out. You don't have to let out much. The barest spark will do for the purpose of this lesson."

"I don't think that is a good idea."

"Why?"

"Because I don't think," Clare said, choosing her words carefully, "that you understand what a spark can *do*. What it *wants* to do."

Marquin frowned. "You have let it out before to specific results. No one could call the actions at the mages' stables random."

"No." Clare swallowed. "They were not *random*, but..."

"But?"

"The Song and I were in accord at the time. We were angered by the same thing. We wanted the same things."

"And you are not in accord now?"

"No."

"What does it want?"

"To destroy this room."

"And what do you want?"

"Nothing."

"Nothing?"

"I want to be left alone." *I want to be free, but freedom doesn't exist.*

"You want the power itself to leave you alone?"

I want everything to leave me alone.

The smell of the marsh invaded her nostrils. Thick, squelching mud and the brittle crack of bones beneath bare feet. The long, piercing cry of a loon, as if to say, *That was alone. Did you like it so much?*

She shrugged the memory off. "Does it matter?"

It was dangerous, this freedom to speak as she pleased.

Marquin sensed her shutting down and returned to the previous subject. "And when you are not in accord, you have no trouble holding the power in check? It is only when you want what it wants that you lose your grip on it?"

"Not exactly." Clare thought on the puzzle, and that was new enough. She avoided thinking about the Song as much as possible, wary her thoughts might call it forth.

"Anger," Clare breathed. That had been the catalyst, had it not? That moment in a wet, filthy room in Renault County, her stomach squeezing itself to death from hunger, the air outside too frigid to sleep in the relative safety of hidden outdoor hovels, her grip on the shard of mirror in her hands turning frozen, knowing the escape she had effected would be short-lived, and she would be found and taken back to him.

And when the latest threat had approached, her limbs had been too rigidly locked in place to move. She had waited for the fear, but it had refused to come, and in its place had risen nineteen winters of repressed rage. Anger she had been too scared to feel because fear kept you alive, kept you moving even as if it fed on you, but anger…

Anger was your own recognition that the whole of your life was a series of injustices not of your own making and well, how could you live acknowledging that if you couldn't *do* anything about it?

In her memory a hand reached out and plucked the excuse-for-a-knife from Clare's motionless fingers. Rage rose like the flames of Ferrian's fires, and a younger Clare opened her mouth and *screamed*, the sound harsh and hoarse. The careful tethers inside her had snapped, loosing the Song on a Renault County ill-equipped to withstand the force of its regard.

Clare jerked backed to the present, gained her feet and bowed to Marquin with all the formality she possessed. "Thank you. This has been most instructive."

Marquin frowned. "Clare, I have not really taught you anything," he began, but she was already striding from the room, following the curves of hallways that led her to the back patio door, out into the cool winter sunshine, feet taking her to the ancient tree whose brokenness had so profoundly bothered her upon her arrival.

She closed her eyes and fell inward until she came to press against the walls of the cage she had built for the Song. She could not open the door because, should it allow her to enter, so too would it allow the Song to leave. She traced invisible fingers along the walls, envisioning those walls as a specific substance, one that would allow *her* to move through it, but would not allow the Song the same privilege. The walls turned liquid, enveloping her, accepting her into their bounds and depositing her on the other side.

Darkness. Emptiness, and the unfeeling cold of a power a thousand times more ancient than the tree before her.

All of this, and…surprise?

You came to see me? Its voice, raw and unfiltered by the layers of its prison, hit Clare with the force of high tide crashing against Renault County's cliffsides. *Why?*

She buckled under the force, ears ringing as she answered. *Fix it.* She gave it, without quite knowing how, the image of the tree.

Let me out, and I will.

No.

Then why would I help you, little one?

Because you are lonely.

A soft sigh of air in the motionless void. *If I help you, you will leave and I will be lonely again.*

Help me, Clare answered, *now and in the future, and I will not shut out your voice again. I will listen, though I may not speak, and my sight will be your sight.*

For she did understand, now, walking into this place inside of herself, what she had done to the Song. Unable to see the world, its voice falling only on her own deaf ears, able only to feel what she felt, and of the things she felt, only anger was strong enough for it to latch onto and temporarily break the bonds of its confinement.

Clare had forced it to live as she had lived. But she was walking a small path from the darkness, and perhaps she should take it with her. Because if Marquin was right, she couldn't keep it contained forever.

A long, ponderous silence filled the prison, then a spark of light blossomed in the abyss.

Take this, then, and let us see.

Clare clutched invisible fingers around the spark and traveled up, out of the darkness. As she breached the walls of the cavern she trailed behind her a thin line from the spark, a channel from the prison to her mind.

Clare opened her eyes to sunshine and an ancient, dying tree. Warmth fluttered and squirmed in the palm of her hand, and the presence of the Song looked out behind her eyes.

Place it on the tree.

Outside of herself the Song's voice was blessedly muted, featherlight inside her mind where its voice, when they were both inside its prison, had been a roar.

She stepped forward and placed the squirming warmth against the silver trunk. The earth groaned and the tree shook. Roots gone dormant long ago woke and burrowed, old leaves cascading to the ground as new ones grew. Bark knitted across the trunk's horrible cleft, sealing over the festering wound, expelling a stink of blackened, septic sap before it closed over entirely, hale and hardy.

She stood, the soft wind teasing at the edges of her hair, the silver of the tree's bark gleaming in the sun, and felt an odd sense of peace.

"Clare." Marquin's voice, unsteady. "What have you done?"

"As you instructed. I negotiated."

Marquin watched Clare disappear into the house, mixed feelings of pride and dread inside chest. Had he helped the woman, or simply damned them all? He pressed his hand in wonder against the warm bark of the tree, now whole and thriving.

The tree that had been slowly dying for the last twenty-one winters, its sickness beginning the day the last girl to bear Clare's power had been buried beneath it.

He closed his eyes, felt the power echoing beneath the bark, and knew everything he and Verol had done up to this point would not be enough. That however much Verol hoped otherwise, she was too strong to be hidden forever.

But was she strong enough to kill a man who had made himself more god than king?

CHAPTER

FORTY-THREE

THE OFFICIAL TITLE

Clare's awareness of the Song's gaze, looking out at the world alongside her own, gave her vertigo. Given that she was due to go riding with the Taellan proconsul in less than an hour and could barely walk straight, this was problematic.

I could fix it for you, the Song offered.

I don't need your help. She thought the words more harshly than the offer warranted. Felt the Song's mirth as its laughter rumbled through her.

Is not my help precisely what you made this bargain for?

Yes. When I ask for it.

And I am never to offer?

I don't trust your offers.

You do not trust me at all.

Clare stopped trying to walk and pressed one hand to the hallway outside her room for support. *Is there some reason why I should?*

I have saved your life. Each word was a soft brush against her mind, a gentle caress. *More than once.*

Clare shook her head. *You saved yourself. Do me a favor, Song, and keep your offers and your opinions to yourself for a bit. The last thing I need is Proconsul Miriam thinking I am insane.*

She's going to think you're drunk if you cannot walk better than that. I shudder to consider how you will stay on the horse.

She didn't have double-vision precisely—she was not *seeing* the Song's sight as if it were alongside her own—it was more that she *felt* its sight, slightly out of step with her own, and the awareness tilted her off-balance. Clare gritted her teeth and focused on *her* vision, on remembering the way it felt, honing in on it until her awareness of the Song was only a faint buzz in the background of her senses.

It gave her a splitting headache, but she managed to straighten and walk steadily into her room. The hibiscus plant crowding the glass of her window caught her attention. She'd avoided looking at it, when she'd ridden in, had done the same when she'd tossed her clothes in here before settling down to work with Marquin.

But now... She walked to the window, flipping the latches and sliding it open. The plant was as hale and beautiful as when Numair had first coaxed it from the earth. She could still remember the feel of his magic flowing through her into the ground. She'd never felt anything that pure, and the memory of it finally banished the phantom touch of Alaric's magic from that same hand.

On impulse, she plucked four flowers before closing the window. After changing, she wove one of the flowers into her hair, so it rested above her left ear, a deep red contrast to the black diamond below it. The others she took with her to the stable and, braiding Kialla's mane into a sleek plait down the crest of her neck, wove the other flowers in to match.

When Clare approached with the pad and saddle, Kialla decided she wasn't in the mood for them. She shifted as much as her tied rope allowed, swinging her hindquarters from one side of the fence to the other. Clare got the pad on, only to have it dislodged by the mare's constant shifting each time Clare stopped holding her still long enough to reach for the saddle.

Eventually Clare put her foot down—letting Kialla determine fully what she would or would not allow was a recipe for disaster. If she thought she was the more dominant of the two of them, she would fight Clare at every opportunity, and when push came to shove, she wouldn't trust her. But dominance—leadership—didn't have to come from harshness. So Clare wasn't harsh, but she *was* firm, and Kialla settled and let the saddle be placed with a sigh.

"There, that wasn't so bad, was it?" Clare murmured as she finished tightening the girth. Kialla blew out a long breath that fluttered her lips. "But since you so obviously *aren't* in the mood, you can go without it today."

Clare wasn't much in the mood for the restraint of the saddle either, so she removed it with quick efficiency. "But you get to explain to His Princeliness if he asks where his expensive tack wandered off to."

"Is 'His Princeliness' the official title these days?" Alys had come up some time in the middle of Clare's argument with the horse, and she leaned now with her forearms on the wooden fence railing.

"Yes." Clare carted the saddle toward the gate.

"You can leave it on the fence, I'll put it in the tack room."

Clare did. Divested of gear, she was left on display for Alys's perusal. It was a thorough perusal, one that took in both her, her outfit, the hibiscus flower in her hair, and then subjected Kialla to the same inspection before snapping back to Clare with a snort. "You look like you're riding off to be the flower goddess's virgin bride."

She wore a pair of dove gray riding breeches Chalen had embroidered with what could have been maiden's breath-on-the-vine, or artistic daggers, depending on visual interpretation. Clare appreciated the ambiguity. She also appreciated that the pants were spelled against wear, and to shed the dirt that would otherwise cling to her after a bareback ride. Even if the cost of such attributes had made her head spin at the time of commission. Her riding shirt was a gray-blue festooned with enough fashionable embellishments to hide its practical nature, and it contrasted nicely with the rich darkness of her hair.

She had chosen the ensemble with care, to evoke just the type of innocent correlation Alys had made.

"I had no idea Veralna had a flower goddess."

"It doesn't. But if it did, you'd look like her virgin bride." She stepped next to Clare, pulling a length of fine, slender brown ribbon from her pocket, from which dangled a delicate, filigreed clasp for holding small letters or mementos. "Many people ride the king's trails this day of the month."

"So I have heard."

"You owe me a favor."

"So I do."

"Wear this today." Alys wrapped the ribbon deftly around Clare's left wrist, tying it on the underside in a pretty knot that Clare studied with an eye towards being able to reproduce.

"Only wear it?"

"Yes. Unless the right person comes along, in which case I trust you to ensure that there are no misunderstandings."

"A difficult order as I've no idea who the person might be, or what they might misunderstand."

"You'll figure out what you need to know." A delicate shrug. "Or you won't, in which case I have grossly over-estimated your intelligence and made a poor bargain for your services." She hoisted Kialla's discarded saddle and pad into her arms and walked away.

Clare watched her go, realizing with a start that the unfamiliar feeling echoing through her was sheer, unadulterated amusement. She *liked* Alys, she realized. She didn't trust her, but she liked her.

Miriam Aula, the proconsul of Taella, rode a smart little bay mare, fourteen hands at the most, by Clare's guess, with a narrow, fine-boned face and a pretty white star between her eyes. Kialla greeted the mare nose-to-nose, trading breaths as horses were wont to do, her neck arched and nostrils flared. No doubt she would have proceeded to posture and squeal in typical mare fashion had Clare not settled her with a firm but gentle hand.

"It seems they are taking each other's mettle." The proconsul laughed, her voice melodious and deceptively soft.

"As do their riders."

Miriam Aula smiled, and it was all bone-white teeth against deep black skin. "And do I measure up to your scrutiny?"

"We both know the real question," Clare answered, "is do I measure up to yours?"

Miriam tilted her head in what could have been acknowledgment and nudged her mount down one of the palace's many riding paths. The acreage on this side, between the inner and outer walls, was all carefully curated, and the bay picked her way delicately down a trail that, though Clare hadn't the faintest idea what the signpost for it read, she assumed was something like Butterfly Trail, given the painted insects dotting the sign. Not that she expected to see any of the pretty fliers at this time of year.

"You know, I was very much like you once." Miriam stroked her hand absently against the bay's neck, the mare's head lowering fractionally under what was obviously a familiar touch.

Clare waited for the woman to elaborate. The phrase did not, to Clare's mind, mean much of anything at all. It was natural for people to see themselves in others, and easy enough for a smart person to know that saying as much made most people feel as if they had been approved of in some way. In the end, what might or might not be useful to Clare was *what* self-reflection the woman saw in her.

"Did you know that Marquin Delaun—Marquin Arrendon, now —hails from my province?"

"I did not."

"Our paths never crossed in Taella, but here at court we have become allies. And friends, of a sort. Here, where I have none of my own people with me, he is a comfort."

Clare wondered *why* the proconsul had none of her people here. The bringing of them, she was certain, was not prohibited by the king's requirements.

"Do you know what they call him here? What they whisper behind his and Lord Verol's backs?"

"Yes." A simple answer, no curiosity or anger, though Clare felt both, and it caused Miriam to look up sharply.

"It is how the court thinks of Taellans, you know. As barbarians."

"Why?" A question as simple as her previous answer had been, and Clare could tell it grated on the woman a little. But in the end, the proconsul chose to be indulgent.

"When Alaric came for our province, his soldiers outnumbered our warriors ten to one. By the time he finally took my kingdom we had narrowed that difference to five to one." Miriam flashed Clare a grin. "We terrify them, Miss Brighton. And they are horrified that our women fight alongside the men."

"Did you?"

Miriam's face shuttered. "I wanted to. But I was fifteen at the time, and my parents refused to allow it." Her voice deepened with old rage and sorrow. "Alaric slit their throats in front of me, and then he told me I had a choice. He could do the same to every one of my people, or I could swear fealty to Veralna and take up the mantle of proconsul."

"You saved your people."

Miriam's fingers tightened into a fist in her horse's mane. "I enslaved them to a monster. And they allowed it because their new Majiin told them to."

"You *were* fifteen," Clare pointed out.

"Indeed. Has telling yourself the age you were when you did something ever helped you to sleep at night?"

"No. Why are you telling me this?"

The proconsul sighed. "For one, because it seems one talks more than one means to around you. As for the other....it has been a long time since Verol took an apprentice." Meaning, in those words, but easily missed if one didn't know what they referred to. "I want you to know that our king is the true barbarian, the true butcher. Now that the world is his, he wants to make a new image of himself.

"He wants us to think of him as some benevolent unifier. He wants us to *appreciate* what he's done, as if now that the bloodshed is over we ought to be grateful. He wants to be loved. I want *you* to remember that no matter how eloquently he speaks or how he talks of peace and prosperity, his throne is soaked in the blood of my people and every other province in this land. I want you to remember that however tame a jackal may look, it always bites in the end."

Clare mulled it over before asking, cautiously, "And why do you feel I should be the recipient of this...information?"

"Because you're *Verol's* apprentice." The implication was all too clear. So this was why Miriam had invited her to ride, then.

Fingers of ice wrapped around Clare's spine. Miriam might have had no fear of talking of the king so openly, but Clare had not forgotten in whose forest they rode, and the last statement could not go unaddressed.

"I don't know what that should have to do with anything. I could be any mage's apprentice, and only ended up Verol's by chance. And my master serves the king."

Clare only smiled brilliantly in response to the narrowing of Miriam's gaze, and in the end the proconsul only murmured, "So he does."

They rode in cautious silence for a time after that, and becoming lost in the scenery was no difficult task. It must have taken the careful attentions of dozens of unseen gardeners to craft the nature around her, nature that *looked* so beautifully wild it could only be meticulously ordered. True wildness had its ugly sides, like every-thing in life. There were patches in the wilderness that were snarled knots, where the flowers that the butterflies flitted to and from were half-dead or dying, and whole swathes where the flowers were too unimportant to bother naming at all.

Here, the wildness was a pattern that only appeared uncurated at first glance. It was as lush as a winter landscape could be without the constant interference of nature mages—though she saw some of that influence, to be sure, in a few flowers that were not known to be winter-blooming—the carefully chosen foliage thriving in defiance of the cold that nipped at Clare's skin. They crowded together in a semblance of free growth, yet were so carefully manicured that no limb or vine entangled with another unwanted. Everything lay masterfully placed so the exalted members of high society could pass through it and claim they appreciated that which was natural, when what they had really done was broken nature to their image of what it should be.

It *was* beautiful, and Clare loved it with the fierceness born of a life filled with ugliness. But while she loved it, she held no illusions about what it was. It was this singular difference between her and the kingdom's courtiers that made her want to throw every single one of them into Renault County's Howling Woods with nothing but their own skin and let them tell her then how much they *appreci-ated* nature.

Something of it must have showed on her face, because Miriam asked, "Do you know what you are in for, dabbling in this society?"

Three horses appeared from around a bend in the trail ahead, and she recognized Numair on Hellack before placing the other two. Lady Dahlia and—surprisingly, given her earlier state—Lady Meraland.

"Unfortunately," Clare answered, "I rather think I do."

FORTY-FOUR

NOT HER TYPE

Miriam watched the riders approach, murmuring quietly, "If you need help separating yourself from Prince Numair—"

"I don't need to separate myself from my friends."

Lady Aula gave her a sharp look. "That boy is no one's friend."

Clare met the gaze, pointedly, so there could be no doubt or confusion as to her immovability on the subject. "He's mine."

Miriam sighed. "That must be why Lady Dahlia looks so pleased at present. She wants very much to be *Princess* Dahlia."

The would-be princess, her horse keeping pace with Numair's, had already trained on Clare a look that good breeding was desperately attempting to prevent from becoming a scowl. When Numair's face broke into a grin and he urged Hellack into a trot to meet them, good breeding was defeated.

"Proconsul Aula, Miss Brighton, how delightful to run across you. Do you have room for three more in your party?"

"My lord," Dahlia objected, for her horse had caught up to his just in time for her to hear, "they are traveling in the opposite direction. We would not want to ask them to retrace their steps."

"Well, I did ask to join *their* party, so it would be us doing the retracing."

Clare covered her laugh with a feigned cough. "By all means, join us," she said, since he already was. Hellack executed a partial turn on the forehand, hindquarters swinging around neatly to settle him alongside Kialla. On a trail only wide enough for three to ride abreast, it forced Lady Dahlia and Lady Meraland to turn around ahead of them, becoming the de facto leaders of their little party.

This didn't even last long enough for Numair to speak. Ahead, Dahlia was engaged in fervent murmuring to Lady Meraland who, while clearly having more wits than she'd had a few hours ago when Clare ran into her in the hallway, still looked mostly dazed and out of sorts.

Eventually, sounding confused rather than confident, Lady Meraland called back, "Won't you ride with me, Proconsul Aula? I wish to talk to you about..." She trailed off, looking helplessly at Dahlia.

Disgust was written in every line of Dahlia's body. "Honestly, Ella, you are acting completely *odd* today."

Lady Aula let out a long-suffering sigh and trotted ahead to join Lady Meraland, while Dahlia naturally made noise about giving them privacy and dropped behind to join Clare and Numair. The latter kept Hellack so firmly on the far left of the path that Dahlia had no option but to take up the empty space on Clare's right. The lady made a single attempt to guide her horse between Kialla and Hellack, but when Kialla pinned her ears, head snaking out, and bit at her horse's face, she decided it wasn't worth the trouble.

"I don't understand why you've never done anything about that horse," Dahlia snapped to Numair. But she was looking at Clare when she added, "She needs to be made to understand her place."

"Oh, I don't know," Clare said breezily, "I find her spirit refreshing."

"I didn't ask *you*, did I?"

Riding with Dahlia of Moria, Clare decided, was going to be a true delight.

"She's too beautiful to tame," Numair said. He was, naturally, *not* looking at the horse when he said it. His gaze fell to the hibiscus flower tucked into the small braid behind Clare's ear. "Nice flower." At least he had the good sense, when he reached out, to touch one of the blooms on the horse.

Since he looked entirely too satisfied with himself, she answered, "Nice scarf."

"Isn't it?" He looked down at the green scarf, as if he'd possibly forgotten he was wearing it. "I think I'm rather fond of it."

Dahlia seemed to recognize some level of subtext was occurring, but as she couldn't discern what it was, she resorted to what Clare suspected was her default response of derision. "Why *are* you wearing that thing again? You wore it two days ago and it looks like you bought it in the Midtown markets."

He leaned conspiratorially towards Dahlia—which the woman might have appreciated had it not, in this particular instance, meant it was Clare he was getting the closest to—and whispered theatrically, "That's because I did."

Dahlia blinked, looking so astonished at the thought that the second prince of Faelhorn might debase himself in so vulgar a fashion as to shop in what she viewed as an inferior marketplace, that she was momentarily speechless. She at last recovered. "I suppose it *is* a form of charity to shop among the less fortunate."

Which was a sentence that made absolutely no sense to Clare, until the woman continued talking and it became clear she'd only made the comment as an excuse to segue into talking about her *own* charity work. She launched into the subject with a genuine pride and enthusiasm that made Clare want to slap her.

Clare recalled, from Alys's briefings on various court persons, that appearing charitable was the latest trend among young noble women, and Dahlia had taken to the field with all the enthusiasm her father's pocketbook could provide. Still, Clare could have overlooked the fact the charity was only being enacted for the sake of accolades, had it been carried out in a useful manner.

Unfortunately, it soon became clear that Dahlia's idea of "helping the less fortunate" was to make them *look* better. Which would have been all to the good, had that meant supplying them with decent clothing. Clare actually listened to the woman blather on for half a bell to determine that, no, what Dahlia had done was commission various ribbons and other accoutrement-type items to make the recipients of her beneficence "look more festive" and to "improve their cheer".

Clare angled her head slightly to turn a disbelieving look on Numair, certain something had fundamentally broken in her brain and she was hearing this wrong. Numair rolled his eyes.

Unable to help herself, Clare interjected, "And you don't think their cheer might be more improved by, say, a winter coat than a pretty ribbon?"

Dahlia—in a much better mood now that everything was, to her mind, all about her—missed the blatant sarcasm in Clare's voice. "I can see how, if you haven't engaged in any charity work before, you might think so. But if you simply *give* them things like that—things they need to survive—they won't work for anything. They'll become dependent on handouts. Like when you start feeding wild animals and they forget how to hunt for themselves. But things like I provide them—nice, pretty things—allow them a taste of what they can aspire to if they only work hard. It gives them an incentive to rise above their meager stations.

"It's that sort of effect a person like me can have on them, and I do think it is so important to help the less fortunate. Don't you agree?"

For a moment, Clare was back in Renault County in rags and dirt, her stomach snarled up in knots and her feet covered in cuts, and her tongue itched to demand just what Dahlia thought she knew of the "less fortunate". The anger was tempered by the part of Clare that felt herself a traitor for the fineness of the clothing she now wore, for the happy satisfied state of her stomach, and for the lack of dirt ground into her skin.

She felt guilty, simply for *having*. As if the fact she was not currently in abject need somehow made her an impostor inside her own skin.

Her hands tightened on the reins so that Kialla tossed her head in irritation, and she instantly relaxed her grip. It wasn't as if she had any special fondness in her heart for "the poor", as they were all lumped in together. Poverty did terrible things to people, and she had been done too much harm by those of her own former lot in life to have any special pity left for them. She only retained a general sense of the wrongness of poverty as an idea, and that someone— society at large—ought to do something about it.

What was it about money that turned people wicked? Lack of it and excess of it had near the same effect. Those without had so little to lose that fearing the repercussions of their actions was pointless— they could hardly fall any lower—and the latter had so much afflu- ence they simply purchased their way out of those repercussions.

She forced herself to make some general noise of agreement in

Dahlia's direction, and was relieved when Proconsul Aula called back to suggest they break for lunch.

The mystery of where lunch was to be found was solved when they exited the Squirrel Garden—she'd only caught a few glimpses of the typically industrious little rodents in the trees, their activity curbed by winter's chill—and entered a meadow littered with gazebos on one side and corrals on the other.

Lined up along the outer edges of the gazebos were carts that bore a semblance to the food carts that could be found in the busy market streets. Clare chose to consider it a mere semblance because, where the market carts were humble creatures, these were painted and gilded and so clean they could have driven through a noble-woman's parlor and she might never be the wiser.

The horses that had carried the carts here had been unhitched and corralled far away before the preparation of food ever began, and of course the customers here could not be expected to stand in line to order. Instead, Clare noticed boys and girls in clothing matching the color of one or another of the carts. They darted between gazebos, taking orders and returning from the carts with food.

She followed Numair's lead as he stopped at one of the corrals, where they left their horses before setting off on foot toward an empty gazebo. They were halfway to it when Clare felt someone's gaze on her. Or rather, on the wrist with Alys's ribbon bound around it. She followed the feeling to a young woman with brown skin and eyes covered with thick black lashes. It was several moments before the woman's gaze lifted from the ribbon to Clare's face. It did not linger long before her eyes widened and she turned away, though she didn't do so quickly enough to hide the hurt skittering across her features.

Clare was quite certain, then, that she knew exactly what sort of misunderstanding Alys meant her to prevent. Now she simply had to prevent it while also divesting herself of the ribbon without being noticed. All in a wide, open expanse of high society in which everyone was watching everyone else while pretending not to. She had no reasonable excuse to approach the woman and no idea who she was. Her clothes, while well-made, were not quite fine enough for the company she mingled in at present, though the clothes of her companion most certainly were.

Said companion towered above the woman by a good foot and a half. Gray peppered his hair, though he didn't look old enough to truly warrant the color. He had the same nose and eyes as Alys.

To Miriam, Clare quietly asked, "Who is that?"

Miriam followed her gaze, lips thinning. "Geoffrey Megadari. The soon-to-be Duke of Wake if no one can find his sister."

Everything about him set Clare's teeth on edge. He had the same effect on the young woman, if the way she held her body arched away from him was any indication. For his part, he seemed ambivalent to her presence at his side. No, that was not quite right. It was more that he was barely aware of her presence, as if she were an accessory he'd put on. So why had he brought her?

But then, she was obviously important to Alys. Alys, who did not want to be found. Alys, whose brother enjoyed the status granted him by her absence, and who would not *want* her found. At least, not publicly. He might well benefit from finding her on his own, quietly, and to that end the presence of the woman beside him became obvious. She was a lure. A lure, or a warning, or perhaps both.

Clare kept an eye on the woman throughout the lunch, waiting for an opportunity to arrive. Numair was the only one to notice where her attention went. Dahlia and Lady Meraland—Ella, Clare supposed, as she found titles onerous—were keeping their own conversation, which pointedly excluded Clare, who couldn't have been happier about the fact. The proconsul of Perish Province, which bordered Taella, had joined their party, and so had taken most of Miriam's attention.

For his part, Numair was pretending to be halfway to drunk. She suspected it was partially in dedication to maintaining his reputation and partially because, after his second glass of wine, Dahlia got an irritated look on her face and ignored him. The woman clearly had a dedication to obtaining a royal title since, to all appearances, she disliked everything about Numair and didn't bother to hide it. She didn't *have* to, since absolutely no one had any respect for him.

For Clare's part, when she wasn't watching Alys's mystery woman, she was trying to figure out where the copious amounts of alcohol Numair supposedly consumed actually went. She didn't think he was surreptitiously dumping it in the grass somewhere, because it wasn't the kind of strategy that could be employed in every situation. She was relatively certain it was actually alcohol because, though she was sure he could manage to have a servant at every function, ready to provide him with colored water instead, she was also certain one of them would eventually talk.

Nor were his beverages disguised by glamour. She could *always* see through that, even when the Song was being as quiet as it was now. It hadn't fully abandoned her, as it did within the walls of Alaric's palace, but it was keeping to itself here, in the king's gardens. Besides which, glamour was yet another strategy too risky for long-term employment. The right mages could see past it if they paid enough attention. So how was he doing it?

She was no closer to an answer when he seemed to ascertain the purpose of her attention. He lifted the wine glass at her in a mocking salute and drained the remaining half of its contents. Well, it had definitely all gone into his mouth.

In her peripheral vision, Alys's mystery woman rose, and Clare's attention shifted, watching as she walked down to the corral. Her horse—and Lord Megadari's—were in the corral next to Kialla's, and the woman began adjusting cinches that had been loosened for comfort while their riders ate.

Clare reached across the table and plucked the apple Numair had purchased but not eaten. "May I?"

"You already have. I don't mind, but Hellack might. It was meant for him."

"I'm sure he won't mind sharing with Kialla, then. He's terribly smitten."

"That he is," Numair answered, with just enough suggestion to set Dahlia to scowling again.

Clare shot him a you're-going-to-make-her-insufferable look and took the apple down to the corrals, entering Kialla's enclosure on the side closest to her target. The woman did not fully turn as Clare approached, but the stiffening of her posture made it clear she knew who had arrived. Something about her nagged at Clare, as if the woman were a puzzle piece designed to fit with something else in the world, but she couldn't for the life of her fathom what. It was one of those slivers of certainty she was now accustomed to receiving from the Song, ones destined to never have an answer.

Although, now that she'd renegotiated her position with it, she wondered if it would solve the mystery for her, if she asked.

She slid a knife from her boot and neatly divided the apple into thirds. One-third went to Kialla and another to Hellack. Then, as if just noticing the other woman, she turned and held out the remaining apple over the fence, prominently displaying her ribbon-wrapped wrist.

"Would you like it?"

The woman held her gaze, the tight bronze curls of her hair moving gently in the wind. "No."

Clare marveled at how well she managed to make the single syllable sound like, "Go throw yourself in Ferrian's flames." She thought Clare was taunting her. Clare opened her mouth to set things straight, but the Song flared up with such insistence it strangled the words in her throat.

We are not the only ones who listen.

Clare considered ignoring it, but she had never been stupid simply for spite.

What do you mean?

Listen.

So she listened with the Song's ears and heard an eerie, high-pitched keening that led Clare's gaze to the bulge of an armband beneath the shirt on the woman's right bicep, and behind that hidden ornament she *felt* the prying attentions of Alys's brother.

Subtlety, then. "Are you quite certain? I think she would like it, if you take it." Clare slipped between the fence rails and stepped forward so that her hand, apple and ribbon included, were shielded from any watching eyes by the woman's own body. She pulled her hand up, transferring the apple to her palm at nearly the same time she loosed the ribbon and deftly transferred it to the woman's tunic pocket.

The woman's mare reached out and delicately lipped the apple from her hand. Clare stepped back and stroked the horse's neck.

"She is quite lovely, but not my type, I'm afraid." Clare put just enough pressure against the mare's shoulder to get her to sidle a step away from her and towards the woman, without appearing to have done anything more than pet the horse. "Ah, and you see I am not her type either. She is very obviously taken with you."

Slowly, bit by bit, the woman's shoulders relaxed. "She and I have been together a long time," she said carefully. "She ran away once, when she was injured."

"And no doubt she made her way back to you as quickly as she could."

Footsteps approached, intentionally noisome.

"Are we to feed every horse in the valley?" Numair asked loudly. Clare turned, seeing he approached only a few paces ahead of Lord Megadari.

"Not unless you have bought a bushel of apples instead of the one," Clare answered lightly.

Lord Megadari wasted no time in gathering his horse and swinging into the saddle. The woman followed without a single glance passing between them, and as they rode off she was wise enough not to cast a backward glance at Clare.

"You seem to be missing your pretty ribbon," Numair said.

"Do I? Missing it implies I don't know where it has gone."

"I knew someone who had one just like it, once."

Clare decided, then, that it was not *her* fault if Alys had underestimated the attention to detail that others might be capable of.

"Indeed, you probably did."

Numair checked Hellack's cinch as the rest of their party approached. "Is she all right?"

"Yes." Clare led Kialla to the corral fence and climbed a couple rails to slide smoothly onto her back. "And that is all I will be saying on the matter."

"I can help her," he said, his voice low.

"*I* have no doubt that is true. I do not believe she will feel the same."

Those shutters of black ice, so adept at hiding Numair from the world, closed once more over his eyes. "I see."

The rest of their party drew within earshot, leaving Clare no chance to offer pretty soothing words, if indeed any could be found. Numair played his role, for whatever reason, and because he did, the woman he still considered a friend would never accept his help. Would never believe him *capable* of helping.

He was moody and morose the rest of the afternoon, playing his drunken persona for all it was worth, and his sour mood infected her own. She had to work twice as hard to keep up her own facade of joviality, and couldn't help but wonder if the role she played among these people would poison her as thoroughly as Numair's seemed to have poisoned him.

A week ago, she would have said it didn't matter. What was a little more poison in the wellspring of it that was the world they lived in? But a person seemed to be coalescing inside of her where before there had been only a starving creature hellbent on survival. And that nascent person, it seemed, had objections to a lifetime of emotional misery.

CHAPTER

FORTY-FIVE

REAPER

On her return, Clare cornered Alys in the stable. A feat made easy by the fact Alys had obviously been intent on cornering *her* the second she returned.

"Did you get it to her?"

Clare waved her bare wrist. "One ribbon delivered."

"And is she—was she all right?"

"Oh, she was delightful. Practically arm-in-arm with your charming brother. I don't think she's thought about you at all."

Alys just stared at her.

"Your lover is in good health, if poor spirits."

"She's not my—"

"Oh, please." Clare rolled her eyes. "The jealousy when she thought you'd replaced her with me was palpable. I had to use a very clever demonstration with a horse and an apple to dispel that misunderstanding, I'll have you know."

"A horse," Alys repeated, "and an apple."

"I even had the horse do a little acting. So, tell me about her."

"She's none of your concern."

"On the contrary, you've involved me, so now she is my concern. I can start you off, if it's helpful. You love her. She loves you. Your brother keeps her because controlling her controls you, which implies he is the very thing you are hiding from. So why don't you just go home and get her back?"

"If it were that simple, I would have already done it."

"Is it that wretched thing on her arm that stops you? Because I can take care of that."

Alys's head jerked up. "Excuse me?"

"I can take care of it," Clare repeated.

"You don't even know what it is, but you can take care of it?"

"Tell me a story," Clare purred, "and I'll show you I can."

Alys paced back and forth in short, frustrated steps before turning on Clare and saying, grudgingly, "Her name is Lina. We've been friends since we were eight."

"That's an excellent start. Tell me more."

Alys shot her an annoyed look, but did. "My parents knew her parents, though we weren't in quite the same social circles. So when her family died, my parents took her in. We grew up together. Somewhere along the way we fell in love. Everything was fine until my parents died last year." Alys paused, fingers curling into fists. "Geoffrey and I never got on well. He hated us both, but I think he hated Lina more, because I was afraid of him and she never was. She used to antagonize him terribly when we were younger. She'd cut the pockets in his coats, or line his shirts with itch-flower." Alys's face softened as she spoke. "I was never brave enough to stand up to him, but *she* was."

"You hardly seem like a shrinking violet."

Alys shrugged. "People change."

"So what happened?"

"Understand that my brother is a truly frightening individual. I lived through more than one occasion in my youth when I thought he might kill me. When I turned fifteen winters and he seventeen, he strangled me because I laughed at him, and the only reason I am not dead is because Lina broke a vase over his head and the resultant noise brought the rest of the household.

"My parents sent him away after that. Various schools and military institutions they believed would *cure* him, as if his actions were born of some disease and not his own wretched soul. Yet they must have somewhat understood his nature, because they left the estate, in its entirety, to me, with the stipulation that I would continue to provide for Geoffrey. There were also stipulations that, in the event of my death, the estate would revert to a trust that would pay for housing and staff, and allow Geoffrey a fixed allowance. They did not wish to humiliate him, so the particulars of the inheritance were sealed from public knowledge, and only Geoff and I were present for the reading.

"When Geoffrey did not cause a scene after the news, I thought perhaps the various rigors of military life *had* cured him, as my parents hoped. I hadn't seen him in years, by that point. I realized how wrong I was as soon as I returned to the manor. Because the reading of their will was private, only Geoffrey and I were allowed to attend. Lina stayed at home. I was delayed in town by some business I now recognize he planned for, and he returned to the manor before me. When I came back, he had Lina. Are you familiar with binding bracelets?"

Clare shook her head.

"Well, *that* is the 'wretched thing on her arm' that stops me. They were made in pairs, two bracelets cut from the same chunk of white dreamstone, the bound slaved to the master bracelet. It is illegal to make them anymore, but of course there is always a market for antiques, if one has money and a taste for that type of sordidness.

"If Lina so much as steps a foot outside of Megadari Manor without Geoffrey's consent, the bracelet will kill her. She cannot run away, and I cannot take her." Alys took a steadying breath. "He wanted me to sign control of the estate over to him, but even if I was willing to, I don't have the authority. The will was very clear on that point. So instead, I became his puppet, with Lina's life always subject to his moods. It is no way to live, and Lina and I were not going to do it.

"I tried to steal the master bracelet while he slept. He woke and gave me this." She indicated the jagged scar running diagonally across her face. She grimaced. "I'd never wished to have been born a mage so fervently as in that moment. I spent a week tied up in the unused groundskeeper's cottage while my face grew infected and my brother examined legal loopholes, the predominant one being that nothing in my parents' will explicitly stated what happened to the estate if I went missing but did not die.

"It only took the right lawyer to tell him what he wanted to hear: if I were missing for long enough, but not dead, he could gain control of the estate. When I learned *that*, I knew I had to leave.

Geoffrey would keep me tied up for the rest of my life with Lina as security. As it is, if anyone sees me, I have no doubt he will kill her."

"Why didn't he just kill you outright and tell everyone you were missing?"

Alys laughed. "You're direct, aren't you? Well, I am sure you will be shocked to hear this, but the nobility are quite accustomed to scandals, treachery, and backstabbing. As such, any family worth anything pays to have their children entered in the Book of Life at birth. It takes a single drop of blood, the power of which is consumed entirely by the spell that places it in the book, so one need not fear it being used for nefarious purposes. While a person lives, their name in the Book of Life is written in red. When they die, it fades to black. To date, the book has never been manipulated, so all of Veralna City knows I am alive, if they choose to look.

"Naturally, certain people suspect my brother of having a hand in my disappearance. Those who prefer me to my brother ensured Megadari Manor was searched, as were his other holdings, and the staff questioned, but the only person who knows anything is Lina, and if she speaks of it, she will die."

"You must have powerful friends, why not go to them?"

Alys hesitated. "I don't have any I trust enough with this."

"Verol and Marquin?"

"Have already risked enough for me."

"They don't know, do they?"

"Not the particulars. And you will take care to keep it that way. So long as I remain hidden, Lina is safe. If she dies, he knows nothing will prevent me from coming forward. But if he hears that I *am* coming forward, he will kill her simply to hurt me, even if he can't stop me."

"So all you really need," Clare reasoned, "is this bracelet destroyed?"

Alys laughed. "You don't understand, Clare. The bracelets cannot be destroyed. Only the person who possesses the master bracelet can remove Lina's, and since my attempt to take it from him, Geoffrey has taken certain precautions to ensure that if anyone attempts to remove it, it will destroy her. When you said you could take care of it, I assumed you had an actual plan."

"I do." Clare lifted her hand and, at Alys's tight-lipped nod of consent, placed her fingertips to Alys's cheek. The Song unfurled inside Clare, reached out through her fingers, and drank the magic of Alys's glamour down. The doing of it filled Clare with a soft warmth, as if the glamour's magic were something she had given away long ago and come to regret the giving of, and now it was being returned to her.

The action seemed to Clare a simple enough one. So simple, in fact, she had doubted the Song's insistence that this show of ability would convince Alys of anything at all, much less that Clare could free Lina of the binding bracelet.

Alys's response was to stumble—inasmuch as anyone with Alys's court-trained graces could be said to stumble—back two steps, her face blanched of color. Trembling fingers slipped into the pocket of her breeches and she pulled out a little compact mirror, opening it to stare at her face, and the wholly visible scar upon it.

When she closed the compact her hand was steady once more, fright hidden beneath layers of frigid control. "I need to arrange a few things. Once I have, you will come with me and free Lina, and in return for your help and your own silence, I will do you the favor of never speaking of *this* again."

She walked away, as if frightened to stay any longer in Clare's presence, and climbed the stairs to the living quarters above the stable.

Why is she scared?

The Song purr-hummed in response, its self-satisfaction evident. *Because we do what only one other can.*

Clare did not miss how much 'we' sounded like 'I' in the Song's voice. How long, she wondered, before it failed to remember she was here at all? How long would she maintain control, before she ceased to be, and only the Song remained?

CLARE STORMED into Verol and Marquin's study, expecting to find only Marquin, but not displeased to find Verol as well. Two opinions were always better than one, and Verol's expressions were easier to read. "Give me something with magic. Something small that you don't care about."

Two perplexed faces looked up at her, Verol's from his journal, Marquin's from what looked like an accounting ledger.

"I can choose for myself if you like." She reached for a small wooden box on Verol's desk. One inch wide by two inches long, she could feel the magic engraved into its lacquered surface.

"Not that." Verol snatched it away, and she wondered what it did. He tucked it into a drawer and instead handed her a small glass apple.

"Why is *this* so terrifying?" she asked, and though the Song was feeling recalcitrant, its desire for the small magic in the apple was clear, and it did not require much nudging on her part to make it reach out and take it.

Both men went still. Verol recovered first, rising to take the apple from her fingers, turning it over and over in his own, as if he would come to some different conclusion if he performed the motion enough times.

When he spoke his voice was calm and cold, and it sent a shiver through her. "Clare, who have you shown this to?"

She did not answer him. "*Why* is it frightening?"

"Because" Marquin said gently, "it is something only Alaric can do."

Clare swallowed, hard, the movement sticking halfway down her throat because Marquin's voice, while gentle, held the same undercurrent of cold dread as Verol's.

He was frightened. They were *both* frightened. Of her. Just like Alys.

A sense of distance opened between her and them, a pang of *something* twinging through Clare's chest.

"What does it mean?"

"It means that, among other things, Clare, you are a Reaper."

"She can't be a Reaper." Though Verol's tone said he didn't believe his own words. "She's a Songweaver. Reaper doesn't coexist with other disciplines."

"We have seen she is a Healer, too. Another discipline that does not coexist with others, but you did not raise the problem then."

"I did not because—"

"What," Clare interrupted, voice much calmer than she felt, "is a Reaper? I have never heard of them."

"That is because they were ruthlessly culled two centuries ago by royal decree. Any living Reaper was killed and their entire family line sterilized."

"And the Mages Guild allowed this?" The brutality of it didn't surprise her, but she had thought that, for the sake of self-preservation, the Mages Guild would balk at allowing the death of their own kind.

"They didn't allow it, Clare, they executed it. Even in the guild, reapers were—"

Abominations.

"—feared. They don't simply possess the ability to take magic from a spell or an item, which is in itself impressive, but can reap it directly from a mage."

An inkling of understanding spread through her, but she asked anyway. "What happens to the mage?"

"If the Reaper is merciful? They kill them. If they are not?" Quin shrugged. "Magic is what a mage is. Without it, they are only a shell. They go mad. If they retain any agency at all, most kill themselves."

"And Alaric? How does he exist?"

A bitter smile twisted at Marquin's lips. "It seems his great-grandfather, who ordered the annihilation of the Reaper talent, knew it ran in his bloodline. He didn't order the destruction of the talent because he feared it, but because he wanted a world where that talent existed only in royal hands. He must have been sorely disappointed when it didn't manifest to any offspring in his lifetime."

She thought of the magic coating Alaric, thick and viscous, layer upon layer of foul, putrid power, and understood where the scent of decay that lingered on him originated. How many people, she wondered, had Alaric reaped?

I saw the future, Numair had said, *and it is a monstrous thing.*

"Can a Reaper only reap a mage?"

"Clare—"

"Just answer the question. Please."

"Everyone has a spark of magic. And a Reaper can take that. But non-mages never survive a reaping."

She had a feeling she knew what had happened to the people of El-Dennon.

"I'll see you back at the palace." She left, hardly able to hear the calls they made after her. No, it was Madame Aria's voice she heard, laden with disgust, repeating in her mind.

Abomination.

It was becoming increasingly difficult to convince herself she was not.

FORTY-SIX

COME WITH ME, AND YOU WON'T

Verol slumped in his chair. His eyes had that glassy, vacant look they'd had after Marie died. Quin should reassure him. Should tell him that he wasn't going to lose Clare too, except he didn't think he could fake the sincerity well enough. Not this time. Not after what they'd just seen.

Verol jerked suddenly and the glass covering his eyes shattered, replaced by a feverish light. "We have to leave. Investigate the most recent tip from Phoenix. If they're right and we get the gatestone for them, we'll finally have one that's worth something."

Marquin dragged his hand across his face, feeling wearier than ever, and knowing talking Verol out of this wasn't going to be easy. Phoenix, the anonymous source they'd been in communication with for almost a decade, wasn't in the habit of sending them toward the ancient magical artifacts he and Marquin hunted. The information Phoenix sent them typically skewed political. But they knew Quin and Verol looked for those items that, if enough were collected, might help them oppose Alaric, and their most recent note had said they knew where one might be found—but they would need a gate-stone to reach it.

Since there hadn't been a Gatekeeper born in over three-hundred years, the surviving gatestones were difficult to find and almost impossible to pay the price to obtain. He and Verol knew where only a single one was, and they had resolutely refused to pay its price for the last fifteen years. Even after Phoenix's note, Verol hadn't considered it. Until now.

He was ignoring Quin, standing and shuffling through half a dozen books, looking for Ferrian alone knew what. "During the journey we can see what might be done to draw him away from the palace without causing any actual damage."

"Verol—"

"And it's time to start pushing harder on the political front. Possibly with Taella first. Miriam's always understood where we stand, and she has her own vendetta. Besides, she likes you, so even if she doesn't *agree* with our methods, we can likely count on her support."

"Verol—"

"I'd take on another apprentice if I thought it would confuse Alaric, except he'd likely see right through that and I—"

"*Verol.*" The deep boom of his voice finally halted Verol's manic energy. "She's too strong to hide. What she did with the tree this afternoon proved that. You only felt the echoes of this Song's power. That was nothing compared to what I felt when she spoke with it."

Verol frowned. "I understand that. It's why, more than ever, we must accelerate our plans and keep his attention divided across the kingdom. We have to kill him, Quin."

Quin stepped around the desk. He removed the book in Verol's hand and set it aside, taking his hands. "No, love. *She* has to kill him."

Verol pulled back, as Quin had known he would. Just as Quin had anticipated the horrified, reproachful look he was now on the receiving end of.

"She's barely more than twenty winters," Verol said.

"She isn't a child. And she isn't your daughter."

"Is there a point buried in those words somewhere?" So much ice, in his voice.

Quin had thought he and Verol had already passed through the crucible that might break their marriage. Now he wondered if it had only been the first. If Marie hadn't broken them, but Clare yet might.

"The point is that she is bigger than us. The point is that *we* cannot kill Alaric. You *know* we can't. How long have we been searching the provinces for artifacts he hasn't already found and Reaped? How many have we located?"

Verol set his teeth and didn't respond. He knew how unimpressive the answer was. That they'd found several lesser items, worth keeping out of Alaric's hands, but none strong enough to offer any real threat to the king.

"If we believed we had a chance in Ferrian's hells of defeating him, we would have tried it already. Open your eyes, Verol. *She's* that chance. I don't say that because I want to use her. I say that because she is her own best hope of survival, once he finds her out. And it's only a matter of time before he does.

"She is untrained and volatile, she is prone to impulsive and angry outbursts, and though I don't think she realizes it, that leash she keeps her power under is so tight it's bound to snap."

Verol jerked his hands free of Marquin's. "She isn't a feral animal. And it isn't her responsibility to fix this. She never asked to be born with the power she holds."

"Neither did you. But you can't avoid it any more than she can."

Verol shook his head. "It was different for me. I had a life, before this. I…don't think she did. She deserves to now, however much of a one she can have."

Sensing a thaw, Marquin stepped into it. "What good is a month or six of an idyllic life if it means she doesn't have one at the end?"

But Verol didn't relent. "What good is her survival if at the end of it she's done too much to *enjoy* living? You think I don't understand how poor our chances are? You think I have suddenly forgotten that it would take a miracle to destroy him?

"I haven't. But don't ask me to ask this of her. Don't ask me to trick her into it, to train her for it while pretending I am not. I can't give her that weight. I won't."

Marquin didn't answer. He didn't know how to. He didn't want to put this on the girl either. Verol thought him harsh, but he was trying to protect her in the only way he knew how. When decades of bitter experience and failure told him that he and Verol could not win this fight for her, and common sense said she could not hide forever, it only made sense to prepare her.

But Verol thought he only wanted to throw her at Alaric like a battering ram, and he clearly took Quin's silence for disagreement.

"I know that I am not the easiest man to live with. This power, this Kinthing, would be no partner's joy. Yet knowing that, you broke the moral codes all mages live by to keep me here when I would have faded."

The heartstone in his staff pulsed in response to the mention of its creation.

"So I will ask you this only once. Do you want to lose me, Marquin?"

This was what it came down to, then. He would give anything for Verol, and Verol would give anything for the girl. The potential of the world forever falling under the rule of a self-made god-king, because Verol would never put her at risk.

It didn't change his answer. "You know I don't."

Verol nodded jerkily and headed for the door. "I'm leaving in one hour. Come with me, and you won't."

Quin would go. Of course he would go. But he had a different agenda. They could hunt these relics of legend more relentlessly than they ever had before. They could dig up the provinces' mages of rare and unique abilities, and try to convince them they had some chance of defeating Alaric. They could sow the seeds of political rebellion.

But while his husband sought to build Clare an army to protect her, Marquin would be the more realistic, if less kind, guardian. The only army that might protect her was the one she led herself. And if Verol had forbidden him from suggesting she take the helm of this fight, Quin had little doubt she would come to the conclusion herself, eventually.

He simply had to hope that, in between now and then, she was as clever as he thought her. Clever enough to survive.

He started to rise, to begin the preparations for their travel, when his gaze fell on the box they used to communicate with Phoenix. He settled himself behind Verol's desk and wrote a brief note.

Verol and I will be gone for some time. His apprentice, Clare, will remain here. I do not know if you are in a position to do so, and I am not requesting any information about your station but, if you can, watch out for her. She is…important.

He dropped it into the box before he could overthink the wisdom of it. Phoenix had been careful with their correspondence with them over the years, never giving any hint as to their identity. It had made trusting them difficult, in the beginning, but the relationship was so well-established at this point that if they'd harbored ill-will toward the Arrendons, they'd had more than a few opportunities for betrayal.

The risk felt different this time, though. Because it wasn't himself or Verol he was trusting Phoenix with. It was *her*. It felt like a fist had squeezed tight around his heart. He'd told himself, all these years, that it was Verol who had never gotten over Marie. Had told himself mere days ago that it was Verol he was worried about, should anything happen to Clare.

But Marie had called *Quin* Father, too. He'd been there when she'd taken her first steps. He'd been just as sleep-deprived as Verol as the two of them figured out how to be unexpected parents to an orphaned infant. And when she was older, when she'd woken from nightmares in the middle of the night, he was always the one she'd expected to check under the bed and in the darkened corners for lurking monsters.

He had told himself he didn't trust Clare. He'd convinced himself she couldn't *be* trusted, this young woman who was so different from the child they'd lost before. But the truth was, he'd actively kept his distance from her. Because Verol wasn't the only one who might not survive another Marie.

CHAPTER
FORTY-SEVEN
I PROMISED YOU THAT MUCH

Verol and Marquin never returned to the palace. Clare had waited up the entire night for them and she hadn't even known why. She'd passed the time with Numair's reading books, and once the sun rose she went into the suite's common room, intending to have breakfast sent up. But when she entered the shared space she found Fitz occupying it, and he'd already ordered what looked like enough food for four people.

When he nodded to the seat across the table, where a clean plate and utensils were waiting, she decided she really had no cause *not* to join him. She filled her plate, but when she went to pour a cup of coffee there was barely enough left to fill her mug a third of the way.

She glared at him. "You drank *all* of it?"

He shrugged.

"The entire carafe."

"I ordered it, didn't I? Order your own."

She didn't. It seemed wasteful to have someone walk all the way up here to deliver a damn carafe. "The Arrendons are still out?" she asked casually, spreading butter onto a biscuit.

He grunted in response.

"Do you know when they'll be back?" It wasn't that she *wanted* to talk to them, precisely. It was more that she couldn't help feeling like they were avoiding her. Not that she cared, obviously, it was only that if they were having second thoughts about her, she needed to be prepared.

The looks on both their faces—on Alys's—yesterday, and that single word: *reaper.*

"Not for a couple weeks at best. They're away on business." She could tell, from the way he said it, that he knew where they were and wasn't going to tell her.

She drank a swallow of her one-third cup of lukewarm coffee. "You think he likes me best, but you're the one he tells things to." *You're the one he trusts. I'm...* What was she? Anything more than an obligation? Fitz had been Verol's apprentice in truth. Verol wasn't even bothering to *pretend* to train her. And after yesterday, she didn't think Marquin would be doing so again either.

She didn't look at Fitz's face for a response, and he didn't give a verbal one. A few minutes of twitchy silence later, he tossed a stack of envelopes at her. "These arrived for you this morning."

She set them aside. After a night spent on practicing her reading, she was done with it for a few hours, and the letters would give her an excuse to ride back to the Arrendons to ask Alys to help her with them. She was curious to find if the Duchess of Wake was as eager to avoid her as the Arrendons seemed to be.

"So, Clare. Where are you from?"

She didn't spare the question more than an irritated flick of her gaze.

"What did you do before you came to the Arrendons?"

She bit into the buttered biscuit, which was ridiculously delicious, and continued to ignore him.

"Because I find it interesting that you deduced what *I* do so quickly. And I admit, it's made me curious about something." The too-smooth easiness of Fitz's voice was the only warning Clare got before he was lunging at her, the dagger in his hand arrowing for her stomach. She barely reacted in time, her body moving one way, her hand lashing out to strike at his wrist. It shunted the blade aside, but didn't make him drop it.

She looked for his next attack but it didn't come immediately. He stood there, laughing. He was saying something, but she couldn't hear it. The wheels of memory shifted in her, accelerating her heart rate, telling her it didn't matter *why* he'd paused, only mattered that she took advantage of it. The veneer of civilization, of the woman she was pretending to be, fell away. She was back in Renault County, a creature of instinct, every one of them telling her to kill him, kill him quick, before he killed her. She lost herself to that frenzy.

The only thing of coordination in her attack was that she'd fought enough to know where to strike with the dagger she pulled from her boot, the only thing of strategy the certainty that she had to hit and hit hard, with everything she had. To keep him off his stride because he was physically bigger and stronger than her and the Song wouldn't help her, not here in Alaric's palace, and *fuck* she didn't want to die now.

She forced him across the room with the wildness of her onslaught, and when his back hit the far wall, opportunity reared its head and she struck, right between the ribs, with everything she had...and her knife shattered. Like Fitz was made of stone and the blade of spun glass.

She kicked and punched after that, the skin of her knuckles breaking against the magic that coated Fitz's body in invisible iron, and all the while he was yelling at her but the fear and the rage in her ears was too much to let the words in. Her strength flagged and he grappled, bearing her to the ground and pinning her.

Her chest heaved, her breaths coming in jagged, painful gulps. It was supposed to have been safe here. Marquin and Verol, they were supposed to be safe, and *Fitz* was supposed to be safe because they'd left her with him, and how could she have been so stupid?

"*Clare*, it's okay. I'm not trying to hurt you, I don't *want* to hurt you." Fitz's words didn't register, were almost unintelligible over the words she was screaming, over and over.

"*Don't touch me, get off me, don't you fucking touch me.*" Somewhere in the back of her mind she realized he wasn't doing anything *but* stopping her from attacking him further, realized she was able to get her knees between them and kick him off because he didn't fight it.

She rolled onto all fours, shuddering and panting. Her stomach squeezed and contorted and she retched, her body trying to purge her terror.

"Fuck, Clare, I'm sorry. I'm so sorry. I wasn't trying to kill you, I wasn't even trying to hurt you, I thought—I thought you might have been like me."

She sat back, shaking too hard to hold herself up, his words barely cutting through the panic still flooding her mind. He'd thought she was like him. An *assassin?* What, because she'd been able to recognize it in him? And he'd decided to test that theory by attacking her?

His face was white, and he looked sick. "The blade was dull-coated, it wouldn't have hurt you if I was wrong. But I didn't think I was wrong. You had that look people like us get and you knew what I was. I never thought..." He squeezed his eyes shut, tears leaking out the corners. Like *she'd* scared *him.* Like *he* had a right to be upset. He opened his eyes. "I never would have done that if I'd had any idea what you've obviously been—"

"*Fuck you.*" She shoved to her feet, a rush of dizziness surging through her.

He took a step toward her. "Clare, I—"

"Stay the hell away from me." She darted for the door, yanked it open and ran into the hall. She hit the stairway before she realized how she must look. Food was splattered on her shirt from when he'd lunged across the table. Sweat saturated her clothing. Her hair was mussed and wild, her hands bleeding, and while she hadn't vomited on herself, the remnants of her sickness lingered in her mouth.

She forced herself to calm down, enough to take the edge off her flight. She hadn't passed anyone in the halls yet. No one had seen her like this. She should go back to the suite and change her clothes. But the thought of going back there right now, even knowing that Fitz had never intended to do anything worse than test her skill with a blade, was unbearable.

The claws of Renault County were digging into her, reminding her of who she was. Of *what* she was.

Mine, min quellea. *You'll always be mine,* that old voice promised, its acrid, poisoned words dripping down her throat.

She shuddered and almost threw up again right there, on the richly carpeted steps of the palace. It was never going to end. She'd thought escape would be enough, but she was never going to stop feeling like this until *he* was dead.

"You'll die," she whispered, to a person who wasn't *here* and yet wouldn't leave her alone. "I don't know how, and I don't know when, but I promised you that much."

CHAPTER

FORTY-EIGHT

HE ISN'T HOME

She snuck her way out of the castle, darting through hallways, slipping into nooks and shadows to avoid being seen, and pulled Kialla from the stables. It was only once she was on the horse, only once she'd passed through the Outer Gate and Kialla's stride was a rhythmic canter beneath her, that the tightness in her chest eased enough for her to breathe normally.

It was also when the Song crept forth, and she snapped at it. *Good to know that if I'm dying, you'll only help so long as Alaric isn't within screaming distance.*

She detected the faintest sense of embarrassment from it, which was perhaps why its reply was so caustic, as if she was the one worthy of reproach. *You were in no danger.*

But she hadn't known that. And the Song, who well knew what lurked in her memories, hadn't even been able to overcome its cowardice long enough to *tell her.*

Her hands throbbed, the knuckles bruised and skin torn from battering against the unyielding, invisible armor that had coated Fitz's skin. As if in penance, the Song reached for those wounds. She let it. She'd made this fool's bargain with it, so she took the advantages as it knit the flesh back over her knuckles to gleaming wholeness, let the cool tide of magic wash away the heat and swelling.

She reached the Arrendons' manor and left Kialla to graze in the empty paddock while she went inside. All of her new clothes were at the palace—she'd have to rectify that oversight—but her one decent set of breeches and tunic from her original clothing was cleaned and mended, and she gratefully changed her current stained and sweat-soaked clothing for them.

A sweep of the grounds and stable proved Alys was nowhere to be found—which was fine, because Clare had left all her letters in the palace suite, and wasn't in the mood to deal with them besides —so she mounted Kialla and rode to Numair's. She had the ridiculous notion that seeing him would somehow soothe the jagged edges Fitz's ill-advised "test" had sharpened to razor points.

Hellack was in the paddock where she'd first met Kialla, so she untacked the mare and left her with him. But though his horse was here, Numair didn't seem to be. After he didn't answer the rocks she tossed at his window, she opened the hidden door and went wandering—he *had* said to stop by any time. She made it through all of the first floor and part of the second before she encountered a single person. She'd had this idea of the homes of wealthy people as bustling places, always filled with staff or visitors or family. Numair's home was like a place he'd hidden away from the world —a haven he expected no one to find him in—and it settled her.

The house felt safe, in a way the Arrendons' palace suite now never would. Its silence, its dark, muted colors and its carefully chosen comforts, wrapped around her and she thought if only she could stay here long enough, some of the peace it exuded might finally absorb into her bones.

She was in his library, running her fingers over tomes she might someday actually be able to read because of him, when she saw it. Resting on a random bookshelf like a mere decoration, was a small one-inch by two-inch box, an exact twin to the one she'd seen yesterday in Verol's office, identical down to the magic she felt imbued into its making.

It was in her hands before she could think better of the impulse, but when she opened it, nothing happened. It was just an empty box, the interior lined with soft blue velvet. Disappointed, she placed it back on the shelf when she sensed someone staring at her. An older woman stood in the doorway, and Clare recognized her as the woman who had met her carriage the night of Numair's nameday celebration.

That evening, the impression Clare had gotten from her was one somewhere between suspicion and contempt. The impression she received now was something softer. A cautious, weighing look, almost…. Clare groaned internally. Almost *hopeful*. First Lian, now this woman. Why did people keep looking at her like that?

"He isn't home," the woman finally said. "And I wouldn't expect him before tomorrow."

"I see." It didn't seem like the woman wanted to kick her out, necessarily, so she said, "I'm Clare."

The corners of the woman's eyes crinkled. "I know. Numair mentioned you might wander in at some point. I'm Ida."

Pleasantries upon meeting someone weren't a thing in Renault County. But the Song had shoved enough of various people's memories at her on the road to Veralna that a few of the phrases stuck in her head, and she found herself finally wanting to try one out. "It's nice to meet you, Ida."

Ida nodded. "You can borrow that one, if you like."

Clare looked down at the book she'd picked absently off the shelf. "Oh, that's all right. I just liked the picture." Etched on the soft cover was a serpent-like red dragon, so different in body from the stone one she'd met on Firedrake Mountain. The only word she could read of the title was a basic "the" and she felt suddenly self-conscious, aware she couldn't do a fundamental thing this world seemed very dependent on.

I could help, the Song offered. When she was at the palace, when she was near Alaric, it disappeared deep within her. But since the pact she'd made with it at the Arrendons, since they'd healed the tree, whenever she was elsewhere, its presence behind her eyes was constant. She hated it, the ever-present reminder that she was never alone in her own skin. That she didn't belong only to herself.

I wish you wouldn't think of it that way, the Song said sadly.

There is no other way to think of it. And I'll learn to read on my own. She knew the Song's solution to this problem: to infect her with another person's memories, another person's life. She'd only know how to read as long as she kept that other person around, and she wasn't going to let someone *else* live in her body, too.

She could attempt the same trick she'd pulled to learn how to ride, but she didn't think it would work again, now that the Song had slightly more agency. It had been so angry when she'd severed the war maiden's knowledge of horses from her identity and taken the former for herself. As if she'd destroyed something it loved.

She placed the book back on the shelf. She'd learn to read on her own. "I should be going."

"Before you do, I have something for you." Ida crossed the room, opening a large drawer in a wooden desk and pulling out a stack of slim books. Six in total, tied together with a pretty two-toned black and green ribbon. "He made these for you yesterday."

Clare took them, recognizing the feel of the magic from the first ones he'd sent her, and knew that every word she ran her fingers over would be spoken in his voice. She looked up sharply at Ida, but there wasn't any condescension on her face. Just that same, odd, hopeful expression.

"It's quieter here than at the palace," Ida said. "You could stay for a while, if you wanted. I could bring you some tea."

It felt less like an offer meant for Clare than something Ida herself wanted. And if Clare didn't know *why*, she wanted to know more about the woman. So she stayed, and she worked through the first book while Ida sat on a couch opposite her and embroidered. When they'd been there long enough for the silence to become comfortable, when the moment was right, Clare asked, "How long have you been with Numair?"

Ida hesitated only a moment. "Since he was born. Since before then, I guess you might say. His mother and I grew up together. She was my closest friend, a sister in everything but blood. When she took ill…" Ida paused, taking a sip of tea long gone cold. "Evaleen made me promise I would always look after him."

Ida wasn't an employee at all, then. She was family.

"I'm afraid I haven't done a very good job of it."

Clare had no idea what to say to that, so she didn't say anything. She left shortly after, and Ida insisted on walking her to the door, pressing a container of cookies into her hands as she did.

"Will you be coming back?" Ida's voice contained far more hopefulness than someone like Clare warranted. But she thought she understood why.

"I will. I don't know when, but I will."

Ida nodded. "He's—I know what he looks like. I know what everyone thinks. But he's a good man."

"I know," Clare said softly. "I know." And she pretended she didn't see the tears filling up Ida's eyes because she had no idea what to do with those, either.

348

FORTY-NINE

HEY, NEW GIRL

The quiet steadiness she'd found in Numair's home left Clare when she left it. Her uneasiness returned, hammering home the sense that she still wasn't in control. Of anything. Oh, she'd made things happen since she'd arrived in Veralna. It was a direct result of her actions that had forced her into the apprenticeship with Verol, that had resulted in Numair's hiring her for the event that had further catapulted her onto the royal scene.

But she wasn't yet in control, there. Her popularity and her future with the nobility remained dependent on their whims. Her proximity to Alaric, her new knowledge of the Song and his desire for it, was an ever-present reminder that she still wasn't safe.

She wanted a sense of further stability, another place in which to plant a foothold. And she just so happened to have a meeting with a certain violinist that evening.

She wasn't certain she intended to do anything more than annoy Madame Aria, but she'd known, even without Numair's warning the other night, that annoying her carried risks. So she spent the afternoon in Hightown, building further on the information she'd already gathered about the operation of the Musicians Guild.

The stranglehold the guild had on musical performances in the city had been built carefully over time, until it was so entrenched a thing that uprooting it would be next to impossible. At its inception, Madame Aria had marketed the guild as a guarantee of quality of performance to anyone looking to hire, an easy way for businesses to have fresh artists on rotation while guaranteeing their competency.

Perhaps even once it had only done that, and been successful at it. So much so that it became a draw for businesses to assert that they only hired Musicians Guild licensed artists. Initially, when the licenses hadn't been so expensive, it had even been an affordable way to guarantee a more steady income—which meant musicians themselves hadn't fought the guild.

But, as with all things, give an enterprise enough time to run and its greed deepened. The licenses became more expensive, as did the standard fees to hire a licensed performer. Unless, of course, a business signed an exclusivity clause with the Musicians Guild, agreeing not to hire any performer unaffiliated with the guild in return for steeply discounted pricing on those performances.

The business who didn't sign the contracts didn't fight the guild's gradual encroachment either. After all, the Musicians Guild had set the standard for what a talented musician was—one who could pay them to belong—which meant any non-guild affiliated businesses now had an excuse to pay the unlicensed singers they hired mere pittances for their performances. If they were *good* musicians, they would be licensed. Unlicensed, they were clearly inferior and, subsequently, ought to be grateful they were getting hired at all.

It was an extensive racket, and she might have been impressed by its range if she hadn't detested it so much. As it was, by the time she finished her afternoon's reconnaissance, she was seething with a quiet fury. The emotional side of her was already plotting Madame Aria's destruction, while the cold, practical side of her whispered that it wasn't her problem. That *she* had escaped the misfortunes the Musicians Guild could cause for people like her, and she should take that escape without looking back. Without trying to pull anyone else free with her.

The two desires warred within her as she met Amarrah the violinist at the agreed-upon spot.

The woman looked her over from head to toe. "If you're trying to pass for one of us the clothes work, but the coat's too fine."

The clothes were the old ones she'd put on at the Arrendon manor. The coat was Numair's. She'd returned to the palace to leave

Kialla in the stables, taking a rented carriage back into town, and had risked dipping into the suite for the coat. She was accustomed to being cold and she could handle it, but she didn't *like* it, and the coat always managed to keep her at the perfect temperature.

She bared her teeth. "I'm not trying to look like anything."

Amarrah shrugged. "Just remember that you paid me to bring you along tonight, not to make you any friends."

Clare followed her through the streets, to an out-of-the-way bar that looked as if it belonged in Lowtown rather than High. A sign above the door read *Fool's End,* in rough, thrown-together letters. They walked into a rowdy, boisterous room and it was clear, by the way Amarrah stopped the second they were inside, that she expected Clare to recoil from the noise and disorder in ladylike horror.

Clare shoved her hands into her coat pockets, the fingers of her left hand brushing reassuringly over the smooth top of the bone knife, tucked into its cleverly sewn-in sheath. The coat had come with this useful feature—and a different knife, but she found something comforting about the simplicity of the bone blade, so she'd swapped them out—and the familiarity of the weapon had a grounding effect on her as she studied the room's inhabitants. The majority were younger, those who hadn't yet given up on making this life work. Those who *were* older mostly came in the weathered but jovial variety, people who had, impossibly, kept an optimistic outlook on life despite its trials.

When it became clear that Clare wasn't going to run screaming back out the door, Amarrah led her through the packed room toward the bar. Stares followed them openly, blends of curiosity and distrust. She sat at the bar, ordered a beer and pretended to drink it until the sounds around her returned to some semblance of normalcy.

She had no doubt Amarrah had forewarned everyone about the woman who'd paid her too much money to bring her here tonight. They'd been braced for a woman with more money than sense to walk in and try to take over the place. So she ignored them all while surreptitiously observing them, waiting for curiosity to get the better of someone.

She didn't mind the wait. The oddest feeling was in her chest, growing stronger the more she watched everyone around her relaxing, settling back into drink and conversations, bursting into impromptu singing every now and then with random people grabbing for instruments to accompany. They laughed. They played. They threw darts at targets tacked to the wall. They danced and they flirted.

It was only once she identified the strange feeling that she realized it wasn't her own. The Song was content. Almost more than content, almost...happy. It hummed in her veins with a deep satisfaction, of a kind Clare had only ever felt in fleeting moments, when a set of chords or lyrics finally came together in her mind in just the right way.

It irritated her, that the Song should be capable of feeling such a thing, and in a place such as this. It wasn't as if it had *made* this camaraderie that stretched around her. It wasn't as if it was a part of it. It didn't belong here any more than she did.

I don't have to belong to appreciate.

She nearly jumped at the Song's voice in her mind. She still wasn't entirely used to the small measure of freedom she'd granted it, and she disliked this reminder of it. The reminder that it *knew her*, deeper even than the bone, because it knew her thoughts and her fears and her horrors.

The damn thing laughed at her irritation. *Though* you *could try to belong. It might make both of our lives more interesting.*

I don't want *to belong.* A truth or a lie, she wasn't certain. She was only certain that she never *could* belong. Oh, she could observe the crowd and mold herself into a person who pretended to belong, and whom everyone would like and accept. But that person would not be her.

"Hey, new girl!" The shout came from a woman with dark skin and long locs spilling over her shoulders. She looked happy and bright, surrounded by friends, and Clare was suddenly, intensely, jealous of her. "Amarrah says you sing."

"A little," the man beside her who, if the resemblance was any indication, was a relation of some sort, broke in. "She told Amarrah she sings *a little.*"

Laughter rippled through the bar, but it wasn't mocking like the laughter the court gave Numair, nor was it harsh and cruel like the laughter of her childhood. It was just...laughter. Maybe it would turn into something that indicated a judgment if she failed whatever test was sure to be thrust upon her but, for now, it was a nebulous thing.

"I suppose I do," she answered. Then added, "A little."

"Well then, new girl who sings a little, you owe the bar the newcomer's tithe. Sing us a song."

She wondered if there actually was a newcomer's tithe tradition, or if she was being thrust into the spotlight because she was a stranger who'd bought her way in here. Like the reasons behind most things in life, she supposed it didn't matter. She closed her eyes and sang. The itch to Songweave scraped at her, but she resisted it.

If she won the respect of these people, she didn't want to do it through her magic. She wanted to do it by herself, by coming to them on their terms. And a true musician didn't *need* magic to make the recipients of their song feel. Music, in the hands of the adept, was its own magic. The way the artist's emotions bled into their work, felt in where they chose to give emphasis, where to speed or slow, when to soften to the point of barely being heard.

She gave this song that purest version of herself, the her that was stripped to the bone, bare of Songweaving, bare of the Song, only her voice and her drive and her soul in the words. The noise and business of the room quieted, until she could feel the tension of the breaths held all around her.

The final note poured out of her. She let it linger, let it fade, and opened her eyes. Triumph curved her lips at the shocked stillness that surrounded her. *She* had done this. Not her magic. Not the Song.

Her.

Amarrah was staring at her, brown eyes filled with a suspicious understanding. "You never told us your name." The soft words were yet loud enough to carry through the silent room.

"It's Clare." She lifted her hand to her hair, tucking the brown waves behind her ear to reveal the black diamond. "Clare Brighton."

FIFTY

NOT NICE

Clare was exhausted by the time she stumbled back to the Arrendon manor. As she'd expected, the musicians at the Fool's End bar had not been struck with awe at the revelation that Veralna's black diamond Songweaver had taken it upon herself to visit their humble meeting place. Her reputation was, after all, all of a week old.

But the fact that she'd sung for them without the weight of that title, that she had impressed them without it, had counted in her favor. Especially when the magic sensitive among them had attested that it was only her voice, and not her power, that she had used.

And despite them declaring her a probationary new member of The Fools—as they had apparently named themselves after the bar —she was well aware they considered her presence that evening an oddity. That they were looking for a reason to exclude her from their ranks. She couldn't blame them. They had worked daily, for years and some of them for decades, to scrape a living together and here she had come, an unknown, who had cut through the muck straight to the pinnacle of Veralna's society in a matter of days.

She would hate herself too, were she them. So they'd offered her inclusion with a caveat: if she truly wanted to be one of them, she could sing with them. On the streets the next evening.

They'd expected her to refuse. She hadn't.

She had no problem lending her voice and her title to the street performers. In fact, that part of her that vindictively wanted to quash Madame Aria *liked* the idea of a public show in which she clearly distanced herself from the Musicians Guild.

She locked the Arrendons' front door behind her, knowing she should return to the palace suite, but unable to just yet. It wasn't even the thought of Fitz being there that bothered her. He'd made an unbelievably stupid gambit, but seeing his reaction to her terror, she was not afraid of him.

She was afraid of herself. Of every raw, repressed feeling she'd relived in those moments before she'd understood what was actually happening. Of the cruel, stark reminder that it took so little to make a person helpless.

She had fled Renault County but it refused to leave her, its lessons carved into her bones, stitched into her skin. It was the furnace that had forged her, and though she had shattered herself and crafted a new person in her place, the common core of both was the same. The memories couldn't be erased, only buried, until a storm hit and the earth turned soft, and they clawed their way back to the surface.

Her day had been spent reburying as many of them as possible but she still felt them, writhing and unsettled, turning in the soil. If she went back to the palace tonight, she did not think they would stay buried, and the only thing worse than Alaric thinking she was avoiding the room he'd made her would be if she jumped out of her own skin and proved all his suspicions correct.

She entered the bedroom—hers, she supposed she was to think of it now—and locked the door behind her, even though a sweep of the grounds and barn had proved that Alys was still nowhere to be found. She supposed the woman was completing whatever preparations one made when planning to rescue one's lover from one's traitorous brother.

The bed taunted her from its position in the corner. It promised sleep and rest—a rejuvenation from the exhaustion that plagued her —but she knew she would find none of those things if she sank into its depths. Her mind was too busy.

I can quiet it, the Song whispered.

"And no doubt I wouldn't have a mind *left* once you've finished," she muttered.

You always think the worst of me.

"Because I know you." Because she knew what it truly wanted, knew what desires she kept caged by caging it.

She lay down on the bed, if only to spitefully prove to herself that sleep would elude her. The house felt strange, empty of its lords, and the perfectly fine bed with its perfectly soft mattress did nothing to lull her into sleep. The silence seemed to have a voice that wouldn't be quiet.

She knew where she wanted to be, where she might be able to sleep, but given what Ida had told her that morning, there was no point in going back to Numair's. Because what she wanted wouldn't be there. Outside, the wind blew, slapping the branches of the hibiscus plant against the window.

Getting up, she eyed the distance between the bed and the window. Grabbing hold of one of the bedposts, she pulled. Nothing happened. The frame was massive, carved of solid, heavy wood. Gritting her teeth, she set her weight into her legs, took a firmer grip, and strained. The post slid a scant inch.

I suppose you don't want my help with this either? the Song rumbled, amused.

"That depends"—Clare strained, moving the post another inch—"on what you mean"—another heave, another inch—"by 'helping'."

Only this.

She gave another forceful pull just as the Song's power flared, and both her and the bed shot six feet across the room. She stumbled from the unexpected movement and let go of the post, her back slamming into the wall as momentum continued to carry her. Annoyed that she couldn't even glare at the Song—at least, not without looking in a mirror—she shoved herself off the wall…and found herself halfway across the room.

Glaring, even though it *couldn't* see, she very carefully walked back to the bed and very carefully slid it lengthwise against the wall, the center of it beneath the window.

There, was that so awful? The Song retracted its power and Clare's unnatural strength ebbed.

No, it *hadn't* been awful. That was the problem with the Song. It was always tempting her with things she knew better than to rely on. As she'd been reminded only that morning, the Song wasn't always there when she needed it.

She ignored the entity within her and climbed onto the bed,

opening the window six inches to feel the crisp bite of winter flood in. The hibiscus plant was still alive, still flowering, not a hint of frost burn on its petals, nor any other sign of nature taking the toll it exacted from all its inhabitants. Just the pure, unmarred beauty of the flowers that shouldn't be blooming.

"Damn you, Numair" she whispered. For what, she wasn't sure. Her fingers brushed one of the blossoms and it curled against her, as if recognizing that she had been there at its inception, that Numair's magic had flowed through her and into the seeds from which it had been born.

When she retracted that hand, the bloom followed, its branch lengthening as it grew to extend its reach into the room. She crossed her legs, settling her back against the wall, and cupped it in her palm.

"I'm not nice," she told the flower. "And it's stupid to be both beautiful and trusting." As if a *flower* were capable of trust. She had the violent urge to pluck the blossom, to crush it in her hands and see her skin stained red with its destruction.

One of the petals moved, brushing against her, and she sighed. She could always destroy it tomorrow.

FIFTY-ONE

NEVER AGAIN

Clare woke before the dawn, face and fingers chilled from the frigid air that had been allowed to creep in all night through the partially open window. The branches of the hibiscus plant had grown unnaturally more in the night, curling around her head like some kind of living crown. She gently pushed them back through the window, sliding the glass barrier closed.

She'd slept unexpectedly well, and the hours of rest had resettled her unpleasant memories down deep where she preferred them. She crept back into the palace before most of its inhabitants woke, returning to an empty suite. Judging by the mess that remained, Fitz had left directly after she had, and the palace's staff took the Arrendons' ban on entering their suite, even to clean, quite seriously.

The phantom hands of panic reached for her, grasping, reminding her of the unexpected surge of violence, of hands holding her down. She brushed them off and tidied the space, removing the physical reminder of the previous day's events. Once she'd gathered all the scattered letters Fitz had handed her yesterday, she took them to her room and set about deciphering them with the aid of Numair's books.

She suspected, as she worked through them, that she was learning more quickly than she should. Yesterday, she'd hardly been able to make out a single word on the cover of the book she'd picked up in Numair's library. Today the words were difficult, and she found herself having to sound them out in a way that felt childish to her, but she *could* make them out.

As if it was an old, forgotten skill she was dusting off, rather than one she was learning fresh. It had the feel of familiarity to it, and she wanted to be angry with the Song, as she suspected its hand in her improved literacy, but it had gone as silent as it always did once she'd walked through the palace's doors.

By the time she'd finished reading through them all, she was irritated she'd bothered. The majority of them were stuffed full of flowery, circuitous language that amounted to one thing: where she was concerned, Veralna's court had decided to wait and see.

At least, all of them save Proconsul Miriam Aula, whose letter informed Clare that the western solarium was pleasant in the afternoons, and Miriam hoped she would join her there tomorrow at the fourteenth bell. Since the letter had been sent yesterday, tomorrow was now today, and a glance at the clock revealed she hadn't yet missed the invitation, though it was a near thing.

She was approaching the solarium entry when a group of people in her periphery vision caught her eye, and she made the mistake of glancing in that direction. Alaric walked with two of the resident proconsuls. His manner was light and charming, in that way people who have no conscience can effortlessly slide into, and it had clearly put his companions at ease.

She didn't have time to look away before he sighted her. The mask of joviality fell, his stare an empty, assessing thing, like staring into an abyss so deep she doubted it had any end. The pulse of stolen magic and rotted lives roiled off him. How did he stand it, being covered in it every minute of every day? How did the people next to him not *feel* it?

She forced herself to give his own stare back to him, to hold it for a full second before continuing into the solarium, leaving the Jackal King behind. Tension clung to her as she searched the room for Miriam, finally spotting her on the far wall, near the doors that led to the inner courtyard.

Clare strode directly for the woman. Her back itched, deep between her shoulder blades, as if from outside the room the king's stare could burn her skin. She walked by Lady Meraland, surprised when the other woman didn't halt her progress. But Ella only gave her an inscrutable look and let her pass by, and Clare wondered if she even remembered that day in the hallway, when Ella had been so out of sorts.

She took in the quiet chatter of those around her as she progressed, catching Numair's name more than once. In her brief time here, she'd already determined that discussing him was one of the favorite pastimes within these walls, the comments speculative or derogative, and often both at the same time.

She didn't know how he stood it. Or why each mention made her want to punch someone.

Clare reached Miriam and the woman's eyes cooled. It took her a moment to realize the proconsul's gaze was fixed, not on Clare, but on something over her shoulder. Something that had made a hush fall over the room. That grease-slick of foulness drew close, but Clare refused to turn, to admit she knew who now stood at her back, who had done her no favors by ignoring the rest of the room's occupants and walking straight to her.

"Take a walk with me," Alaric said.

Her heart thudded in her chest. She had hoped he would forget her. Had hoped that the white throne and her white room were all he would bother with after getting no outward reaction from her. Had hoped, with Verol gone, that she would not even be useful as something to needle the mage with.

Clearly, she'd wished in vain.

She turned, as if the king of the known world wanting to spend time with her should be the most natural thing in that world. "Of course."

Several of the women didn't bother to hide their glares as Clare exited in the king's wake. Did these foolish women really think they wanted this kind of attention? Nothing *good* ever came from catching the eye of a powerful man.

The Song, which was as difficult to feel as it always was when she was inside the palace, seemed to remove itself even farther, as if it could somehow inhabit negative space.

Coward, she told it. *She* had to be here. *She* had to endure. Why did it get the luxury of escaping whenever it wished?

Either the king desired privacy, or he held her own contempt for whatever temperature the season chose to bestow, because he led her to the outdoor garden paths. He had the absence of guards a man certain of his absolute superiority was bound to exhibit, and they walked in silence for ten minutes before he spoke.

"Do you like my palace, Miss Brighton?"

Indifference, she reminded herself. To anything he might have to say. She shrugged. "It's very nice, as I suppose any palace is."

"There are no others." A slight edge to the words, coolly delivered, looking for the barest flicker of response from her. Because he'd torn down the palaces in every province on the continent after he conquered it. Because there was only one palace he hadn't managed to claim, and that one lay in the heart of Renault County, built of shining white stone and bleached-white bone, and he was waiting to see if she would flinch.

The throne and her room weren't a fluke. He *knew*. So why hadn't he done anything yet? "Of course not, Your Majesty."

"I did tell you to call me Alaric, didn't I?"

"And I did tell you I wouldn't, didn't I?"

He'd expected the reply, because he had his own ready. "And yet you seem quite comfortable calling my nephew Numair."

She had only a second to decide how to reply. Derision was the safest avenue for her. Derision, but delivered teasingly enough that his pride couldn't be pricked *too* hard. "Why, Your Majesty, are you jealous of a man half your age?"

He wasn't. She knew jealousy. She knew men. The game he was playing with her wasn't sexual or romantic—it was mental.

"Isn't everyone jealous of youth, once they age?"

As if he didn't look decades younger than his age. As if the foul layers clinging to him didn't hold that age at bay. As if Numair wasn't closer to a quarter of his age than the half she'd said.

"I suppose in a few decades, I could let you know."

He laughed. "You've hardly spent any time here, and yet you're all anyone can talk about. Why is that?"

"People like new and shiny things. They'll forget about me soon enough, if you don't keep pulling me away for clandestine walks. You should be careful, Your Majesty. They'll worry you intend to marry."

"You sound certain I won't make an offer."

"Kings don't make offers—they make demands."

"And you have no wish to be a queen?" Was she imagining the tone of his voice? The way it seemed less a question than a taunt.

Queen. How she hated that fucking word. *Min quellea. My queen.* She dug deep inside herself, found a laugh and forced it out. "No. For one, the political position seems tedious, and for another, I have no wish to marry at all."

"I thought all women wished to marry."

"May I be blunt, Your Majesty?"

"Please do."

"No woman wishes to marry. They may wish for love or money, power or station, public acknowledgment or lifelong companionship. They may wish for the attention of the wedding day. But they do not wish for marriage itself—marriage is simply the set of shackles that allows them to attain their desires. Whatever things I desire, I will acquire some other way, or do without."

Alaric laughed. "I think I begin to understand his obsession with you."

The unease simmering beneath Clare's skin intensified at the vagueness of that pronoun. It could mean Numair. It could mean someone else. "Was there something in particular you wanted to speak with me about?"

He let her change the subject. "I heard you went riding with Proconsul Aula. What did the two of you talk about?"

Unease crept down her spine and she was grateful, more than ever, for the vagueness of her own words in that conversation. "I don't recall."

"No? Do treasonous words stick so lightly in your memory?"

Her shoulders stiffened, and he laughed.

"People speak too freely in my own court, it seems. But do not worry for her. She's useful where she is. For now."

"Then why bring it up?"

"Because she told you a simple story. About a king who spilled blood to take her land. But all stories have two sides. I wager she failed to mention the history of her own province. Her lands were soaked in the blood of the fallen long before I spilled any there.

"The Taellan Province was once several countries, you know? But the Taellans waged war ruthlessly, until they formed the kingdom they were when I came.

"You see, people only have a problem with subjugation when it happens to them. They only believe people have a right to their own beliefs and systems and rules when *they* are the ones in

danger of being subsumed. When they are at the top of the hierarchy, however, I assure you they have no difficulty believing
their rules and mores ought to be imposed upon the lesser
masses."

"And what am I to take away from this lesson, Your Majesty?"
Clare stopped—the garden path had looped back, reopening into
the mouth of the palace's back courtyard—and faced him.

"Only that I have not done anything that others have not been
doing for centuries. The singular difference is that I have succeeded
where they have failed. I do not deny that my actions have killed
many. But the world is now at peace. Is a temporary sacrifice not
worth it, to attain a better state?"

"Why should my opinion matter?"

Anger flashed in his eyes. "Because they love you. And they
hate me."

Miriam had been right. Alaric *did* want his people to love him.
And he couldn't understand why they didn't, because he didn't
have the faintest idea *how* to love.

"What is love worth? You hold all the power over them. Any
woman in that room would marry you if you asked. Any courtier
would debase themselves for you, any proconsul kneel."

He laughed, as if she was hopelessly naive. "Love *is* power. It
shackles people to each other. It destroys them. And all without you
ever having to lift a finger to make it happen. I hold power over
them, yes. But I am forced to remind them of it at every turn. They
will only kneel so long as they haven't had enough distance to think
perhaps they do not have to.

"But you...when you sing, they love you. When you sing, they
would do anything for you, and do it happily."

"They may love me while I sing, but they forget me easily when
I am silent."

"Because you allow them to. Because your...charms are
constrained by the rules that govern magic's use. I can remove those
constraints."

To anyone else, it might have been a tempting offer. Anyone else
might have asked if it would be so bad to be beholden to one man, if
doing so meant that everyone else was beholden to *her*. But a leash
was still a leash, no matter how long the line. No matter if only one
person was ever allowed to hold it.

"If you think I can make a kingdom love you, Your Majesty, you overestimate my charm."

"Do I?" She didn't miss the sudden sharpness of his gaze, the new hardness in his tone. "Did you not once do the same for someone else?"

Ice crept down her spine. Memories she didn't want pushed at her mind, but they were hers this time, and she couldn't force an absent Song to take them away. "I have no idea what you mean, Your Majesty." And he was wrong. What she had done at another's behest had not been to create love. Not even a twisted approximation of it. "Thank you for the walk." She bowed and turned.

"Did I get the throne right? And your room? Did they make you feel at home?"

She held her tongue and kept walking. Power clamped around her and it took her half a second to understand what it was supposed to do. Half a second to know that, as she should have been brought to her knees at Numair's nameday celebration, she should be incapable of movement now.

She froze. But she'd taken a step before she did. Had he seen the hesitation between his command and her obedience? Would she walk out of this courtyard alive?

"There is an acquaintance of mine. An old rival, I suppose you might say. He's missing something. The interesting part is, that something he's missing looks a lot like you—a young, pretty, scarred little songbird." Phantom fingers skated up the scars marring her back and she couldn't stop it—she flinched.

The Jackal King laughed. The magic surrounding her spun and she forced herself to spin with it, to face him. Forced herself, when he crooked his finger, to walk to him. His fingers closed on her chin in a bruising grip, forcing her head up.

"What do you think Simian Hensa would give me, if I gave you back to him?"

Her vision blurred at the periphery, sound and sight narrowing to the rushing of her blood in her ears and the king before her.

He tapped his index finger against her cheek, as if in contemplation. "But perhaps the better question is, what would *you* give *me* to avoid going back?"

Never again. She closed her eyes as the words echoed in her head, over and over. Insistent. Undeniable. *Never again. Never again. I said never again.*

Never again would another person control her life. Never again would she bend. Never again would she break. Never. Again.

She opened her eyes. "Know this, Your Majesty. I will open my throat to the bone before I ever return to Renault County." There was no longer any point in hiding. Not with him. "If you want me to do the impossible for you, find something better to threaten me with."

"Perhaps I will." His magic dissipated and she turned, walked three steps before he said, "I'm curious. How did you get out? Even Simian can't leave that place. Not anymore."

Without breaking stride, she said, "It's simple. I died."

She passed through the courtyard and into the solarium. It had grown markedly more populated in her absence, and its inhabitants now rushed to look as if they were engaged with each other, rather than in watching her and their king.

Someone spoke to her, but she didn't hear the words. She didn't care what that scene had looked like to any of these people. She only knew she needed to get out of this place before she tried to claw her way out of her own body.

She realized Numair was now among the solarium's occupants when he took one look at her face and stood. Dahlia had literally been in his lap this time, and she tumbled sideways at his abrupt ascent.

He followed Clare without a word, until they were out of the palace, out of the stables, past the outer wall. Until they arrived at his home, and they'd dropped Hellack and Kialla in the paddock. And when he did speak, he didn't ask her what had happened. He didn't ask her if she was okay.

The Ferrian-cursed, brilliant man made a *joke*. "You may want to buy actual battle armor before you return to the palace. No doubt rumor has already spread that both my uncle and I have fallen madly in love with you. Half the court women may try to kill you."

The laughter that burst out of her was unexpected. It took the edge off her anger, enough for her to remember how to speak. "Next time, you might try *not* dumping a woman on the floor to run after me."

He shrugged. "She deserves far worse than being dumped on the ground."

Then why are you sleeping with her? She wanted to ask. But she knew that was one of those questions she could never give voice to, in the same way he knew not to ask her what his uncle had said to her. Their new friendship was built on unspoken rules they both instinctively recognized the boundaries of. And she didn't want to ruin it.

When they stopped outside the hidden door to his home she said, "I don't think I can be inside right now." She wanted to run. And run. And run. To run until her lungs and legs burned with the strain and her soul, if she had such a thing, left her body.

"Humor me for a moment. I have something I think will help. If it doesn't, I won't keep you."

He led her up to the third floor, to a wide, airy room with a row of windows overlooking the paddock. The floor was covered in soft mats, and he led to her a corner, where a bag hung suspended from the ceiling. "What am I supposed to do with this?" She poked it and found it was heavy but semi-pliant, as if filled with sand.

"You hit it. And then you keep hitting it, until you feel better."

So she hit. And she kept hitting, until the skin flayed from her knuckles and she left bloody imprints on the bag, and if she didn't feel *better* she at least felt...quieter.

FIFTY-TWO

AS IF HE BELONGED TO HIMSELF

Numair watched her hit the bag and tried to shove down how desperately *he* needed to hit something. He figured only one of them got to let their rage overtake them at a time, and at the moment she was the one with a right to need it more.

But he couldn't stop the earlier scene from replaying in his head. Walking into the solarium and seeing her in the courtyard with him. Forcing himself to pretend he didn't care, to sit down and let Dahlia practically climb all over him.

There was a disjointedness to watching something unfold and knowing that everyone around you was seeing one thing, while you were seeing another. The courtiers muttering that yes, Clare was pretty enough, and young enough, and talented to be sure, but where precisely had she even come from? Why was Alaric so taken with her?

As if that hand gripping her chin had been a caress and not a demand for submission. As if they thought Alaric had spoken words of endearment to her rather than threats. As if the flush on her cheeks had come from excitement, rather than anger.

It had taken every shred of the self-control he'd been cultivating since he was fifteen to not ask her what his uncle had said. Because it hadn't only been anger he'd seen in her eyes. There had been a blankness there too, as if Alaric had carved deep into her and hollowed something out and, with its withdrawal, the Clare he knew had been replaced with a doppelganger that thought only in terms of survival.

Whatever had passed between her and the king, Numair didn't think it had to do with the power he suspected she possessed. Alaric wouldn't have let her walk away from that conversation. She wouldn't have responded to it so...personally.

Her breathing was ragged, her hands bloodied, her shirt soaked through with sweat, but he didn't try to stop her. He didn't try to tell her it was enough. It was never enough, would never *be* enough. He knew that better than anyone. Knew the only reprieve was exhausting the body until it was too tired to express the physical symptoms of fear.

And she *was* afraid—just not of Alaric. Or at least, not only of him.

Her hands finally fell away from the bag. Streams of crimson flowed down her fingers, *plink plink plinking* onto the mats that covered the floor. For a moment he saw the bright white of exposed knuckle bones. Then that cold, foreign power shivered through her and her skin was whole, quicker and neater than any healer could have managed.

Irritation crossed her face, as if the healing had been unwanted, and he had the sudden, ludicrous desire to leave with her. To just... walk out of this house, out of this city, and see if she would go with him.

As if either of them had that freedom. As if the world didn't belong to Alaric and they could hide somewhere in it. As if Numair's most minor absence from Veralna didn't have to be planned and approved. As if he belonged to himself.

Her gaze went to the clock on the far wall. "I have something I promised to do. Put on a different face and come with me?"

"I'd like to."

"But you can't?"

He shook his head. He was already going to have enough to fix, following her out of the palace like that. But he couldn't bring himself to regret it.

She turned to go, stopped, turned back. "If I come by tonight, will you be here?"

He wished she hadn't asked that. "No."

She didn't leave, and now he wished she would. Wished the knowledge of what that *no* meant wasn't sitting between them. Wished he was a different person.

"When will you be?"

"*Clare.*" He closed his eyes. Opened them to find her kneeling in front of where he sat.

"When will you be?" she pushed.

Her liquid green eyes were intent on him, and he searched them for judgment. Relented when he found none. "I don't know."

She gave a sharp nod and rose, making him realize she'd taken the truth he'd given her for a brush-off.

"I don't know," he repeated. "But I'll tell you when I do."

She smiled. The first one he'd seen from her that didn't look like a warning or a promise or a presentation. It just looked like…her.

Then she was gone and he was sitting there, staring at her blood drying on the floor and wondering if she had any notion of how much messier she'd made his already complicated life.

FIFTY-THREE

WHO YOU ARE

Something dark and chaotic churned in Clare. Something the strain of exhausting her muscles on the bag had tempered, and Numair's *no* in answer to her question had coaxed from a diminished ember back to a raging fire. The flames licked at her bones, a deep burn that needed an outlet.

How fortunate for her that she had one. She'd promised to sing with some of the musicians from the Fool's End tonight. She knew that all they wanted from it was a simple test—to see if she would meet them on the streets, in the community she claimed to want to be a part of.

That was what she had promised and it was, initially, all she'd planned to do. Then Alaric had happened. Alaric, who had made her feel as if she'd escaped one prison only to have stepped halfway into another, and if she wasn't careful, she would fall wholly through and the door would slam shut behind her. Alaric, who had threatened to send her back to *him*. Like it was nothing.

Alaric, who had said, *They love you when you sing,* and, *Love is power.*

Alaric. Alaric. ALARIC.

His name was a curse buried beneath her tongue, was the vitriol burning through her veins, was the fuel that had her urging Kialla faster toward the city.

If love was power, then she would make them love her. If love was power, then she would be more powerful than he could ever be.

But it wasn't love that had her walking into business after business, every one she could find that might ever need to hire a singer or other musician. It wasn't love that drove her into the normal businesses after that. It wasn't with love that she delivered, to every person in those establishments, the black diamond in her ear on full display, the same message: *I'll be singing tonight, in the city park, at the nineteenth bell.*

By the time she walked into the Fool's End, her rage had subsided to a steady simmer—manageable, but ready to return to a boil at a moment's notice.

The bar went briefly silent at her entry—possibly because of the look on her face—before Marcus, the brother of the woman who'd asked Clare to sing the night before—broke it. "Told you all she'd show."

The groans and shuffling of coins told Clare a fair amount of betting had taken place on whether she would or wouldn't appear this evening. She ignored it. "There's been a change of plans."

Marcus's sister snorted. "And I told you she wouldn't actually sing with us."

Clare ignored that too, taking in the packed bar. "I'm going to need all of you. And we're going to the park."

A hush blanketed the room.

"The law doesn't forbid us from playing in the park," came a soft voice, from a girl who looked perhaps fifteen, "but they don't like us there. They always find a reason to make us leave."

"They won't make *me* leave."

An older man spoke up next. "There's a reason we don't all get together and put on a concert. There's not enough money once you split it that many times."

"You'll all make a night's worth of Musicians Guild wages, or I'll pay it myself. Now"—she found Amarrah, standing by the bar, and flipped her a coin—"you need to hire me to Songweave. On behalf of everyone here."

Amarrah turned the coin over, but her eyes were on Clare. "What am I hiring you to do to us, exactly?"

Clare smiled. "To show you exactly who you are."

Amarrah contemplated it, reading the room before tossing the coin back to Clare as payment. "Then show us who we are."

So she did.

SONGWEAVING WAS a resource Clare had once made use of daily, in that lawless place where the only curbs on magic use were those put in place by whomever was stronger than you. She realized she'd missed it, having not exercised the power since she'd made the king feel heartbreak. The twist and lull of the magic in her voice, how achingly good it felt to use it. Like stretching a muscle that had been begging for use only to be ordered to rest.

She worked it now, sussing out from each person in this room what had drawn them here. What made them unique, what the one thing was they brought to their art that no one else could bring, and she reminded them of it.

Nothing could be won without confidence, so for this one night, she gave them the confidence of who they were. Of who they could be. And when they were ready she led them out of the Fool's End, through the streets to the park, where already so many were gathered.

She'd counted on her name, on her novelty, to draw the first crowds, and she was not disappointed. She sang, and the musicians at her back played. The crowd swelled around them, until the city guard did indeed make an appearance. But they, like the crowd, only listened as she poured herself into the music, and every person with her did the same.

She knew she'd accomplished what she wanted when she spotted Madame Aria at the edge of the crowd, flanked by two red-clad Hounds. But there was nothing for those Hounds to find as Clare sang. Her magic was tucked away, her voice only her voice. She smiled at Madame Aria as one of the Hounds shook his head.

The look the woman gave her in return promised that this wasn't over, that she could be every bit as vindictive as Numair had warned. Clare welcomed it. She was going to need something to occupy her time.

FIFTY-FOUR

I KNOW BAD MEN

Clare didn't even pretend she should return to the palace that evening. If Verol thought it wouldn't be a problem that she wasn't with him now, as the apprenticeship's terms stated she should be, then she couldn't see how it would be a problem if she stayed here, rather than in the palace suite. And after today...well, she wanted to stay as far away from Alaric as possible.

She wasn't foolish enough to think he would forget about her. Now that it was out in the open between them—Renault County and Simian—she knew better than to hope he would leave her alone. But he was a king. One for whom the foulness stitched to him meant he would live a very, very long time. So surely he had more important things to do than wonder, immediately, where *she* was.

The only real problem was that, once again, her wardrobe was in the palace suite. She would go by Chalen's tomorrow, she decided, and see if the rest of what she'd ordered was finished. Bring it here to the Arrendons'. At least this time she'd had her coat on when she'd left. She drew it closer around her—it still smelled faintly of Numair, a mixture of floral tones and earthiness she equated with his nature magic. It was...oddly soothing.

She pulled the garment tighter after murmuring a soft goodnight to Kialla, who was sniffing at the wood-chip bedding in her stall with that look that said she was trying to find the perfect place to lie down. Clare was halfway to her room's window—it felt like a more natural entrance to her than the front door—when she realized something was bothering her about the house.

That something was the light glowing softly from the kitchen window. A form paced on the far side of the room. Her first thought was Fitz, but then she realized the silhouette was too slender, a hair too short.

She changed course, entering through the back door and walking into the brightly lit kitchen.

"Where have you been?" the Duchess of Wake snapped. And oh, did she *sound* like a duchess, having dropped all pretense of a common accent, tone rife with the kind of aristocratic self-importance that one had to be born with to have it come so naturally.

Clare arched one eyebrow at the haughty demand, shoved her hands into her coat pockets, and leaned back against the wall, adopting an insouciant air. "A thousand apologies, Your Ladyship. Had I realized I was now a vassal of the Duchy of Wake, I'm certain I should never have left this kitchen, in case you should possibly need to speak to me for any reason."

Alys looked about to snap out an agreement that that was precisely what Clare should have done. Then she closed her eyes and took a deep breath before opening them again. She didn't apologize, but Clare hardly expected her to.

"You promised you would help. You *owe* me."

"I did and I will." She took some issue with the matter of *owing*, but she decided to let it pass unremarked on, given how…volatile Alys looked. "Do you have something for me to help with, then?"

"I'm trusting you," Alys warned. "With something far more precious than my life. If you don't deliver, if she dies, I'll kill you."

"You could try," Clare purred. "But don't worry. I'll make certain you never need to."

"Then I need you tomorrow night." Perching on one of the kitchen chairs, she motioned for Clare to sit. She then proceeded to talk, going over and over the plan for the next two hours. She probably would have gone over it until the sun rose, had Clare not put her foot down and said, "I'm going to sleep. You can follow me if you truly feel the need to reiterate the plan to my unconscious form, but I'd hate to have to tell Lina that you spent the night before her rescue in bed with another woman."

Alys looked affronted.

Clare rolled her eyes. "Get some sleep, Lady Megadari. You clearly need it."

"Wait."

Clare groaned, then almost jumped at the sound—at her ease making it, the same ease with which she'd rolled her eyes seconds ago. She could not remember the last time she had been comfortable enough around anyone to have uncalculated responses. Between Alys, Numair, and the Arrendons, she hardly knew what was happening to her.

When Alys deduced that Clare was, in fact, waiting, she said, "What did you do to Fitz?"

Clare's voice cooled a few degrees. "What did I do to *him*?"

Alys didn't miss the anger in her voice, but she clearly missed the seriousness behind it. "Yes. He's—I haven't seen him like this since I met him."

"Do yourself a favor, Alys. Stay out of business that doesn't concern you."

"It *does* concern me. I need him tomorrow night. But when I told him you were coming, he said I had to ask *you* if it was okay, or he wouldn't."

Clare made a frustrated noise. Life had never been complicated in *this* way before, this way that seemed to involve so many emotions and relationships, things she had shoved down and avoided. It occurred to her that she should just go back to avoiding them. She schooled her voice into dismissive neutrality. "It makes no difference to me if he comes."

"What happened between the two of you?"

"That would be none of your concern." No one, absolutely no one, needed to know how helpless he'd managed to make her feel. How helpless she'd *been*, with the Song hiding away. What kind of magic let a man coat his body as if in stone?

In retrospect, she could have Songweaved. Distracted him. Her response to the attack had simply been too animalistic for the rational part of her brain to remember that. So tonight she would sit in her room and relive that moment over and over again, until she accepted it, so that the next time, she would not panic.

She'd allowed herself to become complacent in all too short a time, had let herself relax. It was almost a relief to realize she shouldn't. When everything was a threat, it was also less complicated.

But Alys seemed intent on making it complicated. "Fitz is my friend," she warned. "And he's been through enough. Don't trifle with him." Softer, she said, "I'd rather you didn't with Numair, either."

It took a nudge from the Song, filling in the gaps between the words, for Clare to understand what she meant. Once she did, she didn't bother to stop her laugh. "What exactly did Fitz say to you?"

"*Nothing*. That is what's so strange about it."

The woman wasn't going to let it go. Clare shouldn't care what she thought. Told herself she didn't care, but that it would be easier —neater—if Alys didn't hold a grudge against her because of a misunderstanding.

"Fitz hates me," she told Alys plainly. "Based on that feeling, he did something that had consequences he didn't expect. Now he feels guilty about it. I imagine he'll recover from the feeling in a few days and return to an uncomplicated view of me. As for Numair, he's my friend."

"And that 'friendship' has nothing to do with the fact that he's a prince?" Skepticism coated Alys's words.

If it wasn't for the fact that, underneath the skepticism, it was obvious the woman still cared about Numair—and for the fact that he still cared about her—Clare would have snapped out something cutting and left. As it was, she had to put it in a way Alys would understand. "Do you think I am stupid?"

Alys blinked. "No."

"Then understand that *I* understand there are no material advantages to being his friend. Everyone will think he's bedding me. If they think he's not, they'll worry he actually likes me, which will be even worse.

"I am not trying to use him, Alys. I am not trying to marry him." Inadvertently, a truth she hadn't realized slipped free. "I need him. And he needs me. Interfere and you will regret it."

It was the threat that seemed to finally convince Alys, to make her smile. "Then I suppose I won't."

"You could be nicer to him, you know? When you come back. He never stopped being *your* friend."

Alys blew out a breath. "My parents were the ones who forced me to quit that acquaintance, though I can hardly say I blamed them. Now that they're gone...we'll see. You have not been here long. You have hardly scratched the surface of his reputation."

Clare deliberated, choosing her words with care. "I'm disappointed. I would have thought you, of all people, could tell the difference between a reputation and a person. I'll see you tomorrow night."

She left Alys in the kitchen and went to her room—to find the object of their previous discussion lounging on her bed. Apparently, she wasn't the only one who had a propensity for sneaking in through windows. Given her and Numair's earlier conversation, she hadn't expected to see him so soon, and wondered if the only reason she was now was *because* of that conversation.

He had one knee drawn up to his chest, looking out the window as Alys strode across the lawn to the stables. If he'd overheard any of their conversation, it didn't show on his face. His voice came out a little hollow, a little tight. "Figured I'd find you here. Didn't figure I'd find her. Has she been here the entire time?"

"As far as I know. She does a terrible job of playing stable girl."

He didn't laugh. He had that same pensive, wounded expression he'd worn when he'd first realized Clare knew where Alys was. "Is she all right?"

"She will be. Once we solve her little...problem."

His jaw clenched, mouth setting in a firm line. "I want to help."

She opened her mouth to tell him he couldn't. Not because she didn't want him to, but because Alys would likely abandon the plan if Clare arrived to their meeting the next evening with him in tow.

But Numair looked oddly vulnerable, sitting on her bed, his boots discarded nearby on the floor, his hair tousled. Dark circles lurked beneath the glamour on his face. She had the sense that he needed to do something—something helpful that he could feel good about—and she didn't know what it would do to him if she told him no.

"I can't tell you what we're doing. I made a few promises, where that is concerned. But I can tell you that, should you happen to find yourself in the vicinity of the Megadari's estate tomorrow evening around the twenty-third bell, you might find a way to make yourself useful."

"Thank you." He reached for his boots.

"Stay." The word came out less of a request than a command.

His fingers paused above one boot. "You're exhausted."

She didn't point out that, beneath his glamour, he looked worse than she felt. "Doesn't mean you have to go."

"I'm in a piss-poor mood."

She snorted. "Then shut your princely mouth and go to sleep. You look awful."

"Verol won't take it kindly if he finds out."

"I won't tell him if you don't. Any other concerns you'd like me to allay?" She took the second pillow off the bed and pulled a spare blanket from the armoire, making the kind of bed she was far more accustomed to.

"I can take the floor," Numair offered.

"It's fine."

"I don't mind."

"I sleep better this way." She hated how much more natural the hard surface felt than a mattress did. And Numair didn't argue with her, after that.

She turned off the room's magelights and settled in, still wrapped in his coat. In the darkness the sounds of their breathing were amplified, and she knew he wasn't any closer to sleep than she was, the air thick with two people thinking too much.

"Clare?"

"Hmm?"

She heard the rustle of sheets as he turned on his side, looked up to find him peering down at her in the moonlight. "She wasn't wrong. You *haven't* scratched the surface of my reputation."

Which answered the question of whether or not he'd heard them talking. She wondered when he'd come in, if he'd even needed her to tell him where to find them the next night.

The moonlight seemed to intensify every aspect of his face— lines he was too young to bear, eyes too haunted by things he'd seen and done and rather wouldn't have.

This was why she needed him. This was why he needed her. Because they were the same.

She half-rose, propping herself on her elbows, coming to the edge of that personal physical boundary neither of them crossed without permission and intention. "I know bad men, Numair. You aren't one of them."

Her statement went without response, dissolving into the silence of the room, for long enough that she lay back down.

"Why is it," he said softly, "that you're the only person who believes that?"

"I thought you knew by now—I'm smarter than everyone else."

She stayed awake, until his breathing evened out and she knew he slept. As it turned out, the second prince of Faelhorn snored. It made her smile, for some reason, and she fell into an almost-peaceful sleep.

When the sun's rays spilled through her window the next morning, the harsh glare waking her, he was gone.

CHAPTER

FIFTY-FIVE

IN WANT OF A PUBLIC DISTURBANCE

Clare spent another evening in Hightown, singing with the Fools, before slipping away to meet Alys outside the Megadari estate. It was another of those not terribly far from the Arrendons' or Numair's. The Duchy of Wake included Veralna City as part of its domain, so naturally the Megadaris had built their dwelling as close to the seat of ultimate power in the area as possible.

The primary difference between this estate and those other two was the large contingent of guards present on its grounds. When Clare had asked about it, Alys had helpfully pointed out that, "Everyone knows Numair is never home, and furthermore no one is willing to risk crossing Alaric by killing his favorite nephew. Especially when Numair has never engaged in politics. There's no value in killing him.

"As for the Arrendons, people *are* occasionally stupid enough to try and kill them. They always die bloodily and painfully. Handling it personally like that—it reminds people that walking into the house of two diamond-ranked mages is a truly terrible idea.

"My family is neither politically unimportant nor are we mages. Hence, guards."

So it was that Clare found herself slipping along the shadowed edges of the Megadari estate, recalling the mental map of the layout, and the guard schedule Alys had spent the last few days acquiring.

She climbed the exterior wall and slunk silently down the other side, the mottled brown-gray-green of her chosen breeches and coat doing well to blend her into the nighttime landscape. She reached the house without incident. Its facade had not been built with the ease of scaling its walls in mind, the stones laid flat and even and polished to a shine. So it was a good thing she found easily enough the hidden door Alys had said let into the kitchens, the door she swore her brother did not know about and therefore could not possibly have tied into the home's wards.

She wondered if every large house had such hidden entrances. Despite Alys's certainty, Clare was still mildly surprised when she slipped inside the dark kitchen without incident.

I could have disabled the wards, the Song said, in what was perilously close to a grumble.

No, Clare answered, *you couldn't, because we need them to contact Alys later.*

It did not say what Clare suspected, which was, *I could put them back together, too.*

She slipped through the kitchen, reciting memorized directions in her head in Alys's voice as she moved quietly through the house.

Left at the hall after the kitchens. Servants' staircase three doorways down on the left, fourth, sixth, and eighth steps creak.

She continued following Alys's directions until she arrived onto a mezzanine floor, then moved down the east wing to the door at the end of the hallway on the right, which was not locked because why bother when the person inside it could be killed with a thought?

Lina was being kept in the family rooms like the prized hostage she was, and she slept fitfully as Clare crept silently into the room. She watched the woman for a moment, feeling odd, for she had never before watched a sleeping figure she had not intended to kill. How many nights had she stood by the piled rags in the one-room hovel in Renault County, watching the labored strain of alcohol-riddled breaths wheeze in and out of her mother's bare chest while the latest nameless male snored heavily next to her?

She could still feel the smoothness of the bone gripped in her then-small hands, its tip shaved to a point, longing to sink it into the heart of whatever man shared her mother's bed. Because even at four and five and six, she had known the way they looked at her was wrong. She had never done it because she'd known killing one would not make the men stop coming while her mother lived, and she had not yet been cold enough to kill her own mother.

Had she been, things might have turned out differently. Some, Clare reckoned, might even argue that the failure of that moment was the one that led her to *this* moment, this room, but Clare knew it had begun earlier than that. It had begun, really, in her being born. Of all the selfish things Clare's mother had ever done, bringing Clare into the world was perhaps the worst of them.

But she was here now and, having been born, had no intention of dying. So she stood watching Lina sleep without waking her because something about Lina's and Alys's situation distressed her greatly. Prior to their current circumstances, the two women had had an abundance of money and influence between them. They were beautiful and clever and yet, somehow, they had still been made near-helpless.

How?

But the answer was obvious. It lay in the look Lina had given Clare when she'd seen Alys's ribbon about her wrist. It had expressed itself in the nerves Alys had barely contained prior to letting Clare sneak onto the estate, when she had wanted so badly to do it herself.

Alaric's voice rose, unbidden, in her mind. *Love is power. It shackles people to each other. It destroys them. And all without you ever having to lift a finger to make it happen.*

She didn't truly understand love, she realized. Her only experience with it came from songs and ballads, where the truth of how it happened hid somewhere between the lyrics. If she was going to avoid it, to avoid *this* situation, she needed to suss out those truths.

But first, she had a job to do.

She scuffed her toe deliberately on the stone floor and Lina jerked upright, her wild gaze falling on Clare. Her eyes widened and she shook her head, hand moving frantically to the white bracelet on her arm.

Clare gave the woman a look that said, *Be still,* and before Lina could even think of protesting Clare clamped her own hand over Lina's, the tip of her middle finger brushing the foul warmth of the band beneath. The Song unfurled eagerly and latched on. With a sigh of such relish it was nearly disgusting, it drank and drank and drank, leaching the bracelet of warmth and power, until the white band crumbled into ash.

Ignoring the awkward feeling of the Song's satisfaction, Clare reached for the cat-shaped crystal Alys had told her to look for, knocking it from its pedestal atop the bedside stand. Magic pulsed through the walls, the wards shrieking, and Megadari Manor came alive with noise and activity.

"What have you done?" Lina stared at the crumbled bracelet and fallen ward-tripper, clearly unsure if she should be grateful or angry.

"Let your lover know it's time for her to do *her* part."

Lina's eyes narrowed. "And what is her part?"

"Alas, her ladyship did not see fit to inform me of it." Which she suspected had more to do with Alys not wanting Lina involving herself in that part, as opposed to not trusting Clare with it.

Lina untangled herself from twisted bedsheets, moving with haste for the door. Clare considered parting from her and slipping from the home the same way she'd entered. Her part here was done, her duty carried out, and as she did not know what Alys intended, the safer course was to leave the woman to it.

It was the smart thing to do. It was what the Clare who'd first arrived in Veralna City *would* have done. But she didn't. She couldn't. An uneasy fear beat in her chest, a fear that she would leave and wake tomorrow in a world Alys and Lina were no longer a part of.

This is how it starts, a cold part of her whispered. *With caring if people live or die.*

But she followed Lina's frantic rush down the hall to the open mezzanine area. The inside of the manor was now ablaze with magelight. Lina stood still as death, one hand on the balcony railing, and Clare stopped silently beside her, looking down at the scene below.

Everywhere, men lay dead, dying, or fighting. Every single one of them wore the Megadari crest, but only some wore a thin black band about their left wrist, and at the head of their force were Fitz and Alys. Their banded men fought with the brutality and single-mindedness of those whose job it was to kill, and who were adept at their profession.

Mercenaries, Clare realized.

None of this was what had stopped Lina, however. Her gaze had caught on Alys's brother, on the unnerving quickness with which Alys spotted him and *moved*. He held no blade in his hand. His face held no fear for his life.

Stupid man, thought Clare.

He looked at Alys and smiled. Magic thrummed through the armband on his bicep. It glowed, hot and white, before crumbling to ash as its twin had so recently done. The confusion on his face brought relief to Alys's.

She pulled a fresh dagger from the sheath at her hip, not pausing for speech or negotiation. No, she simply closed the distance between them while Geoffrey realized too late that he should have been moving. She gripped his shoulder in her left hand, thrust her dagger between his ribs with her right and shoved deep, sliding between ribs to reach the heart.

Too late, his hands reached for her, trying to strangle, but with a cry of sheer primal rage Alys heaved him against the wall, the dagger inside the man making a noise Clare could hear even on the mezzanine floor above as its small hilt caught against flesh, crunched into bone. Alys held until his weight sagged against her, then slid the dagger free, letting Geoffrey's limp bulk fall to the floor.

Lina made a strangled sound that jerked Alys's gaze up. Then she was sliding down the balustrade and Alys was catching her. Their arms came around each other and they were kissing, Alys's bloody hands stroking madly through Lina's hair, and neither one of them seeming to mind the mess.

Clare was busy studying the facets of this emotional entanglement, ostensibly in order to best identify how its dangers might be avoided, when Numair walked in.

The two women on the ground floor, surrounded by dead, dying, and wounded bodies, stilled.

Numair surveyed the wreck of the foyer, took in the mercenaries in House Megadari crests and said, "Hostage negotiations gone awry, I take it?"

Clare suspected it was Numair's very obvious sobriety, and the confident, assessing tone that kept Alys from immediately berating Clare for his presence.

"I'm afraid," Alys answered, "that my brother was killed

attempting to secure my return. He was unprepared for a double-cross."

"Who killed him?"

"His Second, the same man who kidnapped me." She jerked her head to where Fitz had men rearranging the scene. Two of them came forward to move the body of Geoffrey's Second next to Alys's fallen brother, setting the body into place just-so, and placing in his hand the knife Alys had used to end Geoffrey.

"How did you escape?"

"Reinforcements arrived."

The remaining men, Clare noted, had stripped the identifying black bands from their wrists, indistinguishable now as anything but house guards.

Numair nodded. "Are the wards tied in to alert the city guard?"

Alys nodded.

"Then you need a little more time to set your scene." He looked up to the mezzanine floor. "Clare?"

Clare, because it had looked like a great deal of fun when Lina did it—slid down the balustrade to land nimbly by his side.

Alys looked at them in confusion. "How are you going to delay the guard?"

"My prince," Clare said, "you do look indecently drunk and in want of a public disturbance."

"Don't I always?"

They were at the door when Alys called, "Numair."

They paused, turning.

"When you're finished doing what you're doing…come talk to me."

Clare felt him hesitate, recognized a coming refusal on his lips. So she gave him a look that said, *Don't be a coward.*

His return look said, *Don't be an ass.* But aloud, he said, "If I can."

FIFTY-SIX

DO YOU HAVE TO?

Numair stood in the rising dawn outside the Megadari estate, trying to make up his mind. Go in, or leave. Stay with what was comfortable, what was safe, or see if he could find anything better.

Don't be a coward. The words had practically been written on Clare's face, as if she'd known he was going to refuse Alys's invitation.

But was it really an invitation if Clare's prodding at Alys was the only reason he was receiving it? Was there truly anything better to be found in a grudging friendship based on one party's sufferance of the other's behavior?

He sighed and walked through the gates, up to the heavily guarded front doors. It didn't have to be the start of something. He could just see that she was all right. Her and Lina both. They'd been inseparable as children, and he'd had a good notion of the direction they were heading in before either of them had figured it out.

One of the few benefits of his obnoxious title was *not* having to wait at the door. He was led to one of the sitting rooms, which Alys, Lina, and Fitz appeared to have done their best in the last few hours to make comfortable rather than formal. The low table between the *L* formed by the couches was strewn with an assortment of breakfast items, the decorative throw blankets had been put to actual use, and Lina was lying with her feet in Alys's lap.

Fitz, who had been lying on the adjacent couch, sat up. Numair gave the man a hard once-over. He only vaguely remembered him from when he'd been Verol's apprentice. He was several years older than Numair, and since Verol hadn't been much in the public eye at that time, Fitz hadn't been either.

Numair had never really given the man much thought, save a vague curiosity when he'd returned to Veralna last year. In that time, it was almost like Fitz had retreated into the role of the apprentice he no longer was. Like he'd been lost and come home, but still hadn't found himself.

After what Numair had heard between Alys and Clare the other night, he found his curiosity had increased. What had Fitz done to Clare that could drive a man who'd always struck Numair as cold and indifferent to not even be willing to be in the same sphere as her without her permission?

Several possibilities came to mind, and he didn't like any of them.

A look passed between the three and Lina and Fitz departed. Lina with a brush of her lips to Alys's, Fitz with a glance at Numair that he couldn't parse out. Then he was left alone with his one-time friend and it was…awkward.

The last time he'd spoken to her at any length they'd had the argument that had effectively ended their friendship. Or rather, *she'd* argued. It had involved a lot of colorful language and the by-then familiar refrains of *Why are you being like this?* and *You need to grow up* and *Don't you have* any *self-respect left?*

Mostly, he'd stood there and let her yell at him. It wasn't as if he could say anything in his own defense. But he was pretty sure it had been him laughing and telling her to relax and calm down, followed by asking her if she wanted a drink—it had been barely an hour after dawn—that had made her descend from angry concern to cold disgust.

Her parting words had lived in his mind ever since. *My parents were right. You aren't who I thought you were. You aren't anything. And you're going to die sad, alone, and worthless.*

He shoved his hands into his pockets. "It seems as if everything turned out like you wanted."

She nodded, sharply. "It did."

"I'm glad you're all right. I'm glad she's all right."

Another nod, her hands twisting together, her mouth pressed in a tight line.

In his pockets, his hands curled. This—coming here—was a mistake. Maybe last night she'd felt a small remembrance of the friendship they'd shared when they were young and life wasn't so complicated. But dawn had a way of shining light on those complications. He shook his head and moved for the door.

"I didn't mean to abandon you." The words tumbled out of her, so fast they were almost one word.

He halted.

"I shouldn't have said what I did to you. I didn't *mean* to say it."

He didn't know what to do with that. She might not have meant to say it, but she'd meant the words, and he couldn't even blame her for them.

"And after…I was ashamed, and I didn't know how to talk to you. And you—you didn't seem to care that I was gone. Your life wasn't any different without me in it."

His life had been completely different without her in it. She'd been the last person who'd truly given a damn about him. And then she hadn't. "If you honestly believe that, then you never knew me at all."

"I *thought* I knew you. And then you became"—she waved her hand at him—"this. I tried to understand. I'm trying to again. But I can't."

"Do you have to?" He couldn't stop himself from adding, "She doesn't."

"I don't understand *her* either. But I don't seem to hold it against her like I do you." She scrubbed her hands over her face and exhaled heavily. "Lina and I are getting married. In two months. Will you come?"

It was a small offering, that invitation. But it was a start. It was a chance. "Of course I will."

When he left, Fitz was waiting for him outside. "May I have a moment of your time, Your Highness?"

Numair wondered how much it had cost him to get the "Your Highness" out. Having come up under Verol's tutelage, Fitz had likely heard Numair disparaged in the most colorful language possible.

He shrugged and continued walking, and Fitz fell into step

beside him. They'd never spoken before, so it didn't take a great deal of deductive reasoning to figure out why the man was approaching him now. But he was quiet until they moved beyond the estate's grounds.

"Is she all right?" The man sounded downright tortured.

Numair halted, rounding on him. "What exactly did you do to her?"

Fitz winced. "What did she tell you?"

Nothing. She'd told him nothing, hadn't even mentioned it, because that was the unspoken agreement between them. That they didn't demand the right to know anything about the other. Maybe he was breaking that agreement in some way, now, but he couldn't stop himself.

"I'm asking *you*. Did you hurt her? Did you *touch* her?"

Fitz paled. "Not…like that."

"Then like what?" He wasn't sure how he ended up with his forearm at Fitz's throat, pinning him to the estate's exterior wall. The transition was lost in the haze of anger thrumming through him. "Like *what?*" he demanded, pressing harder against Fitz's throat.

"I made a mistake," Fitz rasped. "But I swear I didn't hurt her. Not physically. But I…triggered her."

Numair didn't release him. He understood, now, why she'd said nothing. He could guess well enough the types of things that lay in her past. Knew that, for her, having such a thing exposed would be worse than any physical harm.

"Here's what you're going to do," he said evenly. "You don't talk to her. You don't touch her. You don't look at her."

"I promised Verol I'd keep her safe."

"Then you already fucked that up, didn't you?"

Fitz swallowed. "Would you just…tell her I want to talk to her? On her terms. Wherever she wants, whenever. I'll be there."

The part of Numair that hadn't been allowed to feel protective of another person in over a decade wanted to refuse. But that same part whispered that Fitz had once been Verol's apprentice, and the record showed that none of Verol's were ever harmless. If he'd left Fitz to protect Clare, then he must have had some reason to think him capable of doing so.

"I'll tell her."

CHAPTER

FIFTY-SEVEN

THE PRACTICAL BENEFITS

Clare jolted awake to a thunderous banging on the front door. Trepidation skimmed phantom fingers up her spine. No one should be knocking on the Arrendons' door for her. Numair would have come in through the window. Alys or Fitz would have simply come in.

Someone could be looking for the Arrendons, but—

The knocking sounded again, more insistently. "Miss Brighton!"

She gained her feet, grateful she hadn't shed the habit of sleeping fully clothed, and padded to the front door. A glance through the peephole showed two members of the royal guard. For a heart-stuttering moment she wondered if this had something to do with last night, and Alys—or with her activities with the Fools. But if that were the case, it would have been the city guard, not the royal.

She felt for that connection to the Song, feeling, for the first time in her life, reassured by its presence. She opened the door.

The guard's gaze flicked to the black diamond in her ear rather than asking confirmation of her name, then held out a white envelope. Message delivered, he snapped a short bow and then he and his companion remounted their horses, leaving her behind.

She stared at the envelope, knew the Song had done even more to speed the progression of her reading, because she had no trouble making out the two words written in thick black ink: *Little Songbird.*

It felt as if all the blood in her body chilled. Her fingers trembled slightly as she broke the wax seal and pulled the letter out. And when she gave a growl of frustration as the letters jumbled together in her sight, a flash of searing heat from the Song coursed through her mind and reading suddenly wasn't *any* difficulty anymore.

It seems our conversation the other day has driven you from the palace, and I find I miss your presence. Since you so kindly reminded me that kings demand rather than ask, here is one such a demand for you—return to my court, little songbird. You will spend Verol's days here, while he is away.

Dinner is held at the nineteenth bell in the dining hall. Be there. Amuse my court with your presence. Amuse me. Or I might decide to find out if you truly do prefer death to going back.

The paper crumpled in her fist. There was no outlet, this time, for the rage that pulsed and turned on itself within her. No bag to punch until the pain of damaged knuckles and the exhaustion of muscles wore her down. No Numair to make her laugh. No immediate threat, as there had always been an immediate threat in Renault County, to eliminate and release the tension.

There was only her, and the endless power that looked out from her eyes, that had read the words of Alaric's letter with her. That was a thousand times more terrified than she and filling her with the cloying, panicking feel of that terror.

It swelled within her. That thin tendril of escape she'd allowed it in their bargain thickened and intensified, straining against its bonds. She gritted her teeth and clamped it tight.

I can stop this, the Song whispered. *I showed you long ago that I could stop this. Let me.*

No. Because the "this" they referred to had not been then, and was not now, Alaric. Was not *only* Alaric. The Song's price for what it called protection, for what it called deliverance, was too high. She had refused to pay it in her childhood. She had refused to pay it with Simian. She would not pay it for Alaric.

But her rage was a storm inside her, growing as the Song fought her for control as it had not fought her in years, and they both fed off that rage. It swirled and howled, whipping itself into a tempest and crashing against the vessel that was Clare.

NUMAIR WAS TURNING Hellack off the road, onto the Arrendons' estate to deliver Fitz's damn request, when he felt the storm of magic. It was that same signature he'd felt when Clare had spoken to the innkeeper at the Hawk and Scepter, when she'd placed her palm upon a stone dragon and told him it was lonely.

Hellack balked, every muscle in the horse's body going tense. He half-reared, pivoting, and only a spear of Deirdren Blessed magic kept him from bolting. Numair dismounted, removing Hellack's bridle and murmuring to the horse with another whisper of magic. "Go home, boy."

Both of them bolted—the stallion for the safety of home, the man for the source of the storm. He shoved the front door open and almost tripped over himself, having expected resistance and found none. The energy of magic was thick around him, heavier and more potent than any he'd ever felt save Alaric's.

It spilled from Clare, who sat on the foyer floor, her legs crossed, her eyes closed, a crumpled paper clutched tight in her fist. An envelope lay beside her, two words written on the white paper in an all-too-familiar script: *Little Songbird.*

His gut twisted. "Clare?"

No response. He had to stop this—whatever this was. He'd felt her magic all the way out at the road, and it had been spreading, like a rolling fog. If it reached far enough that anyone *else* felt it...

He dropped to his knees in front of her. "Clare?"

She didn't so much as twitch, not a single indication that she'd heard him, that she was aware of his presence. He tried twice more, to the same effect.

"I'm sorry," he said. And then he covered her hands with his.

Her eyes flew open. The normally green irises glowed an incandescent white. He was struck with the inexplicable certainty that something other than Clare looked out at him. It was cold, and ancient, and it did *not* like him. The furious wave of its—Clare's?—power pulsed...and lessened.

Her hands shifted beneath his. The crumpled paper dropped to the floor and she gripped him tight in return, the brilliant blaze of her eyes dimming. She blinked and the brilliance retreated further, leaving *her* eyes, only a little brighter than they should be. Power swept past him, into her, as if the liquid contents of a spilled glass were being sucked back into it.

And then it was only Clare looking at him, no trace of what he'd felt before lingering in the air. As if a candle had been extinguished, plunging the room into darkness. She looked down where their hands linked, but she made no move to pull away. He didn't either.

"What happened?" His words were barely more than a whisper.

Anger compressed her mouth into a thin line, and a flicker of that other magic surged. Determination lit her eyes and it died.

A clatter sounded as someone surged through the open doorway —Fitz. Ferrian's hells, hadn't Numair *told* him he would deliver his damn message? The man was panting, out of breath, his eyes fixed on Clare. "I felt..." He swallowed.

Cold washed over Numair. He surged to his feet, no real plan of what he was going to do, save knowing that if Fitz had felt her, felt that magic, the man couldn't leave here with the knowledge.

But Clare had moved with him, in perfect tandem, and her hands tugged at his, holding him back. He stared at that connection. Such a small, simple one, and yet his ease with it wasn't simple at all.

"You felt like her." Fitz sounded uncomfortably like he was addressing a god, had the same adoration on his face Numair imagined the devout reserved for their deities.

Clare scowled. "I'm *not* her."

Fitz swallowed again and lost a little of the dazed expression. "I know." Then he echoed the same question Numair had asked. "What happened?"

She sighed and, with the slightest squeeze of Numair's hands, removed hers. She bent, retrieving the envelope and the letter. "The king desires entertainment, and he has found me acceptable for it. He expects me at dinner, and to keep Verol's schedule in the palace." She said it evenly and without inflection, a simple relaying of facts.

But there was more to it than that, Numair was certain. Something else rested in the ink on that crumpled paper, something that had sent her spiraling into that power she hid so carefully.

"I can help," Fitz said.

She laughed. "What are *you* going to do against *him*?"

He didn't answer.

"I think I preferred it when you hated me. You want to help? Then whoever it was I reminded you of, who makes you feel all that guilt when you look at me now? Remember that I'm not *them* any more than I'm *her.* And *stop* looking at me like that."

Fitz's face closed off, his expression going blank. That it could do so on command was…interesting. "I'm returning to the suite," he said carefully. "I'll stay out of your way."

She shrugged, as if it didn't matter, and Fitz left. Numair watched her stalk out, presumably to her room. When she returned she was wearing his coat, a bag slung over her shoulder.

Numair walked with her to the stables. Tension had her shoulders in a death grip, and if she was any more rigid she was going to shatter. Kialla approached without any prompting from him, huffing a gentle breath against Clare's cheek. He'd been right to think they would suit.

She closed her eyes, resting one hand on the mare's neck, and spoke so quietly her lips barely moved. "Don't ask."

"I won't." Even if he wanted to. Even if how *much* he wanted to scared him. The trap that was Clare Brighton had caged him neatly, and he hadn't even felt it spring.

It had been easy, before, not to care about anyone. Because no one cared about him. No one even pretended to—not without demands, not without a goal in mind. But now here she was, and he cared, and he couldn't help her because he couldn't even help himself. She was caught in the same poisoned web they all were, with Alaric the spider at its center, and no one could help anyone because they were all trapped at different points.

He hesitated, but in the end, he had to say it. "I won't be any help to you. The opposite, in fact. I won't blame you if you cut me loose."

Her eyes flashed with obvious irritation. "If you don't stop offering to let me out of this friendship, I'm going to start thinking you don't want to be in it."

He sighed. "If I didn't want to be in it, I wouldn't be."

"And if I thought you were more trouble than you were worth, I *would* cut you loose."

He choked out a laugh. "You know, that is possibly the nicest thing anyone's ever said to me."

She glared at him. "I'm not nice. I'm practical."

"Ah, so you keep me around for the practical benefits. I'm dying to know what those are."

"You make me feel human." The words held a raw honesty, and judging by the way her teeth clicked when she snapped her mouth shut, she hadn't meant to say them. "I need to go. I have to... prepare. I'll see you tonight."

She stalked off to the barn, presumably for Kialla's tack.

You make me feel human.

"Me too."

Almost.

CHAPTER

FIFTY-EIGHT

MORE IMMEDIATE CONCERNS

Quin and Verol had been on the road barely more than three days when the message from Phoenix came through. Typically, Verol checked the box for them—the correspondence between them and their unknown information source had given Verol a sense of purpose when he'd desperately needed it—but Verol's attention was firmly entrenched in getting them to their destination. Which meant he was driving the wagon while sifting every mind in the nearby vicinity for information, and to ensure that nothing and no one interfered with their journey.

So Quin checked, and once he'd read the short note, he was glad it was him and not Verol who'd found it.

If there is any way for you to get the king to leave Veralna, do it. He has hired Clare for the court's entertainment until he sees fit to release her.

He jotted out a quick reply and placed it in the box. *Is she all right?*

He waited for a response, hoping it would come soon. The problem with communicating with someone via notes dropped into a magical box was that, if you weren't checking that box frequently, you had no idea how long ago a message had come through. Therefore, you had no idea if the person you were replying to was likely to see it any time soon.

He and Verol made a point to check it once a day, because

Phoenix was typically the one initiating correspondence. On the rare occasions they had had cause to message first, several days would sometimes pass before they received a reply.

But he waited now, despite the unlikelihood of a response, because he did not want to go to Verol with this news without some reassurance. Because *he* needed reassurance.

He popped the lid of the box open every few minutes, and on his tenth check, found a reply.

Physically, she is fine. I do not believe he will cause her bodily harm.

There was an unspoken "yet" at the end of the sentence, a thick blot of ink on the page, as if Phoenix had debated writing something more before sending it through as it was.

Quin took the letters and exited through the front of the wagon, sliding onto the driver's box beside Verol. His husband's gaze was unfocused, and Quin was never clear on how he managed to steer while his mind was flitting in and out of *other* minds, but Ver always said the mundanity of the physical task helped him focus.

He placed a hand on his arm and Verol blinked, coming fully back to his surroundings.

"The gatestone is going to have to wait." He traded Verol the letters for the reins. "We have more immediate concerns."

CHAPTER

FIFTY-NINE

WHAT IS YOURS IS ALSO MINE

Clare didn't intend to confront the king of Faelhorn. She intended to sing at his dinner that evening, smiling all the way through it so he would never be able to tell she was rattled, and then leave as soon as was politely possible. But his unusual habit of being so…available within the walls of his palace meant she saw him on her way to the Arrendons' suite.

He was in one of the meeting rooms, lounging on a couch while in discussion with the same two proconsuls she'd seen him with a few days ago—Balenze and Perish provinces, she thought. He noticed her, noticed the bag clutched in her hand, and satisfaction lit his eyes.

She halted abruptly, turned on her heel and walked into the room. "A moment of your time, Your Majesty?"

She'd spoken right over the Balenze proconsul—Tridian Vidal—and he turned a sharp, disgusted look on her. "You can see that he is in the middle of a conversation, can you not?"

"If you didn't want to be interrupted, you should have closed the door."

Alaric's laughter boomed out, cutting off Vidal's reply. "I always have time for one of Verol's little projects. He does tend to bring me the most interesting things."

Vidal's neck reddened with irritation. "We are not finished discussing—"

"Yes," Alaric interrupted, "we are." He waved the proconsuls off. When they were gone, he lifted an eyebrow at Clare. "Not going to close the door?"

The thought of being in a room with him with the door closed made her skin crawl. It was strange, the difference a three-foot by seven-foot slab of one-inch-thick wood could make. Locked or unlocked, it was hardly more than a symbol. But it was what the symbol implied. Left ajar, it implied that what occurred within the room was something anyone might witness without concern. Sealed tight, it conveyed that what occurred had reason to be hidden and wondered about and remarked upon.

The truth, of course, lay nowhere near that mark. The door's physical position meant nothing to Alaric. He could do whatever he wished, whenever he wished, and if someone happened to see it and he didn't want them to, well, he could always have Verol wipe it from their mind. So the open space at her back should offer her no comfort, and yet it did.

"I have no intention of taking up quite so much of your time that complete privacy should be necessary."

He had one arm stretched long across the top of the couch, and he drummed his fingers idly against it. "Ah, but perhaps I intend to take up yours. Perhaps," he said with a smile, "I don't wish to be interrupted. Shut the door, Miss Brighton."

She gritted her teeth and did. She also remained by it.

His gaze dropped to her bag, the one she still clutched in her hand as a statement to her intent to leave as soon as possible. Amusement lit his eyes. "You received my letter, I take it?"

As if the guard who'd delivered it to her would not have reported as much. As if that hadn't been the entire reason he'd sent it with a royal guardsman rather than a courier.

"Yes. I came to inform you that I don't work for free." When she'd walked into this room, she'd had no notion of what she would say. But now that she'd made the declaration, it felt vitally important. Because what he'd demanded of her—playing on his whims, here at his beck and call—was all too close to what she'd run from.

His fingers stopped drumming. "At the risk of sounding self-important, you do if I say you do." The words might be vaguely self-deprecating but his tone, laced with a dangerous edge, was anything but.

She needed to tread carefully. So she set her bag on the floor, a concession to his ability to keep her here however long he wanted. And she took a step—a single step—toward him. "You want their affection. Not simply the courtiers, but the entire kingdom. Do you think you will gain it if word spreads that you all but hold me captive here for your amusement?" Another step toward him. "The courtiers won't care. But the rest? They're starting to like me."

He leaned forward, resting his forearms on his thighs. "Is that why you've been doing your little performances in the city? I told you I wanted them to love me, so you've decided to make them love *you* instead?" He chuckled. "An industrious little songbird, I see. But you know I could simply keep word of your...situation from ever spreading."

"I'm sure you have better uses for Verol's magic than containing word of *me*." She paused a beat, then said what she'd puzzled out on her own, what she'd been wondering ever since he'd shown an interest in what she could do for him. "And he is only one man. Tired, at that, and getting older. I imagine his reach has all but exceeded your grasp these days."

And he would not live forever, this man whose magic was a glue Clare suspected kept much of Alaric's "peace" in place. And here she was, that man's apprentice and potential successor.

His eyes narrowed, tension thickening the air. "I appreciate backbone." He said it in a way that implied he might also appreciate crushing it. But then he leaned back once more, his hand returning to its previous idle drumming, and the tension broke. "Very well. Consider yourself hired in the traditional sense, then. I'll have the payment details taken care of by the afternoon."

The very dismissiveness of his answer kept her from feeling as if she had won anything. She felt, instead, like he was humoring her. She wanted to take a step back but forced herself not to. It was enough, she told herself, that he had leaned away from her. "What precisely am I hired for?"

"Not so very much. One song an evening, before the dinner is served. Put that useless little Songweaving talent to work for me. Since you've already proven it isn't such a useless thing, after all. I want my court careless, Miss Brighton. I want to know what they think and say when they do not have the common sense to hold their tongues. Do you think you can manage that?" He didn't wait for a reply. "But leave Numair from your grip. He's already been careless enough of late, don't you think?"

It wasn't quite a threat. She didn't know what it was, and he wasn't giving her any signs by which to determine it. He was gazing past her, over her shoulder, as if she simply wasn't worth looking at directly.

"He seems always careless," she answered lightly. "And you? Do you wish to be careless?"

That brought his full attention back to her. "Power only affects me when I wish it to. And having allowed one song under your influence, I find the experience will last me quite some time."

"Then I'll see you tonight." She turned for the door—

"One more thing."

—and froze.

"I expect you to be more present while you are here. Spend time in the public areas. Get to know my people. And if you hear anything interesting, bring it to me."

She swallowed. "I don't presume to know what you would find interesting, Your Majesty."

He made a *tsking* sound. "Oh, I think you'll recognize it when you hear it. Things like what Proconsul Miriam spoke so openly to you about. In this endeavor, consider yourself to have free rein to use that voice of yours as you see fit."

Her pulse thudded angrily in her temples. She hated being told what to do with her time. How to do it, *when* to do it. What she was and wasn't allowed.

She choked on her rage as she swallowed it down. Voice deceptively mild, she asked, "And the rest of my time?"

"What of it?"

"I talk to your court and I sleep within your walls. Am I to be confined within them the rest of the time?"

He shook his head. "Spend your spare time where you wish. If you're asking for permission to continue your street performances, I've no objection. In fact, I wholeheartedly approve of your bid to win the affection of the masses. But, little songbird?" He stood, crossed the space between them so he towered over her. "Do not forget that what is yours is also mine, and there will come a day when I will expect what you win to be given back to me."

Anxiety clawed at her insides, and something in her snapped.

She was tired—so Ferrian-fucking *tired*—of always living on the cliff's edge of fear. She tilted her head up, meeting his gaze. "What is mine is *mine*. Anything you succeed in taking from me will only ever be stolen."

She turned on her heel and grabbed her bag. The sound of his laughter followed her out.

CHAPTER

SIXTY

HAPPINESS

Carelessness was not the easiest state to induce. Carelessness was not an emotion, and emotions were the thread with which Songweavers wove. She had to come at the problem from the side, and it was difficult since Alaric had only given her one song to do it with.

After thinking on the problem the remainder of the morning and half the afternoon, she'd settled on the right song—he'd never said it had to be a short one—and set about having a piano located and moved to the dining hall. She preferred the guitar, but playing it meant being on display. It meant having to see the people she played for, and being seen by them in return.

The benefit of the piano was that one could hide behind it. She didn't want to see or be seen because she didn't feel the message of her song, and the hypocrisy would be written on her face. She walked into the dining hall five minutes after the nineteenth bell.

Part of the intentional lateness was spite, but most of it was not wanting to have to talk to anyone before she'd sung them into a better mood. She wore another of Chalen's creations, the pants and shirt a gaudy array of shining silver this time, so she practically shimmered as she walked into the room.

The piano had been staged in the center of the room, and therefore in the center of the dozen tables arrayed throughout it. She walked confidently through those tables, a smile on her face that could be directed at everyone or no one. The space was loud, filled with the idle chatter of so many people.

She didn't attempt to quell their speech with words. At least, not with words spoken directly to them. She slid onto the padded piano bench, her fingers finding position on the keys, and played. She didn't even attempt subtlety. She was not, as she recalled, being paid for subtlety.

Magic rose, crested, and poured out of her in a tidal wave as she played the happiest song she knew. Because happiness was what made people careless. Happiness and safety, acceptance and security. Only once material danger and mental despondency were removed did a person feel like they *could* be careless.

So she sang of those things, and she convinced people they were true, and her magic echoed out a single resounding promise: *Happy. For tonight, you are happy, and because you are happy you will feel free and honest.*

And because she didn't know what Alaric would do with her if she failed, she emptied herself into that promise, squeezing every drop of her Songweaving power into the words, until she felt hollowed out. Had she bothered to look up at any point in the performance, had she not given herself, as she always did, to the music, she might have discovered that everything she had to give was, perhaps, too much.

Because when she played her final note, the hall maintained silence for all of a second before breaking into chatter all at once. It was as if a floodgate had been lifted on the mouths of the people surrounding her, as if they were all drunk senseless except they were perfectly coherent enough to speak and couldn't wait to do so. Laughter rang around her, undignified peels of it she doubted the hall had ever heard the like of.

No one seemed content to remain in their chairs. They stood and milled about, wreaking havoc on the poor servants attempting to navigate their way through the mess. She stood from the piano and nearly knocked over a woman she'd never seen before.

The woman giggled, like she was twelve instead of the thirty or so Clare guessed her at, and nearly spilled the glass of wine in her hand. "I *loved* your song. It was so…so…*happy*. Honestly, I thought what I heard about your performance at the prince's nameday celebration had to be exaggerated, but you're wonderful."

"Thank you," she murmured. The area around the piano was growing more and more crowded, and Clare could feel the space shrinking in on her. She moved, needing to get out *now*.

"Wait"—the woman grabbed her wrist—"we haven't even gotten to—"

Clare jerked her hand free so viciously the woman stumbled, spilling her drink on her skirts.

The woman frowned, staring down at the red stain. "Ordinarily, I would be very upset about this, but I'm too happy tonight."

A hand brushed the small of Clare's back and she jumped, spinning, to find the crowd of people had pressed in so closely she could barely spin a stationary circle. Her heart pounded, her body unpleasantly aware of everyone's breathing, everyone's scent, everyone's *presence*.

The world narrowed to a pinprick and all she wanted was *out*. Out of the press of bodies, out of the attention and then—

The two people closest to her were shoved aside and Numair was in their place. The crush of bodies filled in around him like water filling a tide pool, shoving him against her, his chest flush against her back.

"Sorry," he muttered.

"It's okay."

"Let's get you out of—"

"Are you already in his bed?" The woman—the same one who had grabbed Clare earlier—said it loud enough to draw the attention of everyone nearby. She didn't sound judgmental, she sounded envious. At least, as envious as one *could* sound beneath that much magically induced jubilance. She continued, talking to Clare like Numair wasn't present. Like he was a thing instead of a person. "I have been trying for *months*. I thought it was my age, but he's been with women twice as old."

Numair went tense against Clare's back.

"I actually even heard he—"

"Shut *up*," Clare snapped.

The woman smiled uncertainly, her unease alarmingly discordant with her happiness. "I'm sorry, what?"

Clare didn't bother to repeat herself, and since she and Numair were already touching she turned and wrapped her arm around his waist, dragging him with her as she plunged into the crowd. She didn't care if she was supposed to stay for the duration of dinner, she wanted out. She wanted *Numair* out.

She wanted them both away from the hands that grabbed indiscriminately at them, that seemed not to view either of them as people. But moving through them was a slog, and no matter how fiercely she scowled or how vehemently she batted away hands, no one gave them space.

"Calm down," a deep voice said, stilling the crowd. "It wouldn't do to suffocate Miss Brighton, now would it?"

The Jackal King, it seemed, could do what nothing else could— temporarily blunt the happiness she'd infected them all with. They parted just enough to open a path from her to the king, and though she knew she should, she didn't let her arm fall away from Numair. She had the distinct impression that if she let go of him, the barely contained crowd would swallow him.

All Alaric did was say, mildly, "Your dinner is getting cold."

"Walk in front of me," she told Numair softly, grateful when he didn't argue, because it got him out. Even if out meant both of them seated at Alaric's table across from each other.

"Well," the king said, "this is so much more than I could have hoped for. You've set the bar quite high for yourself, little songbird. I hope you don't disappoint me in the future." He leaned against his chair, arm resting across its back as he surveyed the room, far more pleased than any king should be at having their court thrown into utter chaos.

He looked that way the entire evening, while people once again swarmed around them. Sitting next to Alaric proved enough of a buffer against random touching, but nothing could buffer against the things that were said. The things they all heard. Things that made the first woman who'd spoken to Clare sound positively proper, that made it so Numair wouldn't even meet her eyes anymore.

And that—she had a feeling Alaric enjoyed that, too.

SIXTY-ONE

I STILL DON'T THINK I LIKE YOU

Clare was getting tired of waking to the sound of pounding at her door. She sat up, a headache throbbing behind her eyes. After the disaster of a dinner had ended, she'd ridden into town to sing with the Fools precisely because she hadn't wanted to. Then she'd stumbled back to the palace suite where no level of exhaustion could convince her body to sleep.

She'd pulled the still-unwilted hibiscus flower from the drawer of the nightstand, placed it on the tabletop and stared at it, absently mapping the curves of the petals, reaching out every now and then to feel the thrum of Numair's magic coursing through it like water.

Predictably, her body had finally decided to sleep once the sun came up.

The knocking rattled through the suite again and she stalked out to greet it, opening the door to find Alys, Lina—and Fitz. He hung behind the two of them and Alys said, "He'll go if you want him to."

"It's fine."

"You look terrible," Alys noted as Clare stepped back, allowing them all to enter. Her scar was on full display, without a trace of glamour to cover it. "But then, I imagine I would look terrible too if I'd caused the end of no less than six marriages last night." Honesty and carelessness had a price, it would seem. "What did you do?"

Clare couldn't summon even a false smile. "What I was ordered to. I don't want to talk about last night, so if that's why you're here, you can leave."

"My my, someone's prickly." Alys settled onto one of the couches and Lina came with her. When Fitz remained standing, Clare took the other couch.

"Don't you have duchess things to do?" Clare suggested. "Holdings to oversee, other nobles to flatter? That sort of thing."

"I dedicated yesterday to looking into how much of a mess Geoffrey made of my duchy and delegating a start on the changes. I am here today to flatter other nobles. Are you satisfied?"

"It's still unclear what any of that has to do with you interrupting my"—she glanced at the clock—"four hours of sleep."

"It's hardly my fault if you failed to retire at a reasonable hour."

"Didn't I do you a rather large favor a mere two days ago? Gratitude might be more in order than a critique of my sleep schedule."

Alys opened her mouth, a mischievous gleam in her eye, and Lina clapped a hand over it. "Gratitude is *precisely* why we are here. I wanted to thank you. For everything."

"I like her better than you," Clare told Alys.

Alys snorted. "*I* like her better than *you* too."

"However, why do I feel like the gratitude is actually a prelude to a request?"

Lina blushed. "We wanted to ask if you would sing at our wedding."

"You're getting married? When?"

"In two months."

"I wanted to sign the paperwork and be done with it now," Alys grumbled.

Lina's expression hardened. "And I want to shove all their faces in it. So will you? Sing for us?"

Clare didn't know anything about weddings, but she supposed she had two months to rectify the fact. "If you do me a favor in return. As it turns out, I'm expected to socialize while I'm here. Keep me company while I do?"

Lina smiled. "We would have done that anyway."

And Clare would have sung at their wedding anyway. But she suspected they already knew that.

"Do you want to come with us now? We were about to go down."

Clare did not want to go down. Alaric might have been pleased with the result of her previous night's work, but she was still unsettled, still...raw. She didn't know how these people would react to her today, and she didn't know how she would react to them. She'd forced too much honesty out of them, and hadn't liked what she'd learned.

She had understood before, of course, the benefits afforded by the company of others. Understood the protection that could be provided by having others claim you, in public, as part of their number. But she had never thought to see a time when that connection was more beneficial than it was problematic. She had never thought to see a time when she trusted enough to make such an alliance.

And she did, on some level, trust Alys and Lina, she realized. Alys, for all her snarling and bluster, was honest in a way that few people were. Lina was...open, in the way her face seemed to reflect whatever she was thinking. And the connection between the two was, despite how much Clare knew she should avoid finding herself in any similar situation, intoxicating.

"Let me change," she told them finally, because they were waiting for her answer.

Fitz shuffled his feet. "Before you do, could I speak with you?"

She smothered her instinctual reply of *There's nothing to talk about*. Better to let him say whatever he needed to say to make himself feel better, so he could stop reminding everyone by his behavior that *something had happened*. "Fine."

"We'll come back in half an hour," Lina said, rising and pulling Alys out the door.

Fitz still wore that completely genuine mix of contrition and guilt she found so irritating. Because the two things always wanted something out of the person they were aimed at: absolution.

"Stop looking at me like you're a puppy I've kicked."

"I'm—"

"—sorry," she finished for him. "I've gathered as much. The thing about that, though? You're the one who's making this a problem. I don't want your apology or your explanations. I don't want to hear your sad story about whatever woman in your life you watched horrible things happen to, so you can assure me you *would never*."

His eyes widened, almost comically. Like it wouldn't be obvious *why* he'd cried after she'd reacted the way she had when he'd attacked her.

"Your damage is your own. I'm not taking it on to make you feel better. I'm not forgiving you. You made a judgment about me and you did something incredibly stupid as a result. Live with what you did. Ferrian knows the rest of us have to."

She waited while he processed. Finally, he said, "You want me to act like nothing happened?"

"I want you to learn from it and move on."

He ran a hand over his face. "You…aren't who I thought you were."

"People rarely are."

"I still don't think I like you." The words lacked conviction.

"I still don't think I like *you.*"

"Then we're back to…not liking each other."

She beamed at him. "Precisely." She went to her room to change, calling back, "Make yourself useful and have breakfast sent up. You owe me a carafe of coffee."

SIXTY-TWO

SOCIALIZING IS HELL

Socializing was every bit the hell Clare had imagined it to be. Everyone today had flocked to one of the inner gymnasiums, in order to watch... "Fencing?" Distaste laced the single word.

Alys made a noise of sympathetic agreement. "You know how much men love to poke things," she said, making Lina snort. "Personally, I long for the days the history books describe, when the nobility had to learn how to actually fight, rather than this fancy-stepping artful mimicry of it. But I think our illustrious leader prefers his lesser rulers complacent and lacking in the martial arts."

They stood just inside the gymnasium door, drawing a fair number of gazes with their entrance.

"What do you think they're more upset by?" Alys mused to Clare. "My face, Lina and I's engagement, or you?"

"Does it matter?"

"Of course it matters. If my face doesn't win, I'll be sorely disappointed."

"You have the strangest sense of vanity," Lina said affectionately.

A peel of laughter drew Clare's gaze to the right. Numair, surrounded by a small crowd, was gesticulating wildly about something. A new woman stood too near him today, closer to Verol's age than Numair's, though her glamour did its best to hide the fact.

Alys followed Clare's gaze, her mouth tightening. "I don't understand him."

"Do you have to?" The words came out more irritated than she'd intended them to.

Alys's eyebrows rose. "You know, he asked me the same thing, and I...don't know. I can't condone what he does."

"No one is asking you to."

"And it doesn't bother you?"

Of course it bothered her. "Why should it?"

Alys shrugged. "No reason."

Across the room, the apparently abandoned Dahlia of Moria glared daggers at Numair while she stood within a protective coterie of friends. Clare was certain, by the sly looks being sent the woman's way, that Dahlia was the subject of much discussion that morning. She just couldn't ascertain what kind without hearing it.

"Could you explain something to me? What exactly are the social mores concerning..." She trailed off.

"Fornication?" Alys offered. "Attempting to sleep one's way into the royal family?"

Clare's teeth clenched. "Yes. That." No one seemed to care beyond it being fodder for gossip or an excuse to laugh about or shun someone they already didn't like.

"There aren't really any. Our king is the law, and our king does not care. If one had to guess by the way he indulges Numair, he practically approves. That isn't to say the older families can't be more puritanical on the subject of virtue, but it's become a private matter these days.

"And though people are typically more circumspect, when it comes to Numair...well, I'm sure he's had lovers who didn't broadcast the fact, but most of them do, and their families approve. They're all certain they'll be the one that convinces him to settle down and make them princess, right until he doesn't."

That seemed, to Clare's mind, a poor bet. Even if she hadn't known what she did about him.

"Of course, people weren't quite so desperate before Prince Brennan took sick, even when it looked certain he would propose to Lady Meraland."

Clare frowned. "Prince Brennan?"

"The *first* prince of Faelhorn," Alys said slowly, giving Clare an odd look. "Where did you grow up that you don't know that?"

Clare could have kicked herself. "I only meant I haven't seen him at all."

Alys made a disbelieving noise, but she let it go. "About six months ago he took dreadfully ill. The healers are at a loss. He occasionally manages an appearance, carefully monitored, of course, but otherwise no one is allowed to see him."

"It's why Lady Meraland's been such a delight to be around," Lina chimed in. "Apparently, she actually likes the man, as opposed to simply wanting to marry him."

She remembered Lady Meraland's dazed confusion that day in the hallway, her hollow, *"I went somewhere I wasn't supposed to."* Had she managed to see Prince Brennan? If Verol had manipulated her memory that day, was this why? And if so, what about the first prince's condition necessitated the secrecy?

Aloud she only said, "I wonder they don't all simply bypass the princes and try for the king."

Lina and Alys gave her twin looks of incredulity. Alys said, "Even excepting the fact that King Tolvannen earned his moniker getting his hands dirty, and responds to the slightest rebellion with crushing force—there are, after all, some women who find that sort of thing appealing—you *do* realize he doesn't talk to anyone, don't you?"

"He talks to people," Clare muttered.

"Outside of business and ordering people around."

"He talks to *me.*"

"So I've heard. And that is why everyone here hates you, wants to be you, and will say anything if it means they can be seen in your company." Alys nodded to their right. "Look, your first hopefuls are headed our way."

They were indeed. A group of two women and three men, to all appearances merely wandering the outskirts of the gymnasium, though it wasn't difficult for the practiced eye to guess their true aim. Clare mused darkly upon the difference a king's attention could make. Yesterday they'd all been waiting to see who would pick her up next, and if she was worth associating with. Now, they were apparently willing to pretend she hadn't been responsible for the social fiasco the previous night had been, and all because they were stupid enough to think Alaric's attention was synonymous with his favor.

"I don't feel like talking to them." Despite the fact that talking to them—to everyone here—was precisely what she'd been ordered to do. The thing about that was, she didn't appreciate taking orders. She might perform as she had to, and she would do just enough to placate Alaric, but she had no intention of throwing herself into this role. The bonds he'd placed on her were already chafing, and she had a tendency to rub herself raw against restraints.

She turned in the opposite direction of the approaching group, and made her way to Numair's instead. He noticed her approach but wouldn't meet her eye again, as he'd refused to all last night, and the thin line of tension in his body suggested he was waiting for her to treat him as everyone else did. The green scarf around his neck said he was hoping she wouldn't.

She inserted herself into his surrounding circle and said to him, without preamble, "I'm bored."

She'd talked over a woman who now fell silent, waiting for Numair's response. He finally met her gaze, and the tension in his body melted at whatever he found there. "Bored," he repeated.

She nodded. "I can't see how anyone finds fencing interesting. I'm told it's because I lack the male inclination to poke things."

No less than three of the surrounding individuals choked on thin air.

"When you put it that way, it does seem like a lesser sport." A smile curved Numair's lips. "So I suppose we should find something more interesting to do."

The trepidation that crept onto the surrounding faces said that when Numair suggested they do "interesting" things, the results were often questionable.

CHAPTER

SIXTY-THREE

SURVIVING

T he following days dragged on in a grinding, repetitive fashion, each one drawing the net Clare was caught in a little tighter. She found herself once again hating what she did. In that brief time she had spent with Marquin and Verol on the journey here, and then in those first few days in Veralna, her music and her talent had finally felt like they were hers. Even though she'd been playing for others, the music had still been *hers*. Because she had been in control. She had chosen—what to sing and when, and she'd had a goal. Something to strive for and attain.

Now...now, on the surface, everything she wanted had been dropped at her feet. She couldn't rise any higher than playing for Alaric, and yet this wasn't what she had wanted. It was a facsimile of it, because she had not shaped its creation. She had not laid the careful groundwork and watched it come to fruition. She had not felt the triumph of success.

She had been outmaneuvered—run into a dead-end alley and trapped. She had not come to Veralna to belong to a man, and though Alaric had not claimed ownership of her in any technical sense, he might as well have. Nothing she had now was hers, no matter how ridiculously Alaric paid her, which was a form of mockery in itself. Everything she had, from her money, to her job, to her social status, to the rooms she lived in, was his. If the situation possessed a key difference from the one she'd fled in Renault

County, a difference that made this one more bearable, it was yet still a cage she was unwilling to reside in forever. But she once again found herself unaware of how to escape it.

So she took the only ready escape she had, the only control she could. After each day spent in the palace, wasting hours of her time on frivolous people and acting ridiculous with Numair—because that was the only way he *could* be, and she refused to let him alone in it—and after each evening turning Alaric's court into whatever he wanted of them, she took to the streets in the later hours.

The Fools began to joke that she was a demon rather than a woman, for she never seemed to sleep. She wasn't sleeping. She ran herself ragged performing in the city—Hightown, Midtown, Lowtown, she didn't care—and Veralna had a betting pool on where she would appear next. She was succeeding in diminishing the prestige provided by the Musicians Guild licensing system—and angering Madame Aria, who never failed to show up, when she could, with Hounds from the Mages Guild, intent on finding some use of illegal magic—but that wasn't why Clare was doing this anymore.

She needed it—the act of proving herself over and over again, without Songweaving, without the Song—the knowledge that she was worth something. Something that could not be quantified by money or desire, but only by the rapt attention of an audience, by adoration. By the questionable love of strangers for an icon they could never hope to touch or know or have. And if she found some camaraderie in the musicians she worked with, it wasn't the same kind of camaraderie they had between each other. They had put her on a pedestal, this woman who had managed to grant them the legitimacy that had been denied them by their inability or refusal to pay the Musicians Guild. She was more a god to them than a peer, and she did not want to be a god.

On the two nights of the week that Verol—and therefore she—was not required to stay in the palace, she would stumble from the streets of Hightown to Numair's estate. But he was never there. He was running himself as ragged as she was. They were both growing more and more tightly strung, like threads caught between competing spindles, pulling them in separate directions. Always, always Alaric watched them, but she didn't know what he was watching *for*. She had only the distinct impression that he observed them like a scientist might observe the stages of an experiment and she couldn't help but wonder, once he considered the experiment concluded, what he would decide to do with the results.

It was, therefore, a relief when she woke to find the palace in a state of shifted energy, because Alaric was leaving. Unrest, it seemed, was brewing in Trin Province, adjacent to the Veralna Province boundary, and he would be seeing to it personally. He took a quarter of the First Army with him, leaving her with a parting note that said only, *I leave the court's evening mood in your hands, little songbird.*

She'd heard nothing from Verol and Marquin since they'd left, and when she'd asked Fitz if he knew when they were coming back, he'd shrugged and said only that they likely wouldn't return until Alaric did. And she told herself it didn't matter—that they'd all but dragged her into their lives only to completely exit hers—but there was still this odd feeling of...abandonment? She'd never felt it before, because to feel abandoned, you had to first feel as if you were wanted. She had never felt wanted before. Not in any healthy sense of the word.

It was another thing she ignored, like she ignored her building resentment each night she continued to perform her one song for Alaric's court, even in his absence. Like she ignored the harsh, hot claws of anger that ripped at her each time some woman ran casual touches over Numair and she saw his revulsion in the barely perceptible stiffening of his body while they never noticed. Like the ever-increasing pulse that beat within her own body, wanting action and release. Because now that Alaric was gone, the Song no longer hid deep within her, but took the full measure of the small freedom she'd granted it.

She'd had three weeks now of its constant presence, and she still wasn't accustomed to it. Even now it looked out through her eyes, a heavy weight between her temples as she stood, layered in shadows, on the mezzanine that overlooked the dining hall. There was no denying her performances—and their results—had become less dramatic with Alaric's absence, and the truth was that tonight she didn't know what to make them feel. The possibilities seemed both too few and too many—a base set of emotions, but a thousand nuances of each—and yet she wasn't inspired to any of them this evening.

"You get the most interesting expressions on your face when you observe the world." The soft, velvet voice was a few feet to her right. He sounded more distant—more a stranger—than he had since that first day she'd talked to him in Galina's dress shop.

But then, she'd hardly seen him alone since Alaric left. Had felt a subtle difference between them, as if that distance she felt was literal. Part of her wanted to ask him what the hell he was doing. But the other part was too glad he was here, even if it was only for a moment, to make her not feel so alone.

"Maybe I'm trying to discern how they can all be so content. How they can sit there night after night and continue being...*that*. Or"—she paused for effect—"maybe I'm trying to decide if it's worth ruining their facade of happiness for the evening."

"Maybe you should."

She sighed, the Song throbbing behind her temples, and leaned against the wall. "To what end?"

He finally came and stood beside her. "It might be worth it, just to make it all change. Even if it's only for a night."

"What good is a night? What good is a temporary change? What does it accomplish?"

The remainder of that distance that had been growing between them broke, and he finally smiled for her. "I think it makes you feel better."

"I don't want to feel better. Toleration breeds complacency and I won't be complacent. I won't forget what I'm here to accomplish."

"And what exactly is that?"

She smiled, a baring of her teeth because she needed to remind *herself* of what that was. "Everything."

He huffed out a small laugh. "Then I'm sure everything will be yours."

She wasn't so sure. Not anymore.

"And you? What are you trying to accomplish, Numair?"

He hesitated and for a single, stupid second, she thought he might give her a real answer. But then he said, "At the moment? Hearing the way you say my name seems accomplishment enough."

The anger that statement lit in her expressed itself so viciously on her face that he couldn't mistake it. "Don't," she said harshly. "Don't lie to me like you lie to *them*. I'm *not* like them."

His face lost what little humor it had regained. He lifted his hand to her face but halted just shy of touching her. Always, always, he was so careful not to touch her, unless she'd given him permission. It didn't fit. Nothing about who he was with *her* fit with who he was with *them.* He let his hand fall.

"I'm not." He swallowed, and that sadness that swam perpetually in the deep, dark waters of his eyes came closer to the surface. "I've never lied to you."

She measured him. "Never?"

"No."

"Then tell me something." She reached out and tugged the end of the green scarf hanging from his neck. "Why do you always wear this?"

"Because you told me to wear it when I think of you. And I'm always thinking of you."

Her heart and her stomach did things they shouldn't, things she was still desperately trying to pretend she didn't understand. So she asked the question she wasn't supposed to. "And what are you doing out *there*?"

He swallowed, pain shattering those almost-black eyes. "Surviving."

Guilt hit her. It was a new emotion, one that had had no place in her life when she was the one only surviving. But he'd tried to *stop* surviving, and she was the reason he was still here. And she still didn't know if he resented her for it.

"I'm not like you," he said finally. "I can't have everything. I can't have anything."

He walked away and she let him, certain she should have said something and equally certain she had no idea what that something would have been. She watched from above while he walked into the dining hall, and then she shoved off the pillar and followed. For once, in the palace, she played what she felt, and her melancholy spread like a disease, infecting everyone her voice reached. And when she was finished, she bypassed her table, with its seat across from Numair, and walked out.

CHAPTER

SIXTY-FOUR

LET'S GET OUT OF HERE

For once Clare ignored the call of the city and went directly from the dining hall to Numair's, even knowing there was no point. That she'd left him in the palace and he wasn't likely to make an appearance later. He hadn't any of the other nights she'd come.

But she found Ida in the library, as she had so many other nights, and they settled into their typical routine: Ida made tea, they both chose a book, and then they read in silence while never once discussing their one mutual connection.

When Ida retired for the night, Clare went up to Numair's room. She didn't mean to fall asleep. She didn't expect him to walk in late in the night, barely visible in the soft blue light from the wall flowers that illuminated the room, and she didn't mean to wake silently at his entrance. Waking silently was an ingrained habit, and it wasn't until he pulled off his shirt that it occurred to her to tell him she was there.

But the words of greeting never left her mouth because the fingernail marks down his back made something feral come out of her throat. He spun as she sat up and she saw the mark on his collarbone, another on his neck, saw the red flush that hit his cheeks, the shame that lit his eyes before he shut his emotions down and grabbed a clean shirt, pulling it on.

"What are you doing here?" he bit out. The caustic in his voice could have melted flesh. It bounced off her harmlessly. She understood it, that instinctual response to shame, even if she didn't understand why the shame came in the first place.

Except she understood it was a response to her, to that sound she'd made, to the sudden urge she had to walk out of this room and hold his latest lover by her hair above some fathomless precipice. Until this moment, she'd never grasped why people who saw her scars wanted to get rid of them. The marks couldn't harm her anymore. The pain they had caused had been gone long ago.

But she finally realized that they could hurt others. That seeing them could cause others pain. But even understanding didn't change her resolve to never let the Song take hers from her, so she quelled the itch in her fingers that begged her to touch her fingertips to Numair's skin and heal every single one of those marks.

"Well?" he demanded, his gaze unflinching, blood seeping through his white shirt from the scratches.

She shrugged and fell back against his pillows, forcing herself into the easy, taunting dynamic they spent most of their time together in. "I didn't realize you had calling hours now. Should I leave and come back once I've sent an official letter requesting to see you, Highness?"

Her eyes dared him to say yes, because what she was really asking was, "Do you not want me here anymore?" and they both knew it. Was his renewed connection with her earlier only a misstep in that distance growing between them?

"No." His shoulders sagged. "No, just...let me know you're here, next time."

Next time. "Okay."

His jaw clenched, a muscle feathering in his cheek. "I'm sorry." He wasn't looking at her, and she didn't think he realized it when his hand came up to cover the mark on his neck. "You shouldn't have to see that."

She was off the bed and across the room before she realized she was moving. She didn't touch him, but she stood close, until she looked up and his eyes couldn't avoid her own. "Don't you *ever* apologize to me for them. You understand? Not ever."

He inhaled sharply, his lips parting, but he didn't speak. His mouth pressed back into a line and he nodded.

"Good," she said.

His eyes flicked from her to the bed, exhaustion written in them. "I'm tired."

"Then go to sleep."

"Will you be here when I wake up?"

"Do you want me to be?"

"Yes."

"Then I will." She forced him to take the bed by the simple expedient of claiming the chaise before he could. And she didn't sleep again until she was certain that he was out, that he wasn't faking the steady rise and fall of his chest.

And she stared at that fucking mark on his neck until it felt branded into her memory.

* * *

CLARE WOKE to a very different Numair than the one she'd gone to sleep with. He was practically manic with energy, an almost boyish excitement on his face.

"What is wrong with you?" she asked, grumbling, as he deposited a tray with coffee and breakfast pastries onto the table beside her.

"Let's get out of here."

She shoved an entire chocolate pastry into her mouth and waited to see if his exuberance would lessen. It didn't. She swallowed and said, "You want to go for a ride?"

He shook his head. "I want to get out of here. Out of the city. Away from everyone."

"Camping?" she asked. "Because I must inform you, I am fond of the amenities of civilization."

He grinned. "Not camping. Well, okay, there will be a night of camping to get to where we're going, but I promise you'll have an actual room and some amenities once we get there."

After the chocolate kicked in, she finally managed to put his words together. "You want to go somewhere...overnight?"

"It's a day-and-a-half ride. Then we'll stay a couple nights. Come back."

She stared at him. "You want me to leave with you? For almost a week? Have you lost your mind?" That excitement in his eyes flickered, like maybe half the manic energy had been building himself up to this ask, and she'd effectively kicked him in the gut. That was also when she realized the mark on his neck was gone, that he'd clearly had a healer take care of it, and likely the others, too. So before he could back away from his statement she said, "Fine. I suppose Alaric can't wonder where I am if he isn't here." Undoubtedly, he had someone watching her but...but she wasn't *tolerating* the situation, she reminded herself. And if he'd left the gate of her cage open, she was damn well walking out of it for a time. "Where are we going?"

The smile Numair gave her—one of those rare, honest ones—was worth everything. "It's a surprise."

"Please understand the great honor I do you in allowing you to *surprise me*."

"Consider me honored. Eat your breakfast and pack."

She did both and, after an internal debate as to the wisdom of leaving without any word, finally penned a brief note to Fitz, ensuring it would be delivered after she was well enough away from Veralna that he wouldn't be able to follow.

Then she and Numair were off, leaving the city and all of its problems behind.

CHAPTER

SIXTY-FIVE

HE ISN'T YOURS TO TALK TO THAT WAY

Clare had been patient yesterday, assuming that, despite promises of their destination being a "surprise", Numair would tell her where they were going once they were far enough away from Veralna. He hadn't. After a full day of riding they'd spent the night in a tent, which had been significantly less awful than she'd thought it would be, because practically every piece of Numair's camping equipment came with heating spells. In the morning Numair had made surprisingly decent campfire coffee, and when they'd packed up and started riding again, he'd said it was a little less than half a day's ride to their destination.

It had now been almost half a day, and she was getting anxious. Because *he* was getting anxious. The Numair riding next to her was a side of him she'd only caught rare glimpses of. He'd lost the rigidity he carried at court, lost the jaded glaze to his eyes and the dark twist to his lips that always said he was waiting for the worst to happen, and he was determined to find it amusing when it did.

He looked younger. He looked…happy. He also looked nervous. Yesterday, he'd been excited. What did it mean that he was nervous now?

"Are you ever going to tell me where we're going?"

He hesitated before finally saying, "A village."

She waited, but he didn't elaborate. "Is it a very special village?"

He was the second prince of Faelhorn. The position might come

424

with far more ills than positives, but when it came to entertainment, privileges, or goods to be purchased, there was nothing he couldn't afford. So what could a village a day-and-a-half's ride from Veralna have to offer him that he couldn't find within the city?

"Yes. More special than any other." His voice was soft and serious. Enough so that she didn't press him further. Not that there would have been time, had she decided to. They crested a hill, a deep valley spread before them, and in that valley lay Numair's promised village.

It was a farming community, with the town and most of the housing located in the center, and what would be cultivated fields when the warmer weather hit sprawling out around them. More people than she'd expected were out, bundled up against the cold, doing repair work on fencing and outbuildings. Most were too busy to look up as she and Numair rode by but a boy—may seven or eight—who was tagging along after an older woman and clearly hindering more than helping, looked to the road and let out a whoop of excitement.

He came running at them full-speed, so fast and unexpected that Kialla snorted and danced, her neck arching. Who was this child, and why was he so excited? Had he mistaken them for someone else?

If anyone, child or not, had come running at Clare like that in Renault County, she would have already sent a dagger flying for their throat. It was still her first instinct, her fingers itching for the blade hidden inside her boot, a lifetime of bitter experience telling her that this boy was either mad or drugged, or simply pushed too far and hoping the appearance of being crazed would lend him an advantage in theft or survival.

The instincts gripped her so deeply she almost didn't register the broad smile breaking across Numair's face.

"Uncle Numair! Uncle Numair!" The boy shouted the greeting as he approached, and he said Numair's name differently, turning it from a flat, two syllable word into a rich, rolling, three syllable affair. Nu-my-ir instead of Nu-mare.

The boy finally reached his target, flinging himself exuberantly at horse and rider like this *wasn't* the notoriously ridiculous, notoriously drunk second prince of Faelhorn.

Uncle? To her knowledge, Numair had no siblings.

Numair laughed, catching the boy as he tried to jump onto Hellack and helping him scramble on behind him. Poor Hellack took a knee or two to the stomach and rump in the process but, paragon of equine virtue that he was, handled it with nothing more than a backward twitch of his left ear.

The boy didn't stop talking during the whole process. "We didn't know you were coming! Mom said you wouldn't be back until the spring, but I volunteered to help Nari in the fields because I thought you'd come sooner and look! Now I get to ride back on Hellack, and who are you?" The boy asked the question as if it flowed from the rest of the sentence, squirming around to look at Clare and kicking Hellack another time in the process.

"Settle down before you give Hellack bruises," Numair admonished.

"Sorry." He wilted the tiniest fraction, and Numair twisted in the saddle to ruffle his hair. "Tomlin, this is Clare, Clare this is Tomlin."

"Hi Clare! It's nice to meet you." The kid said everything with an abundance of enthusiasm, as if he'd never been hurt in his life.

She…didn't know what to do with it. At court, most of the nobility's children were kept out of sight, the responsibility of nursemaids and tutors. She hadn't truly interacted with someone so young since she'd left Renault County. And no one was actually young in Renault County.

The kid—Tomlin—stared at her expectantly. She swallowed, but her throat was stuck. This wasn't... What was she supposed to *do?* She looked at Numair helplessly, certain that her confusion and terror was, for once, written all over her face.

The joy in his eyes dimmed as he registered that something about this was causing her stress. She hated the disappointment in his eyes. She knew it wasn't disappointment in *her*. It was disappointment in himself, in thinking he'd done something wrong, but she was the one there was something wrong with. He'd been so excited to bring her here and now she was struck incapable of speech because a child was *happy*, and she'd never seen that before.

Talk. Open your mouth and speak words, Clare, it isn't that difficult.

But it was. More so the longer she was silent.

Tomlin squirmed again, looking up at Numair. "Did I say it wrong? I've been practicing my Common like you said, but it's harder than I thought."

"You didn't say it wrong." There. She had managed words. But the kid was still staring at her expectantly.

He blinked. "Oh, are you—what's the word?" He launched a rapid sequence of syllables at Numair that Clare didn't understand. Numair answered in the same language and the kid turned back to her. "Shy. Are you shy? It's okay if you are, my friend Elsie is too."

She couldn't help but laugh, her tension finally easing. This child was strange and foreign to her with his openness and his happy nature, and she was half-convinced he couldn't be real, but it was impossible not to be put at ease by him. "Yes, I suppose you could say I am."

Tomlin gave a serious nod. "Numair's good with shy people. He lets Elsie follow him around even though she never says anything. Do you follow him around?"

She arched an eyebrow at Numair. He just grinned back at her, a little color rising in his cheeks. "I'll tell you a secret," she told Tomlin, her voice dropping into a confidential tone. "Most of the time, Numair follows *me* around."

Tomlin's eyes widened. "He does?" He turned back to Numair and went to talking at rapid speed again in his native tongue.

The color in Numair's cheeks deepened and he shook his head, breaking back into Common. "Let's go before your mother accuses me of not coming to see her quickly enough."

"Can we gallop?" Tomlin bounced up and down excitedly.

"What did I tell you last time about bouncing on horses?"

Tomlin sighed, stilling himself with visible effort. "Not to do it because it's bad for their backs."

"No more bouncing and we can canter."

"Gallop?" he asked again hopefully.

"Canter," Numair said firmly.

"Okay." He drew the word out in obvious disappointment and wrapped his arms around Numair's waist. His mood improved immediately when Numair kissed to Hellack, and he let out a whoop of happiness as the horse glided into a gentle lope.

Kialla blew out a breath and twitched her ear back at Clare, as if to say, "Are we really getting involved in this?"

Clare stroked her neck. "It's two days, girl. Surely we can approximate normal that long." She squeezed her legs and Kialla leapt into the gallop Tomlin had wanted, her long legs eating up the ground between them and Numair. She reached Hellack's side as the road reached the first buildings, and the sound of thundering hooves drew attention from the village's inhabitants.

Clare eased Kialla to a walk as Numair did the same with Hellack. The stallion acquiesced without the fit of crow-hopping Kialla engaged in, the mare clearly unhappy to have her run cut so short. She nearly bolted a second later when a gaggle of screaming children came running around one of the buildings, shouting Numair's name. Her head was high in the air, nostrils flared, the line of her body one tense muscle.

"Me too, girl," Clare murmured. "Me too." She backed the mare up a few paces, leaving Numair to the mob. He helped Tomlin down, then slid off Hellack with a flashy leap he would never do at court, but which was good for another round of shrieking and laughter from the children. They swarmed, clambering over him like he was a climbing tree. He ended up with one on each hip, one clinging to his back, and the rest darting around him in circles.

None of them paid Clare the slightest bit of attention, which she appreciated. It occurred to her, as she watched, that no one in Veralna City would let children this age anywhere near Numair. In Veralna, he was a drunk and a debaucher. Certainly no one who could be trusted not to harm a child from inattention or ineptitude.

She didn't yet know how he was connected to this place, but she did know why he'd brought her. Because she'd been seeing too much of the side of himself he had never wanted her to see, and here he was a version of himself he was never otherwise allowed to be. Here he was...happy.

The realization sparked something uncomfortable inside her. Something that made her want to shrink into herself, to turn Kialla and leave before he noticed, because *he* might belong here, but she didn't. She would never smile like he did now. She would never be able to forget the darkness in her life, even temporarily, the way he seemed able to forget his here. Hers was too much a part of her, the way the Song was.

It felt her discomfort and her instinctual desire to run, and it whispered its encouragement that she should. That if she stayed, Numair would realize that she might be a good enough friend for the dark prince no one respected, but she was no fit company for the man before her now. That he needed her there, but he didn't need her here.

It was that sense of urging, the knowledge that the Song didn't like Numair—or, at the very least, didn't like her *near* Numair—that made her swing her leg over Kialla's back and drop to the ground. Children stepped back as she came forward, as if they knew she wasn't approachable in the same way Numair was. That, or it was Kialla snorting like a dragon that had them wary.

Numair turned to her but didn't get a word out before the door of the house nearest them opened. A sturdy woman stepped out, her black hair falling over her shoulder in a thick braid. A smile tugged at her lips when she saw Numair. Then her gaze landed on Clare and the smile disappeared, the warmth in her expression replaced with ice.

Her voice whipped out, authoritative but not unkind, and a collective groan went up from the children. She hadn't spoken in Common, but it wasn't hard to guess she'd said some version of, "Leave Numair alone so the adults can talk."

Tomlin volunteered to take the horses to the stable, but Clare found herself unable to unclench her fingers from the reins. Kialla wasn't looking any more enthusiastic about leaving than her mistress was about letting her go. Numair—free of clinging children now—stepped up to her.

"It's okay," he said softly. His hand hovered over hers, waiting for permission. When she didn't shake her head, he gently peeled her fingers off the reins. A whispered word to Kialla, born on a spark of his magic, had the mare condescending to allow Tomlin to lead her off.

Numair gave her a rueful grin. "In retrospect, surprising you might not have been wise."

"I'll survive." She attempted to say the words with optimism, but they came out tight and forced, a rigid vow of endurance.

He winced. "Give it a chance. If you hate it, we can leave tonight."

"Where *are* we?"

"This is where my mother was born. She used to bring me here, before..." Before she'd died. Before he'd become what he was now.

She tightened her fingers on his, a brief squeeze. "I'll be fine," she said, managing to sound more like she meant it this time. "It was just…unexpected. The children. There are a lot of them and they are…enthusiastic."

"I take it you aren't that fond of children?"

Better he think that than the truth—that she had no idea what to do with any of them. That she had never been that innocent and didn't know anyone who had. That she had hated being a child because it had meant being smaller and weaker than everyone around her, and she didn't know how to look at children and not remember feeling that way.

But he was waiting for a response so she said, "I'm not *not* fond them."

"It's okay if you aren't. It isn't a test."

The woman who'd ordered the children off cleared her throat loudly, and Numair let Clare's hand drop. "Come on," he said. "She doesn't like waiting."

She followed him to where the woman waited outside her home. Her face was still set as if in stone, and it didn't relax any as they approached. She looked Clare over, dismissed her, and spoke to Numair in her native tongue. It was a long, berating speech, which Numair attempted and failed to interrupt twice.

Clare snapped. He might be willing to let this woman talk over him, but she wasn't. He was talked over and ignored enough at court, and she was sick of it. She couldn't do anything about it there, but here she didn't have to let it stand.

"He isn't yours to talk to that way." Those…were not quite the words she'd intended to say.

The woman leveled a cool gaze on her and replied in Common. "And I suppose you think he's yours, to intercede on his behalf?"

Clare crossed her arms and returned the look. "I think I haven't seen you anywhere near the capital in the time I've been there. He puts up with enough from the infernal courtiers. I was under the impression he comes here because he finds it relaxing, though given this welcome, I can't imagine why."

The woman's eyebrows crept up a fraction. "I'm assuming you didn't understand a word I said to him?"

"I understood the tone."

"Am I allowed any voice in this conversation?" Numair asked lightly.

"No," they replied in tandem.

He held up his hands in surrender. "I'll be in the kitchen. Consider yourselves welcome to find me whenever you're finished sorting this out."

They watched him go, and only once the promised sounds of kitchen rummaging reached them did the woman turn back to Clare with a sigh. "I...think I might have mistaken you for something you're not."

"Such as?"

"One of his court women."

"I am *not* one of *them*."

"I'm beginning to understand that. What are you, then?"

I have no idea. "His friend. What are you?"

"His aunt."

Clare blinked. She had been under the impression that Numair had no living family aside from Alaric. But if his mother was from here, she'd clearly married above her station, and maybe he simply hadn't wanted anyone to know about this place.

"His aunt," she repeated, the knowledge fanning the dregs of her anger.

The woman nodded.

Just to be certain there wasn't a miscommunication from Common not being the woman's first language, she said, "And he has other relatives here?"

Another nod.

Anger burst into glorious flame inside her. "You're his family. You clearly understand what his life is like, and you let him endure what he does *alone*?"

The woman's lips thinned. "I told my sister if she married that man, she'd regret it. But she loved Numair's father, and nothing we said was going to stop her. Prince Navarren wasn't a bad man. If he had been, he might have lived." She said it like she was expounding on some unimportant philosophical point. "The king killed him when Numair was twelve. Told Evaleen—his mother—to leave Numair with him and run home to her little village. She didn't. I'm surprised she lived the three years she did, after that."

"So that's your excuse for leaving him there?"

His aunt sighed. "There is no excuse for that. But he became the king's when Evaleen died. Ida was allowed stay with him, because Ida would no more hurt anyone or scheme than a blade of grass would. But the rest of us are not welcome there. By the king *or* Numair.

"We are his escape, when the king allows it. We—some of us— have some understanding of what his life is like. But we don't *see* it. He doesn't want us to."

Her anger lessened. Because she did understand that there was a difference in knowing a thing theoretically and seeing it firsthand. Understood that Numair came here to have a temporary semblance of a normal life. One that he couldn't have if their pity constantly reminded him of what he came here to forget.

"Fine," she allowed grudgingly. "But don't talk to him again like you were. I don't like it."

"Do you have a name?" his aunt asked stiffly.

"Do you?"

She shook her head, but in exasperation rather than refusal. "Lorna."

"Clare."

"Well, Clare, you're as difficult as a drought in the growing season. He clearly has the same taste as his mother."

"Taste?" Clare echoed. It wasn't that she didn't understand the phrase, it was that she didn't understand how it related to her and his mother.

Lorna surveyed her, as if trying to determine if Clare truly didn't grasp the meaning. Then she rolled her eyes, muttered something in her first tongue, and followed it with, "Never mind," in Common.

On that promising note, Clare followed her inside.

SIXTY-SIX

WATCH ME

Numair watched the kettle heat on the mage-stove he'd finally bought for Aunt Lorna despite her insistence that she didn't need it, while his stomach twisted itself into knots and he wondered if he'd made a terrible mistake. He'd never wanted Clare to see him like she had two nights ago, when he'd come home and hadn't realized she was there. Hadn't realized how badly he hadn't wanted it until it had happened, and he'd been overcome with the desperate need to show her something else. To show her the one place people didn't think he was useless.

He had been thinking about himself—about how he felt here, and who he was allowed to be here. He hadn't considered how different it might be for her. But even if he had, he wouldn't have predicted her reaction. He knew, from her scars and her aversion to touch, that she had damage. But he didn't know anything about it, save the obvious that could be inferred, and he never would have guessed she'd respond as she had.

He'd asked her if she didn't like children, but whether she did or didn't, her reaction had been deeper than like or dislike. She'd looked at them like she couldn't understand them in any capacity. Like their behavior—their openness and happiness—was something she'd never encountered. Like their very existence ran counter to some fundamental law. Like being presented with this normal, peaceful place was horrifying.

He remembered what he'd thought of her initially, watching her flit her way through the Midtown market as if she had no understanding of the value of currency, and considered that his first instinct on where she came from might have been right. He hadn't known, then, what she likely was. Hadn't known that if anyone could leave that place alive, it would be her.

At least she'd seemed to find some normal footing, bickering with Aunt Lorna. She likely had no idea what she'd implied, interrupting his aunt like that. His mother's people were traditionally matriarchal, and traditionally possessive. By those metrics, at least, Clare would fit right in.

He heard the door shut and they walked in just as the kettle whistled. He took it off the stove, giving them both exaggerated once-overs. "Well, I don't *see* any blood or other signs of physical violence."

He received identical scathing looks in return.

"She can stay," Aunt Lorna said. "But you're going to have to share Tomlin's room and you get to explain to him why he has to share a room with his cousins."

Numair groaned. "Nissa's fighting with Arlan again?" Lorna's only daughter, Nissa often wound up back here, along with her two daughters, whenever she and Arlan weren't happy with each other.

"When *isn't* she fighting with Arlan?"

"You know this is a small house," Nissa's high voice shouted from the direction of the guest room. It sounded a little shrill, like it always did when she'd been crying. And half the time he visited, she was crying. "I can *hear you.*"

"Then consider coming out and being polite," he yelled back. "I brought company." Utter silence greeted this announcement. Then a door opened and his cousin stalked into the kitchen.

One look at her and he knew that this time, her and Arlan were *really* fighting. It was midafternoon and the only concession to dressing she'd made was to put on her most well-worn, tattered robe. Even with the heating spells he'd "accidentally" bought for every house in the village, his aunt's home was still plenty chill, because she refused to fully utilize said spells, and Nissa's skin was prickled with gooseflesh. Her eyes were red-rimmed, her cheeks puffy, and she looked like she hadn't brushed her hair at all in the last two days.

"You look awful," he lied. Nissa was one of those people who could fall into a mud pit and somehow still come out looking effortlessly beautiful. Most of the village had been in love with her at one point or another, but true to his family's seemingly innate sense of obstinance, she'd gone and found a husband from three villages over.

She drew herself up, eyes flashing. "You don't exactly look like a fresh blossom yourself. I can smell the travel dirt from here." She looked around him at Clare, who was more or less attempting to fade into the shadows. "Company, hmm?"

"Nissa, this is Clare. Clare, this is my cousin Nissa."

"Hi, Clare." She crossed her arms. "Why are you here?"

Numair covered his face with his hand. Clearly, he hadn't thought any of this through. "She's here because I invited her."

"No," Nissa said slowly, "she's here because she accepted the invitation, and I want to know why. I don't know many court women who enjoy visiting farming villages in the middle of the cold season."

"You don't know *any* court women," he pointed out.

"Yes, and I'd been hoping to keep it that way."

"She isn't a courtier, she's"—he'd been about to say "a singer" but he hadn't brought her here to make her perform, and that would definitely happen if they knew she could sing—"my friend."

Nissa raised her eyebrows skeptically and drew out the word, "Right." She pointed at the kettle. "Were you going to make tea with that or let the water go cold?"

He let her have the kettle—she made better tea than he did anyway—and faux-whispered to Clare. "I promise I thought it would be nice to bring you here, but now I can't remember why."

"What's nice about Deleen Village?" Nissa objected. "Especially in winter? Honestly, Numair, this is not the place to bring a woman you're trying to impress, and I would expect a prince to know that. Unless you're trying to run her off." She peered at Clare. "Is he trying to run you off?"

Clare swallowed. She didn't look *precisely* like a horse about to bolt, but she did look like one strongly considering the option.

"I have to check over the horses," he said abruptly. "Ollie's knee was still giving him trouble the last time I was out, and Clare needs to come with me." He herded her toward the door.

"Oh no you don't." Nissa attempted to gesture proprietarily with her tea mug. "You don't get to bring home the first woman you've *ever* brought home and then abscond with her."

"Watch me." He reached around Clare, opened the door, and they escaped.

CHAPTER

SIXTY-SEVEN

SPECIAL OCCASIONS

Clare was not entirely certain what had happened. Other than that she had stood there, in the midst of so much chaotic energy, and said absolutely nothing. Lorna, she had felt compelled to respond to. She was the type of woman Clare understood. Nissa was...not.

She had never seen anyone willing to wear their pain so openly. Clare did not cry. If the impossible happened and she did, she would never let anyone see it. Because that required trust, and trust was the thing she'd found so confusing in that house. It had been there in the easiness between the three of them, willing to speak so openly with each other, as if unworried about how their words might be used against them. And while she hadn't quite been a part of it, she hadn't been excluded either. As if they were willing to include her if she took the right steps.

It made her feel like she stood before a lone, starving wolf, and if she made the right choice, she could join it to form a pack, but if she made the wrong one it would eat her.

"Are you okay?"

Clare realized they were not in the stables. She'd followed Numair blindly, which was worrisome in and of itself, and now they stood at the edge of a frozen lake, his dark eyes looking down at her with concern.

"I...don't know."

"I meant it when I said we could go. Say the word and we will."

She shook her head. "I don't want to go."

"But you aren't okay."

How was she supposed to explain? "You just grew up like this?" She couldn't define "this". How did she define something so totally opposite of her own experience?

"Sometimes. A lot of the time, when I was younger." His voice softened. "You didn't."

It wasn't a question, not really, but: "Never." She stared out at the lake. Everything was so placid in winter, so suspended. Numair didn't push her, he just waited. "I understand the rules in Veralna," she said finally. "I know what I'm supposed to do, even if I don't always do it. I don't understand the rules here."

"There aren't any. You don't have to make yourself into someone you aren't here. I don't want you to. Just be honest. They might not understand you, but they will accept you. They're good people."

Something tight lodged in her chest. "I'm not." And she didn't want to be. Good people…well, nothing good ever happened to them in her experience.

"We might have to agree to disagree on that."

She blew out a breath. "And what if I don't know how to be honest? What if all I ever am is what I think people want me to be?"

"Is that who you are with me? Whoever you think I want you to be?" Buried underneath it was another question: *Has everything you've ever shown me been a lie?*

She could fix everything, she realized, by saying yes. Maybe he would believe her and maybe he wouldn't. But she was certain it would hurt him enough that he would let her walk away. And then she wouldn't have to feel him pulling away from her ever again, like he had the last few weeks, because she would have done it first, and more cleanly.

That was how she would avoid being trapped like Alys and Lina had been by Geoffrey. That was how she would ensure she never felt again like she had when she'd woken in his room as he'd come home.

That was how she would avoid ever living a single moment of the life she had wanted to build. The life she didn't know how to build because her old one still had its hooks sunk deep into her chest, and no matter how hard she pried, they never came loose.

Maybe…maybe this was how they started to. "I've never pretended with you."

He exhaled heavily, like he'd been holding the breath. "Then let's go back, and not pretend."

She started to move away with him, then stopped. There was one more thing she wanted to know. "Your name. No one pronounces it right in Veralna, do they?" His aunt and his cousin had said it as the child had, three syllables rather than two.

He shrugged. "Everyone in Veralna speaks the Common tongue. They use the Common pronunciation of the name."

"Does it bother you?"

"It used to. When I was a child. Now… Now, in Veralna, I'm Numair." Two syllables. "Here, I'm Numair." Three syllables. "I prefer it that way."

She understood that need for separation. But it bothered her that all this time, she hadn't truly known his name. "And what do you prefer I call you?"

"You," he said slowly, holding her gaze, "can call me anything you want."

She had no good explanation for why she suddenly felt hot when she was standing next to a frozen lake. She shook her head and started back the way they'd come. "I suppose I'll save the one for special occasions, then."

His soft laugh curled around her in response.

CHAPTER

SIXTY-EIGHT

DISHES

Life in the small village did not grind to a halt simply because the second prince of Faelhorn had arrived, and she suspected that was another part of its allure for Numair. If anything, rather than slowing down, everyone seemed to be in a fervor of activity.

She simply observed it for a while as Numair went through the barn, whispers of magic flowing from his fingers as he scratched the neck of this or that horse, rubbed the muzzle of another, checked feet and legs for soundness. An anxiety Clare hadn't realized she carried eased when she saw Kialla and the mare gave her a soft nicker in greeting.

They left the relative warmth of the barn for the surrounding fields, where she was surprised to realize things were actually growing. A small selection of plants, the Song whispering something about hardy winter crops, and Numair walked through the tidy rows, magic slipping from him into the ground, bolstering it all.

We could help, the Song said.

It was such an unexpected offer that she stopped walking. *You don't even like him.*

I like them.

She'd felt as much, the Song taking from this place the measure of peace she hadn't quite managed to grasp for herself yet.

Ahead, Numair realized she'd stopped and turned back, eyebrow lifted in silent question.

She bit her lip. *You won't hurt him.*

The Song rippled through her like a sigh. *You wouldn't let me if I tried.*

She closed the distance to Numair. "I think I can help. If you want."

"How?"

It came together in her mind with the quickness of a lightning flash. She knelt on the cold ground and he mimicked her. "Like with the hibiscus plant," she said, "but reversed."

Understanding swept across his face and he put his hand on the ground. She placed hers on top of it.

"What now?"

"Do what you were before, and I'll do the rest."

Magic trickled out of his fingertips, burrowing into the earth, and the Song joined it. She felt its power twine with his, amplifying the magic he'd been carefully allotting and dispersing. A trickle became a flood, seeping through the ground and spreading out.

As it stretched into the earth, she felt it all—every worm and bug that crawled in the soil, every root stretching down deep into the ground to anchor the plants above. She felt the pulse of the earth as if it were a beating heart comprised of dirt and rocks and plants and water. And in that moment, the Song having pushed Numair's power to the boundaries of the fields, entwined with his and wrapped around everything she felt, she knew that if she wanted, she could squeeze that heart and crush it.

Carefully, she drew the Song back. It came willingly enough, for once, until there was no magic between her and Numair, only her hand covering his. She met his gaze and his lips parted.

The sound of a small, trampling animal came toward them. "Uncle Numair!" Tomlin tried to halt his forward momentum, failed, and crashed into Numair, who pulled his hand from hers to right the boy. "Lorna—I mean Mom—says the two of you need to stop mooning at each other and come inside for dinner."

His message delivered, he took off at top speed across the field again. Numair laughed quietly. "I suppose we've been summoned. It's best not to test her patience."

They walked while Clare puzzled over the first thing the boy had said. "Lorna's his mother?"

"She is now. His parents died last fall. She simultaneously complains about being too old to raise an eight-year-old while contradictorily saying it keeps her on her toes and makes life interesting."

She frowned. "Then why does he call you his uncle? Shouldn't he be calling you cousin?"

"Apparently, he's always wanted an uncle. Using the logic of children, he determined that if Lorna could be his new mother despite not actually being his mother, there was nothing preventing me from filling the role of uncle. We decided he had a point."

<hr>

DINNER WENT BY FAIRLY EASILY, if only because the three children wreaked enough havoc to keep their respective parents from focusing too much attention on Clare. Which was a relief, even if after a bit Clare started to feel awkward when the two girls would repeat, like clockwork every few minutes, that they missed Daddy and wanted to go home. This inevitably made Nissa's eyes water until Numair, after quietly asking if Clare was okay on her own for a bit, dragged them squealing into the common room to play some kind of children's game.

Nissa watched him playing with them and then promptly burst into tears, at which point Lorna's apparent irritation got the better of her. "If he makes you so miserable, why don't you just leave him?"

"Don't," Nissa snapped. "Don't start with that again. He is a good man and a good father."

"If he's so wonderful, then what are his wife and his children doing back in my house for the second time this month?"

"If you don't want us here—"

"That's not what I meant and you know it."

Clare, as unobtrusively as possible, slid her seat back and stood. For a moment she had no idea what to do with herself. Joining Numair in the common room was unthinkable. The children were there, and she did not want their undivided attention. They were not quite as frightening as they'd been when she'd first seen them, but they were still something she preferred to not directly engage with. Much like the argument unfolding between Nissa and Lorna, which had all the cadences of one repeated often and to the same end result.

What was she supposed to do with herself?

Dishes, the Song offered, providing a further explanation of what that entailed because the Song knew, as always, the extent of her ignorance. It wasn't like she'd ever had dishes in Renault County, and since she'd come to Veralna, they had always been someone else's problem.

For once, she took its suggestion without grumbling, because she was grateful to have something to do. And there was something soothing in the methodical clearing of plates from the table, the scraping of food remnants into the bucket for that purpose that the Song had been able to guess the location of on its second try.

Eventually Nissa and Lorna stopped arguing long enough to be horrified—but somewhat approving—that she was doing everything. It hardly took any time to finish once they joined her, and once it *was* finished, Nissa bestowed upon Lorna a stiff, formal, "Goodnight, Mother," and a slightly less stiff, "Goodnight, Clare, I'm glad you survived the day."

She went into the common room, collected all three of the children and took them down the short hall to their room.

Lorna sighed as Numair came back into the kitchen. "She never would listen to reason, at any age. You were much more well-behaved." She let out another world-weary sigh, this one sounding slightly manufactured. "I'm too old for this. Don't either of you cause me a heart attack before the morning."

With that she departed, turning out all but a single magelight on her way. In the remaining dim light, Numair led her to a smaller room off the kitchen, turning on the magelight within. He stood in the doorway, rubbing at the back of his neck. "So, ah, it is a child's room."

Which meant, she realized, that in addition to being small in general it also had a very small bed, the mattress of which rested directly on the floor as opposed to on a frame of any sort. And while they weren't unaccustomed to sleeping in the same room, the layout of this one meant that whichever one of them took the floor might as well be on the bed for all the space that separated them.

"I'll take the floor," they said at the same time.

They bickered about it back and forth before Numair insisted they settle the matter by playing some ridiculous game involving hand gestures and rocks and scissors, which she naturally lost.

"This is a bad idea," she muttered, kicking off her boots.

"I don't think anyone's ever grumbled so much about *not* having to sleep on the floor."

"You have. Less than a minute ago." She flopped onto the mattress, handing him the extra pillow and blanket Lorna had laid out at some point. "If I accidentally roll off this bed onto you in the middle of the night, don't blame me when the unconscious version of myself decides to punch you in the throat again."

CHAPTER
SIXTY-NINE
WE ARE WHO WE ARE

The sound of approaching feet registered in Clare's subconscious a moment before a rap at the door startled her awake. Her body and her mind were disjointed, the latter having not quite caught up with the former.

Where was she?

Panic set in as she tried to see through the total darkness. She felt the smallness of the room—air always moved differently, the smaller the space—and when the knock at the door came again and she felt someone stir beside her, she reacted on instinct. She pulled her slim bone dagger and rolled on top of the threat, pinning arms and legs, the blade of the dagger pressing against a soft throat.

Her hand trembled, her brain scrambling to understand why she hadn't pushed the blade home. Threats had to be dealt with quickly, efficiently. But this body beneath her did not feel like a threat. Even if it *was* male. A soft wash of magic came from the man, bringing the scent of earth and growing things.

On the other side of the door, a boy's innocent, "Uncle Numair?" finally made her mind catch up with her body. She shook, horrified, but she couldn't move.

The magelight in the room flared to life, bathing her and Numair in a soft glow.

"We'll be out in a minute, Tomlin," Numair said, pitching his voice to carry. He smiled sleepily up at her, like there wasn't a knife pressed to his throat or a thin line of red coming from it. "Morning."

Morning? She was probably cutting off the circulation to his arms and legs, and he went with *Morning?* "I'm sorry," she whispered. She wanted to let the knife go, but she had this terrible fear that if she tried to pull back her body would do the opposite and push forward. And she realized in that moment that, of all the terrible things she'd done in her life, this would be the worst.

This would be the one that would *matter*, the one she couldn't come back from, the one that meant nothing else would ever matter again. If she pressed that blade forward, if Numair was no longer here, then she might as well give the Song what it wanted.

Which was precisely *why* she couldn't move her hand. Her fears were never born from absent things, though often they *were* born from things she couldn't immediately identify the root of. This one —the fear that she would drive the blade in rather than pull it back —was born from the Song. It didn't like Numair, and she finally understood why. It had nothing to do with him, and everything to do with what he was to her. With what his absence might finally allow the Song to convince her to do.

Numair shrugged off her apology. "It isn't the worst way I've ever been woken up."

Her fingers still wouldn't let go. She squeezed her eyes tight before opening them again, and she wondered what they looked like, if the Song was burning out of them the way it felt like it was.

She didn't know if she'd ever felt as vulnerable as she did when she admitted, "I think I need you to help me."

"All right. I'm going to move my arm, okay?"

She exhaled. "Okay."

The pinning she'd done on his arms was a poor job, because it was the knife at his throat that was the real threat, so it wasn't too difficult for him to work his arm free. He did so slowly and—just as slowly—covered her hand where it gripped the knife.

"Good so far?"

Her arm trembled. She steadied it and nodded.

"What about now?" His fingers curled around the back of her hand. She nodded again and he drew her hand away. Her fingers finally loosened, knife clattering to the ground. She took a deep, shuddering breath and dropped her forehead to his chest.

"I'm sorry." She'd never said those words to anyone but him, and now she'd said them twice in a span of minutes.

"It's all right."

"It's not. I don't want to be like this with you." It was one thing, what had happened with Fitz. That hadn't been unprovoked and, if he couldn't have predicted her response, it had still been his fault. But this had just *happened*. Because she hadn't known where she was when she first woke and it had been dark and she'd heard a noise. A simple, stupid noise.

"We are who we are, Clare. I don't blame you for it."

"Maybe you should."

"And maybe *you* shouldn't."

She ignored that bit of advice. "I promise I'll get off you as soon as I can move." Pinning a person to the ground required far more physical contact than they ever shared, and she didn't want to be another touch he didn't want, but her limbs wouldn't unfreeze.

He spoke, his voice a little odd. "I don't mind so much."

"I don't either." She'd answered without thinking, but the realization that she *didn't* mind was like a plunge into ice-cold water. Suddenly every part of her body was working perfectly fine, and she vaulted off him.

What in Ferrian's name was wrong with her? What was this nice place with its nice people and its seeming lack of atrocities doing to her?

Numair sat up, dragging a hand through his hair.

I don't mind so much? Where had that come from?

He'd realized how it probably sounded the second it left his mouth, but then she'd said *I don't either* and he'd thought maybe it hadn't been the worst thing to say after all. Except then she'd leapt across half the room to get away from him.

Silence with her had never been awkward, and he didn't like the way it was morphing into that now. For lack of any better idea, he swiped the makeshift knife off the ground and offered it to her. She took it but didn't immediately put it away, staring down at it instead.

"I can't sleep without a weapon." She finally stowed it away. "So I'll sleep in the tent tonight."

He understood the reaction. He would be having it himself were their positions reversed. But… "You didn't have an issue on the way here, and you don't at home. So what's the problem? The darkness? The small space? The unexpected noise?"

She got that cross look on her face that, if he was being honest with himself, he absolutely loved. Then she blew out an irritated breath and said, "The darkness. The space wouldn't be a problem if it didn't feel so…dead. Your room has the night flowers, and mine has a window and the hibiscus. Without those, the noise was… instinct awakening."

"So some night flowers and a little extra light would probably fix the problem?"

She huffed out a breath. "You don't have to do this."

"Do what? Make you comfortable when I'm the one who dragged you out here without any explanation?" In retrospect, that had been a terrible idea. But he hadn't told her where they were going because he hadn't wanted her to say no. It had been selfish, but here they were.

"I'm the one who agreed to come without any explanation." She broke eye contact. "I don't want to be a problem."

"It's never a problem to make you feel safe."

She shook her head. "I shouldn't need it. I don't *want* to need it."

"We need what we need."

She smiled bitterly. "Like we are who we are?"

"Like that, yes."

She looked like she'd bitten into something sour.

"If you'd rather sleep in the tent that's fine." Even if there was no explanation he would be able to give Aunt Lorna for *why* Clare had decided to sleep outdoors. At least, not one that would make any sense to her. People like her—people who'd never been through the worst life had to offer, or who had never seen its effects up close— couldn't really understand it. But he didn't tell Clare any of that because he didn't want her to feel pressured to stay inside. "But if you want to stay here, I can fix the problem."

She took a moment to answer, finally saying, "It depends."

"On?"

Her lips curved up. "What kind of flowers you bring me."

He laughed. "I'll do my best not to disappoint you."

CLARE WAS, for the first time since they had arrived here, relieved by the amount of chaos and energy that greeted her when they exited the room. She wanted to be distracted, and there was plenty to distract. She'd barely taken a step outside the room before three children unevenly screeched "Happy Solstice Day!" at her before dissolving into giggles and fleeing.

"Solstice Day?"

He grinned. "It's kind of why I wanted to come so suddenly. It's the Winter Solstice celebration."

She hadn't noticed the passing of time, hadn't marked this date. Ordinarily it would have meant nothing to her. But this time—this year—it meant something it never had before. Something she hadn't known until Marquin and Verol had told it to her.

Today was her nameday.

Numair sensed her change in mood, as only he seemed able to, and shot her a questioning look. She only smiled and shook her head. If she told him, he would probably want to do something for her, and she didn't want him to. Besides, despite how strange and unsettling this place could be for her, his bringing her—his *wanting* to bring her—was the best gift he could have given her.

"Numair only condescends to visit us on holidays," Nissa said as she breezed into the room, clearly having caught Numair's explanation. Unlike yesterday she was fully dressed, cosmetics artfully concealing the puffiness of her eyes. "I think it's for the food."

One of her daughters ran over, stretching her arms in a silent demand to be picked up, which Nissa did.

"Is Clare going to help us decorate?" the little girl asked.

"I don't know," Nissa said, "you'd have to ask her."

Clare sent Numair a please-tell-me-what-to-do look and Nissa laughed.

"Did he tell you *anything* before he brought you out here?"

"No."

"We spend the entire day setting up for tonight, so everyone is either cooking, cleaning, decorating, or doing anything else that needs to be done. You can pick whichever one you want, but you have to do one."

"What are you doing?" Clare asked Numair.

"Cooking. I make better pies than anyone else."

Nissa rolled her eyes. "And if it wasn't true, we'd never suffer his hubris."

"I can't cook," Clare said.

"You don't need to. Join decorations with me, and I'll keep the curious at bay."

"The curious?"

"I *did* say you were the first woman he's ever brought home, didn't I? People let you be yesterday out of politeness, but don't expect that to last into today. Especially once the cider starts flowing. Stay with me and I'll protect you."

"But she won't protect you from herself," Numair warned.

Nissa sniffed. "I'm a delight."

In the end Clare went with Nissa, both because she didn't want to need to feel as if she could only function in this place if she was at Numair's side, and because how difficult could decorating be?

CHAPTER

SEVENTY

IN ANOTHER WORLD

Four hours later Clare was dizzy from climbing up and down ladders and following instructions of "Move that garland there," and "A little to the right" and "No, back to the left after all."

They were in the village's common building. On normal days, Nissa had explained, it saw a continuous line of people from the village making use of the communal kitchens for what they weren't equipped to make in their homes. But today the building's kitchens bustled with so many people that Clare had taken one look inside and been grateful she hadn't attempted to learn how to cook. How did they work in there, all packed together? It was like a choreographed play, people shimmying and sliding past one another to get to here or there. More baffling was how happy they'd all seemed.

Decorating was a much more reasonable, if tedious affair. Nissa directed it all with the utter certainty of a woman who knew precisely what she wanted and would settle for nothing less. Clare had to admit the end result was pretty, even if she couldn't understand putting in so much effort for a single day's enjoyment.

Half of her followed directions while the other half of her observed this strange event. She was trying to sort everyone's behavior into the neat categories that allowed her to navigate a social space, once they were learned. But she'd never seen people act the way they did here.

Perhaps it was that she only had two places to compare them to —Renault County or Veralna—and those two had more in common with each other than one would ever imagine at first glance. They were both ruled by power—who had it, how did they wield it, and how could someone else get it—albeit Veralna was less open about the fact.

Clare struggled to find that same structure here. It wasn't that there was *no* hierarchy—leaders of various small task groups were deferred to, as Clare and the other decorators deferred to Nissa's instructions—it was that no one seemed unhappy to have those people above them. Nor did the ones in charge abuse that authority —as if it wasn't a particularly coveted thing to have, and if they should find themselves swapping places with someone else, they wouldn't find it an issue.

These people were...happy. They were comfortable. They were not walking as if on broken glass, waiting for a tide to shift and anticipating how best to keep from being submerged by it. Even when someone wandered over, obviously intent on talking to Clare, and Nissa chased them off, no one ever seemed bothered by Nissa's briskness. As if they were willing to listen to her without fearing her.

The more Clare watched, the more it appeared the egregious amount of work being done now, for this one day, was simply an excuse to bring them all together, joined in a single goal. She couldn't understand what it was that could make people act this way.

Community, the Song said, stirring from the lazy contentment it had been riding all morning. *Family.*

And what would you know of those two things? she snapped.

They are what I dreamed of in the darkness. Clare felt the weight of the word—darkness. As if the Song meant a far more weighty, ancient thing than the years it had lived within Clare's body.

Her own darkness had not had such happy dreams. She'd had no understanding of them to dream about. She had dreamed instead of what she knew, and what she knew was power. But this... perhaps it wasn't such a bad dream. For someone else. Someone unlike her.

A bell clanged through the building, shifting the mood from easy camaraderie to eager anticipation, and everyone began putting hurried, finishing touches on whatever they were doing. Nissa dismissed everyone under her command with a, "That will do," and motioned for Clare to join her.

"What next?" Clare asked. "Are we draping the entire village in garlands?" She was only half-joking. Nissa was formidable, and extremely dedicated to aesthetic presentation.

"Now," she said theatrically, "we change and waste time being pretty because we can. Mother has the girls, and I'm taking full advantage."

Nissa walked so fast back to the house that she was almost jogging. They were of a same height, so Clare was almost jogging beside her.

"What is the rush?" Clare asked as Nissa dashed inside.

"The rush is that you should get dressed and come to my room before Numair sees you. We'll get ready together and not ruin the reveal." She danced off down the hall before Clare could object, though what she would object to, specifically, she didn't know. Deciding it was easier to do as instructed, she searched her pack for the one nice outfit Numair had told her to bring.

She had been confused as to its necessity when she'd discovered their destination, but now she understood, and she was grateful to have it. There was no joy in being inappropriately dressed for an occasion, unless you had done so with purpose and intent.

She'd packed one of the finer pants and shirt sets Chalen had made for her. They were a light silvery-blue and so comfortable it should be impossible that they looked formal, but Chalen was a master of their craft and it showed in this production, as it did in all of them.

Even so, when she went to Nissa's room and the woman looked her over and gasped, she wondered if the outfit, while not truly daring for Veralna's circles, might be considered so here. Nissa wore a light green dress that flattered her figure without being ostentatious, and Clare wondered if she should have brought something more like it.

Nissa practically leaped across the room. She reached out, then stopped herself at the last moment. "I love this—where did you get it?"

"A designer named Chalen Mora."

Nissa bit her lower lip. "I suppose it's custom made and horridly expensive, then?"

"More or less."

She sighed. "Ah, well. Maybe Serah—our local seamstress—will attempt something like it for me, if she isn't too scandalized by the idea. Now sit." She pointed to a padded stool in front of a vanity that held a small mirror. An array of cosmetics littered the wooden surface.

Clare managed not to outwardly grimace. She was better with women than men, but she still didn't particularly like being touched. But she'd managed it when Alys had helped her, and Nissa was obviously excited. It was one night, and then she was never going to see this woman again. She could survive it.

Nissa seemed oblivious to Clare's discomfort, so at least this place had not so unsettled her that she couldn't still hide her true feelings. She sat on the stool. Nissa surveyed her face, as if it were an artist's canvas and she was deciding what she wanted to paint.

Clare found herself staring at Nissa's chest, where a pendant dangled from a thin gold chain. The pendant was the same gold as the chain, a long slender rectangle with symbols etched onto the surface. There was something about it—the simplicity or the elegance of the etchings, she wasn't certain—that appealed to her.

"I like your necklace."

Nissa studied Clare, as if looking for sincerity or an ulterior motive. Then she shook herself and said, "Thank you. It's...from Arlan." She tucked it behind her shirt and Clare had the sense of having made a misstep. But how was she supposed to have known it was from the husband Nissa was fighting with?

"Now," Nissa said, forced brightness in her voice, "I think I know just the look for you." She proceeded to paint Clare's face, then moved on to twisting her hair into an elaborate upsweep, chattering endlessly the entire time. Clare only half-listened. Numair's cousin had a pretty voice, and she found herself focusing on the cadence and tone of the words rather than the content.

It was only once that cadence halted, and she found Nissa looking at her expectantly, that she realized she'd missed a question. "I'm afraid I missed that."

"You and Numair—how did you meet?"

I watched him pickpocket a man, then followed him to an inn, then punched him in the throat a few days later because he was following me. Then he helped me scheme my way into getting noticed by all of high society, and then I discovered he was the second prince of Faelhorn. "That is... a long story."

"I love stories."

"Yet I'm afraid I'm not much of a storyteller."

Nissa's hands paused, having put the final pin in the delicate twists she'd formed in Clare's hair, her eyes meeting Clare's in the mirror. "I care about my cousin. As much as he allows us to. I don't want to see him hurt."

Clare had a deep suspicion she wouldn't like where this went.

"I don't want *you* to be hurt, either. And if the two of you could be here, if he could be who he is here, I wouldn't warn either of you away from each other. But you're both returning to Veralna tomorrow. And I know a thing or two about wanting a man who feels like he can't be who he truly is. It's not something I'd wish on anyone."

Denial was a hard kick in Clare's stomach. For the first time in her life, she thought she understood how a person might end up spluttering, though she had no intention of allowing herself to do so. She took a moment to be sure she wouldn't and then said, in calm, measured words, "Numair and I are friends."

"And I am suggesting that that is what you stay. For both of your sakes." Nissa smiled, a little sadly. "For what it's worth, Clare, I like you. And in another world, I think you could have made him happy."

NISSA'S WORDS wouldn't leave Clare's head as she paced back and forth in the small common area, waiting for Numair to come out of their room. She'd left Nissa to finish her own preparations, hoping to hurry them along. She wanted to be moving, leaving, and to that effect she'd put on her coat—Numair's coat. It was pulled tight around her, and she clung to it as she'd never clung to anything but her guitar in her life.

She wanted to go back half an hour and un-hear Nissa's opinion. And then she told herself it didn't matter, because Nissa was wrong. Clare had never expected, never wanted, anything more from Numair than friendship. He didn't want anything more than that from her. So she didn't need to panic or feel like she stood on a rug that was being pulled from beneath her, because nothing had changed. Nothing *would* change. So there was nothing to worry about.

I don't mind so much.

I don't either.

Their door opened. Her gaze snapped to it and everything in her settled. Numair looked good, in the black he almost always wore, but with detail work in silver threading. But it wasn't his clothes or how he wore them that made her stare, unable to draw her gaze away. It was the way he looked at her—open and unguarded as he never was in Veralna, and staring in return, a smile curving his lips.

Nissa's door opened. She stepped into the hallway, looked between them and sighed. "We should go before we're last in line." She marched past them, opened the door, and let out a startled, "Oh."

A man stood on the threshold. He was easily a foot taller than Nissa, with broad shoulders and biceps the size of saplings. For all his bulk, the immediate impression Clare got from him was, oddly, gentleness.

"Hey, Niss."

"Arlan," she said softly.

"Are the girls here?"

Nissa shook her head. "With my mother, at Averna's."

"Can I come in?"

Nissa bit her lip. "Numair is—"

"Leaving," Numair said firmly, nodding to Clare, who took the hint and followed him to the door. They slipped out, but ten paces from the door Clare stopped, looking back at the house where Arlan was disappearing inside.

"Are you sure she'll be all right?"

"Neither one of them would ever physically hurt the other, if that's what you're concerned about." It was. "Trust me, I know precisely what's wrong with their marriage, and it's nothing like that."

"How do you know what the problem is?"

"She wanted my advice a year or so ago, told me all of it. Apparently, since I grew up mostly in the city, I am supposed to be open-minded and free-thinking."

"I would say you are both of those things."

"Yes, but it has nothing to do with growing up in the city."

She heard the celebration when they were still well away from the common building—music playing and the boisterous sounds of merriment.

"If you need a break from it all, let me know. Or if you want to leave, let me know that, too."

She clenched her hands, glad they were hidden in her coat pockets. "What do we do?"

"Whatever we want. Eat. Drink. Dance. Talk to people. Or don't. Pretend we're human."

They reached the building. His hand was on the long metal door handle when she blurted out, "You won't leave me alone?"

The smile he gave her…she didn't have the words to describe it. "I wouldn't dream of it."

CHAPTER

SEVENTY-ONE

REMEMBER ME LIKE THIS

Clare was not drunk—she'd specifically followed Numair's lead to find the non-alcoholic cider—but she felt like she imagined it did to be drunk. Lightheaded from the noise and all the heat produced by so many bodies crammed into the same space. A little…giddy, almost, but relaxed, too.

The night had stopped feeling stressful an hour or so in, once she realized that when people came up to talk to her and Numair, it wasn't a test. They weren't asking the cleverest questions, waiting to see if she could come up with an equally clever remark quickly enough. They weren't attempting to trick her into revealing something they could use against her.

It wasn't that they were entirely uncalculating—they were curious about her, and she had no doubt whatever she and Numair said was working its way through the crowd—it was only that none of it felt malicious. It was that they didn't press too hard, and she could tell most of them were doing their best to let her be.

And they weren't *all* interested in her. Plenty of people were stopping to talk to Numair. Half of that, interestingly enough, was questions about plants and soil conditions and the like, things she would have thought he'd have no need to know. That his magic simply grew what he wanted, regardless of his knowledge of how.

You couldn't Songweave if you didn't understand how to sing, the

Song pointed out. *He can't grow something if he has no idea how it grows.*

It made a certain amount of sense. While Numair talked ideal planting conditions, she found her gaze wandering the room. She caught sight of several more necklaces similar to the one Nissa had worn. All were the same basic design, though the colors and symbols varied.

When Numair's conversation ended and they were once again as alone as they could be in a crowded room, she found herself asking, "The necklaces so many of the women have—does someone in the village make them?"

He froze, almost in the same way Nissa had when Clare had remarked on hers. Honestly, if she wasn't supposed to notice them, why were they all worn so openly?

"Yes," Numair said finally, "there are two people in the village who make them. Why?"

She shrugged. "They're pretty."

He finally relaxed again, grinning at her. "And you like pretty things, even if you shouldn't?"

She'd said that, hadn't she? "Maybe I could buy one, before we go?"

"Oh." He looked away. "I don't think—that is, they're usually custom made. And with us leaving in the morning…"

She felt a flush creep up her neck. It was obvious what he wasn't saying. That they weren't for outsiders and that she, however much she'd been welcomed for a brief time, was an outsider. "Of course. Forget I mentioned it."

They lapsed into a brief silence, which he broke by asking, "Do you want to leave?"

"No."

"Then do you want to dance with me?"

Surprisingly, she did, only, "I don't know any of the dances."

"The next one will be slow."

"How can you be sure?"

"Because I asked them to play it earlier. Slow dancing is more drifting than dancing, so will you?" He held out his hand as the current song concluded. She placed hers in it and let him pull her onto the floor.

It was a very slow song and the number of dancers, which had steadily been declining as the evening wore on and people grew tired, was renewed as everyone took advantage of the opportunity to, as Numair had put it, drift rather than truly dance.

Part of that drifting was toward each other. The more they swayed in lazy circles, the closer she and Numair came, the space between them diminishing until there was almost none left. She found herself staring at the hollow of his throat, acutely aware of him beneath her hands, of his arm around her back.

The song was more than halfway through before either of them spoke.

"I know I should have been more transparent about where I was bringing you," he said. "But I'm very glad you're here."

"So am I." Though she couldn't help but compare the differences between their pasts. In Veralna they were both trapped in similar versions of an unpleasant present, and he had brought her here to show her a different side of himself. One he thought was better.

She had no better side to offer him in return. She had only pain and blood and death, and if she ever told him the truth of it, if he ever *saw* the truth of it, would he remain at her side? Would he still be understanding then and tell her, *We are who we are*, or would he choke on the horror of it and run?

He swallowed, and the movement of his throat drew her out of those dark thoughts.

"Would you do something for me?" His hand tensed on her back as he asked, and she tilted her head up to find his face inscrutable. "When we leave here—when we're back there—would you remember me like this?"

The rawness in the request made it feel like something cracked in her chest. And she hoped he recognized the truth in her words as she answered, "I thought you knew—I always see you like this."

His breath hitched, his head dipping a fraction toward hers.

The song ended, but they didn't move. Not until she realized no other song had started, and practically the entire room's attention was shifting to the entranceway. Reluctantly, she and Numair looked away from each other, following everyone else's gazes.

Nissa stood just inside the doorway. The fingers of one hand were threaded with Arlan's, the other with another man's. Nissa lifted her head in defiance at the silence that had taken over the room. "We're getting married."

Numair let out a soft laugh and muttered, "Finally."

The silence remained a bit longer, and then someone shouted, "Congratulations!"

More followed after that, along with a few inquiries of, "How does that work?" A woman ran up and pulled Nissa into a hug, and then the group was surrounded, the loud clamor of the hall returning.

"So the marriage problem was that she was in love with both of them?" Clare asked.

Numair shook his head. "The marriage problem was that they were all in love with each other, but she was the only one willing to admit it."

"At least we aren't the center of attention anymore."

"There is that. Should we escape while the opportunity is here?"

She nodded, and they retrieved their coats and slipped through the crowd. Clare snuck a glance at Nissa as they left. She was smiling. She looked happy. Clare was, inexplicably, happy for her. Back at the house, Numair paused in front of the door to their room, his palm flat against the wood.

"You'll have to tell me how I did."

For a moment, she didn't know what he was talking about. Then he pushed the door open, and she remembered she'd vowed to sleep in a tent tonight, depending on what kind of flower he brought her, because she was staring at one of the most beautiful ones she'd ever seen.

It rose from a wide planter, its stems and leaves black. The one opened flower in the center was a brilliant, luminescent purple veined with white. Numair stretched out his hand and the six other buds on the plant blossomed, unfurling their petals.

She reached out, gently stroking a petal. "What's it called?"

"Night's solace."

She smiled. "It even has the perfect name."

"Does that mean I don't have to ready the tent for you after all?"

The soft velvet of the flower petal stroked against her skin. "I suppose not." But she insisted on taking the floor that night.

CHAPTER

SEVENTY-TWO

SHE'S GONE

Quin's exhaustion had nothing to do with traveling, though he tried to convince himself that was the case as the wagon rumbled back into Veralna City. Trin Province had been...difficult. It didn't make him feel any better, that what had happened there had been inevitable. That long-term there was nothing he or Verol could have done to prevent it. That it happening this way meant Verol had been able to take the pain from so many as they passed.

So why had hastening the inevitable made him feel so vile? Verol was likewise affected, sitting stone-faced beside him, his emotions so muted Marquin hardly felt them through the heartstone. Perhaps it was only that nothing of this scale had been required of them since the Mages War, and they had managed to forget the worst of the deeds that had made them into the Butcher and the Barbarian. They had been allowed years in which to merely dislike themselves, as opposed to actively loathing themselves.

He and Verol were nearly drained, magically and physically, so perhaps it was good that Alaric had ordered them back to Veralna. Even if it meant that concocting a reason to leave and retrieve the gatestone later would require more time and finesse. At any rate, it was a relief when the horses finally clopped up to the stable at their estate.

It was a short-lived relief. He had the first hint of something amiss when Alys did not come out to greet them. Neither he nor Verol expected her to actually work for them in return for harboring her—they'd tried to simply put her up in the room that had instead become Clare's—but Alys was militant about "not taking advantage of their generosity". Given that leaving the estate was not something she did often, she tended to come out immediately upon their return.

When she didn't, and when Fitz came out of the house instead, his expression grave, worry gnawed at Quin's gut. "Alys?"

"She is fine. Her brother is dead, and she's reclaimed the duchy."

Alys had forbidden them, under the strictest of oaths, from interfering in her situation. One she had refused to ever explain in any detail. "And…how did that happen?"

"My help, to some degree." He hesitated, then: "But mostly Clare's."

The worry intensified, and he couldn't tell anymore if it was his or Verol's or simply theirs. "And where is Clare?"

"Gone."

"What do you mean gone?" Verol demanded. "Where?"

"I don't know. This was all she left." He handed them a letter that contained only three sentences. *I'll be back in five days. Four by the time you receive this. Don't even think about trying to follow me.*

"She had it sent the day after she left. I *did* look for her. I couldn't find any trace of where she'd gone, but…"

"But?" Verol asked icily, as if he'd already guessed.

"But Prince Tolvannen appears to have left at the same time."

Verol swore. "Why aren't you out looking for her?"

"For one, because it is a large kingdom and I've no notion of where Numair Tolvannen would go outside of Veralna City. But the more important reason is that I do not want to draw attention to the fact that she is gone. The king didn't precisely order her to remain here in his absence, but I believe it was heavily implied."

Verol's mouth tightened into a thin line. "Has he noticed she's gone?"

"Yes. He sent a summons to the suite for her. Given that he ordered her to keep your schedule, she is not required to be in the palace today, and if she keeps to her note she will be back tomorrow, but if she is not…"

Quin could already see where Verol's thoughts were going. "She clearly left of her own volition," he pointed out, "and she has stated an intention to return. Searching the streets for her will only further draw Alaric's attention, and ensure you are not here when she returns."

Verol's eyes closed. "You wish me to wait?"

"Yes."

"While she is with *him*?"

"Yes." He felt it flicker through the heartstone, the resignation as Verol realized Quin was right.

"Set a ward for her at the edge of the estate. I want to know the moment she returns."

"They won't work for her. Not any more than they do for Alaric."

Verol's lip curled. "Then set one for His Highness."

Quin blew out a breath and walked for the woods. One day, he had a feeling, his husband was going to regret the contempt with which he treated the second prince of Faelhorn. And it wouldn't be because of the man's station or any threats he made. But Quin would never be so foolish as to ever voice that suspicion to Verol.

SEVENTY-THREE

I'LL RISK IT, IF YOU WILL

For once in Clare's experience of mornings, the next one came too soon. It wasn't that she wanted to stay, precisely. She would never belong in a place like this, no matter how nice the people. Their well-meaning inclusivity would, she suspected, drive her to madness. But there was a type of peace to be found in the temporary escape, in pretending she belonged, for a time.

By unspoken agreement, she and Numair packed and left the house before anyone else woke. After a moment's hesitation, Clare had carefully folded the outfit she'd worn to the solstice celebration, leaving it on the bed with a note that said only *Nissa*. The two women were close in size, and a skilled tailor could alter it to fit.

They had the horses saddled and Clare had just swung atop Kialla when Numair handed her Hellack's reins. "I forgot something. Wait for me a minute."

He wasn't gone terribly long—ten minutes, at the most—but he wasn't carrying anything with him when he returned. If what he'd forgotten was a physical item, then it fit in a pocket. She didn't ask and he didn't offer. They left the village in silence, and remained that way most of the first day's journey.

What peace they'd found leeched from them the closer they came to Veralna. By the time the sun was high the next day, and they approached the woods outside the Arrendons' estate, only a thin sliver of it remained. She couldn't remember the last time either of them had spoken, and the horses stopped of their own accord just inside the woodland boundary, as if sensing their riders' reluctance to continue.

Suddenly, Numair said, "I got you something." He turned Hellack, sidling him next to Kialla but facing the opposite direction as the mare, so Numair faced Clare. His knee nearly brushed hers as he reached into his pocket and pulled out a necklace. It was the same style as the ones she'd seen in the village, the rectangle a matte black, the symbols etched in gold, but more ornate than any she'd seen there, with small chips of amber set around the etchings.

He held it out to her, his eyes dark and oddly vulnerable. "If you want it," he said softly. "They *are* usually custom-made, and you weren't able to choose this one, but—"

"Yes." She blurted the word out before she could overthink it. "Would you...?" She lifted her hair, holding it off her neck. He slid the thin black chain around, linking the clasp at her nape.

He swallowed and let the chain fall, but one hand hovered by her face. His eyes met hers. "Can I...?"

She nodded, her breathing short and shallow, and his fingertips brushed her cheek. The rough pads caressed her skin and before she could think about what she was doing, she leaned into it, until his hand cupped her face.

In another world, I think you could have made him happy. But they didn't have another world. They only had this one, and if she still wasn't convinced she knew what happiness was, she knew being with him was the closest she'd ever come to it. She knew being with her was the only time he ever looked free. She knew the warmth of his hand on her skin was making her pulse pound too fast, but not with fear.

She swallowed. "I think there's something wrong with my heart."

He laughed, short and raspy and nervous. "Mine too." He held out his free hand and when she put hers in it, he placed it on his chest, where his thundering heartbeat was a twin to hers. His next words were so soft they could have been a whisper in the wind. "I really want to kiss you."

Her breath caught. This was a terrible, stupid idea. "I really want you to kiss me. But I might punch you if you do. Reflex."

His hand shook against her cheek. "I might throw up."

And she knew, then, that if they did this, it wouldn't only be the first kiss *she'd* chosen—it would be the first one he'd chosen, too. The first one either of them had been allowed to experience without coercion, without agenda.

She didn't care what Nissa thought. She didn't care what anyone else thought. She never had. She knew what she wanted. "I'll risk it, if you will."

And then the distance between them was gone, his lips a featherlight brush against her own. Once, twice, both of them trembling like leaves in an autumn wind.

"I didn't hit you," she whispered when they broke apart.

His thumb brushed across her cheek. "I didn't throw up."

Every nerve ending in her body was on fire in a way she'd never experienced and she leaned back in, chasing that feeling.

A throat cleared and she startled, jerking so badly that Kialla spooked three steps sideways. Verol sat astride Skye ten paces off, his expression unreadable. Numair turned Hellack to face him, and for a moment they all waited in silence, tense and awkward.

Then Verol broke it. "Could I have a word, Your Highness?"

"There's nothing to—" Clare began, but she cut off when Verol lifted his hand.

"It won't take long."

She hesitated, and when she looked at Numair all his walls were firmly back in place. He gave her a tight nod. Some innate instinct told her not to leave, warned that if she did the moment would be gone and she would never get it back. But the moment was already gone, because that was what a moment was—a brief instant in time that couldn't be held.

But there would be new ones, wouldn't there?

She felt as if she shouldn't leave. But she did.

———

As Verol had promised, his talk didn't take long. The anger and dislike Numair usually felt from him was absent, as if it had melted into resignation. Verol only looked at him and said, "Don't promise her things you can't give her. Don't hurt her."

He knew it was over then, knew it even before he went home and found Alaric's summons waiting for him.

CHAPTER

SEVENTY-FOUR

CAN'T AND DOESN'T ARE TWO DIFFERENT
THINGS

It didn't take long, only the short ride back to the house, for doubt to creep in over the spinning in Clare's head. For the time away to feel like it had happened to someone else, for her to wonder what in Ferrian's flames she and Numair had thought they were doing in the woods.

If he regretted it. If she should. She'd tucked the necklace pendant beneath her shirt but she couldn't stop touching the outline of it.

She was so off-balance it took her twice as long as it should have to untack Kialla and brush her down, and Verol came back while she was at it, completing the same job with Skye in the time it took her to finish. Neither of them spoke. He wasn't angry and she almost wished he was. She knew how to deal with anger because he didn't *get* to be angry about her choices. She didn't know how to deal with this...sadness? Fear? Regret?

They walked into the kitchen and Marquin was waiting for them. He rose abruptly as she walked in, something she would have sworn was relief crossing his face. "Are you all right?"

Her brows drew together in confusion. "I'm fine. Why wouldn't I be?"

"We returned and you were gone," Verol said. "We had no idea where you were or if you were safe. I know we are not your parents." At the look on her face, he hastened to add, "And I know

469

you think you are too old to need any. Perhaps you're right. But we do care about you. Did you give any thought to how we would feel that you'd left with barely a word and with no hint as to where you were going?"

"Did *you*?" Something she told herself was anger but felt more like hurt bubbled in her chest. "When you left me here without a single word, when I had to find out from Fitz that you were gone, did *you* give any thought to how *I* would feel?"

They shared a wordless look, as if, no, it had never occurred to them.

"You just *left me here*. You found out I was a Reaper and then you left without a word." As if they hadn't been able to stand being near her any longer. "*I* had to navigate this court without you, *I* had to deal with what I am without you and *I* had to deal with Alaric without you. You didn't even bother to write. So forgive me if I didn't realize you would even notice I was gone, much less care."

"Clare..." Verol began, then trailed off, as if her outburst was unexpected and he had no idea what to say.

She shook her head and walked past them, heading for her room.

"Wait," Quin said. "Alaric returned a day ahead of us. He was not pleased to find you gone and wants to see you."

"Then I suppose I should clean up and attend my king," she said acidly.

"We should discuss where you were," Verol said. "It might be better if he believes you had our blessing for this excursion, and that requires us to present a united front."

"That would require us to have one. Don't trouble yourselves on my account. I have been handling His Majesty without you these last weeks. I don't imagine it will be too much of a strain to continue doing so."

She left, and she didn't know if she was grateful or disappointed when they didn't follow, when they didn't try to apologize or explain.

She filled the tub in her bathing room with water so hot it turned her skin red and scrubbed until the dirt of travel turned the water murky. Then she drained it all and did it again, cleaning every inch of skin, under every nail, scrubbing her scalp until not a remnant of grit remained.

She couldn't control Alaric's summons, but she could control this—her body. How it felt, how it looked. And she did so obsessively.

QUIN RUBBED his hand over his face. "That...did not go well."

"I never thought..." Verol dropped into a chair. "She never much seemed to care—if we were here or not."

"I don't think it's ever been safe for her to care, before. Certainly never safe to express it. I imagine she's feeling like it wasn't, again."

Verol was quiet a moment. "Was it like that for you?"

"When I met you?"

Verol nodded.

"In some ways. But it's often easier, if perhaps more foolish, for people like us to trust a lover than a parental figure." It was a gentle request to know what had happened when Verol had found her. Quin certainly hadn't seen a trace of Numair when Clare, and then Verol, had returned.

Verol drummed his fingers on his thigh. "She can't trust him."

"Can't and doesn't are two different things, my love."

"She *shouldn't*."

"I am begging you not to push her on that. You do remember what it was like to be that age, don't you? If I recall, your parents hardly approved of me. You didn't speak to them for a year after."

"This is different."

"How?"

"They didn't approve of where you came from. It was a baseless dislike. Numair is Alaric's nephew. It would be only too easy for Alaric to use him to get to her. The Kinthing hasn't calmed since she came to us. It is *always* worried. When Alaric was here *and* once he was gone.

"And don't even ask me to contain my anger over him dragging her away like that. It was reckless and Alaric's demand to see her only proves that. Even if Numair doesn't harm her intentionally, he's bound to do it through his sheer idiocy."

NUMAIR WOULD NEVER HURT ME. It was Clare's first and only response to the words the Song pulled from the common room, carrying them down the hall to her ears.

She understood why it had brought them to her, brought her Verol's conviction that she wasn't safe with Numair because the Kinthing didn't feel she was safe. But Numair wouldn't hurt her.

You think he will not, the Song said, *but how can you be sure?*

Because I know him. And I know you. And it is to you the Kinthing answers.

If you're certain, then, it replied, in that casual manner intended to instill doubt in the person it answered.

But she knew better. Numair was her friend. And she was his. Nothing was going to change that. Not even the fact that she could still feel the featherlight brush of his lips against hers, the touch of his hand on her cheek. Not even the beating thrum of anxiety that already whispered, *Did we ruin everything?*

She stood, water cascading down her body, and ignored both the Song and her own concerns. When she dressed, she intentionally chose the plainest of her outfits and left her face unpainted, her hair unstyled. Then she left through the window, saddling Kialla and riding for the palace before Quin or Verol could stop her.

SEVENTY-FIVE

THE FIRST PRINCE OF FAELHORN

The Song retreated within her as she passed through the Outer Gate. It had been with her so constantly these last few weeks that its abrupt departure was jarring, a harsh reminder of who had returned to these grounds since she'd last left them.

She had barely walked through the palace's front entryway when one of the guards broke away from his station, halting her with a brief bow. "His Majesty asked to see you the moment you arrived. If you would follow me."

With little choice in the matter, she did. He led her to the second floor, to the end of a hallway and a set of wide oak doors. He rapped smartly, the doors opened, and Clare choked on the sudden, intense need to vomit. The sickly sweet stench of Alaric's magic permeated the room, inundating her nostrils, coating her skin with the oil-slick taint. It was far more potent than it had been the last time she'd seen him, when she had almost inured herself to its feel.

Nor was that the only thing different about the Alaric that stood before her now and the one who had left. He had easily dropped ten years, looking more like a man in his early thirties as opposed to his forties, the lines about his eyes lessened, the salt and peppering of his hair having reverted to an undiluted brown. He no longer looked like the urbane king. He looked like what he was: a general of war who had conquered the world with magic, brute force, and bloodshed, and yet found that his stranglehold on power had not lessened his fear that it could all be taken away.

She felt herself staring into his eyes as if she looked through a mirror in time, a portal into a future in which she stood precisely where he did now. She had wanted wealth and status, certain they would insulate her against fear, but they had done neither. Because the fear was in her, in the past, and in him, in the present, and she didn't know how to destroy either of them.

He held her gaze, as if he knew exactly what she was thinking. If he'd returned to Veralna yesterday, he didn't appear to have slept or changed clothes in that time. The soldier's leathers he wore were dirt-stained and flecked with blood, and she felt as if she was seeing the true king of Faelhorn for the first time. He stood at the head of a table, across which was spread a map of Faelhorn. El-Dennon, at its southern-most tip, was a blacked-out, ruined space.

Next to Alaric stood the two proconsuls who had been with him when she'd marched in and demanded to speak with him before, along with another four people she didn't recognize. None of them looked pleased to see her, especially when Alaric told them to, "Continue without me," and cut a path across the floor to her.

"Walk with me." He held out his arm and Clare forced herself to take it, to not cringe as his magic caressed and stroked against her skin. Stolen magic. Magic that whispered of death and atrocities far more recent than the ones he'd left with.

He led her down the stairs, out of the palace to that same garden path they had walked before. She felt his magic snuff out the heating spells, allowing winter's chill full rein, as if he wanted her cold. "Have you reconsidered what we last spoke of here?"

A woman who was smarter than she was stubborn would have prevaricated. "No."

"Do you know how many people I have had to kill since I left Veralna?" There was an edge to his voice, as if he laid the necessity of each one of those deaths at her feet. As if he had decided she was the missing puzzle piece in his plans, and he only needed to push her until she fell into place.

"I am not an antidote to war, Your Majesty. I am not a flower you can pin to your collar and make the world see a benefactor instead of a conqueror. If you truly wish to reform your image, to make them love you, why don't you marry? Everyone loves a love story. So fall in love, Your Majesty. With a commoner, perhaps."

"This is your advice to me?"

"It is as likely to work as anything else."

"Perhaps I'll take it. Perhaps the love story this kingdom will cherish is yours and mine. Is that the threat that will bend you to me?"

Cold that had nothing to do with the temperature gripped her spine. "You can force my hand in marriage, but you cannot force my smiles or my song. A marriage is nothing to people if a woman does not sell it for you."

"I thought you might say something like that. You told me, before, to find something better than Renault County to threaten you with. I should warn you, not to challenge a man like me to do so. I will succeed and you will not like the results."

"There is nothing you can take from me that has not already been taken."

"Is that so?" Three words, spoken with derision. Three words that indicated she was wrong.

The weight of Numair's pendant burned against her skin.

"I want to show you something." He turned, leading her out of the gardens and back to the palace, to a wing she'd never entered. On the upper floor he opened a door and led her into a room. It was a suite much like the Arrendons, and a man stood on the other side of the entry room, his back to them.

His build was similar to Alaric's, his hair the same shade of brown. He turned at their entrance, revealing a man closer to Numair's age. Bloody gashes raked over his face, down his neck, and she realized, from the red covering the tips of his fingers, that he'd caused the damage to himself. He saw Alaric and a manic light came into his eyes. When he launched himself across the room at the king there was no finesse, no subtlety. It was like a wild animal driven to savagery.

Clare took multiple steps back. Alaric simply stood there, his hands clasped behind his back, as the man ran at him and drove what looked to be a piece of sharpened cutlery deep into the king's chest. Alaric didn't so much as flinch. His power unfurled almost casually, gripping the man and dragging him back a step.

Clare was not in the slightest bit confused about the message being sent as Alaric calmly gripped the shaft of metal embedded in his heart and pulled it free: *See how little I fear death.* And why should he, when she felt one of the many souls clinging to his frame extinguish as the wound closed in his chest, not a single drop of blood on his shirt, the hole in the fabric mending itself.

"Allow me to introduce you to my other nephew," Alaric said lightly. "Brennan Tolvannen, the first prince of Faelhorn."

Brennan dropped to his knees. For a moment, Clare thought Alaric had driven him there, but then she realized he had collapsed all on his own, sobbing. He crawled to Alaric's feet, holding the king's ankle and resting his face on his boot. "Please," he said. "Please *please please.* Give it back. Or kill me. I'll do anything. Anything you want." It went on, the same words repeated over and over again, and Clare understood she was looking at what happened to a mage who had had his magic Reaped.

"What did he do?" Clare made herself ask.

"Attempted to usurp me," Alaric said in a confiding voice. "It was a shame. He had his uses."

"Why leave him like this?" she asked, trying not to show the horror she felt. "Why not kill him?"

Alaric shrugged. "He's the heir to the throne. As you have pointed out, I have no wife, no children. Besides, I had to put too many of my court down after his little insurrection. And then Verol had to work for months to make everyone forget it had ever happened, because I don't want to deal with the number of them I'd have to destroy if a succession war occurs.

"I do adore my other nephew, but no one in their right mind would think Numair could lead this kingdom. So I kept this one." Alaric raised his hand, power flooding from him and lifting Brennan to his feet. The gashes on his cheeks healed over as if they had never been. "He's convalescing from an unspecified illness, at the moment, but I bring him out on the necessary occasions. It keeps things from getting too…messy."

Clare swallowed the bile rising up her throat. "You mean to tell me your court hasn't figured it out?"

"Figured what out?"

"That there will never be a succession to the throne of Veralna. You look a decade younger than you did when you left. What is your true age?"

He sighed. "I see Verol hasn't monitored you as he ought. Of course they haven't figured it out. It's one of those facts that simply…slips from their minds as it needs to. As for the other, it's quite impolite to ask."

"Are they even your nephews?" Part of her strongly did not want for Numair to be related to this man.

"Great nephews, technically, though you'd be one of the few now that can remember the fact."

She swallowed. "Why are you showing me this?"

"Because I wish you to understand something, Miss Brighton. There are things worse than death. I am one of them. And for you to choose death over service to me, I would first have to *allow you* to die.

"Think on that. Mull it over. This does not have to be like it was for you before. Simian was always short-sighted, ruled by baser desires. It's why he always broke everything. I would not do the same, can assure you I have no interest in you in that manner. You are little more than a child compared to me.

"I will force your hand on this matter if I must, but this would be easier for us both if you would simply come to reason. I'll give you some time to consider it."

He walked out, leaving her with the raving husk that was the first prince of Faelhorn, and the question of why? Why *not* simply force her hand? Why give her time at all?

She couldn't come up with an answer, and the failure made her suspect she wouldn't like it once she did.

HER FIRST THOUGHT was to find Numair, and because it was she ignored it, going instead to the suite. She wasn't surprised to find Quin and Verol waiting.

"I'm alive, as you can see."

"That truly isn't funny," Verol said stiffly. "What happened?"

She shrugged. "That's between me and Alaric."

"We cannot help you if we do not know what is going on."

She arched her eyebrows. "Even if I needed your help, precisely how long will you be around to give it? A few hours? A few days?

Do I get a calendar of the times at which you'll be available so I can schedule my difficulties around it?"

"Clare…" Verol rubbed wearily at his temples. She finally looked at him—really looked—and saw the exhaustion in him. The dark circles bruising the underneath of his eyes, the way his already thin frame had lost weight. Marquin didn't look much better. "We didn't mean to make you feel abandoned. We didn't mean *to* abandon you. I didn't consider how it might look to you, us leaving after the Reaper bit came to light. You didn't seem to need or want us—"

"I don't."

"—and I was frightened. Not of you, but for you. I selfishly want to believe you can be hidden beneath Alaric's nose forever, but I know that is unrealistic. He is already too interested in you.

"We left because we were trying to protect you. We will leave again for the same reason, and there are things I will not tell you because I do not want you to bear the weight of them. But I can do far more to protect you out there than I can here. All the more so because my absence makes it seem as if I care less for you. As if you are perhaps not what Alaric knows my magic seeks out, and simply a broken man's attempt to replace the daughter he lost. Whatever we can do to draw him away from here, we will."

A bad feeling spread through her. "He left suddenly because there was unrest in Trin Province. Was that you?" Verol's eyelids fluttered shut briefly, and her stomach turned. The wealth of new foulness she'd felt clinging to Alaric's body… "How many?"

"How many what?"

"How many people died to distract him from *me*?"

Verol's voice was weary. "It would have happened anyway. Not this quickly, but rebellion there was inevitable, and it would have ended the same. I simply…allowed it to happen at a more advantageous time."

"How many?"

He exhaled audibly. "What number would be acceptable? One? One hundred? One thousand? You are not responsible for them. Only he is."

"You could have stopped it."

"No," Quin said, finally wading into the argument with a gentle squeeze on Verol's shoulder. "He could not have. He cannot change who people fundamentally are, what they want. Once they chose their path, he could at most have delayed what happened, and that is if he spent himself to the dregs. It is far easier to nudge people in a direction they already wish to go than it is to haul them back from a decision they have already made."

That doesn't make it right. She didn't say the words. Since when had she ever cared about what was right? When had anyone else ever cared about the rightness of what was done to her? She was not certain she even knew what the word meant. She only knew that this didn't *feel* right, and it was made all the worse by the fact she wasn't certain she *would* have cared, if she hadn't felt every sundered life clinging to Alaric's body just now.

"There is a reason," Verol said softly, "that they call me the Butcher. A mind can only be cut into so many times, can only be nudged and rearranged so many times, before it falls apart. What I do for Alaric here—doing it without destroying anyone?—it takes the majority of my focus."

"What else does he have you hide besides his age? Brennan Tolvannen?" They shared another one of those wordless looks, the kind where she suspected they were speaking where she couldn't hear. "He took me to see him."

"When? Why?"

"Just now. I believe he wanted to prove a point."

"What point?"

She shook her head. "You have your secrets, and I have mine. That's what you took from Lady Meraland, wasn't it?" Alys had said the woman was in love with the first prince. "She found him in that...state, and you had to take it from her."

Verol sighed. "It wasn't the first time. It won't be the last. I told Alaric to send her away, but he wants her here."

She sat with it for a minute, trying to reconcile a lifetime of knowing that the only thing she could do was look out for herself with this nascent sense that, while that might have been the only way it was possible to live in Renault County, the wider world was more complicated. The sense that the difference in her societal place in this world had altered her culpability in ways she didn't fully understand.

A selfish part of her wanted it all to be simple again. Wanted the only answer to be that she had to take care of herself, because no one else would do it for her, and everyone else was doing the same for themselves. Except there were holes in that theory, in the form of Quin and Verol, Alys and Numair and Chalen.

"And if I asked you to stop doing things on my behalf?" she asked.

Verol's only answer was a sad smile.

"Does it even matter? If he's distracted for a few weeks or a few months? Even a few years? He is eternal." She didn't realize how much she was hoping Marquin would deny that conclusion until he didn't.

"We are…working on the issue," Marquin said carefully.

"But you won't tell me how?"

"No."

"We'll be more open with you about when we leave. And we'll be *here* as much as we can. That is what we can offer you."

A week ago, she might not have taken it. She told herself she only did so now because it was practical to, but the truth she wouldn't quite acknowledge was that something in her had shifted during that brief time spent in Numair's village, and she wanted things she hadn't known to want before.

SEVENTY-SIX

JUST LIKE ALL THE REST

The first hint of something wrong came at dinner that evening. She sat across from Numair, as she always did, and he was…vacant. He was always vacant with everyone else, though they never noticed, but he'd never been that way with her, even in public. The difference was in his eyes, in his voice, in the content of his responses that had always before been curated to appear perfectly vapid while containing undertones just for her.

It was as if all of that had been struck from the man. One night passed, then two, then three, and it was as if everything that had made them *them*—Clare and Numair, Numair and Clare—had been devoured by a lurking beast that had left no crumb behind. Her imagination offered a dozen explanations in lieu of the one she feared, all of them stemming from Alaric, or in her darker moments even Verol, but none of those accounted for one thing: he never wore that green scarf anymore.

The one no one knew the meaning of, save her and him. The one even threats or interference would not necessitate him dispensing with, because she was the only one who knew it meant he was thinking of her.

By the end of the fifth day, even the court had noticed the difference. She and Numair usually joked and played off each other, and she always found some reason to take him away from whatever woman he was with at the time—to give him the only respite from his role that she could offer.

But her early attempts to reclaim that ground had been met with such lackluster responses that she quit making them. He never found any reason to be alone with her. No letter arrived by Celerian runner to explain this sudden change in behavior. To reassure her.

Twice, as she'd returned from singing in the city, late at night, she'd ridden by his estate. But the rocks she tossed at his window went unanswered. Anxiety was a constant shadow at her back, whispering over and over a single fear: *Did I ruin everything?* Had he seen too much of who she was while they were gone? Had he finally realized just how deeply her damage ran?

But why kiss her in the forest, if that was true? It didn't make any sense. It had to be Alaric's magic, or Verol's, except there was a dark voice that wouldn't stop whispering, *He's had a little distance from you now. You saw how he was, what he came from, and it is nothing like you. Perhaps for a while he thought you were similar, but you were too foreign to even understand* family. *He is not broken in the same way you are. Why* would *he want to stay with you?*

The court was beginning to whisper it too. That she wasn't so special after all, just another dalliance, and now he was done with her, like he was eventually done with all the others. And they delighted in mocking her for it, now that no favoritism was shown to her to stand in their way. Especially since Alaric had likewise stepped back, allowing her the promised time to think on his demands.

Half the courtiers gossiped that Numair must have finally bedded her and found the experience lacking. The other half claimed he'd been in love with her, but her constant attention to Alaric had finally driven him off.

It was not lost on her that nowhere in any of these explanations were Numair or Alaric to blame. It was always, in one way or another, her fault. Because even in this court where no laws prohibited consensual carnal activities, where in theory a woman could not be held accountable for them when a man could not, in practice society still made it so. A woman was always easier to blame than a man, no matter how reprehensible the man's behavior. A woman was always easier to shame.

If it weren't for Alys and Lina and Proconsul Aula, she might have been completely ostracized. Verol and Quin never frequented the social spaces in the palace, and they had sent Fitz away, to do something they refused to tell her about. As it was, the company she *did* have was getting difficult to be around, because Alys wouldn't stop asking her *What in Ferrian's hells is going on with you and Numair?* and *Do I need to kick him in the balls because I will.* That was actually easier to deal with than the knowing, sympathetic looks Lina and Proconsul Aula kept giving her, as if she was some naive storybook damsel.

She broke down and sent him a letter by Celerian runner, hardly blinking at the exorbitant cost. Then she sent a second, and a third. He never sent one in return.

By the time the week's five palace days were up, and she and Verol and Quin were headed back to the Arrendon estate for the weekend, she was strung like an overtightened guitar string, ready to snap at a too-firm pluck. But it was when she went to her room and found the hibiscus plant, dead and desiccated against her window, that everything came to a shattering crescendo inside her.

She must have made a sound, and a terrible one, because Verol and Marquin both came running.

"What is it?" Verol demanded.

She had the window open, hands cupping dead blooms that hadn't yet fallen off. "It's dead."

Verol looked between her and the plant several times, his tension melting to confusion as he gradually understood that, yes, she was upset about a plant. "It isn't native to this region. Or adapted to this season. We thought *you* were making it grow. Like you did with Marie's tree."

She didn't correct him. She couldn't. Because despite everything, Numair's secrets were still hers to keep, and she would choke on them if it killed her.

I could make it grow, the Song told her. Hesitant, like it didn't understand her reaction any more than Verol did.

The memory of Numair's hand covering hers, him telling her *Not everything beautiful has to be marred.*

Her harsh *Then it's just going to die.*

I won't let it. I promise.

Except he had let it. They'd grown it together and now it was dead. The Song's magic reached for the plant, intent on breathing new life into the dead stalks. She cut it off.

Don't bother.

It wasn't the plant she wanted. It never had been.

She turned on Verol. "I need to ask you something and I need you to tell me the truth."

Wariness crept into his eyes. "All right."

"What did you say to Numair in the woods?"

Verol reevaluated the plant, as if connecting it to the subject of her question, even if he wasn't sure how. "I told him not to promise you things he couldn't give you. I told him not to hurt you."

"That was all?" Her fingers clenched around the brittle blooms, crumbling them.

"Nothing more."

"Did you threaten him?"

"No."

"Did you reach into his mind?"

Verol jerked back like she'd slapped him. "Clare—no."

The crisp petals crackled between her clenched fingers. There had to be an explanation. This wasn't right. None of this was Numair. Something else was going on. Something was wrong. Even with the way he'd been acting, he wouldn't just let it die. Not unless...not unless he was hurt. Hurt so badly his magic had drained, that he didn't have the strength to spend it on a plant.

He hadn't been in the palace today.

She rattled off some excuse to Quin and Verol and rode Kialla to Numair's. Dropped the mare in the paddock with Hellack and went straight to the hidden door. It was gone. Not a changed lock, but *gone*, its seams mortared over. So she climbed the window to his balcony and, when the sliding door wouldn't open, broke the glass so she could reach inside and unlatch it.

It took her fifteen minutes of searching the house before she found him, in that room with the bag she'd once hit until her knuckles bled. Where he was doing the same thing right now.

Fine. Physically, he was fine. By the time she'd accepted that fact she'd been watching him long enough to grow angry at how he was pretending she wasn't there. Pretending he hadn't seen her reflection in the windows. As if his ignoring her long enough would make her disappear.

The pain that had been festering in her chest for the last week bubbled up, boiling over, until she was striding across the room and placing herself between him and the bag so he couldn't pretend away her existence anymore.

He reared back, throwing his entire body into the movement to keep his next punch from landing. "What the *fuck*?" he spat. True anger laced his words, of a kind Clare had never heard directed at her. Not from him.

That increasingly bad feeling spiraled in her chest, stoking the flames of her anger, her confusion. "I could say the same thing to you."

He stalked away, to the water pitcher that rested on a bench on the other side of the room. Poured a glass and went right back to pretending she wasn't there. He'd never ignored her like this. Never treated her like…like one of those other women at court. Like she was contemptuously beneath his notice, even when he was paying her attention.

Her stomach clenched. "It's been a week."

Nothing.

She bit her lower lip until she tasted copper. "I was worried about you."

He laughed. It was cold and harsh and utterly unlike him. He put his hand to his heart. "I'm so touched. Did the unanswered letters and the walled-over door not tell you I don't want your concern? How did you even get in here? Oh, wait." He snapped his fingers. "I forgot. You like to climb walls like a gutter rat."

She flinched. He made her *flinch*. Her hands curled into fists, but he wasn't finished.

"Ferrian's flames, do I have to hire a contingent of private soldiers just to keep *you* out of my house?"

"No." She laced the word with violence and promise, hurt and confusion. "I told you once the only thing you needed to keep me out of here was your words."

He drained the rest of the water and slammed the glass down hard enough it cracked. "Then get out."

Something was wrong. Something different than what she'd feared and yet, when she told the Song to *look*, and it grudgingly obeyed, there was no magic wrapped around Numair that was not his own, nothing forcing him to act this way.

She closed the distance between them. "Look at me." He didn't. *"Look at me.* Look me in the eye and tell me you don't want me here, and I'll go."

His eyes met hers. His lips parted but the words didn't come out. He looked…wild. So she forced out words she didn't want to say to this version of him, because they were words that made her vulnerable, words that cut to a deep uncertainty in her heart. But her Numair wasn't here, and she didn't know how else to bring him back. "Is this because of what happened? In the woods?"

She saw him. For a second, she saw him. And then he was gone again, a slow, half-smile tugging up the right corner of his lips. He leaned in. "Because of what *happened,*" he said mockingly. "Do you honestly believe a shadow of a kiss has me so confused that I'm running away from you?"

She took an involuntary step back.

"Don't flatter yourself. Or are you so naive that you thought you were different from all the rest?" He advanced and she let him move her, until her back hit the wall and his hands pressed against the plaster to either side of her face, and he leaned in to whisper, "You're *just* like all the rest. Wanting the same thing as all the rest because that's what I'm good for, right?"

His voice dropped, low and seductive, and she wanted to punch him in the throat again. Wished she had when he said, "Do you want me to kiss you now? Do you want me to show you how good I can make you feel? To put my head between your legs and—"

"Shut up." She couldn't breathe, yet she was breathing too fast. "This isn't you."

He drew back, until his face was in front of hers again. "Oh, this is *exactly* me. This is everything I am. Isn't that why you're really here? I have to admit, you chased me longer than most. Irritated you got cheated at the final step?"

"I don't give a damn if you never kiss me again," she said vehemently. "I'm here because I miss my friend. I miss my *best friend.* And right now I don't see him even though I'm staring at him."

He shook his head. "If I'm your best friend, you're more pathetic than I am."

She shoved him back, then, because she couldn't stand to be this close to him when he was already so far away. Her hands flew without thought to the clasp of her necklace. She held it out, the matte black absorbing the sunlight, the soft gold reflecting it. He'd looked so unsure, so hopeful, when he'd given it to her. So careful when he'd fastened it around her neck. She didn't know what it meant to him, but it meant something.

"Pathetic would be keeping this. So take it back."

His eyes fastened on it. "No."

"Why not?" Her voice was sickly sweet. "I'm just like all the rest, aren't I? So give it to the next one that comes along." She opened her hand, letting it fall.

He broke, lunging for it. His knees hit the floor as he caught the pendant, looking like she'd knocked the air from his lungs. "Take it back."

She knelt in front of him. "Why?"

But he only shook his head. "I can't." Agony laced the perfect black of his eyes. "I can't change for you. I told you that first night in my room I couldn't change for you."

"I *never asked you to.*"

"You ask all the time. You ask every day, every minute, just by existing." His voice was hoarse. "And I'm a selfish prick for telling you that."

Yes, he was. And the ground was broken and the bridges were nowhere in sight and he'd set all the rules on fire, so she asked the one question she was never supposed to ask him. "Why do you do this? You hate them. I see it in your face when you talk to them. You hate it when they touch you because I notice you flinch when they never notice. So *why?*"

He drew in a jagged breath, his eyes shining, and something in *her* broke. Something she hadn't realized was whole enough *to* break. She reached for him and he reached back, and this time when they kissed it wasn't soft, or hesitant, or a *shadow.*

It was her lips almost bruising his and him returning in kind. It was her hand curled into the fine silk of his hair and the small, surprised moan that came out of her throat when his tongue brushed hers, when his hand fisted in her shirt.

It was him pulling her onto his lap and her legs locking around his waist because she never wanted to let him go. It was the soft drowning of her mouth in his and the way she trusted him enough to close her eyes. It was the tears slipping down her cheeks when she did. It was the saltwater that coated her own hand when she cupped it to his face. It was the labored breathing when they finally broke apart, his forehead resting against hers, the wild *thump thump thump* of her heart insisting that this was what home meant.

Not a city or a house or a room, but *him*.

"Let me help you, Numair."

Every line of him tensed and she knew she'd lost him. "You can't." His lips brushed her forehead, her nose, her mouth. He pressed the necklace into her palm, curled her fingers around it, then gently slid her off his lap. Then he stood and walked away. "Goodbye, Clare."

She screamed. Still on her knees, the first tears she'd cried in a decade running down her cheeks, she screamed. It was a raw, ruthless sound and the Song screamed with her, rattling the walls, the floor, the ceiling.

Shaking the foundation of the house.

The chains holding the punching bag snapped and it fell, and Numair—he *still* wasn't afraid of her. He just turned back, so much sadness in his eyes, and waited. For whatever she needed to say.

And the brilliant thing she came up with was, "When you realize how much you fucked up here today, don't come begging at my feet for forgiveness."

She rose and stormed out, so angry that she went down the main staircase, out the main doors. Footsteps sounded behind her, a pleading call for her to wait. She wanted it to be him, coming after her. But the footsteps were louder than Numair's ever were, the voice female.

She made herself stop and let Ida catch up to her, but she knew the expression on her face wasn't anything kind, and she couldn't force it to change.

Ida wrung her hands together. "Please don't give up on him."

"I didn't. He gave up on himself. He gave up on *me*."

Ida just stood there, that crumpled look on her face. And Clare remembered drinking tea with her in the library, remembered the kindness she'd shown that she didn't have to. Clare wasn't fooling herself. That kindness to her had been for Numair's sake, not hers. But Ida had still given it.

"If he wants to answer the question I asked him today, I'll listen. If he wants my help, I'll give it. That's all I can promise you. The rest is up to him."

SEVENTY-SEVEN

TOO KIND-HEARTED

The next week proved itself a different kind of hell than the previous one had been. It was as if that moment in Numair's home had never happened. She saw him, finally, as he must have been for the last ten years, before she'd come along —completely alone—and she understood why he'd wanted to finally be done with it all the night of his nameday celebration.

The fear that he might still make that decision warred with her anger and her hurt. She wore the pendant tucked carefully away, so not even the chain showed, not wanting him to know she still wore it. Her days she spent Songweaving recklessly in the palace. Sometimes at Alaric's behest, but most of the time simply because he'd given her the freedom to do so. A freedom he had not yet taken away, despite her failure to tell him anything of interest she'd learned with it.

The king's easy patience frightened her more than threats would have. Threats, direct ones that asserted specific consequences, could be responded to. This couldn't. She could almost be lulled into thinking he wanted nothing from her, were it not for the fact he watched her constantly. But he never interfered, not even when she sowed the kind of chaos among the courtiers that made Alys pull her aside and ask her if she'd lost her mind.

It was rude, she supposed, to drag people through so many

emotions that half of them didn't come out of their rooms the next day, and the half who did spent it glaring at her as if they wanted to murder her in her sleep. She wasn't sure when she'd gone from wanting to win them over for practical reasons, to wanting to see just how desperately she could make them hate her.

Had Marquin and Verol been here, no doubt they would have intervened. But they were gone again, and if they had at least told her this time, been candid with her over what they would and would not tell her, their absence was another layer to her growing isolation.

She needed something to break, something to change. So she kept pushing, because without Numair to distract her, she too keenly felt the bars of her new cage. Even if the man who held the keys was, for now, indulgently allowing her to run roughshod over some of the most powerful people in the kingdom. Sometimes, she thought she wanted them to hate her because if she made them hate her enough, Alaric couldn't possibly believe she could turn around and make them love him.

Nights were more difficult than the days. She had never been a creature that slept well, and the condition only seemed to be getting worse. If she stayed in her room, the single hibiscus flower taunted her from the nightstand, refusing to wilt or die. As did the red envelope tucked into the nightstand's drawer. She'd almost broken the seal on it a dozen times in the past week, to finally know what it said, what Numair had written her when he'd barely known her. But in the end, it wasn't his ghost she wanted talking to her.

She spent as much of each night as possible in the city, singing in the streets and the parks. Madame Aria and the Mages Guild Hounds were never far behind. *She can be vindictive*, Numair had said. Clare suspected the woman was planning something and by the fourth night, when Madame Aria arrived in the palace at Lady Dahlia's invitation, she knew it.

Knew it, and welcomed it. Anything to break the pattern she seemed to be stuck in. She held nothing back, either in her performance at that evening's dinner, or the next afternoon among the courtiers in the solarium. When Madame Aria left that afternoon, shooting Clare a look of smug triumph, Clare wondered how long she would have to wait to find out what the woman thought could be done about her.

Familiar laughter broke out to her left, grating on her nerves. She couldn't bring herself to look at Numair, to see what was happening. She walked out, waving off Alys's offer to accompany her. She wanted to be alone, and so found herself walking the garden paths of the inner courtyard. The heating spells that had once been welcome, even if they'd felt like an absurd luxury, now felt stifling.

She wanted the cold and the welcome numbness that came with it. Heat—warmth, comfort—made it too easy to feel. She blamed that for why, sitting on a stone bench in one of the path's recesses, she tugged the pendant out from beneath her shirt. She'd resisted the Song's offers, when they were outside the palace, to tell her what the symbols meant. She'd resisted the urge to ask the palace librarian if she had any books on Deleen Village. She'd resisted the urge to ride to the top of Drake Mountain and hurl the damn thing off the cliff.

"A necklace shouldn't make a person so sad, little songbird."

She startled to her feet, fist clenching around the pendant as if she could hide it. There were few people in this world who could sneak up on her. Numair was one. Unfortunately, Alaric was another.

He held out his hand. "Let's see it."

She clenched her fist tighter. He grabbed her wrist, squeezing with bruising force. She didn't let go. His other hand pried her fingers loose one by one, fine muscles screaming as she fought to clamp them back down, until he *tsked* and said, "Don't make me break them."

She glared at him. "Why shouldn't I?"

He laughed. "Oh, little songbird." With those words she knew what he would do before he did it, and it was only the intuition that made her fingers snap open in time as his magic pulsed through her hand.

She wondered why he hadn't started with magic. Why he'd bothered prying her fingers back with brute force at all. If he simply enjoyed her obstinance, or if…if that was a calculating gaze he was giving her now, trying to determine if her fingers had opened at her command or his.

A chill swept through her. He didn't know—he couldn't know—that his magic swept through her without effect. Because if he knew *that*, she wouldn't still be alive. Would she?

He plucked the pendant from her palm, and she hated him for touching it. Hated him for having found a way to force her to *let* him touch it. Hated that he was running his thumb over something that was far more to her than the piece of carved stone it was to him.

"Ah." He made a fist of his own around the piece and yanked. The chain bit into her neck, tore her skin before the clasp gave and it ripped free.

She grabbed for it before she could stop herself, hand catching on one of the dangling chains.

"I'm surprised you want it back, given what it is."

She was too raw, and her confusion showed for a split-second before she smothered it.

"So you don't know what it is, then." Amusement dripped from his voice. "Walk with me."

She was growing tired of walking places with Alaric. She never liked where the paths he chose led. Today's led back inside, to a room just off the palace's grand foyer. The hall of royal portraits. It wasn't an area she'd been interested in exploring before. Paintings, most of them of dead people, weren't to her taste.

She passed Brennan Tolvannen's and suppressed a shudder, remembering the manic desperation in his eyes. Remembering that he was still there, in that same room, in that same state.

"Here we are." Alaric drew her in front of him, pointing her at a painting of a woman. She recognized the eyes, the lift of the eyebrows, even before she saw the name written beneath it: Evaleen Tolvannen. Didn't need Alaric reaching around her, holding the pendant up to the painting, where its likeness was draped around Evaleen's neck, to understand why he'd brought her here. Why he'd been so amused that she didn't know what it was.

Numair hadn't given her any necklace—he'd given her his mother's. The rest of it fell into place easily enough. His discomfort when she'd asked if she could buy one, how he'd told her they were always custom made. The fact that only the women in the village had worn them. Nissa's brief *It's...from Arlan* when Clare had pointed out hers.

Alaric's other arm reached around her, tapping his way down the symbols on the pendant. "Honesty. Loyalty. Sacrifice. Hope. Tell me, little songbird, has he kept any of those vows to you?"

She didn't answer. Her body shook with rage, and she didn't know if it was at Alaric, Numair, or herself.

"I would have thought," he said, his voice almost tender, "that you would have known better than to let a man hold sway over you again. Men are such weak creatures."

"And what are you?"

"A god. Self-created, in my own image. And you could be one, too." He took her hand and turned it over, dropping the pendant into it so the chain spilled over the edges of her palm. "You simply need to let this go." He left. She remained, until she felt the weight of his power pass beyond the door, then she too went to leave.

She stopped abruptly at the room's threshold. The palace foyer was crowded, everyone who usually passed time in the solariums or other rooms now filling this space. She and Alaric had been in the portrait hall how long? Five minutes? Certainly not long enough for everyone to congregate here naturally, where they never did. They were here for a reason, and it was her misfortune to be exiting a room just after Alaric.

She felt the open speculation, the whispers. Her face, ordinarily so compliant to her wishes, refused to smooth back into neutrality. She felt it like a whip-crack through the air, the moment Numair saw her. The moment he recognized where she'd come from, his face going ashen as his gaze dropped to the broken chains dangling from her clenched fist.

His eyes darted to hers and he started to shove off the wall he was leaning against. Then he froze and she watched him take hold of himself, as she herself had done so many times in her life, and relax once more. She was tempted to do something unforgivably foolish. Like walk across this room and drag him out of here, when she suspected he would refuse to go.

It was a good thing, then, that she didn't get the chance. The palace doors opened, and Clare immediately knew why everyone was here. She wouldn't have to wait, it seemed, to find out why Madame Aria had looked so happy so short a time ago. The woman strode in, four Hounds at her back, along with six mages in black—the guild's internal enforcers.

Madame Aria took stock of the room before landing on Clare. She smiled smugly, addressing her loudly in the now-silent room. "Clare Brighton. You are hereby accused of illegal use of magic on the following counts: use of magic against the nobility of Veralna without their consent. Use of that magic in ways that can be considered harmful and disruptive, and which shows a blatant disregard for the laws of the Mages Guild, which are designed to ensure the safety of both the magical and non-magical citizens of this kingdom. You will be remanded into the custody of the Mages Guild, until such time as a trial can be set."

Across the room, Alys took an angry step forward. Clare gave her a subtle shake of her head—this was not a situation Alys could fix, and for Clare to fix it, she needed to appear as unruffled as possible. She arched her eyebrows at Madame Aria. "Permission for that use—dare I say encouragement of it—was given to me by the king. Whose authority, unless I am very much mistaken about the nature of kings, supersedes the guild's."

Madame Aria nodded, as if having expected this rebuttal. "Yet if the Mages Guild has reason to believe a mage poses a danger to the king himself, or that his permission for your activities was not freely given, we do not have to honor that permission. From the moment you stepped into these halls, you have held an unnatural sway over the ruling family." She slid a scroll from her inside cloak pocket. "I have here a document signed by no less than twenty of Veralna's most influential nobles attesting to the unusual behavior of both the king and the second prince since your arrival here."

Clare laughed. "Well, it certainly sounds as if I have been busy." It wasn't a terrible plan. By publicly casting doubt on the freedom of the king's behavior, any appeal she made for him to intervene would be met with suspicion. That wouldn't stop his word from overruling the guild's, but only if he bothered to intervene, which Madame Aria no doubt knew he wouldn't.

Not without proper motivation.

"Will you come willingly, or must you be made to comply?"

"Oh, I don't believe either will be necessary. We can clear up this little misunderstanding directly." She could feel the weight of Alaric's power on the mezzanine floor above her, still within hearing range. She raised her voice and called, with emphasis on each syllable, "Alaric."

The Hounds shifted, trading glances, but there had been no magic in her call for them to detect. The only pull that had the king answering her command lay in her finally using the informal address to which he had once invited her, and using it so publicly. His name was a lie on her tongue that said, *You see you've rattled me, Your Majesty, and I am considering your offer.*

He appeared above them, leaning against the railing that lined the mezzanine. "Yes, little songbird?"

She finally determined what it was about that nickname she so despised—the adjective coupled with something most people already considered small and harmless. An address meant to remind her, constantly, of how small she was. Mere minutes ago, he had suggested she become a god at his side. She was, presumably, not supposed to recognize, or at least not to care, that if she did he would always view her as a lesser one.

It served her purposes well enough in the moment. Though she had no doubt he'd overheard Madame Aria's accusations, they had been related in a way that made Clare appear brilliantly manipulative, as opposed to making him look weak and gullible. Put in the former light, he would certainly let her rot in the custody of the Mages Guild. If she directly asked for his help, he would probably take it as an excellent time to remind her that he had made her an offer she had yet to accept.

If she wanted him to allow her the demonstration she needed to make, she needed to prick his pride. Gods, from what the legends would have a person believe, were easily insulted creatures.

"I'm embarrassed on your behalf, Your Majesty. Your own Mages Guild seems to think me capable of ensorcelling you beyond reason."

"Do they now?" A dangerous edge laced his voice.

She made a sympathetic noise. "A good number of your courtiers, too, as they've signed statements to that effect. I thought I might prove the ludicrous nature of the assertion now, with your permission. I would hate to miss dinner tonight, and I hear the guild inquisitions can be lengthy and tedious."

He waved his hand in a dismissive, by-all-means gesture.

Clare gave Madame Aria a cold smile. "You are the *second*-best Songweaver in the kingdom, are you not?"

Madame Aria gritted her teeth. "I am."

"So when I sing, you can tell what I am trying to induce."

"Yes."

"And you"—she turned to the Hounds—"are capable of verifying that I am using magic, and how much of it?"

They nodded.

"Delightful." She tilted her head up to Alaric. She did not sing, as such, merely let three words, imbued with command and all of her Songweaver's magic, arrow at him. "Come to me."

She had only used the full extent of her Songweaving talent that first dinner. Then, her magic had been spread across a multitude of people, and it had still driven them to nearly maul her and Numair. Now all that power, a reservoir so deep she almost couldn't spend it all within the confines of the short command, gushed out of her in a torrent, hitting the king of Faelhorn square in the chest.

When Clare's magic worked, she could feel it—where it wrapped around people, where it coaxed and cajoled. It did not wrap around Alaric now, did not feed little bits of information back to her. Instead, it was severed from her in the span of a second, too quick for her to determine *how* the king had done it.

Power only affects me when I wish it to.

Alaric looked bored. "Not now, little songbird. But perhaps in the future." His gaze switched to Madame Aria. "I believe that was desire she struck me with?"

Madame Aria's assent sounded like it was dragged out of her throat. "Yes, my king."

His gaze flicked to the Hound beside her. "And the entirety of her magical reservoir?"

"Yes, my king."

Alaric steepled his fingers, resting them a moment against his lips. "I find it concerning, how impotent you must all think me, if you believe a girl with a pretty voice could usurp the entirety of *my* will."

The court flinched as a single entity.

"I find it *more* concerning that even my Hounds have come here on such a ridiculous supposition. Clearly, I have left the Mages Guild too long in peace to run itself. It is an oversight you can rest assured I will rectify immediately. As for those of you foolish enough to actually bring this here, to my own halls, no less, that will be settled now."

He turned to Clare. "They've insulted you as well, Miss Brighton. What would you have done with them?" *See what it can be like*, was the message beneath the offer. *You had no power where you came from. So feel what it is like to wield mine.*

It wasn't nearly so tempting as he thought. Because it was *his* power, *his* authority, and it would only be hers when it suited his whims, would only protect her so long as it amused him to do so. The only power she had was what he granted her, and she had lost far more in this exchange than he had pretended, publicly, to give her.

Because she had started the lie of *I am considering your offer*, the lie of *Give me time and I will bend to you.* Lies required careful tending. They could only be maintained for so long when they promised something, as this one did. This particular lie also required that she not bore him. Because she was, by virtue of the authority he'd granted her in this moment, representing him. And no man appreciated being thought boring.

And she would enjoy part of this. To Madame Aria she said, "The Musicians Guild no longer exists. Its offices are closed, its accreditations are worthless, and no business of a similar nature can be reformed."

Madame Aria's face went bloodless, but she wasn't reckless enough to protest. Clare addressed the Hounds and the guild's enforcers next. "You no longer work for the Mages Guild. You no longer work in *any* magical capacity. Your ability will never again contribute to your financial well-being."

"You are too kind-hearted," Alaric said lightly. "I would not have been so lenient. But it will be as you wish. And what of my noble subjects? The ones so concerned for me that they petitioned the guild without my consult?"

"They are banished from your court, for the next year." It was not a punishment, and she knew it. After the spectacular degree to which this had gone poorly for them, anyone whose name was on that document would want nothing more than to disappear from Alaric's sight in the hope that he would forget them.

She had riled them too much lately and, as she'd started this farce of considering Alaric's offer, she could no longer afford for him to think she couldn't deliver on it. Fortunately for her, the court's opinion was a fickle thing, and so long as they understood that *she* understood what she did with this "punishment" she should be well on her way to shifting that opinion in her favor. So she added, "Because I am, as our king says, too kind-hearted."

She left before anyone else could speak to her, went directly to the stables and saddled Kialla. There were a few hours yet before she was expected at dinner that evening, and after what had just happened, she had work for Chalen Mora.

CHAPTER

SEVENTY-EIGHT

SHE HAD A RIGHT

Clare wasn't surprised when Alys and Lina practically pounded down her door the next morning. They'd taken to eating breakfast with her in the Arrendons' suite and, since she'd intentionally avoided them all of yesterday after the Madame Aria event, she was actually surprised they'd been patient enough to wait until dawn to ambush her.

She hadn't been able to sleep, so when they walked in she was fully awake and wearing one of the pieces Chalen had been able to send her home with yesterday. Alys stopped so abruptly that Lina ran into her back.

"No," Alys said flatly. "You are not wearing that."

Clare smoothed her hands over the fabric. "You don't think the cut flatters me? Chalen tried something different with the waisting this time."

"You know exactly what I don't like about it. Wear something else."

"Hmmm." Clare tapped her index finger against her chin. "Let me think on it—no."

"*Clare.*"

"Alys."

"He isn't worth mourning."

Veralna, being a melting pot for the provinces, had a wealth of cultures with various mourning practices and Clare, by virtue of

499

never having told anyone where she was from, was free to choose whichever of them suited her purposes. As it happened, Dunen Province had two different mourning practices. The first, and the one she had chosen, wasn't for the dead but the dying. The base color of the garments worn during this period was a dark gray, accented with black that increased as the mourned's condition did, or with silver if they showed improvement.

"It isn't him I'm mourning." Numair wasn't what was dying. It was the tie between them—the friendship they'd grown that he was starving of water, strangling to death in the slowest way possible, and he wouldn't even tell her why.

She had a right to mourn that. She had a right to make him feel it die.

"Even if I believed that, which I don't, everyone will *think* that's what you're doing."

"Everyone will be too busy tiptoeing around the king after yesterday to care. And this will give me an excuse to not be around them as much. I can hardly be expected to socialize happily while in mourning."

More importantly, it was a calculated move to buy her time with Alaric. *You simply need to let this go.* Let him think she was. He was being patient with her because he was certain she would come to the conclusion that willingly accepting his offer was the only way forward, and she intended to use that patience to find an alternate route.

The focus of Alys's ire predictably shifted at mention of the previous day's events. Unfortunately, it shifted in a direction closer to the truth than Clare would have liked. "The king's interest in you —does he know you're a Reaper? Is that why he's so obsessed with you?"

"I would appreciate it if you didn't use that word again, especially in the palace, and he is not obsessed with me."

"I know the Arrendons well enough to know not a single word spoken in their rooms is going to leave it, and he *is*. King Tolvannen is practically an island unto himself. He has connections, yes, and working partnerships. He interacts and he knows when charm will keep certain people happy and when threats will keep others in line.

"But he does not have friends. He does not have confidants. He does not have lovers, and please take a moment to appreciate the magnitude of that last one. In all the years of his rule, no one has heard a whisper of him taking a lover or indulging with a prostitute. And now he's taking leisurely strolls with you in the gardens and the royal portrait hall, allowing you to use magic on his court in any way you see fit, and having you dole out punishments in his stead. *You* are the one who called him by his given name in front of the entire court. You're too intelligent not to understand how that looks."

Clare grimaced. "Of course I understand how it looks. But it is not obsession." Alaric's obsession was reserved entirely for his kingdom, his interest in her only a means of further maintaining it.

"It is—"

"What would you have me do, Alys? I cannot ignore him, I cannot reject him, and I cannot escape him. If you know the easy answer here, I would love for you to give it to me."

Alys's mouth opened, clicked shut.

"This"—Clare indicated the mourning clothes—"is me buying all the time I can."

"To do what?"

That was the question, wasn't it? "I don't know."

CHAPTER

SEVENTY-NINE

DON'T YOU DARE COME TO MY WEDDING

Alys didn't *mean* to do what she did. But she was, as her mother had often bemoaned while Alys was growing, loyal to a fault, and Clare had earned her loyalty. The woman was strange—so cold at times she almost felt like a non-human entity rather than a person—but Alys had also found her honest in a way few people were. With what she was—and the question of how a Reaper other than Alaric had survived was one she still hadn't put together—Clare had never *had* to bow to any of Alys's demands. But she'd helped her anyway.

For getting Lina back, Alys would have been loyal to Clare even if she'd been a murderer on par with Alaric's bloody history. For all Alys knew, she was. But it seemed unlikely. The Arrendons trusted her, Fitz had gone from hating her to treating her with an almost-brotherly devotion, and Numair—well, her once-childhood friend was the current object of her search.

"*Please* do not get imprisoned for regicide three weeks before our wedding," Lina begged, trotting to keep up with Alys's determined strides.

"It's only regicide if I kill a king. A prince is simple murder."

"I know you think you're helping, but if she wanted us to intervene, she would have asked."

"Clare wouldn't ask for help if she was drowning and we were dry land."

"At least don't do this in public. You'll only make it worse for her."

Her fiancée had a point there. She finally found Numair—everyone was in the gymnasium again today—surrounded by his usual entourage. He saw her coming and straightened.

Too late to run, she thought. "You and I need to talk." She grabbed a fistful of his shirt and dragged him out, down the hall and into the nearest room.

Lina raised her hands in the doorway. "I went with you to get him because I don't want everyone thinking you're sleeping with him before our wedding, but I am not going to be a part of this. I'll see you at home." She shut the door and walked out. Lina had a policy of keeping her hands clean whenever something didn't fit with her deeply ingrained sense of right or wrong. It was one of the things Alys loved most about her.

Numair shrugged out of her hold. "To what do I owe the honor of being dragged into the cleaning closet?"

"What in Ferrian's hells is wrong with you?"

"You'll have to be more specific. The list is a little long, at this point."

"She's your friend. She's your *only* friend. And you abandoned her like she was nothing. I want to know why."

He slipped his hands into his pockets and leaned against the door. "I got bored with her. Women always grow tiresome, after a while."

She moved before she had the conscious thought, her hand cracking against his cheek. Sharp anger lit his eyes, replacing indifference. He flexed his jaw and the anger extinguished, smothered once more beneath bored indifference. "If she's having difficulty being jilted, tell her to deal with it like all the others do, instead of sending you to harass me. I hear publicly mocking me is quite therapeutic."

She could not understand him. She could not understand what Clare had seen in him. "I sent myself because she won't even tell me what happened. And no matter what you've done, *she* would never treat you like they do."

His gaze wandered off, like the conversation couldn't hold his attention. More likely he was already too drunk to focus. She snapped her fingers in his face. "You liked her—there's no use lying,

I know you did. So what happened?" For Clare's sake, Alys would like to believe there was a reason this time. "Did your uncle threaten you?"

He sighed. "You want to know what happened?"

"I just said that I do," she gritted out.

"I did like her. And then I kissed her"—he leaned toward her—"and I realized I've had better. Wasn't any point in keeping on after that." He opened the door and stepped out. "Stop fighting other people's battles for them, Alys. Neither side appreciates it."

"She's mourning you, you bastard." He stopped, his back to her, his hands clenching into fists. "Like you're on your deathbed and you actually deserve the attention."

His hands uncurled, fingers flexing. Curled back into fists. He walked away.

"Don't you dare come to my wedding," she yelled after him. Not after that.

CHAPTER

EIGHTY

YOU DON'T GET TO MISS ME

The mourning clothes helped—and they didn't. Alaric had cast a single glance at her in them the first day, given her a knowing look, and proceeded to let her be. The court had likewise been happy to have an excuse to murmur sympathies—while never once bothering to ask who she was mourning—and then leave her alone, ostensibly out of respect for her pending loss.

As for Numair...he hadn't had a reaction. Not surprise, not anger, not sadness. When she entered a room, he looked right through her, if he bothered to look at her at all. But even when he did, he wasn't *there*. It was as if he'd vacated his body, leaving an automaton in his place that laughed and spoke and played his part without his input.

She hadn't expected her actions—this display—to change anything. He'd made it clear, when they'd last spoken, that he wouldn't change his mind. That they wouldn't be going back to what they were. But she would have settled for a hint of regret. For the slightest indication that he felt *anything*.

Because no matter how she tried to cover it up with anger, there was a raw, festering hole inside her where he used to be, and as the weeks leading up to Alys and Lina's wedding dragged by, there was little to distract her from it. She stopped circulating in public aside from the dinners she was still required to attend, because she couldn't stop herself from looking for him. Every room she walked into, he was the first face she sought, and every time his gaze slipped by her like she wasn't there, it cut something open inside her.

Sometimes she wondered if she'd imagined it all. Then she'd return to her room, where a single hibiscus flower, still refusing to wilt and die, proved she hadn't. She almost set it on fire half-a-dozen times. She wanted him to let it die, so she could change her mourning clothes from gray to black and put it all to rest. Conversely, she wanted to return to the Arrendons' home on the weekend and find the plant by her window had come back to life.

Neither happened, and after the second weekend, she stopped going. Verol and Quin still hadn't returned. They'd written that they would be back for Alys and Lina's wedding, but for now their estate was empty. She felt like a ghost haunting it, and the reprieve it brought her from being in the same building as Alaric wasn't worth the trade-off of the Song's uninhibited presence. At the palace, it still hid, but outside of those walls, it battered at her ceaselessly.

It was terrified, and she had learned the first time it had spoken to her as a child that it had only one solution to terror. One thing she would never give it, because it would save the Song, but it would not save her. And she still stubbornly wanted to save herself, even if she didn't know why.

A dark voice whispered that this world was no different than the one she had left. That she was no more free, no more powerful, no more hopeful than before. But there were differences. She had the illusion of all those things now, where she hadn't before. And the illusion whispered that she should accept what Alaric offered her, in order to maintain it.

But she had never had it in her to bend, even when it was smart, even when it would keep her alive, and she still didn't. And Alaric had been…distracted the last two weeks. It was more than merely giving her the space to "mourn". Far more runners than normal had arrived in the palace lately, bringing him reports that apparently necessitated delivery no matter what he was engaged with at the time. Several had been brought to him during dinner, and she would often find him looking at her after he read them, as if he wanted to cut her open and find out what was inside. As if he'd thought her a flower, then plucked it only to discover her a mere weed.

By the time Alys's wedding finally arrived, Clare's uncertainty around Alaric, combined with the isolation she'd spent the last few weeks in, had turned her half-back into that mad creature that had roamed the swamps. Especially since one of those reports had finally drawn Alaric away a few hours ago, a fact she'd known before anyone else, because the Song had flooded in behind her eyes once more.

Its returned presence made her temples throb, and she had certainly not arrived at Alys's estate in any fit mood for a wedding. A fact that hadn't gone unnoticed by Alys, who had taken one look at her and told her to, "Have an emotional crisis when it isn't my wedding" and "I'll still kick him in the balls for you if you give me permission, but he better not show his face here."

So she'd done her best to force herself to be the Clare she'd become in Veralna. Now she was standing off to the side of the stage, fiddling with the voice crystals despite knowing they were perfectly tuned. She'd spent the last week combing through the palace library's archives of the Veralna Times, scouring the society pages for information on weddings, because she'd never seen one before and hadn't really had any notion of what she was supposed to do at one. She now knew entirely too much on the dreadful affairs, though apparently the cake was something to look forward to.

Unfortunately, she didn't think she was likely to get a slice of it. She was to sing the first ten dances before giving way to a purely instrumental group, but by then she doubted there would be any cake left. The dessert in question sat atop a ridiculous pedestal, a crowning, six-tiered marvel of chocolate perfection with piped blue icing and the Megadari house crest ostentatiously repeated on each tier.

"I confess myself dying to know what it is about that cake that puts such a look on your face." Numair's voice came from behind her, soft and tired and worn.

Her heart thudded so hard she was surprised the cage of her ribs didn't break. She was angry with him. So unspeakably angry. For leaving her alone and being able to do it so easily.

And she missed him just as fiercely as she wanted to tell him to go drown in Ferrian's hells. It wasn't that she couldn't be alone. She knew how. She'd always known how. She'd just preferred to be alone with him.

She waited to answer. Waited to see if she *wanted* to answer, trying to feel in the silence between them what had made him approach her tonight. But she couldn't find the answer. If he'd said anything else to her, anything that wasn't a blatant plea for her to remember that first day in Galina's, she didn't know if she would have responded.

"It's the manner of acquiring a piece," she replied finally, moving to fiddle with another voice crystal that lay closer to the sound of Numair's voice. He stood behind one of the foliaged trellises gracing either side of the stage, foliage that had grown noticeably larger and thicker so as to more easily conceal a person who wanted to stand behind it unnoticed.

All it took was a single look at his face for everything she thought she knew to spin from its axis. He looked like hell. Oh, his face was so well-glamoured that no one save her would see, but she *did* see. She saw the sunken darkness beneath eyes devoid of their usual brilliance, saw the harsh prominence of his cheekbones. Money could buy newly tailored clothes that fit perfectly as a body changed, but they couldn't hide the fact that he'd lost weight—too much weight, in too short a time.

She took quick stock of the area and slipped behind the trellis when no one was watching. Her eyes roved over him, catching on a glamour-covered bruise peeking out from the collar of his shirt, dark purple covering the entirety of his neck up to his left ear.

He realized where her gaze lay riveted and grimaced. "I should have guessed you would be able to see through glamour."

Her anger at him gave way to anger for him—she could return to the former once she'd fixed this. "Who did this to you?"

"It doesn't matter."

"It matters to me." Anger stirred the Song inside her and it rose on a howling wind of fury. Overhead, clouds moved to blot out the sun, shadows creeping over the wedding scene.

There was nothing normal or human in her voice, the Song echoing in the pauses between her words as she demanded, "Who. Did. This?"

Numair's eyes widened. His hand snaked around her waist and he pulled her further from the stage, greenery growing around them with haste to form an enclosure that hid them completely from sight.

It was the physical contact, the fact he'd touched her without asking, that made her realize thunder now rumbled in the skies above, and the darkness that coiled about her was unnatural. She closed her eyes and made the Song relent. The skies cleared, the darkness receded, and he breathed a sigh of relief.

He started to let her go.

"Don't." Barely more than a whisper from her, but he froze, his hand on her back. She wished he hadn't heeded her command, wished he'd ignored her and left. Because this—being this close to him, seeing the real *him* again—was bad for her.

She looked up, into his eyes. "Why now?" *Tell me you changed your mind. Tell me you'll let me help you.*

His free hand touched the hibiscus flower she'd woven into her hair that morning. She'd arranged it carefully, so the petals brushed her face. She shouldn't have worn it. But he wasn't supposed to have been here, and she hadn't been certain she could stand being around so much happiness without it.

"This is…distracting," he confessed.

She jolted. "You can feel it?"

"It's my magic. Of course I feel it. Every touch." He brushed his fingers across the petals, then lightly down her face. "Every time."

Every time she'd picked it up since he'd left. Every time she'd held it for hours when she couldn't sleep. Every time she'd held a lit match an inch away and tried to make herself touch the flame to the petals. Every time she'd missed him.

Every. Single. Fucking. Time.

And he'd let her. He'd kept it alive, he'd felt *her*, and she'd had nothing but his absence and his public indifference.

If the announcer's voice hadn't cut through the silence, calling for the guests to take their seats, she would have ripped the damn thing out of her hair and crushed it in front of him. As it was, she was so incapacitated by rage that he slipped away from her, disappearing and reappearing on the other side of the sea of chairs, a chameleon adept at becoming a part of a crowd without anyone noticing his arrival unless he wanted them to.

If Alys saw him, she might become the first bride to attempt committing murder at her own wedding, and Clare wasn't certain she'd stop her. She forced herself to focus, to watch the ceremony, and not Numair. It was simple and beautiful, and she supposed she could understand why people liked weddings. So full of hope and promise, and for a day, at least, the belief that everything could be as perfect as a moment.

So when she took the stage, she sang for that moment, for the looks in Alys's and Lina's eyes when they looked at each other. She sang for Marquin and Verol, who had slipped into the wedding on the verge of being unforgivably late, and slipped out again after her first song. Later in the evening, relieved of her duties, she made her way to the punch table, taking a cup from the non-alcoholic side. The cake was, predictably, gone.

She watched Numair dance with some girl she didn't care to recall the name of, and who was so busy chattering on that she didn't notice the ticking of the muscle in Numair's jaw as he clenched his teeth, or the stiffness with which he held her. Clare was debating the various merits and drawbacks of finding an opportune moment later in the evening to spill punch on the silly chit—for reasons even she could admit came down to jealousy, pure and simple—when the dance ended and Clare found herself directly in the path of the third son of the Marquis of Venatas, with no avenue of quick escape.

A rumor had surfaced that the Arrendons intended to legally adopt her. Diligently as she'd worked to discover its source, she never had. And as it turned out, the Arrendons were not only wealthy, they were obscenely wealthy. Between that and the Arrendon title that would pass to her if this adoption rumor proved true, she found herself in the unfortunate position of looking like a good marriage prospect. And since Alaric had shown no further public favoritism toward her since she'd gone into mourning, every second and third son of every semi-important family had decided it was worth the risk to develop an interest in her.

She was, presumably, supposed to be dumb enough to believe them infatuated with her, allow them to sweep her off her feet, and marry one of them as soon as possible, handing them the Arrendon title and wealth as soon as this supposed adoption occurred. Dealing with them tactfully was a challenge she was rapidly losing the will to accomplish.

The one who walked toward her now—Julian? James? No,

Joseph, Lord Adlington—both bored and offended her in equal measure. And it appeared, given the rearranging crowd at her back, cutting off escape, she would have to allow herself the honor of being bored by him for an entire dance.

She handed her now-empty punch glass to a passing attendant, straightened her shoulders, and steeled her resolve.

"If I might have this dance?"

The voice did not belong to Lord Adlington, who had stopped five feet from her with an inscrutable expression on his face.

She very nearly told the second prince of Faelhorn precisely where he could shove his dance invitation. But it was him or Lord Adlington.

"Delighted." She turned and took Numair's hand. He was cautious as he led her onto the dance floor, obviously sensing her anger. He was just as obviously straining for that old easiness between them when he said, "Have I saved poor Lord Adlington from the sharper side of your tongue?"

"He's so dull he wouldn't recognize the sharper side if it cut him to the bone." She couldn't yell at him here, in this sea of people. She didn't want to cause a scene at Alys's wedding. And she couldn't get past the bruise peeking out of his collar, the too-thin feel of him beneath her hands. "What happened to your neck?"

He stiffened. "I'm a drunk. I tripped and fell on something."

"And how many times have you tripped and fallen on things lately? How many times did Chalen have to remake your clothes because they don't fit you anymore? How many—"

"*Stop*," he said harshly. Then his voice softened. "Please, just… stop."

"Why should I? If you aren't here to be honest with me, then why are you here?"

"Because I miss you."

Bitterness laced her words. "So you get to come to me like this when it's convenient for you? When you have a moment of weakness? Like I don't know that tomorrow if I see you, it'll be like I don't exist all over again?"

"I—"

"You don't get to *miss me*." Her voice was low, hard. "Not like this. Not at my friend's fucking wedding where I can't even yell at you. Do you think I haven't missed you every day? The difference is that when I missed you so much it hurt, I didn't get to feel you through a damn flower and know you hadn't forgotten me. I didn't have the luxury of slipping into your life like you did into mine tonight, because when I looked for you, you *weren't there.*"

"I'm sorry." His arm tightened on her waist, and his forehead dropped onto her shoulder. "I never meant for any of this to happen. I never meant for *you* to happen."

He'd never meant for this to happen? She had a magic flower and a necklace that said otherwise. But she didn't want to see him wince, or tell her they were both mistakes, so she didn't point it out.

Her rage battled with her sadness and her terror, with the unknown of what was happening to him. With the knowledge that something more than her wearing said magic flower had brought him to her tonight. If that was all it took, he'd have been at her side countless times before now.

Something was wrong. Or something had changed. Or he was desperate. "Please let me help you."

He lifted his head. "You can't."

"Because you won't let me."

His mouth tightened. "It isn't that simple."

"Then explain it to me in small words so I can understand."

He just looked at her.

"I know," she said bitterly, "you can't." The song ended, the dance over. "And until you can, you can go back to missing me, Your Highness. Without this." She plucked the flower from her hair and slipped it in the breast pocket of his suit. Let him see what it was like to miss her in the same void she'd missed him in.

She walked away without looking back, ignoring the stares of people who'd stopped bothering to pretend they *weren't* staring.

CHAPTER

EIGHTY-ONE

PHOENIX

Clare went back to the Arrendon estate, but wherever Quin and Verol had gone when they'd slipped out of the wedding, it hadn't been home. The house was empty, the only sign that anyone had been there at all a small parcel on the dining room table. A note on the top—Fitz's handwriting, so presumably he'd returned to Veralna with Quin and Verol—stated that it had arrived for her by courier not long before.

She knew immediately who it was from, the black box with the black-and-green ribbon. She ignored it at first, debating whether she would open it at all. Because if he'd sent her that damn flower back she *would* light it on fire. She went to her room to change out of her dress. Obstinance had her sticking to her mourning clothes, selecting a simple pair of gray pants and a tunic. Once changed, her curiosity got the better of her. She returned to the kitchen and the black box, untying the ribbon with a single tug. Inside lay one decadent slice of wedding cake, slightly squashed as if it had been wrapped in a handkerchief and hidden away.

"Bastard," she whispered under her breath, opening the letter that had come with it.

I can hear you calling me a bastard. She refused to laugh. Because if she laughed, she was going to cry, and crying once in a decade was enough for her. *I know I don't deserve it, but don't mourn me in black just yet. You can't help me. But I'm trying to help myself.*

Her fingers tightened on the letter, unease coiling in her stomach. This was unreasonable. He didn't get to do this. She wasn't going to *let* him do this. She folded the top of the box back over the cake, carried it to the cold box and placed it inside.

She turned out the magelights and walked in comforting darkness to her room, intent on finding shoes and tracking Numair down somewhere she *could* yell at him and demand an explanation. Halfway down the hall she heard the unmistakable sound of the front wards unlocking, and she slunk instinctively against the wall, unable to break the habit of hiding, no matter how long she'd been here.

Quin's and Verol's voices floated through the darkness—they had not seen it any more fit to turn on a light than she—and she molded herself into stillness, into silence, listening.

"It is out of our hands now," Marquin was saying. "All we can do is wait."

"We do not have time to wait. You read the report. Madame Aria tried to have her arrested and Alaric is showing her far too much favor. I don't know what he is planning, but I want him away from here. Away from *her*."

"We have planted enough seeds of doubt across the provinces. If he can be drawn away, he will. She needs us here, Verol. We leave her alone too much."

"I would know if something was wrong," Verol said defensively.

"You would know if her life was in danger. That is not the same as knowing she is all right."

Since it sounded like this was an argument they'd had many times before, and which could go back and forth for hours, she flicked the hall magelight on. They blinked at her in surprise.

"We should talk," she said mildly. "And this time, I am not interested in being spared any moral burdens."

She gestured them to the kitchen. They went almost meekly, sitting at the table while she prepared a pot of coffee. She settled it, along with the attending accoutrements, on the table and took the seat directly across from Marquin. She judged him the less likely of the two to talk around issues out of a desire to spare her feelings.

"Let's begin with what you've been doing while you've been gone."

"It's safer for you if you do not know," Verol began.

"Safer?" she echoed. "There is nothing safe about my being here. There is nothing safe about my being kept in the dark. I have been stuck here walking the tightrope of this infernal court and Alaric's attentions, while the two of you have been who knows where doing who knows what in the supposed name of my protection, and I want to know what those things are." She needed to know if they had any chance of working. If there was anything she could do to *make* them work.

"Spreading rumors, mostly," Marquin said, reaching to pour three cups of coffee and slide them to everyone, since no one else had.

"Rumors," Clare said flatly.

"Yes," Verol said, giving in. "Rumors about power. As far away from here as we can without being obvious." He took a long drink of coffee, without the addition of cream or sugar, and Marquin took over.

"There are certain…events that tend to happen around the person who bears your power. Miraculous healings. Sudden bounties of harvest in typically barren places. We have been causing things like that."

It was certainly better than hastening rebellions as a distraction, but… "Neither of you are healers and rumors alone are easily seen through."

"It is easy and harmless enough for a mindmage to convince people they have witnessed something miraculous," Marquin said. "And it takes little enough money to bring bounty to a place that has practically nothing. The trick is in hiding the source. We've been ensuring word of the happenings reach Alaric, while making it look as if we're trying to obfuscate them."

At least now she knew what had been in all those reports Alaric had been getting. Why he kept looking at her so oddly after he received them. And whatever news he had received today had finally prompted him to leave the palace to investigate. One thing, however, still didn't make sense. "If you are trying to convince him the real Song is out there, that I don't matter, why would you let all these rumors circulate that you plan to adopt me?" An untrue rumor was the last thing a mindmage ever needed to suffer. And just like that, the answer was startlingly obvious. "You're trying to make him think *I'm* the decoy. That you found the Song somewhere else, so you brought me back to court to take his attention."

Of course they hadn't *actually* wanted to adopt her. What would be the point? She was an adult. She didn't need guardians. She didn't need fathers. Hadn't she said so enough?

"Yes."

"You've certainly distracted him," she admitted. "But though he's hunting the trail you've laid, it will eventually run out. What is the plan, after that?"

Verol shook his head. "I don't want you involved in the rest of it. It's too dangerous."

"It's too dangerous if I *don't* know."

"We are planning," Marquin said softly, "to kill him."

She looked at them, incredulous. "How are you going to kill a man who could Reap the city with a breath? A man who can take a dagger to the heart and pull it out without even staining his clothes?" She'd been hoping they had some plan to contain him.

They were quiet for so long that she finally understood. "Me. You intend to point *me* at him."

"No," Verol said. "Absolutely not."

But Marquin said, "It would be a lie to say you don't have the best chance of success."

Verol turned on him. "You *promised me*. You promised me you would not ask this of her."

Marquin smiled sadly. "I promised I wouldn't ask *you* to ask it of her." He turned to her. "And *I* am not asking it of you now. But you stand to lose more than any of us."

"*Quin*," Verol warned.

"He isn't wrong," Clare said. "Not about what I stand to lose. But as of this moment, I do not believe I have the best chance of success. The Song won't fight him. It's terrified of him and hides like a child in his presence."

The Song seethed within her, but she didn't care. She hadn't said anything that wasn't true. "So if you point me at Alaric, it will only be me. And I can tell you from recent experience that everything a black diamond Songweaver has to throw at him didn't even make him blink." They shared a look. "So since one of you, at least, had no intention of relying on me, how *did* you plan to kill him?"

"By creating mages strong enough to counter him."

She frowned. "Creating?"

Verol rubbed at his temples. "His initial power came from his Reaper ability, but the rest of it—everything that he has become in the years since—is from magical objects he has acquired. Many of them from countries that no longer exist. He Reaps them and absorbs their abilities."

She remembered a room, objects displayed behind glass cases, her sense that they were all missing something. Numair's explanation that it was a collection, and her failing to understand what any of the pieces had in common.

"We have not only been misdirecting his attention when we're gone—we've been tracking legends. Every legend about every item of immense power. While we don't have a Reaper of our own"—he carefully didn't look at her—"were we to acquire enough of them, and find a mage capable of mastering each, we might have a chance of defeating him."

Possibilities sprang to life in her mind. Chances that hadn't been there before, a narrow exit opening from her cage. "How many of these objects have you found?"

It was clear they had been hoping she wouldn't ask that question.

"Of the kind that hold the power we are looking for? One," Verol admitted.

She didn't bother to hide her disappointment. "One. Alaric has Reaped hundreds." And hundreds—thousands—of lives. "I've seen the room."

"He has Reaped hundreds of lesser artifacts," Marquin corrected. "What we are looking for—they are all artifacts we believe the Song created throughout history in the other people it has inhabited. They would possess far more power than anything Alaric has acquired."

Far more power than any ordinary mage could wield, the Song said with satisfaction. At least that answered the question of whether they were as powerful as Marquin and Verol hoped.

Then I will wield them, she snapped back. As if she would be foolish enough to leave Alaric's destruction—and her survival—in the hands of someone else anyway.

"I would like to see it."

"What?"

"The one you've found. I want to see it."

Verol hesitated. "We've located it, but it is difficult to reach. It is currently being retrieved by an associate."

They didn't even have it yet. Not growling in frustration took significant effort. "Who is doing the retrieving?" When they didn't answer, she said, "If you honestly think you cannot trust me with this, then I wonder that we are having this conversation at all."

"It isn't a matter of trust," Marquin said. "It's that we don't actually know."

Now Clare was the one rubbing at her temples. "How can you *not know*?"

"They're an informant of ours. One we know only by the name Phoenix," Marquin said. "Whoever they are, they are well-connected, and we've been in contact with them for enough years to have established trust. They have given us information in the past that has been invaluable. Along with information that has allowed us to save several lives. What Alaric asks of Verol within the court is never pleasant. Phoenix has sometimes been able to give us information that allows Verol to…manipulate those tasks."

Well-connected. In Alaric's court. Her heart slowed, then sped up. "So it's someone close to Alaric?"

Verol nodded. "One of his generals, I suspect. But in truth, it's better if we do not know. For them and for us."

One of his generals. But how much would a general know of the intimate details of the courtiers whose minds Verol altered at Alaric's whim? She thought of a lacquered box sitting on Verol's desk, of its twin in Numair's library. Of the way they'd felt linked, as if…as if what you put into one ended up in the other. The perfect method to send letters between people working together against a king.

She thought of his most recent letter to her. *You can't help me. But I'm trying to help myself.*

She thought of the name, Phoenix. A creature that died to be reborn. Like a man who might be allowed to be reborn as himself… if a king died first.

She stood, pacing the length of the table. "The item Phoenix is after. Where is it?"

Another shake of Marquin's head. "We don't know."

She was growing exceptionally tired of the number of things they didn't know. "Then *what* is it?"

"It's called the Siren's Tear."

She dropped her coffee cup. The fine porcelain shattered on the dark wood floor, splashing hot liquid over everything.

"Clare?"

She stepped around the mess of broken china and spilled liquid. "I have to go."

Because she knew the legend of the Siren's Tear. That it lay in a cave beneath Siren's Cliff, the very same one she'd sung of at The Musicale House. The song Numair had heard. The one that held all the clues to the location of Siren's Cliff, if one knew what to listen for.

She ran to her room, hastily pulling on her boots while the Arrendons followed like shadows.

"What is going on?" Verol asked. "Talk to us."

She shook her head and brushed past them, down the hallway, pausing in the front doorway. "If Alaric comes looking for me, tell him"—she looked down at her mourning clothes—"tell him my uncle in Dunen Province has taken a turn for the worse. I've left to be at his side."

"You don't *have* an uncle in Dunen Province," Verol said, following her outside, Marquin on his heels.

"I could." Long, almost-running strides carried her to the paddock where Kialla waited.

"Well, yes, but what does this have to do with the Siren's Tear? Why do you need to leave?"

"Because I know where it is, and Phoenix can't go there. I have to stop them." She pulled Kialla's halter and lead off the gate, slipping through the rails to collect the mare.

"You know who Phoenix is?" Verol asked.

She haltered Kialla and looped the lead around her neck, tying it to the metal ring beneath the halter in a set of makeshift reins. "I don't have time, I have to go."

"Then we'll come with you—"

"*No.*" She cut Verol off. "You can't." Numair wouldn't want him to know.

"Clare, they aren't traveling by traditional means, you may not be able to follow."

Marquin squeezed Verol's shoulder. "Let her try." He opened the paddock gate for her. "Be careful, but be fast. Verol's right. You'll need to reach them before they leave. I'll write them a note, but they tend not to check our method of communication too regularly. I'm sorry."

With those last two words, she realized he knew. Who Phoenix was. Or he at least suspected. Just as she knew Verol would never suspect, or probably even believe her if she told him. "Thank you."

She vaulted onto Kialla's back and galloped out of the stables, her entire being focused on a single, fervent hope. *Don't let me be too late.*

FOR THE FIRST TIME, Clare didn't bother with subterfuge, going directly to the front door of Numair's house. She pounded on it and didn't stop until a wide-eyed Ida opened the door.

"Where is he?"

Ida hesitated.

"Where?"

"Not here."

Clare squeezed her hands into fists. Marquin had said he wasn't traveling by traditional means. Would she still be able to catch him?

"How long ago? Which road did he take out of town?"

"I can't. I'm sorry."

Clare looked at her, this woman who had been like a second mother to Numair. Who had done her best to be there for him when no one else could. Who had been so welcoming to Clare simply because Numair liked her. A woman like that would never have let him leave without argument if she'd had any idea where he was going.

"Ida, I need you to hear me. He is going to Renault County."

All the blood drained from the woman's face.

"So which road did he take?"

"He didn't," Ida whispered. "He used a gatestone."

Clare's confusion prompted an explanation from the Song, a burst of understanding sending fresh fear cascading through her. "Where did he use it? Show me."

Ida led her to the library, to an open area where Clare still felt the residual traces of magic.

"Is he going to be all right?"

"Yes. He's going to be fine." She refused to accept the alternative. "But I need you to do something."

Ida nodded.

"I need you to close me in here and lock the door. Don't let anyone in this room if you can help it. If anyone comes looking, I was never here and you don't know where Numair is. Can you do that for me?"

"You're going to bring him back?"

"Yes."

"Then I will."

Clare's facade of calm evaporated the moment the door closed and the lock clicked. She knelt on the floor, feeling the gatestone's residual magic, feeling where it led, and her body shook. Chills swept her, and her stomach churned.

He couldn't be there. After everything that had happened, after everything Renault County had ever taken from her, it couldn't be taking *him* too.

She took a deep breath, opened her mind to the Song, and made her demand before she could think about it. *The portal he left through —recreate it.*

Silence. Then, *No. It would be uncaring of me to allow you to return to that place.*

You don't make my choices for me.

You have made that abundantly clear. But you do not make mine for me either. And my answer is no.

Her trembling turned to rage. As much as she didn't want to go back, the idea that she couldn't, that she might lose him, was untenable. *Do you think you will* ever *taste freedom if you refuse me this? Do you think I will ever let you know peace if he dies? Recreate the portal, or I will make the first prison I built for you look like a palace.*

If you want it so badly, trade me for it.

What do you want?

If I open the portal, if I aid you until you find your prince, you will give me what I wanted the first day we spoke.

Clare hesitated. It was a fine line. One so easy to cross. So difficult to cross back from. *You may have the* first *thing you wanted that day,* she allowed. *If you get me to Renault County in time. Help me find Numair, keep him safe, and alive. And you allow me to deal with Simian. Then you get what you want.*

Pondering silence, the seconds stretching out. Then: *Very well. We have a deal.*

The Song rumbled inside her and Clare embraced it. Magic tore from her, the gate yawning open to reveal the dirty streets of a place Clare had never wanted to see again. Her stomach revolted, and she barely had time to grab a nearby wastebasket before she was throwing up everything in her stomach.

And when she was done, she wiped her mouth with the back of her hand and passed through the gate into hell.

CHAPTER
EIGHTY-TWO
WELCOME TO MY HOME

The stench hit her first. The smell of urine and septic waste, of dankness and mold, of sickness and rot curling into her nostrils. There were no safe places in Renault County, but the Song had spit her out in the closest approximation of one that existed here, on the east rooftop above what had once been a market square.

But an approximation of safe wasn't actually safe. Her knife was in her hand and she was turning the instant she registered the soft scuff behind her. She struck, the blade jabbing into soft neck tissue then carving a line out. Blood gushed as she wrenched the knife free, and the body was falling before she'd even registered what the person looked like.

Young. Male or female, she couldn't tell. Rail-thin and the hair shorn close to the skull. Vacant brown eyes stared up at her, but they didn't try to speak as the lifeblood poured out of them. Rarely did anyone in Renault County have dying words. She felt a trace of something—guilt? Remorse?—that had never been present in her time here before. If you couldn't kill in Renault County, then you couldn't live.

A commotion drew her attention back to the square below. The market was a remnant of a time when Renault County had still been accessible to the outside world. Legend had it that at one point a few merchants had still dared to travel here. Legend had it that at one point, you could even leave, if you were willing to pay the exit cost. But the guards at that gate wouldn't tell you what the cost was until you'd agreed to pay, and you weren't guaranteed to survive the price.

But as long as Clare had been alive there had been no guards, and no market visitors. Because to step outside those gates, to touch the ground on the other side, was to die. It was the easiest escape out of Renault County, and the corpses of those who found such a death preferable to life within were piled on the other side.

In the absence of merchants, the market had become more theater than trading place, and it was ruled by Jaol's gang. Jaol himself had been dead so long that no one Clare encountered had ever actually met the man, but the figurehead changed so frequently that no one bothered to learn the new names. If you ruled the market square then you were Jaol, and that was that.

The Jaols never lasted long—the people who made the market their home expected entertainment out of their leader, and entertainment was difficult to provide in a place where people thrived on cruelty and debauchery, and every form of both had already been seen a thousand times. Yet tonight the square below her teemed with people, excitement thick in the air, as if finally, *finally*, something new had come their way.

Dread was an iron band around her chest as the crowd below, looking like nothing more than rats packed into a tunnel, made a thin opening on the eastern side. Through it the current Jaol strode, two men behind him hauling a body between them.

She recognized the clothes, the fall of silky black hair. His head lolled limply as they dragged him, and the world came to a crashing halt, the noise of so much vermin beneath her fading out. She didn't hear what Jaol said as he motioned to the guards and they hurled Numair into the small space that had opened in the center of the crowd.

He didn't move, and the silence she'd erected was pierced by a high ringing. Then she saw it—a small, quick slip of his hand into his pocket—and the sound came crashing back in on her.

You promised, she told the Song.

I have not forgotten, the Song answered, and its power inundated her.

She opened herself to it and jumped from the roof. As she plummeted she realized what Numair had taken from his pocket—seeds —because a violent burst of greenery erupted around him in a protective enclosure of brambles. The band around her chest eased. Fine. He would be fine until she reached him.

She hummed as her feet hit the ground, using the Song's power in the only way she knew how—the same way she wove emotions, only now she wove something different, power cushioning her landing. A three-foot hollow opened in the ground beneath her, wide cracks radiating out from it all across the square. The noise halted. Prior to this day, Clare could not have thought of a single thing that would cause Renault County's inhabitants to collectively turn silent and focus on one thing. Clare landing at the edge of the market in a haze of magic and splintered earth, did.

She sang a high, eerie note and the twenty people nearest to her dropped. The gathered crowd stared at her. She bared her teeth. They swarmed at her...and hit a wall of magic.

She trilled her next notes instinctively, feeding the barrier, every body that fetched up against it sliding lifelessly off it. They were piled six bodies high before the tide of people stopped madly rushing in. In the lull, Clare dropped the note, sliding into a song. Without the first note in play her barrier was down, but the song she had given it up for was more versatile, more useful. As her voice spun the words, her mind spun ribbons of power, floating them out to ensnare those closest to her. She spun and trapped, spun and trapped, gathering the inhabitants of the market in the Song's magic.

But the channel from the Song's prison was too narrow—she could not pull the power fast enough, and as the horde pressed in on her, she knew it wouldn't be enough. So she widened the channel. The subsequent influx of power was intoxicating, a high euphoria that enveloped her as she sang, until every single living thing in the market, save one, was hers. They rocked back and forth in unison, feet locked in place, swaying gently in her thrall.

She felt each and every presence held captive to her and marveled at how simple, how *easy*, it was to hold them. The Song liked it too, wanted to take the lone individual she had not sought to bend to her. The one that waited beyond the sway of bodies, encased in a living shelter of thorns.

He's mine, she told the Song. *You promised.*

She waved her hand and people swarmed over each other to open a path from her to Numair. She went to him. Seeing him through the brambles, bruised and bloodied but alive, was a cold check to the heady feeling of so much power pulsing in her veins like blood. He'd taken no small amount of damage in the short time he'd been here—Renault County had given him its best—and growing this enclosure had clearly taken what little strength remained out of him. He was slumped over, his eyes closed and his breathing labored.

She crouched beside him. "Numair?" The Song answered her need, sluicing over him, closing cuts, erasing bruises, mending broken bones.

He bolted upright, eyes flying open. "Clare?" Panic laced his voice. Before she even realized what was happening he'd opened a hole in the enclosure, jerked her inside and reclosed it around them. Like *he* was trying to protect *her.* Her lips curved up.

"What are you doing here?" he asked. "*How* are you here?"

"I'm here for you. As for the other…" She shrugged.

He started to talk and then stopped, cocking his head, as if finally realizing the world had gone silent around them, save for the gentle shuffling sound of so many bodies swaying together.

She touched her fingers to the brambles. "You can let this go, if you want. I have it under control."

He peered through the vines at what lay around them and swallowed. "This is you?" He put an emphasis on the last word, and she knew what he was really asking.

"Yes. And no."

He squeezed his eyes shut. "You shouldn't have come."

"No, *you* shouldn't have come. You have no idea what this place is like."

"But you do?" He asked it quietly, as if he already knew the answer.

Her stomach clenched, and she wanted to undo his being here. His seeing her here. But she knew she couldn't. Knew, deep down, that it was always meant to come to this. Hadn't she understood it, dancing with him in Deleen? Understood that no one could know her without knowing this, just as she'd understood that no one could possibly know this and accept it?

"Yes. Welcome to my home."

He took a deep breath and the brambles folded down, giving an unobstructed view of the people surrounding them. Jaol stood less than two feet away, swaying lightly, and Numair's face turned livid. "Don't take this the wrong way, but I don't much care for your home."

At least he wasn't yet looking at her like she was something sub-human. "Neither do I. Do you still have the gatestone?" They worked twice. Once to take a person to a place, and once to bring them back. He nodded. "Then go home. I have something to take care of here."

"So do I."

"No, you don't. I'll get your rock for you."

His gaze narrowed. "How do you know about that?"

"I made the Arrendons tell me about their mysterious correspondent. It wasn't so difficult to figure out it was you. Phoenix? Really?"

He winced. "I was sixteen when I picked it. And actually drunk that time. Did you…"

"Tell them? No. That's your decision. I would never take it from you."

His shoulders sagged in relief. "Thank you."

"You're welcome. Now go home."

He shook his head. "Don't ask me to leave you here. I won't do it and we'll fight. Recent experience has shown I don't like fighting with you."

She wanted to send him back anyway. Before he saw the worst this place had to offer. Before he saw the worst of her. But the Song did not trust her any more than she trusted it. And it wasn't sending Numair anywhere until it got what she'd promised it.

"This isn't going to be pretty," she warned him. "You won't like what you see."

"I see things I don't like every day."

"And what if you don't like me by the end?" *What if you see what made me, what I was, and you don't miss me anymore?* What if Renault County—if Simian—made her lose the first good thing she'd ever found?

"Look at me." He waited until she did. "In the last three hours I have seen things I never wanted to. I have been beaten and tortured, and the only reason nothing worse happened is because I was being saved for public spectacle. You knew what you risked coming here for me and you still came."

"It's not the same. You've barely scratched the surface of this place."

"Clare...I once told you that you'd barely scratched the surface of what *I* am. You've seen most of it now. And you've never looked at me any differently. There is nothing you can show me that will make me see you differently. We are literally sitting in a mass of people you've hypnotized. I haven't run away yet."

He's lying, the Song whispered. *He doesn't know he's lying, but he is. He wasn't there. He wasn't* here. *I was. No one could understand this. No one could accept this. But if you want him, I can give him to you.*

The Song plucked a single thread of power from the rest, offering it to her. It was a variation of what held the crowd in thrall around her, a thread that would twine around Numair, instilling trust and admiration and devotion. He would never look at her and be horrified. He would never want to leave her side again.

He wouldn't be able to.

She took that shining thread, felt the weight and balance of it, how seductively it was spun—and snapped it. *After all this time together, you still don't understand me if you think I could ever do that to him.*

Irritation laced the Song's response. *He would never know the difference.*

Perhaps not. But she would. And she didn't want a lie.

She realized she'd been quiet too long when Numair said, "Do you honestly want me to go? Do you truly want to be here, in all this, alone?"

"No."

"Then don't be. Let's finish this and go home."

Finish this. Yes, she needed to finish this. She needed to finally make the nightmares end. "All right."

They stood, and Numair eyed the people around them. "Are they...coming with us?"

"Yes." She sang and they shifted, forming a living, protective circle around her and Numair. "They're going to help me keep a promise."

CHAPTER

EIGHTY-THREE

MIN QUELLEA

lare's swarm grew as they walked, the Song's tendrils reaching out to ensnare any newcomer who dared walk out and touch the borders of her living barricade. Both she and Numair's destinations lay on the other side of the county. As they walked through it, she forced the horrors they passed to slide off her like water off well-oiled leather. Numair, after a few cautious glances, kept his gaze straight ahead, his lips compressed into a bloodless line, and didn't speak.

When the ground to the left of the dirt path they walked fell suddenly away, revealing a deep, yawning chasm half a mile wide and twice as deep, he broke his silence. "What is that?"

Clare spared a glance at the monstrous wound in the earth's flesh. The entirety of it was covered in thick white dust, as were the people who scurried about in its depths. They descended into tunnels punched into the pit's sides and climbed back up on cobbled rope ladders, laden down with bags of hard white stone, going about their duties with a mindless, broken focus.

"Those are the quellstone mines."

Numair stopped walking, forcing Clare to stop with him. "I thought quellstone was a myth."

"It is. Everywhere but here. I understand it's why Alaric never took this place." Simian had told her the story once. How Alaric had saved Renault County as the last conquest on his map. Because

Simian had never been interested in extending his own borders, and Alaric had thought it safe to let it wait.

But by the time the Jackal King had come, the borders of Renault County had been walled over with quellstone. It amplified Simian's power—and negated anyone else's. Alaric's magic couldn't pass beyond the border. If his soldiers went in, they became lost to the madness that infected everyone here. Simian's madness.

In a fit of rage, Alaric had Reaped the ground surrounding the county, turning it into a wasteland. Turning Renault County into an island that no one came to and no one left. Because no one crossed Reaped ground and survived.

"I thought the stone had to be claimed by a mage before it quelled another's magic."

Clare started walking again, Numair and the swarm falling in with her. "It does. All of that"—she pointed at the mines—"every chunk they carve out and bring up was claimed years ago."

"By who?"

"The self-appointed king of Renault County."

"You're telling me there is a man behind the madness in this place?"

"Isn't there always a man behind atrocities?"

"Who?"

Why did people always want a name, as if naming a person would somehow make them less terrible? "He is called Simian Hensa. And he is the sickness that plagues Renault County. As I understand it, long ago this was a place people came to live without magic. No mages were allowed in, and any born were killed or exiled.

"Simian was born here, but no one recognized what he was. Not until it was too late. He projects his emotions, his desires. People feel what he feels, becoming reflections of him. And once he found the quellstone, discovered what it could do, with no other mages to oppose him?"

She shook her head. It had been far too late, by that point. "The founders of Renault County misunderstood the stone, because of the name. They thought it quelled magic, period. But it amplifies the power of the mage who claims it. Only once claimed does it quell the magic of others."

Except hers. Just as possession of the Song alone caused Alaric's magic to slide past her, it had done the same with Simian's. It was the first thing about her that had fascinated him. And that was before he had learned that she could sing with her own power, and though it couldn't affect him, because the quellstone was his, he could pour what she made *into* what already belonged to him.

The sun had almost sunk below the horizon when Clare and her swarm came to a halt at the twenty-foot-high walls that held such an unpleasant place in her memory. They were as imposing as she remembered, pure white blocks formed from quellstone. And between them, a gate made of bone, with guards posted at the entrance.

"I had a choice," Clare said softly, as she drew the guards into her Song, "around the time I was fourteen. Death in the quellstone mines, or walking through these gates. I walked through."

As she did again, now. When Numair stepped forward with her, she hesitated. "You came this far. You don't have to come the rest of the way." *You don't have to see this. I don't want you to see this.*

He gave her a hard look. "Where you go, I go."

She turned and met his gaze, looking straight into night-black eyes. "I am not a good person. I am not a *forgiving* person. This will not be pleasant."

"I've never had much time for forgiveness. I've always found it damages too much the person it's asked of."

He was insane, this man. Or he was her mirror. Perhaps he was both. Perhaps *they* were both.

"Welcome to the Castle, then." Simian had named his stronghold to fit what he thought he was: a king.

A monster.

She was a monster too, she supposed, if only of a different breed.

Clare walked through the gates. She couldn't bring herself to allow them to close behind her. Instead, she left her swarm there, filling that break in bone and iron and quellstone, because the people could never hold her in. She took the gate guards with her, along with any others she met. Any of the Castle's ordinary workers who came within her radius fell into her thrall, and she sent them to join the rest of her swarm.

She and Numair walked the stone path through the vegetable garden, where half-starved skeletons dug at the hardened earth, planting seeds or pulling weeds, or stumbling along its surface with buckets of water pulled from Simian's well, their lips cracked and bleeding and their skin ashen with dehydration. Many were the people she had seen too hungry and thirsty to resist stealing a carrot from the ones they pulled, or a handful of water meant for roots. Many were the dead buried beneath Simian's bloodfruit trees in the back orchard, and many more were the screams that had been her macabre lullaby through endless nights.

The guards hauled open the wide, front doors of Simian's Castle, and Clare passed through them. Like the first time she had done so, it was like entering a different world. In the rest of Renault County, the ugliness was out in the open. Here, the twisted hid beneath a veneer of fine, decadent beauty.

Magelight sconces were set into the walls, patterned between elaborate tapestries. Plants, that most elusive of life in Renault County, draped tastefully over standing planters. Porcelain tile of a soft gold formed the floor of Simian's receiving room, all the way up the seven steps to the carved white throne that sat atop a layer of thick, white fur rugs.

Numair's gaze locked on the empty throne. "Is that made of..."

"Human bone," Clare finished for him. "Yes."

Numair looked warily to the guards. He clearly didn't like the idea of going any farther into the building. "Can you send them to search for him?"

"There's no need. He will come to us."

Clare led them through the door to her right, the guards following at her heels. The halls were as familiar as they were terror-inducing, panic and adrenaline flooding her body in waves. She locked both away from her, as she had done in order to survive her years in this place. That severed piece of her screamed and wailed in terror, while the rest of her remained cold and empty.

She climbed the stairs to the second floor, took the right wing to the room at the end of the hall.

Please let it be empty. Please let it be empty. Please let—

The door swung open at the brush of her fingertips. It was exactly as Clare remembered. The pale wood four-posted bed with the thin, gauzy white curtains, a bed she had never been allowed to sleep in. The wardrobe filled with court finery, each dress a thing impossible to get into or out of without help; the memory of rough hands on her day in and day out, dressed like a doll and posed like one. The corner of the room with the chains drilled into the wall, the circular drain set into the floor. Fire arced across the scars on her back and she swallowed hard, stifling her reaction.

The girl lay propped in the corner. Blood ran down her legs, dripping steadily to the floor, flowing to the drain. Her head lolled to the side against one wall. With the fall of dark hair obscuring her face, she might have been Clare's double. She was the right height, the right size.

How many dark-haired girls had been buried in Simian's orchard since Clare left?

The dress the girl wore was one Clare had worn often enough, gold brocade with tight, fitted sleeves and a plunging neckline. Dark red stained the bodice until it wasn't gold anymore, so much that Clare thought the only reason the girl was still alive was because the tight lacing of the dress was compressing her wounds, slowing the bleeding.

Simian hated ruining things. People, he didn't mind ruining, but his things? He must have been truly angry to damage the girl with the dress still on her. His anger was like the ocean, a massive reservoir of endless potential. Rarely ever was it completely calm, and even when it was, ripples broke the surface at random, could grow into tidal waves without warning.

The girl's head turned, and the fall of hair fell away, revealing a bleeding, broken mass where the left side of her face had once been. The cheekbone was caved in, the white of bone visible through the skin and the blood that was going tacky, and the left eye…

"You're her." The girl slurred the words like a benediction. "The one he lost."

It had taken years of planning to break out of Simian's Castle. Years, and the only place she had had to escape to was the rest of Renault County. It had only taken Simian's men two months to find her, and as bad as the rest of Renault County was, it was the idea of going back to the Castle that had sent Clare into the madness she'd spent the next two years in. Because that in-between place, where nothing touched her and lived, had been the only way to survive the trek out, across Alaric's reaped ground, without fully surrendering to the Song.

"Please." The girl lunged at her wildly. The movement should have been impossible for someone in her condition, but the hazy sheen in her remaining eye spoke of the liberal dose of Glaze Simian must have shoved down her throat. He would have wanted her awake—awake to feel everything he did to her, and awake after to reflect on it.

The girl's hands closed around Clare's ankle. Her good eye looked out from the ruin of her face.

"Please kill me."

Clare didn't need to contemplate her answer. As she crouched, the girl relaxed, her hands sliding off Clare's ankle.

"Thank you." She died with a smile on the working half of her face as Clare's knife slid into her throat, piercing the artery, the remaining burden of her blood swirling quickly down the drain.

Where did the drain go? Was the girl's blood even now mixing with Clare's own deep below? With the blood of all the other girls who had come before and after her?

Numair gently extracted the knife from her hand, and only then did she realize the hand was shaking so badly she'd almost sliced her own thigh.

"It was a mercy," Numair said softly. "She would never have lived."

Clare didn't tell him what she knew and he did not. That the Song could have fixed her body—that it even might have, if she had asked it to, had been willing to pay whatever price it demanded—but it could never have fixed the girl's mind.

Sometimes people broke, and they could never go back together again.

Had she put herself back together, or was she still broken? She didn't know.

Numair wiped the knife blade clean and offered it to her. She took it, sliding it back into its sheath, and crossed the room to the door at the opposite side. The adjoining room was a mirror to Simian's receiving room downstairs, all gold tile and tones, expensive rugs and magelight sconces. No throne occupied this room, and for that Clare had been grateful. She had enough memories of the things he had made her do on the one downstairs.

In appearances, this room actually looked like an ordinary music room, instruments sitting in stands, gleaming. Guitar. Violin. Harp. Flute. Lyre. They lined the edges of the room, and in the center sat the piano.

This room, more than anything else, was the reason Simian had chosen her. For her hands, picking at the battered strings of a guitar. For her voice, foolishly singing somewhere she'd thought no one would hear.

"Stand there." Clare pointed Numair to a place where he wouldn't immediately be noticed by anyone entering the room. "And don't interfere. He is mine to deal with."

"If you need help…" He trailed off, gaze going to the brutish guards standing passively in her wake, shook his head, and went to stand in the shadows near the lyre.

She sat at the piano, settled her fingers into position, and played.

This room was the only thing she had never fought Simian on. He could twist everything else in her life, but she could not allow him to twist what she was, and *music* was what she was at her core. Her music was not always pretty, and it was never innocent, but it was her. So she did not fight him here because this room was the only reason she had survived him for five years.

For all he had no interest in leaving Renault County, Simian wanted to believe himself a king equal to Alaric. Better than Alaric. For that, he had an obsession with having a queen. Once Clare had arrived, she became that obsession to him.

So she wore the dated court clothes that had arrived before Renault County had become inaccessible by traditional means. She learned the lessons taught by one of Alaric's cast-off courtiers that had arrived even earlier. A man who well knew that the only thing keeping him from the true horrors of Renault County was his usefulness to Simian, and that usefulness lay in making Clare into a lady. It also lay in Clare never getting it quite right, though, because if Clare was ever perfect, then there would be no need for him anymore.

Young as she had been when she first came to the Castle, it had taken her some time to figure that part out—that she could never be perfect enough to escape punishment. Not from her tutor, because he needed her imperfection. Not from Simian, because he simply enjoyed punishment.

This room was the only time she could ever escape them. It had not taken her long to take what she knew of the guitar and apply it to the other instruments in the room. In that first year, Simian had brought her anyone he could flush out of Renault County who had musical ability—remnants from before the county was closed off—and Clare had taken the basics they had been able to give her and moved far beyond them.

This was the one arena where no one could try to justify their continued presence by claiming she had not learned well enough. Because when Clare played, when she sang, even the monsters in the room fell silent. She was not always allowed to come here, was not always allowed to sing. But when she was, sometimes, if she played until her fingers ached on the keys or bled on the strings, until her voice was nearly gone, *sometimes* then, Simian was so enthralled that for a few days he forgot to be sadistic.

Sometimes he would even let her sleep on the floor of the room that was supposedly hers, instead of shoving her back into rags and sending her down to the cellar room with the iron bars and the rats, and the insects always scritching, scratching, scrabbling.

Her fingers trembled on the keys and she turned it into a trill, twisting the notes, the rhythm, to meet her demands.

She knew the moment he entered the room. His presence was a dark, oily film spreading through the air, settling onto her skin, clogging her pores. She wanted to spit out the taste of him, to expel all the air from her lungs and rid herself of his scent, his taint.

The final notes of the song echoed in the air. Simian exhaled in ecstasy as Clare's hands slid from the keys to fold in her lap, her head demurely bowed.

"Min quellea." Anyone unfamiliar with him might be forgiven for thinking the words a lover's endearment. They meant *my queen,* in the language of Simian's people, but it was a slippery language, and *quellea* was a word that had a trifold meaning: queen, slave, torment.

She had been the first two, in Simian's mind. Today she would be the third.

"You came back." He spoke the words both as if he couldn't believe them and as if their truth had always been a foregone conclusion.

"Yes." She stood, graceful, sliding the piano bench back without making a sound. "I came back. I made you a promise the day I left." She turned, taking in the sight of him. The last two years had not been kind. The blond hair was shot through with gray, the yellow eyes sunken into the sockets, the hollows below them deep and prominent, as if he hadn't eaten, hadn't slept, much since she left.

She hoped he hadn't. She hoped his obsession was such that he had been locked in endless unrest.

Her gaze took in the perfectly tailored shirt and trousers that couldn't hide the weight he had lost, traveled to rest on the white gloves covering his hands. The remembered feel of them on her skin made her gag, but it was when he took them off that things became worse.

"Do you remember what that promise was?" she asked him.

His gaze roved over her, his tongue licking out to wet his lips. "You made a mistake. You'll be punished, of course, but it's nothing that can't be forgiven."

"I promised you that I would make you feel everything you had ever done to me, and that I would only grant you death when you begged me for it."

Simian's eyes turned hard, that mix of anger and erotic stirring that always preceded some of his most imaginative horrors.

"Take her to her room," he ordered the guards. "Throw the other girl out."

Simian waited. No one moved.

Clare smiled. "They don't belong to you anymore. They belong to me." Her eyes rose to the guards. "Seal the room. He doesn't leave."

Two of them closed the wide double-doors at Simian's back.

"I didn't expect this day to come so soon," she said, walking toward him in that slow, bored manner he had so often approached her with. "I thought it would take years, decades, before I had any chance of coming back here in a position to keep that promise. But fate is an unpredictable thing, and I find I am glad to be here now."

Simian watched her approach, his gaze flickering briefly to the guards, then back to her.

"I don't know what you've promised them, but don't think this will end well for you. You may hold them, but I hold the county." He wasn't worried. No, he was *excited*. Because everything was a game to Simian, and since he believed he held the upper hand, this game promised to be fun. Interesting. That was why he had said he would keep her forever, wasn't it? Because she always made things *interesting*.

"Just when I think I have you broken, you cobble yourself back together

on me, and I get to break you all over again. That's what I love about you, min quellea. How repairable you are."

Always she had been *min quellea* to him. Her mother never named her, and no one else had seen fit to either, Simian included. He liked her that way, a nameless slate he could write himself onto. But she had named herself. Clare Brighton, a name that meant so much more because she had chosen it for herself and hidden it away in the deepest recesses of her heart. She had never shared it with anyone in this place because if she never shared it, it could never be taken away from her.

Alone at night, in the darkness of the prison cellar with the rats and the bugs crawling around her, she could take that name out and hold it, and imagine what it would be like to be Clare Brighton. During the day she could chant the name in her mind, and tell herself the unspeakable things being done to her were not really being done to *her*, because Clare Brighton was who she truly was, and Clare Brighton was not yet alive.

No, Clare Brighton had finally been born when she'd met two lords on the outskirts of the Valedon Swamps, and their light had drawn her back from the madness. She'd had a choice to make, then, on who she would be. Who she would become. And now that Clare Brighton was alive, she was never going to be hidden away again.

Clare stopped within touching distance of Simian, and the Song rumbled in her chest, as eager as she. It had lived through him with her, after all, and Clare considered for the first time what her years here must have been like for the Song, feeling everything she felt and yet unable to do anything. Trapped, as she had been trapped. Was she as bad as Simian, locking it away in a cage and only letting it out when it was useful to her?

Even as she thought it, she knew there was a difference. She had had no choice in the Song's being a part of her, and she knew that if she let it out, let it free, there would be no more Clare Brighton. There would only be the Song. She was not willing to die. For the Song to be free and she to live, it would have to view her as an equal.

We are not equal, Clare. The Song's voice was not unkind.

You believe we are not, and so we fight. But we are of the same mind right now, are we not? The Song had lived this hell with her. The Song hated Simian as much as she did. In this experience, in this vengeance, they were united.

We are, the Song agreed. And when Clare stepped forward, reaching out her hand to Simian's cheek and smiling, the Song smiled with her.

Simian Hensa's face went bloodless. Clare's fingertips touched his skin, and the Song's power flowed from her.

"Live, Simian. Live everything you have done to me, and when you cannot stand it any longer, beg Clare Brighton for release."

She had never heard Simian scream before. Screaming was not, in general, a sound that she liked. But she found she enjoyed his screams very much. As justice played out before her, she settled onto the piano bench and bore witness to his torment.

Min quellea.

Be careful what you have named a person, she thought, *for they may one day become it.*

He started begging when he had barely lived half a year of her time. For a man who enjoyed inflicting pain, he was startlingly incapable of bearing any himself. When he tried crawling to her, the Song brought up a wall, invisible but solid, keeping him back.

Numair left his place by the lyre and came to stand next to the piano bench. She didn't know what she saw in his face, couldn't name the emotions hovering just beneath the court mask of Numair Tolvannen. But she knew what she didn't see: Disgust. Pity. Fear.

She slid to the edge of the bench and Numair sat beside her. When he laid his hand between them, palm up in offering, she placed her own into it. And when Simian's screams finally subsided into sobs, when her promise was kept, when he stopped calling her *min quellea* and remembered her name, she was holding Numair's hand when she granted Simian the death he begged for.

CHAPTER

EIGHTY-FOUR

A PROMISE OF DESTRUCTION

S iren's cliff lay on the north-eastern end of Renault County, accessible only by a near-vertical climb two hundred feet up to the brink. The ascent had killed plenty of people over the years Clare had lived in this place, so much so that it was colloquially known as Suicide Cliff. People only climbed it if they wanted the kindest death Renault County could offer, and so they didn't mind if that death came from falling on the climb up, or casting themselves off to the sea on the other side.

Clare had made the climb more than once, and she found she remembered the best way up easily enough, feet and hands finding carefully chosen protrusions. She had first been called to it not longer after her mother died, and she had been looking for a place to hide. A brutal storm had swept through, and the resultant rain and winds had woken the siren stones above, their haunting sounds driving Clare to climb in order to discover what made them.

She crested the brink, Numair scrambling up behind her. The clifftop was long and narrow, ending on the eastern side from where they had come up in a hollow at the base of an overhang. The hollow, the overhang, and its base for twenty feet in all directions, was pure glittering siren's rock, broken only in one place where a tree had been dying for as long as Clare had known it.

Though siren rock was named for the man who had died here, it occurred naturally enough in other parts of the world, and Clare might even have believed this deposit was natural, that the legend of the siren's death was exaggerated, had she not heard their haunting cries as the rain swept over them. Had she not curled into the hollow as a child and dreamed his death as she slept. Had she not seen what lay on the other side.

She crossed the narrow width of the clifftop and looked down at the broken skeletons of ships, piled atop the rocky shore and rammed into one another. They were worn now with age and torn apart from the ceaseless battering of the ocean waves, but they were there, standing sentinel for all who might come after them, giving silent testimony to man's capacity for inhumanity to their fellow man.

She let Numair take in the sight, lulled into a state of near-trance by the hypnotic calm of the ocean, and went to the Siren's hollow. There, on a small ledge a foot up, where she had tucked her head as a child and stared at its beauty, Clare plucked the Siren's Tear free of the rocks that held it. They broke from it gently enough, as if simply waiting all this time to set it free.

"Numair."

He jumped, shook his head ruefully and turned from the grave-yard of ships, arching one brow at her.

"How did you hear of this?" She cradled the Tear in her cupped hands, its power curling against her. So much power, born of death.

"It was something my uncle said when I was younger. That he had once put something he wanted forever out of his reach. The only thing Alaric wants is power. I didn't put it together until..."

Until she sang the siren's song at The Musicale House. How foolish of her, to have brought him here. To have brought herself here.

She tucked the stone into her pocket and returned to the cliff.

"We don't need to climb back," he said, pulling the gatestone from his pocket. She turned and placed the Siren's Tear in his hand, closing his fingers around it.

"*You* don't need to climb back. Take this and go."

"I'm not leaving you here."

"I made a bargain to come here. I have a price to pay, and I can't delay it much longer." The Song kept building and building inside her, testing the limits of that wider channel she'd made from its prison.

"I'm not leaving."

Foolish, stubborn man. She started climbing, the Song's pressure growing stronger with each handhold, until they reached the top once more and it threatened to bleed out of her eyes.

She didn't have time to tell him, again, to leave. Not with the impatient, churning violence inside her. She managed a single word, and it was barely her voice at all, the Song's overlaying it.

"Run."

She stood atop the cliff, looking over the wretched sinkhole of Renault County, her eyes blazing with a fury, a presence that was not wholly her own, and yet was in its entirety.

She opened her mouth and a promise of destruction poured out.

LOOKING AT CLARE, feeling the power emanating from her, Numair did not doubt that she was right.

He *should* run.

Dust stirred at her feet, the ground far beneath them rumbling and groaning as the air grew thick and magic-charged. A great fissure split the ground at the cliff-base, cracking the earth through Renault County all the way to the heart of the quellstone mine. It spiraled out from that white heart, carrying quellstone dust with it, snaking white-dusted wounds in ever-widening concentric circles until the faults in the earth encompassed the entire county.

He watched the figures of the guards, small as ants from this vantage point, this distance, flee in terror, only to fall into the ravine that opened to swallow their escape. The inhabitants of the county, released from Clare's thrall, scurried about like cockroaches. Some simply ran, panicked, in the first direction they found. That, Numair could understand. What he couldn't—didn't—understand were the ones given over to a spree of butchering, as if they knew their world was ending, and all they desired was to commit one or two more injustices before they were finished.

The earth stilled, and for a moment, it was quiet. But it was the kind of quiet that heralded the coming of a greater noise, a greater work.

He should run. But running from her was beyond him.

He stepped to her right, leaving a couple feet of distance

between them. Close enough to offer support, to bear witness, but not close enough to get in her way. Not close enough to be seen, by the thing giving its power to this act, as a threat.

Clare's eyes were opened wide and they held a sheen of rapture, whether hers or its he didn't know. But when she spoke, her own voice was a bare thread beneath the other's, the cadence of speech bearing no similarity to Clare's.

"Did you know, Prince Tolvannen, that it takes heat one thousand times hotter than that of mages' fire to set quellstone alight?"

Numair did not answer, as the thing clearly did not wish a reply.

"Once burning, no water, no smothering, can quench its flames, and it is a long-lasting fuel source." Clare's lips pulled back into a grim baring of teeth. Her arms bent at the elbows, hands lifting from her sides, palms up. "Renault County is going to burn for one-thousand and twenty-seven years. And I am going to savor every one of them."

Clare's hands began to rotate, moving around each other as if she wound a massive, invisible spindle. The concentric faults in the earth began to rotate around each other in mimicry, until the whole of the ground beneath the cliff was one giant mass of shifting, spinning ground coated in white dust. Then heat blossomed in the air and fire burst into life, the flames so high the ones nearest licked upwards a foot from the clifftop, turning Renault County into a sea of writhing flame.

Numair knew that as long as he lived, he would never forget the screams that issued forth from that ocean of fire, nor the look of sleepy pleasure from the thing inside Clare before the air around her whipped into a frenzy and flung him away.

***

CLARE HAD MADE A MISTAKE. In striking her deal with the Song, she had been forced to allow it more egress from its prison, and the once-thin path from that cage was now a wide channel down which the Song's power rampaged.

It had helped her get Numair out, and in return she had given it the death of Renault County. They had each given the other what they'd promised, but in the doing she had lost much of the Song's prison, much of her control, and nearly two decades of pent-up power and frustration now raged against her.

The winds howled and her feet left the ground, her body buoyed up by the incandescent fury of the entity within. She contained it by sheer force of will, the clash between her own desires and the Song's creating the contest that bent the air around them.

Give. Up. Her voice, a silent growl inside her own mind, pushed against the flood of power streaming from the Song's prison.

You do not even understand what I want, the Song answered, sounding faintly amused. But beneath that amusement, Clare detected a hint of strain.

I know that you would use me to do it. This is my *body.* And she was tired—so, so tired—of having it violated. An image of Simian rose unbidden in her mind.

The Song recoiled and Clare pounced on the opening, holding the exodus of power in check.

You would compare me to him? Me?

He may have raped my body but he could not rape my soul. You violate me just by being here. You know what I think, what I feel. And whenever it is convenient for you, you seek to use me for your own ends.

And do you *not seek to use* me *for yours?*

Maybe I have. But I have only sought to use what was forced upon me. I had no choice in your presence. But you chose me. You chose to be born into me. She knew it for the truth, felt it deep within her bones.

Yes, I chose you. Shall I show you where your life ended had I not *chosen you?*

Her vision clouded over with memory, the Song taking her back to a moment that was, objectively, not the worst in her life, but that felt as if it was because she had lost, then, the last shred of illusion that she had control.

Closing her eyes did not staunch the assault on her vision, her senses. She saw and felt everything as markedly as the night it had happened. The dimly lit hovel surrounded by the smell of musty rags. The rough, oily hands pawing at her, the warm press of flesh and the sick-sweet smell of rotting breath pouring over her nose.

Her small hands fumbling for the bone shard kept always beneath the pile of rags she slept on because she had known, instinctively, that the way he looked at her was dangerous. Wrong.

She whipped the shard out, sinking it into his eye with a frightened yell. His cry of pain mingled with her mother's howl of rage, and the memory was twice as painful re-lived because she knew how foolish the relief in her younger self's mind was. Relief that her useless, drunken mother was coming to help her.

But her mother, when she leapt, did not leap on the man but on Clare, knocking the bone shard from her hand, bony fists slamming into her face again and again and again.

"Stupid bitch." She howled, the blows landing one after another, frequent as raindrops in the wet season. "All you had to do was lie there."

It went on until Clare's vision blurred and she saw, through the Song's eyes, the moment she would have died had its power not snapped out of her and crushed first her mother's throat and then the man's. Had it not closed over Clare's wounds and taken the pain.

Standing whole in the falling down hovel that was her childhood home, staring at the dead who would have killed her, seven-year-old Clare had built the Song's prison. Had she been in the habit of lying to herself, she would have said she built it because she was horrified by what the Song had done.

But she had built it because she'd reveled in it. In the power and freedom and lack of fear, and she had felt just enough of its penchant for destruction to know that if she let it run free, it would burn the world down.

Not burn it, the Song whispered to her now. *Unmake it.*

She felt the storm inside her once more, what it had been whispering in her mind since her childhood. A ceaseless, endless song of destruction.

Clare roared her fury at the Song. *I did not survive Renault County, survive Simian, simply to be unmade. For it all to mean nothing.*

That is…not how I see it. The world I made has become unkind. It is time to wash away that unkindness. That hurt.

If you can wash it all away, why not fix it?

Because I cannot.

NUMAIR SCRABBLED FOR PURCHASE, finding it just as the wind knocked him over the cliff, his hands grabbing onto rough rock that sliced into his palms, slicking his hold with blood. He heaved himself back onto the clifftop and grasped another rock, pulling himself forward while the winds buffeted and tore at him.

Twenty feet ahead Clare hovered, her feet six feet off the ground, arms held out by her sides, her face an incongruous mixture of serenity and rage. For a moment both emotions flickered and the winds lessened. He gained his feet, sprinting for her even as the momentary lull eased and the winds renewed, their efforts redoubled for the brief respite they had taken.

His magic cast out, searching for anything living to come to his aid. It found answer in the gnarled shell of a tree atop the cliff, its branches sweeping to catch him behind the back and send him hurtling into the calm of Clare Brighton's storm.

———

You mean you will not, Clare accused.

A parent cannot intercede every time their child makes a mistake, else the child has no life of its own. Should the child become a monster outside of control, the parent must accept that they have failed, and destroy the atrocity they have made.

And I am the atrocity in this story? Verol? Quin? Numair?

No. Not everything made has turned rotten. But that which has outweighs that which has not.

So we suffer twice? We live through their horrors and we have our perseverance brought to nothing so we can pay for their deaths with our lives?

Try not to think of it as death. You will return to what you were before. What you all were before.

It hit Clare, then, why part of the world was destroyed every time the Song was born into a person. *Part of you.*

Yes.

Why? Why now?

I was…lonely when I cut off a piece of myself to make this world. The power its creation, its sustainment, took from me meant that I could not take part in it. So I slept, and I was content to watch in my dreams that which I had made.

Images filled Clare's mind of a world she understood must be this one, and yet it teemed with more life than she could ever have imagined. A great beast roamed the skies, its scales iridescent silver in the sun, massive wings spread wide. A chimera creature flitted next to it and the two spiraled down toward the ground, nipping and chasing in play.

They landed next to a horse with a horn sprouting from its forehead, standing at the side of a great fall of water several hundred feet high. The city built into the cliffs beside that fall took Clare's breath away. Hanging gardens cascaded from rocks and cracks in the cliffside, and nestled between them were thatched outcroppings teeming with the cheerful bustle of contented people. They moved between dwellings via rocky outcroppings or long, looped rope ladders.

Birds darted this way and that, and it was all so idyllic that it did not seem to Clare like a real place at all, but simply someone's idea of a perfect place.

Halzhenna, the Song whispered, *the first city of humankind. This is what I hoped for, when I tore myself apart to make this world. And it was beautiful, for a time.*

Halzhenna faded, replaced by a place Clare only knew because the Song knew it. Aidenmarra, the city where the slave trade first came to life.

I gave so much of myself to make this world that to walk wakefully in it, I must take something back. When I dreamed of what was happening in Aidenmarra, I took the city back, and I walked this world through Ilara's eyes. She was the first to bear me in this world and she bore only a fraction of the power I hold in you. We destroyed the slave trade, and when she died, I gave back what I had taken, returning to sleep, confident that I had fixed what had gone wrong. That all would be well again.

But Clare saw that it was not. Before her eyes the eons flashed by, revealing a litany of humanity's penchant for cruelty. Slavery returned, this time in Densara. The caste system grew in Maharan. War upon war shed rivers of blood and all that she saw covered only the global scale of humanity's depravity. It did not cover the everyday lies and abuses, rapes and murders, thefts and starvation.

Over and over the Song came into the world, correcting errors, then disappearing. But always, always, the corruption returned.

I could not fix it, the Song whispered sadly, the images fading.

Clare laughed. The sound never left her lips, only reverberated inside her, for the Song's ears alone.

Of course you could not fix it. You do not even see why, do you?

The Song was silent for a brief time, in which the winds around Clare almost completely died.

Are you telling me that you *do?*

It would seem, she told it, *that even you have something to learn.*

As if to prove her right, it howled, and the winds howled with it. Clare was amused enough in that moment that she might have shattered its prison and let it reclaim the world, just so it could spend a few eons of loneliness pondering why the world it created was part good, part bad, until lack of an answer drove it to recreate Clare just so she could tell it the answer.

But something fell to the ground below her, and she opened her eyes.

Numair.

She snapped the Song's power back, shoving it into its cage as if it were water poured through a funnel. Pain split her skull as it fought her, but she had rattled it with her laughter, and she held on through the pain, through the blood that poured down her nose and out the corners of her eyes, until she slammed shut the doors of the Song's prison.

With its departure she fell abruptly out of the air, landing awkwardly and collapsing onto all fours beside Numair. He didn't speak, only found the gatestone and took them home.

EIGHTY-FIVE

STAY WITH ME

They returned, not to the library but to Numair's bedchamber. She stood in the center of the room with her fists clenched, waiting for…what?

Judgment, she finally realized. He'd walked with her through Renault County, he'd sat with her through Simian's death, and he'd stood with her on the cliff and watched her past burn, but she was still waiting for judgment. Waiting for him to realize, now that they were back here, that he shouldn't have done any of those things.

His eyes searched her face. "Are you hurt?"

"I should be asking you that."

"I think, of the two of us, you had the harder time." He gave her a shaky smile. "I really don't like that thing inside of you."

She barked out a laugh. "It doesn't much care for you, either."

"Why?"

"Because I do." The words fell heavily between them, a truth she'd never voiced. Given the tortured look he was giving her now, she wished she hadn't. But the words had just fallen out, and it wasn't as if he didn't already know. It wasn't as if she expected him to return the sentiment. But maybe he thought that was why she'd said it?

She scowled. This—everything—was confusing. Her gaze caught on his palms—scraped and torn—and she was grateful to have an excuse to change the direction of the conversation. "Give me your hands, you're bleeding everywhere."

He lifted them. "You don't have to—"

But she already was, taking his hands in hers, the Song reluctantly doing as she bid it. She used the cuff of her sleeve to wipe away the blood, verifying that his skin was once more whole beneath it. Her own skin was likewise bloodstained. It wasn't her own, or his, but that of the person she'd killed almost as soon as she'd arrived in Renault County.

Something like regret washed over her and she felt unclean in a way that had nothing to do with dried blood or dirt, but she wanted both off her. "Can I use your washroom?" she asked abruptly.

"Of course. Are you…" He trailed off, and she was glad of it.

Because no, she was not okay, and she didn't want to lie to him but she didn't want to talk about it either. She dropped his hands and escaped to the washroom, shutting the door. This space, like Numair's room, was a reflection of him. Black and gray stone tiles covered the floor and walls, brightened by plants that dripped from hanging pots and wall planters so it looked more like a jungle oasis than a washroom.

The tub sunk into the center was the size of a small pool, and she turned on all four of its taps. While it was filling she went to the sink, rinsing her mouth. First with water, then with a mouthful of the peppermint-heavy healer's rinse from the jar on the vanity table. Only once the ashen film in her mouth was gone did she gulp down handfuls of cold water, soothing a throat that was rough from the power that had expressed itself through her voice. In the vanity mirror her eyes stared back at her, the weight of the Song flashing behind the green depths, bloody tear tracks down her face.

She turned away from her reflection and went to the tub, stripping out of her clothing and sinking into the scalding depths. It was a too-familiar process, scrubbing her skin clean of blood. She wondered if she should feel remorse—not for Simian, but for the girl in her old room, and the nameless person in the market square, both dead by her own hand. For the thousands of nameless others consumed by the licking flames of the Song's rage.

And to some degree, she did. Simian was what had made Renault County its worst, and she had destroyed him. Who was to say that without him, its denizens couldn't have made something better of themselves?

They could never have returned from the mire in which they were sunk, the Song said with certainty. *They never do.*

She could argue with it, but what would she say? She was not a creature of hope, not a creature who believed in humankind's better nature. She did not honestly believe that Renault County would have improved, if left to its own devices. But she would not have chosen to destroy them all on the basis of that belief. Choosing how they ended, deciding that they weren't capable of improvement, it made her feel like... like Alaric. So smugly confident that he knew what was best for everyone else.

But it didn't matter what she *would* have chosen. Because though it had been the Song that burned her birthplace, it had been her choice to let it happen. Her choice, to trade the lives of everyone there for Numair's. And she would make it again. If that made her a terrible person, then she could live with that. Because he was still here, and right or wrong, there was nothing she wouldn't do to ensure that he was *always* here.

Even if that meant she never stopped seeing the blood on her skin every time she closed her eyes.

She climbed out of the tub and dried off, but she couldn't bring herself to put her old clothes on. They smelled of smoke and death and she didn't want to crawl back into them. She spied one of Numair's shirts, thrown over the back of the vanity chair, and shrugged into it instead. The hem hit midway down her thighs, and she had to roll the sleeves up twice so they didn't cover her hands, but it smelled faintly of him, and being wrapped in his scent eased her tension.

The bedroom was empty when she stepped out of the wash-room. She bit her lip, wondering if he would care if she rummaged through his dresser in search of pants. She was still debating whether it would be an invasion of his privacy when he walked in. He had on different clothes and his hair was damp, so presumably he'd gone to clean up in one of the half-a-dozen other washrooms the house likely boasted.

He stopped short just inside the doorway and sucked in a breath, his eyes raking over her before snapping back to her face. "That's— are you wearing my shirt?"

Heat flooded her cheeks. "My clothes were dirty."

"Of course." His voice sounded strained and a muscle ticked along his jaw.

She crossed her arms defensively over her chest. "I didn't think you'd mind." He had dozens of shirts, what was this one to him? But he certainly *looked* as if he minded, his hands clenched and his eyes hot with—*oh.* That wasn't anger in his gaze.

She squeezed her eyes shut. She hadn't meant... "I'll put mine back on."

"Don't," he said roughly. She opened her eyes to find his were softer now, his body less tense. He exhaled heavily and gave her a rueful smile. "I'm sure you feel like burning yours."

"I might have considered it, but you were all out of matches."

He didn't laugh, but then it wasn't much of a joke. He reached into his pocket and withdrew a small cloth bag. She could make out the shape of the Siren's Tear within it, the magic sewn into the bag masking the stone's power. He offered it to her. "Here. You should take it to Verol and Marquin. I wanted it for them—for you." He swallowed. "For...us."

She stared at it, trepidation a hollow in her gut. "If I take it, are you going to disappear on me again?"

Shadows fell across his eyes and he dropped the bag onto the dresser, his shoulders slumping. "I don't know."

She clutched her arms tighter to her stomach, her fingers digging into her ribs. "How can you not know?"

He dragged a hand through his hair, looking more tired in that moment than she'd ever seen him. "There are things I need to tell you. Things I don't know how to tell you and don't want to, and I... can't tonight. Not after everything."

She understood. Or thought she did. But her patience had limits. She closed the space between them, until she had to tilt her head to look up at him. "When can you?"

He was silent for a time, and she gave him the space to weigh his answer, because she knew that if she did, the one he gave her would be the truth. "In the morning," he said finally.

"Promise?"

The corner of his mouth quirked up. "If you stay, you can hold me to it."

"Do you want me to?" After weeks of him ignoring her, she

needed to hear him say it. Needed the reassurance, even as she hated how that need felt like vulnerability.

"I always want you to." He lifted his hand, gave her time to refuse before he brushed her hair back and said, softly, "Stay with me."

"Okay."

She pushed onto her tiptoes, bringing their faces level, needing something more and not knowing how to ask. But she must have asked it by the way her gaze fell to his mouth, because all he said was, "Yes."

So she kissed him. Their lips met, somewhere in between the shadow of their first kiss and the violence of their second. Somewhere that might be halfway close to normal. And she marveled at the way she could close her eyes and not feel the darkness. The way the gentleness of his mouth moving against hers could blot out the pain that had so recently been dredged up again. The way the slide of his tongue against hers could stir an ache inside her she'd never expected to feel.

Her hands tangled in the fine silk of his hair and his slid around her waist, drawing her closer. She wanted him to keep touching her and never stop. And it scared her, because she wanted everything, and she didn't. She drew back, her breathing shallow and rapid. "I don't know that I want— I don't think I can—" She couldn't finish either sentence, didn't know how to explain. But she didn't need to. She never needed to with him.

Because while her own want was mirrored in his eyes, the thing that held her back was there in them, too. "I know," he said softly. "I can't either. Not yet." He pressed the lightest of kisses to the tip of her nose. "But I also don't want to let you go."

Her heart beat heavy in her chest. "Then don't."

He led her to the bed, drew her down until they lay face to face, his arm sliding once more around her waist to draw her close. It was awkward at first, until she found the way she fit against him, the place where her head fit in the crook of his shoulder. He smelled like he always did—like his magic—of earth and flowers and the unique sweetness of horses. He was warm and solid, and every part of her relaxed against him.

She didn't mean to fall asleep.

CHAPTER

EIGHTY-SIX

DON'T TELL ME WHAT I CARE ABOUT IS
CHEAP

She woke in Numair's arms, not because of the sunlight streaming in through the glass balcony doors, but because something was different. Wrong.

He woke with her, his eyes opening into hers, a question in them. And then she heard the footsteps down the hall and realized that what had woken her was the Song's abrupt withdrawal to its prison.

"Alaric," she whispered. Why hadn't she stopped to think that as soon as news of Renault County reached his ears, he would return to Veralna? And that he'd been gone so short a time that his return would take none at all?

Magic tore from Numair. The vines on the wall surged with new growth, reaching for her, pulling her flat against the wall, covering her mouth. Another vine grabbed the bag with the Siren's Tear and placed it in her hands before the rest grew completely over her. She couldn't move or blink, so tightly and thickly were they woven around her, binding her to the wall and hiding her from view. Her only sight came from the tiniest slit between vines in front of her left eye.

Numair vaulted out of the bed, hastily throwing the covers over the pillows to hide the indentation of her head in the pillow next to his. She watched his anxious energy melt into an air of casual, bored indifference. He began lazily unbuttoning his shirt, as if he'd been out all night and only just returned home. He was two buttons down when the door to the outer suite exploded inward with a cracking of wood, and the Song recoiled within her as Alaric Tolvannen strode into his nephew's room.

He appeared calm, for all that he'd just shattered a door as if in a fit of pique, and Numair was mirroring that calm. Alaric's gaze roved over the room before settling on him. "Where is she?"

Numair lifted one eyebrow, as if unaware of the fury that lurked beneath the king's facade. "I am afraid you'll have to be more specific. There are so many they tend to all run together."

"You know precisely to whom I am referring. And think very carefully before you tell me she isn't here. That bloody mare is in the paddock."

Numair shrugged. "Marquin dropped the horse by yesterday. Something about Clare going out of town. Per her lease agreement, Kialla stays in my stables if she leaves Veralna. The horse is worth too much to be treated like a pack animal."

Alaric did not speak. He simply advanced until his nose was an inch from Numair's, threat and magic coalescing in the air around him.

Numair's eyebrow lifted impossibly higher. "Very well, then. If you are so convinced she is here, perhaps I hid her in the wardrobe."

The wardrobe exploded outward, slivers of black wood sinking into various walls. The greenery deflected most of them from Clare, but two made it through. One thudded into the wall a hairsbreadth from her left eye. The other buried itself in her shoulder. She could not move to inspect it even had she dared, but she did not *think* it had hit anything vital. Its continued presence in her shoulder meant it would not bleed more than the vines could obscure.

The Song trembled from its hiding place far, far within her, its terror trying to leach out into her.

Take hold of yourself, Clare snapped. *Or are you so afraid of what you have made?*

The Song did not answer. It did stop trembling.

Numair looked about the room as the dust settled, his gaze intent. "Not in the wardrobe? Perhaps she is under the bed."

The bed flew across the room, breaking against the opposite wall.

Numair snapped his fingers. "I must have tossed her in the cedar chest, then."

The chest levitated into the air, flipped over and dumped its contents.

"Or perhaps," Numair continued, his voice calm, cold steel, "she is not here."

Alaric ignored this. The room continued to tear apart beneath his fury, every drawer and door opening, every item in the room shifting its locale, the plants the only things he did not deem worth searching.

Only once the entire room lay in splinters did Alaric's magic turn directly on Numair, pulling him to him, the king's fist wrapping around Numair's throat. "I gave you the opportunity to make this easy on yourself. On both of you. You could have had everything you wanted."

"I told you. I don't want her."

"You can't hide the way you look at her, boy. She could have been your last. I would have let you quit all the others, for her." His fist squeezed. "Would it have been such a burden to make her love you? To fuck her until she'd do anything for you? Until she'd tell you every secret rattling around in that pretty head?"

Numair's voice came out strained. "She's a simple girl from some simple nowhere village. She wants pretty things and for people to like her. The only secrets she's likely to tell me are silly dreams."

Alaric laughed. "Sometimes I wonder if I made you too well. If I didn't know better, I'd think you believe that. But you know what the problem with that is?" He leaned in. "The second I left, you just couldn't stay away from her. I'd have thought you'd have more sense than to dance with her in public. Because I told you, if you aren't talking to her for *me*, you aren't talking to her."

Magic sizzled on the hand wrapped around Numair's throat and the smell of burning flesh hit the air. "No doubt you've fully undone any progress I made with her. So I'm giving you this one last chance to change your mind. Take her. Convince her to show you what's truly lurking under that pretty voice, and I'll forgive everything."

Numair's answer was a hoarse, clipped, "No."

Alaric's first slammed into Numair's face. Drew back and

connected again. And again. And again, each strike made with cold, methodical precision.

Clare knew the stupidity of revealing herself, but the part of her that lived only for her own survival broke at the smell of burned flesh and copper-bright blood. She strained against the vines but they only gripped her tighter, wrapping about her like a caress and holding her fast. The only noises she could make came out muffled against the thick padding of vegetation covering her mouth, and what did escape was lost to the rhythmic sound of Alaric's grunting as his fist connected over, and over, and over.

Desperate, Clare reached for the Song, only to find it had deserted her entirely, locking the doors of its prison from the inside. Her body trapped in vines, her only power locked inside a cage of her own making, Clare could only watch as Alaric spent his fury breaking Numair's body.

When she couldn't watch anymore, when her own fury rivaled Alaric's, she dove inward and found the Song. She could not force it from its prison, but neither could it keep her out of it.

You are afraid of Alaric.

The Song bristled, but it did not deny her.

Why?

Silence.

You made this world. I watched you burn Renault County to the ground. Why fear him?

Because as much power as I have reclaimed being reborn into this world, there is still more required to sustain it. Alaric has gathered much of that power to himself. I am…not certain which one of us is stronger.

Clare went cold. *So he could kill you?*

In a manner of speaking. If he kills you I will be forced to return to my dormant state. There is not enough left of the world for me to transition once again to wakefulness, and if I cannot wake, I cannot be reborn. Neither can I unmake the world while I only dream.

What aren't you saying?

Hesitation, then, *While I dream, though I do not have physical form, or agency, I can be reached through this physical plane. I have no doubt that should you die, Alaric will find me, and he will absorb my power into himself.*

So he'll be like you are with me, now?

No. You and I are two consciousnesses existing within the same vessel.

I have watched Alaric pull power from this world time and time again. His methods are brutal. He would rip my power from my consciousness and I, as I am within you, would cease to exist.

Can you not simply take his power from him?

Not without killing him first. He has bonded that power to himself. To take it from him would require unmaking the pieces of the world that power belongs to. But a single piece of the world cannot be unmade. It is like cutting a hole in a blanket—eventually, the rest of the blanket will unravel. The only solution is to unmake everything.

But you have destroyed pieces of the world before, and we are still here.

Think of the world as a collection of squares, sewn together. If you sever the threads connecting one square to the others, you may destroy that square without harming the rest. You no longer have the original whole, but what you have done will not cause the rest to unravel, and you could, should you desire it, sew a new square on to replace the one you have destroyed.

The Faelhorn Provinces, the Song continued pedantically, *are the last remaining square. Allow me to unmake it, Clare. There are people who should not have to suffer the world that Alaric would make if he consumes me.*

And what then? How long until you grow lonely again, and the cycle simply repeats itself?

I made an error in the creation of this world. I will see the error is not repeated in the next.

The thought of Clare's laughter echoed softly in the Song's prison. *The error, dear Song, is* you.

She felt it absorb her response, felt its bafflement.

I do not understand.

You created this world from yourself. It, and everyone in it, is a reflection of, a part of, you. It is neither all good nor all bad, because you are neither all good, nor all bad. The true battle you fight lies within yourself. To be better than you are.

Destroy this world and make a new one. Your optimism at the fresh start will ensure that initially it will be as beautiful as you imagine. Give it a few ten winters, a few hundred, and you will become complacent, and the corruption will slip in. You will see it and it will enrage you, and that will only fuel the downward spiral. Watch and see. In a few centuries your new world will be right where this one is now.

The Song's silence was a cold and terrible thing, and it drew another soft, internal laugh from Clare.

Oh Song, this is not your first world, is it? Dare I ask how many others there have been?

The Song did not answer.

May I take it this is the first time anyone has had this conversation with you?

It is, the Song finally answered.

Some advice from my childhood? You may destroy yourself only so many times before you must recognize that you are what you are. Save yourself, for once. Or destroy yourself again. The choice is yours, I suppose.

It was only when Alaric's anger was vented, when he stood, blood dripping from his fists, that the Song asked, tentatively, *What do you suggest we do?*

What anything does when backed into a corner, Clare answered, her hand clenching around the cloth-wrapped form of the Siren's Tear. *We adopt his tactics, and we fight.*

Alaric wiped his hands on a shredded remnant of the bedspread and tossed it onto Numair's bloody, supine form. "If you're alive when the healer comes in the morning, you can go back to work." He shook his head, and his next words sounded almost genuinely regretful. "You should have taken her, boy. Now *I* have to handle things, and she won't like it."

He started to leave, then paused in the doorway and turned back, his head canted as if listening. She quit breathing. She hadn't moved, hadn't made a sound. Had she? He looked directly at the wall of vines—and turned and walked out.

Her heart beat so loudly it thudded harshly in her ears, the pulse painful. He couldn't have seen her. If he'd seen her, he wouldn't have simply left. She strained against the vines but she was so tightly captured that movement was impossible and she was forced to wait. To listen to the sounds of Numair's labored breathing and just *wait,* until the Song unlatching the doors of its prison told her Alaric had left the estate.

I think, it told her, *that I would like to fight. But Clare? If we should be on the verge of failure, understand that I will destroy this world before I will let Alaric have it.*

Only then did the vines let Clare go, and it was the Song's magic freeing her, because Numair was too weak.

She pulled out the wood sliver pinning her to the wall, the Song sealing the wound closed as she did, and ran to kneel at his side, her hand reaching for his face. Power flickered over her palm, the Song's shame making it unusually willing to acquiesce to her desires. Magic flowed and the bones of Numair's cheek began sliding back into their proper places.

"Don't." Numair's hand caught her wrist, trembling and slick with his own blood. "He'll send the healer in the morning."

"You will be dead by the morning." Her voice was harsh and guttural.

Numair shrugged, as if it didn't matter. The indifference infuriated her, more so because she understood that if Alaric's healer arrived to find Numair perfectly fine, that would likely mean his death too.

She touched her hand once more to his cheek and bid the Song to work. It suffused Numair with warmth, searching for the injuries that were immediately life-threatening while leaving the superficial, physical remnants of his mistreatment. His cheekbone finished mending, bone sliding together with a crunch before melding back into a whole unit. The Song probed further, found the ruptured organs inside him and mended those too, staunched the flow of blood that moved internally where it should not.

Numair's eyes cleared and he blinked slowly, hesitantly.

"The pain is gone," she told him, "and the worst of the injuries. But most of the damage is still present, and if you push yourself too hard before the healer's arrival, you can easily still die."

He let her help him to his feet, leaning heavily on her as she helped him to the sitting room just outside the ruined bedchamber. He didn't fight her help as she eased him onto a sofa.

"My thanks," he said stiffly, sinking into the softness of the sofa, letting go of her as if her skin burned.

"Hardly necessary." She answered in tones that matched his own formality, but when he didn't say anything else, when he wouldn't even look at her, she softened. And when she spoke his name, it was with that pronunciation no one else here used. "Numair…"

His jaw tightened, and she had the sense she'd made a misstep. "You know it all now, then," he said bitterly. "What I am."

It wasn't truly a question, but she answered anyway. "I know."

"I'm the king's bloody whore," he snarled, as if she had denied the knowledge. "I sleep with who he tells me to sleep with when he tells me to, until I find out whatever he wants to know that Verol's stretched too thin to acquire. Because no one thinks the drunken idiot who's only good for a good time would ever have the brains to *spy* on anyone."

She fixed him with a pointed stare. "And you think that would change my opinion of you? After what you've seen of my life?"

He shook his head. "You didn't have a choice."

"I had the same choice—the only choice—that you have. Death or survival. And I don't regret that either of us is here."

His eyes flickered shut, reopened. "I can't do this anymore. But I don't get to stop just because I had the idiocy to fall—" His mouth slammed shut so fast Clare heard his teeth click.

Inexplicably her body came all over with pinpricks of gooseflesh, nervous heat coiling restlessly inside her stomach. She felt as unsettled as the first time she'd been struck, and when her hand reached for his, he took it.

"He asked you after we came back from Deleen, didn't he?"

"Yes."

"Why didn't you agree?"

"Because he'd want me to make you do things for him, and glamour can't hide from you the evidence of what happens when he doesn't get what he wants. I've seen how angry you get. Over me. For me. You'd either do what he wanted to make it stop, or you'd try to stop him yourself. I wasn't going to be the reason you either became his puppet or got yourself killed.

"So I thought if you hated me, he couldn't use me against you." He sighed. "But then I fucked that up too, because you didn't believe it and I wasn't strong enough to make you. Today I thought if he was angry enough to finally kill me, well, that would solve the problem too."

Her hand tightened on his. "Don't say that."

"Why not? It's true. And I'm not worth it. I never have been."

"That is bullshit."

"It's—"

"Not." She cut him off. "It's not the truth, and it never has been. You saw what I came out of. I left that and I came here wanting an actual life, but I didn't even understand what that meant. And then

I found you. I wanted *you.* So don't tell me what I want isn't worth it. Don't tell me what I care about is cheap."

"Clare…" He struggled to rise onto his elbow.

She shoved him back down. "And do *not* reinjure yourself."

A hint of a smile finally ghosted his lips. "Is there anything I *am* allowed to do?"

"Yes." Her throat tightened. "Promise me you'll be here when I come back."

The shadows returned to his eyes. "Back from where?"

"Dunen Province. I need to fabricate a dying uncle and make myself difficult to forget." Alaric might know exactly where she was from. But that didn't mean the world did. It didn't mean she couldn't paint a very different picture of her life for them. A life where she'd grown up known and loved and adored. And wasn't it convenient that she'd been in public mourning these last weeks? "And then I am going to fix this." She had legends to track down. And she had a Song that knew where every single one of them was. "So promise me you'll be here."

He looked tired, in that way that only years of hopelessness can make a person, grinding them down day by day. "Does it mean that much to you?"

"It means *everything* to me." For a moment, she was afraid that her deepest truth wouldn't be enough.

But he blew out a shuddering breath and said, "Then I'll be here."

EIGHTY-SEVEN

FOUNDATIONAL MEMORIES ARE TRICKY THINGS

Marquin was not certain what to expect when he and Verol arrived in Farthenam Village. They had come in response to Clare's letter, which had stated only, *My uncle has passed on. I would be grateful if you would attend the wake.*

They had had no other communication with her. She had said nothing of Renault County, which by now the entire kingdom knew was burning. While Phoenix had, in response to his inquiry on the matter, confirmed she was responsible, and that she had the Siren's Tear in her possession, they refused to say anything else about what had happened there.

Alaric had accepted their explanation of Clare's absence with too much unruffled calm, not asking a single question. Had, in response to their own departure for the wake, merely bid them a fair journey. Experience had taught Marquin that Alaric's calm often came before his most violent storms. Yet he couldn't sense the building of this one, could not predict when it might break.

So now he and his husband stood in a small, unremarkable village nestled in the heart of Dunen Province, attending a wake for a man they had never heard of. A man Clare had never met. She had never stepped foot in this village until two weeks prior—if there was one thing the pit of fire that was Renault County proved, it was that—and yet every single inhabitant of Farthenam Village was utterly convinced Clare had grown up within the bounds of their small slice of the world.

Each person he and Verol spoke with had some story about her. Clare running about the village as a toddler, terrorizing everyone and keeping her dearly departed uncle on his toes. Clare racing horses with the other village children. Clare sneaking into Mr. Thompson's apple orchard. Clare singing her first song at seven at their spring festival.

The stories were too richly detailed to have been made up, Clare's "life" here too intimately woven into everyone else's to be the result of even the most careful coaching. It was, none of it, the truth of Clare's past, and yet Verol's careful sifting through minds could produce no hint of a lie, nor mental manipulation. Each person they spoke to believed they told the truth.

And as they had only just arrived in Farthenam in time for the wake, they had not yet had an opportunity to get Clare alone to have her explain. She was relentlessly popular with everyone, who could not stop offering her sympathy, or this or that creature comfort, or this or that amusing anecdote meant to honor her uncle's memory.

All of this was odd enough, but the thing that brought him and Verol to the end of their patience was when the local innkeeper recounted, in vivid and what he believed to be truthful detail, the night Verol and Marquin had "discovered" Clare.

"What a stroke of luck, your carriage breaking down outside our little village, eh? Why, if you hadn't had to spend the night at the inn, you'd have never heard her singing, and I wager the world would be the poorer for it. Why, the way I hear it, even the king himself adores her song."

"Indeed," was the only word Verol could manage in response.

"Her uncle tried his best, you know, but he was never a true father and always in poor health, that one. It's such a relief to us all, knowing she has the two of you looking out for her now."

Marquin murmured a polite response, and Verol seized an opportunity to pull Clare away from a group of villagers. "Could we talk to you in private?"

"Of course." Clare made her excuses and they followed her to a small receiving room.

Verol rubbed at his forehead, as if the confusion of the night were a physical spot on his skin he could simply rub off. "Clare, you did not grow up here," he began, and carried on before she could respond. "These people do not know you and yet they are telling stories about you like they saw you every day of your life. Stories they believe are true. I cannot find a trace of magic on them, not a spell, not a compulsion. The recollections are too detailed and varied for them to have memorized crafted tales, and even if they could have, it wouldn't explain how I can *feel* the memories. What *is* this?"

"It is *a* life," she answered simply. "It is detailed, because it was real. As you surmised, there is no spell compelling them to lie, nor any story for them to memorize. There is no need for either, because they simply remember."

"You…implanted false memories?" Marquin asked.

"Not false. As I said, the memories are real. They simply did not originally belong to these people. The man who died here? My 'uncle'? He was not a good man. He wielded a great deal of power in this village, and he made life difficult for its inhabitants. So I offered them a choice—to keep the memories they had of him, and be miserable, or to take the ones I gave them, and be happy. They chose the latter. Only two parts of their memories are false. The girl whose life this was died of a fever at nineteen, along with her father. I altered things so that she—I—was raised by my 'uncle.' And I replaced the memory of her death with the one where I met you."

Clare made a fist and then opened her hand, palm up. Two dots of pure white rested in the center of her palm. "*This* is that memory. And I am thinking it would be safest if you both had it as well."

Quin didn't move. Neither did Verol.

"Can you do this to anyone?" Verol asked.

Clare shook her head. "Something this extensive must be chosen, or else it will not last. You, of all people, know how difficult it can be to find purchase in a mind. It is why you can only force small changes without shattering a person's sanity."

Verol reached for one of the white dots, his fingers halting just shy of it. "Will we forget how we actually met you?"

"No. It is such a small crossover that it is not necessary. It will be more that you can recall two different versions of the same event, each one feeling as real as the other."

Marquin's hand brushed past Verol's, taking up one of the white dots. "What do I do?"

"Put it on your tongue." Clare smiled. "It tastes a bit like spun sugar."

He did, and Verol followed suit. The memory washed over him in soft waves. Their carriage breaking an axle outside the village, their journey delayed while it was repaired. Staying at the inn and hearing Clare sing. Verol's recognition of her Songweaver talent and his offer to her of an apprenticeship.

He frowned. "I remember it all"—and it was such an odd thing to remember, so clearly, something he *knew* had not occurred—"but I do not feel anything about it. Not the way these people seem to."

He could see the events in his mind as if he had lived them, but there was no emotion attached to it—to her.

She hesitated. "I did not want to force you to feel anything for me. Foundational memories are tricky things. If I created the emotions you supposedly felt upon meeting me here, I could not prevent them from trickling through and coloring our actual history. It might alter how you feel about me now, and I would not induce you to think more kindly of me on the basis of a lie."

Part of Clare had wanted to put those emotions into the memories she'd given them. Because part of her was now living alongside the girl whose memories she'd stolen. It was not enough for everyone in this village to remember Clare being here. To play the part, she had to remember it all too.

It was another life inside her mind, the way the Song had often tried to shove the lives of others at her when it suited its convenience. She remembered being this alternate version of herself. She remembered growing up with someone who had cared about her and done his best to keep her safe and make her happy, while she was surrounded by a small community that adored her.

She remembered being the kind of woman a person could actually love. And though she was not that woman and never had been, the fundamental knowledge of what it felt like made her want the reality of those connections. Made her want the Arrendons' adoption rumors to be true—not a diversion meant to confuse Alaric, but a result of their actually caring about her. She had seen how easy it would be to shift their feelings in her favor. How the right emotions, sunk into an alternate meeting that had never happened, could twist through the memories they did have and make them think of her as a daughter.

But while they might never realize that their feelings weren't real, she would. And she cursed herself, just a little, for being unwilling to live a slightly altered, slightly happier lie, the same way she was unwilling to let the memories she'd absorbed change her. At her core, she was who she was, and for all the grief it might bring her, she was unwilling to be anyone else. She had fought too hard to *be* Clare Brighton, and now she fought to stay her.

It had been the most difficult, in the first few days of taking this other life into herself. A battle every second to partition it off from who she was. To keep it close enough to delve into the memories when they were needed, to slip into the shoes of the Clare the people of Farthenam Village knew, and yet keep those memories from altering *her*.

Only once she was certain she had attained the requisite control had she set the date of the wake and sent for the Arrendons. So she could be certain that she would give them what she had—an emotionless, factual memory they could recall when needed. And once she was done here, she could lock this alternate Clare in a box in her mind and never have to look at her again.

Verol and Marquin shared a look, and if that was pity passing between them, she did not want it. She stood. "I should return."

"Wait," Verol said. "Is this the only reason you wanted us here? A memory could have been handled in Veralna."

Was he irritated, to have been dragged to the southern reaches of the continent simply for this? He didn't *sound* irritated, but she couldn't place what he did sound like. What he wanted her answer to be.

"Not entirely," she said. "But I would prefer to *show* you the other reason, in lieu of an explanation. And that will require the cover of darkness. Meet me at my uncle's house an hour after sunset."

She returned to the wake. Returned to becoming that slightly different Clare while repeating, over and over in her mind, *Not me. This isn't me. This will never* be *me.* Nothing could have proved it truer than when, twenty feet from her "uncle's" home, the Song went silent, and she walked in to find Alaric Tolvannen in the receiving room.

CHAPTER

EIGHTY-EIGHT

TWO THINGS YOU NEVER WANTED

Only the Song's desertion of her kept Clare from doing something truly stupid. She could still see Alaric's fists breaking Numair's body. The casual way he'd wiped the blood off his hands and left.

She forced calm, indifferent words out. "Your Majesty. To what do I owe this honor?"

"I came to thank you. For Renault County."

Cold stole through her. "I don't know what you mean."

"Oh, come now. We are so very far past denials." He gripped her chin in his hand, as he had that day in the garden, looking into her eyes as if he could see through her to the Song and asked it, "Do you recognize me?"

The Song did not rise to the bait. Seconds passed, her blood rushing wildly. Adrenaline demanded action while logic demanded stillness. She had watched Brennan Tolvannen drive a blade into Alaric's heart and felt the remnant of another person take that death. To kill the Jackal King would require doing so thousands of times. She alone could not do it, and the only thing that had any hope of accomplishing it now cowered within her.

For someone who said they would destroy this world before they let Alaric have it, you can't even look at him, Clare snapped at the Song. *If he tries to kill us, are you even going to protest?*

No answer—and then there was. Only it wasn't in words. It was

569

death with Alaric's face, coming for her over and over again. She stood there, with his hand gripping her jaw, living and feeling every time he had killed the Song.

It was, she realized, in shock. Caught in a loop of death and terror, this immensity of power that had made itself mortal time and time again, only to die as mortals so easily did. It would be of no use to her in this moment. Without it, she had what she always had: herself.

When Alaric saw no traces of what he sought, he let her go.

She tilted her head up and didn't let a trace of fear show. "How long have you known?"

"Since that day in the gardens. One footstep too many, little songbird."

That first day in the palace gardens. It felt like a lifetime ago. So long. He'd known what she was practically from the moment they'd met. "Why didn't you kill me then?"

"Kill you?" He shook his head. "Why would I do that, when it would destroy everything I've built?"

So he understood, then. That each time he killed the Song's vessel, it took a part of the world with it. He thought if he killed her, the Faelhorn Provinces would be destroyed. He didn't know she was the Song's last attempt. That if he killed her, the Song could not rebirth itself.

He studied her. "Did you know that every time I kill one of you, the next one is a little stronger? All that power, in a single shell. I've tried Reaping it, but you can't be Reaped, even at the moment of death. So I kept going, pushing it to grow stronger, until I ended up with you.

"And you should be the strongest, but none of it escapes you. You are...so different from the rest. They were all kind, all innocent. You are neither. It made me doubt, on occasion. Especially with reports of so many unexplained happenings in far-off places making their way back to me.

"But then, just when I was going to explore those happenings, I learned Renault County was burning, and my little songbird was missing from her cage." He tapped his fingers against her collarbone. "You were playing the game so well. What prompted you to show your hand?"

She would have to tread carefully, here where there was no path to follow. He needed a reason he could believe that did not involve Numair. "You told me I couldn't escape the threat of Renault County through death. So when you left and gave me the opportunity, I removed that threat in a different way."

"*You* removed the threat. That is…interesting phrasing." His fingers, still resting on her collarbone, slid higher, his hand curling around her throat. Tightening but not yet squeezing. "I want to feel it."

"What?"

"I want to feel it," he repeated. "You hide it well. Mere inches from you and I don't feel even a whisper. Yet somehow it destroyed a place even I could not reach. So I. Want. To. Feel. It."

She felt that careful line she walked grow even narrower. She spiraled deep inside herself, down and down, until she found the Song hidden far within its prison. *Do as he says.*

The Song responded with blind panic, quivering, making her wish it had a physical body that was not *hers* that she could slap. *He wants to know if we're stronger than him. Or if we are strong enough that we could* become *stronger.*

Because destroying Renault County was something he had never managed to do.

So show him that we're not. Show him enough, more than the last vessel contained, but not everything.

Slowly, reluctantly, the Song rose, opening its prison door and suffusing her with power. It built and built, far more than she'd channeled in Renault County, until it felt like her body would burst from the strain of containing it. So much, and yet the Song had told her Alaric possessed more.

Catching her thoughts, it whispered, *He has carved the world up to become my equal.*

Bitterness swept through her. *As if you didn't butcher it first.*

She wondered if it mattered which of them came out on top in the end—the Song, or Alaric. The rest of them, they were all just pawns in a game between two gods—one born, one made.

"There it is." Alaric's voice was as close to ecstasy as ever she'd heard it. It blazed in his eyes, a deep, burning hunger that could never be sated.

Go, she told the Song. *Now.*

It vanished within her in a blink and Alaric squeezed her throat.

Pressure built in her temples as her blood flow restricted, her breath becoming an audible wheeze. He released her abruptly.

She didn't give him the satisfaction of reacting. Didn't move, didn't reach for her bruised throat.

"You control it," he said. It wasn't entirely accurate, but she didn't disabuse him of the fact. "Good. That should make it easier for you to give me what I want."

"And that is still your people's love?" *Love is power*, he'd said to her. *It shackles people to each other. It destroys them. And all without you ever having to lift a finger to make it happen. I hold power over them, yes. But I am forced to remind them of it at every turn.*

"My wants are not so fickle as the average creature's. They remain constant."

"I wonder that you don't like it," she murmured.

"Like what?" A dangerous edge laced his voice.

"Having to remind them that it is you who holds the power. Or does it simply prick your pride when they defy you?"

His fingers curled, and she suspected he wished they were still wrapped around her throat. "You think I am a tyrant, that the ends I desire are self-serving. Perhaps, to some degree, they are. But not entirely.

"You did not see this world as it was before I molded it into something different. How much discord and chaos reigned. These people decry what I have done as if I took their kingdoms in order to endlessly murder and torture.

"But there is far less death than there was before me. I waged war when it was necessary, yes. I smother rebellions when they occur. And yet all that is a mere drop of blood in the ocean that bathed this continent prior. Twelve provinces, but those provinces only managed to unite within themselves to oppose me. Each held dozens of small collectives before me, miring their people in endless bloody squabbles, wasting lives.

"I have brought them more stability than they could have hoped to find in another ten centuries. I can continue to hold them with the bloodshed that seems to be the only thing they understand. But I want a better way forward."

He sounded so calm and genuine, and she realized it was because he was both. He was a man who felt his vision was the height of morality simply for the fact that *he* held it and had the power to enforce it. And now he wanted everyone else to believe it too. She wondered, if he simply gave it another hundred years, if they wouldn't. Because his sincerity had an almost hypnotic quality to it, and were it not for the lives clinging to him like extra skins, she could see how a person might be persuaded by the words.

Making people love him would not be all that difficult. All she had to do was make them forget. But *she* would never forget. She would never not feel the rot clinging to him, never unsee the look on his face as he broke Numair's body.

"And if I refuse to help you?"

"You already know you don't want to refuse me. This could have been easy—for you and Numair. His...duties have been too damaging for him to understand how readily you would have complied if he'd asked it of you. The two of you could have been happy together. I wouldn't have begrudged it.

"And I might still have convinced him to take that route, if you hadn't been hiding in his room that morning. I *almost* missed you. A masterful touch really, hiding a life behind so much other life. But unfortunate for you, as now you understand that play, you won't yield to it. So I'm afraid you've forced my hand."

He took her left wrist, splayed the fingers of her hand wide, and shoved a band of cool silver onto her ring finger. A small spike on the underside drew blood as it slid. Blood that dropped onto a parchment that appeared, floating in the air beneath her hand. He forced her thumb into the pooling blood, her print appearing next to his own on the royal marriage contract.

"Now you get to be two things you never wanted—a wife, and a queen." She didn't try to hide her anger, and he laughed. "This was your idea, little songbird. You told me to marry a commoner. And you have made yourself one here, with this pretty lie you've woven about your past."

He rolled the contract up, tapped her on the nose with it like she was a dog. "This is settled, between us. But to the world, this is a courtship. Make them all believe you're falling in love with me."

Her blood boiled. "I wonder you don't expect me to actually do it."

He smiled. "I don't imagine you're any more capable of the emotion than I am. People like you and I—we do not love, Clare. We obsess. It can be almost as dangerous—the objects of obsession can control a person every bit as much as love can. That is why I chose the world as mine—because it can be manipulated, but it cannot be used in whole against me.

"It is why I do not mind that Numair is yours. Because I do control him. And I will use him as I need to. I'll give you a few days to conclude your business here. Then I expect you to leave for Veralna."

His hand was on the door when she said, "And if I don't? If I decide he isn't worth it?"

"That would be very unfortunate for Numair. Because the thing about obsessions? They're even harder to let go of than love. And I would have to dedicate all of my creativity to ensuring you had truly let that one go. Two weeks, little songbird, or I'll make what I did to him while you hid and watched seem like nothing. You would be surprised, what I can do to a man and keep him alive."

He opened the door. Verol and Marquin stood rigid on the other side, held motionless in the grip of his power. He looked at Verol, as if something had just occurred to him. "I suppose I ought to have asked your blessing. But then, I was never much given to the customs of the old country. But don't worry, the public wedding ceremony is still several months off, I imagine. Plenty of time for you to come to terms with giving her away."

Verol's face lost what little color it had held, and when Alaric's power finally released him, once the king himself was long-gone from sight, Verol took a halting step toward her. "Clare?"

She shook her head, too angry to speak just yet.

I've seen how angry you get. Over me. For me. Numair had no idea. She was incandescent with fury.

People like you and I—we do not love, Clare. We obsess. Perhaps Alaric was right. She had never loved before. It seemed improbable that she should begin now. Obsession made so much more sense.

But whichever it was, Numair was *hers*. And no one, she decided, harmed what was hers.

Alaric Tolvannen could not fathom how deeply he would regret making her his *wife*. How much more deeply he would pay for Numair.

574

CHAPTER

EIGHTY-NINE

THE LAKE OF A THOUSAND SORROWS

Clare refused to discuss what had happened, no matter how Marquin and Verol pushed. Later, she would have to. Later, they would plan. But at this moment she needed to act, not talk. So she led them, under the cover of silken darkness, down the single lane that led out of the village. When they came to the end of it she stepped off the path, walking through the scrubby vegetation that lay beyond. She followed a stone path only she could see, one that had been buried beneath centuries of change.

Marquin and Verol let her keep her silence, following without question until they came to a sheer, inland-facing cliff. The clifftop was so high above them they would have had difficulty seeing it even in the daylight. At first glance, no part of the cliff face looked any different from the rest. But the Song knew precisely where to draw her gaze so she might find the seams of a gate, its doors each spanning twelve feet in width and towering to a height of fifty feet.

Her hands trembled in anticipation. When she had asked the Song for its legends, she had never dreamed this one was true. Or that it would be in Dunen Province, and she could choose to weave the lie of her beginnings in the small village that was a remnant of a time when the gate had been ever open.

She approached, placing her hands against the stone and murmuring soft and low, in a tongue old enough these lands had nearly forgotten it. Thin tendrils of light snaked from her fingers,

575

falling into grooves etched so lightly into the stone that they were difficult to see in the daylight, impossible to find at night. They shone with the light gifted to them, a brilliant glow in the darkness, illuminating the boundaries of the gate and the etchings high above.

"Are those words?" Marquin asked, finally breaking the silence.

"Indeed." And since she knew what he wanted, she translated them for him. "Pass through this gate, all you who are troubled, and leave your sorrows with the lake."

A mighty crack appeared in the center of the stone, stretching vertically along it. Dirt and rocks tumbled down, the earth shaking as the stone split in two, and the great doors opened with a terrible groan.

Clare led them through, came to a stop at the place where land met water. Here, the darkness required no magelight to illuminate it, for here the bright orange luminescent shapes flitting anxiously beneath the water lit the night.

"Welcome," she said softly, "to the Lake of a Thousand Sorrows."

This was my first failing in this world, the Song confided. *My belief that if people could simply give away their deepest sorrows, they would live peaceful lives. Instead, I found they were worse for the absence.*

Of course they were worse—sorrow was a teacher. It taught you what you valued. What you could make other people feel when you took what they valued from them. It was not pleasant, but without it, it would be too easy to value nothing. If the pain of a loss could be removed without cost, then loss itself became unimportant.

Ferrian had known that. Ferrian, whom the legends claimed had been so heartbroken that she had come here to lay her sorrows down...and gained a thousand more instead.

Was she real? Clare asked. *Did Ferrian truly come here?*

Yes. She was my most-beloved vessel in this world, and I will tell you now what I told her then. Turn back. There are other ways to fix what has been broken. This lake and its contents are not for you.

She survived.

She almost did not. I cannot protect you here.

I understand. And she did. Understood how unacknowledged sorrow could tear a person to pieces. To calm sorrow, one had to embrace it. To make it a part of oneself. To acknowledge what mattered, and the fear of losing it. *But I need to do this.*

She just needed to do one other thing first.

She reached into the pocket of Numair's coat and pulled out a red envelope. The color was faded slightly around the seal, from the number of times she'd almost broken it since learning to read. She'd always decided not to at the last moment, certain that any words he could have written when they first met, given to her with a dress when he didn't know she understood who he was, would have little bearing on her now.

She would have been wrong.

Battle armor suits you. And unfortunately, you'll need it in this place. If they manage to cut you, don't let them see you bleed. If they make you bleed, make them hurt. Never let them see you flinch. And forget, entirely, about me.

Carefully, she refolded the note and slid it back into the envelope, the envelope back into the coat. She would not forget. He was the only one who had ever seen her flinch, seen her bleed. Before this was done, she would make Alaric hurt. And if she had armor, now she needed a blade.

She slipped off her boots, shrugged out of the coat and handed it to Marquin. "Hold onto this for me."

He took it reflexively. "What are you doing?" he asked as she waded into the lake.

"Reclaiming history." She dove beneath the surface. The cool waters enveloped her, the taste against her lips briny, as if the lake truly had been born from humanity's tears, as the legends claimed. Bright sorrows slithered through the currents like eels. She sang, her voice garbled beneath the water, and called them to her.

They noticed her at once, ceasing their lazy serpentine movements, and swarmed. At the shift in their attention, she swam upward, breaking the surface of the lake once more, inhaling a deep breath as the first sorrow reached her. It twined around her ankle, up her calf, and then she was falling into it.

Loss washed over her, a flurry of emotions and distress, of suffering and longing and endless nights of weeping. The person whose sorrow it had been had lost their son, and they had come to the lake to forget. She did not try to fight the feelings, to bury them. She had heard Ferrian's legend enough times to know better, to know that sorrow could be neither fought nor destroyed. It could only be lived.

So she lived it, and in so doing, bought that sorrow a moment of peace. Its form stilled in the water, no longer battering at her. The relief was brief, a mere handful of seconds before the next one gripped her. A lover, this time. Lost not to death or disloyalty, but to a slow fading of passion. To long years of tiny miscommunications and small hurts that seemed like nothing at the time and yet, strung together, caused an end. She lived that slow separation that was heartbreak and desolation.

A third sorrow was more intricate, a loss of a different kind, born from secrets and betrayal and slow-plotted revenge. It was, surprisingly, the sorrow of the person who had hidden and schemed and brought the plans to fruition, rather than the sorrow of the person who had been harmed. And she knew, from the Song's sadness in her mind, that the moment they had laid the sorrow for those actions down, they had gone out and done it all again.

The fourth that came to her was born from failure and uncertainty. From all the ways a person could allow fear to keep them from ever living a moment of their life and how they might, near the end of it, understand as much. Just as Clare understood that, had they not given the sorrow for it to the lake, they might have found the strength to finally live.

Then the fifth came, and the sixth, and the seventh. On and on it went. So many sorrows, all different and yet all the same, an inundation of hurt and tragedy. Her limbs grew leaden, her breathing labored, and she struggled to keep her head above water as the weight of a thousand sorrows tried to drag her under. And when they didn't, when she had acknowledged the final one and the sky was beginning to lighten on the horizon line, the lake tried to convince her to give them back. To give them back and lay down one of her own alongside them.

Wouldn't it be easier, the lake seemed to ask, if she did not have to carry the weight of all those choices she had made? All those deaths? If she didn't have to feel the consequences of the cage she'd made for the Song when she was so young. The one that had locked away from her the only power that could have saved her from the years of torment that had been Simian. The one even she hadn't been able to open until she'd finally broken, and it had cracked the cage, and then to keep herself intact she'd had to break the tether to her body.

Wouldn't it be easier if she hadn't spent two years in madness, in the muck and mire of the swamp, her mere touch a death sentence to anything living? Easier if she hadn't come back from it, hadn't found the Arrendons and Chalen, Alys and Lina, Kialla and Numair? Her greatest sorrow was that she had come to care and, having never cared for anything before, she did so all the more fiercely now.

But more than that, she *was* sorrow. She, who had seen so much of life's depravity. She, the lake promised, belonged here. She had once nearly lost herself beneath the waters of one of its sisters, and it had tasted her and found her welcome. Why should she want to leave, carrying the burden of a thousand sorrows with her, when she could remain here?

Stay, the lake whispered, *and be my lady. Stay, and we will neither of us be lonely again.*

And Clare felt the lake's sorrow then, for it had once made the offer to another, but Ferrian had refused it. And like Ferrian before her, Clare could not be swayed by the tranquility she knew would be hers if she let the waters claim her. If she became the lady of this lake. For her heart was not a thing made for tranquility and forgetting. Hers was a heart designed for rage and vengeance, and no force in this world would quell it.

She had lived her own sorrow. She had lived a thousand more. And there was power in sorrow. In surviving it.

She called them to her now, every now-quiescent bit of soothed pain. They rushed to her, filling the space between her hands, folding in on themselves in order to fit. Once she had them all, she drew her hands together, compressing them into a small sphere of brilliant orange light.

She clasped the sphere to her chest and dove, willing tired eyes to stay open, tired lungs to hold breath. Down and down and down she went, until her ears and lungs both felt as if they would burst from the pressure. Until one questing hand found the lakebed, and the light of the sorrows finally washed over the hilt of a sword.

It rose vertically from the rocky floor, the tip plunged deep into solid stone, the hilt pointed toward the surface. The blade was impossible to discern beneath layers of algae and aquatic buildup, the hilt eaten bare of its former wrapping, mussels latched onto its frame like ornaments.

She teased a single sorrow from the sphere and fed it to the sword. The mussels fell away, algae sloughing off the blade in chunks that broke apart and turned the water to a cloudy haze. The sorrow she had fed into the sword called to the others in her sphere, dragging the next to join it, and the second called to the third. So they went, one after the other, all connected to each other like a rope made of so many sashes tied together.

As they slid into the sword rust fell from the metal, the ragged, cracked edges of the blade repairing themselves, the tattered remnants of the hilt-wrapping growing once more supple and whole. With each sorrow absorbed, the sword's black blade shone with orange light, until it took in the last sorrow and, vibrating with heat and energy, the rock holding the sword blade began to melt. She reached out, curling her fingers around the hilt, and pulled the sword from the stone.

It was a wicked, undulating thing with a flamberge blade, each dip and curve like flames sprouting from the sides. The hilt felt right in her palm, as if it fit with her. She clasped it to her chest and kicked for the surface, her vision blacking and her head thrumming with the incessant need to breathe. Every inch of her body screamed at her to open her mouth and inhale, to let out the breath trapped inside her lungs and trade it for another, pulse hammering against her temples until she thought her skull would split from the pressure.

She kicked furiously, bursting above the lake's surface and sucking in great heaving breaths. Ferrian's sword cast an orange, sun-dance glow, lighting her way as she swam for the shore, her teeth chattering with wet and cold. When her feet at last found purchase and she walked out of the lake, Marquin and Verol were there. The former wrapped her in Numair's coat, the spelled warmth of it driving away the water and its chill.

Verol stared at the blade in her hand. "Is that…?"

"The Sword of a Thousand Sorrows." It hissed and sparked as the sorrows burned the water from the blade, and Clare slid it into the sheath that appeared in her left hand. She buckled it around her waist and its weight there also felt right. Familiar.

She closed her eyes and saw the last battle this blade had fought. Saw it through the eyes of a woman several centuries dead. A woman who had also lived a thousand sorrows so that she might claim vengeance as her own. A woman whose bloodlust now clamored in her Clare's veins, whose memories now pressed at the back of her skull.

She inhaled deeply, the faint scent of flowers and rich earth that lingered on Numair's coat grounding her back in the present. She opened her eyes, letting go of Ferrian's ancient battle to focus on the one ahead of her. Her lips curved, offering the Arrendons a smile that was all promise and no comfort.

"Come," she said. "We have work to do."

About the Author

Michelle lives in a desolate land with a dark wizard, a unicorn, and a feline overlord. Despite certain stereotypes you may be familiar with, the dark wizard is not holding her captive, nor does the unicorn require virgin riders. The feline overlord, however, may well be evil.

You can find Michelle on her website: Michellemanus.com or join her newsletter for updates on new releases, and to receive exclusive bonus content.

ALSO BY MICHELLE MANUS

The Song Duology

A Song to Wake a Thousand Sorrows

A Song to End the World

The Aspect Society Trilogy

Siren's Song

Valkyrie's Call

Truthfinder's Promise

The Nyx Fortuna Series

Guardian of Chaos

Guardian of Shadows

Guardian of Madness

Guardian of Torment

Guardian of Defiance